# LIFE OF THAD STEVENS

*What part of
" All men are created equal "
do you not understand?*

## KATHY BRABSON

COVER DESIGN BY
BRAD ADAMS

YURCHAK PRINTING, INC.
LANDISVILLE, PA

Life of Thad Stevens / by Kathy Brabson

ISBN 978-0-9834797-7-2

10 9 8 7 6 5 4 3 2

Printed in the United States of America.

# CONTENTS

**Part IV- Thad Seals His Legacy: His Final Days**

**Appendix**

# ACKNOWLEDGEMENTS

Many individuals have contributed immensely to the successful completion of this project. Alex Munro and Sophie Weibel, of the Thaddeus Stevens Foundation, first encouraged me to write about Thad Stevens. Sharon Lakey, executive director of the Danville Historical Society, and Lorna Quimby, curator of the Peacham Historical Association, provided, on-site, colorful background about Thad's years in Vermont. Suzanne Waddell, librarian at Thaddeus Stevens College of Technology (TSCT), and Dr. Deborah Grove, retired curriculum supervisor from Williamsport Area School District, offered wise recommendations for editing my manuscript, as did Ginger Shelley, author of several history books for children, and retired director of library services at LancasterHistory.org. Ross Hetrick, president of Thaddeus Stevens Society, reviewed the text for historical accuracy. (I alone am responsible for any inaccuracies that remain.) Brad Adams and Abby Cook, of the TSCT Graphic Communication and Printing Technology department, configured the cover and formatted the text, respectively. Paul Hoffer, TSCT trustee, recommended me to John Yurchak, who offered to print this book. Gail Tomlinson suggested innumerable development concepts. To each I offer my deep and humble appreciation.

Most importantly, I thank my husband Chip, my daughter Terri, and my granddaughter Maddi, for their unfailing love for, faith in, and patience with me, throughout this journey, and always.

# INTRODUCTION

Have you ever wondered how some people get to be famous heroes, and others do not? After all, your great-great-great-grandmother probably was a seamstress, just like Betsy Ross was. And was Paul Revere the only person who ever rode around town on a horse shouting about imminent danger? What is it about these individuals that helps them to become celebrated and remain celebrated?

Do you sometimes think that maybe you hold some characteristics in common with people who eventually became or will become memorable heroes? You, no doubt, always tell the truth. So might you become a well-known hero like George Washington, who could not tell a lie about the fallen cherry tree?

Do heroes have only good traits? Isn't it true that Thomas Jefferson owned slaves? Didn't we hear that Christopher Columbus actually ordered the destruction of Native American villages?

Have you ever asked yourself whether a particular family background might influence a person to become a notable hero? Maybe you were born in a log cabin, just like Abe Lincoln was?

In this book we reflect on these questions as we examine the life of Thaddeus Stevens-- savior of Pennsylvania free public education, activist for abolition of slavery, conductor on the Underground Railroad, advocate for civil rights of the freedmen after the Civil War. At the same time, we study his antics as an orator who used his sharp tongue to wound his rivals, as an attorney who consistently discredited the Freemasons with his brittle reasoning, as a U.S. representative who fought to impeach a U.S. president on admittedly weak grounds.

We look at deprivation in Thad's childhood home and dysfunction in his early family; we consider his voracious consumption of schooling, his 'loner' perspective on community, his independent approach to athletics, his teenage triumphs and his youthful exercise of poor judgment. We witness the growth of his political skills as he moves into a Gettysburg lawyer's office, into the Pennsylvania Assembly, and into the U.S. House of Representatives. We view his tireless commitment to his causes, his years of deteriorating health, the final silencing of his speech making.

As readers and as students, we wonder which of his days measured as milestones toward his maturity; which values, experiences, and contacts were most influential in forming his future; which ideas and deeds most shaped his legacy of achievement and of fiasco. We question whether all heroes are flawed; indeed, whether any heroes are real.

Finally, we are inspired to ask ourselves if we have "what it takes" to perform meaningful deeds. We wonder what qualities in ourselves we need to develop further. We think about how we can prepare to accomplish something important for our own future lives, or something significant for the future of others.

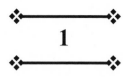

**1**

# Thad Encounters Bullies 1800

Thad pressed his tears down inside him. He hobbled toward his doorstep, his spruce-limb cane clenched in his right fist, his twisted left foot dragging behind, his threadbare shirt stretching taut against his bony, 8-year-old back. He was conscious of still being in full view of the boys across the roadway. They were bellowing and cheering each other. They wouldn't notice if he began to cry now, as his mother opened the door and rescued him with warm arms and sad eyes. He gave the tears permission to rise behind his face, then overflow, first as a trickle, then as a torrent.

Inside the one-room cabin, 3-year-old brother Baby Alanson stared blankly at him, and then returned his focus to his faceless ragdoll. Six-year-old brother Abner, also curious to see what the bawling was about, peeked down through the slats that edged the boys' loft. He, too, recognized the familiar scene, and turned his attention back to his business at hand.

Sarah Stevens moved her needlework from the chair by the fireplace, and gently nudged her sobbing son into the seat. She lowered herself to her knees and leaned into him, and he muffled his weeping in his mother's chest. Neither did she need to ask what had happened. She knew it was a repeat of last week's incidents, and last month's, and last year's. Sometimes at different places, sometimes with different characters, sometimes with different words, but really always the same:

*"Ma, Ben and Tom and John are outside just hanging out. I'm going out."*

*"Okay, Thad. But don't over-exert yourself; you're just getting over your bout with fever," she had cautioned.*

*Once again, he had ventured over to the other boys who lived in or near their hamlet of Danville Center: Ben, whose dad worked as a clerk at the Strobridge Hotel, and who was his nearest neighbor; Tom, son of the storekeeper and the toughest of the group; and John, whose family lived on a farm in Danville Green. James, whose father was Caledonia County's delegate to the Vermont House of Representatives, sometimes was with them.*

*Thad had reasoned that if they were not playing "Roll the Carriage Wheel," nor racing to the old mill pond, nor doing any other activity that required the use of two strong legs connected to two normal, straight feet, they might--just might--let him sit on the barrels with them, tell some jokes, or shoot some marbles, or chomp some apples.*

*Nevertheless, this time was like any other. Ben would try, at first, to be friendly.*

*"Hey, Stevens, how's it going?"*

*But the others would have nothing of it. Tom would begin with something like, "Hey, look, it's Stevens, the lame duck! When ya gonna tell us, Stevens: What'd your mama and papa do to earn ya that devil's foot?"*

*"Maybe it was 'cause your drunken daddy don't like to work?" John would shout.*

*Thad had no answers to their questions. He would push his lower lip forward, remember his mother's advice, then try to distract them from their taunts: "Hey, did you guys see that ole' black bear wandering through the village last night?"*

*"Or was yer mama bein' punished for smilin' at that man from France back in that year you was born? That's what my mama says," was Tom's response.*

*"And besides," offered John, "my dad says your dad ain't paid his taxes, and that's against the law."*

*Try as he might to be strong, Thad's courage would always be derailed by yet another insult. Occasionally, Tom would even kick his cane from under his fist, sending it flying. When the confrontation got to this point, Ben's mother would appear on her stone stoop, frown on face and hands on hips. Ben would glance at her and retrieve the walking stick for Thad, and murmur to his pals, "Aw, gee, let the cripple be." Then they would turn their backs to Thad and wander away, mimicking his gait, and giggling.*

Thad's sobs subsided. His mom gingerly moved away from him to wrap a tattered quilt around Baby Alanson, now napping on the braided-rag rug disguising the packed dirt floor.

The door opened, noisily drawing in Joshua Junior, with his two walking sticks, a sack slung over his shoulder, and a loud voice.

"Ma," he announced. "Mr. Weeks gave me a scrap of leather that he had left over from a pair of boots he made, and I'm going to try working it into a pair of moccasins."

Thad turned, tilting his head in a way that his older brother might not see his flooded face.

"Shhh," their mother scolded. "Don't wake the baby."

"I'm going to stitch a pair of moccasins," Joshua Junior corrected his volume, and was gone to the work corner of the cabin, adjusting his cobbler's bench to receive more light through the bottle-glass window.

Their mother returned to her second son. "Thaddeus," she offered with her arm around his shoulders, "if you could only let those boys go from your mind. You don't need them. You have your three brothers to be your friends.

"Can't you be more like Joshua Junior? He's accepted his condition; he's content to just be with family. He's happy to let your daddy teach him a different shoemaking skill each time he's home." She looked directly into his eyes. "Let's pray that the Lord give you strength to overlook those boys who won't overlook your condition."

"Just leave me alone; that's my prayer!" Thad shouted, this time not caring about drawing Joshua's or the baby's attention, and pulling briskly away from his mother. "Why did I have to be born a cripple, with this disgusting, deformed, devil's foot?" he despaired as he clumsily climbed the notched-log ladder to the loft. "It's not fair!"

Abner reached an arm to comfort his brother, but was shoved away. Thad buried his face in his straw mattress, and sobbed for a long time.

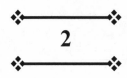

**2**

# Thad Meets a Doctor 1801

On a Sunday morning, Thad slipped on his freshly washed trousers, his frayed shirt, and his tight woolen jacket. He scowled as he snatched his spruce-limb cane, and scurried to catch up with his mother and brothers who already had begun the quarter-mile walk to the Danville meetinghouse that served on Sundays as the Baptist Church. He joined his family on their usual bench.

Thad intermittently considered the Reverend Adams' sermon. "Love thy neighbor...," he heard him say. "...We are called to love our enemies..." His mind lingered on the incidents with the other boys in his village.

The final chorus of "Father We Wait to Feel Thy Grace" sounded, and the worshipers filed outside. Thad watched an intriguing man approach his mother. He was wearing black breeches with silver buttons, a linen jabot beneath a fine jacket, and silver buckles atop his shoes. Thad couldn't take his eyes from his cane made of polished maple with a silver handle. The gentleman introduced himself.

"Good morning, Madam. I am a physician from St. Alban's Town, making my way to Boston, and then to Switzerland to study children's bone growth. I wonder if I might have a word with you."

Thad, curious, observed his mother respond with a nod.

"I apologize for my intrusion," the doctor continued, "but I have noticed that two of your young sons appear to be afflicted with *talipes equinovarus,* also known as 'clubfoot.' Might I take some of your time to examine the lads? I should like to gather more details about their condition, which may enhance my studies when I arrive at my destination. And perhaps I may be of some assistance to them, as well," he added.

His mother glanced expectantly at Thad as she said, "Yes, that would be fine." She added that she had no money to pay his fee, and he assured her there would be no fee.

That afternoon, Thad and Joshua Junior and their mother passed more than an hour with the gentleman in the brick building that had transformed itself back into the meetinghouse. The brothers cautiously cooperated as their feet and legs were probed and prodded and pushed and pounded. Next, the boys answered questions about their daily activities, about how they passed their time; what they liked to do, ways they helped their mother.

Finally, the specialist addressed Thad's mother. "Your sons are suffering from the most common congenital abnormality of the foot. Clubfoot may occur in several forms, but *talipes equinovarus* is the most common. In this case, the foot turns downward and inward." He paused, apparently pondering Thad's bare foot.

"There is a physician, a Dr. Jean-Andre Venel," he resumed, "who has pioneered a new field called orthopedics. A few years ago, Dr. Venel established in Switzerland a hospital dedicated to the treatment of children's skeletal deformities. His experimentation and publications have vastly increased knowledge of muscular functions and of the growth and development of bone. He has demonstrated much success in adjusting the bones of…"

Thad could feel his heart pumping furiously as he anticipated the doctor's next statement.

"…of newborns with the condition, but obviously it is too late for that treatment for these young men. I fear, also, that your boys' conditions have progressed such that any of the known treatments would be ineffective."

Thad shoved his lower lip forward, pressed his tears down inside him, and looked toward the window.

The physician noted that it was fortunate that Joshua, as a 10-year-old with two clubfeet, was reconciled to his affliction, because his deformity was so severe that he would never be able to perform any kind of physical labor.

He added that Thaddeus, too, needed to accept his fate in life, because, although he had the condition in only one foot, he would be quite limited in his future, and would best come to terms with it.

Thad's mother spoke in a low tone to the physician, several times diverting her eyes from the doctor to Thad. The doctor, too, rested his gaze frequently on Thad's face, and nodded.

When the whispering stopped, the physician proceeded, "Young man,..." He had a long talk with Thad; he explained that his clubfoot was just a physical deformity, a medical anomaly; that it was not the devil's work, nor was it the Lord's punishment; and that the nasty notions that some folks had about the origin of his deformity were just folklore. Raising his silver-plated, polished maple cane for emphasis, he added that bullying was some people's response to their own fears and insecurities.

The doctor advised Mrs. Stevens that her boys--especially Thad-- had good heads on their shoulders, and he wished her success in helping them find a way to employ their brains for their livelihood, for they certainly would not be employing their legs.

Thad was not hungry for supper that evening. Instead, he climbed awkwardly to his loft, then tossed and turned on his straw mattress for a long time.

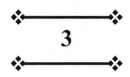

# 3

## Thad Confronts the Bullies 1801

Several days later Thad spied, through the window, the Loud Lads (as the brothers had secretly named them) loitering near his house. He put on his wraps without saying a word.

"Oh, Lord, not again!" his mother prayed aloud. "Why does he forever put himself through this?" She moved toward Thad as he struggled out the door, almost forgetting his cane.

The meeting began in the usual way; however, this time when the boys asked how Thad and his parents had earned his devil's foot, he answered them.

"My clubfoot is just a physical deformity, a medical anomaly. It is not the devil's work, and it is not the Lord's punishment," he added. "It is the most common congenital abnormality of the foot. Clubfoot may occur in several forms, but *talipes equinovarus* is the most widespread. In my case, my foot turns downward and inward."

The boys listened momentarily. Ben was the first to laugh. "Oh, so your clubfoot's a 'medical anomaly'?"

Tom snickered, "That don't change nuthin'. Yer daddy is still a drunken good-fer-nuthin, and yer mamma's still a saucy one!" The boys' merriment was as loud as ever.

Thad raised his voice above theirs, "The most effective form of treatment of congenital *talipes equinovarus* for infants is orthopedic splints and..." calmly, articulately, and logically sharing what he had learned from the traveling physician.

The boys eventually turned their backs and wandered away, but this time no one had kicked Thad's walking stick. And this time he did not stumble into his house crying. Instead, he sat on a rock, lay his cane on the ground, and stared at the road ahead, for a long time.

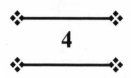

# 4

# Thad Learns About Education 1804

The Vermont winters that followed were long and raw, but the Stevens family managed to get by with enough food. Thad's mother had planted a few potatoes in the rocky soil behind the cabin; she harvested them, then stored them in the cool dirt cellar that she had dug just beyond.

There was plenty of milk, too, for several years: Thad's dad had brought a cow--they had named her Nelly--with him once when he had come home to visit. They housed Nelly in Ben's family's shed, in exchange for sewing that Thad's mother provided for Ben's mother. They fed Nelly with hay that they also had laid up in the shed.

From time to time the Reverend Adams even brought the family a freshly killed rabbit or squirrel that had been donated by a member of the congregation.

In the afternoons, when the light was bright enough, Joshua Junior would follow the steps to cobble a boot, as his father had demonstrated. Thad would imitate Joshua Junior's maneuvers with the straight last, but with less success. Too frustrated to concentrate on shoes, Thad often let his mind wander.

"Mother, what did James Fisk's dad do to become a famous person?"

"I think he's a member of the Vermont House of Representatives," she answered.

"What does House of Representatives mean?" he posed.

"I'm not really sure," was her reply.

"Where do laws come from?" was one of his common questions. His mom responded that she didn't really understand the process herself.

Most evenings, after a satisfying soup, Mrs. Stevens wrapped her boys in cozy coverlets, sat them in front of the toasty fire and haltingly read to them from the Bible. Baby Alanson usually was the first to succumb to the soothing sound--however faltering-- of his mother's speech, drifting into sleep. Thad usually was the first to scramble to a perch behind her shoulder and ask for the meanings of words. He also was the first to show off to his siblings his limited reading skills by taking over his mother's Bible recitations.

On a frozen February morning when Thad was almost twelve, he and his mother walked to the general store, while Joshua Junior and Abner stayed in the cabin to keep an eye on Baby Alanson. Sarah had sewn and delivered three aprons for the village innkeeper, and altered a new suit for the Reverend Adams, and stitched several gingham skirts for the Widow Murphy. Now she had a few coins to buy flour to make bread and biscuits.

"Mother, I miss Father," Thad ventured as he wobbled along the frost-encrusted cobblestone. "We had so much fun last summer when he took us to Boston. It was great to tour the Old State House, and to see where the Battle of Bunker Hill was fought, and to meet those old patriots who had rioted in the Boston Tea Party. My favorite part of the trip, though, was learning about the Boston Latin School, the first public school in America; I remember that Dad said it was founded in 1635, way back before I was born."

His mother answered, "Yes, it was a fine trip. It also was good that your father was able to buy us some dried fish and a block of salt to bring back.

"And don't forget the rum and tobacco!" Thad added joyfully. His mother lurched on the icy roadway, and she seized his arm to support them both.

"But, then, as soon as we got back home, he went away again." Thad's voice grew thin. "Why do you think he left, Mother? Do you think he will come back to live with us again soon? He promised us that next summer he would take us on a family trip down to New York." Thad and his mother tottered unsteadily on the slippery stones as they approached the mercantile.

Suddenly, a post rider burst past them. He slowed his steed just enough to toss his sack of mail to the man who appeared at the doorway of the store, and to receive a sack in exchange. When Thad and his mother entered the building, the storekeeper, who was Tom Martin's father, already was scanning the newest issue of *The Hartford Courant*, the weekly newspaper that arrived from Connecticut via St. Johnsbury. A few farmers were warming themselves around the Franklin stove. They had gathered to hear the news from one of the few Danvillians who could read.

"Them there slave owners down in Virginny and Maryland, they're gonna get ther come-uppance one o' these days, they are," Mr. Martin offered a teaser. After silently studying the paper, he summarized, "Looks like they're tryin' to catch their runaway slaves again, and, because of that there Fugitive Slave Act of 1793, they want good folks up here in northern states to cooperate in capturin' 'em and deliverin' 'em back to ther southern plantations."

Young Thad peered at Mr. Martin as he read directly: *"The U.S. Constitution guarantees the right of a slaveholder to recover an escaped slave. The Fugitive Slave Act of 1793 elaborates on that right. It stipulates that slave owners or their agents may arrest and return escaped slaves from any territory or state, provided that proof be given to a magistrate that the apprehended blacks are indeed fugitives. It empowers slaveholders to seize fugitives who have crossed state lines. The law makes every escaped slave a fugitive for life, unless manumitted by the owner, ... "*

At this phrase, Thad cocked his head and squinted his eyes.

The reader continued with his text, *"who can be recaptured at any time anywhere within the United States, along with any children subsequently born of enslaved mothers."* [1]

Mr. Martin punctuated with, "I say, 'Run, slaves, run! As fast as you can, and don't look back!'"

Ben Lewis' dad added, "Why, back in 1777, when us Vermonters constituted our own independent country, we totally abolished slavery. We even said all males--even Negro-folk--can vote. Way before we became the 14th state of the United States of America in 1791, we already knew that 'All men are created equal.'"

"Yeah, but ar U.S. lawmakers from Vermont, like Senator Israel Smith and Senator Stephen Bradley and Representative William Chamberlin--down there in Washington--they don't seem to believe that," remarked John Cook's dad. "They ain't doin' nuthin' to reverse that Fugitive Slave Law, and help the slaves. All they care about is gainin' power to tax decent law-abidin' citizens to pay for their high-flyin' salaries and their arguin' about what oughtta be controlled by federal government."

Thad inserted, "Mr. Martin, what does 'manumitted' mean?"

Mr. Martin looked up from the paper, noticing Thad and his mother. Ignoring the question, he added, "And them state legislators over in Windsor, they keep levyin' more taxes to pay for common schools. All's they wanna do is charge us to open more schools for waifs and paupers and them whose parents don't even take care of 'em. The government ain't got no business givin' out education, even if families do haf to pay half o' the bill. That academy they opened down in Peacham Corners in '97-- it's just a drain on the taxpayers' pocketbooks. Fer what good is it? Boys in these parts don't need no education."

"Mr. Martin, what does 'state legislators' mean?" Thad again interrupted.

"You wouldn't understand, there, kid."

"What about 'waifs?'" he tried again.

"I said you wouldn't understand this stuff," he persisted, his lips curling into a small grin. "Now, what do you want today, Mrs. Stevens?"

"In addition to my regular items, I'd like a cord of leather, so the boys can make some new boots for little Alanson; he has grown out of his already."

Thad studied Mr. Martin closely as he gathered the flour, eggs, thread, fabric, and leather, and penned on a pad of paper five prices. He watched him add the two columns, and jot a new number at the bottom.

"That'll be...." Mr. Martin began to say. But Sarah Stevens, also studying the ciphers, interjected. "I do believe you made an error there. Shouldn't this number here be a three instead of a four?"

"Well, yeah, I guess it should," he mumbled awkwardly. "My mistake."

Thad tried to carry his mother's basket of goods as his cane supported his shuffle along the icy street, but his mother, fearing for the safety of her eggs, took over. Thad thrust his lower lip forward. After that, he and his mother walked in silence.

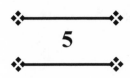

# 5

# Thad Challenges His Mother 1804

That afternoon, back in the Stevens's cabin, squirrel meat was stewing in the black kettle over the hearth. Mrs. Stevens was paring potatoes and dicing them into the pot. Joshua Junior was tinkering at the cobbler's bench that had been his father's in better times, trying to perfect his skill at stitching a straight seam. Abner and Alanson were sampling the still-warm biscuits from the tin on the table.

The flames from the fireplace were reflecting in Thad's eyes. He began to speak. "Mother, I want to learn how to read better and to write. I want to learn how to cipher numbers. I want to be able to understand the newspaper and learn about 'state legislators' and 'waifs' and 'manumitted.' I want to learn about the world. I want to go to school."

His mother remembered what the traveling physician had told her about her boys being sharp-minded, and his recommendation that they get an education. She knew he was right.

"It's not fair," Thad whined. "Why can't everyone be allowed to know what's happening in Washington and Virginny and Maryland? Why do we have to have secrets that some people can't know about?

"Thad, you are right; education is a good thing," his mother reassured him, "but there are no schools near here."

"But, Mother," he countered. "I heard Mr. Martin say there's a school in Peacham."

"That's over seven miles from here," his mother argued. "Maybe someday, in a few years, we will have a school in Danville."

"But I want to learn NOW!" Thad was adamant.

His mother explained again why schooling for him would be impractical--in fact, impossible--at least in the near future. For a long time, though, Thad insisted that his mother enroll him in school, offering many arguments to carry his case.

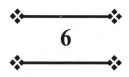

# 6

## Thad Stumbles onto a Solution 1805

With the first robin sighting in April came a knock on the Stevens's door. It was Sarah's young cousin, James Morrill, dropping in to wish Thad a happy 13th birthday. James reported that he had spent the day in St. Johnsbury, where he had purchased a new axe blade and a new plow to fell trees and till soil on his newly purchased farm. Thad and his brothers were delighted when their mom invited her cousin to stay for a dinner of venison and beets--and overnight--before resuming his journey.

After the boys helped their mother clear the empty dishes from the table, they joined James in relaxing near the hearth. James elaborated to his relatives about plans for his farm in South Danville, a town a bit larger than Danville; he told them about the crops--corn, beans, and peas—that he would be growing. He informed them of his intention to raise a flock of chickens and a few cows. James added that he wished he had a good wife who would keep house for him.

Later, while Cousin James entertained Abner and Baby Alanson with a game of Hide-and-Seek, Thad was thinking. He remembered that his mother had lost a good part of her seamstress income since the inn had closed right after Christmas. He remembered that since Nelly Cow had died in February, he and his brothers had not had a regular supply of milk. He also remembered that South Danville was about five miles closer to the school in Peacham!

Thad was the first to propose that his family move to South Danville to live with Cousin James on his farm. Mother, naturally, could cook, sew, and launder for all of them, he advocated, with more food than was available here in Danville. Abner and 'Baby'

Alanson were old enough and strong enough to help with plowing and planting and harvesting. Joshua Junior was getting good at making shoes, so he could sell them in the new community, and Thad himself could help his mother in the kitchen--in addition to attending school, of course.

The adult cousins hesitated about approving so dramatic a change in their lives. Before long, however, they agreed that the move would be a gain for everyone involved. Well into the night, Thad and his family excitedly discussed plans for packing their belongings, leaving word of their whereabouts with neighbors for when Joshua Senior would come to see them, and migrating down the corduroy road toward Peacham Academy.

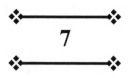

# 7

# Thad Hobbles to School 1805

The two oldest Stevens brothers, already able to demonstrate the required basic reading and arithmetic skills that they had learned from their mother, were easily admitted into Peacham Academy, also known as the Caledonia Grammar School. Because they were residents of Caledonia County, tuition was free, but other fees totaled one shilling per term. Their mother paid those costs as her first priority when she earned a few coins by sewing for her new neighbors.

Thad was delighted to trek only one and one-half miles along the Bayley-Hazen Military Road between his new home and his school two times a day. Thirteen years old himself, he had about one hundred schoolmates from ages 8 to 20.

During one of Thad's first weeks at school his class took a spelling test. "Lame duck," Schoolmaster Wilcox recited. "President John Adams was a 'lame duck' president from election day in November, 1800, until Thomas Jefferson took office on March 4, 1801. Lame duck."

Thad was shocked by this new information! Before he knew it, his mouth was calling to the teacher: "Does that mean President Adams had a clubfoot like me?"

The class exploded in laughter.

"No, Master Stevens," replied the schoolmaster, icily. "President Adams did not have a clubfoot like you." Thad's classmates struggled to suppress their amusement. "On the contrary," the schoolmaster clarified, "a lame duck is an elected official who is passing the short time between the election of his successor and the day that his successor will take his office. He no longer carries the power or respect that comes with his office. Hence, he is lame, like a duck who is a cripple."

Thad's lower lip quivered; he focused his eyes on the floor, slid deep into his seat, and mentally closed his ears to the seemingly endless din in the classroom.

After that, Thad was not interested in finding friends at his school. To the other students, in fact, the feeling was mutual. They chuckled when he tried to run and tripped over his clubfoot; they cackled when he attempted, clumsily, to join his schoolmates in a game of horseshoes; they chortled when he stuck out his lower lip like a pouting toddler. They labeled Thad as disagreeable, stubborn, and obnoxious.

Thad quickly discovered that Schoolmaster Wilcox was stern and demanding. Thad witnessed some of his schoolmates being expelled for violating the strict behavior code. Blasphemy, perjury, cursing, tavern tippling, card games, and dice games were among the banned activities. Everyone who attended the school was expected to be in his bed by 9:00 in the evening. Another regulation forbade students from performing a tragedy play by candlelight.

Even though Thad thought the rule against performing a play by candlelight was bizarre, he, in general, did not care about the regulations. The only thing he did care about was learning. He began to study grammar, spelling, Latin, and arithmetic. He mined his books as if he had discovered the motherlode, partly because he was required to participate regularly in exhibitions of his knowledge, but mostly because he just wanted to know!

One afternoon following dismissal, Thad, to distract himself from the weary way home, was examining the architecture of the local buildings. As he trudged through the town, he was staring at a large and beautiful house when a man leaned out of the window and shouted to him, "Well, my boy, do you think you are in Paradise?"

Thad retorted, "I did until I saw the devil looking out of the window."[2]

The gentleman laughed heartily, came outside, and congratulated Thad for his quick wit. He introduced himself as Judge John Mattocks. They bantered for a while, and the judge invited Thad to call on him if he ever needed anything. Thad made a mental note to do that.

Thad searched at Peacham Academy for a physical activity that needed neither friends nor teammates, and in which his mangled foot would be no handicap. He eventually found a sport that called to him: horsemanship. He began in earnest to work with the instructor. He wanted to learn how to manage a horse, so that one day he could ride, instead of hobble, to where he wanted to go.

Two years later, Cousin James married, so the Stevens family moved from James' homestead to another small farm, known as the Graham Place, which was even closer to the school. Thad was thrilled to be able to continue his studies more conveniently. In fact, now that he and his brothers shared a larger room, he organized a library in his home, from which he lent books to his schoolmates and neighbors.

Tucked inside one of his books, Thad found a folded rendering of the Constitution of the United States of America, which he studied day and night. He was spellbound by the structure of the government of the 31-year-old United States: three branches of government—Legislative, Executive, Judicial; two chambers of the Legislative, or lawmaking, branch—Senate and House of Representatives, together known as Congress; terms of service— six years for Senators, two years for Representatives; Executive branch led by the president and his cabinet of advisors; Judicial branch headed by the Supreme Court; powers and duties assigned to each branch; system of checks and balances among the branches. He was struck by the Bill of Rights enumerating all citizens' rights in ten amendments; the right to trial by jury; the right to life, liberty, and pursuit of happiness; the ratification process for subsequent amendments. Thad devoured all of it whenever he finished his school assignments!

At night, he frequently dreamed of standing in a courtroom, unfolding unarguable arguments to twelve fascinated faces. In his dreams, he had no cane, and two perfectly formed and functioning feet.

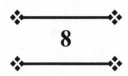

# 8

# Thad Meets Mortality 1810

Over time, several boys who were repeat borrowers of Thad's books would initiate conversation with him about a volume they returned or sought. Thad himself soon felt comfortable enough to offer comments. By the time he was 18, he had formed a few friendships at the academy.

One evening, Thad and a fellow student decided to celebrate their good fortune at having achieved a perfect score on a killer Latin test. The partiers met at the Jonathan Elkins Tavern in Peacham, and each drank a pint of ale. Thad's companion, however, dared to down several more; he became quite inebriated. He was unable to walk to his boarding house, so Thad carried him, struggling with his weighty burden, his own limp leg, and his cumbersome cane, all at the same time. He rested his classmate on the settee in the landlady's parlor. Within minutes, Thad witnessed his classmate's death.

Thad was traumatized. He pushed his way out of the home, staggered to Graham Place, and retreated to his room, where he sobbed on his pillow for a long time. When he awoke, he despondently told his family what had happened. He vowed to his mother, "I will never again risk my life by drinking alcohol."

Although Thad indeed had broken the rule about tavern tippling, he managed to maintain the focus and sympathy of the trustees toward his unfortunate deceased friend. Thus, he escaped attention to himself, and expulsion from Peacham Academy.

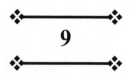

# 9

# Thad Escapes Expulsion - Again 1811

When Thad was 19, he had studied for six years at Peacham Academy; he was ready for graduation. Several days before his scheduled commencement, he and a dozen other students were expected to present their exhibition, a play, early in the day, to an audience of the trustees. Thad and his buddies, instead, in an act of defiance, chose not to appear. The officials grew impatient and angry as they waited, and finally left the theater. To make matters worse, the would-be graduates chose to perform their play later that evening, after dark, in a field near the school, blatantly breaking the rule against performing a play-- a tragedy-- by candlelight.

The irate officials, when they learned of the further insolence, voted to expel the thirteen actors. Ultimately, though, they calmed themselves, and demanded, instead, that each of the young men sign an apology-- or be denied his diploma.

Thad considered his options, and then stubbornly asserted, "I will not apologize for presenting a play in the evening."

His friends had a different notion; they promptly signed, and thanked their benefactors for their mercy.

Thad soon relented. "Okay, I'll sign, but I won't mean it," he begrudgingly muttered. He graduated with his class from Peacham Academy, as scheduled, on September 5, 1811.

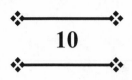

# 10

# Thad Tackles College 1812

Thad announced, "Mother, my goal is to become a lawyer."

Sarah calculated that the cost of sending him to college would be approximately $150 for his first year. Having recognized her son's longing, she already had been saving money for his education.

With her encouragement, Thad applied for admission to Dartmouth College, a new school in Hanover, New Hampshire. To be admitted to Dartmouth, he took exams in arithmetic and Greek, and he translated English passages into Latin. Many students often studied for a year before taking the entrance tests; for Thad, it was a piece of cake. His scores were so high that he was invited to skip his freshman courses, and to begin college as a sophomore.

As soon as Thad received word that he was accepted at Dartmouth, he traveled forty-two miles by horseback to his new state and his new school. The money his mother had given him was enclosed in a leather pouch his brother had crafted for him. He found a room in a private household, which he rented for $15 for the year. The college supplied meals at $1.20 per week. Tuition was $20 a term. He used the remainder of his cash for his books and other expenses.

Thad found the curriculum at Dartmouth to be both rigorous and rigid. In spite of the fact that he wanted to study law, he had to follow the same course as his one hundred classmates. He invested most of his time boosting his knowledge of Latin and Greek, and the rest of his time learning grammar, logic, geometry, algebra, trigonometry, surveying, astronomy, and philosophy—everything but law.

During his first term, Thad heard that during the 8-week winter break many students typically returned to their country schools to teach. He decided to try it, too. Like his classmates, he was easily hired, via written correspondence.

At the end of the term, he ventured back to Vermont to teach at Peacham Academy and earn some dollars. After reporting his college adventures to his brothers, Thad quietly asked his mother, "Have I missed a visit from father?"

"I have nothing to tell you," she answered sadly.

As Thad was approaching the close of his first year in college, he read in *The Dartmouth*, the school newspaper, that the United States had declared war against Great Britain because of shipping issues. Congress was calling it the War of 1812. Thad was concerned when he saw that fighting had erupted between the British forces just across the border in Canada, and the U.S. Army in the northeast, near where he was attending college.

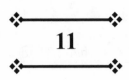

# 11

## Thad Escapes Expulsion - for the Third Time 1813

For Thad's junior year, hoping to study the subject of his choice, he applied to transfer to University of Vermont, in Burlington. Again, he easily met the admission requirements, including that he prove himself to be of good moral character and that he pass exams in Latin and Greek, including four speeches of Cicero, six books of Aenid, and the gospels of Matthew, Mark, Luke, and John.

For the most part, Thad cooperated this year with the rules at the college, including that he attend chapel every Sunday--morning and evening. As always, he found easy academic success.

During winter break Thad again returned to Peacham to teach. Again, he asked his mother for news of his father. This time, she solemnly shared that a soldier, who had fought under a General Winfield Scott in the October Battle of Queenston Heights in Canada, reported to a neighbor that a Joshua Stevens from Danville, Vermont, had been killed in battle. Thad sat by the hearth, the warmth drained from it, his lower lip protruding, for a long time.

When Thad returned to college, he scripted a play, 'The Fall of Helvetic Liberty.' His professors were impressed, and they invited him to produce it. He scheduled the performance for the day before commencement, for an audience of the senior class.

Thad and a friend were scurrying to Johnson House for a rehearsal of his play. "You must put more emotion into your portrayal of Napoleon. You must demonstrate his sagacity…," Thad was advising. He was so focused on his production that he didn't notice the wedge of cow manure into which he slammed his cane. The cane slipped through the slop, his mangled foot entangled in the cane, and down he went.

"These damned farmers and their unholy cows!" Thad wildly wailed, as his companion helped to wipe the goo and the stench from his trousers. "It's high time our Burlington neighbors respected our property and kept their bloody bovines and their repulsive cow-pies off this campus. The filthy farmers don't even take heed to the authorities' notice about possible consequences," he ranted, his lower lip curled into a snarl.

"We ought to give the creature a consequence," conspired Napoleon's player, as the pair spied the suspected perpetrator grazing nearby.

After dark, following rehearsal, Thad and his comrade returned to the scene, now with an axe they had boldly borrowed from a fellow student-- a senior who was about to graduate. They found the cow under an elm tree and approached her. "May she graze on green grass in the great pasture in the sky," they intoned.

A few minutes later, they speculated, "That will teach our farmer friends to honor our college campus." Then they brusquely bolted back to their rooms.

Thad lay awake for a long time that night, contemplating what he had done, and already regretting it.

Early the next morning, the cow carcass was discovered, and the nearby gory axe was gathered as evidence. When the owner of the instrument of brutality was identified, the university president pronounced the senior unfit to receive his diploma!

Witnessing the results of their actions, Thad and his compatriot agonized about how they could reconcile their situation, and that of their innocent schoolmate, with no one being expelled.

At length, they approached the owner of the cow and confessed their guilt. "If you help us," they promised, "we will pay you two times the value of the cow we slew."

The farmer agreed to their proposition, and staged "new evidence" that British soldiers in the area had used the axe to kill the cow. Thus, the trustees cleared the accused student and allowed him to graduate, and Thad and his actor friend escaped notice.

Relieved, they, as agreed, paid the farmer. A few weeks later, Thad and his friend received a hogshead of Vermont cider from the man in return.

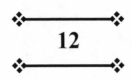

# 12

# Thad Completes College 1814

Thad was getting ready to return to University of Vermont for his senior year, when he was notified that U.S. troops had taken over the college, and the school was closing to students. The Army had determined that the campus was a desirable location for them to set up a base of operations to sustain the soldiers fighting the British, just across the border in Canada.

Thad's only choice was to return to Dartmouth College. The school now permitted him to drop his studies of the classics to learn about philosophy, theology, speechmaking, and his favorite- -political law.

Thad's compulsory routine was harsh: He appeared at the unheated chapel at 5:00 every morning. Next, he was expected to contribute in recitation. Finally, he joined his classmates for breakfast, then study period. He participated in a second recitation at 11:00, and then another period of study. He attended afternoon classes beginning at 3:00, and at last joined the student body for prayers at 6:00.

Thad spent as much time as he could practicing and perfecting composition and public speaking. His routine included speech delivery every Wednesday. He performed impeccably in the quick give and take of debate, discovering that his brilliant use of language illuminated the room.

As a senior, he was excused from classes on Saturday afternoons, but on Sundays his attendance at chapel was demanded in both the morning and the afternoon.

During winter break this year, instead of returning to Peacham, Thad joined classmate Samuel Merrill in traveling to Calais, Maine, where they worked as instructors at a boys' academy. Of the lessons Thad taught, his favorite was 'How a Bill Becomes a Law.' On large slates he prepared diagrams with boxes and arrows to illustrate the process for his students.

"For a bill to become a law," he lectured, "it must be approved by the U.S. Senate, the U.S. House of Representatives, and the U.S. President.

"A bill starts as someone's idea," he proceeded. "That person writes a letter to his representative in the House. The representative may choose to write and sponsor the bill. If so, he talks to other representatives about it, in hopes of getting support.

"The next time the House meets," Thad continued, "the representative introduces the bill by placing it in a box called the hopper. The clerk assigns the bill a number, which, because it was introduced in the House of Representatives, begins with H.R. The bill is read to all the representatives, and it is sent to one of the House committees. Each committee is made up of representatives who become specialists on a topic. The committee may make changes to the bill, and then vote to accept or reject the changes. If the committee rejects the changes, they may send it to a subcommittee for research. The subcommittee collects expert opinions on the bill. Based on this information, the subcommittee makes changes in the bill and sends it back to the committee. When the committee approves the updated bill, they send it to the House membership.

"Now the bill is ready to be voted on by the House. Representatives vote 'yea' (if they back the bill), 'nay' (if they are against it), or 'present' (if they don't wish to vote on the bill). If more than one half of the representatives vote 'yea', the bill has passed in the House.

"Next, the bill is sent to the Senate, where it goes through many of the steps it went through in the House. The bill is discussed in a Senate committee. Then the senators vote on the bill. If a majority of senators vote 'yea', the bill has passed in the Senate.

"Now the bill is sent to the president. He has ten days to decide what to do with it. He has three choices: sign it, veto it, or pocket it.

"If the president chooses to sign the bill, it becomes a law.

"If the president refuses to sign, or vetoes the bill, he sends it, with his reasons for vetoing it, back to the House. The bill may yet become a law, however. The House and the Senate can vote on the bill again. This time, if two-thirds or more of the senators and representatives support the bill, the president's veto is overridden, and the bill now becomes a law. If less than two-thirds of the representatives and senators support the bill, it does not become a law. The bill has reached the end of its journey.

"If the president chooses to do nothing," Thad closed, "he 'places the bill in his pocket.' The president may want to do this if he is expecting an adjournment of Congress within ten days. That way, he is actually effectively vetoing the bill, but without taking the chance that Congress might override his veto. Thus, he has killed the bill." [3]

The school trustees in Maine were pleased with the teaching of Thad and Samuel, and they paid them generously. When Thad returned to Dartmouth, he applied all of the cash he had earned toward his tuition bills, and he began his final term of studies.

Thaddeus Stevens graduated from Dartmouth College in August 1814, after only three years of study. Like many of his classmates, he still owed the school a significant sum of money. Leaning on his cane, Thad signed an interest-bearing note before his diploma was given to him.

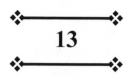

# 13

# Thad at Last Learns Law 1815

After the commencement, Thad returned to Peacham, where he promptly was hired, again, as an instructor at his first alma mater. His next order of business was to contact his old friend, Judge John Mattocks, the 'devil' who had yelled to him from his window on the main street of Peacham ten years earlier. Thad explained to the judge that his plan was, in addition to teaching, to pursue his interest in law, and would the judge consider advising him as to how to study?

Thad felt honored that Judge Mattocks consented to serve as his mentor. The judge shared his books with him, assigned him readings, and then conducted recitations with him, on evenings and weekends. Studying his assigned text, *A Manual of Parliamentary Practice for the Use of the Senate of the United States,* written by Thomas Jefferson in 1801, Thad was intrigued to learn, among other procedures, the process for impeachment of a U.S. president.

The Constitution empowers Congress, Thad learned, to remove a president from office on impeachment for and conviction of "treason, bribery, or other high crimes and misdemeanors."

Judge Mattocks noted that leading legal minds interpreted the Constitution to mean that Congress may decide for itself what constitutes an impeachable offense. "An impeachable offense is whatever a majority of the House of Representatives considers it to be at a given moment in history," he emphasized.

Thad recited, during his examination by the judge: "Jefferson's *Manual* states that impeachment of a president is set in motion by charges made by the House of Representatives. The charges may rise from facts reported by an investigating committee of the House.

   "The impeachment process is a two-step procedure," Thad
progressed. "The House must first pass articles of impeachment,
which constitute the formal allegations.

   "Next, the Senate tries the accused. To convict the accused, a two-
thirds majority vote of the senators present is required. Conviction
automatically removes the president from office."[4]

   Passing his examination with flying colors, Thad mused to
his instructor that he could not imagine a time when impeaching
a president of the United States would be an advisable course
of action.

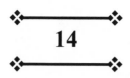

# 14

# Thad Aces the Bar Exam 1816

Several months later, Thad's reading about Constitutional law was interrupted when his mother handed him some mail that had been delivered to the Peacham Post Office. It was from Samuel Merrill, who had been a member of his study group at Dartmouth.

Samuel had moved to York, Pennsylvania. His letter encouraged Thad to join him there; it reassured him that he would have lots of opportunity to learn law and practice it 'here in York.' In the meantime, he mentioned, Thad could teach at the York Academy, a boys' school, which was advertising for a teacher.

So, assuring his mother and brothers that he would write frequently, Thad headed south in February 1815. His exciting new town had paved sidewalks. The brick buildings were more modern than the lumber structures in New England. Thad had a feeling that he was beginning a great adventure in his life.

After he settled in, Thad asked his friend why the families, instead of the communities, paid tuition for the schooling.

Samuel clarified, "York Academy is a private school, attended by boys whose parents can afford the tuition. Public schools for the poor have been available here in Pennsylvania since 1790; however, few students enroll in these schools, also known as pauper schools, because parents are reluctant to publicize their poverty by signing the necessary papers. Many destitute families prefer to say that their children have no need for education."

Thad reacted with a puzzled expression.

At the York Academy, Mr. Stevens sat on a platform and heard student recitations from a primer. He taught his students English, Latin, Greek, science, mathematics, and moral values. When the pupils misbehaved, the schoolmaster freely administered corporal punishment.

At the same time, Thad pursued his individualized study of law with the help of a distinguished local attorney, David Cassat. By August of 1816, Mr. Cassat certified that Thad was prepared to take the examination for admission to the bar association. Membership in the bar association would make him an official lawyer in Pennsylvania!

Thad discovered, however, that the York County Bar Association recently had passed some new rules: One specified that to be admitted to the group, an applicant must have lived in York for longer than he had; another one regulated that an applicant may not have practiced any other profession while studying for the bar exam.

Thad's friend Samuel told him he suspected that the bar association had enacted the rules just to prevent Thad from becoming a lawyer. "They are jealous of your intelligence, and feel threatened by your potential for attracting their clients," he surmised.

Nevertheless, Thad knew he had to look elsewhere for admission. He knew that Pennsylvania exercised an agreement with Maryland, such that a lawyer certified in one state could practice law in the other state as well. He decided he would take the test in Bel Air, Maryland, just across the border, and he made an appointment for September 14. With $45 in his pocket, he journeyed to Bel Air on his horse, Morgan. Promptly at 7:30 p.m., Thad presented himself to the evaluating panel.

Thad and the committee dined together, and then the head judge asked him, "Are you the young man who is to be examined?" Thad eagerly nodded.

The judge continued, "Mr. Stevens, there is one indispensable prerequisite before the examination can proceed. There must be two bottles of Madeira wine on the table, and the applicant must provide them." Thad laughed and hurriedly shuffled to the nearest tavern to secure the wine.

Another gentleman asked Thad what law books he had read, to which he responded impressively. A few more questions by others followed.

Presently, the lead judge was thirsty again; he interrupted, "Gentlemen, you can see this candidate is all right. I will give him a certificate." He signed the certificate, then addressed Thad: "I cannot hand it over to you until you have delivered two more bottles of wine."

The newest lawyer, the judges, and other witnesses then celebrated. They drank the wine--with Thad pretending to imbibe--, munched on fresh bread and cheese, and played cards during most of the night. When the sun rose, Thad had only $3.50 left, but he was ecstatic. He signed a document affirming his belief in the Christian religion, and now he officially was permitted to practice law in Maryland and Pennsylvania!

Smiling broadly, Attorney Stevens saddled Morgan and set out for Pennsylvania to find a place to start his law practice. He approached the new bridge at McCall's Ferry, where he would cross the Susquehanna River. Morgan suddenly shied as he encountered the bridge, unhinged for repairs. Losing his balance, he stumbled toward the swiftly moving water. A workman impulsively grabbed the horse's reins and pulled him back, saving both horse and rider from death by drowning.

Thad breathlessly thanked the worker, and made his way to the next town, Lancaster, where he settled Morgan in a livery stable to recover from the traumatic incident. He then rejoiced in his own good fortune by spending his last $3.50 on dinner at the Conestoga Inn, on the east edge of King Street.

Thad asked the innkeeper, Abraham Witmer, if Lancaster was a good place to live.

"I love Lancaster!" Mr. Witmer gushed. "Our town is the seat of one of the wealthiest counties in Pennsylvania, and it is surrounded by rich farmland. Lancaster was settled in 1718--almost one hundred years ago--and we served as the capital of the state from 1799 until 1812."

He pointed through a window to the span across the Conestoga River. "We built that toll bridge just 15 years ago, so now we have easy access to Philadelphia," he added. "This improvement alone has been bringing much more business and industry to the Lancaster community."

After dinner, Thad limped from the east end of King Street to the west end, noting to himself that he was in a fine and prosperous place. He observed regular streets crossing at right angles. He spied a jail, a marketplace, a brick courthouse at the center square, churches of all denominations, and taverns with clever names. He saw signs directing visitors to Franklin College and to a museum. He spotted a building with 'Masonic Hall, Lodge No. 43' imprinted on its façade; puzzled, he jotted, "Note to self: Research 'Masonic

Lodge No. 43.'"

Thad, leaning on his spruce cane, made his way back to the barn where he had stabled his horse. He reflected about whether he should establish himself here. At length, decided this thriving setting of Lancaster was not for him. He needed to begin in a more modest and less privileged place-- something like Gettysburg, he thought. Heading west and crossing the river again, Attorney Stevens went to his home in York to spend the night.

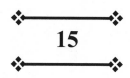

# 15

# Thad Launches His Law Practice 1816

The next morning, Thad departed for Gettysburg, the seat of Adams County, Pennsylvania, to establish his law practice. He rented a room in which to sleep, and a room in which to practice law. He placed an ad in the local paper: "Thaddeus Stevens, Attorney at Law, has opened an office in the Gettysburg Hotel…"

But no one in Gettysburg seemed to need a new lawyer! Weeks and months went by, during which Thad represented very few clients. The cases that did come his way tended to be unimportant. As he plodded between his office and his rooming house, he became more and more discouraged.

In the spring, Thad, at age 24, was watching others dancing at a church social. Leaning on his walking cane, he confided to his friend Samuel, "I am ready to 'hang it up' in Gettysburg. I am thinking seriously of moving to another city."

Then, in the summer, a tragic event occurred: A Gettysburg farmhand named James Hunter killed a fellow laborer, Henry Heagy, with a scythe. Mr. Hunter had become enraged when Mr. Heagy's father earlier had called him names and helped to arrest him. Charged with murder, James Hunter asked several attorneys to defend him, but they all declined because they believed they surely would lose the case.

James Hunter then asked the hungry young attorney, Mr. Stevens, to defend him. Thad accepted. He tried to reduce the charge from premeditated murder to involuntary manslaughter, claiming the defendant's decision to maim the victim was spur-of-the-moment. But Thad was unsuccessful. His client was found guilty, condemned, and executed.

The judge and jury, and others in the courtroom, nevertheless, commended Attorney Stevens for his handling of the case. "Your arguments," they flattered, "were inspired, eloquent, forceful, and witty." They spread the word that he had done an excellent job!

"At last!" Thad sighed. "Finally, my law practice will grow by leaps and bounds." And he was right.

One of his first acts with his real income was to replace his spruce-limb walking stick with a cane fashioned from polished maple and sporting a silver handle—just like the one carried by the doctor he had met that long ago Sunday in Danville, Vermont.

Thad continued to be hired as a competent and ever more successful Gettysburg lawyer. In 1819, five years following his graduation from Dartmouth College, Thad sent the last of the money he owed to the school. As he passed his banknote to the postmaster, he embarrassed himself by dancing a little jig, and tripping over his silver-plated cane.

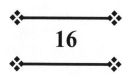

# 16

# Thad Sells Out a Slave 1821

In 1821, a Maryland slaveholder, John Delaplaine, brought an appealing case to Attorney Stevens. Mr. Delaplaine angrily stated that he owned a slave named Charity, who, several years ago, had escaped to Pennsylvania, married a free Negro named Henry Butler, and now had two daughters. She periodically traveled to Maryland with her free husband.

Thad was very much aware that for the past several years many slaves had been escaping from their owners in Maryland, fleeing north to the border, and crossing into Gettysburg. He also knew that Pennsylvania never did tolerate slavery. In fact, state laws had been passed in 1780 and 1788, pronouncing that if runaway slaves arrived safely in Pennsylvania and stayed for more than six months, they could declare themselves free. When Maryland slave owners found that their slaves had fled to Pennsylvania, they usually tried desperately to retrieve them before the six months had passed.

"I caught up with Charity Butler, and took her and her two children back to Maryland," Mr. Delaplaine revealed. "Now her husband is claiming freedom for her and her daughters, saying they had lived in Pennsylvania for more than six months. He also is claiming that the girls never were slaves. I want my slaves back. I am signing you, Mr. Stevens, to win them back for me."

Thad accepted the challenge. He argued before the Gettysburg court that the residence of Charity had not been continuous, as a result of her periodic visits to Maryland. Thad interpreted for the court that uninterrupted residence was the requirement by the Pennsylvania law. At first he lost the case, but then he argued all the way to the state Supreme Court, and finally won.

Attorney Stevens watched as Charity and her children wept uncontrollably as they were peeled from husband and father, and shoved into a carriage to be returned to Maryland to live again as slaves.

Suddenly, the evil of Thad's deed slapped him in his face: His work was loathsome and indefensible!

He did not sleep well for a long time after that—not until he decided how he would atone for what he had done to Charity Butler: He resolved, from then on, to defend, for free, any slaves who fled from Maryland to Pennsylvania, were caught, and were being forced to return to the South.

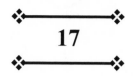

# 17

## Thad Buys a Slave 1821

Shortly after that, Attorney Stevens folded $300 into his leather pouch, and was on his way to Baltimore to buy some books. He stopped for lunch at a Hagerstown, Maryland hotel, where he knew the owner. A slave took his horse to the stable to feed him.

When Thad limped into the hotel, a crying slave woman told him that the man outside who was caring for Morgan was her husband, and that the owner was going to sell him. She begged, "Please, Mr. Stevens! Don't let your friend sell my husband!"

Thad talked to the master. "Are you not ashamed to sell a human being and separate him from his family forever?" he asked.

The innkeeper replied that he didn't want to sell him, but he needed the money.

Thad, remembering his resolution to help to free slaves, offered, "I will pay you $150, half of the going price, for the slave."

The innkeeper hesitated.

"Fine! I'll give you the full price," Thad yielded. He immediately set his new purchase free.

The man traveled to Pennsylvania as a manumitted person, committed to earning money and returning to buy freedom for his wife. Thad returned to Gettysburg without his books. But he slept very peacefully that night!

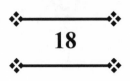

# 18

## Thad Pursues Politics 1824

By 1824, Thad, as a result of reading newspapers and listening to speeches and talking to colleagues, had become interested in state and national politics.

He read about a Tennessee lawyer and slave owner named Andrew Jackson, and his followers who called themselves Jacksonian Democrats. Thad learned that these Democrats sympathized with the slave owners, and that they believed that blacks were inferior to whites, and therefore blacks should be slaves for whites, and should hold no legal rights. Thad instantly and bitterly disliked Andrew Jackson and his Democrats.

Thad also heard about John Quincy Adams, who was from Massachusetts. Mr. Adams led a group who believed that slavery was wrong. They called themselves Anti-Jacksonians. Naturally, Thad joined the Anti-Jacksonians, and did everything he could to spread support for them.

Before long, Andrew Jackson and John Quincy Adams were running against each other for U.S. president.

Thad talked to his friends and neighbors. "Let me tell you why you want to vote for Mr. Adams," he began.

"Excuse me," he interrupted strangers as they entered or left work at the carriage-making shops. "I'd like to tell you why I am favoring John Quincy Adams for president."

"Are you aware that Andrew Jackson holds non-Christian beliefs?" he informed worshipers as they entered or left the Presbyterian, Methodist, and Catholic churches.

"The Democrats do not uphold the U.S. Constitution," he lectured to students who were entering or leaving the Gettysburg Academy and the Lutheran Theological Seminary.

"Good evening! Have you been following the race for president?" he initiated conversation with guests in the lobby of the Gettysburg Hotel.

Many of these citizens agreed that Thad made good points. They indicated that they would vote for John Quincy Adams.

Following Election Day, Thad read in *The Gettysburg Compiler* that John Quincy Adams had received the most votes, becoming the sixth president of the United States.

Thad beamed. He congratulated himself for having helped President Adams to win. He resolved that he would persist in assisting political candidates who shared his own moral convictions.

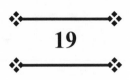

# 19

# Thad Advocates Abolition 1826

Thad was dismayed a short time later to read in the Gettysburg newspaper that slavery was popular and profitable even in the nation's capital, Washington, D.C. He was disgusted to learn that many U.S. congressmen themselves owned slaves, many of whom were serving their masters in their city residences, and were transported during legislative breaks back to labor on their plantations and farms, then back again to D.C. to work when the new lawmaking sessions began. Thad decided that Washington was the first place where slavery must be abolished. He told his friends and his colleagues what he thought.

In March, 1826, Thad read another news report that, in his mind, was a good beginning. The article quoted a law that had just been passed in Harrisburg. It was named the Pennsylvania Fugitive Slave Act. This law forbade bringing an enslaved person into Pennsylvania to work, and it forbade returning a runaway slave to his 'owner' in another state, six months or no six months. Thad applauded the new law.

He noted, however, that this new Pennsylvania law did seem to contradict the federal Fugitive Slave Act of 1793, and the U.S. Constitution, as well. He elaborated at a Gettysburg Bar Association meeting: "The federal Fugitive Slave Act requires, simply, that fleeing slaves be returned to their owners, in whatever state." He continued, "Article IV of the U.S. Constitution also states that a person who is charged in any state with a crime, and flees from justice, and is found in another state, must be delivered back to the state having jurisdiction of the case." He added, "And in those 'other' states, slaves are guilty of a crime when they escape from the state."

Thad concocted a hypothetical scenario: A slave escapes from Maryland to Pennsylvania. Someone captures that slave, with the goal of returning him to his master, to receive a reward. The state of Pennsylvania notes that the capturer has broken Pennsylvania law, captures the capturer, and finds him guilty of violating the Pennsylvania Fugitive Slave Act of 1826.

"Now, what would happen," Thad wondered aloud, "if that capturer appeals to the federal law, saying that the Pennsylvania law is unconstitutional, that the U.S. Constitution does not allow for a state to interfere with the slave trade?"

Thad concluded that an appropriate amendment must be made to the Constitution. His audience reflected on his message.

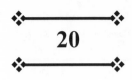

# 20

# Thad Defies the Masons 1826, 1827

Besides slaveholders, Thad began to disrespect another group--the Freemasons, also known as the Masons. Having satisfied his curiosity about the Masons following his 1816 visit to Lancaster, Thad knew that the Masons were members of a secret society who met frequently and demonstrated intense loyalty to each other. He learned that they admitted only wealthy, prominent, and 'physically undamaged' men into their group. He voiced that he did not trust the Masons because of their secrecy and their sense of elitism.

Then, in September 1826, Thad followed an unsettling news story about a man named William Morgan, who disappeared after he tried to join the Masons. According to the newspaper article, Mr. Morgan had been angry when members in Batavia, New York, declined his application for admission to the group. Mr. Morgan then announced that he would publish a book entitled *Illustrations of Masonry*, which would be critical of the Masons and would describe their secret activities in great detail. He disclosed that he had learned these secrets from a former Mason, David Miller.

Some members of the Masons responded to Mr. Morgan's and Mr. Miller's 'betrayal' by publishing an advertisement blasting them. In addition, several attempts were made to set fire to Mr. Miller's printing office.

The account continued on September 11, when a group of Masons gathered at William Morgan's home, claiming that he owed them money. The sheriff, who accompanied the group, arrested Mr. Morgan, to hold him in debtors' prison until the debt was paid. Later that night, Thad read, someone appeared at the jail, identifying himself as a friend of Mr. Morgan and offering to pay his debt and have him released. Mr. Morgan next was taken to a carriage that was waiting for him. And then... he disappeared!

Thad—and others to whom he talked--came to a conclusion: They believed that the Masons killed William Morgan to prevent him from publishing the revealing book. Thad and his associates denounced the Masons; they pressed for the elimination of all Masonic lodges. They formed an Anti-Masonic movement, which rapidly developed into the Anti-Masonic political party.

During the next year, Thad found himself in a court case arguing against an attorney from Lancaster. His opponent's name was James Buchanan. Thad had heard of James Buchanan before; he knew that Mr. Buchanan was a Jacksonian Democrat who was not interested in eliminating slavery. In addition to that, he was a prominent Mason!

While the jury was deliberating, the two attorneys, one leaning on a silver-handled cane, took a stroll down a lane together and sat on a fence. Mr. Buchanan, as he lit his cigar, remarked, "Mr. Stevens, everyone can see that you are a brilliant attorney. May I suggest that you join the Democratic party? We then will be willing to help you to get elected to public office."

Thad did not think long before he replied sharply, "No, thank you, Mr. Buchanan! I will not be changing my views on slavery or Freemasonry."

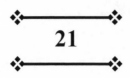

# 21

## Thad Is Elected to Public Office 1833

In 1832, Thad involved himself again in the presidential election contest. Three candidates appeared on the final ballot:

Andrew Jackson was the leader of the Jacksonian Democrats whom Thad had deeply disliked in 1824. He also was a Mason, and a slave owner from Tennessee. Mr. Jackson had lost the election in 1824, but had won in 1828, and now was the U.S. president. He was nominated as the Democratic candidate for re-election. Thad surely did not want to see him re-elected!

Henry Clay from Kentucky was the Anti-Jacksonian candidate. --He and many Anti-Jacksonians began to call themselves Whigs during this campaign-- Although Henry Clay ran as an Anti-Jacksonian/Whig, Thad did not like him either, because, just like Andrew Jackson, he was actually a slave owner and a Mason.

The Anti-Masons presented a candidate for president-- William Wirt, of Maryland. Mr. Wirt, in fact, was a "reformed" Mason, regretting that he ever was counted among their number. Amos Ellmaker, from Lancaster, Pennsylvania, was the Anti-Masonic candidate for vice president, also known as Mr. Wirt's "running mate." Thad enthusiastically embraced the Anti-Masonic ticket, and heartily fought for Misters Wirt and Ellmaker to win. He paid for posters, letters, newspaper advertisements, and rallies on their behalf.

Nonetheless, Andrew Jackson was re-elected. Thad extended his lower lip.

In addition to assisting political candidates of his choice, Thad used some of his money to show his indebtedness to his mother for her dedication to his education. He bought her a farm with a barn and fourteen cows back in Peacham, Vermont. A dairy farm would assure her of a proper diet and a regular income, as well as a productive way to occupy her time, he reasoned. She welcomed his gift.

Thad also contributed much money and time to causes and activities in his community. He served on a committee that founded a library in Gettysburg; he was selected to be a member of the town council; he was appointed to be a trustee of the Gettysburg Academy; he was chosen to be a leader of the Temperance Society, which disapproved of drinking of alcoholic beverages.

By 1833, Thad had made many friends, and he managed a thriving law practice. He had formed himself as an appreciated citizen of Adams County. He was an outspoken believer of the Anti-Masonic political party. It seemed a natural progression that Thad himself should become a candidate for public office.

The *Gettysburg Anti-Masonic Star* printed an editorial encouraging Thad's candidacy: "Who is Thaddeus Stevens? He is widely known by the splendor of his talents, which have raised him from indigence to comparative wealth, and the highest honors of his profession, but he is still more widely known by his charities and benefactions, which have earned him a noble reward...in the blessings of the poor. The powers of his mind are as great as they are diversified—his judgment is profound..." [5]

On October 14, 1833, 41-year-old Thad Stevens was elected to serve as Representative from Adams County to the Pennsylvania Legislature. He bore a broad smile for a long time.

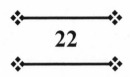

# 22

# Thad Rescues Public Schools 1834, 1835

In December, Representative Stevens traveled for the first time as a legislator from Gettysburg to Harrisburg, the capital city of Pennsylvania. Crossing the Susquehanna River by way of the Camelback Bridge, he remembered his near-disaster eighteen years earlier when he had crossed at McCall's Ferry. He recalled that when his startled horse Morgan almost sent him flying into the river, he was penniless, unknown, and unprincipled. Now cushioned in a classy carriage and clutching his silver-plated cane, he envisioned the great achievements he would score in his new life: He would abolish the Masons; he would free the slaves; maybe he even would become U.S. president!

Thad also was recollecting the sacrifices his native Vermont county had made in the form of taxes so that he could have the basic education he had so desperately desired; he wished that same opportunity would be offered to all Pennsylvania children; he knew that education was the key to a successful citizenry and a flourishing state.

One of Thad's first acts as a lawmaker was to team up with Governor George Wolf (He could hardly believe he could find common ground with a Jacksonian Democrat Mason!) and Whig Representative Thomas Burrowes to provide free schools for Pennsylvania children, boys and girls, wealthy and poor, black and white.

In spring 1834, the Free Schools Act passed. Thad expressed pride that this law immediately would establish one thousand common schools in the state.

The legislative session closed for the summer. The term of office for state representatives was one year, so Thad and his colleagues stayed in their home districts to campaign for re-election. Surprising to Representative Stevens, many of the Pennsylvania communities, including his own, were unhappy with the new law! Taxpayers were assessed higher taxes to fund the schools, and they were angry. They demanded that the legislators cancel the law, or be voted out of office. Some towns and boroughs totally ignored the law, and others, to display their displeasure, actually closed the schools they already had in place.

Thad was surprised, but overjoyed, when he was re-elected to the Pennsylvania Assembly in October.

During the following legislative session, the Pennsylvania Senate, responding to the uproar about taxpayer-provided education, voted to repeal the law. Now, if the House would vote the same way, the newly-created free common schools of Pennsylvania would be history.

The representatives met secretively in Harrisburg, and decided to copy the senators by voting to abolish the school tax, in order that they might continue to be re-elected by the enraged citizens. Representative Stevens did not attend that meeting because he was out of town, but when he returned to Harrisburg, his friends ran to tell him of their plan. He was not happy.

He knew what he had to do, and he did it: On April 11, 1835, he delivered a persuasive, unforgettable, and long (lasting two hours) speech to his peers in the House of Representatives--as well as to members of the Senate and news reporters and private citizens who had congregated in the standing-room-only gallery. Thad exclaimed that education was necessary for good government, and that it produced great scientists and philosophers. He reminded his spectators that reluctant school-tax-payers also paid for jails and courts, so they should be willing to pay for schools, which would be a better use of their money. He urged his colleagues to vote "...that the blessings of education shall be conferred upon every son of Pennsylvania, shall be carried home to the poorest child of the poorest inhabitant of your mountains so that even he may be prepared to act well his part in this land of freemen..." [6]

The chamber exploded in wild cheers! Almost everyone who listened to Representative Stevens's speech was inspired by it. His words were convincing and moving. When the House members voted, they changed their plan and upheld the Free Schools Act; the senators returned to their chamber and did the same thing.

Now, schooling could continue, for free, to every boy and girl in the state. Thad was sure that the taxpayers would grow to accept the expense as a right and a privilege of all children.

In addition, Thad observed that many Pennsylvanians were seeing him as a talented politician and a gifted speaker. Because of his winning speech, people began to call him the "Savior of the Common School Movement." He speculated to his colleagues that restoring public education in Pennsylvania might be recorded as the most significant achievement of his life.

Again, when the session closed for the year, Thad campaigned for re-election. Again, he easily was re-elected to the Pennsylvania Assembly.

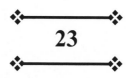

# 23

# Thad Creates Enemies 1836, 1837

During the 1835-36 legislative session, Representative Stevens delivered numerous speeches in the capitol and in the community. He called for the emancipation, or setting free, of all enslaved people. He preached that the ownership of human beings is immoral, and must be abolished. He reminded his audience that the Declaration of Independence declares that 'All men are created equal,' and that equal rights for all is the cornerstone of the Constitution.

In 1836, Martin Van Buren, who had been Andrew Jackson's vice president, was running for president, nominated by the Jacksonian Democrat party. Of course, Thad would not endorse him.

General William Harrison, from Ohio, was running against Mr. Van Buren. General Harrison was of the Anti-Jackson/Whig party. But Anti-Jackson and Anti-Slavery were not enough for Thad; he also advocated Anti-Masonic.

Thad and his Anti-Masons were unable to identify an appropriate candidate from their third party to run for president this year, so he tried to convince Whig General Harrison to defy and decry the Masons. General Harrison refused to endorse Anti-Masonic beliefs, so Thad refused to endorse General Harrison.

Thad was re-nominated for the Pennsylvania Assembly in September, but the Whigs were unhappy with him for not promoting General Harrison for president. They repeated hateful things about him, and urged people not to vote for him. Thad lost the contest this time, to Democrat William McCurdy.

Thad had never lost an election before, and he was miserably disappointed. He sulked in his armchair for several days, protruding his lower lip. Finally, he decided it was time to re-focus on his law practice. But…he resolved to stay active in state politics and national issues, too.

In 1837, a convention was organized to draft a new Pennsylvania constitution. Private citizen Thad Stevens was selected to participate. In the meetings, he promoted his anti-slavery convictions. He asserted, "…Slavery in this country is the most disgraceful institution that the world has ever witnessed, under any form of government, in any age…" [7]

Thad wanted the constitution to declare that all men residing in Pennsylvania have the right to vote. Other members of the convention wanted the constitution to state that only white men were qualified to vote. Thad argued long and hard with them. In the end, he lost the battle, and, joined by two others, he refused to sign his name to the revised document.

But the debate did serve to bring Thad's name before the public again. He was re-nominated for the Pennsylvania legislature in September 1837. The race again was nasty, but he won.

During the next legislative session, Representative Stevens proposed a bill to provide state financial help to colleges. Many people who favored education in general did not agree with giving public money for colleges. They thought higher education was appropriate only for wealthy folks, who could and should pay for it themselves.

"Yes, higher education does indeed cater to the rich," Thad pointed out. "This is the very reason that the state should provide colleges."

His bill passed.

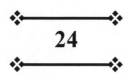

# 24

## Thad Delivers Drama in the State Capitol
## 1838, 1839

Thad invested a mass of money into his next campaign, 1838, and again, he won the election. Shortly after Election Day, Thomas Burrowes, representative from nearby Lancaster County, informed his friend Thad that in eight of the voting districts in Philadelphia County, both parties were claiming victory. Thad and Thomas conspired to defend the Anti-Masonic/Anti-Jacksonian faction of the fighters; they accused the Democrats of cheating.

When it was time, December 4, for the Harrisburg legislative session to begin, Thad and his pals refused to allow the Democrats from Philadelphia to take the disputed seats. A mob from Philadelphia, bearing bowie knives and double-barreled pistols, arrived to defend the Democrats. The Philadelphia gang jumped over railings and chairs and desks to attack the Anti-Jacksonian leaders. Thad and Thomas and others dove through a window behind the Senate chamber, escaping with their lives—and snapping a maple-limb, silver-handled cane in the process.

The controversy continued for several more weeks, in the form of arguments, speeches, and newspaper editorials. Finally, near Christmas, the issue was resolved: To Thad's dismay, the Anti-Jacksonians in charge recognized the Democrats, and invited them to take the seats!

"I am disgusted that you folded!" Thad, his lower lip stretched downward, shouted to his party leaders. "I hereby resign from my elected position!"

Thad's friends eventually convinced him to return to his own seat in the House chamber. Now it was the Democrats in charge who said he could not return to his seat! The Democrat Speaker of the House authorized a special election in June, just prior to the end of the session. Thad asked his constituents to vote for him again, which they did.

State Representative Stevens thanked his patrons, and several days later when the session adjourned, he returned to Gettysburg. He thought for a long time about whether his bright leadership and dazzling influence in the Pennsylvania legislature had faded already.

Discouraged, Thad did not seek re-election in the fall, for the 1839-40 term. Instead, he visited his family in Vermont.

He found his mother, now 73 years old, to be in good health, happily working the small and picturesque dairy farm that he had bought for her in Peacham. Youngest brother Alanson, now 42 and a bachelor like himself, was living with their mother and helping her with the farming.

Brother Abner was 45 years old and practicing medicine in St. Johnsbury, about fifteen miles from their mother. Abner and his wife Lucy proudly had named their first son after Thad, calling him Thaddeus Junior. They had named their next son Alanson, after another of Abner's brothers. Now, they and their two unruly sons were struggling to make ends meet.

For several days the relatives celebrated their history together. They exchanged memories about the "olden days," reminisced about the depth of their poverty, wondered why their father had deserted them, updated their individual stories, devoured old Mrs. Stevens's cooking, and wished that brother Joshua Junior, now a cobbler in Indiana, with a wife and children, could be there with them.

Before Thad left, brother Alanson whispered to him that he had accrued some personal debts. Thad thanked him for watching over their mother, and caringly gave him a sizeable sum of money. Thad also thanked Abner for looking after their mother, and passed him some cash, as well.

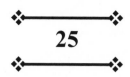

# 25

# Thad Pursues Peace 1840, 1841

When Thad returned to Pennsylvania from Vermont, it was time to think about the 1840 presidential election. He was haunted by his memory of how he had alienated the Whigs during the 1836 campaign, and how it had cost him his own election.

The Whigs nominated General Harrison again. Thad concluded that he might have the best chance to successfully pursue his own abolitionist goals if General Harrison were elected, so he decided to cooperate with the Whigs this time. He backed General Harrison both verbally and financially; he worked hard to help him.

Thad was not pleased, however, when General Harrison named John Tyler, a slaveholder from Virginia, as his running mate. Incumbent President Martin Van Buren, with no running mate, ran against them on the Democratic ticket.

When Election Day arrived, the Harrison/Tyler combination prevailed.

Thad journeyed to Washington and watched with his friend Thomas Elder in the cold pouring rain as William Harrison took the oath of office on March 4, 1841, as ninth U.S. president. President Harrison wore neither an overcoat nor a hat, and delivered a two-hour inaugural address. Thad laughed, and broadcast to everyone within earshot that the prepared speech had already been shortened, with the help of fellow Whig Daniel Webster!

When President Harrison walked past Thad and Thomas in the inaugural parade through the wet wintry streets, Thad waved to him. He speculated to Thomas, "Our new president is grateful for all of the work I did to get him nominated and elected. I think he will offer me a position in his cabinet, or at least some other high position in his administration. Maybe he will nominate me to be his Postmaster General, or his Secretary of State. Who knows? Maybe he will select me as his Attorney General."

Thad was sorely shocked and deeply disappointed when he did not find his name on the list of appointees to be confirmed by the Senate! He felt little consolation when he learned that President Harrison also neglected to offer positions to others who had helped him.

Abruptly, President Harrison died--one month after his inauguration! He had developed a cold, which progressed to pneumonia, and he succumbed to it on April 4!

Vice President John Tyler succeeded him as president. Citizen Stevens knew that his struggle against slavery now would suffer a severe setback. He curled his lip for a long time.

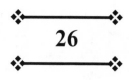

# 26

# Thad Seizes an Opportunity 1842

Thad realized that if he were ever to achieve his goal of abolition, he must run again for his old seat in the Pennsylvania House of Representatives, and now was the time to do it. He ran, still on the Anti-Masonic ticket, against Democrat John Marshall. His campaign was a fierce battleground, and he had to borrow money to pay for it. When he received the endorsement of the Temperance Society, his chances of winning advanced significantly.

In fall of 1841, following a break of two years, the Adams County voters again sent Thad Stevens to represent them in the Pennsylvania Assembly.

Thad, in Harrisburg, was considering how he would proceed in his fight against slavery, when, in early 1842, a legal case, *Prigg v. Pennsylvania*, beckoned to him. Thad reviewed the case with his colleagues:

"A colored woman named Margaret Morgan," he narrated, "had been a slave to a Maryland man named John Ashmore. Mr. Ashmore, at some point, no longer thought of Miss Morgan as a slave, and allowed her to do as she pleased. He, however, never formally freed her. Ten years ago, in 1832, Miss Morgan freely moved to Pennsylvania.

"Five years ago," Thad continued, "Mr. Ashmore's family decided to re-claim her as a slave, and they hired slave-catcher Edward Prigg to recover her. On April 1, 1837, Edward Prigg and his partners kidnapped Margaret Morgan and her children from her York County home, arranging to take them to Maryland to return them to John Ashmore's family.

"Clearly, Miss Morgan had lived in Pennsylvania more than the six months required by our state law to make her free," Thad emphasized. "Invoking the Pennsylvania laws of 1788 and 1826, both protecting the safety of former slaves, Pennsylvania police arrested Mr. Prigg and his men," he explained.

"The men pleaded 'Not guilty.' They argued that they had been hired legally to arrest and return Miss Morgan to her owner. In 1839, the York County Court convicted Mr. Prigg and his cronies.

"No one was surprised when Mr. Prigg appealed to the U.S. Supreme Court," Thad added. "Mr. Prigg argued that Pennsylvania law cannot trump the federal Fugitive Slave Act of 1793, nor the U.S. Constitution, both of which declare that slaves rightfully must be returned to their owners.

"The Supreme Court," Thad summarized in March, "now has ruled in favor of Edward Prigg. It has decided that the recapture of fugitive slaves is a purely federal concern."

Representative Stevens next advanced a bold idea: "I suggest a bill to repeal all Pennsylvania laws relating to fugitive slaves. This will support our cause!"

His Whig and Anti-Mason friends were confused!

Thad explained his reasoning. "Logically, it is not what we really want, but if we and other states refuse all cooperation with the federal Fugitive Slave Law, no assistance will be offered to those wishing to recapture slaves, and runaways will not be caught or imprisoned!

"Such a dramatic refusal to uphold the Fugitive Slave Act will be seen as brazen," Thad conceded, "but, by discouraging state cooperation in returning fugitive slaves, this Prigg Decision, with our help, will actually undermine the Fugitive Slave Act of 1793."

Thad's fellow legislators were intrigued by his vision. He formally proposed the bill, and they voted to approve it.

Afterwards, Thad revealed further thoughts to his fellow abolitionists. "The Supreme Court is right," he acknowledged. "The Pennsylvania laws of 1788 and 1826 do indeed contradict the United States Constitution. The Constitution, by the way it is worded, implies that each state has the right to decide separately whether it will allow slavery.

"The obvious solution is to change, or amend, the Constitution," Thad urged, "in such a way that individual states will not have that right." He added, "The Constitution also contradicts the primary principle of our Declaration of Independence, 'All men are created equal.'"

When the legislative session ended, Representative Stevens went home to Gettysburg. In spite of his successful leadership following the Prigg Decision, he was pessimistic about his prospects for abolishing slavery.

Of more immediate concern, he found himself deeply in debt, owing $217,000, the result of his large losses in business investments, the effect of his substantial financing of political competitions for himself and others, the outcome of his generous donations to charities, and the consequence of his giving less attention to his law practice.

He resolved to make a change in his life. He decided to not run for another term in the state assembly, but to revive his law practice by moving to a bigger town than Gettysburg. He considered Lancaster, remembering his impressions from the first time he had visited there, back in 1816.

"Yes," Attorney Stevens mused to himself, "my potential for earning money is great in a community like Lancaster, one of the largest, richest, and most populous counties in the state."

**Thad's Home and Office, 45 and 47 South Queen Street,
Lancaster**
*Courtesy of LancasterHistory.org, Lancaster, Pennsylvania*

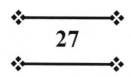

# 27

## Thad Thrives In Law Practice
## 1842-1844

On August 24, 1842, Thad hung his shingle above the door to his new office in Lancaster, Pennsylvania. Next, he located his advertisement in the weekly publication of *Intelligencer Journal*. It read: "Thaddeus Stevens, Attorney at Law, Office on Central Square, in the home formerly occupied by James Hopkins." He wondered who would be the first client to respond to it. He waited patiently. Later, he waited not-so-patiently.

Although Thad had been admitted to the Lancaster Bar Association on August 11, he had received a less-than-warm welcome from the other lawyers who had attended the social that evening. "I suspect my reputation has preceded me," he considered. "My colleagues undoubtedly fear my competition," he moaned to himself as he limped to his rooming house at 38 South Queen Street.

Finally, Attorney Stevens received a visit from some potential clients. They were from nearby Columbia--five free Negro men who had been charged with assault and battery. He accepted the challenge to defend them in court, and he charged no fee. Similar to his first big trial in Gettysburg, Thad lost the case, but it brought him much attention, and he quickly made up for the money he had turned down.

Now, new clients drifted into his office daily. They hired him to defend their situations involving real estate and religious freedom. They employed him to plead the cases of accused thieves and murderers. They engaged him to restore freedom to fugitive slaves who had been caught.

Thad earned so much money so fast that he made huge monthly payments against his debts. In addition, in April, less than a year after moving to Lancaster, he bought adjoining properties, 45, 47, and 49 South Queen Street, at sheriff's sale for $4,000. He used the first of the two-story brick buildings for his lodging, and the second as his workplace. The third was the Kleiss Tavern, from which he collected rent.

Christopher Dice and his family operated a grocery store at 43 South Queen Street. After no time at all, Thad and Christopher became good friends. During evenings, Thad and other neighbors regularly gathered around the grocer's counter to complain about the Masons, slavery, and various political candidates.

With his neighbors' encouragement, and with money to spare, Thad injected himself into the presidential election contest of 1844. James Polk became the Democratic candidate. Henry Clay became the Whig candidate, just like in the 1832 election.

Thad still found Henry Clay to be a distasteful nominee, because he was both a Mason and a slaveholder. He pushed, instead, for a third-party candidate, General Winfield Scott. General Scott had led U.S. troops, apparently including his father, in the Battle of Queenston Heights. More importantly, he endorsed the anti-slavery movement. Thad fought for Winfield Scott, on the Anti-Masonic ticket, to be elected president.

Thad soon saw that very few people were listening to what he was saying as he canvassed on behalf of General Scott. He became frustrated. He observed that in Lancaster County-- indeed in Pennsylvania--, most folks were bearing witness to the Whig candidate.

Thad began to re-think his position: He knew that if he were to succeed in his long-term goals, he would want the Whigs on his side. In time, he realized he had no choice but to set aside his anti-Masonic ideas and his anti-slavery ideals (temporarily), and to back the Whig candidate, Henry Clay. Which he did.

Now he was so busy with his defending and his campaigning that he was neglecting his properties, including his own home. His rents were uncollected, his clothes were rumpled, his dishes were dirty, his home was messy. He knew that he needed help, but he was too busy to seek it.

On Election Day, 1844, in spite of the energy Thad had expended for the Whigs, James Polk beat Henry Clay. Thad was disheartened.

**Thad's Housekeeper and Friend, Lydia Hamilton Smith**
*Courtesy of LancasterHistory.org, Lancaster, Pennsylvania*

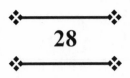

# 28

# Thad Inherits a Family 1847

It was early March, 1847; a letter arrived for Thad from Vermont.

"To our Dear Uncle, Attorney Thaddeus Stevens," it read, "We regret to inform you that our beloved father, Dr. Abner Stevens, fell ill on March 1, and met his Maker on March 4. Our loving mother Lucy has been inconsolable, and is crying for your presence and encouragement at this time. With sincere affection, and with trust that you will respond appropriately, your faithful nephews, Thaddeus Junior and Alanson."

Thad promptly traveled to St. Johnsbury to tend to his brother's affairs, and to offer consolation to his brother's widow.

No sooner did Thad return to Lancaster than he received word in August that his brother's widow, Lucy, had died. Now Thad returned to St. Johnsbury to tackle the question of what to do with the boys: Should they go to a boarding school, live with old Mrs. Stevens in Peacham, or come to Lancaster to live with him? Thad concluded it would be in the best interests of all involved for the boys to live with him.

Back in Lancaster, Thad acted to get his nephew Thaddeus Junior admitted to his own alma mater, Dartmouth College. He arranged for Nephew Alanson to attend a school in town.

Finally, Thad's home unkempt, his foster sons undisciplined, and his businesses in disarray, he focused on finding a housekeeper and property manager. Soon, he hired a lady from Gettysburg. She was Lydia Hamilton Smith, a mulatto widow with two children, William and Isaac. Mrs. Smith's boys became quick and congenial playmates for Thad's nephew Alanson.

Thad was pleased that Mrs. Smith immediately showed herself to be not only a good mother-figure and a good employee, but also a good friend. He insisted that his nephews address her as 'Mrs. Smith' or 'Ma'am.'

During dinner with his enlarged family one evening, Thad referred to Speaker of the House John Davis. Thaddeus Junior asked if the Speaker of the House was a person who answers knocks on the door of a home, and sends away beggars and/or solicitors. Thad laughed. He reverted to his role as a teacher:

"The Speaker of the House, Junior, is the presiding officer of the United States House of Representatives. The office was established by the U.S. Constitution."

Alanson, William, and Isaac interrupted the lecture with a tug-of-war over the last bit of cake. Thad offered them a frown, and Alanson stuffed the handful into his mouth. When the screaming subsided, Thad continued:

"The House elects the Speaker of the House on the first day of every new Congress. Each party nominates a candidate. Whoever receives a simple majority of the votes is elected. The new Speaker is then sworn in by the Dean of the House, the chamber's longest-serving member."

This time the disruption came in the form of whispers and giggles. "Now, what?" demanded Uncle Thad. The three younger boys accused each other of raising a question about the location of the chamber pot in the chamber. Mrs. Smith sternly reprimanded the youngsters. Thad proceeded, with only Thaddeus Junior eyeing him:

"The Speaker becomes the leader of the majority party. He actively works to set that party's legislative agenda, therefore endowing him with considerable clout. He assigns members to serve on important committees. Aside from duties relating to heading the House and the majority political party, the Speaker also performs administrative duties, and represents his Congressional district."

In addition to moonlighting as a parent, Attorney Stevens found himself devoting considerable effort to the Underground Railroad. He taught his young dinner companions, on another evening, about its purpose. "The Underground Railroad," he instructed, "is a system of sympathetic citizens who assist escaping slaves. It is especially important in the border counties of southeastern Pennsylvania, such as our own."

Thad disclosed to the boys that he had hired a heroic spy, Edward Rauch, to carefully watch the activities of known slave catchers--who were paid very handsomely for their services. Thad told the boys that Mr. Rauch had shrewdly deceived the slave catchers into believing he was one of them. Mr. Rauch collected information about their schemes, and without being noticed, entered the Dice's grocery store. Here, he quietly communicated to the owner the facts he had learned. Mr. Dice then secretly relayed the info to Thad, his next-door neighbor.

Thad cited a specific example: He had received a message from Mr. Rauch, in January, that some slaves who were hiding in the cellar of Quaker Jeremiah Brown, in Fulton Township, twenty-five miles south, were in immediate danger of being caught. "I speedily penned a dispatch to my friend Jeremiah," he whispered. He recited it from memory:

*"I learn that the manstealers of Lancaster have taken means to obtain authority from Maryland to arrest and take into slavery two colored girls who have lately lived with you and your brother. Will you see that they flee to an immediate city of refuge? They should not stop short of Canada.*

*There is a regular chain of agents and spies of the slaveholders in this and all the adjoining counties. I have a spy on the spies and thus ascertain the facts. These are the eighth set of slaves I have warned within a week."* [8]

Thad swore his incredulous surrogate sons to secrecy.

In December, on the 31st, Thad's 51-year-old unmarried brother, Alanson, died. Thad visited Vermont briefly, this time to assure that his mother was well disposed. She insisted that she would thrive, though quite alone, on her dairy farm.

Several months later, Uncle Thad happily learned that nephew Thaddeus Junior was accepted by Dartmouth College; he saw to it that young Thad began his studies there as soon as possible.

He also sent nephew Alanson to Caledonia Forge, to learn the blacksmith trade. Thad had opened the ironworking business 14 miles northwest of Gettysburg ten years earlier, and named it after his beloved county in Vermont. He hoped that young Alanson, who was totally disinterested in schoolwork, might enjoy smithing with hand tools.

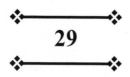

# 29

## Thad Conducts
## on the Underground Railroad 1848

During the hot and humid Wednesday afternoon of August 23, 1848, Thad, resting in the parlor of his Lancaster home, heard Mrs. Smith respond to a rap on the front door. His reflecting about the approaching presidential election interrupted, he strained to understand the urgent conversation that ensued. Mrs. Smith silently ushered a group of sixteen young blacks, thin, wearing sweat-soaked, dirt-laden rags, and clearly desperate, to his presence. She stood in the background expectantly as Thad rose to greet them.

The delegated speaker, who introduced himself as Ben, revealed, "We were directed to call at 45 South Queen Street and we would find a lawyer, who was a friend to slaves. We are looking for work and we heard that you give work to colored people."

"How far have you come?" inquired Thad.

"A right smart ways, sir," Ben answered, as his companions focused on their shuffling feet.

"Can you walk several miles farther?" asked the master of the house. When the youths assured that they could, indeed, Thad invited them to have a meal before they proceeded. Mrs. Smith prepared ham and potatoes as they shared their story with Thad.

This time, Oliver Gilbert, 16 years old, was the spokesperson:

"We are owned by Dr. William Watkins of Anne Arundel County, Maryland. We were attending a camp meeting with some other slaves on Sunday. We saw an opportunity, and we planned among ourselves, and we fled. We ran through fields and forests and orchards and streams and creeks. We were chased by hunters and bloodhounds, but finally we were able to throw off our chasers.

We ran northward, tracking the sun by day, and the North Star by night. Yesterday, we swam across a river, and we thought we must be in Canada, but a Negro man told us, 'No, this is the Susquehanna River, and you are in a town called Columbia, Pennsylvania.' He told us that, although in this state whites do not own slaves, we are in danger of being captured and sent back to Maryland. He was the one who told us to run ten miles east into a city called Lancaster, and to talk to you."

When the young men had eaten their fill, Thad wrote on a paper and handed it to them. He directed them to a village seven miles farther east. "Go to Bird-in-Hand and give this note to Daniel or Hannah Gibbons and they will find you work. Just before you get into the village you will see a white painted house sitting back in the field, then go up the lane and ask for Mr. or Mrs. Gibbons, or their son Dr. Joseph Gibbons." [9]

Thad and Mrs. Smith sent them on their way, tucking packages of biscuits and ham under their arms, and bidding them safe travels.

Before nightfall, Thad received word from his contact, Edward Rauch, that slave catchers from Maryland again were on the trail of the sixteen freedom seekers, with warrants for their arrest. Thad hastily dispensed a messenger to the Gibbons, hoping the alert would arrive before the pursuers.

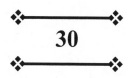

# 30

# Thad Befriends the Whigs 1848

Late in the summer of 1848, the Democrats nominated Lewis Cass as their presidential candidate. Thad again promoted General Winfield Scott for the Whig nomination, but still no one was paying attention to him. Eventually, he understood that he, once again, had no choice but to promote the official Whig candidate--and Louisiana slave owner--Zachary Taylor. Which he did.

Finally! The Whigs were ready, willing, and able to believe in Thad. They gave him the Whig nomination for member of the U.S. House of Representatives from the district that included Lancaster County. He ran his campaign on an anti-slavery platform.

Candidate Stevens received a letter from Congressman Abraham Lincoln, a Whig from Illinois serving in the House. He reminded Thad that they had met at the Whig convention. The writer explained that he was "looking for the undisguised opinion of an experienced and sagacious Pennsylvania politician" [10] to tell him how the state was likely to vote in the presidential election, and Thaddeus Stevens was that man.

Answering promptly, Thad confessed that it was hard to say how his state would vote. He had some hopes, but they were not too strong.

Whig Thaddeus Stevens was victorious in the race for U.S. representative in October 1848. And Whig Zachary Taylor was victorious in the race for U.S. president in November 1848. Thad and his Whig friends were ecstatic on both counts!

In August 1849, Zachary Taylor, twelfth president of the United States, passed through Lancaster. Thad and the local Whigs staged a splendid banquet at the White Swan Hotel to honor him. Thad addressed the gathering of cheering Whigs, praising the president and his achievements.

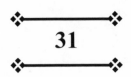

# 31

# Thad Rejects Compromise 1850

Thad had to wait over a year to be sworn in as a member of the Thirty-First Congress. He took the oath in December 1849 in Washington, D.C. He could hardly believe that he now held a position that he had dreamed about during his youth. And he pledged to use the position to lead the country to abolition of slavery! Conscious that his strong opinions sometimes led him into trouble, Thad supposed that he would be more effective if he could hold his tongue publicly for as long as possible, to avoid making enemies.

Thad noted that the size of the country was expanding, as recently-acquired and recently-developed territories were applying for statehood. He--and the rest of the country--sensed that tensions were rising between the northern and southern states over which territories would be admitted as free states, and which would be admitted as slave states. Slavery-induced stress was swelling the disagreements between sections of the country. Thad kept his mouth closed, and thereby was inducing stress of his own.

Henry Clay, now a senator, suggested a compromise that he hoped would ease the national nervousness. He was trying to please both sides by drafting several pieces for peace. He suggested:

- Admission of California as a free state, which would end the balance of free and slave states;
- A statement that the territories of Utah and New Mexico had the right to decide about slavery for themselves;
- Prohibition of slave trade, but not ownership of slaves, in Washington;
- A more strict Fugitive Slave Law; and
- A declaration that Congress did not have the authority to interfere with slave trade between states.

Both the Senate and the House spiritedly debated the merits of the proposal. By February 20, 1850, Thad could restrain his voice no longer. He delivered his first speech to the Thirty-First Congress; it was in opposition to Senator Clay's compromise.

Congressman Stevens's address was to the point: He thundered that slavery was an issue for no kind of compromise. Slavery was wrong in every form, in every place. The only compromise he would accept, he said, was that he would honor the U.S. Constitution, which seemed to allow slavery in states that chose to allow it; but he hoped that the Constitution quickly would be amended to outlaw slavery across the country.

Now that Thad had broken his silence, he was not to be stopped! In June, he further boomed, "If slavery is such a blessing as the Southerners maintain, then let all slaves who want to be free exchange places with free laborers choosing to be slaves." [11]

President Taylor also opposed the Compromise of 1850. With the president on the anti-slavery side, Thad was hopeful that the Compromise would not become law. In July, however, the president became ill with a stomach ailment, diagnosed as 'acute gastroenteritis.' To the shock of Thad and the country, President Taylor died on July 9, sixteen months into his term!

Within hours, Vice President Millard Fillmore took the presidential oath. Hoping to avoid conflict, President Fillmore favored Henry Clay's proposition. In September, the Compromise of 1850 was enacted.

Thad was angry, but he also had generated anger among many of his constituents by his refusal to compromise on the slavery issue. He was astonished that his Lancaster County committee re-nominated him for his seat in the House, and he was further astonished that his Lancaster County voters re-elected him.

Before the next Congressional session began, Thad bought a subscription to a Washington newspaper for his mother in Vermont. Now she would have the opportunity to read, with pride, his speeches, in a timely manner.

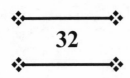

# 32

## Thad Embraces a Clash
## in Christiana 1851

Abolitionist Stevens continued to observe the strain that was mounting between the slave states and the free states. He knew that the pressure would soon burst into a substantial test case, and he anxiously awaited it.

In September 1851, an incident in Christiana, Pennsylvania, involving some freedom seekers and a man named William Parker, grabbed Thad's attention. He researched the backstory:

William Parker had been a slave in Maryland. He had escaped when he was 17, and settled in Christiana, which was just north of the Maryland line. He became a husband, a father, an innkeeper, and an anti-slavery activist. He joined the people in the region who had linked themselves to the Underground Railroad, and he assisted many runaway slaves.

Innkeeper Parker also organized a 'mutual protection society,' or militia, consisting of members of the Christiana community. The group developed an effective intelligence network to know when slave catchers were in the area looking for freedom seeking slaves. This mutual protection society would readily spring into action to protect any captives before they could be taken back across state lines by hunters. The members pledged that if the laws of the country would not protect them, their family, their friends, and their neighbors, then they would protect each other.

Thad gathered the details of the current story: During the evening of September 11, Mr. Parker received communication that a slaveholder from Maryland, Edward Gorsuch, his son

Dickinson, a federal marshal named J.H. Kline, and some slave catchers were on their way to Christiana carrying a warrant to recover Mr. Gorsuch's four escaped slaves who were hiding in the inn. As the Gorsuch party approached, Mrs. Parker sounded a horn alerting neighbors that slave catchers were there and that help was needed. Many militia members speedily arrived at the inn and stood nearby.

Slave-owner Gorsuch demanded that the escaped slaves present themselves. He proclaimed that the law was on his side, and that the ownership of slaves was his legal right. Citizen Parker and the other Negroes inside warned the slave catchers that they would defend themselves.

Two local Quakers, Castner Hanway and Elijah Lewis, were among the bystanders. Federal Marshal Kline issued an order to the crowd to assist in the capture. Most of the locals ignored the marshal's order. Quaker Hanway tried to calm some armed blacks who also had arrived.

Mr. Gorsuch entered the inn and attempted to take the fugitives! Someone fired the first shot, and turmoil ensued! In the end, Edward Gorsuch lay dead and his son was severely wounded. William Parker and his family fled into the night.

Thad announced that this was the case he had been waiting for! He predicted that the incident would have a grave effect on the federal Fugitive Slave Law.

Thad followed the subsequent events closely: He learned that after an extensive investigation, a group of 38 men, including the Quakers, were cited for treason because of their defiance of the federal order. Federal officers concluded that Castner Hanway was the leader of the resistance, so he would be the first to be tried for treason. The prosecutors felt that a strong first win would make wins on the remaining cases easier.

Attorney Stevens threw himself into the center of the case. He represented Castner Hanway in the trial, which was held in Independence Hall in Philadelphia. Thad worried when Judge Robert Grier was announced as the presiding official, as the judge was reputed to be prejudiced against blacks.

Thad engaged his defense strategy: He introduced evidence that Edward Gorsuch's agents had taken part in recent kidnappings; he demonstrated that the prosecution's chief witness, Marshal Kline, was known to be a liar; and he showed that his client actually had reached the scene late, prevented more bloodshed, and assisted Dickinson Gorsuch in removing his father's body, all of which hardly constituted treason.

Thad held his breath while the jury deliberated. He finally exhaled when they returned, finding the Quaker "Not guilty." As a result, all of the accused eventually were released.

Thad appreciated the implications of having won this case. It represented a major triumph in the fight against slavery. He believed that the Fugitive Slave Law now was essentially unenforceable-- in fact, destroyed. He believed that the victory would strengthen the resolve of abolitionists across the country.

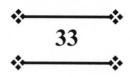

# 33

## Thad Crosses the Whigs - Again 1852

In summer, 1852, Franklin Pierce won the Democrats' nomination for president. Mr. Pierce was a pro-slavery lawyer from New Hampshire, and Thad christened him "Doughface." To Thad, any Northerner who supported slavery and other Southern beliefs was weak and could not think for himself; he was malleable and pliable, like half-baked dough-- a doughface.

General Winfield Scott received the Whig nomination for president. Although Thad was pleased that the General-in-Chief of the Army--whom he had been promoting for president since 1844--finally was nominated, he was amazed and unhappy that the party as a whole still defended the Fugitive Slave Act.

The Whig leaders asked him to deliver a speech championing the Fugitive Slave Law at a scheduled political rally. Thad answered no, he did not feel well. He was not surprised, then, when he was not re-nominated to retain the seat he had held in the House for only four years. He knew it was because, once again, he had angered the Whigs by his lack of full validation of their platform.

Thad, actually, was more upset that Democrat Franklin Pierce, a.k.a. "Doughface," won the election, becoming the fourteenth president of the United States.

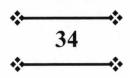

# 34

## Thad Monitors His Family 1853, 1854

In March 1853, Lydia Smith received some mail from Littleton, New Hampshire, near Dartmouth College. It was from her boss's nephew, Thaddeus Junior. In the letter, he revealed that he had been expelled from college, and professed that he accepted full responsibility for it. He confessed that he had not been taking his studies seriously, and, in fact, had been partying a lot. Since then, he noted, he has been counseling with a minister in town, and he expected to return to college in May. Although he had originally planned to write neither to Mrs. Smith nor his uncle until he was actually back at school, he was so sure of returning that he wanted her to know at once. --And would she please tell her uncle the news?

When Thad read the confession, he tore it to shreds and tossed it. His temperament improved when he learned in May that Junior did re-enter college. In August, Uncle Thad mailed a letter back to Junior, reminding him to study hard and not to drink.

When he was not ministering to his troubled nephew, private citizen Stevens was investing his time trying to defeat Senator Stephen Douglas' Kansas-Nebraska Bill. This bill would allow slavery in the territories of Kansas and Nebraska, and it was embraced by "Doughface," the pro-slavery President Pierce. Thad delivered speeches, printed editorials in his own newspaper, the *Independent Whig*, and authored articles for other papers. In spite of his efforts, the Kansas-Nebraska Bill passed into law in May 1854.

The good thing, however, in Thad's opinion, was that as a result of the struggle, the Whigs lost influence, and two new anti-slavery groups, the Republican party and the Know-Nothing party, arose. Thad himself again did not run for re-election to the House, but he sponsored a Know-Nothing, Anthony Roberts, investing his own money to finance the campaign. Thad was proud when Mr. Roberts won the 1854 election!

Several days later, Thad received word that his dear mother, at age 88, had passed away on October 5, after stepping into a hole while looking for a lost cow. Thad and nephew Alanson journeyed from Pennsylvania to Vermont to give mother and grandmother a proper burial, and to sell the farm. Thad's older brother, Joshua, traveled from Indianapolis, Indiana, to join them. Nephew Thaddeus Junior arrived from Dartmouth College for his grandmother's funeral, offered indecipherable mumbles in response to inquiries about his schooling progress, and departed as soon as she was lowered into Peacham Cemetery, saying he needed to return quickly to college.

Despondent, Thad revealed to his relatives that he felt responsible for his mother's death. "I was the one," he mourned, "who bought that farm for her! What was I thinking, condemning an older lady to operating a farm by herself?"

Neither Thad nor his nephew spoke much during the train ride back to Lancaster.

Late in October, Uncle Thad was available to tend to Thaddeus Junior and his schoolwork --or lack thereof. "They again say you are lazy, inattentive, absent, and unprepared in your studies," he wrote. "I have been informed also that you will lose you student status unless you change your ways. This is bad enough, but I have reason to believe that you also love rum. If this is so," he cautioned, "the sooner you are abandoned, the better, for there is no hope for one who ever tastes strong drink. It shall be up to you, Nephew, to make your choices. Possibly you could attend the Lancaster County Normal School, which is slated to open to students next year in nearby Millersville, whereupon I and Mrs. Smith could keep closer watch over you. Or possibly a trade would be better for you," Thad advised, "in which case further outlay of money for college would be a waste." Closing, the uncle threatened that he might never want to see his nephew again. [12]

Thaddeus Junior responded with a note assuring that he would take heed to the warning, and would re-focus on school.

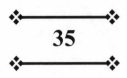

# 35

# Thad Delivers Drama
# in the National Capitol 1859

During the 1856 presidential election year, Citizen Stevens worked to unite all of the anti-slavery groups in the country. He influenced them to join forces and submit a single anti-slavery candidate for president. This, he thought, would offer the clearest pathway to victory over slavery.

John Fremont, a Western explorer, who was know as 'The Great Pathfinder,' became their nominee. Candidate Fremont ran on the new Republican ticket that had emerged two years earlier during the struggle over the Kansas-Nebraska Bill. Abolitionist Stevens was brimming with optimism about the country's future!

James Buchanan, from Thad's own Lancaster, became the Democrats' nominee. Candidate Buchanan defended continuation of the Compromise of 1850 and opposed federal interference in slavery. During the campaign, Thad spitefully slurred James Buchanan as "a bloated mass of political putridity." [13]

In the end, James Buchanan narrowly beat John Fremont, to become the fifteenth U.S. president. Now, Abolitionist Stevens could not have been more disheartened about the country's future!

In 1857, Attorney Thaddeus Stevens took on an assistant in his office: Thaddeus Stevens Junior, who finally had graduated. The older Thad was happy to have help, as his practice was busier than ever, and the younger Thad was happy to have a job.

In August 1858, the Lancaster County Republicans re-endorsed Thad for Congress. His platform, as before, embraced the abolition of slavery. He proclaimed that he opposed slavery everywhere because it was wrong, oppressive, and barbaric. He began to develop a reputation as a radical because the opinions he held were extreme, sweeping, and uncompromising. Radical Candidate Stevens acknowledged the lack of federal authority to interfere with slavery in states where it already existed; however, he maintained that Congress did have the power to remove slavery forever from the territories that were not states.

Thad expected to win the election, even though President Buchanan was motivated to defeat him. In October, Thad did win.

This time, when Representative Stevens went to D.C. to begin his new term, he immediately immersed himself into the action: He nominated fellow Pennsylvanian Galusha Grow for Speaker of the House. Then Representative Keitt of South Carolina belittled Representative Grow, and threatened violence. Thad returned with a sarcastic comment about the South's addiction to slavery. Next, Representative Crawford of Georgia gathered other Southern Democrats and pushed toward Thad.

Thad spied Edward McPherson, a friend from Gettysburg, hastily gathering other Republicans. The gang of Republicans approached the mob of Democrats. Representative McPherson's hand clutched what appeared to Thad to be a gun. To save the day, someone made a sudden call for adjournment! Thad drew a deep breath when he realized the assembly narrowly had avoided bloodshed in the Capitol!

The dispute, nevertheless, dragged on for months. Finally, William Pennington from New Jersey was selected to be Speaker of the House. Republican Speaker Pennington assigned Thad to serve on the Ways and Means Committee. Thad understood that membership on this committee offered him major power because its main purpose was to evaluate the financial requests of the government.

As the Thirty-Sixth Congress progressed, Thad observed that Democrats seemed to fear him. He read an editorial in the *New York Evening Post* that commented, "There is probably no man in the House who has such perfect command of himself as Thaddeus Stevens. This gives him great influence and control." [14] The piece added that Southerners did not know how to deal with him. Thad grinned broadly.

Thad's amusement was short-lived. He soon received a message from Mrs. Smith in Lancaster that her older son William, in his early twenties, had died. Cleaning a gun, he accidentally had shot himself.

Thad immediately returned to Pennsylvania to console his friend, and to help her bury her son through her house of worship, St. Mary's Catholic Church.

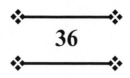

# 36

## Thad Witnesses the Founding
## of the Confederate States 1860

Congressman Stevens next occupied himself with the coming 1860 presidential contest. Abraham Lincoln of Illinois was campaigning to be nominated for president. He spoke against the expansion of slavery beyond the states where it already existed. Thad rallied to assist him. He knew that he and Abe both had the same goal: abolition of slavery. Mr. Lincoln won the Republican nomination.

Thad followed the Democrats' developments: They were unable to agree on a single nominee. Instead, Senator Stephen Douglas, Vice President John Breckinridge, and Senator John Bell, each holding a different degree of support for slavery, and each representing a different part of the country, faced Abraham Lincoln.

Many pro-slavery Southerners threatened to withdraw their states from membership in the United States of America if a Republican were elected president. "We will secede!" they pledged.

In the meantime, Thad himself was re-nominated for his own seat. He snickered when he discovered that the Democrats, certain they would lose, did not even bother to nominate an opponent for him.

Republicans in Thad's district were so proud of him that in July, during a meeting in Lancaster, many of his admirers gathered at Central Square, and proceeded one block down to 45 South Queen Street to honor him. Thad briefly appeared at the window, smiled, and waved appreciatively to his constituents.

Both Thad Stevens and Abe Lincoln won their respective elections in the fall. The new president, with Hannibal Hamlin as vice president, was scheduled to begin his term in March 1861.

Southern Democrats, however, did not wait for March. The South Carolinians, on December 20, were the first to follow through on their threat to secede from the Union if Mr. Lincoln were elected. Thad was not surprised when six other states, Alabama, Florida, Georgia, Louisiana, Mississippi, and Texas, promptly followed. They said they were forming a separate country, and they called themselves the Confederate States of America, or for short, the Confederacy.

Thad looked to the departing president to fiercely condemn the so-called Confederacy. Lame-duck President Buchanan, apparently unsure of what to do, delivered a speech. He acknowledged that secession was illegal, and he apologized that he had no power to do anything about it.

Representative Stevens could hardly believe his ears! The president was totally and pathetically spineless! He was allowing some states to call themselves a separate country, rejecting the Constitution of the United States of America, all because they feared losing their tradition of slavery!

Thad engaged in conversations about removing James Buchanan from the Presidency several months early, but he soon acknowledged that dealing with the crisis of the seceded states at this time was more important than pursuing the legal process of impeachment.

Many other congressmen offered compromises to resolve the situation and preserve the United States of America. Thad criticized these attempts. On January 29, he delivered a powerful speech. He declared that rather than negotiate with the rebels, he would prefer to see the government "crumbled into ten thousand atoms." He remarked that he did not want war, but assured that, if it happened, the United States would crush the rebels. He stressed that compromise, concessions, and further humiliation of the Union were not options.

In a repeat of earlier scenes, during Thad's speech, enraged Southerners in the chamber "rose to their feet and rushed toward him with curses and threats of personal violence." [15] Just like before, many of Thad's Congressional friends gathered around him as a display of protection and a symbol of solidarity.

Finally, Abraham Lincoln took the oath of office on March 4, 1861. In his inaugural address, President Lincoln vowed that he would make absolutely no compromises that would allow the spread of slavery. Thad breathed a long sigh of relief.

Thad's mood of hope did not last long. Five weeks later, on April 12, at 4:30 a.m., Confederate forces attacked the U.S. military base at Fort Sumter in South Carolina. After thirty-four hours of relentless shelling, the federal troops surrendered. Thad proclaimed that a civil war was set in motion, and that it probably would be long and bloody!

President Lincoln reacted by calling for a volunteer army from each state to recapture the federal property. This led to declarations of secession by four more Southern states: Arkansas, North Carolina, Tennessee, and Virginia. Thad was impressed by the western part of Virginia, which refused to accompany the rest of the state in its departure from the United States.

As of July 4, Representative Stevens was no longer just a member of the Ways and Means Committee; he now was its head. Because the committee tackled the financial needs of the country, he believed he could influence the war progress significantly.

Chairman Stevens and his committee at once set to work finding money. They knew they would need at least $320,000,000 to fight the Confederate States. They determined that the best way to start would be to increase taxes on tea and coffee. The bill they proposed also included a tax on liquor, as well as an income tax of three percent.

Thad ensured that the law passed before the month was over. His colleagues immediately recognized him as an effective and efficient leader of the Ways and Means Committee.

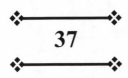

# 37

## Thad Distrusts the President 1861

When the Confiscation Bill of 1861 was introduced in the House, Thad endorsed it. This law, if passed, would provide for the confiscation, or taking by the government, of all property, including slaves, used against the United States. Enemies of the bill pronounced that such a law would be unconstitutional because Congress did not have the authority to confiscate the slaves. Radical Republican Stevens proclaimed that those who did not honor the Constitution in the first place could not ask for its protection. He added that, anyway, according to internationally accepted rules, Congress was entitled to confiscate slaves being used to aid a rebellion.

The Confiscation Bill passed in the House, and it passed in the Senate. Representative Stevens was excited! At his urging, President Lincoln signed it into law in three more days.

Thad was surprised to learn, though, that the president gave no instructions on enforcing the Act. "Hold on!" Thad criticized. "That means that, as a result, few property confiscations actually will occur!" He suddenly was no longer convinced of the president's commitment to the abolitionist cause.

Another incident, this one involving Major General John Fremont, further fed Thad's suspicion: General Fremont, who had run for president in the 1856 election, now was serving in command of the Army's Department of the West, which included the state of Missouri. Missouri was a "border state," officially neutral in the conflict between the North and South. General Fremont ordered his general, Nathaniel Lyon, to formally bring Missouri into the Union cause. General Lyon ejected the governor of Missouri and installed a pro-Union government. Then General Lyon was killed in battle, so General Fremont took over. He issued orders to confiscate secessionists' private property and to free slaves.

President Lincoln asked General Fremont to revise the orders, but he refused to do so, claiming that he was enforcing the legally-enacted Confiscation Act. The president responded by publicly annulling the orders and relieving the general of his duties.

Representative Stevens challenged the president. "Why are you doing this?"

The president expressed to Thad, "I am concerned that General Fremont's order will end the delicate balance with Missouri, pushing that state--and other slave states still in the Union--to the Southern side."

Thad was not buying it!

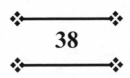

# 38

## Thad Maneuvers toward Manumission of Slaves 1861

Thad, in his distrust of and disgust for President Lincoln, concluded he would use his own resources to move the country in the direction he wanted. Like the farmers he knew in Lancaster County, who worked the soil, planted the seeds, watered the sprouts, nourished the saplings, pruned the trees, and finally, harvested the fruit, Thad himself would perform the many chores that were necessary to yield abolition of slavery.

With his speeches he would plow the soil; he would dig up the dirt, tossing it in chunks, aerating it, preparing the land to sustain a healthy field and a healthy yield.

Thad also would capitalize on his duties as chair of the Ways and Means Committee. Some of his jobs were to arrange the order of business in the House, indicate the hours of adjournment, and fix the time for reconvening sessions. The position gave him much control over the topics to be addressed during the meetings of the legislature. He would use his position to oversee the planting; he would decide which seeds held the greatest potential for growth, and choose when and where to plant them.

He planned also to water and nourish his coveted crop by exerting constant pressure on President Lincoln, by nudging him to take larger and faster steps toward emancipation of all slaves. He resolved to use all of his influence to meet his goal!

As informal leader of the radical Republicans, Representative Stevens selected yet another tactic to champion his cause: He would pull all weeds which may draw nutrients from his desired fruit. He tried to exclude from the House all members-elect from the seceded states, who might promote slavery. Horace Maynard, for example, appeared in Washington to be seated as the Tennessee Representative. Although Thad knew that Mr. Maynard personally believed in the Union, he, nevertheless, hailed from a state that had seceded. Thad moved that the qualifications of all members from the South be evaluated by a committee to determine if they may be seated. --When Thad learned that Mr. Maynard had been elected prior to the Tennessee secession vote in June, however, he withdrew his objections to his seating.

If there were stone walls marking the boundary of Thad's field, he would plant beyond them, defying the legitimacy of the borders. President Lincoln and others argued that since secession was illegal, the rebelling states were still in the Union. Thad's tactic, however, was to declare their people to be enemies from foreign countries. From this perspective, he would not be restricted in his war against slavery.

On December 2, Representative Stevens raised a resolution, to be voted upon by his colleagues, to free slaves everywhere. Of course, Thad's attempted harvest was premature; his resolution did not pass, but fellow abolitionists throughout the country were thrilled that he had even proposed it.

Thad continued to nurse his private reservations about President Lincoln. He convinced himself that the president was hopeless. He believed that the proprietor was not even interested in the farm's bearing fruit! He proclaimed to friends, "Our Republican party has been sold out in the election of Abe Lincoln; the Northwest has deceived us by labeling this Illinois lawyer a true and sound Republican." [16]

For the December recess, Thad returned to Lancaster. Private citizen 'Mr. Thaddeus Stevens and Guest' received an invitation to attend a dinner party at Wheatland, the manor of former President James Buchanan.

"Mr. Stevens and Guest, Mrs. Lydia Hamilton Smith, accept with pleasure," read the response.

Mr. Buchanan's niece, Miss Harriet Lane, served as hostess at the estate, as she had in the White House. She and head housekeeper Miss Hetty Parker had decorated the mansion with scores of red and white poinsettias before the guests arrived. Christmas melodies by a quartet of musicians resonated in the background.

Following a fine meal, and before dessert was served, conversation drifted to whether amnesty eventually might be granted to Southern leaders who would repent and seek return to the Union. Mrs. Smith noticed that Miss Hetty and some other servers were lingering beyond the door of the dining room, apparently listening to the discussion.

Mrs. Smith inconspicuously slipped into the next room to chat with them. The servants inquired about the meaning of 'amnesty.'

Mrs. Smith spoke in hushed tones. "Amnesty is a legal act by which the country would deal with the Confederate leaders who are guilty of crimes, and re-establish them as innocent persons, but without changing the laws about the crimes." She elaborated, "It actually would be forgiving the criminals without punishing them. But...Mr. Stevens believes amnesty should not be granted to these criminals."

Before the servants could ask more, Miss Hetty thanked her friend, and hustled her staff back to the kitchen. The evening advanced to delightful parlor games and ended with the group singing Christmas carols, accompanied by Miss Lane on the piano.

In a January speech, Thad maintained that the seceded South was in constant contempt of the Constitution. He contended that abolition of slavery was essential for ending the war; he argued that emancipation would force the loss of slave labor, would ruin the rebel economy and, thus, would reunite the country. "Action must be taken; the fate of the nation is at stake!" Thad emphasized.

Many, including some Northerners, thought Thad's thinking was too extreme.

Reinforcing his circle of antagonists, Thad, in February, made uncharitable public comments about ex-President Buchanan. He announced that the former president had used thousands of more dollars than were appropriated for him to furnish the White House, back in 1857, when he first had moved into it.

Thad knew that James Buchanan would be irate. Indeed, Mr. Buchanan publicly recalled that it was just several months ago that he had hosted Thad and his companion for a delightful dinner party at his mansion. He was amazed that Thad would so easily betray his hospitality and friendship.

Thad's answer was that President Buchanan had alienated many in the Lancaster community long ago by his pro-slavery politics.

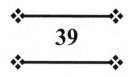

# 39

## Thad Perceives Paltry Progress 1862

Thad's toiling to tug President Lincoln into emancipating the slaves seemed to produce a small fruit on March 6. The president posed a plan for compensated release of slaves. According to the proposal, slave-owners would gradually free their slaves, and would receive some money for their financial loss.

For Thad, this arrangement, though slightly sweet, was simply too small. The rest of Congress seemed to agree: The president's paltry produce rotted on the tree; it was not appetizing to any part of the country. But—at least, the sapling had begun to sprout!

On March 13, a second small fruit appeared on Thad's plant: President Lincoln forbade Union Army officers from returning fugitive slaves to their owners.

As a third indicator of success of Thad's and his radical Republicans' press, a bill to abolish slavery in the District of Columbia, because it was not a state, was presented. Anxious for its passage, Ways and Means Committee Chairman Stevens, on April 10, maneuvered to discuss it with the full House membership —to the consternation of his enemies. He brought the bill to a successful vote in the House, and then the Senate passed it, and then the president signed it!

Thad exulted that now slavery was banned at least in Washington, D.C. --even though the government would compensate slave owners for their financial loss. Thad was certain that it was because of his and other radicals' efforts that the United States of America was able to reap this small harvest in its capital city. Now he was enormously energized!

In spite of his public cooperation with the president, Thad still disrespected him privately. He confided to a friend: "As for future hopes, they are poor, as Lincoln is nobody." [17] For Thad, President Lincoln's progress toward emancipation of slaves was way too slow. Some friends jokingly nicknamed radical, fanatical Congressman Stevens as "Thad-the-Rad."

Thad-the-Rad followed the daily accounts from the war front: Union General David Hunter was commander of the Department of the South. General Hunter was a strong advocate for arming Negroes as soldiers for the Union. He began enlisting black soldiers from South Carolina and formed the Union Army Regiment of African Descent.

In May, President Lincoln ordered General Hunter to disband the group. Thad-the-Rad intuitively predicted, "This will not end well."

General Hunter appealed to Congress; with Representative Stevens's help, the general gained approval to keep the regiment intact. Thad-the-Rad sensed that tension between himself and President Lincoln intensified.

A second storm raged in the same month: General Hunter issued an order freeing the slaves in Georgia, South Carolina, and Florida. President Lincoln rescinded the unauthorized order at once. Thad's impatience grew.

Similar to the General Fremont case the year before, the president explained to Representative Stevens that he was concerned about the political effects that the order would have in the border states. He was uneasy that sudden emancipation in the South might drive some slave-holding Unionists to the Confederacy. President Lincoln repeated his desire that the emancipation of slaves proceed gradually, with financial reimbursement for slave holders who would lose their 'property.'

Thad's response was stern. "I believe the president—and I do not mean to flatter,--is as honest a man as there is in the world, but I believe him too easy and amiable," he announced in a public debate. He added that there could be no peace until slavery was gone; as for him, he would give weapons to the slaves "and set them to shooting their masters if they (the masters) will not submit to this government." [18]

Thad's stifled cooperation with the president in political matters contrasted with his full cooperation with the president in money matters. Relative to financial issues, the president relied on him absolutely; Thad continued to steer taxation bills adeptly through the House.

In July, to Thad's delight, the Second Confiscation Act passed in both houses of Congress, and President Lincoln signed it. The new law:

- Abolished slavery in the territories that were not states;
- Liberated slaves held by rebels;
- Forbade Union soldiers to aid in the return of fugitive slaves, thereby freeing all slaves working within the armed forces;
- Stated that the slaves of any Confederate official who did not surrender within 60 days would be freed; and
- Authorized the recruitment of black troops.

Thad noted, however, a shortcoming of the Second Confiscation Act: It was applicable only to Confederate areas that had already been occupied by the Union army. In spite of the downside, Thad offered to his fellow Republicans, "Dare we venture to suspect that the national mood may be beginning to move against slavery, especially within the army?"

Thad's friends concurred. "The president and Congress, after all, have enacted, in the past year, three laws to severely restrict the practice of slavery." They enumerated: "the Confiscation Act in August 1861, the elimination of slavery in Washington in April 1862, and now the Second Confiscation Act in July."

Late in July, the radical leaders issued 'An Address to the Loyal People of the United States,' in which they praised the Confiscation Act, summoned the people to stand faithfully by the president, and asked for the arming of freed slaves. Thad signed it, with a pleasant smile. Privately, though, he still was alienated by the president's caution; he considered President Lincoln weak, ignorant of the Constitution, and incapable of leading the country in a crisis.

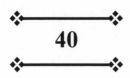

# 40

# Thad is Humbled 1862

By the time Congress adjourned at the end of July, Thad was well aware that he had become perhaps the best-known radical in the nation. He returned to Lancaster, where, continuing to agitate for an end to slavery, he presented himself as a symbol of change for the country.

In September, Representative Stevens was re-nominated by the Lancaster County Republican convention. George Steinman was nominated by the Democrats to run against him. Some prominent Lancastrians, such as Mayor J.P. Sanderson and Alexander Harris, endorsed Mr. Steinman. Mayor Sanderson snipped that Thad was "the most pestilent abolitionist that ever disgraced this district in the halls of Congress." [19] Mr. Harris was an outspoken sympathizer with the Confederacy; he made it clear that he hated Thad personally, as well as politically. But Thad couldn't have cared less what either the mayor or Alexander Harris said about him!

Thad used the election campaign to further broadcast his views. In one speech, he pledged that, if elected, he would vote to pay "not one cent to compensate for any freed slave." To whip up passion for his purpose, he cried, while flailing his cane, "Abolition! Abolition! Yes! Abolish everything on the face of the earth but this Union; free every slave; slay every traitor; burn every rebel mansion, if those things be necessary to preserve this temple of freedom to the world and to our posterity!" [20]

Many Democrats condemned Thad's fiery tirade, fearing that it would be published in the Southern papers and would upset the South even more against the North. Instead, to Thad's delight, it generated increased Northern enthusiasm. A rally of Republicans in Chicago pumped fists and chanted, "Immediate Emancipation! Immediate Emancipation!"

Next, with Thad's coaching from Lancaster, a New York abolitionist, William Patton, headed a delegation who met with President Lincoln in the White House. Mr. Patton and his party urged for emancipation of all slaves. The president replied that he had no Constitutional authority to free the slaves, and he noted that the public, as a whole, was against it.

Hearing Mr. Patton's de-briefing of the meeting, Thad thrust his lower lip forward. He predicted that the president's inaction was "preparing the people to receive an ignominious surrender to the South." [21]

On September 22, the Union won the Battle of Antietam. To Thad's surprise, President Lincoln immediately issued a preliminary Emancipation Proclamation! The president announced that, on January 1, 1863, he would formally emancipate all slaves in all of the states that were still in rebellion as of that future date!

Thad headed for D.C., where he and his fellow radicals celebrated that their persistent pestering had not been in vain!

The next day, however, Thad was deeply embarrassed when he engaged in an exchange with Vice President Hannibal Hamlin. The vice president informed him, "You know, Stevens, the president already had composed the Emancipation Proclamation back in June and July, and he shelved it temporarily to await a victorious battle."

"What are you talking about?" Thad demanded.

"You and your Mr. Patton and your General Hunter and your other radical friends did not convince Abe to free the slaves," corrected Mr. Hamlin.

"I do not understand what you are saying," Thad repeated.

"Don't you get it?" V.P. Hamlin questioned. "In President Lincoln's view, your constant verbal attacks shielded him from the attacks of others. Your very public and very extreme views made the president appear more reasonable, which resulted in his vision being more acceptable to the general citizenry. You and your radical pals paved the way for the president to take the decisive step he had long been planning —issuing the Emancipation Proclamation! President Lincoln let you take the heat until the public was ready for what he really wanted."

Thad's cane slipped out of his hand as his mouth fell open. He had no witty comeback. He was stunned and humbled to know that Abe Lincoln had outsmarted him politically!

Thad returned to his Lancaster home for the election. On October 14, he beat George Steinman, keeping his Pennsylvania seat in the House of Representatives--by a wide margin.

Thad was now 70 years old. His health was declining. Afflicted by rheumatism, on top of his *talipes equinovarus*, he was housebound during most of the fall.

--But, one afternoon, when his strength and the weather permitted it, he tottered through Central Square, following a visit to the courthouse. Turning onto South Queen Street toward his home, he came face to face with his foe, Alexander Harris. Both men stopped in their tracks, blocking each other's passage.

"I never get out of the way of a skunk," announced Mr. Harris.

"Ahh, but I always do," taunted Thad. And with a flourish of his cane, the Congressman stepped aside.

By now, both nephews had joined the army. Uncle Thad stayed in touch with them, sharing his new respect for the president, and cautioning both boys to be careful in the field. He also urged Alanson to dump his Chambersburg girlfriend, who was lying to anyone who would listen that she was his wife.

Late in November, Thad politely bowed to Mrs. Smith, extended his hand, and offered, "Madam, may I assist you into the carriage?" They departed to Washington for a short session of Congress. His home in D.C. was a brick row house at 267 South B Street. During December evenings, they entertained numerous friends there, hosting restrained dinner parties and serene Christmas celebrations. On quieter evenings Thad inched down Pennsylvania Avenue, leaning into his cane, contemplating his strategies.

During the days, he continued his efforts to restore the Union. The western part of Virginia, which had refused to accompany the rest of the state when it seceded in spring, 1861, now was seeking admission as a separate state. Representative Stevens voted to approve the admission of West Virginia.

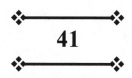

# 41

## Thad Experiences the War - Up Close and Personal 1863

On January 1, 1863, as promised, President Lincoln issued the Emancipation Proclamation. It declared 50,000 slaves instantaneously free, with the rest to be freed as Union armies progressed. By now, Thad was seeing the president's emancipation order as unmistakably inadequate, because it was limited to only the Confederate States. He thought it should affect all of the states. Nevertheless, in fake support, he shepherded a bill for the recruitment of 150,000 black soldiers through quick passage by the House. The Senate quickly passed it as well.

Representative Stevens shared this news with his friend, Lydia Smith. Mrs. Smith shared it with her second son, Isaac, who had achieved celebrity status in Lancaster as a banjo player and a barber. The next morning Isaac enlisted in the Sixth U.S. Colored Troops.

Mrs. Smith bid her son farewell. "I fear for your safety, Isaac, as your brother's death by gunshot occurred just three years ago; however, I honor your decision to defend the Union, and I will pray daily for your safe return."

Drafting an acceptable Enrollment Bill became Congressman Stevens's next pet project. The bill would draft, or demand, every male citizen between ages 20 and 45 to join the Union Army. Its purpose was to provide fresh manpower, and it would establish a quota of new troops due from each community.

Although Thad backed the basic idea of the bill, he did not like the paragraphs about substitution and commutation. The policies of substitution and commutation allowed any draftee to choose not to serve if he would either supply a suitable substitute soldier, or pay the government $300 toward the cost of the war. Both of these practices were created with the intention of softening the effect of the draft on those—such as Quakers--who did not believe in fighting. In spite of Thad's hesitations, on March 3, the plan became law, known both as the Enrollment Act and the Third Conscription Act.

On March 14, Congress called a recess, and Thad returned to Pennsylvania.

Several days later, a large number of citizens assembled at Central Square in Lancaster to listen to a well-known band. The musicians and the crowd, as prearranged, moved down the block to Thad's house. Playing "Battle Hymn of the Republic," they called him outside, then struck up "Hail to the Chief." A quickly-selected spokesperson expressed the citizens' gratitude for his efforts.

Thad saw this occasion as another opportunity: He thanked his constituents for their continued confidence in him, and he charged the Democrats with responsibility for prolonging the war. He was startled when some Democrats from the Cabbage Hill neighborhood pelted him with rotten eggs. The egg-tossers were shoved away, the speech resumed, and the event ended with the playing of a popular patriotic song, 'The Star-Spangled Banner.'

Thad delivered further speeches in Lancaster and elsewhere, clarifying his goals. In early April, he specified: The Constitution must be amended to end slavery; the Emancipation Proclamation must be expanded to cover the whole country; and military tribunals must be set up to sell the lands of the rebels.

Several weeks later, a Union force suffered defeat at Chancellorsville, Virginia. Uncle Thaddeus received word that Thaddeus Junior's horse was shot from under him during that battle, not once, but twice!

In June, Thad heard that the Confederates had invaded Pennsylvania, and that his treasured Gettysburg had been severely assaulted. The part about Gettysburg turned out not to be true, but the military activity in the vicinity was worrisome to Thad. He visited his Caledonia ironworks, near Gettysburg, to implement security measures.

While he was meeting with his manager, John Sweeney, word came that Confederate General Jubal Early was leading a foraging party toward his forge. Thad was hurried away to Shippensburg by a back road, protesting fiercely all the way. General Early arrived at the foundry, and proceeded to destroy the place.

Thad learned later that Mr. Sweeney had pleaded with General Early to have mercy. He claimed that his boss, Mr. Stevens, had been losing money at the forge and would benefit by its destruction while the employees would suffer. The general disregarded his pleas.

While Thad awaited more news on his losses, he was notified, again, that the town of Gettysburg had been violated. This time it turned out to be true.

General Robert E. Lee had led his Confederate army northward, in pursuit of the Union army. He and his high-spirited troops collided with Major General George Meade and his weary Union soldiers at Gettysburg on July 1. By the end of the day, General Lee's corps sent Union troops retreating through the streets of the town.

On the second day of battle, July 2, despite significant losses, the Union defenders held their lines.

On the third day, July 3, the main event was a dramatic assault by 12,500 Confederates against the Union line. The charge was resisted by the Union army, with innumerable casualties suffered by both sides. General Lee finally led his forces on a torturous retreat to Virginia, ending his invasion into the North!

Thad's housekeeper, Mrs. Smith, read newspaper reports that, by the end of the Battle of Gettysburg, tens of thousands of Americans from both armies lay dead, and tens of thousands more lay injured. She instantly notified her employer that she would be leaving her post for a while to tend to the suffering soldiers. Thad urged her not to embrace so dangerous a mission, but in the end, she borrowed a horse and wagon and headed west from Lancaster toward Adams County.

A week later, Thad learned, in a letter from Manager Sweeney, details of the devastation at his Caledonia Forge. The statement itemized the rebels' exploits. They had:

- Seized the horses, mules, and carriages, with their gear;
- Burned a furnace, a rolling mill, and two forges to the ground;
- Pilfered 4,000 pounds of bacon and molasses;
- Taken several thousand dollars worth of corn and other grains;
- Decimated the office and the storeroom, with all the books;
- Hauled off the bar iron;
- Destroyed the fencing; and
- Ransacked the workers' cottages.

Manager Sweeney relayed that, as the violators finished their destruction, they "expressed great regret that they were not so fortunate as to meet the owner..." [22]

Thad wrote to a friend, Simon Stevens: "...But all this gives me no concern, although it was just about the savings of my life...I have, I think, enough left to pay my debts. As to my personal wants, nature soon will take care of them. We must all expect to suffer by this wicked war. I have not felt a moment's trouble for my share of it. If, finally, the government shall be re-established over our whole territory, and not a vestige of slavery left, I shall deem it a cheap purchase..."

Expressing concerns about his employees, Thad added, "I do not know what the poor families will do. I must provide for their present relief."

Simon, to whom he had written, offered financial help. Thad answered that he did not want it. "If necessary, I will retire from Congress so that I might devote myself full time to my law practice to earn the needed funds..." [23]

Thad's losses were widely reported. Some people sympathized with him; his enemies, however, editorialized that 'his chickens had come home to roost.' After all, they said, he had encouraged the burning of every rebel mansion; now he himself was the victim. [24]

Thad visited Adams County personally to view the damage. Next, he traversed the Gettysburg battlefields until he located Mrs. Smith and her wagon. She recounted to him that she had traveled through farms and towns, telling residents about the masses of suffering soldiers stranded on the battlefields and in field infirmaries. She collected donations of food and clothing, and when she reached the makeshift hospitals, she distributed the goods among the injured men. Day after day, she visited homesteads to heap her wagon high, and returned, weary from miles of travel, to minister to the miserable men. She added that she viewed them all, Union and Confederate alike, as wounded humans. She pledged that when her donations were depleted, she would spend her own life savings on the mission, and then, with permission from her employer, she would return to her job in Lancaster. Thad, happy to know that she was safe, gave her some money to continue her mission.

Now, thinking that the turning point of the war may have arrived, Thad was cautiously optimistic. Simultaneously, he was worried about his nephews Alanson and Thaddeus Junior, as well as Isaac Smith, all of whom were actively engaged in the army.

Again, any hopes he had were cut short: In late September, Thad received the news that he was always anticipating in the back of his mind: Nephew Alanson was counted among an immense number of deaths in the Battle of Chickamauga, which was fought along the Tennessee/Georgia border. The battle was second to Gettysburg in number of casualties claimed.

Mrs. Smith returned from her Adams County expedition to console her boss in his bereavement. Thad was despondent both over the loss of his nephew and over the loss of the battle.

Now, he worried night and day about the welfare of Thaddeus Junior and Isaac. He interceded for Thaddeus Junior with the Secretary of War, asking that he might be privileged with a safer position. The Secretary of War yielded to the plea by appointing the young man as provost marshal in his own town of Lancaster.

President Lincoln, in an attempt to foster a sense of American unity, chose to standardize the date of a feast of Thanksgiving for God-given blessings. He pronounced that, beginning this year, Thanksgiving shall be commemorated on the final Thursday of November. The Stevens household, as well as most of the South, declined to participate.

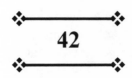

# 42

## Thad Authors a Thirteenth Amendment to Abolish Slavery 1864

Thad found himself reflecting extensively on what was going to happen when the war was over. If the Union wins, he wondered:

- How should the eleven states that seceded from the Union be re-admitted?
- What should be the consequences for the Confederate leaders?
- What rights should be granted to the 4,000,000 slaves who would be freed?
- How would these rights be protected?
- How should the war-torn South be re-built?

He considered these questions himself, and he tried to engage his friends and colleagues in conversations about them over lunches and during dinner parties, throughout meetings and in hallways, in Lancaster and in Washington. His listeners agreed that the questions represented valid and complex issues, but remarked that this was not the best time to talk about them.

Following a prolonged break from official business, the Thirty-Eighth Congress re-convened in December 1863. Thad immediately and consistently focused his attention on two issues.

The first was a Constitutional amendment that would totally abolish slavery. Thad worked closely with radical Republican Representative James Ashley, from Ohio, to develop a draft of a Thirteenth Amendment to accomplish that. But very few House members were interested in it; other issues were infinitely more pressing, they said. Thad placed his amendment in a secure spot on a back burner.

Thad's second focal point was how to deal with the seceded states and their leaders, as it was clear to him that they would be conquered. He referred to this process as Reconstruction of the United States. His rivals and his allies alike accused him of being premature, as the war was far from over, they suspected.

Eventually, Louisiana expressed a desire to return to the Union, and was preparing to send representatives to Congress. Congress now was forced to address the problems Thad had been posing.

Although Thad had supported the seating of the members from West Virginia, he demanded that Louisiana's representatives be excluded. He insisted that Louisiana and the other seceded states were no longer in the Union; therefore, they were subject to being treated the same as if they were conquered countries. In short, he thought the rebels must be severely punished, and he delivered speeches airing his opinions. "We cannot admit to Congress any representatives from these states, even if they were seated in the previous Congress," he maintained.

Meanwhile, on December 8, President Lincoln issued a Proclamation of Amnesty. This was his plan for settlement with the South. It guaranteed forgiveness for those rebels willing to swear an oath of loyalty to the Constitution and agreeing to abide by the Emancipation Proclamation. It stated that when ten percent of those in the 1861 voting population of a state had met these expectations, the state immediately would be permitted to reorganize its government.

"Ten percent!" Thad-the-Rad Stevens exclaimed. "You've got to be kidding!" He found this number to be very offensive because it was so very small.

To end the year, in the interest of racial justice, Representative Stevens introduced a bill to equalize pay of black soldiers with the pay of white soldiers. Negroes had received merely $10 a month, compared to the $13 a month (plus a clothing allowance of $3.50) that white soldiers earned.

A quiet and restful Christmas break nurtured a burst of energy for Thad's new year. On January 11, he presented a formal response to the president's Proclamation of Amnesty. He insisted on harsher terms for the re-admission of the states, as well as confiscation of the Confederate leaders' property. From his point of view, the question was whether the rebellious states, after inflicting great damage on the Union, should be permitted to simply come back and resume their roles in Congress. After all, he reasoned, they had renounced their loyalty to the United States and organized a separate government!

Also in January, Senator John Henderson from Missouri presented a draft of a Thirteenth Amendment to the Constitution, to totally abolish slavery in the United States. His version was slightly revised from Representative Ashley's December draft. Senator Henderson's choice of words received approval by the Senate, but it failed to obtain the necessary two-thirds majority in the House. Thad was one who wanted it to be more strongly stated. Others thought it was already too strong.

Among other radicals, Representative Henry Davis, a Maryland Unionist and a friend of Thad, also was dissatisfied with President Lincoln's Amnesty Proclamation. In February, he introduced a bill that was much more rigorous than the president's 'Ten Percent' plan. Thad did not think even this bill was sufficiently austere, so he ventured a revised version. Thad's colleagues in Congress received his ideas unenthusiastically.

In February, Thad sought to improve the Enrollment Act/ Conscription Act of 1863. Although he originally did not approve of the clause about paying $300 to avoid the draft, he now decided it was a good way to collect money to finance the war. He also knew it was an acceptable alternative for the many Quakers who did not believe in fighting-- and who were his constituents. He voted to increase the exemption price to $400. The bill passed.

On March 28, radical Republican Stevens presented his own wording for a Thirteenth Amendment. Again, he did not succeed in bringing it to a vote.

In the meantime, Ohio Senator Benjamin Wade drafted revisions to Representative Davis' amnesty bill. Now the measure became known as the Wade-Davis Bill. Misters Wade and Davis contended that government should be re-established in the rebel states only when fifty percent of the male white citizens--instead of the president's ten percent--took an oath of loyalty to the Union. Still, Thad did not like it; he thought that the fifty percent requirement still was too low!

On May 4, the Wade-Davis Bill came to a vote in the House. Thad found himself in a dilemma: The bill was at least better than the president's plan, so he actually wanted it to pass. But he couldn't vote 'yes,' because he believed it was not nearly oppressive enough. He reasoned that if he chose not to vote at all, then he indirectly would be helping it to pass, without publicly endorsing it. So he chose to abstain from voting. It passed in the House, without Thad's vote.

On June 28, 1864, thirteen years following the incident in Christiana, Thad saw the Fugitive Slave Law repealed. His joy was small, because it was long overdue.

On July 2, the Wade-Davis Bill passed in the Senate. It moved on to President Lincoln for his signature. The president did not want the bill to become law. He knew that if he vetoed it, he would risk the possibility that Congress would override his veto. Rather than sign it, he chose to 'put it in his pocket.'

The president defended his decision by claiming that it was a question of timing: "This bill was placed before me a few minutes before Congress adjourned. It is a matter of too much importance to be swallowed in that way." [25] And so, the 'Fifty Percent' plan failed to become law. Thad Stevens and his radical Republicans were furious with President Lincoln's 'pocket veto.'

Also upsetting to Thad and his friends, the war was not going well. Union General Grant's offensive against Richmond, Virginia, had resulted in tremendous loss of life; General Butler's assault, also upon Richmond, ended in fiasco; troops in the Valley of Virginia were defeated; and General Sherman was making little progress in his aggression against Atlanta, Georgia.

Meanwhile, 1864 was a presidential election year. General George McClellan became the Democrats' candidate.

Many radical Republicans were talking seriously about replacing President Lincoln. They were discouraged by the gloomy war progress. Impatient as Thad was with the president, he decided it would be best not to abandon him at this time. In May, a convention of Radical Republicans--which did not include Thad -- nominated John Fremont on a third-party ticket.

Thad, instead, publicly and forcefully endorsed Abraham Lincoln, whose Republican party had changed its name to the National Union party. Thad was unhappy, however, with the party's choice for running mate: Andrew Johnson of Tennessee. Andrew Johnson was actually a Democrat, a Southerner, and a Mason.

Thad commented loudly at the June convention, "Can't you get a candidate for vice president without going down into a damned rebel province for one?" [26] He grew pleased, however, when the National Union party promised to campaign with a clear and consistent commitment to create a Thirteenth Constitutional Amendment which would abolish slavery!

Amid pressure to unseat President Lincoln, Thad tried to allay the fray by urging him to make changes in his cabinet. At first, the president refused to cooperate, but by early September, his cabinet was acceptable to Thad and other party leaders.

Next, Union General Farragut took possession of Mobile Bay in Alabama, and General Sherman captured Atlanta, Georgia. Now there was little question that Union victory was close at hand. Suddenly the remainder of the radical Republicans were sufficiently satisfied with President Lincoln. Third-party Candidate Fremont therefore withdrew from the competition, leaving General McClellan and President Lincoln to duke it out.

Thad himself was unanimously re-nominated in September. He thanked his fans for their constant confidence in him. On Congressional Election Day in October, he easily beat his opponent, Hugh North, a lawyer from Columbia.

Thad, not confident that President Lincoln was going to be re-elected, delivered many passionate speeches applauding him. Following Presidential Election Day, November 8, Thad proudly credited himself for having delivered Pennsylvania, indeed the country, to the president.

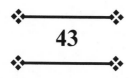

# 43

## Thad Grieves for the President 1865

Representative James Ashley, in January, re-sponsored Thad's proposed Thirteenth Amendment, which had failed earlier. The proposed amendment stated:

*"Neither slavery nor involuntary servitude, except as a punishment for crime whereof the party shall have been duly convicted, shall exist within the United States..."* [27]

This time, President Lincoln reflected that the time was right, and he enthusiastically cheered the statement! With the president's full endorsement of the amendment to abolish slavery, Thad realized that the president possessed some awesome abilities!

Thad recalled the insight he had gained into President Lincoln's thinking when he had issued the Emancipation Proclamation over two years ago. Now he understood, even more clearly, why the president had withheld public affirmation of the Thirteenth Amendment: This was what the president had wanted all along, but he also wanted to be sure the proposal had the support of enough of the country that it could be accepted and enforced! President Lincoln, again, had only been biding his time! Republican Stevens shook his head in admiration.

On January 31, the Thirteenth Amendment to the Constitution, which Thad had had a hand in drafting, received the necessary two-thirds majority vote in the House! Thad, his fellow Representatives, and spectators burst into rowdy applause! All that remained was for the Senate to pass it, and the three-fourths of the states to ratify it. It would then be a part of the U.S. Constitution!

Thad was joyful when, on March 3, President Lincoln signed the Freedmen's Bureau Act, creating an agency to assist freed slaves.

Its purpose was to aid former slaves by providing food, housing, education, medical care, and employment. Congress envisioned that the agency would operate for one year.

At this time Thad also was engaging in discussions about granting suffrage--the right to vote--to blacks, but having learned a lesson from the president about biding his time, he did not push.

On March 4, the day of Abraham Lincoln's second inauguration, rain fell, off-and-on. Vice President-elect Andrew Johnson took his oath of office first. Thad and the thirty thousand others in the audience soon noticed that Vice President Johnson was slurring his words! His speech was incoherent! The listeners quickly concluded he was drunk. They were shocked and mortified. Thad was disgusted and sickened.

A short time later, when President Lincoln rose to deliver his inaugural address, the sun suddenly burst through the clouds. Thad's heart jumped. "Surely, the sun is a good omen. The end of the war is in sight, and Reconstruction will begin smoothly," he prophesied to his companions.

In spite of his positive premonition, during the next week, Representative Stevens resisted the president's effort to complete the re-admission of Louisiana. Louisiana had taken advantage of the president's offer of amnesty by abolishing slavery, and now considered itself ready for restored statehood. But Thad insisted that Louisiana was not eligible to come back into the Union.

After Congress adjourned on March 11, Representative Stevens stopped at the White House to say good-bye to President Lincoln. He urged the president to see the Reconstruction agenda as he saw it. The president listened to his guest, then answered, "Stevens, this is a pretty big hog we are trying to catch and hold onto when we catch him. We must take care that he does not slip away from us." [28]

During Thad's railway ride to Lancaster, he thought for a long time about what the leader of the country had said to him.

April 1865 was an unforgettable month for Thad:

On the 2nd, Union troops took control of Richmond, Virginia, the capital of the Confederate States of America.

On the 4th, Thad marked his 73rd birthday at home in Lancaster, with a small party. Mrs. Smith baked a cake, and invited Christopher Dice and his family to join them.

On the 9th, in a town called Appomattox Court House, Virginia, General Robert E. Lee, with his army of Southern rebels, surrendered to the Union army led by General U.S. Grant. Thus, the Civil War officially ended! The Confederate States of America ceased to exist! Thad rejoiced with Lydia and his neighbors, but he also knew that this was just the beginning of another difficult struggle: the Reconstruction of the country.

A great celebration was hurriedly organized for the next day at the Lancaster courthouse, with Thad as the main speaker. First, he thanked Heaven for the glorious victory. Then he expressed hope that equal rights for men of every race and color might come next. He stated that he might forgive "the ignorant, the poor and the deluded," but cried, "To permit the ringleaders of the South to escape with absolute forgiveness is absolute cruelty. Their riches ought to be seized, their lands confiscated, and the proceeds sold to meet the national debt." [29] He closed by promising he would continue pushing for stern punishment.

On Tuesday, the 11th, the President Lincoln publicly endorsed Thad's petition for the right to vote for intelligent blacks and those who had served in the Union army. Thad was pleased with the steps the president was taking. In fact, he was feeling very happy with life.

On April 14, Good Friday, during the late night hours, loud pounding on the door beneath Thad's bedroom window in Lancaster awoke him. He looked outside to see what was the problem. It was an acquaintance, who was shouting, "The President is dying! The President has been mortally wounded!" Thad rushed down the stairs, hopping on his good leg, and almost fell as he opened the front door. The visitor breathlessly disclosed that President and Mrs. Lincoln were at Ford's Theater in Washington during the evening, watching a play, when gunshots rang out at 10:15, and President Lincoln slumped to the floor! Attending physicians were offering no hope!

Representative Stevens's first thoughts were about the man who would now become president: Andrew Johnson. He remembered the chaos that had ensued when John Tyler and Millard Fillmore had risen from the vice presidency to the presidency under similar conditions. He buried his head in his hands in despair.

Thad spent the rest of the night brooding in his armchair in his parlor. He knew that Andrew Johnson was a Southerner, a native of North Carolina. Like Thad himself, as a youth he had known nothing but poverty.

Relative to education, their backgrounds were different: As an illiterate 13-year-old, Andrew Johnson had been apprenticed to a tailor. It was not until he was a grown man that he had learned from his wife how to read and write. While stitching morning coats for gentlemen, he had listened as she read books to him.

Thad pondered the implications of Andrew Johnson's more recent history: In time, he had moved to Tennessee, where he established a thriving tailor shop, joined the Masons, and entered a political career. Repeatedly elected to his state legislature, he served as governor of Tennessee, and then as U.S. senator. He always was a Democrat, had owned several slaves--even if he did free them in 1863--, and defended slavery on the grounds that the Constitution protected it. Thad, his lower lip trembling, had no reason to believe that Andrew Johnson had discarded the prejudices of his Southern upbringing.

Yet, Thad considered, the president-to-be lived in the Unionist part of Tennessee and demonstrated hostility to the leaders of the secession movement. He had remained loyal to the Union, the only senator from a seceding state to do so. Finally, he had become convinced of the necessity for emancipation, not so much for ideological reasons as for practical reasons--because he thought it necessary to win the war.

In mid-morning, following Thad's angst-ridden hours, a telegram arrived confirming that the president had died at 7:22 a.m. The mayor of Lancaster issued a proclamation suspending all business. Flags flew at half-mast; church bells tolled; newspaper presses rolled.

The next day, Thad read that a funeral train bearing the president's remains would travel in a roundabout route from Washington to Springfield, Illinois, where he would be buried. Thad knew that hundreds, maybe thousands, of officials and common citizens would meet the train everywhere it stopped.

When the processional paused in Lancaster, Congressman Stevens chose not to be among the dignitaries. He told people he was ill, but he watched from the nearby railroad bridge. He leaned heavily on his cane with one hand and tipped his hat with the other.

# 44

# Thad Advances His Brand of Reconstruction 1865

Thad noticed that, at first, President Johnson talked tough about the 'traitors.' When some of Thad's allies suggested that ten of the strongest Confederate leaders be hanged, President Johnson hinted that the number might be greater. He even seemed to be in favor of Negro suffrage. Still, Thad did not trust him.

It wasn't long before Thad saw President Johnson's true colors! In May, while Congress was not in session, the president welcomed Virginia as a restored state. Thad was infuriated! He had stressed that only Congress could set the terms for Reconstruction; the president was merely entitled to make recommendations!

Thad immediately journeyed to D.C. to protest, but the president refused to meet with him. He sent a letter to the president, but the president did not respond. Thad, quite angry, returned to Lancaster.

Several weeks later, with Congress still not in session, President Johnson issued his own Proclamation of Amnesty. In it, he granted pardon to all former rebels who would be willing to take an oath of loyalty to the United States of America. He also authorized North Carolina to call a convention of white voters to reconstitute their state government.

Thad, in denial of his increasingly familiar frailty, was beside himself. "How dare Andrew Johnson recognize rebel states as still being in the Union," he roared, "inviting them to elect representatives, and placing power in the hands of the former rebels! President Johnson is treating them as if they never defied the United States, as if the four bloody years never happened!" --And Congress was not scheduled to be in session until December!

During the succeeding months, President Johnson allowed additional new state governments to be organized throughout the South. Thad was frequently in physical distress, but he stood steadfast against the new president regarding the process of Reconstruction. He and his radical friends concluded that the best thing they could do, until Congress would meet, was to thoroughly inform the public about the president's treachery. They made speeches around the country condemning his actions.

In June, Thad again traveled to Washington to urge the president to change his ways. Again, the president would not see him; again, he wrote a letter, and again, the president disregarded it.

When Thad returned to Lancaster after this wasted mission, early in July, a large crowd greeted him at the train station. They demonstrated their solidarity with him by ringing bells, firing cannons, and displaying a regiment of soldiers. His nephew, Chief Marshall Thaddeus Stevens Junior, led the troops. Across the country, other groups similarly were expressing support for Thad's stance, including outrage against President Johnson. Thad felt encouraged.

In late July, Thad traveled to a spa in Bedford Springs, in the mountains west of Harrisburg, to nurse his health. Immersed in hot mineral baths he plotted--with Representative William Kelley of Philadelphia--some strategies they would use to influence the Republican convention scheduled to be held the next month.

Although the August convention formally endorsed President Johnson's policy, Thad and William led the group to adopt three resolutions that they wanted: The first specified that the Southern states could not be safely entrusted with the political rights they had forfeited. The second asserted that Congress should be in control of the Reconstruction process. The third called for the seizure of Southern property to defray the national debt that had been incurred by the war. These resolutions, of course, did not carry the force of law; they were only statements of belief by the Republican party.

On September 6, Thad summoned the strength to deliver a speech to his fellow citizens at the Lancaster courthouse. He revealed that his purpose was to reshape Southern society. He maintained that the rebel states had defied the Constitution, and therefore must be treated as foreign enemies. Thad's address commanded the attention of the whole nation. He ensured that all members of Congress, as well as newspapers across the country, received copies of it.

On October 3, he delivered a similar speech in Gettysburg. Again, copies were sent to one and all.

In response to Thad's speeches, a number of pleas came from Southern states, asking for his help. He received information, for example, that Confederates were still leading and taking over government positions in some states; freed slaves were being treated in ways little improved from before they were freed. A North Carolinian begged: "Do not let Congress again place us in the power of the men who betrayed us." A writer from Louisiana stated that feelings about the Union presently were more negative than at any time during the war. Folks in Alabama communicated that no loyalty to the U.S. government existed in their community. A government employee who returned from the South reported that the president's policy had caused former Confederates to re-gain power.

Thad considered how he might gain more influence over the Reconstruction process. Both his collection of admirers and his horde of adversaries had been growing as a result of his direct communication of his rigid philosophy. He concluded that if the process of Reconstruction were referred to a committee, and if he were a member of that committee, he might wield more influence than as an individual speaker. He talked freely about his idea before Congress even met, seeking to win enthusiasm for it.

Thad went to the White House once again, on November 29, a few days before the new session of Congress was to open. Finally, President Johnson met with him. He expressed to the president his opposition to pardons for rebels, and told him that few approved of the president's approach to Reconstruction. The president answered with an appeal for harmony for the sake of the country. Following that futile meeting, Thad met with fellow radicals to make plans.

The regular session of the Thirty-Ninth Congress was called to order on Monday, December 4. The events of the first several days were a well-rehearsed performance by Representative Stevens and his collaborators: First, they refused to seat the gentlemen from Tennessee, and then they refused to seat the representatives who had been elected during the summer and fall by the recently-rebel states.

Next, Thad moved to establish a Joint Committee of Fifteen for Reconstruction--nine from the House, and six from the Senate. The committee's purpose would be to investigate and report on the status of the rebel states and recommend whether they were worthy of re-admission. No member from a Southern state was to be seated in Congress, he proposed, until the committee approved that state.

The proposal passed in the House, and several days later, the Senate approved it. The resolution was drafted and adopted in a form such that it did not need the president's signature. As predetermined, Representative Stevens was appointed to serve on the Reconstruction Committee.

Another December 4 event was the president's delivery of his annual address to Congress. President Johnson explained that, from his viewpoint, the states did not secede; they had only pretended to secede. Thus, the secessions were invalid from the beginning. He added that he intended to count the Southern states for the purpose of ratifying the Thirteenth Amendment. Thad reacted by intensifying his intent to prevent the president's plan from being fulfilled.

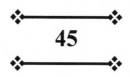

# 45

## Thad Pens Another Amendment 1865

On December 5, Representative Stevens proposed a Fourteenth Constitutional Amendment. His amendment would base the number of Congressional representatives from a state on the number of legal voters in the state. This would force voters to want to include blacks among their numbers, as more voters would equal more representatives. His amendment also would require that state laws apply equally to all citizens, whatever their race or color. The discussion began!

Meanwhile, on the next day, the ratification process for the Thirteenth Amendment was complete. Georgia was the 27th of the 36 states to ratify the amendment, thus meeting the milestone of 75 percent of the states. The amendment prohibiting slavery finally was adopted! "Now," thought Thad, "to keep the energy flowing for the Fourteenth Amendment."

Two weeks later, Representative Stevens delivered a rebuttal to the president's December 4 message to Congress. In expectation of a sensational statement, members on both the Republican and Democratic sides crowded around the speaker.

Thad, in poor health, began with a faint voice. He asserted that it mattered little whether the rebel states were considered in or out of the Union; in either case, they were dead carcasses, and only an act of Congress would permit them to resume their former position, because only Congress had the right to admit new states.

Thad's voice grew stronger as he continued his arguments. "The Confederate states must not be re-admitted until their constitutions are amended to base representation on the number of actual voters," he stressed. He also demanded that those states not be counted toward ratification of the newly proposed amendment. By the close of Thad's speech, his voice was weak again, and he padded slowly to his seat, breathless and shaking.

As expected, Representative Stevens's friends and foes alike received his message as powerful. Many radicals across the country praised him, essentially offering him sainthood. In contrast, at the urging of President Johnson, Henry Raymond, editor of *New York Times*, countered Thad's address, in a newspaper editorial. He denounced Thaddeus Stevens as obsessive and irresponsible. He asserted that no more Constitutional amendments were needed.

Thad sarcastically commented, "A newspaper piece is certainly an unusual path for a president to take to respond to a speech in Congress!"

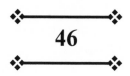

# 46

## Thad Makes Concessions 1866

Following a brief Christmas break, the House of Representatives re-assembled on January 6. Without delay, Thad engineered a subcommittee to visit President Johnson to ask him to refrain from acting on any further Reconstruction matters without approval of the Reconstruction Committee. The subcommittee met with the president, and he agreed to their request. Thad reacted with "Hmph!"

On January 9, Representative Stevens re-proposed his Fourteenth Amendment calling for the number of representatives from each state to be based on the number of legal voters. Representative Conkling, from New York, added the word "male." The draft was not accepted.

Many revisions later, Thad, on January 31, again delivered his recommended amendment to the House. In his speech, he took issue with Henry Raymond's statement, on behalf of the president, that no amendment was needed. "Indeed, Congress has a duty to pass one. Now is the time to rewrite the Constitution in accordance with the wishes of the founding fathers," [30] Thad emphasized.

Thad's speech was dissected across the country. The *Chicago Tribune* tagged it "Stevens's' triumph." Others, however, called it a "disgraceful speech," ranting that his words had shown disrespect to the president. Even some fellow radicals were angry because no mention of Negro suffrage appeared in it. Thad empathized with their issue, but reminded his colleagues that he had learned from Abraham Lincoln that it was politically astute to win one issue at a time.

Thad's wording for the Fourteenth Amendment now passed in the House with the crucial two-thirds of votes. Next, it had to be accepted by the Senate, and then by the individual states.

While the Senate was considering the amendment, the Reconstruction Committee turned to a discussion of the re-admission of Tennessee. Thad, in December, had remarked, "The state of Tennessee is not known to Congress," [31] but now, he was in favor of its restoration to the Union.

In the meantime, Thad backed a bill to extend the life of the Freedmen's Bureau, as it was a minor move to solve simple problems. Both houses of Congress effortlessly passed the Freedmen's Bureau Bill on February 19. To everyone's surprise, President Johnson vetoed it!

This caused another major blow-up between President Johnson and Thad Stevens. Andrew Johnson, stubborn like Thad himself, was totally unwilling to concede even to the smallest demands of Republicans! Thad was so furious that he changed his mind about promoting the re-admission of Tennessee into the Union!

The president then alienated Thad and his radicals even further by his speech on February 22. In it, he snarled that, unlike some men, including "Thaddeus Stevens of Pennsylvania," he was in favor of the preservation of the Union.

The speech caused an uproar in Congress! "Andrew Johnson is actually naming names!" Republicans were shouting. "How unacceptable, how unprofessional, how un-presidential, in a public speech, to personally attack those who express a difference of opinion!"

Amid the furor, a Republican congressman from Massachusetts, Nathaniel Banks, suggested, "A certain fellow representative may have given the president plenty of ammunition for the public assault." [32] All eyes moved to Thad Stevens, who just grinned.

The next day, the Senate approved a Fourteenth Amendment modified from the one that had passed with Thad's wording in the House. Now the House and the Senate, coordinated by a frail Thad, would need to make more compromises until both settled on the same version.

In early March, both houses of Congress passed a Civil Rights Bill. It declared that every person born in the U.S. is an American citizen, without regard to race, color, or previous condition of slavery. It was intended to provide the freed slaves with all the rights possessed by whites. Lo and behold, President Johnson vetoed the Civil Rights Bill! Thad's lower lip shook in anger.

This time, however, the president's veto was overridden by the necessary two-thirds majority in Congress, and the overridden bill became the Civil Rights Act of 1866. With this, Thad believed that life was beginning to improve for himself, his radical colleagues, and his country!

Thad and his committee continued to draft a Fourteenth Amendment that would be acceptable to both houses of Congress. Finally, following many concessions, Thad, the House, and the Senate agreed on the wording, and voted to approve the Fourteenth Amendment to the United States Constitution! The only remaining requirement was that three-fourths of the states --28 of 37-- ratify it.

Thad proudly expounded on the amendment's three sections-- the Citizenship Clause, the Due Process Clause, and the Equal Protection Clause. "The Citizenship Clause," he recited to reporters, "will give citizenship to blacks. The Due Process Clause will prohibit state and local governments from depriving white or black persons of life, liberty, or property without certain steps being taken. The Equal Protection Clause will require each state to apply all federal and state laws equally to whites and blacks." [33]

Next, the Freedmen's Bureau Bill was passed over President Johnson's veto. Now it, too, was law.

On July 28, Congress called a recess. During Thad's carriage ride to Lancaster, he glowed; he giggled like a schoolboy as he considered the recent major victories over the president's pig-headedness. Refocusing his musings more maturely, he felt satisfied that, to some extent, he had triumphed in his quest for robust retribution for those responsible for the rebellion.

What he had not won, he conceded to himself, was the confiscation of Confederate property to give to freedmen or to be sold to allay war costs; nor had he won black suffrage. But he and his radical colleagues had cleared the path!

In addition, he reminded himself, he recently had met his commitment to his employees of his Caledonia Forge, destroyed three years ago: He had continued to pay the living expenses of every last one of them until each was re-established in a new job. As he drifted into a nap, he smiled serenely.

At the Lancaster County Republican Convention in August, Thad was re-nominated for his seat in the House. He set the platform for his re-election campaign by declaring his endorsement of Negro suffrage, and he set his tone for the campaign by blaming President Johnson for the country's difficulties. Throughout the campaign, Thad was hearing complaints, and reminding his electorate, that the president had been appointing his political allies as officials in the Southern states, and in other cases, dismissing generals who were his political enemies.

The *Lancaster Examiner* urged its readers to vote for Thad: "No man in Congress has served the people with a more determined zeal, and with better success, than Thaddeus Stevens." [34] The editorial added that he was clearly the leader of the Republican party in Congress.

On October 9, the citizens of the Lancaster County Congressional District took the newspaper's advice, and re-elected Thad as their delegate to the House of Representatives.

Thad, when he returned to Washington, dramatically warned, "During last winter I was rather conservative, but now I am radical, and I expect to be so for the remainder of my days." [35]

On the opening morning of Congress, December 3, Thad was angered when he saw in the newspaper the text of the president's annual address to Congress. President Johnson had not yet delivered the message in Congress, yet it was published in the paper!

When the session began, Thad directed the clerk of the House, "I call upon you to read the president's message from the newspaper to the entire House membership." [36]

The clerk responded, "Mr. Stevens, the newspaper account is not the official message."

Thad drolled, "I really didn't want to hear it anyway, but I just wanted to call attention to President Johnson's disrespect of Congress!" His comment drowned in a flood of loud laughter!

On the same day, Thad introduced a regulation that he labeled the Tenure of Office Bill. The bill would prohibit the president from firing or hiring cabinet members without the Senate's approval. The House decided to debate the issue.

Next, the Joint Committee on Reconstruction was re-constituted, and, at the urging of Representative Stevens, the Committee decided again to bar all members-elect from the South from taking their seats before they were approved.

After the December break, Representative Stevens introduced a Reconstruction Bill. It would require that Negro suffrage be guaranteed by all states seeking re-admission, and it would prohibit former Confederate officeholders from re-assuming positions of authority. Alas, this bill received little support from Thad's colleagues.

Following much consternation and concession on Thad's part, both houses of Congress passed a revised Reconstruction Bill. This version abolished all Southern state governments formed under President Johnson's plan; it divided the South into five military districts, each commanded by a general appointed by the president; and it provided that the states in question would be re-admitted when they had framed constitutions in conventions elected by black men and white men alike.

President Johnson promptly vetoed the measure, whereupon Congress, without hesitation, overrode his veto. Thad reluctantly and cautiously, because it did not contain everything he wanted, commended the passage of the Reconstruction Act of 1867.

Thad was more fully pleased, however, to witness the final passage of two other bills over the vetoes of President Andrew Johnson, in March: One recognized voting rights for blacks in D.C. The other was the Tenure of Office Act, which required the Senate's approval for all dismissals of officers by the president.

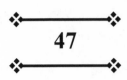

# 47

# Thad Wrestles with the President 1867

In the meantime, Thad and his fellow radicals, fed up by the president's incessant obstruction of Congress's efforts, complained among themselves that he had over-stepped his bounds on too many occasions, and muttered that they ought to charge him with serious misconduct in his official role. They hissed the word 'impeachment.' They knew that the process would involve charging him formally, conducting a trial and finding him guilty; it would be a long sequence with uncertain results. They reviewed the steps specified by the Constitution. "We can do it!" they concluded.

Thad's ally from Ohio, Representative James Ashley, introduced the motion to impeach President Andrew Johnson. The Speaker of the House referred the motion to the Judiciary Committee, instructing them to prepare charges against the president and to report back to the House in July, at which time he would call a vote.

Following the March 3 closing of the Thirty-Ninth Congress, the Fortieth Congress convened on March 4. Thad, almost 75 years old, was exhausted, and needed a break; nevertheless, he had orchestrated this move out of distrust for President Johnson, having no idea what tricks he might pull if Congress were not in session.

Representative Stevens failed in his first effort in the Fortieth Congress: He was unable to reconstitute the Reconstruction Committee.

For his next initiative, in a speech before the House, Thad demanded that the president enforce the Confiscation Act that had been passed in 1862. "The confiscated land should be distributed among the freed slaves, with each family receiving 40 acres," he spat as strongly as he could muster. His physical weakness prevented him from finishing his speech personally, so his friend Edward McPherson read the remainder: Additional Confederate property should be sold, and the proceeds be given to veterans and other loyal citizens who had been harmed. To Thad's dismay, he failed to gain a following for this idea, as well.

In April, Congress passed a second Reconstruction Act, as usual, over the president's veto. Thad's spirits rose. This Act specified the method by which the commanding generals in the South were to oversee registration of voters in preparation for elections. Its purpose was to ensure the participation of Negroes.

Following the law's passage, Thad, widely known as the author of the Reconstruction Acts, received death threats. "Laws providing for Negro rule will cause blood to flow," they warned, "and yours will be among the first." [37] Thad was not the least bit frightened, but he was, nevertheless, discouraged.

On April 20, Congress felt it was now safe to recess. They decided they would re-convene on the first Wednesday of July.

Thad went home to Lancaster. When he arrived, he was so weak that he had to be helped up the stairs to his bed. Mrs. Smith sent a message to Dr. Henry Carpenter, who made a house call at once. Dr. Carpenter diagnosed Thad's ailments as dropsy, dyspepsia, emaciation, and swelling. He prescribed a diuretic, ordered extended rest, and instructed him to eat only small amounts of food at a sitting. Thad humbly followed the physician's and Mrs. Smith's demands.

In the meantime, with Congress in recess, President Johnson interpreted the second Reconstruction Act to mean that the registrars for voting had the power to decide whom to register. As soon as Representative Stevens heard about this violation, he proclaimed that the president had no right to interfere with Congressional directives.

Congress re-convened on July 3, as planned; Thad's health was restored sufficiently for him to participate, though weakly. His first item of business was to present a third Reconstruction Bill, which elaborated on and reinforced the earlier ones. Thad delivered a brief speech from his seat, explaining the bill. Because his voice was barely audible, his fellow representatives gathered around him to hear his arguments. Both houses passed the bill and, once again, overrode President Johnson's veto.

On July 10, the Judiciary Committee, which had been assigned to investigate the misdeeds of the president in preparation for impeachment, reported that it was not yet ready to report, as it had not found adequate evidence against the president. Thad urged them to produce a testimony during the current session, insisting that the group owed it to the country and to the president to come to a speedy conclusion; nevertheless, the House voted to adjourn until October, expecting to hear from the committee at that time.

Thad hardly left the capital when the case for impeachment seemed to build upon itself: President Johnson grew weary of Secretary of War Edwin Stanton, told him he was fired, and appointed General Ulysses Grant to take his place temporarily—blatantly violating the Tenure of Office Act whose passage Thad had fostered recently. The president also removed Philip Sheridan from his job as military commander in Louisiana and Texas, also in violation of the Tenure of Office Act. The president was practicing a policy of removing commanders--without Congressional approval! Thad fumed, but he was not feeling well enough to return to Washington for a confrontation.

# 48

## Thad Prepares His Last Will and Testament
## 1867

Observing that his health was sinking steadily, Thad decided the time had come to compose his Last Will and Testament. He asked Mrs. Smith to summon his nephew, Thaddeus Stevens Junior. With his help, Thad's written words specified that, upon his death:

- Lydia Hamilton Smith would receive $500 a year, or a lump sum of $5000, as well as the right to keep all furniture in his residences in Lancaster and Washington.
- His nephew, Thaddeus Morrill Stevens, in Indianapolis, would receive $2000.
- His niece, Lizzie, in Indianapolis, would receive $1000.
- The son of his business associate, Simon Stevens, would receive $1000 when he came of age.
- The town of Peacham, Vermont, would receive $1000, of which the interest was to be used to sponsor a Juvenile Library Association.
- The trustees of the Peacham Cemetery would receive $500, so that the sexton might be able to plant cheerful flowers at each of the four corners of his mother's grave every spring.
- Thaddeus Junior would receive a gold watch and $800 per year. If he abstained from alcohol, he would receive one fourth of the remainder of the estate every five years, and eventually the whole amount. If he were to die before those twenty years passed, and the estate still amounted to $50,000 or more, then that $50,000-plus would be used to establish a school in Lancaster, which was to be open to needy young men of all races, colors, and creeds.

Thaddeus Stevens signed his will on July 30, 1867; Christopher Dice signed as a witness.

In the meantime, Mrs. Smith's son, Isaac, had returned to Lancaster after the surrender at Appomattox as a damaged, depressed, and drunken ex-soldier. During one of his frequent visits to 45 South Queen Street, he was inebriated, and shouted abusive words to his mother. On November 9, Thad directed a letter to Isaac Smith. He ordered him never to re-enter his residence.

On November 11, Thad added another section to his will. Here he specified:

- If, within 5 years of his death, the Baptist Brethren should build a church in Lancaster, they would receive $100 toward its cost. "I do this out of respect for the memory of my mother...," he added. [38]
- The Pennsylvania College in Gettysburg would receive $1000 for maintenance of Stevens Hall.
- Thaddeus Junior would receive his uncle's house and property if he were to be married prior to his uncle's death.

Thad also made plans for his burial. He knew that many cemeteries in Pennsylvania were segregated; they admitted only whites or only blacks. He chose the Shreiner-Concord Cemetery in Lancaster as his final resting place because it had no such restrictions. He wrote the inscription for his tombstone:

"I repose in this quiet and secluded spot
Not from any natural preference for solitude
But, finding other cemeteries limited as to race by charter rules,
I have chosen this that I might illustrate in my death
The principles which I advocated
Through a long life:
Equality of Man Before His Creator."

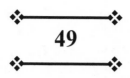

# 49

## Thad Seeks to Impeach 1868

In November, Thad, accompanied by Mrs. Smith, returned to Washington for the next Congressional session. Traveling by train, he presented himself as healthy and upbeat. His appearance in the city created a considerable commotion, and crowds of visitors congregated at his B Street home to welcome him back to town. When the large amount of talking tired him out, Mrs. Smith thanked the guests, saw them to the door, and forced him to rest.

The next morning, Thad read newspaper comments implying that he was on his deathbed and that this session of Congress might be his last--if he were to attend at all. One journalist accused him of enacting a charade: "Although he claimed to be quite well, the luster has gone out of his eyes and he had difficulty keeping awake." [39] Thad bit his lip.

Later that day, he was resting on a settee in a lounge in the Capitol when the time for the session to begin was drawing near. One of his associates offered to help him walk to his seat in the House chamber. He snapped feebly, "I can go alone. I am not as dead as some of my newspaper friends have reported me." [40] As the assembly opened, to the dismay of his enemies, Representative Stevens was in his seat and remained there during the entire meeting.

Energetically resuming his efforts to lead the party, Thad demonstrated that his challenge during this session was to out-maneuver the president, and, if possible, remove him. Thad introduced bills to subdivide Texas into several states, to establish a public school system in the District of Columbia, and to initiate a new method of taxing liquor. He mustered a satisfied smile when he read another news report: "Mr. Stevens, who himself is carried to the Capitol every day…though dying, proposes more bills in one day than any of his colleagues in a month." [41]

The committee that had failed to report on its impeachment investigation in July was now ready, although it had discovered no sensational or substantial infractions of the law by the president. Nevertheless, on November 25, the committee recommended to the House that President Andrew Johnson be impeached for "high crimes and misdemeanors." Thad knew that the charges were largely lame, and he lamented to his friends that the effort would probably bomb.

When the impeachment vote in the House was held, it was defeated. Thad insisted that the results had not changed his mind about his intent to impeach the president. He warned that only the removal of the president would preserve the wins of the war.

The House did finally support Thad's wish to reconstitute the Reconstruction Committee, and appointed him as chair. Thad and his committee quickly introduced a fourth Reconstruction Bill. This would require a majority of actual voters, rather than a majority of registered voters, in each Southern state, to qualify the state for ratification of its new constitution. Thad had devised this bill to block those who wanted to defeat the new state constitutions by not voting at all. The fourth Reconstruction Bill passed. Thad honored that forward step, as well as the New Year, with a small reception in his D.C. home.

On January 13, the Senate acted on the dismissal of Secretary of War Stanton, which the president had imposed in the summer. They voted not to accept it, and ordered the president to restore Secretary Stanton to office. President Johnson refused.

Thad saw this as another opportunity to pursue the impeachment of the president. He convinced the House to transfer the impeachment investigation to his own Reconstruction Committee, and he at once began to re-build the case.

Within several weeks, Chairman Stevens and his committee developed a stronger list of charges against President Johnson. He accused the president of:

- Trying to take over the government after the Confederates' surrender;
- Attempting to organize new states and trying to gain admission for their representatives in Congress;
- Defying Congress when told that his actions were illegal;

- Appointing relatives and friends to important positions for purposes of corruption; and
- Pardoning deserters to induce them to vote for his friends.

When it was time for the committee to vote on bringing the accusations before the House, however, the matter was tabled. Once again, Thad was frustrated in his mission.

Then, on Friday, February 21, while Congress was in session, President Johnson defied the lawmakers further! The president informed the Senate that he was appointing Lorenzo Thomas as Secretary of War. He sent Mr. Thomas to inform Secretary Edwin Stanton, who had stood firm in his office since being fired in the summer. When Thad received news that Secretary Stanton refused, again, to leave his office, and, in fact, barricaded himself inside, he raised his cane and cried, "Way to go, Edwin!"

Congress reacted to the president's defiance with intense anger. The outraged Senate hurriedly passed a resolution denying the president's power to remove the Secretary of War and to appoint a replacement. Now, Thad, leaning on a friend's arm, moved among the groups of indignant Representatives, repeating, "Didn't I tell you so?" [42]

On Saturday, Thad's Reconstruction Committee presented its recommendation for the president's impeachment back to the House for debate. Chairman Stevens limited each speaker to one-half hour, and noted that the vote would be taken no later than 5:00 on Monday.

Thad was the last to speak: He listed all of the examples of President Johnson's misconduct. He was so weak that his voice could not be heard 20 feet away; after starting his speech, he, once again, turned it over to Edward McPherson to be read. He proposed that two committees be set up-- a committee to notify the Senate, and a committee to draw up the Articles of Impeachment. This time, Thad's motion passed, and he was appointed to both committees.

Tuesday afternoon was the appointed time for the notification of the Senate. Too frail to walk, looking pale, emaciated, and death-like, Thad was carried by two young Negro men to the door of the Senate, where he took his maple cane, and grasping Representative John Bingham's arm, walked down the aisle to the president of the Senate, followed by members of the House. Everyone in the chamber silently stared.

"Mr. President," Thad whispered, addressing Senator Benjamin Wade, "In obedience to the order of the House of Representatives, we appear before you, and in the name of the House of Representatives, and all the people of the United States, we do impeach Andrew Johnson, president of the United States, of high crimes and misdemeanors in office." [43] Thad demanded, with a faint voice, that the Senate take order for the president's appearance.

Senator Wade replied, "Order shall be taken." Thad left, to report the proceedings back to the House.

The committee assigned to prepare the Articles of Impeachment expanded the list to eleven charges, without much help from Thad, who was too ill to participate directly and fully. The committee delivered the Articles of Impeachment to the House. The articles generated debate, which flowed into March 2.

Thad, despite his preference for temperance, sipped some brandy to keep himself going while the House voted to accept the committee's articles. The House appointed a committee of prosecutors, to be led by Thad.

Throughout the proceedings, Thad's two brawny black porters carried him to and from his seat. At one point, thin, pale, and haggard, Thad jokingly remarked to them, "I wonder, boys, who will carry me when you are dead and gone." [44]

On March 4, as prescribed by Jefferson's *Manual*, the House delivered the Articles of Impeachment to the Senate. The prosecutors ceremoniously paraded into the Senate chamber, walking two by two, with Representative Stevens carried in a chair. The full House of Representatives followed.

The trial began. Chief Justice Salmon Chase presided. Prosecutors presented evidence, witnesses gave testimonies, defense delivered discourses, spectators stated opinions, newspapers printed repartee. The accused president kept a low profile; he did not appear at his trial, and he made no public comments.

As the trial progressed, the president's defense team argued that he had not violated the Tenure of Office Act because the Act was unconstitutional in the first place, and, besides, it did not even apply to Secretary Stanton, since President Lincoln had appointed him.

It became clear to Prosecutor Stevens that the case against President Johnson had not been developed to its full potential. Too weak to contribute his own natural aggression, Thad observed that his partners were no match for Andrew Johnson's skilled lawyers. The defense emphasized issues, Thad conceded, over which honest people might differ. He recognized that their strategy offered their best opportunity to gain the support of Senators who still were "sitting on the fence."

On April 27, Prosecutor Stevens, with the help of more medicinal alcohol, delivered his best effort: He prepared his argument carefully, having re-written it three times. Then, hardly able to stand, he began to read it. Starting by acknowledging the dignity of the occasion, he pronounced that he would concern himself only with Article 11, which he thought sufficient for conviction. With permission, he sat, and spoke until his voice became so weak that he could barely be heard. He handed his pages to Benjamin Butler, who resumed by stressing that the president, having taken an oath to obey the Constitution, was required to execute, not make, the laws. If he failed to do so, he was subject to removal. Thus, by refusing to obey the Tenure of Office Act, by attempting to remove Secretary Stanton from office, the president clearly had violated the Constitution.

Exhausted, Thad listened to his speech. He was satisfied that he had done all he could do.

Conviction would require a two-thirds vote--36 votes from the 54 members of the Senate. Acquittal needed only 19. The "undecided" Senators experienced heavy pressure from the public. One Maine civilian warned Senator William Fessenden that any Republican who voted in favor of Andrew Johnson need not expect to get home alive.

The critical ballot came on May 16. The Senate began with Article 11. Henry Anthony of Rhode Island was the first to vote.

"Mr. Senator Anthony," recited Chief Justice Chase, "How say you? Is the respondent, Andrew Johnson, president of the United States, guilty or not guilty of a high misdemeanor, as charged in this article?"

Senator Anthony voted, "Guilty."

Senator James Grimes of Iowa, paralyzed and bedridden, came in on a stretcher and spoke, "Not guilty." The roll call vote lasted over an hour, and the outcome was in doubt until the very end.

Senator Edmund Ross of Kansas cast the deciding vote. His voice shaking, he pronounced, "Not guilty."

The final tally was 35 "Guilty" and 19 "Not guilty." President Johnson was acquitted by one vote!

Thad, as he immediately exited the roaring Senate chamber, commented with all the strength he could rally: "This country is going to the devil." [45] Some of his colleagues mumbled accusations that the Masons were behind their defeat. Others spoke of bribery.

Chief Justice Chase called a ten-day adjournment, because of the forthcoming national Republican Convention. The Republicans nominated Ulysses Grant as their candidate for president.

When the convention closed, the Senate reconvened to vote on Articles 2 and 3, with the same result as the vote on Article 11. The Senate held no further votes, and the trial was over.

Thad Stevens went home to B Street, and collapsed into his bed.

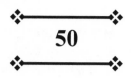

# 50

# Thad Rests His Case 1868

During the next months, Thad rose from his bed, dressed, and joined Mrs. Smith at the dinner table on days when he found some strength. Throughout other days, he stayed in bed, swallowing soft foods and sipping juice offered from the hand of his loyal friend.

On June 2, Mrs. Smith read from the newspaper to Thad that former President James Buchanan had died the day before. He had experienced respiratory failure at the age of 77 at his Wheatland home in Lancaster, the report stated. Recalling earlier visits to Wheatland that had included the president's niece Harriet Lane Johnston, Lydia gently inquired, "Would you like to visit Harriet and her husband at the estate in Lancaster, to pay your respects?" Thad rolled his eyes and shook his head.

On July 10, Mrs. Smith read a happier story to Thad: "Louisiana and South Carolina have voted as the 27th and 28th of the 37 states to ratify the Fourteenth Amendment to the United States Constitution. The country now has reached the required approval of three-fourths of the states to adopt the amendment. Accordingly, all Negroes born in the U.S. are now citizens, equal to whites before the law; all states must now allow Negroes the right to vote. In addition, all those who served the Confederacy are now excluded from holding public office."

Thad smiled and nodded.

By August 2, Thad was so fragile that he could barely sit up. Mrs. Smith fed him spoonfuls of soup and sips of tea, and she summoned Dr. Noble Young to attend to him. Thaddeus Junior came from the forge ruins to help with his care.

The next day, at Thad's request, Mrs. Smith sent a summons for Christopher Dice, their Lancaster neighbor and close friend. He arrived as quickly as possible, and joined those at the bedside. Christopher prayed for God's mercy, and Thad asked him to serve as a pallbearer for his funeral.

By August 9, Thad lay with his hands folded together, his eyes closed, and his lower lip shivering. Only those closest to him were permitted to visit.

On the morning of Tuesday, August 11, Thad rallied a bit as Mrs. Smith sat at the side of his bed. He gazed at his maple, silver-topped cane resting against the foot of his bed. He wondered aloud what had become of Danville's Loud Lads, whom he had never really gotten to know.

Thad's friend Simon Stevens visited, and they talked politics. Thad predicted that General Grant would win the presidential election and faithfully would execute the Reconstruction Acts.

In the afternoon, Mrs. Smith interrupted, "Mr. Stevens, would you have any objections to being baptized?"

He murmured, "No."

At 5:00, Dr. Young checked in on Thad. He suggested that Simon leave. Mrs. Smith asked Simon, as he departed, if he would be so kind as to fetch the Sister of Charity, Loretta O'Reilly, from St. Augustine Church to Thad's bedside.

Two black clergymen from the Methodist church arrived; they received permission to pray with the fading Congressman. "Mr. Stevens," they closed, "you have the prayers of all the colored people in the country." Thad signaled his appreciation. [46]

At 9:00, Dr. Young returned. He informed his patient that he was dying. Thad indicated that he understood. Mrs. Smith fanned Thad's fever, and gave him pieces of ice to wet his tongue.

Sister Loretta and a companion arrived to baptize him. Thaddeus Junior stood beside Thad's bed, holding his hand. Mrs. Smith knelt nearby. The nuns performed their Roman Catholic rite.

At 11:00, Lydia dabbed Thad's forehead with a cool cloth and asked him what else she could do for him. He replied, "Nothing in the world." A few minutes later, he silently gestured for more ice to soothe his dry mouth.

At midnight, August 11, 1868, the maple, silver-handled cane slid to the floor. Thad Stevens breathed his final breath.

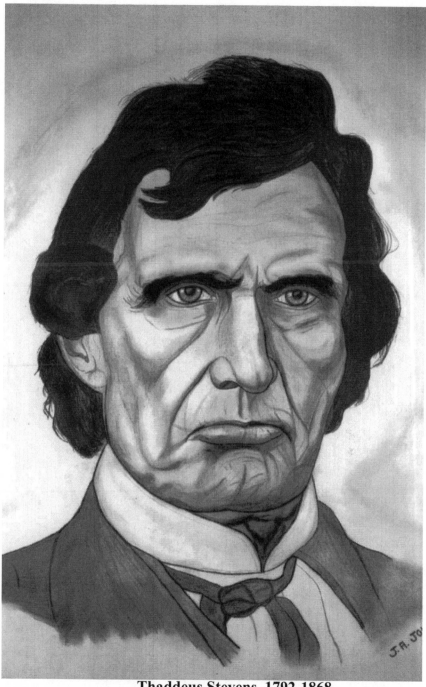

**Thaddeus Stevens, 1792-1868**
*Courtesy of LancasterHistory.org, Lancaster, Pennsylvania*

# QUESTIONS TO THINK ABOUT AND TALK ABOUT

1. What were some of the problems or challenges that Thad Stevens faced in his early life?

2. What were some of Thad's achievements?

3. What were some of the events and opportunities in Thad's early life that prepared him for later success?

4. What were some of Thad's character traits that helped him to become successful?

5. What are some of his characteristic traits that caused Thad to have enemies?

6. What are some similarities between Thad's life and your own life?

7. Should education be provided by the government, or should individual families pay for their own children's schooling? Explain your reasoning.

8. What does "All men are created equal" mean to you?

9. What do you think Thad wanted most in his lifetime?

10. How do you think Thad would respond to civil rights issues if he were living today? Explain your reasoning.

11. What were some of the reasons why Thad was propelled to fame and celebrity during his lifetime?

12. Do you think that Thad was an historically important figure? Provide supporting evidence for your answer.

13. Is compromise good or bad? Explain your reasoning.

14. How might some Southerners have justified their desire to keep their slaves?

15. What might have been the rationale of some Northerners who wanted to quickly and simply re-admit the Confederate states to the Union?

16. Why did Thad think it was important that the Confederate states be treated as "foreign enemies" following the war, instead of as "seceded states"?

17. If you had been a U.S. senator in 1868, how might you have voted on the removal of President Andrew Johnson? Why?

18. Compose your personal definition of 'Hero.' Refer to your definition to answer the question, "Should Thad Stevens be considered as a national hero?"

19. Who is your personal hero? What makes him or her special? Is your hero perfect?

20. What are some traits that you may want to further develop within yourself to become a hero to yourself or others?

# ACTIVITIES TO EXTEND LEARNING

1. Study Thad's instruction about how a bill becomes a law. Draw a diagram or flow chart similar to the one that Thad may have created. Use it to teach the process to others.

2. Refer to information in this story and others to collect and organize facts about the U.S. presidential elections that were held during Thad's public life. Construct a chart or table depicting each nominee and his political party. Include a column indicating which candidate Mr. Stevens supported, as well as another column indicating which candidate won the election. Can you draw any conclusions by studying your table?

3. Plan and conduct a debate arguing whether President Andrew Johnson should have been removed from office. Prepare valid arguments to build your case. Ask some 'judges' to comment on your effectiveness.

4. Select a scene in the story of Thad. Imagine a further conversation between Thad and another character on that occasion. Write and produce a skit depicting your idea of what each party might have said. Invite an audience to view your skit and discuss which of your characters were interesting.

5. Imagine that you are a journalist in the 1860's; you have scheduled an interview with Representative Stevens. Prepare a list of questions you might ask him. Ask someone who has read about Thad to play the role of Thad by answering your questions from Thad's perspective.

6. Select a nationally notable event that occurred during Thad's life. Create and share a patriotic song to commemorate that event.

7. Use technology to develop, produce, and share a summary of Thad Stevens's life.

# GLOSSARY

**Abolitionist-** opponent of slavery

**Affliction-** illness, disease, or medical condition

**Allies-** individuals or groups joined in a mutually supportive association

**Alma mater-** a school from which a particular person has graduated

**Amnesty-** pardon, forgiveness for having committed a crime

**Anomaly-** an unusual situation, with no apparent explanation

**Arbitrary-** random, based on whim

**Atone-** make up for a misdeed

**Austere-** harsh

**Borough-** self-governing town

**Bovine-** cow

**Bowie knife-** single-edged hunting knife

**Bellow-** shout loudly

**Cabinet-** advisors of U.S. president, as described in U.S. Constitution

**Capital-** city in which law-making body meets

**Capitol-** building in which law-making body meets

**Carcass-** dead body of animal

**Cellar-** basement

**Chamber-** meeting place of a legislative body

**Chamber pot-** bowl-shaped container with a handle and lid, kept in the bedroom under a bed, and generally used as a urinal during the night

**Classics-** study of ancient languages and literature

**Cobbler-** shoemaker

**Compensate-** pay money to counterbalance loss

**Congenital-** existing at birth

**Confiscate-** take or seize by the government

**Conscription-** compulsory enrollment for service in armed forces

**Consternation-** shocked dismay

**Constituent-** voter in a particular political division

**Corduroy road-** road made of logs

**Corporal punishment-** physical consequence for student misbehavior, frequently with a wooden paddle

**Declamation-** formal dramatic speech

**Derail-** send or go off course

**Din-** noise
**Draft (1)-** plan, develop
**Draft (2)-** compulsory enrollment for service in armed forces
**Diuretic-** medical treatment to increase urine output
**Elitism-** belief in concept of superiority
**Eloquent-** spoken beautifully and forcefully
**Emancipate-** set someone free
**Espouse-** adopt, support
**Federal-** central, related to national government
**Foe-** enemy
**Folklore-** traditional local stories or legends
**Forge-** furnace for heating metal
**Futile-** useless
**Gallery-** seating area overlooking main floor of auditorium
**Gingerly-** very cautiously
**Gingham-** checkered cotton fabric
**Hamlet-** small village
**Hogshead-** a large cask or barrel holding 63 gallons
**Homestead-** family farm
**Ignominious-** humiliating, embarrassing
**Imbibe-** drink
**Indigence-** poverty
**Indispensable** necessary, required
**Inebriated-** drunk
**Insolence-** disrespect
**Insurgent-** rebel
**Interest-bearing note-** written agreement to pay money owed, plus interest, over time
**Interpret-** make a personal judgment about meaning
**Jabot-** (zhabo) lace or cloth attached to front of a neckband and worn by men in the 18th century
**Journalist-** news reporter
**Lame duck-** officeholder, not re-elected, while serving remainder of term
**Last-** shoemaker's tool
**Lodge-** meeting place
**Majority-** number greater than half of a total
**Manumit-** free from slavery
**Moonlight-** hold a second job
**Mulatto-** person whose parentage is a mixture of black and white
**Notion-** idea

**Orthopedic-** related to study of bones
**Paltry-** insignificant
**Peer (1)-** look closely
**Peer (2)-** person of equal status with another
**Pessimistic-** having a negative outlook
**Plow-** farming tool used to make furrows in soil
**Polls-** place for voting
**Primer-** basic reading textbook
**Proclaim-** announce, declare
**Prosecutor-** attorney who represents government in legal action against accused person
**Putrid-** rotten
**Recitation-** discussion led by a teacher to accompany a lesson.
**Reins-** restraint, harness, bridle
**Retribution-** payback
**Rigid-** firm, refusing to change
**Rigorous-** strict, harsh
**Saucy-** flirtatious
**Scythe-** sharp tool for mowing or reaping
**Seamstress-** woman who sews
**Secede-** formally withdraw
**Seize-** take
**Settee-** bench with a back
**Sexton-** church or cemetery caretaker
**Subside-** lessen in intensity
**Suffrage-** the right to vote
**Supersede-** replace; be held with greater significance
**Suppress-** control
**Surrogate-** substitute
**Talipes Equinovarus-** medical condition also known as 'clubfoot'
**Taunt-** provoke or ridicule
**Taut-** stretched tightly
**Temperance-** abstinence from alcohol
**Threadbare-** worn away to reveal threads
**Tuition-** fee for receiving instruction
**Tragedy-** play with an unhappy ending
**Treason-** betrayal of country
**Trustees-** team who oversees the success of a school
**Torrent-** rush of liquid
**Waif-** abandoned child

# NOTES

1. Wikipedia, Fugitive Slave Law of 1793.
2. Quimby, p.262.
3. Wikipedia, How a Bill Becomes a Law.
4. Wikipedia, Impeachment Process.
5. *Gettysburg Anti-Masonic Star*, October 8, 1833.
6. *Gettysburg Anti-Masonic Star,* April 20, 1835.
7. Trefousse, p.51.
8. *Lancaster Inquirer*, October 27, 1883.
9. LancasterHistory.org, Application to National Park Service Underground Railroad Network to Freedom, p.4.
10. Trefousse, p.77.
11. Trefousse, p.81.
12. Trefousse, p.90.
13. Trefousse, p.94.
14. Trefousse, p.99.
15. Trefousse, p.107.
16. *New York Tribune*, December 10, 1861.
17. Trefousse, p.119.
18. Trefousse, p.120.
19. *Lancaster Examiner and Herald,* October 1, 1862.
20. *Lancaster Examiner and Herald*, September 10, 1862.
21. Trefousse, p.126.
22. LancasterHistory.org, Stevens Papers, Stevens to O.J. Dickey, July 7, 1863.
23. LancasterHistory.org, Stevens Papers, Stevens to Simon Stevens, July 6, 1863.
24. www.mrlincolnandfreedom.org/inside.asp?ID=61&subjectID=3, Civil War, Wade-Davis Bill.
25. *Lancaster Intelligencer*, July 7, 1863.
26. *Lancaster Examiner and Herald*, June 15, 1864.
27. Wikipedia, Thirteenth Amendment.
28. Trefousse, p.157.
29. *Lancaster Examiner and Herald*, April 19, 1865.
30. *Lancaster Examiner and Herald*, February 14, 1866.
31. Trefousse, p.183.
32. *Lancaster Intelligencer,* February 26, 1866.
33. Wikipedia, Fourteenth Amendment.
34. *Lancaster Examiner and Herald*, August 15, 1866.
35. *Washington Daily National Intelligencer*, November 24, 1866.
36. *New York Herald*, December 4, 1866.
37. Trefousse, p.211.
38. *New York Times*, August 20, 1868.
39. *Lancaster Intelligencer*, November 20, 1867.
40. *Gettysburg Star and Sentinel*, November 27, 1867.
41. Trefousse, p.220.
42. Trefousse, p.224.
43. *New York Tribune*, February 26, 1868.
44. Trefousse, p.226.
45. *New York Times*, May 17, 1868.
46. Trefousse, p.240.

# REFERENCES

Bogart, E.L. (2011). *Peacham: The story of a Vermont hill town.* Montpelier, VT: Vermont Historical Society.

Bogart, E.L. (2010). *Peacham: The story of a Vermont hill town.* St. Johnsbury VT: Railroad Street Press.

Burrowes, T.H. *Lancaster County 1845.* Lancaster PA: Adapted and re-published by John Baer's Sons.

Callender, E.B. (1882). *Thaddeus Stevens: Commoner.* Boston: A. Williams and Company.

Clifford, S. (1995). *Village in the hills: A history of Danville, Vermont 1786-1995.* West Kennebunk ME: Phoenix Publishing.

Copeland, P.F. (1975). *Everyday dress of the American colonial period coloring book.* New York: Dover Publications, Inc.

Cornell, W.A. (1990). *Our Pennsylvania heritage.* Lansdale, PA: Penns Valley Publishers.

Foster, G.A. (1964). *Impeached: The president who almost lost his job.* New York: Criterion Books Inc.

Furlong, P.J. (1943). *NEW history of America.* New York: William H. Sadler, Inc.

Gorrecht, F.W. (1933). "The charity of Thaddeus Stevens," Lancaster, PA: Historical Papers and Addresses of the Lancaster County Historical Society. (37: 21-35).

"The great commoner," (1883). Lancaster, PA: *Lancaster Inquirer,* October 20.

Hakim, J. (1994). *A history of US: Reconstruction and reform (Volume 7).* New York: Oxford University Press.

Historic Preservation Trust of Lancaster County. (2012). A place in history: The story of Thaddeus Stevens & Lydia Hamilton Smith.

Hoch, B.R. (2005). Thaddeus Stevens in Gettysburg: The making of an abolitionist. Gettysburg, PA: Adams County Historical Society.

Huden, J.C. (1944). *Development of state school administration in Vermont* Burlington: Free Press Printing Company.

Ketchum, R.M. (1960). *American heritage picture history of the Civil War.* New York: American Heritage Publishing Co., Inc.

Kids in the House. (2012). "How a bill becomes a law." http://kids.clerk.house.
gov/middle-school/lesson.html?intID=17

Klein, F.S. (1964). *Old Lancaster historic Pennsylvania community.* Lancaster,
Pennsylvania: Early America Series, Inc.

Lancaster County Convention Center Authority and LancasterHistory.org.
(2011). *Application to National Park Service Underground Railroad
Network to Freedom.* January.

LancasterHistory.org. (2010). Stevens and Smith Historical Site. "Bridging the
racial divide." www.stevensandsmith.org/ index.php/info/a_place_in_
history the_story_of_thaddeus_ stevens_lydia_hamilton_smith/

Landis, C.I. (1916). "Abraham Witmer's bridge," *Lancaster, PA: Papers read
before the Lancaster County Historical Society, (20:6).*

Lefferts, W. (1913). *Noted Pennsylvanians.* Philadelphia: JB Lippincott Co.

Meltzer, M. (1967). *Thaddeus Stevens and the fight for Negro rights.* New York:
Thomas Y. Crowell Company.

Quimby, L.F. (2005). *Peacham Academy 1795-1971.* Concord NH: Town and
Country Reprographics.

Rhoads, D. (2005). *Thaddeus Stevens: The play.* Lancaster PA: Yurchak Printing,
Inc.

Shelley, M.V. and Munro, S.H. (1980). *Harriet Lane, first lady of the White
House.* Lititz PA: Sutter House.

Singmaster, E. (1940). *Stories of Pennsylvania 1787-1830.* Harrisburg PA:
Pennsylvania Book Service.

Singmaster, E. (1947). *I speak for Thaddeus Stevens.* Boston: Houghton Mifflin.

Sloane, E. (1965). *Diary of an early American boy Noah Blake 1805.* New York:
Ballantine Books.

Switala, W.J. (2001). *Underground Railroad in Pennsylvania.* Mechanicsburg
PA: Stackpole Books.

Trefousse, H.L. (1997). *Thaddeus Stevens: Nineteenth century egalitarian.
Chapel Hill, NC: University of North Carolina Press.*

*Wikipedia: The free encyclopedia.* (2004, July). FL: Wikimedia Foundation, Inc.
Retrieved July 12, 2011, from http://www.wikipedia.org

# INDEX

# ABOUT THE AUTHOR

Kathy Brabson lives in Lancaster, Pennsylvania, with her husband Chip. Her daughter, Terri, and her granddaughter, Maddi, live nearby. Kathy enjoys attending Maddi's many activities, as well as traveling, reading, and spending time with extended family and friends.

Kathy earned her B.S. in Elementary Education from Millersville University of PA, and her M.Ed. and Ph.D. in Curriculum and Instruction from Pennsylvania State University. She is retired from Pennsylvania public education, having served as an elementary and middle school teacher and an elementary school principal. Her favorite students to teach were sixth graders.

# SOLID STATE PHYSICS

## VOLUME 47

# Founding Editors

FREDERICK SEITZ

DAVID TURNBULL

# SOLID STATE PHYSICS

## Advances in Research and Applications

*Editors*

**HENRY EHRENREICH**

**DAVID TURNBULL**

*Division of Applied Sciences*
*Harvard University*
*Cambridge, Massachusetts*

VOLUME 47

ACADEMIC PRESS

San Diego    New York    Boston
London    Sydney    Tokyo    Toronto

Academic Press, Inc.
A Division of Harcourt Brace & Company
525 B Street, Suite 1900, San Diego, California 92101-4495

*United Kingdom Edition published by*
Academic Press Limited
24-28 Oval Road, London NW1 7DX

International Standard Serial Number: 0081-1947

International Standard Book Number: 0-12-607747-9

PRINTED IN THE UNITED STATES OF AMERICA
94   95   96   97   98   99   BB   9   8   7   6   5   4   3   2   1

# Contents

## Homogeneous Nucleation and the Temperature Dependence of the Crystal-Melt Interfacial Tension

### Frans Spaepen

## Cluster Approach to Order-Disorder Transformations in Alloys

### D. de Fontaine

## The Physics and Mechanics of Brittle Matrix Composites

### A. G. Evans and F. W. Zok

### Defects at Surfaces and Interfaces

R. C. POND AND J. P. HIRTH

### Giant Magnetoresistance in Magnetic Layered and Granular Materials

PETER M. LEVY

## Contributors

Numbers in parentheses indicate the pages on which the authors' contributions begin.

D. DE FONTAINE (33), *Department of Materials Science and Mineral Engineering, University of California, Berkeley, California, and Materials Sciences Division, Lawrence Berkeley Laboratory, Berkeley, California 94720*

A. G. EVANS (177), *Materials Department, College of Engineering, University of California, Santa Barbara, California 93106-5050*

J. P. HIRTH (287), *Department of Mechanical and Materials Engineering, Washington State University, Pullman, Washington 99164-2920*

PETER M. LEVY (367), *Department of Physics, New York University, New York, New York 10003*

R. C. POND (287), *Department of Materials Science and Engineering, University of Liverpool, P.O. Box 147, Liverpool, L69 3BX United Kingdom*

FRANS SPAEPEN (1), *Division of Applied Sciences, Harvard University, Cambridge Massachusetts 02138*

F. W. ZOK (177), *Materials Department, College of Engineering, University of California, Santa Barbara, California 93106-5050*

vii

*David Turnbull*

# Foreword

Until the development of wave mechanics in the second half of the 1920s, most attempts to understand the characteristic properties of the various types of solids were *ad hoc* and fragmentary. It was clear that metals and semiconductors must contain electrons that were relatively mobile and that ionic crystals must be bound, at least in part, as a result of electrostatic forces between charged ions. Beyond this, however, everything was guesswork. Least of all, there was essentially no comprehension of the source of the differences between the types of solids.

Then, between 1926 and 1935, as a result of much pioneering work by those concerned with the application of the new quantum mechanics, many major pieces of the puzzle began to fall into place and what was at least a semi-quantitative framework for an integrated treatment of solids began to emerge. The key step was the development of what came to be known as the *band theory of electronic levels,* which was augmented to some degree by an appreciation of the influence of lattice defects.

In 1935, with the special help of my wife, Elizabeth Marshall, I began preparing a volume that would attempt to tie the field together as systematically as possible, displaying both what was known and unknown. I hoped that the process would attract more systematic theoretical and experimental research in the field. The result was *The Modern Theory of Solids,* now scarcely modern, but still a not entirely trivial summary of the state of affairs during the latter part of the 1930s. The war in Europe had begun by the time the manuscript was finished and the world was changing rapidly. Fortunately, with the help of Gaylord P. Harnwell, then the head of the Physics Department at the University of Pennsylvania, and the encouragement of Lee A. DuBridge, then the editor of the McGraw-Hill "green" series in physics, the book appeared in the autumn of 1940, just as the great conflict was beginning to cause major disruptions within the American scientific community.

Perhaps the greatest benefit derived from the book, apart from its usefulness as a reference, was the encouragement it gave to a new generation of scientists in the postwar years to undertake systematic research in the field. New and very powerful techniques of investigation, both experimental and theoretical, were introduced by imaginative and talented investigators. In brief, the field attracted a growing number of investigators on an international scale. It became a major component of the advancing frontier of physics.

The degree of attention devoted to it was significantly accelerated by the invention of the transistor, built as a result of intensive research on

silicon and germanium diodes during World War II, as well as by the significant practical interest in the changes that could be produced in materials when exposed to intense radiation in nuclear reactors. Newly formed federal granting agencies, such as the Office of Naval Research, the Atomic Energy Commission, and the National Science Foundation, joined in sponsoring research in the field.

As the mid-1950s approached, it became clear that the time was again right to provide something in the nature of a comprehensive overview of the field. Several individuals suggested that I consider a new edition of the old book. In fact, some offered to cooperate in such a project. There were two primary objections to this. First, any such endeavor would be truly massive if it was to be comprehensive by that time. Second, the field was in a dynamic state of development and hence open ended. Any such book would need continuous updating. In addition, there were, by that time, several excellent new texts, such as that by Charles Kittel, which satisfied what might be called immediate classroom needs.

During the summer of 1954, while vacationing in upstate New York, I took the opportunity to make several visits to the General Electric Research Laboratories and, among other things, discussed the matter at some length with David Turnbull. We reviewed various alternatives and agreed to get together in the autumn to pursue the preliminary discussions. Then in October 1954, in the immediate wake of a hurricane that had just swept through New York State, we met at his home in the suburbs of Schenectady to focus on the feasibility of establishing a series of volumes devoted to solid state physics that could serve the needs of the growing group of professional scientists involved in the field and be sufficiently flexible that it could be regarded as open ended. We thought of books rather than a review journal in order to provide some element of cohesion to the series. Thus we sought something intermediate between what are commonly called "advances" that have a year-to-year characteristic and a single comprehensive text.

Initially, we thought of the series as perhaps a finite one, but open ended in the sense that it would be terminated only if there were something in the nature of an end to new developments. I note, in reading the introduction to Volume I, that with our understandable limitation of vision, we suggested that the series might involve a dozen or so volumes. Had we been more courageous we might have proffered the expectation that the field would probably not be exhausted within a decade—and indeed it was not. A highly productive period lay ahead as both experimental techniques and theoretical developments evolved that provided researchers with increasing power and penetration.

I should add that, although the series emerged from the planning car-

ried out by David Turnbull and me, the actual process of publication was catalyzed significantly by the interest and perseverance of the late Alan Liss who was then on the staff of Academic Press and followed our activities on an almost day-to-day basis. He made certain that the sequence of volumes gained a degree of priority as they passed through the process of publication. In this he was supported by Mr. Kurt Jacoby, the senior director of publications at that time. Jacoby was a very interesting man—a refugee from Hitler—who had a great deal of experience dealing with European scientists, particularly the leading physicists. As the former director of publications in a major German firm, he delighted in reminiscing about the stratagems he used to induce leading scientists to come his way when the time for a treatise was ripe. He also savored tales of the complicated "duels" he fought with the old house of Springer-Verlag.

At the time the series was started, Turnbull was involved in research at the General Electric Laboratory, probably then at its prime in the pursuit of basic research, whereas I was enjoying the luxury of a relatively carefree life as a research professor at the University of Illinois—the institution, incidentally, from which Turnbull had obtained his doctorate degree. In those days we shared the burden of selecting authors and editing contributions more or less equally. Times changed, however. In 1962 Turnbull joined the Harvard faculty and began that particularly brilliant phase of his career which made him a truly distinguished peer among colleagues and a mentor to a long line of devoted students and postdoctoral fellows. In contrast, I became more and more deeply involved in administrative work and the burden fell increasingly upon his substantial shoulders.

To provide a counterbalance, we both agreed that the series required an additional editor and, in 1967, Turnbull's colleague, Henry Ehrenreich, joined with him to share the burden and the pleasures of the work—a very easy and fortunate transition. Then, by 1983, my activities had moved so far afield that the three of us agreed to face reality and I ceased being a significant participant in the new volumes.

In the course of the preparation of the current volume, Number 47, David Turnbull decided that he too should shift the obligation of continuing this series to younger individuals. By agreement of all concerned, his place is being taken by Professor Frans Spaepen, one of Turnbull's experimental colleagues of longstanding, whom I first met long ago when I was visiting his parents on a summer day in Flanders.

Whatever successes the series and its numerous supplements have had in encouraging members of the profession in their work during the 40-plus years of its existence is primarily a result of Turnbull's enduring interest

and detailed knowledge of all that goes on in the field. Isadore Rabi once said that a scientist has done well if he can remain productively at the frontier of his field for 15 years. Turnbull has done so in a most remarkable way for essentially a half century. He will continue as in the past to provide an inspiration to all of us who have had the special privilege of knowing him.

Frederick Seitz

# Preface I

This marks David Turnbull's last volume as editor of the *Solid State Physics* series. Four of its articles were specifically invited for the occasion and are dedicated to him in respect and friendship.

As one of the founders of the series, his influence on its evolution, scope and quality has clearly been enormous. Frederick Seitz's Foreword to this volume describes the genesis and history of the series. It serves in part to illuminate Turnbull's significant contribution to its development. The view is completed by reference to the Preface of Volume 1 in 1955 by Seitz and Turnbull and the Foreword of Volume 38 written in 1984 by Turnbull and Ehrenreich on the occasion of Seitz's retirement as editor. The 1955 Preface stated the intent and goals of this publication. What was said then bears repeating now, for it will continue to define the contents of these books:

"The viewpoints and activities in certain closely allied fields, particularly electronics, metallurgy, crystallography, and chemistry of solids, have been influenced markedly by developments in solid state science. As a result of this expansion of knowledge solid state physicists are finding that, in order to make significant contributions, it is necessary to concentrate their efforts in narrower fields than formerly. Because of this specialization it is desirable that a mechanism exist whereby investigators and students can readily obtain a balanced view. . . . The purpose of the present series is to fulfill this need, at least in part, by publication of compact and authoritative reviews of the important areas of the field. . . . Three general types of articles are solicited: (1) broad elementary surveys that have particular value in orienting the advanced graduate student or an investigator having little previous knowledge of the subject; (2) broad surveys of fields of advanced research that serve to inform and stimulate the more experienced investigators; (3) more specialized articles describing important new techniques, both experimental and theoretical."

The attainment of these standards is even more important today. The conglomerate of "allied fields" addressed at that time has already achieved some unity under the rubric of "materials science." Nevertheless, the series must continue to inveigh against the forces of parochialism that tend to sharpen increasingly the focus of research efforts.

It has been a great honor and opportunity to serve as co-editor with a colleague as distinguished and far-sighted as David Turnbull. I learned much from him and found our association over the many years we served together a continual source of pleasure. Frans Spaepen, his former student, and now also a colleague at Harvard, succeeds him. He has contrib-

uted previously to the series as author and is responsible for one of the articles in this volume. I hope that despite the continually evolving subject matter as fields advance, he and I together can continue in the spirit originally envisioned in Volume 1.

Finally, I would like to thank the authors involved in this volume for contributing to this testimonial for David Turnbull, and for providing their articles in a timely fashion.

Henry Ehrenreich

# Preface II

The first four articles of this volume center on the structural features of condensed phase physics. The first of these, by Frans Spaepen, presents an analysis of the crystal melt interfacial tension and its temperature dependence which emerged from application of classical nucleation theory to experiments on the kinetics of homogeneous nucleation of crystals in undercooled melts. These experiments, reviewed by Kelton in an earlier volume [45, 75 (1991)], revealed that metallic and other simple liquids required remarkably deep undercoolings for the onset of measurable crystal nucleation. This behavior could be interpreted in terms of polytetrahedral models for melt structure, which were reviewed by Nelson and Spaepen [42, 1 (1989)]. It can be interpreted specifically on the basis of a negentropic model for crystal-melt tension, which falls in magnitude with increasing undercooling. In Spaepen's article, this interpretation is developed and applied to the results on the kinetics of crystal nucleation in undercooled liquid Hg.

The second article in this volume, by Didier de Fontaine, might be regarded as an update of the article "Configurational Thermodynamics of Solid Solutions" by de Fontaine in an earlier volume [34, 73 (1979)]. However, since the appearance of that article, great advances in calculational and theoretical methods have been made which have entirely altered our perspective to the point that a true *first principles thermodynamics* of crystalline solids has emerged. These advances have followed first principles electronic structure calculations. The new developments and the resulting perspective are described by de Fontaine.

A major recent development in materials technology has been the synthesis of composites consisting of high strength particles, often in filamentary form dispersed in various solid matrices. Composite bodies so constituted have ranged from golf clubs to auto bodies. The article by Evans and Zok centers on composites in which the matrices, such as ceramics, glasses or intermetallic compounds, are brittle rather than ductile with elastic properties quite similar to those of the embedded fibers. Such fibers impart good tensile strength to the matrices, even in the presence of holes and notches. Emphasis is placed on providing a framework for development of models to facilitate the design of structures optimal for mechanical applications.

As is well known, the growth and plastic flow of crystalline solids under relatively small driving forces are effected by the operation of linear crystal imperfections called dislocations. These defects, either isolated from each other or in various arrays, also play a key role in a variety

xv

of other solid state processes, such as misfit accommodation in forming epitaxial structures, or crystalline precipitates, diffusive transport of impurities, sites for initiation of phase transformation, and electron-hole recombination in semiconductors. The continuum theory of stationary dislocations was presented by DeWit in Volume *10*, 249, and the dislocation mechanisms for plastic flow were reviewed by Gilman and Johnston in Volume *13*, 147. The article by Pond and Hirth in this volume reviews the crystallographic features of dislocations, with emphasis on their topological characteristics as constrained by the symmetry of their hosts. A major part of the article treats interface structures modeled by dislocation arrays.

The so-called giant magnetoresistance effect in transition metal superlattices was discovered in 1988. It awakened immediate interest in view of its magnitude. In iron/chromium superlattices the resistivity was found to drop by nearly fifty percent as an external magnetic field aligns the magnetic superlattice that is antiferromagnetically aligned in zero field. Potential applications to reading heads in magnetic information storage systems were immediately recognized. So was the fact that the physical explanation of this phenomenon was far from obvious. The mystery deepened when this large effect was also observed in a variety of other systems and even granular materials. P. M. Levy reviews the present theoretical understanding of this phenomenon in the last of the articles in this volume. As he points out, the theory is still incomplete. Nevertheless, significant progress has been made in delineating the principal ingredients like spin-dependent conduction electron scattering in these structures, responsible for the effect and the requisite transport theory. In view of the importance of magnetic recording technology, this report of work in progress within the community, with its copious references, will be valuable in providing an entry into the field and in summarizing the present state of affairs.

Henry Ehrenreich<br>
David Turnbull

SOLID STATE PHYSICS, VOL. 47

# Homogeneous Nucleation and the Temperature Dependence of the Crystal-Melt Interfacial Tension

FRANS SPAEPEN

*Division of Applied Sciences, Harvard University, Cambridge, Massachusetts*

## I. Introduction

When David Turnbull started his work on the undercooling of metallic melts in the late 1940s, one of his most distinguished colleagues at the General Electric Research Laboratory in Schenectady, New York, was greatly skeptical about the likelihood of success—and not without reason. The density and bonding of crystal and melt were known to be quite similar, and many regarded the melt as a highly defective crystal or a dynamic assembly of crystallites. The crystal-melt interface, unlike the crystal-vapor or liquid-vapor interfaces, therefore did not appear to be

1

the major discontinuity required for an effective barrier against crystal nucleation. In fact, Turnbull's colleague was so persuaded by these factors that he promised to eat his hat if the melt of a simple metal such as copper could be undercooled more than a few degrees. David Turnbull took this as a challenge, and in a few weeks demonstrated major undercooling of a large number of such melts. At the next group meeting his colleague walked in with a headpiece made of cheese.

These experiments, which culminated in the classic demonstration of homogeneous crystal nucleation in mercury and a set of measurements of its isothermal kinetics,[1] were the basis of two fundamental insights into the structure of liquids: (1) it is fundamentally different from that of simple crystals and (2) it orders substantially near a crystal surface, with the resulting entropy decrease being the main contribution to the crystal-melt interfacial tension (or excess interfacial free energy[2]).

An important suggestion on the first point, directly inspired by Turnbull's results, was made by Frank,[3] who pointed out that the *short-range* energy minimization in a monatomic system favors icosahedral coordination shells. The fivefold symmetry and the predominance of fairly perfect tetrahedral configurations of the arrangement are incompatible with the simple close-packed lattices (face-centered cubic, hexagonal close-packed) that minimize the *overall* volume and energy.

The essential polytetrahedral nature of simple liquids and the ubiquity of fivefold symmetrical local order were confirmed in the analysis of physical models, such as the dense random packing of hard spheres[4] or computer-generated ones,[5] and formed the basis of a formal description of the liquid state in which a four-dimensional perfect polytetrahedral polytope is mapped onto three-dimensional Euclidean space by the introduction of disclination lines.[6]

The study of the structure and properties of the crystal-melt interface

[1]D. Turnbull, *J. Chem. Phys.* **20**, 411 (1952).

[2]The identification of interfacial tension, which is defined mechanically, with the excess interfacial free energy is strictly only valid for fluid-fluid interfaces. For the crystal-melt interface, where one of the phases is solid and can sustain an elastic strain, the mechanical definition leads to the introduction of an interface *stress* [see Ref. 35 and J. W. Cahn, *Acta Metall.* **28**, 1333 (1980)]. In this paper the two phases will be assumed incompressible, so that the interface stress need not be considered.

[3]F. C. Frank, *Proc. Roy. Soc. London* **A215**, 43 (1952).

[4]J. D. Bernal, *Proc. Roy. Soc. London* **A280**, 299 (1964).

[5]For a review, see F. Yonezawa in *Solid State Physics* (H. Ehrenreich and D. Turnbull, eds.), Vol. 45, p. 179, Academic Press, New York (1991).

[6]For a review, see D. R. Nelson and F. Spaepen, in *Solid State Physics* (H. Ehrenreich and D. Turnbull, eds.), Vol. 42, p. 1, Academic Press, New York (1989).

is difficult for a number of reasons.[7] First, direct structural probes, which have been extremely successful in the study of crystal-vapor and, to a lesser degree, liquid-vapor interfaces, are as yet not available. Second, the development of structural models has long suffered from the incomplete understanding of the liquid structure.

In early models, therefore, the specifics of the liquid structure were mostly ignored. Some of those models were similar to those for intercrystalline boundaries (grain boundaries) in that their interfacial tension originates from the excess energy associated with a substantial density deficit or, equivalently, bond breaking.[8] Other authors made the analogy with the crystal-vapor interfaces[9] and used Ising models to predict interface roughening.[10]

The crystal-melt interface, however, is intrinsically different from an intercrystalline boundary. In the latter, all atomic positions are strongly correlated by one or the other of the two adjacent crystals. High-resolution microscopy shows that the two crystals extend right up to a clear dividing surface, and that all atoms can unambiguously be assigned to one or the other crystal (with an occasional shared one). This causes a substantial density deficit.[11] The positional correlations in the liquid phase, however, are not as strong as in a crystal. As a result, the atoms in the crystal-melt interface can adjust their position to the strong correlations imposed by the crystal on one side to minimize the density deficit. This leads to increased ordering of the liquid as the crystal is approached.

David Turnbull[12] first pointed out that the entropy loss associated with this ordering is the origin of the large crystal-melt interfacial tension (or excess interfacial free energy), which creates the barrier to crystal nucleation and allows sizable undercooling. As discussed in detail later (see Fig. 4), he noted that the entropy must rise more slowly than the enthalpy with distance away from the crystal surface.

Since then structural models that take proper account of the nature of the liquid state, such as static physical models,[13–17] in which the transition

---

[7] A review of the early experimental work, modeling, and applications is given by D. P. Woodruff, *The Solid-Liquid Interface*, Cambridge University Press, Cambridge, UK (1973).

[8] A. D. Skapski, *Acta Metall.* **4**, 576 (1956).

[9] W. K. Burton, N. Cabrera, and F. C. Frank, *Phil. Trans. Roy. Soc.* **A243**, 299 (1951).

[10] K. A. Jackson, in *Growth and Perfection of Crystals* (R. H. Doremus, B. W. Roberts, and D. Turnbull, eds.), p. 319, Wiley, New York (1958).

[11] H. J. Frost, M. F. Ashby, and F. Spaepen, *Scripta Metall.* **14**, 1051 (1980).

[12] D. Turnbull, in *Physics of Non-Crystalline Solids* (J. A. Prins, ed.), p. 41, North-Holland, Amsterdam (1964).

[13] F. Spaepen, *Acta Metall.* **23**, 729 (1975).

[14] F. Spaepen and R. B. Meyer, *Scripta Metall.* **10**, 257 (1976).

from crystal to melt is accomplished by enforcing a polytetrahedral structure, analytic models,[18-26] and molecular dynamics simulations,[26-31] have confirmed Turnbull's view of the interface.

The neg-entropic nature of the crystal-melt interface must be reflected in the temperature dependence of the interfacial tension, and hence also in that of the frequency of homogeneous nucleation. Turnbull's original paper[1] already points out that the interfacial tension must increase with temperature if the atomic jump frequency is to have a physically reasonable value. Although the temperature coefficient indeed has a sign that appears to agree qualitatively with the entropy loss, it has thus far not been linked quantitatively to the structural models.

Part of the difficulty is that most of the models provide thermodynamic information on the equilibrium state (i.e., for flat interfaces), whereas the interfacial tension derived from homogeneous nucleation experiments is obtained under strongly nonequilibrium conditions (i.e., for curved interfaces). In this chapter, the temperature dependence of the interfacial tension under both conditions is reviewed. Considerable literature is available on flat and curved interfaces, going all the way back to Gibbs.[32,33] A simple model for the curved interface,[34] based on Turnbull's

[15] D. R. Nelson and F. Spaepen, in *Solid State Physics* (H. Ehrenreich and D. Turnbull, eds.), Vol. 42, p. 190, Academic Press, New York (1989).

[16] A. Bonnissent, J. L. Finney, and B. Mutaftschiev, *Phil. Mag.* **B42**, 233 (1980).

[17] C. V. Thompson, Ph.D. Thesis, Harvard University (1981).

[18] W. A. Curtin, *Phys. Rev. Lett.* **59**, 1228 (1978).

[19] W. E. McMullen and D. W. Oxtoby, *J. Chem. Phys.* **88**, 1967 (1988).

[20] D. W. Oxtoby, in "Fundamentals of Inhomogeneous Fluids" (D. Henderson, ed.), p. 407, Marcel Dekker, New York (1992).

[21] A. D. J. Haymet and D. W. Oxtoby, *J. Chem. Phys.* **74**, 2559 (1981).

[22] D. W. Oxtoby and A. D. J. Haymet, *J. Chem. Phys.* **76**, 6262 (1982).

[23] B. B. Laird and A. D. J. Haymet, *J. Chem. Phys.* **91**, 3638 (1989).

[24] S. M. Moore and H. J. Raveche, *J. Chem. Phys.* **85**, 6039 (1986).

[25] X. C. Zeng and D. Stroud, *J. Chem. Phys.* **90**, 5208 (1989).

[26] J. H. Sikkenk, J. O. Indekeu, J. M. J. van Leeuwen, and E. O. Vossnack, *Phys. Rev. Lett.* **59**, 98 (1987).

[27] J. Q. Broughton and F. F. Abraham, *J. Chem. Phys. Lett.* **71**, 456 (1980).

[28] J. Q. Broughton, A. Bonnissent, and F. F. Abraham, *J. Chem. Phys.* **74**, 4029 (1981).

[29] J. Q. Broughton and G. H. Gilmer, *J. Chem. Phys.* **84**, 5741; 5749; 5759 (1986).

[30] E. Burke, J. Q. Broughton, and G. H. Gilmer, *J. Chem. Phys.* **89**, 1030 (1988).

[31] W.-J. Ma, J. R. Banavar, and J. Koplik, *J. Chem. Phys.* **97**, 485 (1992).

[32] J. W. Gibbs, *The Scientific Papers of J. Willard Gibbs*, Dover, New York (1961).

[33] An excellent review of the thermodynamics of flat and curved surfaces can be found in J. S. Rowlinson and B. Widom, *Molecular Theory of Capillarity*, Oxford Clarendon Press, New York (1982).

[34] F. Spaepen, in *Proc. Int. Workshop on Containerless Processing of Metals—Undercooling and Solidification* (I. Egry and J. Laakmann, eds.), p. 22, DLR-Mitteilung 89-15, Deutsche Forschungsanstalt für Luft- und Raumfahrt, Köln, Germany (1989).

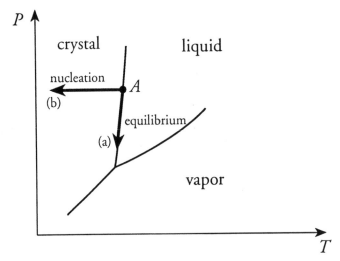

FIG. 1. Schematic phase diagram of a single component system. The change of the interfacial tension with temperature can be considered in equilibrium [path (a)] or in an undercooled melt, as in nucleation experiments [path (b)].

original proposal for the interfacial structure, is introduced, and its thermodynamic properties are related to the nucleation data.

## II. The Equilibrium Interface

### 1. TEMPERATURE DEPENDENCE OF THE INTERFACIAL TENSION: EXCESS INTERFACIAL ENTROPY

The thermodynamic properties of an interface between two phases in equilibrium (e.g., point A on Fig. 1, the phase diagram for a single component system) have been described definitively by Gibbs.[32] The following discussion is based on Cahn's particularly clear exposition of Gibbs's approach.[35] For simplicity, only the single component system is considered.

Consider a system consisting of $N$ moles distributed between two phases, $\alpha$ and $\beta$, in equilibrium, separated by an interface with area $A$. Equilibrium dictates that the interface be flat. The Gibbs free energy of the total system (including the interface) is:

$$G = U - TS + pV, \qquad (1.1)$$

[35] J. W. Cahn, in *Interfacial Segregation* (W. C. Johnson and J. M. Blakeley, eds.), pp. 3-23, ASM, Metals Park, OH (1979).

where $U$, $S$, and $V$ are, respectively, the total energy, entropy, and volume of the system. The Gibbs free energy of the two phases without the interface is:

$$G_b = \mu N, \tag{1.2}$$

where $\mu$ is the chemical potential (the same in both phases in equilibrium). The interfacial tension[2] $\sigma$ can then be defined as the excess free energy, per unit area, in the system due to the presence of the interface, or:

$$\sigma A = U - TS + pV - \mu N. \tag{1.3}$$

Differentiating gives:

$$\sigma dA + A d\sigma = dU - TdS - SdT + pdV + Vdp - \mu dN - Nd\mu. \tag{1.4}$$

Since $\sigma dA$ is the force–times–distance work done by the interfacial tension when the area is increased by $dA$, the combination of the first and second laws of thermodynamics gives:

$$dU = TdS - pdV + \mu dN + \sigma dA. \tag{1.5}$$

Combination of Eqs. (1.4) and (1.5) gives:

$$A d\sigma = -SdT + Vdp - Nd\mu. \tag{1.6}$$

For each of the two bulk phases a similar relation, the Gibbs-Duhem equation, holds:

$$0 = -S^\alpha dT + V^\alpha dp - N^\alpha d\mu, \tag{1.7}$$

$$0 = -S^\beta dT + V^\beta dp - N^\beta d\mu. \tag{1.8}$$

The assignment of the atoms to the two phases requires the placement of a dividing surface, which at this point is arbitrary. The only condition that must hold is, obviously:

$$N^\alpha + N^\beta = N. \tag{1.9}$$

The temperature dependence of the interfacial tension is found by solving the system of three equations [Eqs. (1.6), (1.7), and (1.8)] and three un-

knowns ($dT$, $dp$, and $d\mu$). Following Cahn, this is most conveniently done with Cramer's rule from linear algebra:

$$A d\sigma = - \frac{\begin{vmatrix} S & V & N \\ S^\alpha & V^\alpha & N^\alpha \\ S^\beta & V^\beta & N^\beta \end{vmatrix}}{\begin{vmatrix} V^\alpha & N^\alpha \\ V^\beta & N^\beta \end{vmatrix}} dT. \tag{1.10}$$

At this point, it is convenient to choose the position of the dividing surface such that the excess volume associated with the interface is zero (Fig. 2), or:

$$N^\alpha v^\alpha + N^\beta v^\beta = V^\alpha + V^\beta = V, \tag{1.11}$$

where $v^\alpha$ and $v^\beta$ are the molar volumes of the two bulk phases. Subtraction of the lower two rows from the top one in the determinant in the numerator of Eq. (1.10) then makes two of the elements equal to zero [see Eq. (1.9) and (1.11)] and leads directly to the solution:

$$\frac{d\sigma}{dT} = -S_{ex}, \tag{1.12}$$

where

$$S_{ex} = \frac{1}{A}(S - S^\alpha - S^\beta) \tag{1.13}$$

is the excess entropy, per unit area, associated with the interface (Fig. 2).

It is important to keep in mind that Eq. (1.12) only holds in *equilibrium*, where the variation $dT$ must be accompanied by *a variation in pressure, dp, along the coexistence line* [path (a) in Fig. 1]. It *cannot*, therefore, be applied, as many authors have done[14,36,37] to undercooling experiments, where the external pressure is kept constant [path (b) in Fig. 1]. In that case, only unstable equilibrium at a curved surface can be established, and a different analysis must be made.

[36] Y. Miyazawa and G. M. Pound, *J. Cryst. Growth* **23**, 45 (1974).
[37] G. R. Wood and A. G. Walton, *J. Appl. Phys.* **41**, 3027 (1970).

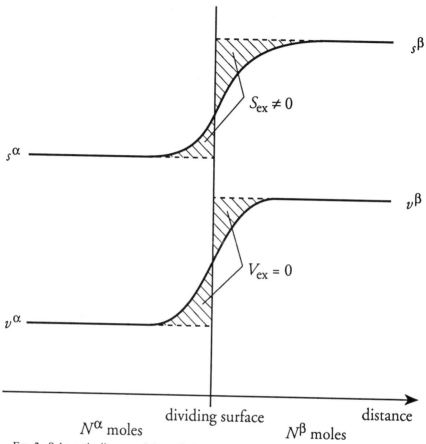

FIG. 2. Schematic diagram of the variation of the molar volume $v$ and the molar entropy $s$ across an interface in equilibrium. The superscripts refer to the values in the bulk phases. If the (negative) excess interfacial entropy, $-S_{ex}$, is to be equal to the temperature coefficient of the interfacial tension, the dividing surface must be chosen to give zero excess volume.

## III. The Interface in an Undercooled Melt

2. THE INFINITELY THIN INTERFACE

If, in the Gibbsian sense, abstraction is made of the interfacial structure and the interface is reduced to a mathematically two-dimensional surface with interfacial tension $\sigma$ separating a crystal and melt with bulk properties, the (unstable) equilibrium condition at a curved surface is established as follows.

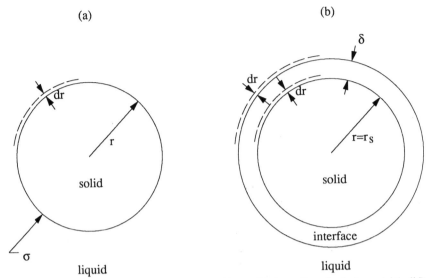

Fig. 3. Schematic diagram illustrating unstable equilibrium of a spherical crystal (solid) in an undercooled melt (liquid) with (a) an infinitely thin interface and (b) a physical interface of width $\delta$.

Consider the case of a single-component, incompressible, spherical, and isotropic crystal of radius $r$, surrounded by its melt [Fig. 3(a)]. The work required to form this crystal from the melt is[32,38]:

$$W_G = \frac{4\pi r^3}{3} \Delta G_{sl} + 4\pi r^2 \sigma, \qquad (2.1)$$

where $\Delta G_{sl}$ is the difference in Gibbs free energy, per unit volume of the crystal, between the bulk crystal (solid) and its undercooled melt (liquid).

The condition for equilibrium is that $W_G$ be at an extremum for a variation $dr$ of the radius:

$$\frac{dW_G}{dr} = 4\pi r^2 \Delta G_{sl} + 8\pi r \sigma = 0. \qquad (2.2)$$

This gives the condition for the radius of curvature:

$$r_G^* = -\frac{2\sigma}{\Delta G_{sl}}. \qquad (2.3)$$

[38] D. Turnbull, in *Solid State Physics* (F. Seitz and D. Turnbull, eds.), Vol. 3, p. 225, Academic Press, New York (1956).

The work to form the crystal in (unstable) equilibrium is then

$$W_G^* = \frac{16\pi}{3} \frac{\sigma^3}{\Delta G_{sl}^2}.$$  (2.4)

We will return to the question of the location of the interface after the discussion of the physical interface of finite width. This requires first a brief review of its structure.


3. STRUCTURE AND PROPERTIES OF THE PHYSICAL INTERFACE

Physical modeling,[13–17] analytic studies,[18–25] and computer simulation[26–31] of the crystal-melt interface in simple systems (hard sphere, Lennard-Jones, or metallic) produce atomic density profiles that are all qualitatively similar to the one sketched in Fig. 4(a). The interface has a thickness on the order of a few interatomic distances and consists of atoms that are localized, to a degree that depends on the distance from the crystal, in layers parallel to the interface.

Note that the apparent width of the interface in simulations of the interface is an upper limit of the intrinsic transition width of interest here. This is due to the formation of crystal terraces, which have only a slight effect on the thermodynamics of the interface. The intrinsic width is more clearly identifiable in static physical modeling, where the planarity of the crystal can be enforced.

Since the structure of the interfacial layers is different from that of the two bulk phases, the enthalpy and entropy in the interface are different from their bulk values in the two phases as well. For example, the localization makes the entropy lower than in the bulk liquid. If the interface had a substantial density deficit, as in a grain boundary, its enthalpy could be higher than that of both bulk phases. If, as is found in most structural models, the density deficit is small, the interfacial enthalpy is expected to be intermediate between the two bulk values.

---

FIG. 4. Schematic illustration of the variation of the structure and thermodynamic properties of the crystal-melt interface with distance across the interface: (a) average atomic density; (b) atomic enthalpy and entropy, in equilibrium at the melting temperature $T_M$; the horizontal lines correspond to the interfacial enthalpy $h_i$ and entropy $s_i$ in the approximate model of a uniform interface; (c) free energy per atom below the melting temperature (crystal in an undercooled melt); $r$ is the distance from the center of the crystal (solid); and (d) the free energy per unit volume for the uniform interface below the melting temperature.

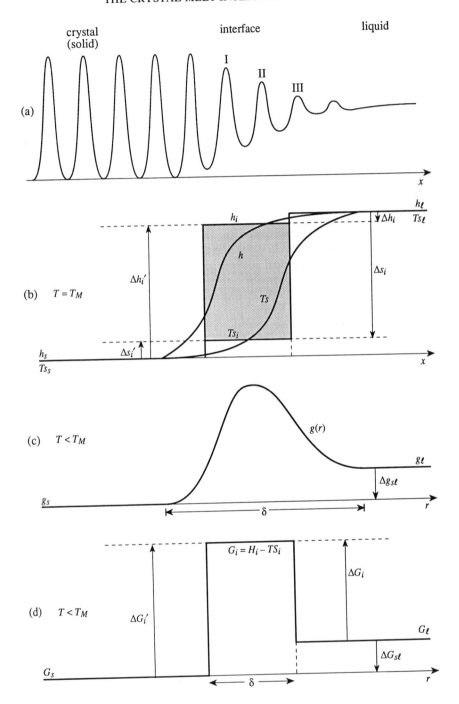

We should emphasize from the outset that the description of the interface as a region with its own thermodynamic parameters does *not* imply that it is being treated as a separate phase.[39] It can only exist between the two bulk phases, and its thermodynamic parameters only have meaning as transition parameters between the bulk values. The approach developed next has, in fact, the same basis as that of the so-called "quasi-" or "local" thermodynamic methods used for the study of interfaces.[33]

Figure 4(b) shows a plausible variation of the entropy and enthalpy, per atom, as a function of position through the interface between the two phases in equilibrium (the bulk free energies, $g_s = h_s - T_M s_s$ and $g_l = h_l - T_M s_l$, are equal and have been made equal to zero). The interfacial tension is proportional to the area between the two curves (normalized by the atomic volume). As Turnbull first pointed out,[12] for the interfacial tension to be positive, and hence for the undercooling of liquids to be possible, the entropy in the interface must rise more slowly with distance from the crystal than the enthalpy.

## 4. INTERFACIAL TENSION OF THE PHYSICAL INTERFACE

The arguments of Section 2 can be repeated for a spherical crystal with a full interface of thickness $\delta$ [see Fig. 3(b)], if the variation of the free energy, per atom, in the radial direction, $g(r)$, is known, as sketched in Fig. 4(c). The approach is similar to that of Cahn and Hilliard for the formation of nuclei with a diffuse interface[40] and has been outlined in an earlier publication.[34] Again, it is assumed that the system has one component, and that the crystal and interface are isotropic and incompressible.

The work $W$ required to create a crystal of radius $r_s$ in the liquid is then the sum of the work to form concentric spherical shells of the crystal and the interface:

$$W(r_s) = \int_0^\infty [g(r) - g_l] \frac{4\pi r^2}{\Omega(r)} dr, \qquad (4.1)$$

where $\Omega(r)$ is the local atomic volume and

$$
\begin{aligned}
g(r) &= g_s & \text{for } r \leq r_s, \\
g(r) & & \text{for } r_s \leq r \leq r_s + \delta, \qquad (4.2) \\
g(r) &= g_l & \text{for } r_s + \delta \leq r,
\end{aligned}
$$

[39] E. A. Guggenheim, *Thermodynamics*, North-Holland, Amsterdam (1967).
[40] J. W. Cahn and J. E. Hilliard, *J. Chem. Phys.* **31**, 688 (1959).

where $g_s$ and $g_l$ are the free energies, per atom, of the crystal and the liquid, respectively.

The radius of the crystal in (unstable) equilibrium with the melt, $r_s^*$, is again obtained by requiring that $W$ be an extremum for a variation of $r_s$ [see Fig. 3(b)]:

$$\frac{dW}{dr_s}\bigg|_{r_s^*} = 0. \tag{4.3}$$

Inserting $r_s^*$ into Eq. (4.1) gives the work needed to create the crystal in equilibrium with the melt:

$$W^* = W(r_s^*). \tag{4.4}$$

This work is now equated to $W_G^*$ of Eq. (2.1), the work required to form a crystal in equilibrium with its melt through a Gibbsian dividing surface, for the same difference in free energy between the bulk phases, $\Delta G_{sl}$:

$$W^* = \frac{16\pi}{3}\frac{\sigma^3}{\Delta G_{sl}^2}. \tag{4.5}$$

Since $W^*$ has been calculated from the properties of the interface, and $\Delta G_{sl}$ is known from the bulk thermodynamics of the two phases, Eq. (4.5) is in fact a *definition* of the interfacial tension, or:

$$\sigma = \left(\frac{3}{16\pi}\Delta G_{sl}^2 W^*\right)^{1/3}. \tag{4.6}$$

The interfacial tension defined this way is also the one obtained from homogeneous nnucleation, since the critical work measured in those experiments is precisely that of Eq. (4.5).

Finally, the position of the Gibbsian dividing surface, $r_G^*$, for the particular interface model used in the calculations is found by substituting the known value of $\sigma$ [Eq. (4.6)] and of $\Delta G_{sl}$ into Eq. (2.3). As shown in Appendix A, the position of $r_G^*$ is such that the excess free energy, computed spherically, with respect to that dividing surface equals $\sigma A_G^*$, where $A_G^*$ is the area of the dividing surface and $\sigma$ is given by Eq. (4.6).

In Appendix B explicit formulas are given for $\sigma$ and $r_G^*$ in terms of the moments of the free energy $g(r)$. The method is actually most clearly illustrated by working out a simple example, as shown in the next section.

## 5. A SIMPLE MODEL: THE UNIFORM INTERFACE

### a. *Calculation of the Interfacial Tension at Constant Temperature*

The interface model under consideration in this section has the following properties [see Figs. 4(b) and 4(d)]: (1) The interface has a thickness $\delta$; (2) the entropy and enthalpy, and hence the free energy are uniform throughout the interface; (3) the entire system—crystal, liquid, and interface—is incompressible; and (4) all atoms in the system have the same atomic volume.

Properties (1) and (2) are the essential features of the model. Assumption (3) is a common, and quite accurate one for condensed phases; it is essential for the formulation of the work according to Eqs. (2.1) and (4.1); it also obviates the need to consider the interface stress[2] and effects of pressure. Assumption (4) is made for computational convenience; it, too, applies fairly accurately to the bulk crystal and liquid phases, as well as to the interface, which has a low density deficit.

The quantities used for the computation of the interfacial tension are indicated on Fig. 4(d). The $G_s$ and $G_l$ represent, respectively, the free energies per unit volume of the crystal and the liquid. Their difference, $\Delta G_{sl} = G_s - G_l$, is negative below the melting temperature. The $H_i$, $S_i$, and $G_i = H_i - TS_i$ represent, respectively, the enthalpy, entropy, and free energy per unit volume in the interface. Two additional free energy differences can be defined. On the liquid side, $\Delta G_i = G_i - G_l$; and on the solid side, $\Delta G_i' = G_i - G_s$. For the interface to be stable, both of these quantities must be positive. It is useful to remember that $\Delta G_i' = \Delta G_i - \Delta G_{sl}$.

In equilibrium, $T = T_M$ and $\Delta G_{sl} = 0$, so that $\Delta G_i = \Delta G_i'$. The interfacial tension is then simply

$$\sigma = \delta \Delta G_i. \tag{5.1}$$

In the following, $T_M$, $\Delta G_i$, and $\Delta G_i'$ are different, and $\sigma$ must be a symmetrical function of both of them. The method outlined in the previous section is now used to determine that function.

The work required to create the crystal and the interface in the undercooled liquid is, from Eq. (4.1) or by inspection,

$$W = \frac{4\pi r_s^3}{3} \Delta G_{sl} + \frac{4\pi}{3} [(r_s + \delta)^3 - r_s^3] \Delta G_i. \tag{5.2}$$

This can be simplified by introducing a dimensionless measure for the driving free energy:

$$a = \frac{\Delta G_{sl}}{\Delta G_i},$$
(5.3)

which is a negative quantity. Equation (5.2) then becomes:

$$W = \frac{4\pi}{3} \Delta G_i (ar_s^3 + 3r_s^2\delta + 3r_s\delta^2 + \delta^3).$$
(5.4)

The condition that establishes the equilibrium radius, $dW/dr_s = 0$ [Eq. (4.3)], becomes:

$$ar_s^2 + 2r_s\delta + \delta^2 = 0.$$
(5.5)

The equilibrium radius is then:

$$r_s^* = -\frac{\delta}{a}(1 + \sqrt{1-a}),$$
(5.6)

which by introduction of

$$b^2 = 1 - a,$$
(5.7)

simplifies to

$$r_s^* = -\frac{\delta}{1-b},$$
(5.8)

Note that the length scale of the problem is set by the thickness of the interface $\delta$—the only length introduced into the model.

The work required to form the equilibrium crystal and its interface is now obtained from Eq. (4.4), i.e., by substitution of Eq. (5.8) into (5.4):

$$W^* = \frac{4\pi}{3} \Delta G_i \delta^3 \frac{b^2}{(1-b)^2}.$$
(5.9)

The interfacial tension is then obtained from Eq. (4.6):

$$\sigma^3 = \frac{1}{4}\delta^3 \Delta G_i^3 \left(\frac{ab}{1-b}\right)^2.$$
(5.10)

This can be put in a more transparent form by eliminating $a$ and $b$ using their definitions of Eqs. (5.3) and (5.7):

$$\sigma = \delta(\Delta G_i \cdot \Delta G_i' \cdot \Delta G_{i,\text{ave}})^{1/3}, \tag{5.11}$$

where

$$\Delta G_{i,\text{ave}} = \frac{1}{4}[(\Delta G_i)^{1/2} + (\Delta G_i')^{1/2}]^2$$

$$= \frac{1}{2}\left[\frac{1}{2}(\Delta G_i + \Delta G_i') + (\Delta G_i \cdot \Delta G_i')^{1/2}\right]. \tag{5.12}$$

Note that the last form of this expression states that $\Delta G_{i,\text{ave}}$ is the arithmetic average of the arithmetic and geometric averages of $\Delta G_i$ and $\Delta G_i'$. Equations (5.11) and (5.12) also have the desired symmetry between the solid and liquid side.

### b. Temperature Dependence of the Interfacial Tension

To apply Eq. (5.11) at different temperatures, the model must be specified further. For example, the following, quite plausible additional assumptions suffice: (1) The interface thickness $\delta$ is independent of temperature; (2) the difference between the enthalpy or entropy of the interface (both per unit volume) and its respective value in the bulk *liquid*, $\Delta H_i = H_i - S_l$ or $\Delta S_i = S_i - S_l$, is independent of temperature; and (3) the difference in specific heat between the liquid and crystal is zero; as a result, the enthalpy of fusion, $\Delta H_f = H_l - H_s$ (positive) and entropy of fusion $\Delta S_f = S_l - S_s$ (positive) are independent of temperature, and $\Delta G_{sl} = \Delta S_f(T - T_M)$.

With these assumptions, numerical computation of $\sigma(T)$ from Eqs. (5.11) and (5.12) is straightforward. For application and generalization, it is useful to have an expression in dimensionless form. The obvious dimensionless variables are:

$$\tilde{\sigma} = \sigma/(\lambda T_M \Delta S_f),$$
$$\tilde{h} = \Delta H_i/\Delta H_f,$$
$$\tilde{s} = \Delta S_{i/\Delta}S_f,$$
$$\tilde{T} = T/T_M,$$
$$\tilde{\delta} = \delta/\lambda, \tag{5.13}$$

where $\lambda$ is an atomic dimension, for example, $(V/N)^{1/3}$ (where $V$ = molar volume and $N$ = Avogadro's number). Keeping in mind that $T_M \Delta S_f = \Delta H_f$, and $\Delta G_i' = \Delta G_i - \Delta G_{sl}$ [see Fig. 4(d)], Eqs. (5.11) and (5.12) yield:

$$\bar{\sigma} = \tilde{\delta} \left\{ (\bar{h} - \bar{T}\tilde{s}) \cdot (\bar{h} - \bar{T}\tilde{s} - \bar{T} + 1) \cdot \frac{1}{4} [(\bar{h} - \bar{T}\tilde{s})^{1/2} \right.$$
$$\left. + (\bar{h} - \bar{T}\tilde{s} - \bar{T} + 1)^{1/2}]^2 \right\}^{1/3}.$$

(5.14)

Of the assumptions made here, (2) is the essential one: It reflects the idea that the interfacial tension originates from the accommodation of the liquid structure to the structural constraint posed by the crystal plane. An alternative assumption, of constant differences in enthalpy and entropy between the interface and the *crystal*, $\Delta H_i'$ and $\Delta S_i'$, would be based on considering the interface as a disordered crystal. Assumption (3) can easily be modified if specific heat data are available, and (2) could then be adjusted so that $\Delta S_i$ would be, for example, a constant fraction of $\Delta S_f$. Keep in mind that the changes in $\Delta H_i$ and $\Delta S_i$ with temperature are linked through the interface specific heat, and therefore cannot be varied independently. Assumption (2) used here, for example, is consistent with the interface specific heat being zero.

A similar model has recently been proposed by Gránásy.[41] It is essentially a special case of the one discussed earlier, in that the interfacial entropy and enthalpy are kept at, respectively, the bulk liquid and crystalline values. The interfacial width $\delta$ then needs to be adjustable and can no longer simply be related to structural models of the interface as is done below.

## 6. THE SIMPLE MODEL AT LOW UNDERCOOLING

The quickest insight into the problem is found by introducing the further simplification of low undercooling. A treatment of the entire problem under these conditions is very brief, and has been published elsewhere.[42] The simplification of the preceding results proceeds as follows.

At low undercooling, i.e., for $T \lesssim T_M$, $|\Delta G_{sl}| \ll G_i$ and $\Delta G_i' \cong \Delta G_i$. Since the geometric and arithmetic averages in Eqs. (5.11) and (5.12) are

[41] L. Gránásy, *J. Non-Crystalline Solids*, **162**, 301 (1993).
[42] F. Spaepen, *Mat. Sci. Eng. A*, **178**, 15 (1994).

the same to first order in their difference, $\Delta G_{sl}$, Eq. (5.11) depends simply on the arithmetic average:

$$\sigma = \delta \frac{1}{2}(\Delta G_i + \Delta G_i'), \tag{6.1}$$

or

$$\sigma = \delta \left( \Delta G_i - \frac{1}{2}\Delta G_{sl} \right), \tag{6.2}$$

or, in dimensionless form,

$$\tilde{\sigma} = \tilde{\delta} \left( \tilde{h} - \tilde{T}\tilde{s} - \frac{\tilde{T}}{2} + \frac{1}{2} \right). \tag{6.3}$$

This is illustrated in the lower part of Fig. 5. Keeping in mind that

$$\frac{\partial \Delta G_i}{\partial T} = -\Delta S_i \quad \text{and} \quad \frac{\partial \Delta G_{sl}}{\partial T} = -\Delta S_f, \tag{6.4}$$

the temperature coefficient at low undercooling is easily found:

$$\frac{d\sigma}{dT} = -\delta(\Delta S_i + \frac{1}{2}\Delta S_f), \tag{6.5}$$

or, in dimensionless form, directly from Eq. (6.3):

$$\frac{d\tilde{\sigma}}{d\tilde{T}} = -\tilde{\delta} \left( \tilde{s} + \frac{1}{2} \right). \tag{6.6}$$

The location of the Gibbsian dividing surface, defined by Eq. (2.3), can also be easily found under these conditions. Keeping in mind the definition of the dimensionless driving force $a$ [Eq. (5.3)], Eq. (6.2) gives:

$$r_G^* \equiv -\frac{2\sigma}{\Delta G_{sl}} = -2\delta \left( \frac{\Delta G_i}{\Delta G_{sl}} + 1 \right) = \delta \left( -\frac{2}{a} + 1 \right). \tag{6.7}$$

Expansion of the expression for the radius of the solid [Eq. (5.6)] to first order in $a$ gives:

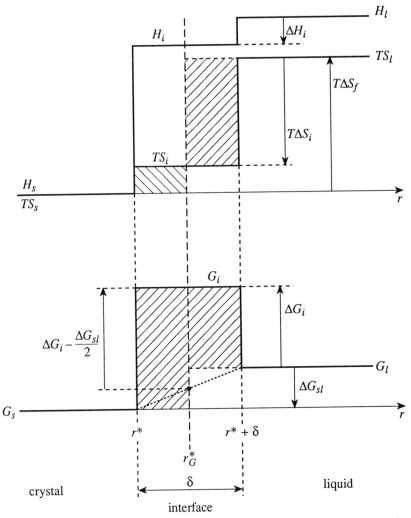

FIG. 5. Schematic diagram of the properties of the uniform interface model at low undercooling.

$$r_s^* = \delta\left(-\frac{2}{a} + \frac{1}{2}\right). \tag{6.8}$$

To lowest order, the two radii are the same and are equal to the classical radius of Eq. (2.3), since to that order $\sigma = \delta\Delta G_i$. The difference between them in the next order shows that the Gibbsian dividing surface in this

model, at low undercooling, lies right at the middle of the interfacial layer:

$$r_G^* - r_s^* = \frac{\delta}{2}. \tag{6.9}$$

Figure 5 shows the location of the surface. Note that the interfacial tension is indeed the excess free energy computed with respect to this interface (cross-hatched area in the lower part of the figure), as discussed at the end of Section 4 and in Appendix B.

Figure 5 and Eq. (6.5) also show that the temperature coefficient of the interfacial tension is the (negative) entropy excess computed with respect to this same surface.

## IV. Application to the Analysis of Homogeneous Nucleation Experiments

7. REANALYSIS OF THE DATA FOR MERCURY

As pointed out in Kelton's recent review in this series,[43] there are only two sets of quantitative data on the kinetics of homogeneous crystal nucleation from the melt in metals: those of Turnbull[1] on mercury and those of Miyazawa and Pound[36] on gallium. Both make use of the emulsion technique to isolate the heterogeneous nucleants.

To establish that homogeneous nucleation has been measured, two conditions must be met[44]: (1) The maximum undercooling should be independent of the nature of the surface of the droplets and (2) the steady state nucleation rate $I$ should be stochastic in volume and time. The latter can be established in two ways: (a) by a detailed analysis of the kinetics on the size distribution of each dispersion or, more convincingly, (b) by showing that for dispersions with *different average size d,* the nucleation probability of a droplet scaled with $d^{-3}$.

In Turnbull's experiments on mercury all of these conditions were met. In those on gallium, however, condition 2b was not met: For reasons that are not understood, $I$ scaled with $d^{-1}$. Nevertheless, similar conclusions on the temperature dependence of the interfacial tension emerged from the two sets of experiments.

[43] K. F. Kelton, in *Solid State Physics* (H. Ehrenreich and D. Turnbull, eds.), Vol. 45, p. 75, Academic Press, New York (1991).
[44] D. Turnbull, in *Undercooled Alloy Phases* (E. W. Collings and C. C. Koch, eds.), p. 3, The Metallurgical Society of AIME, Warrendale, PA (1986).

TABLE I. DATA (FROM REF. 1) AND ANALYSIS OF THE KINETICS OF HOMOGENEOUS
CRYSTAL NUCLEATION FROM THE MELT IN MERCURY

| $T$ | $\log I$ | $\Delta g_{sl}$ | $\sigma$ | $f(T)$ |
|------|----------|-----------------|----------|--------|
| (K) | $(\text{cm}^{-3}\text{s}^{-1})$ | (J/mole) | $(\text{erg/cm}^2)$ | $(\times 10^3)$ |
| Dispersion 1 | | | | |
| 153.62 | 7.105 | 814.50 | 30.270 | 1.0058 |
| 153.89 | 6.970 | 812.10 | 30.277 | 1.0099 |
| 154.34 | 6.686 | 808.08 | 30.308 | 1.0170 |
| Dispersion 2 | | | | |
| 154.15 | 6.948 | 809.78 | 30.244 | 1.0140 |
| 154.36 | 6.790 | 807.91 | 30.268 | 1.0173 |
| 154.64 | 6.592 | 805.41 | 30.294 | 1.0218 |
| 154.91 | 6.444 | 803.00 | 30.303 | 1.0262 |
| 155.12 | 6.244 | 801.12 | 30.340 | 1.0296 |
| 155.40 | 6.077 | 798.62 | 30.354 | 1.0342 |

In the mercury experiments, the steady state isothermal nucleation rate was measured at several temperatures in the range of 153.62 to 155.40 K, and the results are listed in Table I.

In classical nucleation theory, the nucleation rate is determined by the work to form the critical nucleus [Eq. (2.4)] according to the expression:

$$I = I_o \exp\left(-\frac{16\pi\sigma^3}{3kT\Delta G_{sl}^2}\right), \qquad (7.1)$$

where $k$ is Boltzmann's constant and $I_o$ is a prefactor that takes into account the jump frequency across the interface of the critical nucleus.

In the original analysis, a value for $\sigma$ was extracted from the $I(T)$ data, under the assumption that it was independent of temperature and that the difference in specific heat between crystal and liquid was zero. This gave $\sigma = 31.2$ erg/cm$^2$ and $I_o = 10^{42}$ cm$^{-3}$ s$^{-1}$. A theoretical estimate[1] of the prefactor, based on absolute rate theory and viscosity data for Hg, is $I_o = 10^{35}$ cm$^{-3}$ s$^{-1}$. Turnbull pointed out in his original paper that this discrepancy must be explained by the temperature dependence of $\sigma$ and $\Delta G_{sl}$.

We will therefore reexamine the analysis of these nucleation data by taking into account the experimentally measured difference[45–47] in specific

[45] R. H. Busey and W. F. Giauque, *J. Phys. Chem.* **75**, 806 (1953).
[46] J. H. Perpezko and D. H. Rasmussen, *Met. Trans.* **A9**, 1490 (1978).
[47] C. V. Thompson and F. Spaepen, *Acta Metall.* **27**, 1855 (1979).

heat between crystal and liquid, $\Delta C_p$, in the computation of $\Delta G_{sl}(T)$. The undercooled temperature range was divided into three regions; in each $\Delta C_p$ (in J/mole K) was approximated by a linear relation:

$$234.28 \text{ K} - 195 \text{ K} \quad \Delta C_p = 10.274 - 0.0473T,$$

$$175 \text{ K} \quad - 195 \text{ K} \quad \Delta C_p = 13.506 - 0.0604T, \tag{7.2}$$

$$150 \text{ K} \quad - 175 \text{ K} \quad \Delta C_p = 13.679 - 0.0614T.$$

Integration gives the difference in the bulk free energies, $\Delta g_{sl}$, at the undercooled temperature. The molar volume of the crystal at 154 K was computed from crystallographic data[48] (14.086 cm$^3$/mole at 227 K) and the thermal expansion[49] (average value over the relevant range: 14 $\times$ 10$^{-5}$ K$^{-1}$) to be 13.945 cm$^3$/mole.

First, we reconsider the case of a constant interfacial tension. Equation (7.1) can be rewritten as:

$$\log I = \log I_o - \sigma^3 f(T), \tag{7.3}$$

where all the temperature-dependent factors are collected in a function:

$$f(T) = \frac{16\pi}{3} \frac{\log e}{\Delta G_{sl}^2 kT}, \tag{7.4}$$

which is listed in the last column of Table I. A linear fit of $\log I$ versus $f(T)$ for all of the data of Table I gives $\sigma = 33.26$ erg/cm$^2$ and $I_o = 10^{44}$ cm$^{-3}$ s$^{-1}$. The even larger discrepancy with the theoretical prefactor must be attributed to the only remaining temperature dependence, that of $\sigma$.

To find the temperature dependence of the interfacial tension, the pre-exponential factor in Eq. (7.1) is set equal to the theoretical value, $I_o = 10^{35}$ cm$^{-3}$ s$^{-1}$, and $\sigma(T)$ is computed for each temperature. The results are listed in Table I and plotted in Fig. 6. A linear fit to all the data gives:

$$\sigma = 22.46 + 0.0507T, \tag{7.5}$$

where $\sigma$ is in erg/cm$^2$ and $T$ is in K. A fit to the just data from dispersion 2, for which most data were taken, gives, in the same units:

$$\sigma = 16.74 + 0.0876T. \tag{7.6}$$

[48] W. B. Pearson, *A Handbook of Lattice Spacings and Structures of Metals and Alloys*, Vol. 1, p. 683, Pergamon Press, New York (1958).

[49] G. Borelius, in *Solid State Physics* (F. Seitz and D. Turnbull, eds.), Vol. 15, p. 13, Academic Press, New York (1963).

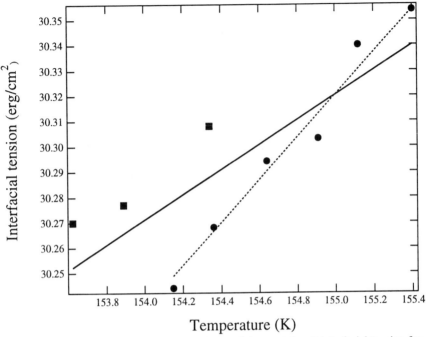

FIG. 6. Experimental temperature dependence of the crystal-melt interfacial tension for mercury, derived from Turnbull's homogeneous nucleation data (Ref. 1). The squares and circles correspond, respectively, to dispersions 1 and 2 of Table I. The solid line is a linear fit to all the data; the dashed line is a linear fit to the data for dispersion 2.

Although the data for gallium[36] do not as unambiguously correspond to homogeneous nucleation, it is still interesting to note that an analysis similar to the preceding one above also gives a positive temperature coefficient (same units):

$$\sigma = 53.8 + 0.055T. \tag{7.7}$$

A positive temperature coefficient of a crystal-melt interfacial tension obtained from homogeneous nucleation data was also found for water[37] (same units):

$$\sigma = -25.67 + 0.211T. \tag{7.8}$$

This case is of interest because the value of the interfacial tension at the melting temperature is known[50]: $\sigma(T_M) = 33 \pm 3$ erg/cm$^2$, in agree-

[50] P. V. Hobbs and W. M. Ketcham, in *Physics of Ice* (N. Riehl et al., eds.), p. 95, Plenum Press, New York (1969).

ment with the linear extrapolation of Eq. (7.8) at $T_M = 273$ K: $\sigma(T_M) = 31.9$ erg/cm². No such comparison can as yet be made for the metals. The linear extrapolation needs to be reconsidered as well.

## 8. Interpretation of the Temperature Dependence of the Interfacial Tension

The uniform interface model of Sections 5 and 6 has three unknowns: $\delta$, $\Delta S_i$, and $\Delta H_i$; Turnbull's data provides two values to fit (both in the narrow undercooled temperature range): $\sigma$ and $d\sigma/dT$ in Eq. (7.5) or (7.6). One of the model parameters must therefore be estimated first. For example, the width of the interface, *assumed uniform*, in a physical hard sphere model of the interface[14,15] is 1.46 monolayers, or 3.69 Å for mercury.[51]

The results of Section 6 can be used by inspection for a first estimate of the remaining interface parameters. Equations (6.3) and (6.6) give $\tilde{s} = -0.70$ and $\tilde{h} = -0.13$ for the data of Eq. (7.5); and $\tilde{s} = -0.84$ and $\tilde{h} = -0.22$ for the data of Eq. (7.6). Note that Eq. (6.6) also implies generally that, since the interface thickness $\delta$ must obviously be positive, a positive temperature coefficient can only be obtained if $\tilde{s} < -0.5$, i.e., if there is a substantial entropy loss.

A more precise determination requires the use the results of Section 5. The numerical determination was made by differentiating Eq. (5.14), which gives:

$$\frac{d\tilde{\sigma}/d\tilde{T}}{\tilde{\sigma}} = -\frac{1}{3}\left(\frac{\tilde{s}}{\tilde{g}} + \frac{\tilde{s}+1}{\tilde{g}'} + \frac{\tilde{s}}{\tilde{g}+\sqrt{\tilde{g}\tilde{g}'}} + \frac{\tilde{s}+1}{\tilde{g}'+\sqrt{\tilde{g}\tilde{g}'}}\right), \qquad (8.1)$$

where

$$\tilde{g} = \tilde{h} - \tilde{T}\tilde{s} \quad \text{and} \quad \tilde{g}' = \tilde{h} - \tilde{T}\tilde{s} - \tilde{T} + 1, \qquad (8.2)$$

are the values of $\Delta G_i$ and $\Delta G_i'$ normalized by the enthalpy of fusion. After choosing a value for $\tilde{s}$, Eq. (8.1) can be solved numerically for $\tilde{h}$. The interface thickness is then obtained directly from Eq. (5.14):

$$\tilde{\delta} = \tilde{\sigma}\left[\frac{4}{\tilde{g}\tilde{g}'(\sqrt{\tilde{g}}+\sqrt{\tilde{g}'})^2}\right]^{1/3}. \qquad (8.3)$$

---

[51] Data used for mercury calculations: CN12 radius: 3.10 Å, which gives an effective close-packed plane spacing of 2.53 Å. $\Delta S_f = 0.70919$ J/K · cm³ at 154 K, using $V = 13.945$ cm³/mole, discussed on p. 22; see Refs. 48 and 49.

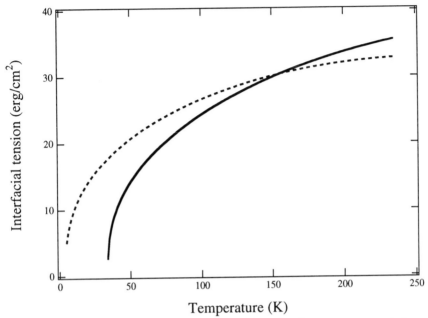

FIG. 7. Temperature dependence of the interfacial tension for mercury computed according to Eq. (5.14) for an interface thickness $\delta = 3.69$ Å. Dashed line: fit to all the data of Fig. 6, with $\bar{s} = -0.55$ and $\bar{h} = -0.01$; solid line: fit to the data of dispersion 2 in Fig. 6: $\bar{s} = -0.68$ and $\bar{h} = -0.10$.

The requirement of a positive interface thickness is satisfied as long as $\bar{g}$ and $\bar{g}'$ are both positive, which is, of course, an essential condition for the stability of the interface (see above). Furthermore, since the left-hand side of Eq. (8.1) is positive, it can only be satisfied if $\bar{s} < 0$, i.e., if there is a loss of liquid entropy in the interface.

Iterative solution of Eq. (8.1) and (8.3) with the chosen value of the interface thickness ($\delta = 3.69$ Å) gives for the two remaining parameters: $\bar{s} = -0.55$ and $\bar{h} = -0.01$ for the data of Eq. (7.5); and $\bar{s} = -0.68$ and $\bar{h} = -0.10$ for the data of Eq. (7.6). Figure 7 shows the temperature dependence of the interfacial tension computed over the entire undercooled temperature range using Eq. (5.14) and the two sets of fit parameters.

The values of the fit parameters can now be compared to those in the physical model chosen to provide the value for $\delta$. The enthalpy in the hard sphere system is, of course, zero by definition. However, since the density of the interface is close to that of the liquid, one would expect

the interfacial enthalpy in the presence of an interatomic potential to be close to the value in the liquid, or $\bar{h} \approx 0$.

The entropy of the static, hard sphere interface was first calculated approximately[14] using an assumption similar to those used by Pauling for proton disorder in ice.[52] A more accurate value was obtained later based on an exact solution for the dimer disorder on a honeycomb lattice.[15,53,54] The results can be summarized as follows.

Since the density of the interface is close to that of the liquid, its vibrational entropy is similar; the vibrational contribution to the heat of fusion in metals is estimated[13] at $\Delta s_v = 0.2$ k/atom. The configurational entropy of the atoms in the first interfacial layer, i.e., the one closest to the last crystal plane and labeled "I" in Fig. 4(a), is very small ($s_I = 0.113$ k/atom). This is because the layer is fully localized in the direction normal to the interface and, because of its high density (close to that of the liquid), derives only little entropy from its lateral noncrystallinity. The next layer in the interface [labeled "II" in Fig. 4(a)] is less localized than the first one; analysis of the model shows that 46% of the atoms in that layer need to be localized, and hence derive their entropy from the configuration of the first layer.[13] The contributions from the next layers (III, etc.) are considered negligible. Since there are, then, 1.46 atoms in the interface per atom in the first layer, the average fractional loss of entropy per atom in the interface is

$$\bar{s} = \frac{s_I + 1.46 \, \Delta s_v}{\Delta s_f} - 1. \qquad (8.4)$$

The entropy fusion per atom, $\Delta s_f$, is close to 1.2 k for metals. Using the value for Hg, $\Delta s_f = 1.17$ k/atom, gives $\bar{s} = -0.76$. This value is slightly higher than the parameters for the rigorous fit. This may reflect the approximation of a uniform interface in the model. Computation of the tension for a layered interface, which is a straightforward extension (see Appendix B), will be undertaken to test this. The interfacial entropy may also be raised slightly by the introduction of crystal terraces, which are not present in the static hard sphere model. Finally, it should be kept in mind that the fit is sensitive to the choice of the interface thickness. For example, if the interfacial entropy is kept fixed at the model value $\bar{s} = -0.76$, the interfacial thicknesses become 2.09 and 3.17 Å for the data of Eq. (7.5) and (7.6), respectively.

[52] L. Pauling, *J. Am. Chem. Soc.* **57**, 2680 (1935).
[53] V. Elser, *J. Phys.* **A17**, 1509 (1984).
[54] P. W. Kasteleyn, *J. Math. Phys.* **4**, 287 (1963).

## V. Conclusions

A classical analysis, based on the Gibbsian description of interfaces, of the temperature dependence of the crystal-melt interfacial tension *at constant external pressure* (i.e., for a finite crystal in an undercooled melt) shows that the temperature coefficients obtained from homogeneous nucleation experiments can be accounted for, as originally proposed by Turnbull, by the entropy loss in the liquid due to ordering near the crystal surface. Analysis of the equilibrium interface[18,19] in the hard sphere system confirms that the interfacial entropy losses are sufficiently large to account entirely for the magnitude of the interfacial tension, since the enthalphic contribution in this system is by definition zero.

Equation (5.14) can be used as an improved expression for the temperature dependence of the interfacial tension in modeling of nucleation. The fit to the nucleation data for mercury suggests that $\bar{h} = 0$, $\bar{s} = -0.6$, and $\bar{\delta} = 1.3$ [see Eqs. (5.13) for the definitions] are reasonable average parameters for close-packed metals.

In a nonequilibrium system, the interfacial tension is only a parameter introduced in the Gibbsian accounting for the work to form a critical nucleus [see Eq. (4.6)], and experimentally only that work can be measured. It is therefore entirely possible to analyze the nucleation data with a model of the interface without explicitly defining an interfacial tension. In equilibrium, however, the tension can be measured directly[7,55] and a determination at undercooled temperatures is then useful for comparison with the equilibrium value. The experiments on water are an example.[37,50] Note that the linear extrapolation that gave agreement between the two sets of measurements needs to be reconsidered (see Fig. 7). Measurements of the tension in equilibrium for mercury, for example, or determinations of the tension from homogeneous nucleation of succinonitrile, for example, would be most valuable to test the models further.

Finally, keep in mind that the analysis presented here has the classic limitation of the Gibbsian approach: It assumes that the bulk properties of the crystal are also valid at least at the center of very small nuclei. Obviously, at the smallest sizes, where all but a few atoms are at the surface, this assumption must break down. In Turnbull's experiments on mercury, there are almost 1000 atoms in the nucleus, so that its center is probably rather bulk-like. The Gibbsian approach is surprisingly successful in the description of the nucleation of liquids from the vapor,[38,56] indicating that the extrapolation of the thermodynamic properties can be

[55] R. J. Schaefer, M. E. Glicksman, and J. D. Ayers, *Phil. Mag.* **32**, 725 (1975).
[56] J. L. Katz, *J. Chem. Phys.* **52**, 4733 (1970).

extended to quite small nucleus sizes. This is confirmed by an analysis of the surface and bulk contributions to the energy of small clusters.[57] The recent enormous expansions in computer power will make it possible to test this on dynamic models of crystal nuclei in the melt.[58-60]

## ACKNOWLEDGMENTS

It has been my privilege to be associated with David Turnbull for many years. He introduced me to the problems of the crystal-melt interface when I was still a graduate student, and I have benefited enormously from his insights on this and many other subjects. I congratulate him on his retirement as editor of the *Solid State Physics* series, knowing that his will be a hard act to follow. I also thank him, Mike Aziz, Peter Voorhees, and John Hirth for useful discussions and comments on this chapter. This work has been supported by the National Aeronautics and Space Administration under contract NAGW2838, and by the National Science Foundation through the Harvard Materials Research Laboratory under contract DMR-89-20490.

## Appendix A: Calculation of the Interfacial Tension as an Excess Quantity for a Curved Interface

These are simple, definitional arguments that will be obvious to many by inspection. For ease of reading, they are spelled out. First, define some volumes associated with the various spherical surfaces in the problem (Fig. A.1): $V_s^*$ is the volume of the sphere with radius $r_s^*$; $V_1$ is the volume between the spheres with radius $r_s^*$ and $r_G^*$; $V_2$ is the volume between the spheres with radii $r_G^*$ and $r_s^* + \delta$; $V_G^*$ is the volume of the sphere with radius $r_G^*$. Hence,

$$V_G^* = V_s^* + V_1. \tag{A.1}$$

The work to form a crystal with radius $r_s^*$ is, according to Eqs. (4.1) and (4.2), with $\Omega$ kept constant for convenience (see also Appendix B):

$$W = G_s V_s + I_1 + I_2 - G_l(V_s + V_1 + V_2), \tag{A.2}$$

[57] An analysis of the energy of small clusters in a Lennard-Jones potential [M. R. Hoare and P. Pal, *Adv. Phys.* **20**, 161 (1971)] shows that the surface tension starts deviating from the macroscopic prediction below about 30 atoms (F. Spaepen, unpublished results).

[58] M. J. Uttormark, S. J. Cook, M. O. Thompson, and P. Clancy, *MRS Symp. Proc.* **205**, 417 (1992).

[59] J. D. Honeycutt and H. C. Andersen, *J. Phys. Chem.* **90**, 1585 (1986).

[60] J. S. van Duijneveldt and D. Frenkel, *J. Chem. Phys.* **96**, 4655 (1992).

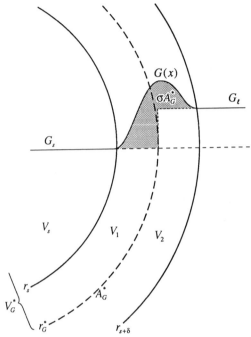

Fɪɢ. A.1. Schematic diagram of the radii, volumes, and area defined in the calculation of the interfacial tension as an excess quantity for a curved surface. The shaded area corresponds to the (spherical) excess free energy with respect to the Gibbsian dividing surface.

where

$$I_1 = \int_{r_s^*}^{r_G^*} G(r) 4\pi r^2 \, dr, \qquad\qquad (A.3)$$

and

$$I_2 = \int_{r_G^*}^{r_s^*+\delta} G(r) 4\pi r^2 \, dr. \qquad\qquad (A.4)$$

The Gibbsian definition of $\sigma$ as an excess quantity is based on the same work being written as:

$$
\begin{aligned}
W &= (G_s - G_l) V_G^* + \sigma A_G^* \\
&= (G_s - G_l)(V_s + V_1) + \sigma A_G^*.
\end{aligned}
\qquad (A.5)
$$

Equating Eqs. (A.2) and (A.5) then gives for the interfacial term:

$$\sigma A_G^* = (I_1 - G_s V_1) + (I_2 - G_l V_2), \qquad (A.6)$$

which is the excess free energy with respect to the Gibbsian dividing surface (shaded area in Fig. A.1).

The interfacial tension is defined in the text based on the work to form a critical nucleus [see Eqs. (4.5) and (4.6)]:

$$W = \frac{16\pi}{3} \frac{\sigma^3}{\Delta G_{Sl}^2}. \qquad (A.7)$$

Equating this work to that defined in Eq. (A.5) and expressing $A_G^*$ and $V_G^*$ in terms of their radii gives an equation for $r_G^*$:

$$r^3 + 3pr^2 - 4p^3 = 0, \qquad (A.8)$$

where

$$p = \frac{\sigma}{\Delta G_{sl}}. \qquad (A.9)$$

The only positive root of Eq. (A.8) is

$$r_G^* = -2p, \qquad (A.10)$$

in accord with the Gibbsian definition of Eq. (2.3).

It is interesting to note that for a *given* $r_s$ and a choice of the location of the dividing surface, the Gibbsian radius, $r_G^*$ of Eqs. (2.3) and (A.10) also corresponds to the *minimum* value for $\sigma$ defined as an excess free energy.[33]

## Appendix B: Calculation of the Interfacial Tension for a General Spatial Variation of the Free Energy

Assume that the atomic volume $\Omega(r)$ in Eq. (4.1) is the same for all atoms in the system, and that the free energy profile as a function of radius through the interface is *independent of the size of the crystal*. The variation of the free energy per unit volume given in Eq. (4.2) can then be specified as:

$$G(r) = G_s \qquad \text{for } r \leq r_s,$$
$$G(r) = G_i(r - r_s) \qquad \text{for } r_s \leq r \leq r_s + \delta, \qquad \text{(B.1)}$$
$$G(r) = G_l \qquad \text{for } r_s + \delta \leq r.$$

Using a change of variables

$$x = r - r_s, \qquad \text{(B.2)}$$

the work to form a crystal of radius $r_s$ [Eq. (4.1)] can be written as:

$$W(r_s) = \frac{4\pi r_s^3}{3} \Delta G_{sl} + \int_0^\delta (G_i(x) - G_l)4\pi(x + r_s)^2 \, dx. \qquad \text{(B.3)}$$

Define the $n$'th moment of $G_i(x)$ as:

$$I_n = \frac{n + 1}{\delta^{n+1}} \int_0^\delta G(x)x^n \, dx \qquad n = 0, 1, 2, \ldots \qquad \text{(B.4)}$$

Define the corresponding dimensionless coefficients:

$$a_n = \frac{I_n - G_l}{\Delta G_{sl}}. \qquad \text{(B.5)}$$

Equation (B.3) then becomes:

$$W(r_s) = \frac{4\pi}{3} \Delta G_{sl}(r_s^3 + 3a_0\delta r_s^2 + 3a_1\delta^2 r_s + a_2\delta^3) = 0. \qquad \text{(B.6)}$$

The equilibrium condition of Eq. (4.3) is then:

$$\left.\frac{dW}{dr_s}\right|_{r_s^*} = 4\pi\Delta G_{sl}(r_s^2 + 2a_0\delta r_s + a_1\delta^2) = 0. \qquad \text{(B.7)}$$

The radius of the crystal in equilibrium with an undercooled melt is the positive root of the factor in parentheses:

$$r_s^* = -\delta a_0(1 + \beta), \qquad \text{(B.8)}$$

where

$$\beta^2 = 1 - \frac{a_1}{a_0^2}. \tag{B.9}$$

The work to form the crystal is found by inserting the value of $r_s^*$ into Eq. (B.6):

$$W^* = \frac{16\pi}{3} \Delta G_{sl} \delta^3 c^3, \tag{B.10}$$

where $c^3$ is a dimensionless factor that depends on the shape of $G(x)$ and the undercooling:

$$c^3 = \frac{1}{4}[-a_0^3(1 + \beta)^3 + 3a_0^3(1 + \beta)^2 - 3a_0 a_1(1 + \beta) + a_2]. \tag{B.11}$$

The combination of Eqs. (B.10) and (B.13) then gives:

$$\sigma = c\delta\Delta G_{sl}. \tag{B.12}$$

The location of the Gibbsian dividing surface is found from Eq. (2.3):

$$r_G^* = -2c\delta. \tag{B.13}$$

SOLID STATE PHYSICS, VOL. 47

# Cluster Approach to Order-Disorder Transformations in Alloys

D. DE FONTAINE

*Department of Materials Science and Mineral Engineering, University of California, Berkeley, California and Materials Sciences Division, Lawrence Berkeley Laboratory, Berkeley, California*

## I. Introduction

This chapter is, in a sense, a follow-up of a review published by the same author in *Solid State Physics* in 1979 under the title "Configurational

33

Thermodynamics of Solid Solutions."[1] That article would never have seen the light of day had it not been for David Turnbull's encouragement and advice and, above all, his infinite patience with a procrastinating author. In retrospect, the title of the article was too restrictive, or perhaps it is the field itself which has evolved and expanded far beyond what its author had envisioned at the time. Hence, it was deemed timely to write an update to the original article, while at the same time altering the emphasis somewhat.

The reason for the change of emphasis is that, since the publication of the original article (to be referred to as I), the field has developed into an entirely new discipline, one that may be regarded as a true *first-principles thermodynamics* of crystalline solids. Classical thermodynamics has always played a fundamental role in solid state physics in the sense that properties of materials, whether metallic alloys, ceramics, or semiconductors, can be described as a function of temperature, pressure, and composition by means of the equations that Gibbs derived more than a hundred years ago. Unfortunately, until very recently, numerical predictions could only be made by appealing to empirical models or to experimental measurements. Recently the situation has changed dramatically: First-principles electronic structure calculations are providing accurate input to statistical mechanical computer codes so that actual predictions can now be made of formation energies and entropies of stable and metastable phases, ordered or disordered, along with reliable values of equilibrium lattice parameters, elastic moduli, and states of order. In other words, modern computational techniques have introduced into Gibbsian thermodynamics what had been missing until now: the role of the electrons. It is this new, predictive aspect of solid state thermodynamics that is stressed here.

But what do we mean by "first-principles calculations of solids"? First of all, we consider here only crystalline solids, i.e., systems for which a lattice framework can be unambiguously defined. Thus, liquids, amorphous solids and grain boundaries, for example, are provisionally excluded. Given those restrictions, what is required is a calculation of the free energy $F = E - TS$ of all important phases, stable or metastable, of a binary $(A, B)$ or multicomponent $(A, B, C, \ldots)$ system as a function of temperature $T$ and average concentration $c$ or chemical fields ($\mu$ = differences of chemical potentials), starting from only the knowledge of atomic numbers $Z_A, Z_B, \ldots$. Energy $E$ has configurational (or replacive) and displacive contributions: The former depends on the nature of atoms $A, B, \ldots$ associated with the lattice sites, the latter depends on the

[1]D. de Fontaine, in *Solid State Physics* **34**, 73 (1979).

displacements of the atoms from these sites, static and dynamic (vibrational). Likewise, entropy $S$ has configurational and vibrational contributions, in addition to electronic and magnetic ones. All of these contributions can be calculated *ab initio,* at least in principle. The task is greatly facilitated by performing configurational and displacive calculations separately, a decoupling procedure that is permissible only under the lattice-framework restriction mentioned earlier.

In I, much space was devoted to the mean-field method, although its inadequacy was already known. Here, the term *mean-field approximation* refers to analytic free energy functions that depend only on "point" configuration variables, i.e., on sublattice averages of atomic concentrations. In all mean-field free energy models (regular and subregular solutions, Bragg-Williams (BW), concentration wave models), the configurational energy is given as a polynomial in point variables and the entropy as a logarithmic function of these variables. Although it was known that the BW method—or that of concentration waves, which is identical to it— could not account, even qualitatively, for frustration effects [for instance, in the case of ordering on the face-centered cubic (fcc) lattice], it was believed that such methods could be used to advantage in cases where the mean-field approximation gave results that were not *qualitatively* incorrect [ordering on body-centered cubic (bcc) lattices, for instance]. Now that *quantitative* results are required, it is clear that the mean-field approach must be abandoned altogether.

What can be substituted in its place? To rephrase the question, is it possible to formulate a statistical theory of configurational disorder (or partial order) that is both mathematically rigorous and tractable? Since the seminal paper of Sanchez, Ducastelle, and Gratias[2] in 1984, the question can be answered affirmatively. The required method is that of orthogonal expansions in cluster functions, a procedure that has its roots in the cluster variation method (CVM), proposed originally by Kikuchi[3] in 1951. The CVM was described briefly in I, but much progress has been realized since then. Today, cluster methods are supplanting the older mean-field approaches, hence, as the title indicates, this chapter intends to summarize cluster methods, and in particular their applications to the calculation of alloy phase diagrams virtually from first principles. Non–mean-field methods are, of course, available: high-temperature, low-temperature expansions, Monte Carlo, transfer matrix methods, renormalization group theory, etc., but since *cluster* methods are to be emphasized here, as they pertain to both the quantum and the statistical aspects of the field,

[2]J. M. Sanchez, F. Ducastelle, and D. Gratias, *Physica A* **128,** 334 (1984).
[3]R. Kikuchi, *Phys. Rev.* **81,** 988 (1951).

these other methods are not considered. The interested reader should, for example, consult the series *Phase Transitions and Critical Phenomena*, edited by Domb and Green.[4]

The phenomenon of ordering is intimately related to the problem of alloy phase stability for the following reason: Crystalline compounds may quite generally be considered as ordered superstructures of a lattice (or sets of sublattices) of some parent disordered phase. The theoretical study of solid state phase stability thus involves the energetics of all relevant lattices, of possible states of perfect order on the various lattices (ground state superstructures), and of states of partial order (and disorder). According to this viewpoint, phase equilibrium in a given alloy system then results from the free energy competition between various *lattices* and, on each lattice, between various *superstructures* of the parent structure.

It is not an exaggeration to state that the technique of orthogonal expansions in cluster functions has revolutionized the treatment of configurationally disordered systems. In addition to offering the most rational and general state-of-order description of alloys, cluster methods provide the rigorous and essential link between quantum and statistical mechanical aspects of first-principles thermodynamic calculations. Previously, quantum and statistical disciplines tended to be treated separately. For example, elaborate mathematical techniques were developed to solve the Ising model, but the interaction parameters of the model were assumed to be known, or were derived from some ill-defined "potentials." Now, a unified treatment is available: *effective cluster interactions* can be calculated by electronic band structure models, and the ECI can then be used as input for approximate (cluster) Ising model solutions. Moreover, ground states of order (ordered superstructures that minimize the configurational energy) can be determined in principle exactly also by appealing to cluster methods. The ground state problem was treated in I, but the new cluster techniques, to be described here, simplify the formalism.

The quantum mechanical aspect of the field of first-principles thermodynamics would, by itself, merit a separate review, which the present author, however, does not feel competent to write. Nevertheless, a tight-binding approach is described here in some detail for the purpose of illustrating in a straightforward manner how quantum and statistical methods can be combined in a coherent whole and used to predict properties of real alloys. Other methods are briefly described along with applications to phase diagram calculations of certain metallic alloys.

---

[4]*Phase Transitions and Critical Phenomena* (C. Domb and M. S. Green, eds.), Vols. 1–11, Academic Press, New York (1972).

One disadvantage of cluster techniques, as opposed to mean-field methods, is that elastic relaxation in disordered systems cannot be handled conveniently. For the present, one still relies mainly on the mean-field treatment of elastic relaxation, which was described in some detail in I. Also, the subject of multicomponent (particularly ternary) systems, covered quite extensively in I in the mean-field context, has not yet been investigated extensively by cluster methods beyond the strictly formal approach. Here, the treatment is limited primarily to binary systems.

In summary, the present chapter is both less and more than an update of I: It turns its back resolutely on mean-field techniques, thereby losing the simplicity and convenience of that approximation, but embraces wholeheartedly the cluster expansion formalism, thereby gaining in accuracy, generality, and rigor. Strictly speaking, the CVM is also a mean-field technique, but the mean-field approximation is delayed, as it were, after the near-neighbor correlations have been treated correctly. Early CVM phase diagram calculations performed in collaboration with R. Kikuchi were mentioned in I, but those performed with J. M. Sanchez, who laid the groundwork for much current investigation, had not been completed at the time. Work described herein includes investigations performed in collaboration with former students and postdoctoral fellows (roughly in chronological order): J. M. Sanchez, T. Mohri, A. Finel, P. E. A. Turchi, M. Sluiter, H. Dreyssé, G. Ceder, and currently with M. Asta, C. Wolverton, and R. McCormack. These collaborators have provided valuable input to this article.

For a detailed background treatment of the material under consideration here, the interested reader can do no better than to consult the remarkable and very recent monograph of F. Ducastelle[5] entitled *Order and Phase Stability in Alloys*. Some even more recent material is presented in the excellent review article of G. Inden and W. Pitsch.[6] Both of these works owe a great deal to the doctoral dissertation of A. Finel,[7] a very complete and authoritative treatment of the CVM and related methods, unfortunately available only in French. A recent review article by the same author is now available in English.[8] A great deal of quantita-

[5] F. Ducastelle, *Order and Phase Stability in Alloys*, Vol. 3 in *Cohesion and Structure*, North-Holland, New York (1991).

[6] G. Inden and W. Pitsch, "Atomic Ordering," in *Phase Transformations in Materials* (P. Haasen, ed.), pp. 497–552, VCH Press, New York (1991).

[7] A. Finel, "Contribution à l'Etude des Effets d'Ordre dans le Cadre du Modèle d'Ising: Etats de Base et Diagrammes de Phase," Ph.D. Dissertation, Université Pierre et Marie Curie, Paris (1987) (unpublished).

[8] A. Finel, to be published in *Statics and Dynamics of Alloy Phase Transformations* (P. E. A. Turchi and A. Gonis, eds.), NATO ASI Series, Plenum Press, New York.

tive work has been performed by the very active group of Zunger and reviewed by him.[9] The interested reader will also profit from the review article of Carlsson,[10] although the subject treated, being primarily that of *pair potentials,* is rather different from that of the *effective* interactions emphasized here.

In the present review, emphasis is on the cluster expansion formalism and related subjects. Derivations are given in a fairly self-contained manner, leaving little space for critical review of the published literature on specific applications. Examples of the formalism are given, but extensive treatment is limited to systems investigated recently in the author's own research group: Recent CVM calculations of transition temperatures will be taken from the work of G. Ceder[11] (Section 9), hexagonal close-packed (hcp) ground state and prototype phase diagrams from that of R. McCormack[12] (Sections 8 and 9), effective cluster interaction calculations from that of C. Wolverton[13-15] (Sections 12 and 15), and structure inversion method calculations from that of M. Asta[16-19] (Sections 14 and 16). Additional pertinent applications are mentioned in Section 17.

## II. Statement of Problem

Here we treat the conversion of the alloy problem, for crystals, into a generalized Ising model. In Section 1, the overall partition function is factored into separate sums over the several degrees of freedom of the system: electronic, vibrational, and configurational. Then, in Section 2,

[9] A. Zunger, to be published in *Statics and Dynamics of Alloy Phase Transformations* (P. E. A. Turchi and A. Gonis, eds.), NATO ASI Series, Plenum Press, New York.

[10] A. E. Carlsson, *Solid State Physics* **43**, 1 (1990).

[11] Gerbrand Ceder, "Alloy Theory and Its Application to Long Period Superstructure Ordering in Metallic Alloys and High Temperature Superconductors," Ph.D. Dissertation, University of California, Berkeley (1991). Available from University Microfilms International, 300 Zeeb Road, Ann Arbor, MI 48106.

[12] R. McCormack, M. Asta, D. de Fontaine, G. Garbulsky, and G. Ceder, *Phys. Rev. B* **48**, 6767 (1993).

[13] C. Wolverton, "Ground State Properties and Phase Stability of Binary and Ternary Intermetallic Alloys," Ph.D. Dissertation, University of California, Berkeley (1993) (unpublished).

[14] C. Wolverton, G. Ceder, D. de Fontaine, and H. Dreyssé, *Phys. Rev. B* **48**, 726 (1993).

[15] C. Wolverton, D. de Fontaine, and H. Dreyssé, *Phys. Rev. B* **48**, 5766 (1993).

[16] M. Asta, "First-Principles Calculations of Thermodynamic Properties and Phase Diagrams of Binary Substitutional Alloys," Ph.D. Dissertation, University of California, Berkeley (1993) (unpublished).

[17] M. Asta, D. de Fontaine, M. van Schilfgaarde, M. Sluiter, and M. Methfessel, *Phys. Rev. B* **46**, 505 (1992).

[18] M. Asta, D. de Fontaine, and Mark van Schilfgaarde, *J. Mater. Res.* **8**, 2554 (1993).

[19] M. Asta, R. McCormack, and D. de Fontaine, *Phys. Rev. B* **48**, 748 (1993).

we show how to handle the configurational aspect as a variational problem.

## 1. SEPARATION OF DEGREES OF FREEDOM

In keeping with the remarks made in the introduction, let us define a *system* as a collection of $N$ "atoms" (including vacancies, if required) of types $A, B, C, \ldots$ *such that each atom can be unambiguously assigned to a unique lattice point.* There shall be exactly $N$ lattice sites, or more generally, $N$ sites on any number of interpenetrating Bravais lattices. The latter extension allows us to refer to the *hexagonal close-packed lattice,* although the true Bravais lattice is, of course, simple hexagonal in that case. Site occupancy will be designated by a site variable $\sigma_p$. For example, in binary systems, it is convenient to take $\sigma_p = +1$ (or $-1$) if site $p$ is occupied by an $A$ (or $B$) atom. In Section 3 a more general scheme, valid for an arbitrary number of atomic components, is presented. A *configuration* is thus specified by $N$ variables $\sigma_p$ ($p = 1, 2, \ldots, N$), and can be regarded as an $N$-dimensional vector $\vec{\sigma}$. Actually, the notion of "configuration" is a sensible one only because, in crystalline solids at temperatures reasonably far from melting temperatures, two very different timescales exist: a slow one for atomic interchanges and a much faster one for lattice vibrations and electronic motions. Consequently, as is shown later, it is possible to perform statistical averages separately over these types of processes.[11,16,20]

Let the number $N$ of lattice points be large enough so that boundary effects may be ignored. For a fixed configuration $\vec{\sigma}$, evolving on a relatively slow timescale, the total energy of the system can be written as a sum of two contributions: a configurational and a "dynamic" one. Since, in this review, we are primarily interested in configurational aspects, let us separate these configurational contributions, $E_c(\vec{\sigma})$, from all others, for example, displacive, magnetic, electronic, etc., which, because of their relatively shorter relaxation time, we shall denote for short as "dynamic." Note that "decoupling" of contributions is not advocated: the dynamic contributions are, in general, very much configuration dependent. The canonical ensemble partition function is then

$$Z = \sum_{\text{states}} \exp(-E/k_B T)$$

$$= \sum_{\text{stat.}} \sum_{\text{dyn.}} \exp(-E_c/k_B T) \exp(-E_{\text{dyn.}}/k_B T). \tag{1.1a}$$

[20] G. Ceder, *Compt. Mater. Sci.* **1**, 144 (1993).

In the applications to be presented later, only elastic displacements (relaxations, index $r$), vibrational ($\omega$), and electronic ($\varepsilon$) excitations will be considered. Let us factor out these dynamic contributions, assuming minimal coupling:

$$Z = \sum_{\{\sigma\}} \exp\{-[E_c(\vec{\sigma}) + E_r(\vec{\sigma})]/k_B T\}$$

$$\times \sum_{\varepsilon} \exp[-E_\varepsilon(\vec{\sigma})/k_B T] \sum_{\omega} \exp[-E_\omega(\vec{\sigma})/k_B T]. \qquad (1.1b)$$

During the lifetime of a particular configuration, electronic and vibrational equilibrium will be attained very rapidly, and the last two sums in Eq. (1.1b) may be performed independently, thereby yielding the electronic $Q_\varepsilon$ and vibrational $Q_\omega$ partition functions, respectively. These partition functions are related to the corresponding free energies by the expression

$$F = -k_B T \ln Q, \qquad (1.2)$$

so that Eq. (1.1) may be written conveniently as

$$Z = \sum_{\{\sigma\}} \exp[-\Psi(\vec{\sigma})/k_B T], \qquad (1.3)$$

where the "hybrid" configuration-dependent free energy

$$\Psi(\vec{\sigma}) = E_c(\vec{\sigma}) + E_r(\vec{\sigma}) + F_\varepsilon(\vec{\sigma}) + F_\omega(\vec{\sigma}) \qquad (1.4)$$

has been introduced, with

$$F_\varepsilon(\vec{\sigma}) = E_\varepsilon(\vec{\sigma}) - TS_\varepsilon(\vec{\sigma}) \qquad (1.5)$$

and

$$F_\omega(\vec{\sigma}) = E_\omega(\vec{\sigma}) - TS_\omega(\vec{\sigma}). \qquad (1.6)$$

In Eqs. (1.5) and (1.6) all energies $E$ and entropies $S$ are configuration dependent.

These arguments show that, under broad and reasonable assumptions (one-to-one correspondence of atoms and lattice sites), the alloy problem may be mapped onto an Ising model.[20]

2. VARIATIONAL PRINCIPLE

The summation over configurational states $\{\vec{\sigma}\}$ in Eq. (1.1) is handled quite differently: i.e., by ensemble averaging. Let $\rho(\vec{\sigma})$ denote the probability of finding in the ensemble a system having particular configuration $\vec{\sigma}$. We must *always* have,

$$\sum_{\{\sigma\}} \rho(\vec{\sigma}) = 1 \tag{2.1}$$

and, at equilibrium, the density function (or density matrix) must be given by

$$\rho(\vec{\sigma}) = \frac{\exp[-\Psi(\vec{\sigma})/k_B T]}{Z}. \tag{2.2}$$

Hence, the expectation value of the total configurational energy may be written as

$$U = \sum_{\{\sigma\}} \rho(\vec{\sigma})\Psi(\vec{\sigma}) \equiv \langle\Psi\rangle \tag{2.3}$$

and the configurational entropy as

$$S = -k_B \sum_{\{\sigma\}} \rho(\vec{\sigma})\ln\rho(\vec{\sigma}) \equiv -k_B\langle\ln\rho\rangle, \tag{2.4}$$

where the familiar shorthand angle brackets notation has been introduced to denote thermodynamic (configurational) averages.

For the function $\rho$ satisfying the normalization condition of Eq. (2.1), but otherwise arbitrary, the free energy can be considered as the functional

$$F[\rho] = U[\rho] - TS[\rho] = -k_B T \sum \rho \ln\frac{\exp(-\Psi/k_B T)}{\rho}. \tag{2.5}$$

The concavity property of the logarithmic function and the fact that condition (2.1) is obeyed guarantees,[5,7] for any function $f(\sigma)$, that $\langle\ln f\rangle \leq \ln\langle f\rangle$, therefore, in the present case,

$$F[\rho] \geq F, \tag{2.6}$$

where the symbol on the right-hand side denotes the *exact* free energy given by $-k_B T \ln Z$. The equality is attained only for $\rho$ given by its equilibrium value [Eq. (2.2)]. Hence, the variational principle: The correct free energy is the minimum of the functional $F[\rho]$ over all possible distributions $\rho$ satisfying $\Sigma \rho = 1$.

In practice, it is of course not possible to minimize over all configurational distributions of (theoretically infinite) systems. Instead, methods are sought that restrict the domain of minimization to subsets of distributions that may be characterized by a small number of parameters. Minimization with respect to these variational parameters then leads to upper bounds for the free energy. The derivation of the CVM equations is based on this principle. As will be explained in Section 9, the configurational entropy $S$ of Eq. (2.4) will be approximated by a sum of terms of type $\rho_\alpha(\vec{\sigma}) \ln \rho_\alpha(\vec{\sigma})$, where $\rho_\alpha$ designates a cluster ($\alpha$) probability.

To obtain the complete free energy, one must then calculate the total configurational energy $U$ of Eq. (2.3) by also expressing the density function in terms of cluster probabilities or, equivalently, in terms of multisite (cluster) correlation functions. What remains is the rather formidable task of evaluating the configuration-dependent energy function $\Psi(\vec{\sigma})$. It is here, and only here, that the physics of the particular alloy system is introduced, as the mathematical form of the approximate $\rho$ function and associated configurational entropy depends only on the choice of lattice (or sublattice) and of cluster variables.

For pure elemental crystals or simple stoichiometric compounds, accurate electronic structure methods have been developed for the determination from first principles of the energy $E_c(\vec{\sigma})$. An essential ingredient in these calculations is the electronic density of states, knowledge of which also provides values for the electronic entropy $S_\varepsilon$. Since the calculation of the energy features integrations over the occupied electronic levels, $E_\varepsilon$ should exhibit a temperature dependence via the Fermi-Dirac distribution function. This effect is not implicitly included in what follows. It is quite troublesome to calculate the vibrational free energy from first principles, even for unalloyed crystals. Molecular dynamics calculations are generally used for that purpose, but that is a topic lying outside the scope of this chapter, which does not consider computer simulation techniques. Other methods are mentioned in Section 16.

What we are concerned with here, however, is the calculation of *configuration-dependent* energies and entropies—recall that the title of I was "Configurational Thermodynamics of Solid Solutions." We argue, in what follows, that the method of choice for carrying out such calculations is the cluster expansion method, as mentioned in the introduction. In principle, if techniques are available for the calculation of energies and

entropies of perfectly ordered crystals, it is possible, by cluster expansion, to obtain corresponding quantities for disordered or partially ordered configurations. This subject, and that of configurational entropy (which is *not* a configuration-dependent function) occupy the remainder of this chapter.

Generally, the most important contribution to $\Psi(\vec{\sigma})$ is the total configurational energy $E_c(\vec{\sigma})$. Since thermodynamic calculations require differences in energy, it was believed, until fairly recently, that contributions from the other three terms of Eq. (1.4) would practically cancel out when taking differences. It is now recognized, however, that this cancellation does not fully occur, so that all contributions must be retained if really qualitatively accurate results are required. However, as shown by Eqs. (1.5) and (1.6), these additional contributions are configuration dependent and may thus be calculated from appropriate cluster expansions. Examples are given in Section 16.

## III. Cluster Expansions

Here we investigate ways of specifying configurations (Section 3), introduce an orthonormal expansion formalism (Section 4), and then apply the formalism to the determination of effective cluster interactions (Section 5).

### 3. CONFIGURATION VARIABLES

In Section 1, the pseudo-spin configuration variable $\sigma_p = \pm 1$ was introduced, $+1$ if an $A$ atom occupies site $p$, $-1$ if $B$. For an $M$-component system, $\sigma_p$ must be assigned $M$ values, which for convenience are taken to be integers: $+1, 0, -1$, for a ternary system $(A, B, C)$, $+2, +1, -1$, $-2$, for a quaternary $(A, B, C, D)$, for example. In general, denote by $\tau_I$ $(I = A, B, \ldots)$ the chosen integers that uniquely identify the atomic species. Values taken by the configuration variable $\sigma_p$ at a particular site (in a "frozen" configuration) are the same as the $\tau_I$ but with a subtle difference: the $\tau_I$ are *parameters*, which are assigned to atom types, the $\sigma_p$ are *variables* actually associated with lattice sites, in a given configuration. Let us also define occupation variable $\Gamma_p^I(\vec{\sigma})$ equal to 1 if an atom of type $I$ occupies site $p$ (in configuration $\vec{\sigma}$), 0 otherwise.

For binary systems, the configuration variables $\sigma_p$ and occupation variables $\Gamma_p^I$ superficially appear to play equivalent roles: The former are variables appropriate for the Ising model, the latter for the lattice gas

model. In reality, however, these variables are very different. In multi-component systems, the $\Gamma$ variables retain their $(0, 1)$ binary character, whereas the $\sigma$ variables take on $M$ values. More importantly, products of $\Gamma_p^I$ at the lattice sites of a cluster of $n$ sites generalize to cluster occupation variables, while products of $\sigma_p$ do not have this property. To construct the necessary cluster algebra, it is essential to express the relationship between spin products (or *configuration* variables) and *occupation* variables. This relationship is embodied in a (generally rectangular) matrix, the configuration (or C) matrix, the nature of which depends entirely on the number of components, the cluster approximation, and the crystal structure.

To construct a quantitative theory of partial order/disorder, it is necessary to attach to each site not merely an arbitrary numerical label, but a set of linearly independent functions of the $\sigma$ variable, there being exactly as many such functions as there are constituents that may be substituted on the lattice sites. The simplest set consists of the successive $M - 1$ powers of $\sigma_p$ $\{\Sigma_p\} \equiv \{1, \sigma_p, \sigma_p^2, \ldots, \sigma_p^{M-1}\}$, as was suggested originally by Taggart[21] and Finel,[8,22] and as presented in a very clear and didactic fashion by Inden and Pitsch.[6] Successive powers of $\sigma_p$ can be expressed by the identities

$$\sigma_p^m = \sum_{I=1}^{M} \tau_I^m \Gamma_p^I, \tag{3.1}$$

where the lowercase symbol $(m = 0, 1, 2, \ldots, M - 1)$ designates an exponent, the uppercase one $(I = 1, 2, \ldots, M)$ a superscript. Equation (3.1) may be written in matrix form as

$$\Sigma_p = T\Gamma_p, \tag{3.2}$$

where $T$ is a matrix whose first row consists of ones, the second consists of the $\tau_I$ integers, the third of $\tau_I^2$, and so on, and where the $\Gamma$ symbols designate vectors consisting of successive occupation variables $\Gamma_p^I$, as defined earlier. The $T$ matrix has a Van der Monde determinant and is nonzero since all $\tau_I$'s are distinct.[6] Hence the linear system of Eq. (3.2) is invertible:

[21]G. B. Taggart, *J. Phys. Chem Solids* **34**, 1917 (1973). For application to ternary systems see also P. R. C. Holvorcem and R. Osório, *Physica A* **152**, 431 (1988) and references therein.

[22]A. Finel, private communication (1993).

$$\Gamma_p = T^{-1}\Sigma_p.\tag{3.3}$$

Designate a cluster of $n$ sites by the collective symbol $\alpha = \{p_1, p_2, \ldots, p_n\}$. The associated cluster occupation variable

$$\Gamma_\alpha(\vec{\tau}; \vec{\sigma}) = \prod_{k=1}^{n} \Gamma_{p_k}^{I_k}(\vec{\sigma})\tag{3.4}$$

takes value 1 (0 otherwise) if and only if the actual atomic configuration $\vec{\sigma}$ of cluster $\alpha$ (denoted by $\vec{\sigma}_\alpha$) corresponds exactly to the specified configuration $\vec{\tau}$, i.e., if atom of type $I_1$ is actually at point $p_1$, $I_2$ at $p_2$, and so on, up to $I_n$ at $p_n$. In Eq. (3.4), the configuration symbol $\vec{\tau}$ stands for the set of indices $(I_1, I_2, \ldots)$. According to Eq. (3.3), each $\Gamma$ variable on the right-hand side of Eq. (3.4) can be expressed as a linear combination of powers of $\sigma_p$ (including $\sigma_p^0 = 1$), so that the cluster occupation $\Gamma_\alpha$ may be written as a tensor product of appropriate $\Sigma_p$ vectors, with $p$ spanning the sites of $\alpha$.

Of particular interest is the expectation value of the occupation $\Gamma_\alpha$ for an ensemble of systems at a particular temperature and average composition (or chemical field). This expectation value is a cluster probability (or concentration), also called a *partial density function*[2,5,7,23]

$$\rho_\alpha(\vec{\tau}) = \sum_{\{\sigma\}} \rho(\vec{\sigma})\Gamma_\alpha(\vec{\tau}; \vec{\sigma}) = \langle \Gamma_\alpha(\vec{\tau}; \vec{\sigma})\rangle.\tag{3.5}$$

Insertion of Eqs. (3.3) and (3.4) into (3.5) yields the general form of cluster probabilities[6]

$$\rho_\alpha(\vec{\tau}) = \sum_{m_1=0}^{M-1} \sum_{m_2=0}^{M-1} \cdots \sum_{m_n=0}^{M-1} (t_{m_1}^{I_1} t_{m_2}^{I_2} \ldots t_{m_n}^{I_n}) \langle \sigma_{p_1}^{m_1} \sigma_{p_2}^{m_2} \ldots \sigma_{p_n}^{m_n}\rangle,\tag{3.6}$$

where the expression in angle brackets is the (ensemble) average value of a product of powers of occupation variables, and the one in parentheses is an element of an $M^n \times M^n$ matrix (configuration matrix). The symbols $t$ designate elements of the inverse matrix $T^{-1}$.

There are just $M^n$ cluster probabilities $\rho_\alpha$, although these are not all independent since they must sum to unity. The cluster $\alpha$ could be the

[23] J. M. Sanchez and D. de Fontaine, *Phys. Rev. B.* **17**, 2926 (1978).

whole system of $N$ points itself; then $\rho_N(\vec{\tau})$ is just the probability of finding the system in configuration $\vec{\tau}$, i.e., it is the density function $\rho$ itself. The $\rho_\alpha$ are then partial densities that are central to the variational solution of the configurational free energy problem, as stated in Section 1. The angle brackets contain products of unity $(= \sigma_p^0)$ and various nonzero powers of $\sigma$ variables located at subsets of the points of the $\alpha$ cluster. Denote these products by $\Sigma_\alpha^{(m)}(\vec{\sigma})$ [as an extension of symbol $\Sigma_p$ in Eq. (3.2)], where $(m)$ is a set of integers [as they appear in the bracketed expression of Eq. (3.6)] and $\alpha$ designates, as before, the "cluster" of points $(p_1 \ldots p_n)$. These average products are called *multisite correlation parameters,*

$$\xi_\alpha^{(m)} = \langle \Sigma_\alpha^m(\vec{\sigma}) \rangle. \tag{3.7}$$

For example (for binary systems), the point correlation $\xi_p = \langle \sigma_p \rangle$, the pair correlation $\xi_{p,q} = \langle \sigma_p \sigma_q \rangle$, the triplet correlation $\xi_{p,q,r} = \langle \sigma_p \sigma_q \sigma_r \rangle$, where $p, q, r, \ldots$, denote subsets of the cluster points, i.e., subclusters ($\beta$) of $\alpha$. For systems of more than two components, expressions such as $\xi_{p,q}^{(1,2)} = \langle \sigma_p \sigma_q^2 \rangle$, $\xi_{p,q,r}^{(2,1,3)} = \langle \sigma_p^2 \sigma_q \sigma_r^3 \rangle$, for example, will also be found, but require rather elaborate notation, not generally in use as yet. The set of $\xi$ variables, excluding the empty cluster correlation $\xi_0 = 1$, form a set of linearly independent variables with respect to which the free energy functional is to be minimized.

The configuration matrix (C matrix, for short) of $t$ products is seen by Eq. (3.6) to relate the subcluster correlation parameters $\xi_\beta^{(m)}$ to the cluster probabilities $\rho_\alpha$. More properly, the configuration matrix is the one that relates the $\xi_\beta^{(m)}$ to the $\rho_\alpha$ when the symmetry properties of the clusters and the lattice have been taken into account in order to reduce, often considerably, the dimension of the linear system of Eq. (3.6). The resulting symmetry-adapted C matrix must be determined for all relevant clusters not only in order to solve the CVM variational problem, but also in order to determine linear constraints for the ground state problem, as is seen in Section 7. When clusters contain more than just a few lattice points (say, 4 or 6), the problem of determining the C matrix soon becomes intractable because of the combinatorial explosion that arises. Computer codes making full use of group theory have been developed[11,24,25] to construct symmetry-adapted C matrices of order 1000.

Helpful illustrative examples of configurations in binary and ternary systems have been worked out in detail in the review article by Inden and Pitsch.[6] Here, let us merely indicate the considerable simplifications

[24] J. M. Sanchez (1984).
[25] A. Finel (1985).

that occur for binary systems. In this case, the tau matrix [**T** in Eq. (3.2)] is a $2 \times 2$, symmetric, orthogonal matrix, which, except for a multiplicative factor of $1/2$, is identical to its inverse:

$$\mathbf{T} = \begin{pmatrix} 1 & 1 \\ 1 & -1 \end{pmatrix} \qquad \mathbf{T}^{-1} = \frac{1}{2}\begin{pmatrix} 1 & 1 \\ 1 & -1 \end{pmatrix}. \qquad (3.8)$$

It follows that the set $\{1, \sigma_p\}$ is already orthogonal in the space of configurations (see Section 4), so that we have, for $I, J, K = \pm 1$,

point:    $\rho_p(I) \qquad = \frac{1}{2}[1 + I\xi_1]$,

pair:    $\rho_{pq}(I, J) \quad = \frac{1}{4}[1 + (I + J)\xi_1 + (IJ)\xi_2]$,

$$(3.9)$$

triangle:    $\rho_{pqr}(I, J, K) = \frac{1}{8}[1 + (I + J + K)\xi_1$

$$+ (IJ + JK + KI)\xi_2 + (IJK)\xi_3],$$

and so on. The expressions in parentheses are elements of the symmetry-adapted C matrix under the assumption that here all lattice points are crystallographically equivalent and that the triangle cluster is equilateral (so that its three pair subclusters are also equivalent). It follows that the subscript notation on the $\xi$ correlations can be simplified, as shown. The point correlation $\xi_1$ is linearly related to the average concentration $c$ of $B$ atoms by $\xi_1 = 1 - 2c$.

To summarize, atomic constituents are labeled by integers $\tau$ and each site $p$ of a "frozen" configuration is associated with a variable $\sigma_p$, taking on any one of the $\tau$ values selected. The configuration of the whole system is given by the $N$-dimensional vector $\vec{\sigma}$. The cluster occupation variable $\Gamma_\alpha(\vec{\tau}, \vec{\sigma}_\alpha)$ takes the value of unity if and only if cluster $\alpha$ has the configuration $\vec{\sigma}_\alpha$, which is identical to that specified by the $\tau$ parameters. Cluster probabilities are obtained by ensemble averaging: $\rho_\alpha(\vec{\tau}) = \langle \Gamma_\alpha \rangle$. At each lattice point, a set of $M$ linearly independent functions of $\sigma_p$ was defined; in the present case, unity and the $M - 1$ successive powers of $\sigma_p$. In the next section, this set is replaced by an orthonormal one. Independent functions of $\sigma$ are defined for selected clusters and are obtained by tensor products whose average values are called *multisite correlation parameters* ($\xi$ symbols). These are the variational parameters for the free energy minimization problem. Any state of order, stable or metastable, can be

described by a set of cluster correlations; average concentration and long- and short-range order parameters, of arbitrary degree of complexity, can be expressed unambiguously in terms of these. The linear relationship between the cluster correlations $\xi_\beta$ and cluster concentrations $\rho_\alpha$ (where $\beta$ is a subcluster of $\alpha$) is provided by the symmetry-adapted configuration matrix, the nature of which depends entirely on the choice of clusters and on the geometry of the lattice or sublattices.

## 4. ORTHONORMAL EXPANSION

Thus far, we have seen that the cluster method has provided a rigorous *description* of partial configurational order/disorder. To be quantitatively useful, this description must be accompanied by a suitable *metric*, i.e., an inner product operation must be defined in the space of configurations. It is the introduction of an inner product and the attendant notion of expansion in orthonormal sets of cluster functions that probably constitutes the major advance in the field, but it occurred too recently to have been reported in article I, although early suggestions are to be found in review articles by Griffiths[26] and by Kawasaki[27] (I am indebted to François Ducastelle for pointing out those references to me).

Let us define the inner product of two functions of configuration, $f$ and $g$, symbolically by

$$\langle f(\vec{\sigma}) | g(\vec{\sigma}) \rangle = \rho_0 \sum_{\{\sigma\}} f(\vec{\sigma}) g(\vec{\sigma}), \qquad (4.1)$$

where $\rho_0$ is a normalization factor that depends on the manner of performing the sum over configurations $\vec{\sigma}$. The meaning of the angle brackets in Eq. (4.1) is, of course, quite different from what it was in Eqs. (2.3), (2.4), or (3.5): in those equations, $\langle X(\vec{\sigma}) \rangle$ denoted an ensemble average of some function $X$ of $\vec{\sigma}$. In previous publications, that distinction was not always emphasized, and seems to have led to occasional confusion.

Unless otherwise specified, the summation in Eq. (4.1) will be taken over all possible $M^N$ configurations, per the original definition proposed by Sanchez, Ducastelle, and Gratias (SDG).[2] For large systems ($N \to \infty$) in equilibrium in a fixed chemical field (differences of chemical poten-

[26] R. B. Griffiths, in *Phase Transitions and Critical Phenomena* (C. Domb and M. S. Green, eds.), Vol. 1, p. 78, Academic Press, New York (1972).

[27] K. Kawasaki, in *Phase Transitions and Critical Phenomena* (C. Domb and M. S. Green, eds.), Vol. 2, p. 465, Academic Press, New York (1973).

tials), it is expected that insignificantly few configurations will be found whose average concentrations deviate significantly from the equilibrium one. Hence, it may appear less wasteful to sum only over a restricted set of configurations—those that strictly conserve average concentration. The consequences of performing such restricted summations were studied in detail in recent publications,[28-30] the results of which are summarized next. In the unrestricted case (U-sum, for short), the normalization factor in Eq. (4.1) is

$$\rho_0 = M^{-N}, \tag{4.2}$$

in the restricted case (R-sum) it is

$$\hat{\rho}_0 = \left(\frac{N!}{N_A! N_B! \ldots N_M!}\right)^{-1}. \tag{4.3}$$

In what follows, the circumflex will designate quantities pertaining to R-sums.

Any function of the discrete configuration variables $\sigma$ may be expanded in a complete sete of basis functions $\varphi_k(\vec{\sigma})$:[2]

$$f(\vec{\sigma}) = \sum_k f_k \varphi_k(\vec{\sigma}). \tag{4.4}$$

If the functions $\varphi_k$ form a complete orthonormal set (CONS), then the generalized Fourier coefficients $f_\alpha$ can be calculated by the inner product formula

$$f_k = \langle f(\vec{\sigma}) | \varphi_k(\vec{\sigma}) \rangle. \tag{4.5}$$

Basis sets $\{\varphi_k\}$ may be constructed in many different ways, one of which is by Gram-Schmidt orthonormalization. Start from linearly independent functions $w_k(\sigma)$ ($k = 0, 1, 2, \ldots$) and iteratively perform the operations

$$\varphi_k(\vec{\sigma}) = \frac{g_k(\vec{\sigma})}{\langle g_k | g_k \rangle^{1/2}}, \tag{4.6}$$

[28] M. Asta, C. Wolverton, D. de Fontaine, and H. Dreyssé, *Phys. Rev. B.* **44**, 4907 (1991).
[29] C. Wolverton, M. Asta, H. Dreyssé, and D. de Fontaine, *Phys. Rev. B* **44**, 4914 (1991).
[30] D. de Fontaine, A. Finel, H. Dreyssé, M. Asta, R. McCormack, and C. Wolverton, in *Metallic Alloys: Experimental and Theoretical Perspectives* (J. S. Faulkner and R. G. Jordan, eds.) NATO ASI Series, Vol. 256, pp. 205–214, Kluwer, Dordrecht (1994).

$$g_0 = w_0, \tag{4.7a}$$

$$g_1 = w_1 - \langle \varphi_0 | w_1 \rangle \varphi_0, \tag{4.7b}$$

$$g_2 = w_2 - \langle \varphi_1 | w_2 \rangle \varphi_1 - \langle \varphi_0 | w_2 \rangle \varphi_0, \tag{4.7c}$$

and so on. We first construct a *local* CONS at point $p$ by taking as starting functions $\{w_k\}$ those of the set $\Sigma_p$, i.e., of successive powers of $\sigma_p$, as defined in connection with Eq. (3.1), and applying to these the Gram-Schmidt construction [Eqs. (4.6) and (4.7)]. Members of the resulting CONS have the form of polynomials in $\sigma_p$, actually discrete Chebychev polynomials,[2]

$$\theta^{(s)}(\sigma_p) = \sum_{m=0}^{M-1} a_m^{(s)} \sigma_p^m \qquad s = 0, 1, \ldots, M - 1. \tag{4.8}$$

The required CONS for the whole lattice of $N$ points is obtained by taking the tensor product of all $\theta$ functions for all lattice points. The resulting set of *cluster functions*

$$\Phi_\alpha^s(\vec{\sigma}) = \theta^{(s_1)}(\sigma_{p_1}) \theta^{(s_2)}(\sigma_{p_2}) \ldots \theta^{(s_n)}(\sigma_{p_n}), \tag{4.9}$$

constitutes the desired set of orthonormal basis functions. As the name implies, each function is associated with a cluster $\alpha$ and with a set of integers $s_i \neq 0$, denoted collectively by $s$. In the product of Eq. (4.9), local $\theta$ functions with $s_i = 0$ are not included since all $\theta^{(0)}$ are equal to unity. In other words, the cluster $\alpha$ contains all points $p$ at which the $\theta$ functions of the tensor product have nonzero index $s$. It follows that the $\Phi_\alpha^s$ cluster functions are expressed as linear combinations of $\Sigma_\alpha^m$, products of powers of $\sigma$, as defined in connection with Eq. (3.7). The change in notation from $\varphi_k$ in Eq. (4.4) to $\Phi_\alpha^s$ merely indicates that, in multicomponents, two collective indices must be used, $\alpha$ for the points of the cluster and $s$ for the particular local $\theta$ function considered. For the empty cluster, with all $s_i = 0$, we have $\Phi_0 = 1$.

For the case of inner products (4.1) defined over the space of *all* configurations (U-sum), SDG proved directly that the cluster functions verify orthonormality and completeness relations:[2]

$$\langle \Phi_\alpha^s(\vec{\sigma}) | \Phi_{\alpha'}^{s'}(\vec{\sigma}) \rangle = \delta_{ss'}, \tag{4.10}$$

$$\sum_{\alpha, s} \Phi_\alpha^s(\vec{\sigma}) \Phi_\alpha^s(\vec{\sigma}') = \delta(\vec{\sigma}, \vec{\sigma}'), \tag{4.11}$$

where the $\delta$'s are Kronecker deltas. Notation for multicomponent systems tends to get rather heavy, so let us look at simple examples.

### a. Binary System (U-Sum)

From Eqs. (4.7a) and (4.7b), there are just two *local* functions: $\theta^{(0)} = w_0 = 1$ and $\theta^{(1)}(\sigma_p) = g_1 = \sigma_p$, since $\langle \varphi_0 | w_1 \rangle \Rightarrow \langle 1 | \sigma \rangle = 0$. Cluster functions are then simply given by the products

$$\Phi_\alpha(\vec{\sigma}) = \sigma_{p_1} \sigma_{p_2} \ldots \sigma_{p_n} \tag{4.12}$$

(in addition to the empty cluster function $\Phi_0 = 1$). In the binary case, the collective index $s$ contains all 1's, so it does not need to be indicated. Expectation values of cluster functions are, in the present case, just the multisite correlation parameters defined previously:

$$\langle \Phi_\alpha(\vec{\sigma}) \rangle = \langle \sigma_{p_1} \sigma_{p_2} \ldots \sigma_{p_n} \rangle = \xi_\alpha \tag{4.13}$$

just as in Eq. (3.7), with all $m$ exponents equal to one.

### b. Ternary Systems (U-Sum)

Now the local functions are[2]

$$\theta^{(0)} = 1, \quad \theta^{(1)}(\sigma_p) = a_1^{(1)}\sigma_p, \quad \theta^{(2)}(\sigma_p) = a_0^{(2)} + a_2^{(2)}\sigma_p^2,$$

with $a_1^{(1)} = \sqrt{3/2}$, $a_0^{(2)} = \sqrt{2}$, and $a_2^{(2)} = -3/\sqrt{2}$. The expectation value of cluster functions is no longer identical to (generalized) correlation parameters, but rather to linear combinations of $\xi_\alpha^{(m)}$, with the collective index $(m)$ representing sets of integers equal to 1 or 2.

### c. Restricted Sum (Binary Systems)

For binary systems,[10] we have $\hat{\theta}^{(0)} = 1$ as before and

$$\hat{\theta}^{(1)}(\sigma_p) = b(\sigma_p - \bar{\sigma}) \tag{4.14}$$

since, for an inner product defined over the space of configurations that conserve the average concentration $\bar{\sigma} \equiv \xi_1$, we have $\langle \varphi_0 | w_1 \rangle \Rightarrow \langle 1 | \sigma \rangle =$

$\bar{\sigma}$. In Eq. (4.14), the normalization constant is $b = (1 - \bar{\sigma}^2)^{1/2}$. Cluster functions are obtained by taking tensor products of the local $\theta$ function so that, neglecting normalization, we have

$$\hat{\Phi}_\alpha(\sigma) = (\sigma_{p_1} - \bar{\sigma})(\sigma_{p_2} - \bar{\sigma}) \ldots (\sigma_{p_n} - \bar{\sigma}). \tag{4.15}$$

The corresponding expectation values are given by

$$\delta\hat{\xi}_\alpha = \langle\hat{\Phi}_\alpha(\sigma)\rangle = \langle\delta\sigma_{p_1}\delta\sigma_{p_2}\ldots\delta\sigma_{p_n}\rangle, \tag{4.16}$$

where $\delta\sigma_p = \sigma_p - \bar{\sigma}$. It therefore follows that the $\delta\hat{\xi}_\alpha$ are *cumulants* in the R-sum approach, rather than *correlations* (as in the U-sum case) although the $\xi_\alpha$ are not, strictly speaking, "correlations," but that term has now been sanctioned by general use in the present context. Proof of orthonormality and completeness of the $\hat{\Phi}_\alpha$ cluster functions is not as straightforward in the R-sum case; in particular, one has to invoke the thermodynamic limit $N \to \infty$.[28] At that limit, the R-sum definition of inner products at $c = 1/2$ ($\bar{\sigma} = 0$) coincides with that of the U-sum.

Regardless of the method of defining the inner product, we may expand in cluster functions the density function as[2]

$$\rho(\vec{\tau}) = \rho_N^0\left[1 + \sum_\alpha \sum_s{}' \Phi_\alpha^s(\vec{\tau})\langle\Phi_\alpha^s(\vec{\sigma})\rangle\right], \tag{4.17}$$

since, by inversion formula (4.5), the generalized Fourier coefficients of the $\rho(\tau)$ are given by

$$\rho_0 = \langle\rho(\sigma)|1\rangle = \rho_N^0 \tag{4.18a}$$

and

$$\rho_\alpha^s = \langle\rho(\vec{\sigma})|\Phi_\alpha^s(\vec{\sigma})\rangle = \rho_N^0\langle\Phi_\alpha^s(\vec{\sigma})\rangle. \tag{4.18b}$$

In Eq. (4.17), and elsewhere in this chapter, the accent on the summation indicates that the empty cluster is excluded from the sum.

Orthogonal expansions of partial density functions $\rho_\alpha(\vec{\tau})$, or probabilities of finding $\alpha$ clusters populated by specified configurations $\vec{\tau}$, may be obtained from Eq. (3.5) by noting that any term of the sum over configurations (restricted or not) is equal to unity if the configuration $\vec{\sigma}$ matches exactly the one ($\vec{\tau}$) specified on $\alpha$ cluster points, 0 otherwise. It then follows from Eq. (4.17) that cluster concentrations, for specified $\vec{\tau}$, are given by

$$\rho_\alpha(\vec{\tau}) = \rho_\alpha^0 \left[ 1 + \sum_{\beta \subseteq \alpha} \sum_s {}' \Phi_\beta^s(\vec{\tau}) \langle \Phi_\beta^s(\vec{\sigma}) \rangle \right], \tag{4.19}$$

where the first summation is performed over all subclusters ($\beta$) of $\alpha$, and where $\rho_\alpha^0$ is the appropriate normalization factor for cluster $\alpha$. Equation (4.19) for $\rho_\alpha(\vec{\tau})$ is equivalent to Eq. (3.6) except that the expansion in (4.19) is performed in an orthonormal basis. For binary systems, the two expressions for $\rho_\alpha(\vec{\sigma})$ should be identical since, as noted earlier, the T matrix of Eq. (3.8) is, but for a constant factor, its own inverse. Moreover, Eq. (4.19) should simply reduce to Eqs. (3.9) for the particular symmetry considered (equivalent points and nearest neighbor pairs).

As noted by SDG,[2] the formalism just described guarantees the self-consistency relations between clusters, i.e., that $\rho_\beta(\vec{\tau})$ is equal to sum over configurations of the $\alpha$ complement of $\beta$, $\beta$ being a subcluster of $\alpha$. For example, the sum over $I$ of the triplet probability $\rho_3(A, B, I)$ must equal the pair probability $\rho_2(A, B)$. There is, however, no guarantee that the expansion for the full density function $\rho(\vec{\sigma})$ will converge. It is only when properly combined with energy and entropy expectation values that rapid convergence can be ascertained, as is shown later.

The notion of orthonormal expansions is of course used a great deal in mathematical physics, but the choice of basis functions is usually dictated by the boundary conditions and by the symmetry of the system. Thus, for crystalline systems characterized by translational symmetry, it is convenient to impose periodic boundary conditions and to use Fourier waves (or Bloch waves) as basis functions. With disordered systems, translational symmetry is lost but, conversely, one may expect that properties may be well described by *local* configurations. Hence, one seeks basis functions that possess local character: These are the cluster functions defined earlier. Usually, it suffices to consider functions pertaining to small clusters: a few near neighbor pairs, triplets, quadruplets, etc., of lattice points, the largest manageable ones today being the fcc 13- and 14-point clusters, for example. The realization that cluster functions could serve as a *local orthonormal basis for disordered systems* provides the essential link between the quantum and statistical mechanics of substitutionally ordered/disordered systems, as is now demonstrated.

## 5. Effective Cluster Interactions

The main objective of first-principles thermodynamics is to solve the variational principle associated with the free energy functional (2.5). In particular, we need to obtain suitable expressions for the energy $U[\rho]$, hence, by Eq. (2.3), for the configuration-dependent "hybrid" energy $\Psi(\vec{\sigma})$ de-

fined by Eqs. (1.4), (1.5), and (1.6). For simplicity, let us denote the configuration-dependent energy by the symbol $E(\vec{\sigma})$ without, at present, specifying the several contributions to the full expression for $U$ in Eq. (2.3). This configuration-dependent energy is a prime candidate for expansion in cluster functions according to the methods outlined in the previous section. Of course, electronic and vibrational entropy contributions could, indeed should, be expanded similarly, but it is particularly instructive to describe the formalism for the energy case.

a. *Types of Interactions*

Equation (4.4) gives the general form of the expansion, written more explicitly here as

$$E(\vec{\sigma}) = \sum_{\alpha, s} E_\alpha^s \Phi_\alpha^s(\vec{\sigma}). \tag{5.1}$$

Since (5.1) is an expansion in *orthonormal* cluster functions, the generalized Fourier coefficients are given by Eq. (4.5), more specifically, from the inner product formula (4.1), by

$$E_0^o = \rho_0 \sum_{\{\sigma\}} E(\vec{\sigma}) \tag{5.2a}$$

and

$$E_\alpha^s = \rho_0 \sum_{\{\sigma\}} \Phi_\alpha^s(\vec{\sigma}) E(\vec{\sigma}), \tag{5.2b}$$

since the cluster function $\Phi_0$ corresponding to the empty cluster is equal to unity. Depending on the method of carrying out the $\{\sigma\}$ summations in Eqs. (5.2), the $E_\alpha$ coefficients will be concentration independent in the U-sum case (since all configurations are summed over), or concentration dependent in the R-sum case (since summations are performed at fixed concentration). In the former case, $E_0^o$ represents a fictitious average energy: the normalized sum of the energies of all possible configurations of the system. In the limit of large $N$, $E_0^o$ is the average energy of a completely disordered system at concentration $c = 0.5$ ($\xi_1 = 0$). In the R-sum case, $\hat{E}_0(\vec{\sigma})$ represents the average energy of a completely disordered system of fixed concentration $\vec{\sigma}$, i.e., a system for which the various atom types are distributed completely randomly over the lattice sites.

The coefficients $E_\alpha^s$, concentration dependent or independent, will be called *effective cluster interactions* (ECI), the computation of which to a great extent determines the degree of success of the first-principles calculations.

The expectation value of the energy is given by Eq. (2.3), so that by (ensemble) averaging both sides of Eq. (5.1), one obtains, with the help of (5.2),

$$E = E_0 + \sum_{\alpha, s}{}' E_\alpha^s \langle \Phi_\alpha^s \rangle. \tag{5.3}$$

The prime on the summation indicates that the empty cluster term is excluded. Note that this expression also could have been obtained by directly inserting Eq. (4.17) for the density $\rho$ into Eq. (2.3) for the average energy. Thus, the treatment is perfectly consistent and formally *exact*.

To illustrate the method, let us examine some simple examples. Consider a binary system $(A, B)$ in the U-sum case. The superscript $s$ in Eq. (5.2b) may then be deleted, and the sum over configurations may be split into two parts: a sum over cluster configurations $(\alpha)$ and one over configurations in the complement $(N - \alpha$, symbolically) of cluster $\alpha$ (which contains $n$ points, say). Let us then adopt the more usual notation $V_\alpha$ for the ECI and rewrite (5.2b) as

$$E_\alpha \Rightarrow V_\alpha = 2^{-n} \sum_{\{\sigma_\alpha\}} (\sigma_{p_1} \sigma_{p_2} \ldots \sigma_{p_n}) \left[ 2^{n-N} \sum_{\{\sigma_{N-\alpha}\}} E(\vec{\sigma}_\alpha; \vec{\sigma}_{N-\alpha}) \right]. \tag{5.4}$$

In this equation, Eq. (4.2) has been used for the normalizations $\rho_0$ and the product (4.12) has been used for the cluster function $\Phi_\alpha$, the form of which ensures that there will be as many products equal to $+1$ as there are products equal to $-1$. This balance between positive and negative contributions to the ECIs is a characteristic feature of the treatment, as discussed later. The expression in square brackets in Eq. (5.4) represents a normalized sum of energies of all possible configurations for fixed occupation of the $\alpha$ cluster. The bracketed term may thus be written as $W_{IJ\ldots K}$, which may be interpreted as the *average energy of all configurations having an I-type atom at lattice point* $p_1$, J *at* $p_2$, $\ldots$ *and* K *at* $p_n$. Thus, for effective *pair* interactions (EPI) we have

$$V_2 = \frac{1}{4}(W_{AA} + W_{BB} - W_{AB} - W_{BA}). \tag{5.5}$$

By (5.4), similar expressions may, of course, be derived for triplets, quadruplets, etc.

For binary systems, Eq. (5.3) for the expectation value of the energy may be written simply as

$$E = V_0 + \sum_{\alpha}{}' V_\alpha \xi_\alpha, \tag{5.6}$$

where $V_0$ is just $E_0^o$ of (5.2a) and $\xi_\alpha$ is the $\alpha$ cluster correlation parameter (4.13). This equation, originally due to Sanchez,[31] is central to first-principles treatments of binary systems. By definition, for a completely random, uncorrelated solid solution, all $\xi_\alpha$ are equal to the $n$'th power of the point variables $\xi_1$. Hence, for such a system, resulting theoretically from an infinitely fast quench of an infinite-temperature mixture, the energy $E_{dis}$ would be given by

$$E_{dis} = V_0 + \sum_{\alpha}{}' V_\alpha \xi_1^n. \tag{5.7}$$

Elimination of $V_0$ between Eqs. (5.6) and (5.7) gives

$$E = E_{dis} + \sum_{\alpha}{}'' V_\alpha \delta\xi_\alpha \tag{5.8}$$

with

$$\delta\xi_\alpha = \xi_\alpha - \xi_1^n, \tag{5.9}$$

where the latter quantities may be called *correlation deviations*. In Eq. (5.8) it was assumed that all lattice points were equivalent; therefore, the first-order term $V_1 \delta\xi_1$, by Eq. (5.9), must vanish and the *ordering energy* expansion

$$\Delta E_{ord} = \sum_{\alpha}{}'' V_\alpha \delta\xi_\alpha \tag{5.10}$$

must start with the pair-cluster term, as indicated by the double prime on the summation sign in Eqs. (5.8) and (5.10). If all lattice points are

[31] J. M. Sanchez, private communication (1978).

*not* equivalent, for example, near an imperfection such as an interface, the point terms must be retained, and would in fact contribute strongly to the phenomenon of surface segregation.[32,33]

The R-sum case (for binaries) gives a very similar expansion:

$$E = \hat{V}_0(c) + \sum_{\alpha}'' \hat{V}_\alpha(c)\delta\xi_\alpha, \tag{5.11}$$

where the concentration dependence of the corresponding (circumflexed) ECIs has been indicated explicitly. The summation in Eq. (5.11) also starts at pairs since the cumulant $\delta\hat{\xi}_1$ vanishes for equivalent lattice points. Note that $\hat{V}_0(c)$ in Eq. (5.11), the average energy of all configurations having specified average concentration $c$, is the same as $E_{dis}$ in Eq. (5.8). Since variables $\xi_\alpha$ and $\delta\hat{\xi}_\alpha$ both form linearly independent sets (with $\delta\hat{\xi}_1 \equiv 0$), energy expressions (5.6) and (5.11) may be identified term for term (in the thermodynamic limit[28,30]) after replacing multisite cumulants by their values in terms of multisite correlations and powers of point correlations ($\xi_1 = 1 - 2c$):

$$\delta\hat{\xi}_\alpha = \xi_\alpha - \xi_{\alpha-1}\xi_1 + \xi_{\alpha-2}\xi_1^2 - \xi_{\alpha-3}\xi_1^3 + \ldots, \tag{5.12a}$$

where $\alpha - 1, \alpha - 2, \ldots$, denotes symbolically clusters with $1, 2, \ldots$, fewer points than cluster $\alpha$. Identification of like terms in the U-sum and R-sum expansions then allows one to express rigorously the concentration-independent ECIs $V_\alpha$ in terms of the concentration-dependent interactions $\hat{V}_\alpha(c)$, thus[28,30] (for $\alpha \neq 0, 1$):

$$V_\alpha = \hat{V}_\alpha(c) + \sum_{\beta \supset \alpha} (-\xi_1)^{n'-n} \hat{V}_\beta(c), \tag{5.12b}$$

where $n'$ is the number of points in the *supercluster* $\beta$ (of $\alpha$). In this expression, the summation is over all clusters ($\beta$) that contain $\alpha$. An expression equivalent to that of Eq. (4.16) may be written for the U-sum quantities $\xi_\alpha = \langle \Phi_\alpha(\sigma) \rangle$ by taking the expectation value of the product of point functions $\Phi_1(\sigma_p) = \hat{\Phi}_1(\sigma_p) + \bar{\sigma}$ [which is Eq. (4.15) written for point cluster $\alpha = 1$]. By expanding the resulting ensemble average, we get

$$\xi_\alpha = \delta\hat{\xi}_\alpha + \delta\hat{\xi}_{\alpha-1}\xi_1 + \delta\hat{\xi}_{\alpha-2}\xi_1^2 + \delta\hat{\xi}_{\alpha-3}\xi_1^3 + \ldots, \tag{5.13a}$$

[32] H. Dressé, L. T. Wille, and D. de Fontaine, *Solid State Comm.* **78**, 355 (1991).
[33] B. Legrand, G. Tréglia, and F. Ducastelle, *Phys. Rev. B* **41**, 4422 (1990).

a summation in *subclusters* that parallels that of Eq. (5.12a). By identification of like terms, as in the derivation of Eq. (5.12b), we obtain another equally rigorous expansion in superclusters (for $\alpha$ beyond the point cluster):

$$\hat{V}_\alpha(c) = V_\alpha \sum_{\beta \supset \alpha} (\xi_1)^{n'-n} V_\beta. \qquad (5.13b)$$

Equations (5.13a) and (5.13b) were proposed by Carlsson[34] for the case of pairs ($n = 2$), from which the equivalence of $c$-independent ECIs and $c$-dependent EPIs was derived in the context of the generalized perturbation method (see Section 13). Because of the equivalence of U-sum and R-sum schemes, it is thus quite immaterial whether one chooses to express energies or other physical quantities in terms of concentration-dependent or concentration-independent parameters.

Equation (5.12a) can be used to provide approximate expressions for correlations $\xi_\gamma$ for clusters not contained in the set of maximal clusters. For large clusters, the corresponding cumulants $\delta\hat{\xi}_\gamma$ may be approximately set equal to zero, which then enables $\xi_\gamma$ to be expressed in terms of subcluster correlations and powers of $\xi_1$. This superposition approximation (called the *renormalized interaction method* by Ferreira *et al.*[35]) will be used in Section 16(b).

Convenient expressions for ECIs in ternary (and higher) systems are more difficult to obtain. The difficulty is that, in order to derive explicit energy expressions suitable for first-principles calculations, we must make use of the inner product formalism, hence of orthonormal sets of functions $\Phi_\alpha^s(\vec{\sigma})$. The resulting expressions involve terms containing the $\Sigma_\alpha^m(\vec{\sigma})$ defined in connection with Eq. (3.7), and such terms must be grouped so as to obtain the balance of positive and negative contributions,[13] which is manifestly apparent in the binary case, as in Eq. (5.5), for example.

b. *Properties of Interactions*

Basic properties of ECIs follow from the formal definition [Eq. (5.4)], or for the explicit special case of (binary) EPIs, Eq. (5.5). If the two lattice sites ($p$, $q$) of a pair are widely separated, then $W_{AB}$, say, may be obtained from Eq. (5.4) by summing all configurations about atom $A$ at $p$ with atom $B$ at $q$. Since half of all configurations about $p$ will have $A$ at $q$, and

[34] A. E. Carlsson, *Phys. Rev. B* **35**, 4858 (1987).
[35] L. G. Ferreira, S.-H. Wei, and A. Zunger, *Phys. Rev. B* **40**, 3197 (1989).

half will have $B$ at $q$, $W_{AB}$ will equal $(1/2)W_A$ plus a correction term that takes into account the fact that the configurations left out in $W_{AB}$ ($A$ at $q$) have energy slightly different from those configurations included ($B$ at $q$, in this example). If the pair spacing is large, the correction term ($\Delta_B$) will hardly depend on the nature of the atom at $p$. Thus we have approximately $W_{AB} = 1/2\,W_A + \Delta_B$. Inserting that expression into Eq. (5.5), and similar ones for the other average energies, gives strictly zero for the EPI $V_2$. One may therefore conclude that the magnitude of EPIs tends to zero as pair spacing increases. More generally, the ECIs for clusters containing one or more points located far apart will tend to have vanishingly small values.

Convergence may also be demonstrated heuristically for ECIs of increasing size (number of sites). Consider the cluster $\alpha$ of $n$ points to which one point is added. If $W_{IJ...K}$ is one of the contributing terms to $V_\alpha$, then the corresponding term for the augmented cluster ($\alpha + 1$) would be, by Eq. (5.4), $(1/2)(W_{IJ...KA} - W_{IJ...KB})$. Hence, for the ECI $V_{\alpha+1}$, we have

$$V_{\alpha+1} = \frac{1}{2}[V_\alpha(A) - V_\alpha(B)], \qquad (5.14)$$

where $V_\alpha(I)$ is a "restricted" ECI for $\alpha$ calculated with $I$ located at the additional point $n + 1$. For any reasonably large cluster, $V_\alpha(A)$ and $V_\alpha(B)$ are expected to be both very close in value to $V_\alpha$ itself, so that ECIs should rapidly decrease in magnitude with the size of clusters.

The arguments just presented do not imply monotonic decay of ECI magnitudes with number of points or separation of points in the clusters. Nor can these arguments provide criteria for how rapidly convergence should occur. To determine actual decay rates it is necessary to perform actual computations. Estimates of convergence have been proposed based on perturbation analysis of the CPA medium[5] (coherent potential approximation). The conclusion was that the concentration-dependent interactions $\hat{V}_\alpha(c)$ (R-sum) derived in this way should provide more rapid convergence than those obtained from concentration-independent interactions (U-sum). That conclusion does not follow from present considerations, certainly not for binaries at the 50/50 concentration; indeed, at that "central" concentration, since $\xi_1 = 0$, the $V_\alpha$ and $\hat{V}_\alpha$ interactions are equal according to Eq. (5.12b), and the rate of convergence for both U-sum and R-sum schemes should be identical. It is possible, however, that away from the 50/50 concentration, the rate of decay of ECIs for clusters beyond pairs should be more rapid for the $\hat{V}_\alpha(c)$ than for the $V_\alpha$.

In most cases, it is found that fully 90% of the *ordering* energy [Eq.

(5.10)] is concentrated in the first neighbor pair (the following discussion is couched in terms of binary systems). The role of higher EPIs and ECIs is essential, however, particularly in lifting ground state degeneracies: Calculations generally do not predict correct ordered structures unless quite a few interactions are included (say, 5 or 10). The *formation energy*, $\Delta E_{\text{form}}$, which is usually larger in magnitude than the ordering energy, is defined as the total energy of a particular $(A, B)$ configuration minus the concentration-weighted average of the pure $A$ and $B$ crystals. This definition is not unambiguous since it is not specified whether the pure $A$ and pure $B$ solids have the same lattice as the parent lattice of the $(A, B)$ configuration in question, with identical lattice parameters. A more general definition is given in Section 14 [see Eq. (14.5)]. For the present simple discussion, we assume that pure $A$, pure $B$, and the configuration considered have *identical lattices*. The formation energy may thus be written as

$$\Delta E_{\text{form}} = E - (E_0 + E_1\xi_1), \qquad (5.15)$$

where $E_0$ and $E_1$ are the half-sum and half-difference, respectively, of the pure state energies $E_A$ and $E_B$. In the U-sum scheme, Eq. (5.15) may be rewritten, according to Eq. (5.6) as

$$\Delta E_{\text{form}} = \Delta V_0 + \Delta V_1\xi_1 + \sum_{\alpha}{}'' V_\alpha \xi_\alpha, \qquad (5.16)$$

where $\Delta V_0 = V_0 - E_0$ and $\Delta V_1 = V_1 - E_1$.

The *cohesive energy*, which is larger still than the formation energy by at least one or two orders of magnitude, may be defined as

$$\Delta E_{\text{coh}} = E_{\text{tot}} - E_\infty, \qquad (5.17)$$

where $E_{\text{tot}}$ is the total energy of electrons and nuclei in the crystalline state, and $E_\infty$ is the energy of an infinitely dilute gas of the atoms of the crystal. Usually, the plain symbol $E$ in previous and subsequent expressions refers to the cohesive energy. One may also define *structural energy differences* by

$$\Delta E_{\text{struct}} = E^I - E^{II}, \qquad (5.18)$$

where $E^I$ and $E^{II}$ are the energies of two different structures at the same stoichiometry, for example, one bcc-based, one fcc-based.

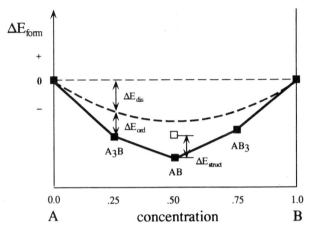

FIG. 1. Formation energy $\Delta E_{form}$ as a function of concentration for an A-B alloy. Energies of formation of three compounds are shown at vertices of convex hull. The dashed line is the formation energy of the disordered A-B solution ($\Delta E_{dis}$). Ordering energy is defined as difference $\Delta E_{form}$ and $\Delta E_{dis}$. The energy difference between different structures at same concentration is $\Delta E_{struct}$.

Various types of energy differences are illustrated schematically in the energy of formation diagram of Fig. 1. By definition (5.15), $\Delta E_{form}$ for the pure A and pure B are zero. Formation energies of other structures are represented by square symbols, stable structures (filled squares) being located at the vertices of a convex polygonal line (convex hull). A hypothetical metastable (or unstable) ordered structure is represented as an open square, inside the convex hull, and separated from the corresponding stable-state filled square by the structural energy difference $\Delta E_{struct}$. The illustrated energy differences are completely consistent with the definition of classical thermodynamics, but $\Delta E_{dis}$ and $\Delta E_{ord}$ introduce new features not *explicitly* taken into account in the classical approach. In the present treatment, a careful distinction is made between the fully disordered state and a state of complete or partial order. If pure A and pure B have the same crystal structure, then the locus of fully disordered state energies may be plotted as shown in Fig. 1 (dashed curve), expressed as a polynomial in the point correlation $\xi_1$, according to the defining equation [Eq. (5.7)]. The indicated difference $\Delta E_{ord}$ conforms to the definition of Eqs. (5.8), (5.9), and (5.10). More complicated cases involving different lattices are described later by means of calculations pertaining to actual binary alloy systems. Typical orders of magnitude of energies are as follows: cohesive, a few electron volts; formation, 1 to 0.1 eV; and ordering, 0.1 to 0.01 eV.

More general considerations pertaining to the distinction between *effective pair interactions* and *pair potentials* and also between *concentration-dependent* and *-independent* interactions are discussed in the next section.

## 6. DISCUSSION OF CLUSTER EXPANSIONS

The cluster expansion method provides a rigorous way of treating configurational disorder on lattices. That relatively small clusters can account for most physical properties and can be understood intuitively based on the idea that, in disordered systems, *local* effects dominate properties. Hence, local bases are the proper ones to set up for deriving an appropriate cluster algebra. Once a cluster function basis has been selected, the expansion coefficients for any physical property that depends on configuration are determined by the inner product operation of Eq. (4.5). The procedure is exact, the approximation being introduced only by the truncation of the expansion.

The choice of a set of basis functions is an important one. The construction of a suitable set in turn depends on the scheme of configuration variables adopted. For binary systems, the natural choice is $\sigma = \pm 1$, and the basis functions for the orthonormal set are a product of point functions 1 and $\sigma$ (in the U-sum case), and a slightly more involved set in the R-sum case. For multicomponent systems, a convenient set is the one described in Section 3, the set $\{1, \sigma, \sigma^2, \ldots\}$. Recently, another scheme was proposed,[36] which provided an elegant geometrical interpretation for linearly independent functions in multicomponent systems. The functions defined by these two schemes are not mutually orthogonal, however. That feature is of no consequence if it is merely required to establish a correspondence between configurational and occupation variables. When computing cluster interactions rigorously from quantum mechanical calculations, it is desirable to use orthonormal sets, however, since ECIs may then be derived from the inner product formalism. Therefore, as proposed by Sanchez, Ducastelle, and Gratias,[2] one must appeal to Gram-Schmidt orthogonalization, leading to discrete Chebychev polynomials, as in Eq. (4.8).

The question of concentration-dependent versus -independent interactions has generated some controversies. It may appear counterintuitive that energies of ordering or formation, say, which generally vary strongly with concentration, could be represented by concentration-*independent*

---

[36] P. Cénédèse and D. Gratias, *Physica A* **179**, 277 (1991).

parameters. What physical meaning could be attached to such $c$-independent interactions? One answer is that the physical meaning of ECIs is of little importance, only the expansion itself has meaning. The concentration dependence of properties is present, of course, in the U-sum scheme, but it resides only in the correlation parameters. In the R-sum scheme, as seen by Eq. (5.11), for example, the concentration dependence of properties is distributed over the $c$-dependent ECIs, $V_\alpha(c)$, and the multisite cumulants $\delta\hat{\xi}_\alpha$. The different types of expansions are completely equivalent, however. In the U-sum case, it is imperative to use multisite (cluster) interactions, beyond pairs, otherwise calculated phase diagrams would be perfectly symmetric about the 50/50 midpoint, which in general they are not.

Admittedly, it does appear surprising that concentration-independent interactions ($V_\alpha$) can be expressed in terms of concentration-dependent ECIs, $\hat{V}_\alpha(c)$. The surprising aspect is that the left-hand side of Eq. (5.12b) is completely $c$-independent, and the right-hand side exhibits two types of concentration dependences: an explicit one through the point correlations ($\xi_1 = 1 - 2c$), and an implicit one through the $c$-dependent interactions themselves. Yet, those concentration dependences do cancel, at least if sufficiently many terms are included in the summation. An example of attenuation of the concentration dependence of interactions is given in Section 13.

Of course, ECIs, whether concentration dependent or not, do have intrinsic physical meaning: They are defined as sums and differences of *energies* (the $W_{IJK...}$), the latter being defined as cohesive energies over the whole system, averaged in appropriate manner. Thus, even the first-neighbor pair interaction, for example, is calculated by means of energy terms that contain full electronic and ionic (or nuclear) interactions of arbitrary range. The meaning and role of ECIs thus differs radically from those of the older notion of *pair potentials* regarded as atom-atom interactions, which, if summed far enough out, would reproduce a fair portion of the cohesive energy.

The confusion over the distinction between effective pair interactions and pair potentials has led to considerable misunderstandings. The EPIs (*a fortiori*, ECIs) are *not* pair potentials. It is well known that cohesive energies cannot be obtained as a sum of pair potentials, regardless of the range of pair spacings.[37] In the EPI description, however, the cohesive energy is contained almost entirely in the empty cluster and point cluster terms, which are evaluated *ab initio* by electronic structure calculations. Pairs, triplets, and so on add a small correction to $V_0$ (and to the point

[37] V. Heine, in *Solid State Physics* **35**, 1–127 (1980).

terms), the subtle correction $\Delta E_{ord}$ being the one that governs the thermodynamics of ordering and that can indeed be obtained as a rapidly convergent series of pairs and cluster interactions. The confusion between pair potentials (appropriate as contributions to total energies) and pair interactions (appropriate for Ising model calculations) was particulaly apparent in certain recent studies of oxygen ordering in the yttrium-barium superconducting cuprate, where it was stated that since Coulombic effects dominated, pair interactions would decay very slowly with pair spacing. That conclusion is erroneous: Coulomb repulsion (and attraction) may well play an important role in the energies $W_{IJ}$ appearing in Eq. (5.5), for example, but the EPI themselves will converge rapidly with spacing because of partial cancellation of energy contributions appearing in the linear combination of Eq. (5.5). It has been shown directly, by total-energy local density-functional calculations, that even Madelung energies, and the Madelung constant itself resulting from charge transfer effects in intermetallic alloys, could be represented quite accurately by rapidly convergent cluster expansions.[38,39]

In the past, as long as generalized Ising interactions were merely conjectured or fitted to empirical data, the precise definition of interactions did not matter. Now that these interactions are being calculated from first principles, it is imperative to start from a precise definition of these parameters. Such a rigorous procedure, in terms of energy differences, is what the orthonormal expansion provides.

## IV. Ground State Analysis

A ground state is by definition one of lowest energy and is therefore the equilibrium one at absolute zero for given pressure and for given chemical field or average concentration (in an alloy). It was originally believed that all alloy ground states should be crystalline, but there are now good experimental and theoretical reasons to include quasicrystalline ground states as well, i.e., states that possess no periodically repeating finite unit cell. The general problem of predicting unambiguously the correct state of minimum energy for a mixture of $N_A A$ atoms and $N_B B$ atoms is an impossible task because, in principle, a non-denumerable infinity exists of possible candidate structures, even if, as is done in what follows, only binary $(A,B)$ systems are considered. In practice, however, certain simple

[38] R. Magri, S.-H. Wei, and A. Zunger, *Phys. Rev. B* **42**, 11388 (1990).
[39] Z. W. Lu, S.-H. Wei, A. Zunger, S. Frota-Pessoa, and L. G. Ferreira, *Phys. Rev. B* **44**, 512 (1991).

structures occur quite frequently in intermetallic compounds, and many of these turn out to be superstructures of some parent "lattice" (fcc, bcc, hcp, . . .). The search for ground state *superstructures* is a much simpler problem (although still a difficult one) and it has been solved exactly in certain favorable cases. The superstructure ground state problem was covered briefly in the author's previous review (I), which summarized some of the pioneering work of Kanamori[40] and of Cahn and coworkers.[41] Recent progress in the field has been covered in the extensive treatments of Finel,[7,42] Ducastelle,[5] Inden and Pitsch,[6] and Ceder,[11] mentioned earlier. Here, only a brief summary of basic results is given for completeness, because the modern treatment of the problem indicates quite clearly the role played by the cluster expansion ideas in deriving the necessary formalism. One recent application is given for illustrative purposes.

### 7. GROUND STATE FORMALISM

In keeping with the general principles set forth in earlier sections, consider $A$ and $B$ "atoms" (particles) uniquely associated with the $N$ sites of a given lattice. It is obviously essential to determine the possible stable superstructures (at zero kelvin) for given sets of ECIs ($V_\alpha$) before attempting to perform nonzero-temperature thermodynamic phase equilibrium calculations for the system envisaged. It is also essential to make sure that *true* ground states have been discovered. Often in the past, various candidate structures were guessed at and their respective energies of formation were calculated and compared. This method, described felicitously by Zunger as that of "rounding up the usual suspects,"[9] may miss true, unsuspected ground states, hence the need for *exact* methods.

The energy expression to be minimized [Eq. (5.6)] is linear in the configuration variables $\xi_\alpha$, but these variables must obey certain sets of linear constraints. Hence, the ground state problem turns out to be one of linear programming, provided that concentration-independent ECIs are used. One obvious constraint may be deduced directly from the definition of the correlation parameters (3.7) (here limited to binary systems): $|\xi_\alpha| \leq 1$. These inequalities do not suffice; it is also necessary to impose the condi-

[40] J. Kanamori, *Prog. Theor. Phys.* **35**, 16 (1966).

[41] M. J. Richards and J. W. Cahn, *Acta Metall.* **19**, 1263 (1971); S. M. Allen and J. W. Cahn, *Acta Metall.* **20**, 423 (1972); S. M. Allen and J. W. Cahn, *Scripta Metall.* **7**, 1261 (1973).

[42] A. Finel and F. Ducastelle, *Mat. Res. Soc. Symp. Proc.* **21**, 293 (1984).

tions that the cluster probabilities $\rho_\alpha$ of Eq. (4.19) lie between zero and unity.

To be more specific, let us modify Eq. (5.6) as follows. Since, by Eq. (5.4), the calculation of the ECIs calls for a sum over all configurations, the $V_\alpha$ necessarily possess the symmetry of the *lattice*, not the lower one of the ordered states. Rather than summing over all possible clusters $\alpha$, as in Eq. (5.6), considering all clusters as distinct, it is far more efficient to group terms that correspond to clusters which are equivalent with respect to the space group of the lattice, and which therefore correspond to the same ECIs $V_\alpha$. The set of clusters equivalent to a given one make up the *orbit* of that cluster.[43] The simplification of Eq. (5.6) then consists in summing, not over individual clusters $\alpha$, but over orbits, to which we attach an index, say, $r$. We simplify further by dividing by the total number $N$ of lattice points, and we bring the term $V_0$ to the left of the equal sign. The convenient form of the (binary) energy expansion is then

$$\frac{E - V_0}{N} \equiv \delta e = \sum_r{}'' m_r V_r \bar{\xi}_r + \mu \xi_1, \qquad (7.1)$$

where $m_r$ is the number of symmetry-equivalent clusters per lattice site and $\bar{\xi}_r$ is an orbit-average of correlation parameters. As in Eq. (5.10), the double prime indicates that the summation contains neither empty cluster nor point cluster contributions. The point term has been written separately in Eq. (7.1) with chemical field symbol $\mu$ as the coefficient.

The same treatment may be applied to Eq. (4.19), which relates cluster probabilities $\rho$ to correlations ($\xi_\alpha = \langle \phi_\alpha \rangle$ for binaries). We have, on using the orbit-index notation:

$$\rho_r(\vec{\tau}) = \frac{1}{2^n} \left[ 1 + \sum_{r' \leq r}{}' C_{r,r'}(\vec{\tau}) \bar{\xi}_{r'} \right], \qquad (7.2)$$

where the summation is over all subclusters $r'$ of clusters of type $r$, indicated symbolically by the notation $r' \leq r$. The coefficients $C$ are elements of the symmetry-adapted configuration matrix, already introduced (in a different form) in connection with Eq. (3.6). For each cluster type chosen, $r$, and for each $(A,B)$ configuration ($\vec{\tau}$) of the cluster, the probabilities $\rho_r(\vec{\tau})$ must be non-negative and less than or equal to one. Actually, since the sum of the $\rho_r(\vec{\tau})$ over all its configurations must equal one, it suffices to impose the non-negativity condition on the $\rho_r$, the upper

[43] D. Gratias, J. M. Sanchez, and D. de Fontaine, *Physica A* **113**, 315 (182).

limit being automatically satisfied. The linear constraints for the ground state problem are thus

$$1 + \sideset{}{'}\sum_{r'<r} C_{r,r'}(\vec{\tau})\bar{\xi}_{r'} \geq 0. \tag{7.3}$$

These inequalities define a convex polytope region in $\bar{\xi}$ space (correlation space), which contains the origin (all $\bar{\xi}_r = 0$, representing the state of complete disorder at $c = 1/2$). All realizable ordered, partially ordered, or disordered states are described by representative points whose $\bar{\xi}$ variables must necessarily lie inside the polytope determined by inequality (7.3). An example of such a polytope, referred to as the *configuration polyhedron* (CP) after the work of Kudo and Katsura[44] who first introduced this notion in the ordering problem, was given in I. Since then, other examples have been given in two- and three-dimensional correlation space by Finel,[7,42] Ducastelle,[5] and Inden and Pitsch.[6]

Let us locate the $k$'th vertex of the CP by the coordinates $\xi_r^{(k)}$. It is then also possible to define a point inside the CP by its barycentric coordinates[45] $z_k (0 \leq z_k \leq 1)$:

$$\bar{\xi}_r = \sum_k z_k \xi_r^{(k)}. \tag{7.4}$$

The $z_k$ are not all independent since we have $\Sigma z_k = 1$, with the summation running over all vertices of the CP. From the properties of barycentric coordinates it is easy to show that the energy $\delta e$ of Eq. (7.1) takes on its minimum value at coordinates $\bar{\xi}_r$, which are those of the CP vertices.[45] One may also give a geometrical interpretation: Eq. (7.1), being linear in the correlation variable, represents a hyperplane whose perpendicular distance from the origin of $\xi$ space measures $\delta e$, and whose orientation is determined by the ECI values $V_r$. Hence, to minimize the energy, at fixed values of the ECI, one must translate the $\delta e$ hyperplane parallel to itself as far away as possible from the origin in the negative energy direction, without however losing contact with the CP. The energy minimum, or ground state, is therefore attained at a vertex, or for particular degenerate hyperplane directions, for an edge or face of the CP. We thus recover well-known results of linear programming theory.

[44] T. Kudo and S. Katsura, *Prog. Theor. Phys.* **56**, 435 (1976).
[45] J. M. Sanchez and D. de Fontaine in *Structure and Bonding in Crystals* (M. O'Keeffe and A. Navrotsky, eds.), Vol. II, pp. 117–132, Academic Press, New York (1981).

The two types of ground state searches are *local* and *global*. The former refer to problems for which the ECIs are known; we then need to find that superstructure which minimizes the energy in a certain range of chemical fields. The Danzig simplex algorithm may be used to find the solution in a very efficient manner: a few pivoting operations will converge on the correct (minimizing) vertex of the CP. The global search is far more involved. Here, we want to find all possible ground state superstructures for given types of cluster interactions: first, second, . . . neighbor pairs, triplets, . . . , for example. In other words, we must now enumerate all vertices of the CP. Algorithms exist for vertex enumeration,[46,47] but one is rapidly defeated by the sheer magnitude of the problem. For example, a global ground state search for binary alloys on the fcc lattice including up to fourth neighbor pair interactions would require, in the 13-, 14-point cluster approximation, the construction of a configuration polytope resulting from a set of 842 constraints in a space of 742 dimensions.[48] For such a cluster combination, only *local* searches have been carried out thus far, in particular for an *ab initio* study of fcc-based ground states in Pd-V.[49]

The CP method is plagued by another major difficulty: it may be that some vertices do not correspond to actually realizable crystal structures. Barycentric coordinates may be used[7] as an aid in constructing crystal unit cells by combining cluster configurations in proportions given by the $z_k$ coordinates, but in many actual cases such a procedure leads to internal contradictions. When that happens, it generally means that the set of linear constraints is not complete, hence larger clusters must be taken into account, and a higher dimensionality space must be considered. Unfortunately, there is no guarantee that large enough clusters will ever be found to ensure that all vertices are realizable. Moreover, since the dimensionality of $\xi$ space also increases with the number of constraints, the number of possible vertices also increases, and does so exponentially fast. The problem thus appears to belong to the "NP-complete" class.[50] In some cases, infinitely many constraints must be added, so that a CP with curved faces results, as discovered by Kanamori for the hexagonal network[51] (see also the description in the book by Ducastelle[5]).

[46] M. J. Carrillo, private communication (1978).
[47] T. H. Mattheis and D. S. Rubin, *Math. Oper. Res.* **5**, 167 (1980); M. E. Dyer, *Math. Oper. Res.* **8**, 381 (1983).
[48] G. D. Garbulsky, P. D. Tepesch, and G. Ceder, *Mat. Res. Soc. Symp. Proc.* **291**, 259 (1993).
[49] C. Wolverton, G. Ceder, D. de Fontaine and H. Dreyssé, *Phys. Rev. B* **45**, 13105 (1992).
[50] A. G. Schlijper, *J. Stat. Phys.* **50**, 689 (1988).
[51] J. Kanamori, *Solid State Commun.* **50**, 363 (1984).

Once realizable vertices (structures) have been constructed, we still need to determine the ranges of interactions for which these vertices are ground states. Because the right-hand side of Eq. (7.1) is homogeneous in the $V_r$ interactions, it is permissible to divide through by one of them, say, the first neighbor pair interaction (call it $V_1$), which is generally the largest in magnitude. Two cases must then be examined separately, $V_1 > 0$ (ordering case) and $V_1 < 0$ ("clustering" case), the former usually being the more interesting one. A given vertex will minimize $\delta e$ for $V_r/V_1$ ratios that lie in a cone made up of the normals to CP faces that meet at this vertex.[5,7,45] Thus, the regions in ECI ratio space that correspond to each vertex will form the faces of another convex polytope, which is the *dual* of the original CP.

In all but the most trivial cases, the dimension of the correlation and interaction spaces will be extremely high, so that the corresponding CP and its dual cannot be represented geometrically. Actually, although large clusters may be required to derive the pertinent constraints, it may be sufficient to test the stability of ground state superstructures with respect to only a few cluster interactions, the first few pairs, for example. In that case, one projects the CP vertices onto a subspace of $\xi$ space, spanned by the cluster correlations used in the energy expression alone (these ECI clusters must, however, be subclusters of the largest cluster(s) used in the constraint inequalities). Out of all the projected vertices, only those forming an outer convex envelope must be retained: the inner (eliminated) vertices pertain to structures that cannot be stabilized solely by the interactions retained in the energy formula (7.1). A method for constructing such convex envelopes in $\xi$ subspaces is given in the appendix of Finel's dissertation[7] and in recent work by Ceder and coworkers.[48] The dual polyhedron must also be projected with the affine-projected faces forming a partitioning of the relevant $V_r$ subspace, each cell of which defines a region where the $V_r/V_1$ ratios stabilize the corresponding vertex structure(s). The resulting partitioning provides the required *ground state map*, or *zero-K phase diagram*. An example is given in the next section.

Although the CP-based ground state search is plagued by serious difficulties, it has yielded much valuable information. Among its advantages is the important one that the method is *exact*, up to the range of interactions considered. If, for a given lattice and given interaction scheme, a set of cluster inequalities has been found to produce a CP in multidimensional $\xi$ space such that all its vertices correspond to realizable crystalline superstructures, then the problem is solved completely. In the limit, when a CP with curved faces is found, one expects an infinity of closely related ground states, or polytypoids, with unit cell dimensions increasing with-

out limit in one or more directions. In such cases, it would be possible to prove rigorously that a quasicrystalline state has lower energy than crystalline ones for some ranges of ECI ratios and of concentrations.

No other ground state method can lay claim to comparable rigor, although certain simpler methods may be more convenient to use in practice. The CP concept, moreover, is conceptually pleasing: A state of arbitrary order is characterized by a point in $\xi$ space inside the configuration polyhedron; the larger the dimensionality of the space, the more detailed the description of order in terms of correlation parameters. As temperature or chemical field changes, the $\xi$ vector in correlation space evolves inside the CP; at very high temperature and zero field the representative $\xi$ point lies close to the origin of the $\xi$ coordinate system and evolves towards the periphery of the CP as the temperature is lowered or the chemical field is increased in magnitude. At fixed concentration, the $\xi$ point is confined to a hyperplane normal to the $\xi_1$ axis so that, at absolute zero, the state of the system must reach a vertex of the subspace formed by the intersection of the constant $\xi_1$ hyperplane and the original CP. The fixed-concentration ground states are then given by the vertices of this reduced CP, which, in general, lie on edges of the original one. Equilibrium ground states are thus two-phase mixtures, as required by the Gibbs phase rule applied to two-component systems at constant pressure.

It was Kanamori[40] who originated the method, which he named the *method of the geometrical inequalities*, the derivation of which was explained by Kaburagi and Kanamori[52] and by Ducastelle.[5] The idea of using the C matrix formulation for obtaining the constraints for the linear programming problem was first suggested by Sanchez and the author,[45] and led in a quite straightforward manner to the set of inequalities (7.3), as explained earlier. The simplicity of the method based on cluster probabilities is a desirable feature, but it does not make the problem of determination of structures any easier. It does, however, have the merit of bringing all basic formulations—energy (and other) expansions, ground state analysis, free energy functional (as shown in Section 9)—into a common framework.

The troublesome problem of unrealizable vertices can be avoided by using a straightforward method of arranging $A$ and $B$ (or more) atoms on lattice sites in all possible ways and calculating by means of Eq. (5.6) the energy of each configuration.[48,53] The energies of the various structures may be plotted in multidimensional $\xi$ space, as for the CP method. Then

[52] M. Kabaragi and J. Kanamori, *Prog. Theor. Phys.* **54**, 30 (1975).
[53] L. G. Ferreira, S.-H. Wei, and A. Zunger, *Supercomputer Applications* **5**, 34 (1991).

the representative points are projected onto a subspace of those $\xi$ parameters that correspond to the set of ECIs considered (i.e., those susceptible of stabilizing the ground state structures). The convex hull of those sets of projected points is then constructed, the vertices thereof constituting *conditional* ground states.[48] The term *conditional* is used since, because the size of the maximum allowable ground state unit cell must be specified ahead of time, certain large-cell structures may be missed. Still, despite that simplification, this enumeration method is very computer intensive in terms of both time and storage. The method of concentration waves, favored by Khachaturyan,[54] cannot be used for ground state determination, but is convenient for analyzing the stability of disordered solutions with respect to ordering-type perturbations, as described in I.

In a real alloy system, stable intermetallic compounds are not limited to superstructures of a single lattice: several lattices may be competing in energy, and the ground states of separate lattices must then be compared with one another to pick out the true equilibrium structure. Moreover, certain stable intermetallics are not superstructures of any Bravais lattice. Such structures as the Laves phases, for example, may be regarded in the present context as interlopers, and there is no other theoretical way to account for their presence than by direct computation (by total-energy density-functional methods) of their respective energies.

An application to hcp superstructures of some of the ground state principles presented here is given in the next section, and numerical examples pertaining to the competition between fcc and bcc superstructures are described in Section 15.


## 8. Ground State Examples

Finel's doctoral dissertation[7] and Ducastelle's book[5] contain extensive bibliographies of ground state searches performed by various authors. Among systems investigated by cited authors are the linear chain, the square, rectangular, triangular and honeycomb lattices, simple cubic, fcc, bcc, bct (body-centered tetragonal), and hcp lattices. Tables in Refs. 5 and 7 indicate, in addition to the bibliographic source, the range of interactions considered and whether the ground state determination was complete or not. Of particular interest are the ground state studies performed on fcc, bcc, and hcp lattices. The first such investigations pertaining to first and second neighbor pair interactions in bcc and fcc crystals were performed by Kanamori[40] and, quite independently, by Cahn and cowork-

[54] A. G. Khachaturyan, *The Theory of Structural Transformations in Solids*, Wiley, New York (1983).

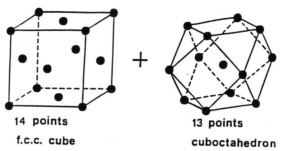

**14 points**

**f.c.c. cube**

**13 points**

**cuboctahedron**

FIG. 2. Clusters for 13-, 14-point approximation on fcc lattice.

ers.[41] Results were reported in I. These studies were extended, for example, to fifth-neighbor pair interactions in bcc by Finel and Ducastelle[5,42] and to fourth-neighbor pair interactions in fcc by Kanamori and Kakehashi.[55] The latter ground state search was incomplete in the sense that first-neighbor pair interactions of ordering type ($V_1 > 0$) were always assumed to be larger in magnitude than other EPIs. In this way, the Japanese authors discovered about 40 ground states (fcc ordered superstructures), whereas only 10 exist for the case of first- and second-neighbor EPI only.[40,41] If the restriction of dominant $V_1$ is lifted, the problem becomes nearly intractable: In a recent study, Garbulsky et al.[48] found that the CP method, based on a 10-point cluster formalism, produced 323,188 vertices in a $\xi$ space of 85 dimensions, with 90 constraints. The enumeration method applied to first- through fourth-neighbor EPIs (with less than 20 atoms per unit cell) produced 468 structures,[48] i.e., an order of magnitude more than those found under the $V_1$-dominant restriction. The Cu-Pt prototype, which was missing from the Kanamori-Kakehashi analysis,[55] was recovered. Of course, additional fcc superstructures may be stabilized by multiatom interactions: By using the tetrahedron-octahedron cluster combination, which spans first- and second-neighbor pairs, Sanchez and the author[45] were able to construct six new structures (out of 26 distinct vertices), which were later rediscovered by an enumeration method.[53] Local ground state searches (given the $V_n$ interactions, find the minimizing vertices) are less demanding than global searches, hence larger clusters may be used, for example the 13-, 14-point cluster combination on the fcc lattice.[49] For this cluster combination (Fig. 2), the number of vertices is not known but must be prohibitively large for global search purposes. The 13-, 14-point cluster combination has been used for CVM calculations, as described in Section 9, where other cluster combinations are shown as well.

[55] J. Kanamori and Y. Kakehashi, J. Phys. Colloq. (Paris) **38**, C7-274 (1977).

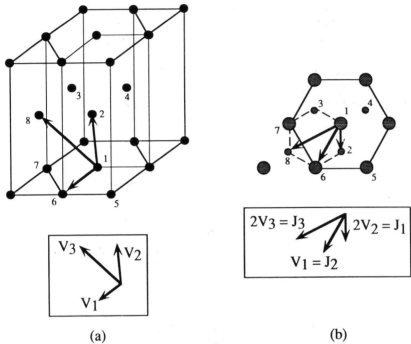

FIG. 3. Interactions and clusters used in hcp calculations: (a) shown in perspective, $V_1$, $V_2$, $V_3$ are first three effective pair interactions; (b) shown in projection, $J_1$, $J_2$, $J_3$ are equivalent two-dimensional EPIs [R. McCormack et al., Phys. Rev. B **48**, 6767 (1993)].

Lower dimensionality lattices are also of interest. For example, the complete and exact solution of the linear chain with convex interactions[56,57] [$V_n < (V_{n+1} + V_{n-1})/2$, all $n$] has been used to predict low-temperature ground states of oxygen ordering in the $YBa_2Cu_3O_x$ (YBCO) superconductor.[58] Two-dimensional lattice ground states were used for determining surface structures and also for YBCO ordered superstructures stabilized by asymmetric first- and second-neighbor EPIs.[59] It was also pointed out by Bichara et al.[60] that the ground states of the hexagonal lattice with anisotropic interactions could be deduced from the ground states of the honeycomb lattice with up to third-neighbor interactions.

[56] J. Hubbard, Phys. Rev. B **17**, 494 (1978).
[57] V. L. Pokrovsky and G. V. Uimin, J. Phys. C: Solid State Phys. **11**, 3535 (1978).
[58] D. de Fontaine, G. Ceder, and M. Asta, Nature **343**, 544 (1990).
[59] L. T. Wille and D. de Fontaine, Phys. Rev. B **37**, 2227 (1988).
[60] C. Bichara, S. Crusius, and G. Inden, Physica B **182**, 42 (1992); Physica B **179**, 221 (1992).

The hcp ground state problem is now briefly described in the light of some very recent results.[12] The hcp structure is shown in Fig. 3(a) and in Fig. 3(b) as a [0001] projection. Effective pair interactions $V_1$, $V_2$, and $V_3$ are also indicated. First-neighbor interactions are isotropic if $V_1 = V_2$, anisotropic otherwise. Previous studies[60-62] considered the first three EPIs; here, $V_3$ is neglected but multiatom interactions out to (asymmetric) first neighbors are included. Although the hcp structure is made up of close-packed planes, as are the $\langle 111 \rangle$ planes of fcc, the hcp stacking is $ABAB \ldots$, that in fcc is $ABCABC \ldots$. It would appear, therefore, that at first-neighbor level, the relevant clusters to be used in hcp would be the same as those of the regular tetrahedron approximation in fcc (see the next section). Actually, the hcp case, because of lower symmetry, requires both the (1,2,3,4) tetrahedron and the basal plane regular triangle (1,6,7). This tetrahedron-triangle (TT) combination was used to derive the cluster inequality (7.3) in the present case. A group theory code[11] provided the required C matrix elements. The resulting configuration polyhedron in the TT combination is formed by 16 hyperplanes in a space of seven dimensions.[12] Vertices were enumerated by means of an algorithm proposed by Matheiss;[47] 18 *distinct* ones were found (those that could not be deduced from one another by $A/B$ atom interchange).

Only 7 out of the 18 vertices were found to be physically realizable. Corresponding structures are listed in Table I(b), including the pure $A$ (or $B$) hcp structure itself. Table I(a) likewise lists common fcc-based ordered structures with pertinent information to be used later (Section 16). In these tables, one finds, successively, short symbols to be used in Section 16, stoichiometric formulas, ordering wave indices (see article I), international table space-group symbols, Strukturbericht designation (if known), conventional unit cell vectors (in units of parent structure), and ratios of lattice parameters corresponding to the ideal close-packed geometries. Open and filled symbols in the structure projections indicate $A$ and $B$ atoms, respectively; large and small circles correspond to atoms separated by one-half of the unit cell vector in the direction normal to the projection plane; half-filled circles indicate sites for which the occupancy alternates along the direction normal to the projection plane. An hcp-based ordered structure not indicated in Table I(b) is the $A_4B_3$ structure, not found in earlier studies, which did not take multiatom interactions into consideration. Its structure is given in projection in Fig. 4. As explained earlier, a ground state map can be derived by constructing the dual to the configuration polyhedron. By projecting the facets of the dual

[61] A. K. Singh and S. Lele, *Phil. Mag. B* **65**, 967 (1992); *Phil. Mag. B* **64**, 275 (1991).
[62] A. K, Singh, V. Singh, and S. Lele, *Acta Metall. Mater,* **39**, 2847 (1991).

TABLE I(A). DESCRIPTION OF FCC- AND HCP-BASED ORDERED STRUCTURES

| FCC | F1 | F2 | F3 | F4 | F5 | F6 |
|---|---|---|---|---|---|---|
| A | $A_3B$ | $A_3B$ | $A_2B$ | AB | AB | AB |
| $\langle 0\,0\,0\rangle$ | $\langle 1\,0\,0\rangle$ | $\langle 1\,1/2\,0\rangle$ $\langle 1\,0\,0\rangle$ | $\langle 1\,1/2\,0\rangle$ | $\langle 1\,0\,0\rangle$ | $\langle 1\,1/2\,0\rangle$ | $\langle 1/2\,1/2\,1/2\rangle$ |
| | | | | | | |
| $Fm\bar{3}m$ A1 | $Pm\bar{3}m$ $L1_2$ | $I4/mmm$ $D0_{22}$ | $Immm$ — | $P4/mmm$ $L1_0$ | $I4_1/amd$ — | $R\bar{3}m$ $L1_1$ |
| $[1\,0\,0]$ | $[1\,0\,0]$ | $[1\,0\,0]$ | $[1\,0\,0]$ | $[1\,0\,0]$ | $[1\,0\,0]$ | $\frac{4-\delta}{6\delta^{2/3}}\left[1\ \frac{4+2\delta}{4-\delta}\ 1\right]$ |
| $[0\,1\,0]$ | $[0\,1\,0]$ | $[0\,1\,0]$ | $\frac{1}{\sqrt{2}}\left[0\ \frac{b}{a}\ -\frac{b}{a}\right]$ | $[0\,1\,0]$ | $[0\,1\,0]$ | $\frac{4-\delta}{6\delta^{2/3}}\left[1\ 1\ \frac{4+2\delta}{4-\delta}\right]$ |
| $[0\,0\,1]$ | $[0\,0\,1]$ | $\left[0\,0\,\frac{c}{a}\right]$ | $\frac{1}{\sqrt{2}}\left[0\ \frac{c}{a}\ \frac{c}{a}\right]$ | $\left[0\,0\,\frac{c}{a}\right]$ | $\left[0\,0\,\frac{c}{a}\right]$ | $\frac{4-\delta}{6\delta^{2/3}}\left[\frac{4+2\delta}{4-\delta}\ 1\ 1\right]$ |
| — | — | $\frac{c}{a}=2$ | $\frac{b}{a}=\frac{1}{\sqrt{2}}$ $\frac{c}{a}=\frac{3}{\sqrt{2}}$ | $\frac{c}{a}=1$ | $\frac{c}{a}=2$ | $\delta=1$ |

75

TABLE I(B). DESCRIPTION OF FCC- AND HCP-BASED ORDERED STRUCTURES

| HCP | H1 | H2 | H3 | H4 | H5 |
|---|---|---|---|---|---|
| A | $A_3B$ | $A_2B$ | AB | AB | AB |
| $\langle 0\,0\,0 \rangle$ | $\langle 1/2\,0\,0 \rangle$ | $\langle 1/3\,1/3\,0 \rangle$ | $\langle 1/2\,0\,0 \rangle$ $\langle 0\,0\,0 \rangle$ | $\langle 0\,0\,0 \rangle$ | $\langle 1/2\,0\,0 \rangle$ |
| $P6_3/mmc$ | $P6_3/mmc$ | $Cmcm$ | $Pmmn$ | $P\bar{6}m2$ | $Pmma$ |
| A3 | $D0_{19}$ | — | — | — | $B19$ |
| $[1\,0\,0]$ | $[2\,0\,0]$ | $[0\,-3\,0]$ | $\sqrt{\tfrac{8}{3}}[0\,0\,1]$ | $[1\,0\,0]$ | $\sqrt{\tfrac{8}{3}}[0\,0\,1]$ |
| $[0\,1\,0]$ | $[0\,2\,0]$ | $\sqrt{3}\left[\tfrac{b}{2a}\,\tfrac{b}{a}\,-\tfrac{1}{a}\,0\right]$ | $\sqrt{\tfrac{8}{3}}\left[0\,-\tfrac{b}{a}\,0\right]$ | $[0\,1\,0]$ | $\sqrt{\tfrac{8}{3}}\left[0\,-\tfrac{b}{a}\,0\right]$ |

76

$$\begin{bmatrix} 0 & 0 & \frac{c}{a} \end{bmatrix} \qquad \begin{bmatrix} 0 & 0 & 2\frac{c}{a} \end{bmatrix} \qquad \begin{bmatrix} 0 & 0 & 3\frac{c}{a} \end{bmatrix} \qquad \sqrt{\frac{8}{9}}\begin{bmatrix} 2\frac{c}{a} & \frac{c}{a} & 0 \end{bmatrix} \qquad \begin{bmatrix} 0 & 0 & \frac{c}{a} \end{bmatrix} \qquad \sqrt{\frac{8}{9}}\begin{bmatrix} 2\frac{c}{a} & \frac{c}{a} & 0 \end{bmatrix}$$

$$\frac{c}{a}=\sqrt{\frac{8}{3}} \qquad \frac{c}{a}=\sqrt{\frac{2}{3}} \qquad \frac{b}{a}=\sqrt{\frac{1}{3}} \qquad \frac{b}{a}=\sqrt{\frac{3}{8}} \qquad \frac{c}{a}=\sqrt{\frac{8}{3}} \qquad \frac{b}{a}=\sqrt{\frac{5}{8}}$$

$$\frac{c}{a}=\sqrt{\frac{8}{27}} \qquad \frac{c}{a}=\sqrt{\frac{9}{8}} \qquad \frac{c}{a}=\sqrt{\frac{9}{8}}$$

The first, second, and third rows give the label, stoichiometry, and special point ordering wave of each structure, respectively. The (001) and (100) projections of the hcp- and fcc-based structures, respectively, are given in the fourth row. Filled (unfilled) circles indicate $B$ ($A$) atoms, and half-filled circles indicate sites for which the occupancy alternates along the direction normal to the projection plane. Large and small circles correspond to atoms separated by one-half of the unit cell vector in the direction normal to the projection plane. The fifth and sixth rows give the space group symmetry and Structurbericht designation, where one exists, for each structure, respectively. In the seventh row the conventional unit cell vectors $\mathbf{a}_1$ (on top of the row), $\mathbf{a}_2$ (in the middle), and $\mathbf{a}_3$ (on the bottom) are given in terms of the unit cell vectors of the parent structure. The values of the lattice parameter ratios corresponding to "ideal" close-packed geometries are given in the eighth row.

77

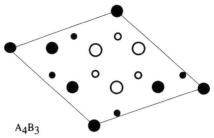

Fɪɢ. 4. Basal plane projection of hcp-derived $A_4B_3$ structure. Filled circles: $A$ atoms; open circles: $B$ atoms. Large circles denote atoms in basal plane; small circles in plane just above (or below) [R. McCormack *et al.*, *Phys. Rev. B* **48**, 6767 (1993)].

onto the $\mu$ (chemical potential difference)–$V_2$ plane, with values normalized by $V_1$ ($>0$), one obtains the zero-K phase diagram of Fig. 5, a modified version of that obtained by Bichara *et al.*[60] The domain of existence of the $A_4B_3$ structure is shown symbolically as a double line: actually, that domain has zero extension in EPI space since the structure can only be stabilized by multiatom interactions; otherwise, $A_4B_3$ is degenerate in energy with a mixture of hcp and $AB$(II) [designated as $H3$ in Table I(b)] structures.

The $A_3B_2$ domain is shown shaded since the corresponding vertex is one of the unrealizable ones. In fact, that is the domain of stability of an infinite set of long-period structures, as predicted in the corresponding two-dimensional honeycomb case of Kanamori.[51] That the stability domain of such an infinite set of structures must be that of an unrealizable vertex is explained as follows:[12] If all vertices were realizable, then all ground state structures would have been found and, since the analysis is exact and complete at that level of interactions, no additional structure, finite or not, could be found. Hence, at least one unrealizable vertex must exist in order to obtain the predicted "devil's staircase." The somewhat paradoxical difference, which is evidenced between hcp and fcc ground states, even at this level of interactions, is discussed further in Ref. 12, where the hcp ground state search has been extended to include all cluster interactions that span the *nnn* distance (multiplet interactions including the octahedron and all of its subclusters). The search yielded 172 vertices, of which 32 physically realizable ground states could be constructed, with stoichiometric formulas $A$, $AB$, $A_2B$, $A_3B$, $A_5B$, and $A_4B_3$. Of these structures, six are stabilized by *nn* pairs, and eight by *nnn* pairs; the remaining 18 structures require multiplet interactions for their stability. Some large unit cells were found, with sizes far outdistancing the interaction range.

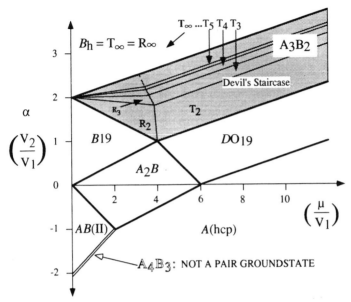

FIG. 5. Tetrahedron-triangle ground state map for the hcp structure. Structures are described in Table I(b) [$AB$(II) (in figure) is structure H3 in Table I(b)]. Structure $A_4B_3$, depicted in Fig. 4, cannot be stabilized by pair interactions alone. Vertex $A_3B_2$ is not realizable; its region of stability (shaded) corresponds to an infinite set of long-period superstructures [adapted by R. McCormack (unpublished) from C. Bichara, S. Crusius, and G. Inden, *Physica B* **182,** 42 (1992)].

## V. Configurational Free Energy

After the ground state superstructures for a given parent lattice have been determined, it is of interest to examine how phase equilibrium between structures may evolve as a function of temperature and average concentration. Such is the purpose of this section, which describes the derivation, from known ECIs, of temperature-composition phase diagrams. A possible procedure for doing so is the Monte Carlo simulation technique. In keeping with cluster methods, however, let us confine our attention only to the CVM,[3] a variational technique that has proved to be both efficient and reliable. A generalized BW or mean-field model was presented in I, along with the method of concentration waves, which is equivalent to it. The BW approach was shown to be quantitatively inaccurate for the case of clustering systems (ferromagnetic transition), although qualitatively acceptable. For ordering systems (antiferromagnetic transition), the failure of the BW model was even more pronounced in

the sense that calculated mean-field phase diagrams were not even *qualitatively* correct, whereas the CVM calculation provided a very good likeness of Cu-Au-type phase diagrams.[1,63] The earlier review presented the pioneering applications of the CVM to phase diagram calculations; it was stated in I that the CVM appeared to hold much promise for reliable and accurate calculations of phase equilibria. That promise has now materialized: Better approximations have been derived in the CVM hierarchy of successive approximations, and efficient numerical algorithms have been developed. It is true that the CVM is, at heart, a mean-field variational procedure, which means that predicted critical exponents turn out to have classical values. However, good estimates of nonclassical exponents may be obtained from the CVM by application of the so-called "coherent anomaly method" (CAM).[64,65]

### 9. CVM FORMALISM

Much of the impetus for recent CVM development has been brought about by the work of Sanchez and coworkers.[23,66-68] An elegant and general derivation of the CVM formalism was given by Sanchez, Ducastelle, and Gratias,[2] and reviewed by Ducastelle,[5] Finel,[6] Ceder,[11] and the present author.[69] Compact derivations of the CVM[8] and of the path probability method (PPM),[70] the kinetic counterpart[71] of the CVM, have appeared recently. The derivation given in I was not sufficiently general, so that a brief account of a more satisfying formulation is given in the following subsections. For didactic purposes, a simple approach is presented, one that is based on the work of Morita[72] in modified form.[73,74]

[63] D. de Fontaine and R. Kikuchi in "Applications and Phase Diagrams in Metallurgy and Ceramics" (C. G. Carter, ed.), NBS Special Publication 496, p. 999 (1978).

[64] M. Suzuki, *J. Phys. Soc. Japan* **55**, 4205 (1986); M. Suzuki, M. Katori, and X. Hu, *J. Phys. Soc. Japan* **56**, 3092 (1987); M. Katori and M. Suzuki, *J. Phys. Soc. Japan* **56**, 3113 (1987).

[65] K, Wada and N. Watanabe, *J. Phys. Soc. Japan* **58**, 4358 (1989); *J. Phys. Soc. Japan* **59**, 2610 (1990).

[66] J. M. Sanchez and D. de Fontaine, *Phys. Rev. B* **21**, 216 (1980); J. M. Sanchez and D. de Fontaine, *Phys. Rev. B* **25**, 1759 (1982).

[67] J. M. Sanchez, D. de Fontaine, and W. Teitler, *Phys. Rev. B* **26**, 1465 (1982).

[68] T. Mohri, J. M. Sanchez, and D. de Fontaine, *Acta Metall.* **33**, 78 (1985).

[69] D. de Fontaine, in *Alloy Phase Stability* (G. M. Stocks and A. Gonis, eds.), pp. 177-203, Kluwer Academic Publishers, Dordrecht (1989).

[70] F. Ducastelle, *Progr. Theor. Phys. (Japan)*, in press.

[71] R. Kikuchi, *Prog. Theor. Phys.* **535**, 1 (1966).

[72] T. Morita, *J. Math. Phys.* **13**, 115 (1972).

[73] D. de Fontaine, unpublished.

[74] Marcel H. F. Sluiter, "On the First Principles Calculation of Phase Diagrams," Ph.D. Dissertation, University of California, Berkeley (1988) (unpublished).

Let us start with the variational principle as expressed in Section 2: we need to minimize the free energy functional $F[\rho]$ of Eq. (2.5) subject to the constraint on the density function $\rho(\vec{\sigma})$ given by Eq. (2.1). For an infinite system it is of course generally not possible to find the correct distribution of configurations that solves the problem exactly. One might at first think of expanding $\rho(\vec{\sigma})$ into cluster functions, as in Eq. (4.17), retaining only a small number of terms, the coefficients of which would be determined variationally. That procedure cannot be followed, however, for the simple reason that the series (4.17) is not convergent, although Eq. (4.19), pertaining to finite-size clusters, contains a finite number of terms and is thus correct.

What is required is a cumulant expansion of the entropy $S$, as suggested by Morita.[72] Consider a very large system of $N$ lattice points, whose density function may be written $\rho_N$. For $N$ large, the expression

$$S_N = k_B \sum_{\{\sigma_N\}} \rho_N(\sigma_N) \ln \rho_N(\sigma_N), \qquad (9.1)$$

will surely provide a very good approximation to the exact configurational entropy $S$ of Eq. (2.4) when $N$ becomes large. Let us then consider successive partial entropies for a single point $(p)$, a pair $(p,q)$, . . . , a cluster $(\alpha)$, . . . , defined as follows:

$$S_p = -k_B \sum_{\sigma_p} \rho_1(\sigma_p) \ln \rho_1(\sigma_p)$$

$$S_{p,q} = -k_B \sum_{\sigma_p, \sigma_q} \rho_2(\sigma_p, \sigma_q) \ln \rho_2(\sigma_p, \sigma_q)$$

$$\vdots \qquad\qquad (9.2)$$

$$S_\alpha = -k_B \sum_{\sigma_\alpha} \rho_\alpha(\vec{\sigma}_\alpha) \ln \rho_\alpha(\vec{\sigma}_\alpha).$$

Let us then try to express $S_\alpha$ for arbitrary cluster $\alpha$ as a sum of subcluster partial entropies by means of successive steps, starting with the pair $p,q$:

$$S_{pq} = S_p + S_q + G_{pq}, \qquad (9.3a)$$

where $G_{pq}$ is a suitable correction term, as yet undetermined. For a triplet of points we have, likewise,

$$S_{pqr} = G_p + G_q + G_r + G_{pq} + G_{qr} + G_{rp} + G_{pqr}, \qquad (9.3b)$$

where the symbol $G$ has been used instead of $S$ for the point terms. This procedure may be pursued until a sufficiently large cluster is reached, the $K$'th one, say, with

$$S_{\alpha_K} = \sum_p G_p + \sum_{p,q} G_{pq} + \sum_{p,q,r} G_{pqr} + \ldots + G_{\alpha_K}. \qquad (9.4)$$

The basic CVM assumption, a reasonable one, is the following: for large enough *maximal cluster* $\alpha_K$, we assume that correlations over distances spanned by $\alpha_K$ become negligibly small. It therefore follows that correction terms $G_\beta$ for $\beta$ "larger" than $\alpha_K$ may be neglected in the superposition approximation of Eq. (9.4). Such arguments turn out to be valid even for rather small clusters except, of course, near second-order transitions where correlations extend to infinity. Hence, depending on the nature and "size" of the maximal cluster $\alpha_K$ retained in the CVM approximation chosen, we expect very accurate results for general phase equilibrium properties except very near a second-order transition.

To proceed further, let us consider the (finite) system as a large cluster of $N$ sites and let us generalize Eq. (9.4) to the partial entropy $S_N$. This expression for $S_N$ should contain correction terms corresponding to all possible points, pairs, triplets, etc., of lattice points in the entire system. The CVM simplification is now introduced: All $G_\beta$ for clusters "larger" than $\alpha_K$ are neglected, i.e., for clusters which are not $\alpha_K$ nor any of its subclusters. In the remaining expression, all clusters and subclusters of $\alpha_K$ (there may be more than one maximal cluster, $\alpha_K$, $\alpha_{K1}$, . . . , which are not subclusters of each other) are grouped into *orbits*, in such a way that all clusters that are equivalent under the space group symmetry operations of the crystal form the orbit of any member of that set. If each cluster type (for example, $n$'th neighbor pair, nearest-neighbor triplet, quadruplet, etc.) is given an *orbit index* of, say, $r$, then the (finite) entropy of Eq. (9.1) may be written symbolically and approximately as

$$S_N \cong N \sum_{r=1}^{K} m_r G_r, \qquad (9.5)$$

where, as in Eq. (7.1), $m_r$ is the number of clusters of type $r$ per lattice site, the approximation coming from truncating the expansion in the correction terms of Eq. (9.4) to a maximal cluster(s) of type $K$ ($K_1$, . . .). The correction terms themselves are derived from Eq. (9.4), which may be rewritten, taking cluster symmetry into account, as the sum over orbits

$$S_r = N \sum_{j=0}^{r-1} m_{r-j}^r G_{r-j}, \tag{9.6}$$

in which the integers $m_n^r$ are the number of subclusters of type $n$ in the cluster of type $r$ with, of course, $m_r^r = 1$. This linear triangular system can be solved recursively for the $G_r$ terms, which are then inserted into expression (9.5). The entropy per lattice site may thus be expressed in terms of the known partial entropies $S_r$, in the $\alpha_K$ approximation, as

$$\frac{S_N}{N} \equiv s = -\sum_{r=1}^K \gamma_r S_r = k_B \sum_{r=1}^K \gamma_r \sum_{\sigma_r} \rho_r(\sigma_r) \ln \rho_r(\sigma_r), \tag{9.7}$$

where the so-called Kikuchi-Barker coefficients $\gamma_r$ are given by the successive formulas

$$\gamma_K = -m_K$$

$$\gamma_{K-1} = -m_{K-1} - m_{K-1}^K \gamma_K.$$

In general,

$$\gamma_r = -m_r - \sum_{j=r+1}^K m_r^j \gamma_j \qquad r = 1, \dots, K,$$

$$\tag{9.8}$$

derived initially and independently by Barker[75] and by Hijmans and de Boer.[76] This convenient algebraic formulation of the CVM is completely equivalent to the original, more geometric derivation of Kikuchi.[3] A very compact and elegant treatment and derivation of the Barker formulas has also been given by Inden and Pitsch[6] and more recently by Finel.[8]

The coefficients $\gamma_r$ may be positive, negative, or they may vanish. In particular, the $\gamma_r$ coefficients vanish for all clusters of type $r$ that are not overlap figures of the maximal cluster $\alpha_K$ with a cluster in its orbit or with another cluster of nonvanishing $\gamma$ coefficient.[2,5] As an example of the application of Eqs. (9.8), consider the two-dimensional square lattice in the square CVM approximation, meaning that the maximal cluster is the $nn$ square $K = r = 4$. Its subclusters are the right triangle ($r = 3$), the square's diagonal ($r = 2$), the edge ($r = 1$), and the point ($r = 0$). The first column of Table II gives the $m_r$ values for the disordered phase,

[75] J. A. Barker, *Proc. Roy. Soc.* **A216**, 45 (1953).
[76] J. Hijmans and J. de Boer, *Physica* **21**, 471 (1955); *Physica* **22**, 408, 429 (1956).

D. DE FONTAINE

TABLE II. GEOMETRICAL PARAMETERS FOR CVM CALCULATIONS IN APPROXIMATION OF 2-DIMENSIONAL SQUARE LATTICE

| INDEX $r$ | CLUSTER | $m_r$ | 0 | 1 | $j = 2$ | 3 | 4 | $\gamma_r$ |
|---|---|---|---|---|---|---|---|---|
| 0 | • | 1 | 1 | 1 | 2 | 3 | 4 | $-1$ |
| 1 | •—• | 2 |  | 1 | 0 | 2 | 4 | 2 |
| 2 | ╱ | 2 |  | $m_r^j$ | 1 | 1 | 2 | 0 |
| 3 | ◿ | 4 |  |  |  | 1 | 4 | 0 |
| 4 | □ | 1 |  |  |  |  | 1 | $-1$ |

Index $r$ designates cluster (here, all subclusters of the square), $m_r$ is number clusters of type $r$ per lattice point, $m_r^j$ is the number of subclusters of type $r$ per cluster of type $j$, and the $\gamma_r$ are the Kikuchi-Barker coefficients.

and the $m_j^r$ values are given by the indicated triangular matrix. Application of the Barker formulas (9.8) yields successively $\gamma_4$ through $\gamma_0$ (last column). As expected, since the triangle and diagonal clusters are not overlap figures of other clusters, their $\gamma$ coefficients vanish.

Intuitively, one expects that progressively larger clusters will improve the CVM approximation. This is not necessarily true in the sense that the approximation does not improve monotonically with the number of points in the maximal clusters; one must also consider the geometry of the cluster. Some progress has been made recently concerning the optimal choices of CVM clusters, following earlier ideas of Schlijper.[77] For instance, Finel[7,78] has proposed criteria based on the proper factorization of the density function $\rho(\vec{\sigma})$.

In a different approach, Vul and the author[79] have shown that a good CVM entropy approximation could be obtained if the approximate and exact entropies deviated as little as possible near the point in $\xi$ space where they are known to be equal, i.e., at the "center" of the configuration polyhedron (see Section 7) where all correlations vanish, that is to say, for the completely disordered state of equiatomic concentration. If the requirement is imposed that the Taylor's expansions of exact and approximate entropies about that point coincide out to third-order terms,

[77] A. G. Schlijper, J. Stat. Phys. 40, 1 (1985); Phys. Rev. B 31, 609 (1985).
[78] A. Finel, in Alloy Phase Stability (G. M. Stocks and A. Gonis, eds.), pp. 269–279, Kluwer Academic Publishers, Dordrecht (1989).
[79] David A. Vul and Didier de Fontaine, Mat. Res. Soc. Symp. Proc. 291, 401–406 (1993).

then a convenient geometrical criterion can be derived.[79] For a given lattice, let us denote the level of CVM approximation by the largest pair spacing $p$ included in the maximal cluster. *The optimal maximal cluster(s) to be used must be such that no point may be added to it that will form new pairs of spacing less than or equal to* p. Figure 6 shows the cluster combinations arrived at by the application of this rule for various lattices and for various pair spacings (or coordination shells) $p$. For example, consider the square lattice [Fig. 6(a)]. If one were to select the right triangle as maximal cluster for the case $p = 2$ (diagonal), it would be possible to add a fourth point, completing the square, which would form with the initial triangle two $nn$ pairs ($p = 1$). Hence, the triangle does not satisfy the criterion, but the square does. Most cluster combinations shown in Fig. 6 do indeed correspond to maximal clusters, which were known from numerical calculations to provide good CVM approximations. To the sets of Fig. 6 one may add two cluster combinations that give excellent CVM approximations and satisfy the criteria of both Finel[7,78] and Vul:[79] for the bcc lattice, the 9-point cube (the bcc cube itself) plus the octahedron, and for fcc, the 13-, 14-point combination shown in Fig. 2 and the quadruple tetrahedron shown in Fig. 7.

The free energy functional per atomic site may now be obtained from the relation $f = e - Ts$ with the entropy $s$ of Eq. (9.7) and where $e$ is the energy, suitably normalized, taken from either Eq. (5.3) (for multicomponent systems), from Eq. (5.6) (more specifically for binaries), or in the symmetry-adapted form of Eq. (7.1). For the latter case, the normalized free energy functional may thus be written as follows:

$$f = \sum_{r'} m_{r'} V_{r'} \xi_{r'} - k_B T \sum_{r=1}^{K} \gamma_r \sum_{\sigma_r} \rho_r(\sigma_r) \ln \rho_r(\sigma_r), \qquad (9.9)$$

with coefficients $\gamma_r$ given by the recursion formulas (9.8). Expression (9.9) is the fundamental one for CVM calculations, the one that, according to the variational principle stated in Section 2, must be minimized to obtain an optimal expression for the equilibrium free energy. As written, it is a hybrid expression containing a summation over correlations $\xi_{r'}$ in the energy term (or over cluster functions $\langle \phi_{r'}^s \rangle$ for multicomponents) and summations over partial densities, or cluster probabilities $\rho_r$ in the entropy term. The entropy summation must in principle contain all clusters up to the maximal cluster(s) large enough to contain the largest cluster effective interaction used in the energy. Hence, in Eq. (9.9), limits (1 to $K$) are indicated explicitly in the entropy summation, although several of the Kikuchi-Barker coefficients $\gamma_r$ may be identically zero. Limits on the

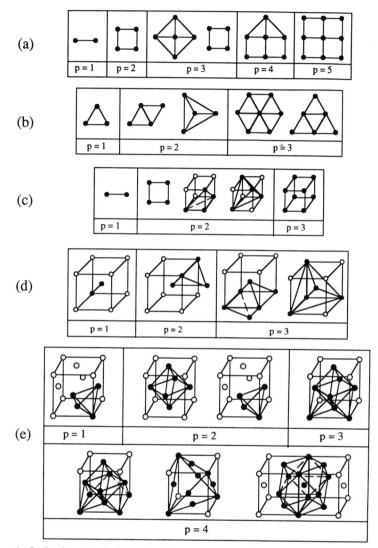

FIG. 6. Optimal maximal cluster for (a) square, (b) triangular, (c) simple cubic, (d) body-centered cubic, and (e) face-centered cubic lattices shown for increasing level of approximation $p$, denoting range of pair interactions: $p = 1$ nearest neighbor, $p = 2$ next nearest neighbor, etc. Sites of the maximal cluster are indicated by solid circles [D. A. Vul and D. de Fontaine, *Mat. Res. Soc. Symp. Proc.* **291,** pp. 401–406 (1993).

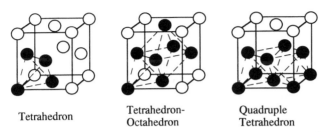

|                | Tetrahedron-  | Quadruple     |
| Tetrahedron    | Octahedron    | Tetrahedron   |

FIG. 7. Tetrahedron, tetrahedron-octahedron, and quadruple tetrahedron clusters used for fcc CVM calculations.

energy summation are left unspecified since all subclusters of $K$ (and $K$ itself) need not be used. One should also keep in mind, following the discussion of Section 1, that the ECIs $V_r$ may be regarded as having been derived from the "free energy" $\Psi$ of Eq. (1.4), and could thus depend on temperature or volume. This complication will not be examined further here, although an example will be given in Section 16.

It is a matter of choice regarding which variables to use to minimize expression (9.9): One may either rewrite the energy term as a function of cluster probabilities $\rho_r$ or rewrite the entropy term as a function of cluster correlations. The former approach has led to the natural interaction method of Kikuchi.[80] Since the probabilities $\rho_r$ are not independent, it is necessary to introduce appropriate Lagrange multipliers to take care of the various self-consistency constraints. The second approach, that of minimizing with respect to correlations $\xi_r$, was introduced by Sanchez and the author;[23] the advantage of minimizing with respect to correlations $\xi_r$ is that these variables form a linearly independent set, so that no Lagrange multipliers are required. Then the derivative of $f(\xi)$ is taken with respect to the set $\{\xi\}$. The relationship between the cluster probabilities $\rho_r$ and correlations $\xi_{r'}$ is a linear one, as given by Eq. (4.19). In the binary case, Eq. (7.2) is the relevant one, featuring the all-important configuration matrix, which embodies the geometrical (or crystallographic) information pertaining to the problem at hand. In Section 7, it was mentioned that, when fairly large clusters are used, the determination "by hand" of the C matrix elements becomes intractable, so that one must rely on appropriate computer codes that take space-group symmetry considerations into account. Such codes may also yield, as by-products, the calculation of the $m_r$ and $m_j^r$ coefficients used in Eqs. (9.8) and hence the automated calculation of the relevant Kikuchi-Barker coefficients.[11]

[80]R. Kikuchi, *J. Chem. Phys.* **60**, 1071 (1974).

The only practical limitation then is that brought about by the infamous combinatorial explosion already touched on: With clusters containing more than about 10 points, the number of independent cluster correlations with respect to which the minimization must be carried out becomes exceedingly large, exponentially so.

The minimization produces a set of nonlinear algebraic equations that must be solved simultaneously, usually by a Newton-Raphson (NR) technique, the initial guess for the iterative solution being obtained by writing cluster correlations as superpositions of point correlations. At low temperatures, the Hessian matrix of the NR method tends to become ill conditioned, a problem that may be remedied by various numerical procedures.[7,74,81]

An intimate relationship exists between ground state analysis (Section 7) and the CVM calculations. To see this, consider the problem of minimizing the CVM free energy functional with respect to the configuration variables $\xi_\alpha$. In principle, one might consider all clusters $\alpha$, of a given number of points and geometry, as distinct, throughout the whole lattice. At each temperature and concentration, the CVM should converge to the correct long-range ordered state in which a large number of the $\alpha$ clusters would have identical correlation values $\xi_\alpha$. In this approach, however, the total number of $\alpha$ clusters would be prohibitively large, hence one must first determine the relevant long-range ordered state(s), for which the crystallographically distinct clusters are known. Hence, it is necessary first to perform a ground state analysis in order to determine what candidate ordered structures to expect; in other words, to determine how to split up the lattice into *sublattices*. For each choice of sublattices, the orbits of clusters split into suborbits, the C matrix elements are altered, and so are the $\gamma_r$ coefficients in the sense that the number of clusters (of type $r$, say) per site will change. All of these modifications can be handled automatically by the C matrix group theory computer codes. In a sense, then, knowledge of the long-range ordered state to which the system will converge, at given $T$ and $c$, is theoretically not required, but in practice is essential in order to reduce drastically the number of independent variables. It may also be necessary to look beyond the strict ground states, i.e., those for which the energy is an absolute minimum on the lattice considered: Some other ordered states, having energy close to the minimum, may become entropy stabilized at higher temperatures, and thus need to be envisaged as well. Otherwise it may be required, for kinetic considerations, to investigate metastable equilibria for their own sake.

[81] J. M. Sanchez, unpublished.

10. PROTOTYPE PHASE DIAGRAMS

From the preceding, it is clear where the "cluster variation method" gets its name; perhaps *cluster variational method* might be more apt. This second version of the name is used by some. Once the parent lattice has been selected, along with the maximal cluster(s) (and the subclusters), the C matrix and the $\gamma_r$ coefficients are calculated, and the minimization can proceed by numerical techniques, provided that the ECIs ($V_r$) have been calculated. Methods for calculating the $V_r$ are described briefly in Section VI, but for now, let us focus attention on so-called *prototype* (or *model*) phase diagrams, i.e., those pertaining to phase equilibria between superstructures of a given lattice, with values of simple $V_r$ ratios chosen phenomenologically.

The simplest interaction scheme is obviously that of first-neighbor pair interaction ($V_1$) only; it was briefly covered in I. Two cases are of interest: $V_1 < 0$ leading to phase separation (ferromagnetic analog) and $V_1 > 0$ leading to ordering (antiferromagnetic analog). For $V_1 < 0$, at $c = 0.5$, the transition is of second-order type, and the CVM critical temperature $T_c$ is calculated by setting to zero the Hessian determinant (second derivatives of $f$ with respect to the independent $\xi$ variables). Values of $T_c$ (normalized by $|V_1|/k_B$) were tabulated in I for different cluster approximations on the fcc lattice. These values are reproduced here in Table III, which now includes some more recent results, namely, those pertaining to the quadruple tetrahedron (Fig. 7), and the 13-, 14-point clusters[11] (see Fig. 2). It is seen that the high-temperature expansion result[82] is approached to within less than 1% by the best CVM (fcc) approximation attempted to date. The order of the transition is also correctly predicted. The BW (mean-field) approximation overestimates the transition by about 20%.

For $V_1 > 0$ at $c = 0.2$, ground state analysis predicts that the $L1_0$ superstructure of fcc will be stable at low temperature (see I for a description of fcc and bcc ordered structures, and also Table I). The CVM correctly predicts the $L1_0$ transition to be first order, whereas the BW method gives a second-order transition whose transition temperature is about two to three times too high. The best CVM approximation (third column of Table III), however, differs from the "best known" by only 0.5%. Of course, first-order transition temperatures are not determined by the vanishing of the Hessian determinant of the free energy, but by matching the appropriate thermodynamic potentials of the two phases in equilibrium.

[82] Sati McKenzie, *J. Phys. A* **8**, L102 (1975).

TABLE III. TRANSITION TEMPERATURE ON FCC LATTICE WITH $nn$ INTERACTION $V_1$ ACCORDING
TO VARIOUS APPROXIMATIONS

| APPROXIMATION | $kT/12|V_1|$    $V_1 < 0$<br>SEGREGATION | $kT/V_1$    $V_1 > 0$<br>$L1_0$ ORDERING |
|---|---|---|
| Bragg-Williams | 1.00000 | 4.0000 |
| Tetrahedron | 0.83545 | 1.8933 |
| Double tetrahedron | 0.84045 | |
| Tetrahedron-octahedron | 0.83394 | 1.81042 |
| Double tetrahedron-octahedron | 0.82999 | |
| Quadruple tetrahedron | 0.82659 | 1.7497 |
| 13 + 14 point | 0.82291 | |
| "Best known" | 0.81638 | 1.741–1.751 |

Normalized transition temperatures for both $V_1 < 0$ (segregation or ferromagnetic case) and $V_1 > 0$ (ordering or antiferromagnetic case) at concentration $c = 0.5$ (or zero field). "Bragg-Williams" designates the mean-field approximation (point CVM approximation), other values are CVM-derived with indicated cluster approximation (see Figs. 2 and 7 for cluster representations) [G. Ceder, Ph.D. Dissertation, University of California, Berkeley (1991)].

For the two-dimensional Ising ferromagnet, Ceder[11] was able to extend the types of CVM approximations suggested earlier by Kikuchi and Brush,[83] and obtained transition temperatures that differed from the exact one by about 2%. Depending on the level of approximation, i.e., the type of maximal cluster selected, the CVM can provide remarkably accurate results, far better than it is usually given credit for.

Of greater interest than critical (or transition) temperatures at zero field (chemical or magnetic) is the determination of the full temperature–concentration phase diagrams, which may also be represented as temperature-field diagrams. The CVM phase diagram construction proceeds as follows. The free energy function is minimized with respect to the independent configuration variables to obtain the best possible estimate of the equilibrium free energy for a given cluster approximation for a given phase. Free energy curves are then plotted as a function of concentration $c$, and common tangents to the curves are constructed wherever necessary. Alternatively, one may look for the intersection of grand potential curves (free energy minus chemical field $\mu$ times its conjugate variable) for various $T$, as a function of $\mu$. For binary systems one then plots the loci of two-phase equilibrium lines and isolated three-phase equilibria. For ternary systems, one generally constructs isothermal sections; some examples were given in I.

[83] R. Kikuchi and S. G. Brush, *J. Chem, Phys.* **47**, 195 (1967).

Review I came out shortly after the CVM had been applied for the first time to (prototype) phase diagram calculations. Hence, only a few results were reported,[63,84-86] those pertaining to ordering reactions on the fcc lattice with $V_1$ ($>0$) as the only pair interaction considered. Use of the CVM in that case was an absolute necessity, since the Bragg-Williams approximation gave unacceptable results, as explained in I, because of the phenomenon of frustrated nearest-neighbor ordering on the fcc lattice. Soon thereafter more complicated problems of greater practical interest were tackled, such as ordering on the fcc lattice with first- and second-neighbor EPIs.[23,66-68] The nature of the resulting phase diagrams in that case now depends uniquely on the ratio $\alpha = V_2/V_1$ of the two EPIs. The maximal cluster in the CVM approximation now had to include both $nn$ and $nnn$ pair interactions, which meant that one had to go beyond the tetrahedron to the tetrahedron-octahedron (TO) combination [see Fig. 6(e), $p = 2$]. This extension was well worth the effort since most of the frequently observed fcc alloy superstructures can be stabilized by $V_1$ and $V_2$ interactions only, at least formally, as shown by the early ground state analyses of Kanamori[40] and of Cahn and coworkers.[41] The first CVM phase diagram in the fcc TO approximation was derived in 1980,[66] a very late date indeed considering that fcc superstructure equilibria with $nn$ and $nnn$ EPIs are of such importance for the general study of alloy phase equilibria. The derived phase diagrams were fairly complex. One particularly interesting aspect of this study was the following: Types of ground states, types of transitions, multicritical points, extent of phase regions, etc., were seen to evolve continuously as the value of the interaction ratio was varied. In particular, for $V_2/V_1 < -1$, ordered superstructures gave way to a miscibility gap because, for large negative $V_2$, the simple cubic (sc) sublattices that make up the fcc parent lattice tend to decouple and the ordering on any one of them is governed almost entirely by the negative $V_2$, which is a first-neighbor interaction in the (decoupled) sc lattices.

Problems of degeneracy abound even in these relatively simple cases, and have been studied in detail by Finel[7,87] and Ducastelle.[5] These authors examined the controversies that surround the $V_1$-only fcc phase diagram, particularly in light of comparisons with Monte Carlo simula-

[84] R. Kikuchi and C. M. Van Baal, *Scripta Metall.* **8**, 425 (1974).

[85] R. Kikuchi and D. de Fontaine, in *Applications and Phase Diagrams in Metallurgy and Ceramics* (C. G. Carter, ed.), 967, NBS Special Publication 496 (1978).

[86] R. Kikuchi, D. de Fontaine, M. Murakami, and T. Nakamura, *Acta Metall.* **25**, 207 (1977).

[87] A. Finel and F. Ducastelle, *Europhys. Lett.* **1**, 135, and erratum **1**, 543 (1986).

tions. Interested readers are referred to these studies, and also to the review by Inden and Pitsch[6] for further details. Ordering on the bcc lattice poses fewer problems because of the absence of frustration, at least for equilibria dominated by large first-neighbor interactions. A study of CVM calculations in bcc was performed by Sluiter et al.[88] in which reference to previous literature can also be found.

Since fcc- and bcc-based prototype phase diagrams have been presented so completely elsewhere, especially in Ducastelle's book,[5] it is not necessary to cover the material again here. Instead, for the purpose of giving the reader some examples of prototype CVM phase diagrams, let us consider the case of ordering on the hcp parent structure. The hcp case is a bit more complicated than the fcc or bcc cases since there are now two "atomic" sites per primitive (hexagonal) unit cell. The results to be presented are due to McCormack et al.[12] and are an extension to nonzero temperatures of the hcp ground state analysis of Section 8. For simplicity, only first-neighbor interactions were considered, including both in-basal-plane ($V_1$, pair 1,6 in Fig. 3) and out-of-plane ($V_2$, pair 1,2) interactions, which, in the hcp case, are distinct by symmetry. The only parameter that enters the CVM prototype phase diagram calculations is the interaction ratio $\alpha = V_2/V_1$, with $V_1 > 0$. For illustration, four diagrams are presented (Fig. 8), corresponding to ratios $\alpha = 1.0, 0.8, 0.5,$ and 0.0. With concentration-independent EPIs, the phase diagrams are symmetric about the central composition, so only the left portions of the diagrams are shown. The *isotropic case*, $\alpha = 1$, is the hexagonal counterpart of the fcc calculation with (positive) *nn* interaction only.[1,89] For all other ratios ($\alpha \neq 1$, anisotropic cases), the hcp phase diagrams will differ significantly from the fcc; even the nature of the ordered superstructures may be different. The case $\alpha = 0$ corresponds to a complete decoupling of the basal planes from each other; the resulting calculated phase diagram should then be identical to that obtained for a two-dimensional triangular lattice.

Three maximal clusters ($\alpha_K$) were used: the *nn* tetrahedron (1,2,5,6 in Fig. 3), the triangle (1,6,7) and the octahedron (1,2,3,8,7,6). This choice gives rise to two possible CVM approximations: the tetrahedron-triangle (TT) and the tetrahedron-octahedron (TO). The TT approximation suffices if only $V_1$ and $V_2$ are considered, although even in that case, the TO approximation should be more accurate, i.e., it will improve the entropy approximation. For the hcp parent structure, both the tetrahedron (1,2,5,6) and the triangle (1,6,7) must be included in a valid cluster ap-

[88] M. Sluiter, P. E. A. Turchi, Fu Zezhong, and D. de Fontaine, *Physica A* **148**, 61 (1988).
[89] C. M. Van Baal, *Physica* **64**, 571 (1973).

proximation, since, unlike the fcc situation, even in the isotropic case, triangle (1,5,6), which is a subcluster of the tetrahedron, and triangle (1,6,7), are not equivalent by symmetry. Hence, both must be included in the TT approximation for hcp. It follows that, even in a first-neighbor approximation, the TT approximation "knows" about the lower symmetry of hcp as compared to fcc. Thus, even the "isotropic" hcp $nn$-only phase diagram should differ, albeit slightly, from the fcc counterpart. Differences were indeed observed,[90] very small but significant.

Results for $\alpha = 1$ are shown in Fig. 8(a) for the TT approximation (heavy lines), for the TO approximation (fine lines), and for Monte Carlo simulations[91] (dashed lines). As expected, the calculated curves are practically indistinguishable from those obtained in the fcc case for equivalent approximations. According to the ground state diagram of Fig. 5, the only two hcp superstructures stable for $V_1 = V_2$ are the $B19$ and $D0_{19}$ structures. Ordered phase $B19$ corresponds to the fcc superstructure $L1_0$, and $D0_{19}$ corresponds to $L1_2$. Also as expected, the TO approximation does somewhat better than the TT approximation, compared to the Monte Carlo calculation. At triple-point equilibria, both CVM approximations deviate appreciably from the Monte Carlo result. This discrepancy was observed for the fcc case as well, although the interpretation of Monte Carlo results at low temperature near $L1_0–L1_2$ coexistence are still somewhat controversial. As emphasized by Ducastelle,[5] the first-neighbor-only case is really more difficult to treat than that which includes higher pair interactions that break the troublesome degeneracy.

Figures 8(b) and 8(c) show phase diagrams calculated by the TT CVM approximation (heavy lines) for the anisotropic cases $\alpha = 0.8$ and 0.5, respectively. The ground state map of Fig. 5 indicates that for $0 < \alpha < 1$, in addition to the $B19$ and $D0_{19}$, the $A_2B$ phase [structure $H2$ in Table I(b)] should become stable at intermediate chemical fields, for stoichiometric composition $c = 0.33$. It is seen in Fig. 8(b) that the $A_2B$ congruent ordering temperature (first-order) is considerably lower than those for $B19$ and $D0_{19}$ phases, while the transition temperatures of the latter phases are reduced with respect to their values for isotropic interactions. Monte Carlo results[91] (dashed lines) are qualitatively similar, although the $A_2B$ phase field is seen to be very broad and, curiously, far from stoichiometry. In Fig. 8(c) ($\alpha = 0.5$), the $A_2B$ transition temperature has

[90] R. Kikuchi and J. W. Cahn, in *User Applications of Phase Diagrams* (L. Kaufmann, ed.), pp. 19–24, ASM International, Materials Park, OH (1987); J. W. Cahn, private communication.

[91] S. Crusius and G. Inden, *Proc. Int. Symp. on Dynamics of Ordering in Condensed Matter* (S. Komura and H. Furukawa, eds.), p. 139, Plenum Press, New York (1988).

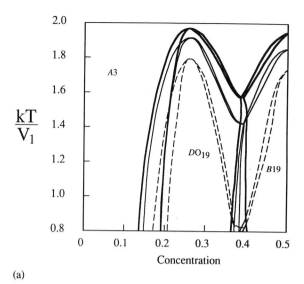

(a)

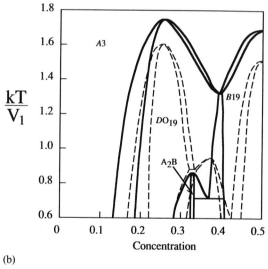

(b)

Fig. 8. Prototype hcp phase diagrams calculated by the CVM for various values of the ratio $\alpha = V_2/V_1$ of *nnn* to *nn* effective pair interactions ($V_1$ always positive). (a) $\alpha = 1$, heavy lines: tetrahedron-triangle (TT) CVM approximation; fine lines: TO approximation; dashed lines: Monte Carlo (MC) simulation. (b) $\alpha = 0.8$, TT approximation (heavy lines); MC (dashed lines). (c) $\alpha = 0.5$, TT approximation. (d) $\alpha = 0$, TT approximation (heavy lines), MC (dashed lines) [R. McCormack *et al.*, *Phys. Rev. B* **48**, 6767 (1993); MC results are from S. Crusius and G. Inden, *Proc. Int. Symp. Dynamics of Ordering in Condensed Matter* (S. Komura and H. Furukawa, eds.), Plenum Press, New York (1988)].

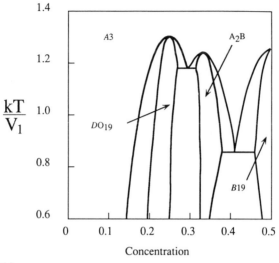

(c)

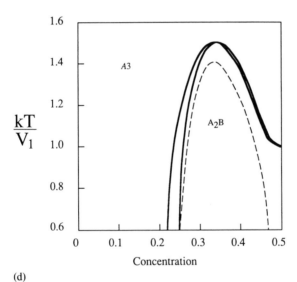

(d)

Fɪɢ. 8—(Continued)

increased even more, and the transition temperatures of $B19$ and $D0_{19}$ have dropped so that all three are now almost at the same level. Finally, for $\alpha = 0$ [Fig. 8(d)], the $A_2B$ phase, which has no fcc counterpart, is the only ordered superstructure remaining. Since the hcp basal planes are now fully decoupled, the resulting phase diagram should be identical to that for the two-dimensional triangular lattice.[5] Monte Carlo simulation results are available for this case[91] and are shown as dashed lines. Here, the discrepancy between Monte Carlo and CVM approximations is more severe, as might be expected for a two-dimensional system. Because of basal plane decoupling, TO and TT CVM approximations give the same result (heavy lines) and incorrectly predict a second-order transition at nonzero temperature at $c = 0.5$; transitions at all other concentrations are weakly first order. In a more rigorous treatment, all transitions should be second order, and that at $c = 0.5$ should lie at the absolute zero of temperature.

It is of course difficult to match the behavior of real systems by using only two EPIs. Nevertheless, prototype systems, such as the one described here, are interesting to study in that they illustrate basic properties in a simple way and point to general trends. For example, the hcp example given here shows clearly that, by varying only a single dimensionless parameter, $V_2/V_1$, resulting equilibria evolve *continuously* from the (isotropic) fcc analog featuring $D0_{19}$ and $B19$ structures (of $A_3B$ and $AB$ stoichiometry, respectively) to the "decoupled" case featuring phase $C49_h$ of stoichiometry $A_2B$.

Comparing CVM and Monte Carlo calculations in a general way would require a separate study, although certain general rules may be deduced from simple examples such as the ones discussed here. Somewhat facetiously, it may be stated that the CVM is precise but not accurate and the Monte Carlo is accurate but not precise, in the sense that the CVM can compute free energies and transition temperatures to high precision, but the results may be inaccurate (off their true values) by the very nature of the variational method employed. Conversely, the Monte Carlo procedure is imprecise because of numerical scatter and finite size problems (the CVM always operates at the thermodynamic limit) but accurate, since the correct partition function itself is, in principle, evaluated. Another difference: the CVM is algebraically intensive but computationally very fast, the inverse being true for Monte Carlo simulations. In that respect the CVM has the advantage: The algebra, though heavy for large clusters, needs to be done only once. Once the computer code is written, the method is very efficient—about 100 times more so than the Monte Carlo.

In terms of accuracy, one must distinguish carefully between different

levels of CVM cluster hierarchies. In the prototype phase diagrams examined in this section with rather modest-sized clusters, CVM first-order transition temperatures lie about 5% to 10% above those obtained by Monte Carlo calculations. Eutectoid (triple-point) temperatures are off by quite a bit more, at least in the isotropic case, but that may be because these particular three-phase equilibria are practically critical endpoints, hence those reactions are close to being of second-order nature. In the two-dimensional case ($V_2 = 0$), the CVM phase diagram is qualitatively incorrect although the predicted weakly first-order transition temperatures, except near $c = 0.5$, are only about 7% away from the Monte Carlo's second-order transition line.

If only first-order reactions are present—and in real alloy systems second-order transitions are very rarely encountered—CVM-derived phase diagrams can be as accurate as those derived by Monte Carlo methods. For example, Finel[8] has used a *mixed CVM* to reexamine the difficult case of *nn* ordering on the fcc lattice, which cannot be handled even qualitatively with point MF approximations. Since no second-order reactions are expected, it is permissible to use different cluster schemes for ordered and disordered phases: The disordered phase required large maximal clusters (the 13-, 14-point cluster, see Fig. 2), but the ordered phases, whose long-range order parameters are close to saturation, can be handled by the simpler TO cluster approximation. We can see in Fig. 9 that the phase diagram (temperature versus chemical field $h$, both normalized by the positive *nn* interaction $J_1$), calculated by mixed CVM (solid lines) and Monte Carlo (dashed lines) methods are virtually indistinguishable. Recent studies[92] have also shown that, at low temperatures, CVM phase boundaries join smoothly with those determined by low-temperature expansions. The reader is referred to work by Binder[93] for further discussions concerning the comparison between CVM and Monte Carlo results. That author concludes that the CVM often does very well indeed but that point mean-field (BW) methods cannot be used in quantitative studies even if, as in the case of bcc lattices, ordering reactions are not frustrated.

The interesting possibility of combining both methods, the CVM and the Monte Carlo, also exists as suggested recently by Schlijper *et al.*[94] Since the MC method is "accurate" and the CVM "precise," it is appealing to use the latter's analytic formulas to obtain well-defined values for the configurational entropy and free energy, but to obtain cluster

[92] G. Ceder, private communication (1992).
[93] K. Binder, in *Festkörperprobleme* (*Advances in Solid State Phys.*) (P. Grosse, ed.), Vol. 26, p. 133, Vieweg, Braunschweig (1986).
[94] A. G. Schlijper, A. R. D. Vandbergen, and B. Smit, *Phys. Rev. A* **41**, 1175 (1990).

D. DE FONTAINE

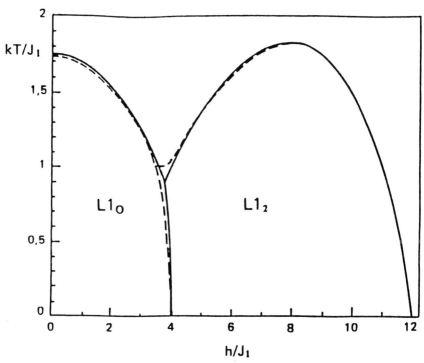

FIG. 9. Phase diagram (reduced temperature $k_B T/J_1$ versus reduced field $h/J_1$) for the fcc lattice with positive *nn* pair interaction $J_1$; solid lines: mixed CVM; dashed lines: MC simulation [A. Finel, to be published in *Statics and Dynamics of Alloy Phase Transformations* (P. E. A. Turchi and A. Gonis, eds.), NATO ASI Series, Plenum Press, New York].

probabilities $\rho_\alpha(\sigma)$ and correlation functions directly by Monte Carlo simulation. An additional advantage of such a procedure is that the free energy does not have to be minimized: The "simulated" correlation function values are simply inserted into the CVM formulas at the desired cluster approximation level. Encouraging results have been obtained,[94] particularly for two-dimensional problems, and it seems that this idea of combined MC-CVM calculation merits further investigation.

Purists may object to the use of the CVM, but its inaccuracies are usually negligible compared to those introduced by attempts to calculate ECIs from first principles: The CVM configurational entropy may be off by 5%, say, but the ECI values *may* be off by 50% or more. Hence, for first-principles thermodynamic calculations, refining the statistical mechanical calculations beyond the CVM approach makes little sense at present. The major effort to be undertaken should clearly be directed at

improving the quantum mechanical aspects of the problem along with vibrational entropy calculations.

Before summarizing the status of first-principles ECI calculations, however, let us briefly mention some results pertaining to $k$ space (or concentration wave) formalisms, which were developed after the publication of the author's earlier review.

## 11. CONCENTRATION WAVES

The term *concentration waves* has been used by various authors in a variety of ways, thereby leading to some confusion regarding the meaning of the term. The simplest meaning is reasonable enough: Given an atomic configuration (consisting of $+1$ and $-1$ occupation variables associated with each lattice site in a binary system, say), one simply computes its Fourier coefficient amplitudes over a *supercell;* the concentration waves are then simply the harmonic components of the configuration. (Here, and in the remainder of this section, the Fourier transforms of a given function, represented by a lowercase letter, will be denoted by the corresponding uppercase symbol, $k$ representing the wave vector.) It is always possible to transform any set of $+1$ and $-1$ values into a set of concentration waves, an operation that involves nothing more profound than a change of basis. What matters is what one does with the configuration in question, now expressed in Fourier (or $k$) space, and whether it is possible, conversely, to manipulate concentration waves in such a way as to preserve the $+1, -1$ constraint. Equivalently, one may ask the following question: For treating compositional order and disorder, is it better to choose, as basis functions, a set of harmonic concentration waves or a set of cluster functions? A decade or so ago the answer might have been "concentration waves," today it is surely "cluster functions." One important reason for the shift in emphasis is that it is easier to impose the $+1, -1$ site occupation constraint in the cluster formalism (by means of the configurational polyhedron concept, see Section 7) than it is in the Fourier formalism. The cluster approach is more difficult to handle, however, so that the concentration wave approach may still be used whenever the cluster formalism becomes intractable. That happens, for example, when effective interactions are definitely long range, leading to long-wavelength concentration modulations that can only be described by extremely large clusters.

The concentration wave method is at its best whenever the configuration-dependent functions of interest can be regarded approximately as quadratic forms in the configuration variables. It follows, as is seen

shortly, that concentration waves of different **k** vectors do not interact and may thus be considered independently. But then, local "site" concentration may take any value between $+1$ and $-1$, which in turn implies mean-field behavior featuring, as it were, the interaction of average atoms. Such an approach is approximately valid for systems deviating only slightly from the homogeneous state, with local fluctuations neglected. More specifically, therefore, the *concentration wave method* implies a perturbation treatment of an artificial uniform configuration, which, applied to electronic structure calculations for disordered alloys, leads to the original (**k** space) generalized perturbation method (GPM) of Ducastelle and Gautier[95] and to the $S^{(2)}$ method of Györffy and Stocks.[96] Applications to configurational free energy instabilities in the mean-field (BW) context were covered in detail in I and in Khachaturyan's book.[54] In both works, but particularly in the latter, one may also find concentration wave applications to coherent elasticity problems.

Following Sanchez,[97] let us now show how to extend the **k** space perturbation method to the CVM formalism. The free energy (9.9), being an analytic function of the multisite correlations $\xi_r$, may be expanded in these linearly independent variables as

$$f = f_0 + f_1 + f_2 + \dots, \tag{11.1}$$

where each term groups like powers of correlation deviations $\delta\xi_r$. Actually, the index $r$ may refer not just to a cluster type in a binary system but also to a given component (in multicomponent systems) or to a given sublattice, for structures with more than one site per unit cell. The index $r$ should then be regarded as a collective index designed to handle these eventualities, which need not be specified further for present purposes.

Stability analysis considers only small variations $\delta\xi_r$ about some reference equilibrium (not necessarily stable) state so that the Taylor's expansion (11.1) may be terminated at the second-order term. Since the first-order term vanishes at equilibrium, the second variation of the unperturbed state may be expressed as the quadratic form

$$\delta^2 f \equiv f_2 = \frac{N}{2} \sum_{r,r'} \sum_{p,p'} f_{rr'}(p,p')\delta\xi_r(p)\delta\xi_{r'}(p'), \tag{11.2}$$

where $f_{rr'}$ is the second derivative with respect to $\delta\xi_r$, $\delta\xi_{r'}$, at the indicated points $p$ and $p'$, of the free energy. Points $p$ and $p'$, which denote the

[95] F. Ducastelle and F. Gautier, *J. Phys.* **F6**, 2039 (1976).
[96] B. L. Györffy and G. M. Stocks, *Phys. Rev. Lett.* **50**, 374 (1983).
[97] J. M. Sanchez, *Physica* **111A**, 200 (1982).

origin of clusters $r$ and $r'$, are considered to belong to the same Bravais lattice. This means that identical clusters on different sublattices are denoted by different $r$ indices.[97] The free energy coefficient $f_{rr'}$ must depend only on the difference of coordinates at $p$ and $p'$ and therefore has the translational symmetry of the Bravais lattice. Hence, a first diagonalization may be accomplished by Fourier transforming over space:

$$\delta^2 f = \frac{N^2}{2} \sum_{r,r'} F_{rr'}(\mathbf{k})\,\delta X_r(\mathbf{k})\,\delta X_{r'}(-\mathbf{k}),  \qquad (11.3)$$

where $F_{rr'}$ and $\delta X_r$ are, respectively, the Fourier transforms of $f_{rr'}(p,p')$ and $\delta\xi_r(p)$. Expression (11.3) may be further diagonalized in cluster space by an orthogonal transformation of cluster variables to obtain:

$$\delta^2 f = \frac{N^2}{2} \sum_r \Lambda_r(\mathbf{k})\,|\delta Y_r(\mathbf{k})|^2,  \qquad (11.4)$$

where $\Lambda_r$ denotes the eigenvalues of the Hessian matrix $\mathbf{F}$, and $Y_r$ are normal cluster modes.

The thermodynamic system under investigation is unconditionally stable toward small perturbations if the quadratic form (11.4) is positive definite for all cluster mode variations, i.e., if all eigenvalues $\Lambda_r$ are positive for all possible wave vectors $\mathbf{k}$. The condition for breakdown of stability is that at least one eigenvalue becomes negative, with marginal stability specified by the vanishing of the determinant of the matrix of the quadratic form

$$\det[\,\mathbf{F}(\mathbf{k})] = 0.  \qquad (11.5)$$

Matrix $\mathbf{F}$ is a function of temperature and concentration so that, for each possible wave vector, condition (11.5) represents a locus in phase diagram space. The locus lying at the highest values of temperature is of particular interest since, for that wave vector, $\mathbf{k}_0$, say, the system will just begin to become unstable as temperature is lowered. By definition, this locus is called the *spinodal,* which may be of the clustering or ordering type. The spinodal concept was described in detail in I. What is new here is that spinodal loci can now be constructed from much more realistic CVM free energies and be plotted on CVM-derived phase diagrams. The labor involved is correspondingly greater, of course, but is indispensable if correct ordering spinodals, compatible with correct phase dia-

grams, are to be obtained, particularly in "frustrated" systems (ordering on fcc, for example).

Let $\Lambda_s$ be the smallest eigenvalue, for given physical parameters, and for a certain range of $\mathbf{k}$ vectors. Then the ordering instability will be found for that $\mathbf{k}$ vector, $\mathbf{k}_0$, which gives $\Lambda_s(\mathbf{k})$ its minimum value, i.e., for $\nabla_k\Lambda_s = 0$, provided of course that $\Lambda_s(\mathbf{k}_0)$ has all three principal curvatures positive at that $\mathbf{k}_0$ wave vector. The extremum condition can occur in principle anywhere in the first Brillouin zone, but at certain points, extrema of any $\mathbf{k}$ space function must be present by symmetry reasons, regardless of the particular values of physical parameters. For Bravais lattices, these *special points* (SP) are found where two or more symmetry elements in $\mathbf{k}$ space intersect at a point, as first described by Landau and Lifshitz.[98]

No attempt was made in I to go beyond the search for SPs in Bravais lattices. For general crystal structures, the problem is more complex, and was described in detail by Sanchez et al.[99] for the case of EPIs of arbitrary range, for structures with an arbitrary number of sublattices, and for any one of the 230 three-dimensional crystallographic space groups. First, it is necessary to construct the space group of the $\Lambda_r(\mathbf{k})$. As was proved in Ref. 99, the required space group is the direct product of the translational group of the reciprocal lattice with the point group of the crystal structure, to which the inversion must be added if it is not already present. Such a group is analogous to the Patterson symmetry group of the crystal, except that the *reciprocal* lattice rather than the direct one is involved. There are 24 Patterson symmetry groups in three dimensions, which are all possible centered symmorphic groups, i.e., those groups that contain no glide planes or screw axes. The procedure for determining special points in general crystal structures is then the following: Look up in the International Tables for Crystallography the relevant centered symmorphic group, obtained by performing the direct product as explained earlier. Then find the Wyckoff positions with fixed coordinates (where symmetry elements intersect at a point). These are the required SP. Table I in Ref. 99 lists all 24 Patterson groups (classified according to the reciprocal space Bravais lattice) and the associated SP in coordinates of the reciprocal lattice. In I, only the SP of the cubic groups Fm3m (fcc) and Im3m (bcc) were given, but with an unfortunate misprint for the former, i.e., for the lattice reciprocal to the bcc. The correct SPs for the bcc direct (fcc reciprocal) lattice are 000, 100, 1/2 1/2 0, 1/2 1/2 1/2.

[98] L. D. Landau and I. M. Lifshitz, *Statistical Physics,* 2nd ed., Pergamon Press, Oxford (1969).

[99] J. M. Sanchez, D. Gratias, and D. de Fontaine, *Acta Crystall.* **A38**, 214 (1982).

It was noted by Ducastelle,[5] however, that in structures with more than one site per primitive unit cell, certain SP determined by the symmetry argument just described may not necessarily correspond to extrema of a $\mathbf{k}$ space function. In such cases, the SP are termed *irrelevant*. The reader is referred to Ducastelle's book for a detailed analysis of the hcp case where such complications arise. The foregoing considerations may of course be applied to two-dimensional structures, as was done, for example, in the case[100] relating to special point instabilities for quasi-two-dimensional ordering of oxygen ions in the superconducting oxide $YBa_2Cu_3O_z$.

The inverse of the Hessian matrix $\mathbf{F}(\mathbf{k})$ is the susceptibility matrix $\chi(\mathbf{k})$, which is positive definite above (in temperature) the highest stability limit and whose determinant diverges at an instability. In the equilibrium regime, away from any instability, the fluctuation-dissipation theorem states that the expectation value of products of cluster wave amplitudes can be related to the susceptibility matrix components according to the formula

$$\langle X_r(\mathbf{k}) X_{r'}(-\mathbf{k}) \rangle = Nk_B T \chi_{rr'}(\mathbf{k}). \tag{11.6}$$

In particular, the point-point correlation gives rise to the pair correlation fluctuation

$$\langle \sigma(p)\sigma(p + q) \rangle - \langle \sigma(p) \rangle \langle \sigma(p + q) \rangle = \xi_{2,q} - \xi_1^2, \tag{11.7}$$

whose Fourier transform is, properly normalized, the short-range order intensity $I_{SRO}$. By Eq. (11.6) we then have

$$I_{SRO}(\mathbf{k}) \equiv \langle |X_1(\mathbf{k})|^2 \rangle = Nk_B T \chi_{11}(\mathbf{k}). \tag{11.8}$$

In the BW approximation, valid in the limit of infinitely high temperatures, Eq. (11.8) yields the familiar Krivoglaz-Clapp-Moss (KCM) formula, since the matrix $\mathbf{F}$ then reduces to the single element

$$\mathbf{F}(\mathbf{k}) = 2V(\mathbf{k}) + \frac{k_B T}{c(1 - c)}, \tag{11.9}$$

where $V(\mathbf{k})$ is the Fourier transform of the effective pair interactions. The BW-KCM approximation was discussed in detail in I for both binary

[100] D. de Fontaine, L. T. Wille, and S. C. Moss, *Phys. Rev. B* **36**, 5709 (1987).

and multicomponent systems. In the case of structures with a basis (the hcp structure, for example), Eq. (11.8) must be modified to contain $n^2$ point-point susceptibilities $\chi_{ij}$.[7,16] An example of $I_{SRO}$ calculated for the Cd-Mg system is given in Section 16; other examples are given by Finel.[8]

Equation (11.8) is formally exact. Unfortunately, except for some very special cases, it is not possible to find exact closed-form expressions for the free energy $f(\xi)$ nor, consequently, for the susceptibility matrix. It therefore follows that, in most cases, $I_{SRO}(\mathbf{k})$ is *not* equal to the Fourier transform of pair fluctuations (11.7). Only for the one-dimensional Ising chain, for which the CVM free energy is exact, can one obtain by Eq. (11.8) the exact SRO intensity.[97] Although the KCM approximation, derived from Eq. (11.9), is very convenient and has been used frequently for analyzing experimental diffraction data, it suffers from a number of drawbacks. For instance, the locus $T_0$ at which $I_{SRO}(\mathbf{k}_0)$ diverges in the KCM approximation is the BW instability limit, or spinodal, which is incompatible, in many cases, with correctly constructed phase diagrams. Also, the integral of $I_{SRO}$ over the Brillouin zone, obtained from Eq. (11.8), with (11.9) for inverse susceptibility, does not remain constant as temperature is varied. This failure of the *conservation of integrated SRO intensity* is not attributable to Eq. (11.8) itself, but to the approximations used in calculating the susceptibility $\chi_{11}$. Clapp and Moss[101] introduced a variable normalization parameter to force conservation of integrated intensity, but that procedure is not really justified theoretically. With CVM approximations for $\chi_{11}$, one can come much closer to conservation of intensity, as Sanchez has shown[97] for the case of two-dimensional lattices, and Mohri *et al.*[102] for fcc crystals. In one dimension (Ising chain), the conservation condition is obeyed rigorously in the CVM.

The BW approximation leading to Eq. (11.9) clearly shows that the $\mathbf{k}$ dependence of the inverse susceptibility is contained entirely in the energy contribution $V(\mathbf{k})$, not in the entropy. In the CVM approximation, the $\mathbf{k}$ dependence is contained in both energy and entropy, thus giving the contours of constant $\chi_{11}^{-1}(\mathbf{k})$ an intrinsic temperature dependence. The $I_{SRO}(\mathbf{k})$ contours calculated in the CVM approximation tend to give sharper peak profiles than in the KCM approximation, as shown, for example, in the case of ordering in an fcc model binary alloy with first- and second-neighbor EPIs.[102] Although detailed comparisons of KCM and CVM approximations for actual alloy systems are not widely available, it appears that the determination of EPIs from experimental SRO intensity gives better fits to the data with fewer EPIs than with the KCM

[101] P. C. Clapp and S. C. Moss, *Phys. Rev.* **142**, 418 (1966).
[102] T. Mohri, J. M. Sanchez, and D. de Fontaine, *Acta Metall.* **33**, 1463 (1985).

approximation.[31] Another cluster approximation for SRO intensity has been proposed recently by Masanskii and Tokar.[103] This *gamma expansion method* (GEM) has been tried out on various systems[104] and was found to perform quite a bit better than the KCM. Comparison of the GEM with the CVM was not attempted, however.

In I, a stability limit for the $\langle 100 \rangle$ ordering wave was plotted on a CVM-calculated Cu-Au phase diagram, in the tetrahedron approximation, with ECIs obtained by fitting.[63] At the $Cu_3Au$ stoichiometric composition, the calculated ordering spinodal was found to lie approximately 170 degrees below the first-order transition (see Fig. 40 of I). Experimentally, it is difficult to determine the position of the ordering spinodal relative to the ordering transition: it is necessary to ascertain at what temperature $I_{SRO}(k_0)$ diverges, which requires that diffuse intensity be measured on samples maintained below the equilibrium transition temperature for a time long enough to perform measurements, but sufficiently short that evolution to the stable phase does not occur. Despite the practical difficulties, Ludwig *et al.*[105] were able to carry out such experiments on $Cu_3Au$ by means of synchrotron x-radiation with very rapid data acquisition. These authors concluded that the temperature difference between the spinodal and the first-order transition was approximately $\Delta T = 35$ K, a much smaller difference than that predicted by the earlier CVM calculation. However, a more recent CVM calculation in the tetrahedron-octahedron and quadruple tetrahedron approximations yielded values of $\Delta T \cong 30$ K in close agreement with the experimental value.[106] It appeared that the instability temperature was much more sensitive to the type of cluster approximation than the transition temperature itself. This may be because the instability $T_0$ is determined mathematically by the vanishing of the Hessian determinant, which would be the condition for a classical second-order transition if there were no intervening first-order reaction, and it is known that high cluster approximations are required in the CVM to predict second-order transitions accurately. This does not mean that changing cluster approximations will eventually bring the difference $\Delta T$ down to zero: It appears that larger cluster approximations for the $Cu_3Au$ calculation actually tend to stabilize $\Delta T$ around the value given by the tetrahedron-octahedron approximation.

Recent results have confirmed these considerations: Finel[8] calculated

[103] I. V. Massanskii and V. I. Tokar, *J. Phys. I (France)* **2**, 1559 (1992).

[104] L. Reinhard and S. C. Moss, *Ultramicroscopy* **52**, 223 (1993).

[105] K. F. Ludwig, Jr., G. B. Stephenson, J. L. Jordan-Sweet, J. Mainville, Y. S. Yang, and M. Sutton, *Phys. Rev. Lett.* **61**, 1859 (1988).

[106] M. Asta, G. Ceder, and D. de Fontaine, *Phys. Rev. Lett.* **66**, 1798 (1991).

both ordering (below $T_t$, first-order transition temperature) and disordering temperatures for the $L1_2(A_3B)$ phase of the system whose phase diagram appears in Fig. 9. The same trend was found: The spinodal (instability) temperatures tended to stabilize with respect to $T_t$ when a sufficiently high $\alpha_{max}$ cluster approximation was used in the CVM. It can be further argued[8,107] that with increasingly higher cluster approximations, the instability lines cannot collapse onto the first-order phase boundaries themselves, for the simple reason that, if this were to happen, the transition would of course be second order.

Clearly, the method of concentration waves can serve useful purposes when used as a perturbation analysis. But even in such a restricted context, the method must be handled cautiously. Actually, the free energy functional to be perturbed should be based on the CVM, not on the BW approximation. In practice, that means giving up the conveniences of the BW simplification, and also means replacing the Krivoglaz-Clapp-Moss closed-form $I_{SRO}$ expression by a more complex one that requires minimization by numerical techniques.

Contrary to what is often claimed, what the method of concentration waves *cannot* do is predict ground states of order or phase equilibrium. Years ago, the present author[108] pointed out that the wave vector $k_0$ of the most unstable wave need not be, and generally is not, part of the spectrum of wave vectors of the perfectly ordered equilibrium structure resulting from the associated first-order transition. As reemphasized in I, such was the important feature of the phenomenon of *spinodal ordering*. Unfortunately, the point seemed to have been lost on some investigators. For instance, one may read in an often-quoted text[54] that "The structure of the highest temperature (and consequently the most stable) superstructure is generated by the star whose ordering wave vectors provide the absolute minimum of $V(k)$," the $V(k)$ being that defined in Eq. (11.9). That statement is seriously in error for several reasons. First, the minor reasons: Structures may be stabilized by effective multisite (cluster) interactions, which are not included in the $V(k)$ of Eq. (11.9). Also, the inverse susceptibility $F(k)$ and the "k space potential" $V(k)$ are minimized by the same $k_0$ wave vector only in the BW approximation of Eq. (11.9). In more accurate CVM treatments, the k space dependence of the configurational entropy may also contribute to $F(k)$ whose minimum may then no longer coincide with that of $V(k)$. The major problem with the quoted statement is that it fails to recognize the "lock-in" effect: Due to the $+1, -1$ site occupancy requirement, most ordered structures must be

[107] A. Finel, private communication (1992).
[108] D. de Fontaine, *Acta Metall.* **23**, 553 (1975).

described by a Fourier spectrum containing **k** vectors belonging to several stars, the "star" of a wave vector being the set of **k**'s equivalent under symmetry operations of the reciprocal lattice. The equilibrium structure is then the one that minimizes a summation over wave vectors such as $\Sigma V(\mathbf{k})|X(\mathbf{k})|^2$. There is no *a priori* reason to conclude that the optimal spectrum, the one that minimizes the summation, will necessarily contain the wave vector $\mathbf{k}_0$, which lies at the minimum of $V(\mathbf{k})$. Indeed, for many known ordered ground states, there is no such simple relationship between instability and ordered phase. In I, it was suggested that, in a given concentration range, the Fourier spectra of the ordered structure should belong to a certain class of wave vectors intimately related to the corresponding unstable wave vector $\mathbf{k}_0$; in other words, the ordered superstructures were said to belong to the $\mathbf{k}_0$ *family*. Such a conclusion is justified in the BW approximation but is no longer valid in a CVM treatment:[109] It was found experimentally, and confirmed theoretically, that in a narrow concentration range in the vicinity of $Pd_3V$, $I_{SRO}$ peaks at $\langle 100 \rangle$, while the stable ordered structure, the $D0_{22}$, belongs to the $\langle 1\frac{1}{2}0 \rangle$ family. The view that ordering proceeds by single-star instabilities has also led to the erroneous notion of secondary, tertiary, etc., ordering for off-stoichiometric compositions.[54]

When the minimum of $V(\mathbf{k})$ lies at some arbitrary $\mathbf{k}_0$, which is not a high-symmetry point in **k** space, there is a tendency for the $\mathbf{k}_0$ wave to "modulate" the structure. Whether or not the structure will be modulated by a quasi-sinusoidal wave of corresponding wavelength will depend on whether the $V(\mathbf{k})$ potential presents a deep and sharp minimum at $\mathbf{k}_0$ or not. In the former case, it is energetically unfavorable to include harmonics of $\mathbf{k}_0$ in the sum $\Sigma V(\mathbf{k})|X(\mathbf{k})|^2$ so that the equilibrium structure, at all but the lowest temperatures, will be represented by a modulation consisting of antiphased ordered regions separated by diffuse boundaries. On closer examination by atomic resolution transmission microscopy, it is found that the diffuse character of the boundaries is actually caused by jogs along their lengths.[110] If the $V(\mathbf{k})$ potential has a rather broad, flat minimum, then there is little penalty in retaining harmonics in the spectrum, and the modulation locks in at definite long-period superstructures with sharp domain boundaries.[111]

It is thus clear that, by itself, the location of the minimum of $V(\mathbf{k})$ does

[109] F. Solal, R. Caudron, F. Ducastelle, A. Finel, and A. Loiseau, *Phys. Rev. Lett.* **58**, 2245 (1987).

[110] S. Takeda, J. Kulik, D. de Fontaine, and L. E. Tanner, in *Proc. XIth Int. Cong. on Electron Microscopy*, pp. 957–958, Kyoto, Japan (1986).

[111] G. Ceder, M. De Graef, L. Delaey, J. Kulik, and D. de Fontaine, *Phys. Rev. B* **39**, 381 (1989).

not determine structure; one must take into account the shape of the minimum even in qualitative descriptions of ordering processes. In quantitative studies, particularly those based on first-principles calculations, real-space approaches must necessarily be used.

## VI. ECI Calculations

The task of calculating ECIs is the most critical one for the successful prediction of alloy properties. The energy $E(\vec{\sigma})$ of a given configuration is given exactly by the cluster expansion of Eq. (5.1) and the expectation value of energy is given by the thermodynamically averaged expression (5.3), rewritten in Eq. (5.6) in simplified form appropriate for binary systems. In all of these expressions, the energy is seen to be parametrized by the ECIs, $E_\alpha^s$ or $V_\alpha$. The average cluster functions, $\langle \phi_\alpha^s \rangle$ or $\xi_\alpha$, on the other hand, are correlation parameters obtained by minimizing the free energy at given temperature and chemical field. The bilinear forms (5.3) or (5.6) hence combine in one expression the 0 K energy parameters, obtained from electronic structure calculations, and the correlation parameters, obtained by CVM calculations. Therefore, the difficult problem of calculating configuration- and temperature-dependent properties reduces, in the present scheme, to *decoupled* quantum and statistical mechanical calculations.

Several procedures have been proposed for computing ECIs from first principles. Often, the derivation of the appropriate formalism starts with electronic structure considerations. The approach taken here is that of pursuing the statistical aspect as far as possible, and turning on the quantum mechanics at the last moment, so to speak. Thus, explicit forms of the ECIs, independent of any choice of Hamiltonian, have already been given in Eqs. (5.4) or (5.5), obtained directly from the inner product definition of Eq. (4.5). Now we need only evaluate the average energies appearing in Eq. (5.4) (term in square brackets) or in Eq. (5.5) (the $W_{IJ}$'s). Such a straightforward and in principle exact procedure leads to the method of *direct configurational averaging* (DCA), which is presented in Section 12. Because such a method requires many repetitive operations, it has been implemented thus far only in the tight-binding (TB) framework. If more accurate, density-functional methods are required, then the configurational averaging must be simplified, for example, by use of the *coherent potential approximation* (CPA). Alternatively, a simple matrix inversion method may be used, as originally suggested by Connolly and Williams.[112] That technique is briefly reviewed in Section 14.

[112] J. W. D. Connolly and A. R. Williams, *Phys. Rev. B.* **27**, 5169 (1983).

## 12. DIRECT CONFIGURATIONAL AVERAGING

The most straightforward way of calculating effective cluster interactions is to perform explicitly the sum over configurations required by the exact expression (5.4). This method of DCA, though conceptually simple, entails some practical difficulties. Since the second summation in Eq. (5.4) is performed over randomly chosen configurations having in general no translational symmetry, the energy calculations must be performed in real space. To minimize boundary effects, the number $N$ of atoms contained in the computational region must be sufficiently large. Moreover, these calculations must be done a number of times to ensure adequate configurational averaging. Finally, the ECIs themselves are obtained formally as small differences of large energies, hence adequate precision is required for the evaluation of the average configurational energies $W$. Procedures for solving these problems are presented here in the TB framework. The method of obtaining the TB parameters will be described in more detail in Section 15, where specific applications are presented. In this section, only electronic band structure energies are considered. Repulsion terms may be included for total energy calculations, but this aspect of the problem is not described here. The cancellation of other contributions to the ECI calculations beyond the empty and point clusters $(V_0, V_1)$ is discussed by Wolverton et al.[15]

For any configuration $(\vec{\sigma})$, the band structure is evaluated from

$$E_{bs}(\vec{\sigma}) = \int_{-\infty}^{E_F} E \mathcal{N}(E, \vec{\sigma}) \, dE, \tag{12.1}$$

where $\mathcal{N}$ is the total electronic density of states and $E_F$ is a configuration-dependent Fermi level. At high temperatures, the Fermi-Dirac electronic distribution function should, of course, be introduced in the defining equation for $E_{bs}$ (see Ducastelle,[5] for example). The inconvenient configuration-dependence of $E_F$ may be eliminated by writing:[113,114]

$$E_{bs}(\vec{\sigma}) = \int_{-\infty}^{E_F} (E - E_F) \mathcal{N}(E, \vec{\sigma}) \, dE + E_F \lambda, \tag{12.2}$$

where $E_F$ is now a suitably averaged Fermi level and $\lambda$, the total charge, is a constant that will drop out when energy differences are taken, and hence need not be retained further in the derivations.

[113]T. B. Grimley, Proc. Roy. Soc. (London) 92, 776 (1967).
[114]T. L. Einstein and J. R. Schrieffer, Phys. Rev. B 7, 3629 (1973).

The important quantity to calculate is thus the total (configuration-dependent) density of states:

$$\mathcal{N}(E, \vec{\sigma}) = -\frac{1}{\pi} \operatorname{Im} \operatorname{Tr} \mathbf{G}(E, \vec{\sigma}) \tag{12.3a}$$

$$= -\frac{1}{\pi} \operatorname{Im} \frac{\partial}{\partial E} \ln \det[E\mathbf{I} - \mathbf{H}(\vec{\sigma})], \tag{12.3b}$$

where the Green's operator $\mathbf{G}$ is the inverse of the operator $(E\mathbf{I} - \mathbf{H})$, $\mathbf{I}$ and $\mathbf{H}$ being the identity and Hamiltonian operators, respectively, all represented by matrices. In Eqs. (12.3), taking the limit as the imaginary part of the argument of the Green's function goes to zero is implied, and so is an appropriate normalization factor. On inserting expression (12.3b) into Eq. (12.2) for the density of states and integrating by parts,[114] one obtains for any configuration

$$E_{bs}(\vec{\sigma}) = \frac{1}{\pi} \operatorname{Im} \int_{-\infty}^{E_{\mathrm{F}}} \ln \det[E\mathbf{I} - \mathbf{H}(\vec{\sigma})] \, dE. \tag{12.4}$$

In Eq. (5.4), the sum over $\sigma$ products times configurational energies may be written symbolically (for short) in operator form as

$$\Delta_n[\ ] \equiv 2^{-n} \sum_{\sigma_\alpha} \sigma_1 \sigma_2 \ldots \sigma_n[\ ], \tag{12.5}$$

for a cluster $\alpha$ of $n$ lattice points. For example, the ECI in Eq. (5.5) could be written $V_2 = \Delta_2 W$, and for triplets

$$V_3 = \Delta_3 W = \frac{1}{8}(W_{AAA} - W_{AAB} + W_{ABB} - \ldots), \tag{12.6}$$

and so on, where the $W$'s are *average* energies, as defined in connection with Eq. (5.5). In practice, the averaging process (normalized sum over configurations) is performed *after* differences are taken, as opposed to what is suggested in symbolic formula (12.6). Thus, a more appropriate notation is that given later in Eq. (12.13). Note that in such expressions the signs are determined by whether the number of $B$ atoms in the cluster is even $(+)$ or odd $(-)$. It is seen that there are as many $A$ symbols associated with plus signs as there are with minuses, and likewise for $B$, this "cancellation" being an important feature of the method. A general

cancellation property, valid for multicomponent systems, is stated at the end of this section.

The cancellation feature may be combined with expression (12.4) for the configurational energy (at least for its band structure contribution) to produce a very stable algorithm for pairs and higher ECIs. This idea was suggested by Burke[115] for the case of ad-atoms on a surface, then applied to the calculation of ECIs in the DCA framework,[13,29,116,117] with numerical computations being carried out by means of modified versions of the Cambridge recursion algorithm graciously provided to us by Nex.[118] As suggested by Eq. (5.4), one writes the Hamiltonian matrix in block form delineating the region in real space pertaining to the cluster ($\alpha$) and to the cluster complement (N $-$ $\alpha$, to be indicated here by the index 0, for notational convenience):

$$H(\vec{\sigma}_\alpha, \vec{\sigma}_0) = \left[ \begin{array}{c|c} H_{\alpha\alpha} & H_{\alpha 0} \\ \hline H_{0\alpha} & H_{00} \end{array} \right]. \tag{12.7}$$

In Eq. (12.7), $H_{\alpha\alpha}$, a matrix of order $n\nu \times n\nu$, where $\nu$ is the number of orbitals, thus represents the electronic interactions of the atoms of the cluster with one another; $H_{\alpha 0}$ and $H_{0\alpha}$ represent the interactions of the cluster atoms with those of the surroundings (complement); and $H_{00}$, a large matrix of order $(N - n)\nu \times (N - n)\nu$, represents the interactions of surrounding atoms with one another. The matrix $(EI - H)$ is to be partitioned in the same way. The calculation of $\Delta_\alpha \ln \det(EI - H)$ is now simplified by making use of the identity

$$\det(EI - H) = \det G_{\alpha\alpha}^{-1} \det(EI - H_{00}), \tag{12.8}$$

where $G_{\alpha\alpha}$ is the top left block, corresponding to $H_{\alpha\alpha}$ in Eq. (12.7), of the inverse matrix $G = (EI - H)^{-1}$. Thus we are left with

$$\Delta_n \ln \det G = 2^{-n} \ln \frac{\displaystyle\prod_{\sigma_\alpha}^{even} \det G_{\alpha\alpha}(\sigma_\alpha, E)}{\displaystyle\prod_{\sigma_\alpha}^{odd} \det G_{\alpha\alpha}(\sigma_\alpha, E)}, \tag{12.9}$$

[115] N. R. Burke, *Surf. Sci.* **58**, 349 (1976).
[116] D. de Fontaine, unpublished work at U. C. Berkeley (1986).
[117] H. Dreyssé, A. Berera, L. T. Wille, and D. de Fontaine, *Phys. Rev. B* **39**, 2442 (1989).
[118] C. M. M. Nex, "The Cambridge Recursion Library," *Comput. Phys. Commun.* **34**, 101 (1984).

and the large determinant corresponding to $H_{00}$ cancels, at a considerable computational saving and improved numerical stability. In Eq. (12.9) the product in the numerator (denominator) is over all cluster configurations containing an even (odd) number of $B$ atoms. For pair clusters ($\alpha = p, q$), for example, Eq. (12.9) becomes more explicitly

$$\Delta_2 \ln \det G = \frac{1}{4} \ln \frac{\det G_{AA} \det G_{BB}}{\det G_{AB} \det G_{BA}}, \qquad (12.10)$$

where $G_{IJ}$ is the leading (top left) block of the inverse matrix $(EI - H)^{-1}$ with Hamiltonian (12.7) appropriate for atom of type $I$ at point $p$ and $J$ at $q$.

Another important simplification is possible, brought about by the method of *orbital peeling*:[13,14,115-119] Consider again the configuration-dependent matrix $A = (EI - H)$, and let $A_k$ denote the matrix formed from $A$ with the first $k - 1$ rows and columns deleted. Let $g_k$ be the leading element of the inverse of $A_k$. Then we have:[115]

$$\prod_{k=1}^{Nv} g_k = \frac{1}{\det A}. \qquad (12.11)$$

The $g$ product in Eq. (12.11) may be used to evaluate the determinants appearing in Eq. (12.9). When that is done, it is observed that the product of $g_k$ for $Nv \geq k > nv$ for given complement configuration ($\vec{\sigma}_0$) cancels. Finally, by combining Eqs. (12.4), (12.9), and (12.11), we have

$$\Delta_n E_{bs}(\vec{\sigma}_0) = \frac{1}{\pi} 2^{-n} \sum_{k=1}^{nv} \text{Im} \int_{-\infty}^{E_F} \ln \frac{\overset{\text{even}}{\underset{\sigma_\alpha}{\prod}} g_k(\sigma_\alpha, E)}{\underset{\sigma_\alpha}{\overset{\text{odd}}{\prod}} g_k(\sigma_\alpha, E)} \, dE. \qquad (12.12)$$

It is seen that only a small number of leading diagonal elements of Green's function matrices need to be calculated. The effect of eliminating successive rows and columns of $G$ amounts to "peeling off" orbitals one by one, hence the name *orbital peeling* given to this elegant technique. Elements $g_k$ are calculated by the recursion technique[119] as explained in Section 15, which gives an overview of the DCA method as it is currently implemented.

[119]R. Haydock, *Solid State Physics* **35**, 215 (1980).

There now remains the task of averaging over complement configurations $\{\vec{\sigma}_0\}$, as required by the general ECI definition of Eq. (5.4). Symbolically, one performs the normalized summation

$$V_\alpha = \langle \Delta_\alpha E(\vec{\sigma}) | 1 \rangle, \qquad (12.13)$$

according to definition (4.1) of the inner product in configuration space. Equation (12.13) emphasizes the fact that the ECIs result from a sum over all configurations, rather than from ensemble averages in the thermodynamic sense. Hence, the $V_\alpha$ are independent of the configuration. It is hardly necessary to sum over all possible configurations; in practice, if $N$ is reasonably large (about one thousand), it suffices to sum over 20 or 50 configurations obtained by selecting site occupations at random. Resulting configurations are then found to deviate little from the average concentration $c = 0.5$.

In principle, any suitable real-space electronic structure method may be used for the DCA formalism, including density functional methods. In practice, since many disordered configurations must be investigated in a region of many lattice sites, thus far, the DCA has been implemented only in the TB framework. Experience has shown (see Section 15) that the TB method can produce very accurate results, particularly for transition metal alloys. For certain alloy systems, for example, those featuring atoms with filled $d$-bands, or with very different $d$-band widths, the TB method fails to give the correct ordering tendencies. Hence, a drawback of the DCA as it is currently implemented is its lack of universal applicability. Nevertheless, the DCA is a highly attractive method, because it comes closest in spirit to carrying out the prescription of the rigorous definition of the ECIs. The method is also highly computationally efficient (in the TB approximation, calculations can be performed on a workstation) and, since it is formulated in real space, highly flexible. In particular, if semiempirical repulsive terms are included so as to treat *total,* not just band structure energies, structural defects that break translational symmetry, such as surfaces, may be handled without difficulty.[32, 120] Local displacements, static or dynamic, should also be amenable to DCA calculations.

Another advantage of the DCA is that ECIs are calculated one at a time, as needed, independently of the others, an advantage shared by the GPM and embedded cluster methods (ECM), which are described very briefly in the next section. The inner product definition of ECI does re-

[120] C. Wolverton, M. Asta, S. Ouannasser, H. Dreyssé, and D. de Fontaine, *J. Chim. Phys.* **90**, 249 (1993).

quire, however, that orthogonal basis functions be used for specifying cluster configurations. For binary systems, the choice of point cluster functions is the obvious one, $\theta = \{1, \sigma_p\}$ with $\sigma_p = +1$ or $-1$. For ternaries, the situation is more complex. In particular, it is not altogether obvious whether an orthogonal set in multicomponent systems will automatically guarantee the cancellation required by the orbital peeling technique. Fortunately, it can be shown that the use of orthonormal sets is a sufficient, though not necessary, condition for cancellation[13]: $M$-component ECIs are given by Eq. (5.2b) with cluster functions defined by Eq. (4.9). Hence, $E_\alpha^s$ or $V_\alpha^s$ in the notation of Eq. (5.4) may be written, for an $n$-point cluster $(\alpha)$,

$$V_\alpha^s = M^{-n} \sum_{\sigma_1} \sum_{\sigma_2} \cdots \sum_{\sigma_n} \theta^{s_1}(\sigma_1)\, \theta^{s_2}(\sigma_2) \ldots \theta^{s_n}(\sigma_n) \langle E(\vec{\sigma}_\alpha; \vec{\sigma}_0)|1\rangle, \quad (12.14)$$

in which the notation of Eq. (12.13) has been used for the sum over all $\vec{\sigma}_0$ (complementary) configurations. By the orthogonality property of the $\theta$ point functions, we have, since $\theta^0(\sigma_i) = 1$ for any $\sigma_i$,

$$\langle \theta^{(s_i)}(\vec{\sigma}_i)|1\rangle \propto \sum_{\sigma_i} \theta^{(s_i)}(\vec{\sigma}_i) = 0, \quad (12.15)$$

for any $s_i \neq 0$. Consider now a cluster with an atom of type $I$ at a particular point $p$. For any cluster containing more than one point, there must be at least one other point $q$ at which the corresponding $s_j$ is different from zero, so that the associated sum (12.15) vanishes. That, in turn, means that the sum of the coefficients of the energy term in (12.14) for atom $I$ at $p$ vanishes as well, since the multiple sum over remaining functions factors into a product of sums such as (12.15). Such is precisely the extension to multicomponents of the cancellation property, which appears explicitly in Eq. (5.5) for pairs or (12.6) for triplets in binary $(A,B)$ systems.[13]

13. METHODS BASED ON THE CPA

Configurational averaging as described in the previous section is obviously a costly undertaking. Not only must one repeat band structure calculations over several configurations, but the computational cell must be a large one (large $N$). Since the running time of current first-principles,

density-functional total-energy calculations is proportional to $N^3$, it is clear that, to go beyond the TB approximation, one must adopt different computational procedures. A major breakthrough occurred when it was found that translational symmetry could be restored to a disordered system while treating correctly the main features of the electronic structure, such as the density of states. To that effect, it was necessary to define a homogeneous average medium, which was characterized by average atoms having on-site energies, or coherent potentials, determined in an electronically self-consistent manner.[121–124] This coherent (single-site) potential approximation (CPA) has proven to be very successful, although the approximation is definitely of mean-field character: It is not the average of properties of systems of an ensemble that is being calculated, but the property of a fictitious average system. The CPA is couched naturally in multiple scattering formalisms and has been adapted to TB, KKR (Korringa-Kohn-Rosktoker),[124] and LMTO electronic structure methods.[125,126] With the muffin-tin density-functional methods such as the KKR-CPA, it appeared that a completely satisfactory (albeit mean-field) first-principles theory of disordered alloys was finally at hand.

For the kinds of properties investigated in this chapter, however, the single-site CPA was inadequate since (configurational) thermodynamic properties depend precisely on *deviations from complete disorder,* all the way up to complete order. It is thus required that the CPA medium be *perturbed* in some appropriate manner. To do that, one then writes the Hamiltonian of the disordered (or partially ordered) system as

$$\mathbf{H} = \mathbf{h} + \boldsymbol{\nu}, \qquad (13.1)$$

where $\mathbf{h}$ is the translationally invariant Hamiltonian of the CPA medium and $\boldsymbol{\nu}$ is the configuration-dependent perturbing operator, which depends on the *difference* between the actual scattering potentials at the alloy sites and those in the uniform concentration-dependent CPA medium. As in Eq. (13.1), the band structure energy also splits into two contributions,

[121] P. Soven, *Phys. Rev.* **156**, 809 (1967).

[122] B. Verlický, S. Kirkpatrick, and H. Ehrenreich, *Phys. Rev.* **157**, 747 (1968).

[123] H. Ehrenreich and L. M. Schwartz, *Solid State Physics* **31**, 149 (1976).

[124] J. S. Faulkner, *Prog. Mater. Sci.* **27**, 1 (1982).

[125] J. Kudrnovsky, B. Wenzien, V. Drchal, and P. Weinberger, *Phys. Rev. B* **44**, 4068 (1991); J. Kudrnovsky, P. Weinberger, and V. Drchal, *Phys. Rev. B* **44**, 6410 (1991); V. Drchal, J. Kudrnovsky, L. Udvardi, P. Weinberger, and A. Pasturel, *Phys. Rev. B.* **45**, 14328 (1992).

[126] P. P. Singh, A. Gonis, and D. de Fontaine, *Phys. Rev. B* **44**, 8578 (1991).

which may be calculated by methods similar to those leading to Eq. (12.4), for example:[5]

$$E_{bs} = -\frac{1}{\pi} \text{Im} \int_{-\infty}^{E_F} \text{Tr} \ln \bar{G} \, dE + \frac{1}{\pi} \text{Im} \int_{-\infty}^{E_F} \text{Tr} \ln(\mathbf{I} - \bar{G}v) \, dE, \quad (13.2)$$

where $\bar{G}$ is the configuration-independent CPA medium Green's function $(E\mathbf{I} - \mathbf{h})^{-1}$. The perturbation term (the second one) can further be written by means of the operators $(\mathbf{I} - \bar{G}_{od}T_d)$, where $\bar{G}_{od}$ is the off-diagonal part of $\bar{G}$ and $T_d$ is a site diagonal scattering operator, which contains the configuration dependence.

The second term of Eq. (13.2) can be expressed in various ways depending on the nature of the perturbation. Three basic approaches have resulted: (1) the $S^{(2)}$ method of concentration waves,[96] (2) the GPM,[5,95,127] and (3) the ECM.[128,129] The ECM is also a real-space technique, and both GPM and ECM take the form of expansions in pair and higher cluster configuration variables, similar to the expansions in correlations or cumulants described earlier.

Relationships between these approaches are described in a very comprehensive paper by Gonis and coworkers.[129] In all of these CPA-based methods, the expansion coefficients are seen to be concentration dependent by the very nature of the embedding medium itself. The GPM and ECM differ in that the coefficients of the latter expansion consist of a regrouping of GPM contributions from subclusters of a given cluster of distinct sites. The resulting coefficients were called *renormalized effective cluster interactions* (RECI).[129] Formally, the ECM expansion is identical to the cluster expansions discussed in Section 5. In fact, the defining equation for ECM pair interactions is practically the same as Eq. (5.5), with average energies $W_{AA}$ [denoted by $\bar{\Omega}'_{ij}(AA)$, etc., in Eq. (3.14) of Ref. 129] defined similarly. Of course, in the CPA-based ECM, the clusters are embedded in an average medium of concentration $c$, thus the CPA-ECM ECIs correspond to R-sum averaging, in the terminology of Section 5 of this chapter. Moreover, the general expression for ECM multiplet cluster interactions, Eq. (4.14) of Ref. 129, is just that given by combining Eqs. (12.4) and (12.9) of the DCA description. We may therefore conclude that ECM-RECIs and DCA-ECIs are formally equivalent, with the proviso that the latter be calculated in an R-sum fashion, i.e., that the configurational averaging be performed at fixed concentration,

[127] M. Sluiter and P. E. A. Turchi, *Phys. Rev. B* **40**, 11215 (1989).

[128] A. Gonis and J. W. Garland, *Phys. Rev. B* **16**, 1495, 2424 (1977); *Phys. Rev. B* **18**, 3999 (1978).

[129] A. Gonis, X.-G. Zhang, A. J. Freeman, P. Turchi, G. M. Stocks, and D. M. Nicholson, *Phys. Rev. B* **36**, 4630 (1987).

generally different from $c = 0.5$. One important difference is that the CPA-ECM (and GPM) relies on a mean-field approximation, whereas the DCA does not. Hence, in the DCA, local electrostatic or displacement fluctuations in principle are included, and concentration fluctuations are included in practice.

Gonis et al.[129] also proposed a more general form of expansion that does not necessarily rely on the CPA medium. The defining equations for the ECIs in this scheme are virtually identical to those proposed here in Eq. (5.4) or (12.14), provided that the probability distribution of the configurations [$P_{J_{Cn}}$ of Eq. (5.5) in Ref. 129] be set equal to the constant $2^{-N}$. With this choice, the proposed expansion, called FRECI (fully renormalized effective cluster interactions),[129] would appear to be equivalent to the U-sum (concentration-independent) ECI expansion described here. The distinction between ECM RECIs and FRECIs thus parallels that between R-sum and U-sum ECIs, respectively. Indeed, the relationship between the latter two types of interactions [$\hat{V}_\beta(c)$ and $V_\alpha$], as given by Eq. (5.12a), clearly shows that the $V_\alpha$ are obtained by an expansion over superclusters, thus taking into account the interaction of a maximal R-sum cluster $\hat{V}_\alpha$ with its surroundings, out to arbitrary order. The perhaps surprising conclusion is then inescapable: For the purpose of calculating ECIs in the CPA context, we need to embed clusters only into the CPA medium at $c = 0.5$. In this way, one automatically obtains a FRECI formulation, provided that interactions beyond the pair terms are explicitly calculated. In practice, however, it may be simpler to calculate only pair interactions at different CPA concentrations, which is what the practitioners of the CPA-based methods generally advocate, in the spirit of the R-sum expansion. As mentioned in Section 5, the relationship between c-independent ECIs and c-dependent EPIs was examined by Carlsson,[34] and the distinction between RECI and FRECI was further explored by Klima.[130] Electronic structure theory is not required to prove the equivalence of c-independent and c-dependent ECI schemes, however; the supercluster expansions of Eqs. (5.12) and (5.13) suffice to demonstrate this equivalence along with the identity of the two types of ECIs at the central concentration ($c = 0.5$, $\bar{\sigma} \equiv \xi_1 = 0$), a property that is not always recognized.

The attenuation of the concentration dependence of (R-sum) $\hat{V}_\alpha$ interactions when "renormalized" by supercluster expansions, as in Eq. (5.12b), is illustrated[30,131] in Fig. 10 for the nn pair interaction in the Ti-Pt system.

[130] J. Klima, Zeit. Phys. 90, 267 (1993).

[131] S. Ouannasser, "Contribution à l'Etude de l'Ordre dans les Alliages Massifs ou près d'une Surface d'Alliage," Ph.D. Dissertation, Université de Nancy I, Nancy, France (1994) (unpublished).

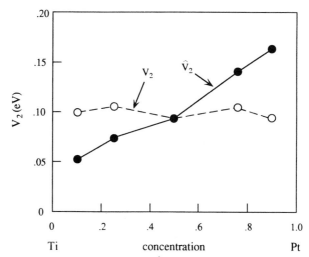

F<small>IG</small>. 10. Concentration-dependent *nn* EPI $\hat{V}_2$ and triplet renormalized $V_2$ EPI calculated by the DCA method for the Ti-Pt system. Renormalization tends to suppress the concentration dependence [S. Ouannasser, "Contribution à l'Etude de l'Ordre dans les Alliages Massifs ou prés d'une Surface d'Alliage;" Ph.D. Dissertation, Université de Nancy I, Nancy, France (1994) (unpublished)].

DCA calculations were performed according to the methods described in Sections 12 and 15 with renormalization [β summation in (5.12b)] being performed over four triplet interactions. Values of $V_2$ and $\hat{V}_2$ are of course identical at concentration $c = 0.5$. It is remarkable that renormalization by only triplet interactions suffices to produce $V_2$ values that have become almost independent of concentration.

Some applications of CPA-based methods are mentioned in Section 17.

## 14. S<small>TRUCTURE</small> I<small>NVERSION</small> M<small>ETHOD</small>

The ECI calculations presented in the two previous sections relied on local perturbations of a (disordered) embedding medium obtained either by configurational averaging or by using a single-site coherent potential approximation. For short, let us refer to these as *direct* methods, since the ECIs are calculated one at a time until suitable convergence is attained. The method to be presented briefly in this section is, by contrast, generally based on calculations of ordered structures: The formation energies of a set of $J$ structures are calculated and expressed as cluster expansions using $R$ cluster functions. Provided that $J \geq R$, the required ECIs can then be obtained by least-squares analysis or matrix inversion.

For short, let us refer to this method as the *structure inversion method* (SIM). Of course, not only ECIs but cluster expansion coefficients (CECs) of any configuration-dependent function can be obtained by such an *indirect* method, indirect because the CECs are *deduced* from a truncated form of the cluster expansion, instead of being calculated directly from the inner product formula [Eq. (4.1)]. Since the example of formation energies is treated throughout this section, we shall continue to refer to ECIs rather than the more general acronym CEC, and shall limit the formalism to binary systems.

### a. *Method of Connolly and Williams*

Following a suggestion by Sanchez that the total energy of an alloy structure could be represented exactly by an expression such as Eq. (5.6), Connolly and Williams[112] calculated by augmented spherical wave (ASW) methods the total energies of the five fcc-based ordered structures of $A$-$B$ transition metal alloys: pure $A$ and pure $B$ (fcc), $A_3B$ and $AB_3$ ($L1_2$), and $AB$ ($L1_0$). These authors could then obtain the five ECIs for empty cluster ($V_0$), point ($V_1$), pair ($V_2$), triangle ($V_3$), and the nearest-neighbor tetrahedron ($V_4$) by matrix inversion. Currently, an expanded version of the original SIM is used, as described next.

Let us return to expression (5.15) for the energy of formation. Quite generally, this energy may be written, for a particular configuration $\{\vec{\sigma}\}$,

$$\Delta E_{\text{form}}(\vec{\sigma}) = E(\vec{\sigma}) - (c_A E_A + c_B E_B), \qquad (14.1)$$

i.e., the total energy of $\{\vec{\sigma}\}$ minus the concentration-weighted average of the energies of the pure states $E_A$ and $E_B$. In Section 5 it was stated that this definition, as it stands, is somewhat ambiguous because the conditions under which the energies have been calculated were not specified precisely. For thermodynamic equilibrium it is clear that each energy to be entered into Eq. (14.1) must be the lowest possible one in the fully "relaxed" state. However, we are interested in much more than individual equilibrium formation energies; Eq. (14.1) is rather to be considered as the starting point for developing a cluster expansion. In that context, it is no longer obvious what constraints should be imposed on the underlying lattice and on atomic volumes in order to generate the system of linear equations to be inverted. For now, let us simply assume that $A$ and $B$ atoms are situated at the sites of the same parent lattice, the purpose of this subsection being that of describing the basic formalism of the SIM. The troublesome problem of "relaxation" will be covered in the next subsection.

With the stated restriction in mind, let us express the formation energy of structure $j$ [defined by configuration $\vec{\sigma}^{(j)}$] by its cluster expansion

$$\Delta E_{\text{form}}^{(j)} = \sum_{r}^{R} \Delta V_r \bar{\xi}_r^{(j)}, \tag{14.2}$$

with $\Delta V_0$ and $\Delta V_1$ defined as in Eq. (5.16) and $\Delta V_r = m_r V_r$. In Eq. (14.2), just as in Eq. (7.1), the summation is over all symmetry-distinct clusters up to the $R$'th (maximum) one, $\bar{\xi}_r$ representing orbit-average cluster functions, and $m_r$ being the number of symmetry-equivalent clusters per lattice point. A set of $J \geq R$ equations such as Eq. (14.2) may be written down, thereby forming a system of $J$ linear equations in the $R$ unknown $\Delta V_r$ (ECI) parameters. The formation energies are calculated by appropriate electronic structure codes, and the elements $\bar{\xi}_r^{(j)}$ form the $R \times J$ matrix $X$ of known correlations, determined by inspection from the $J$ crystal structures (or determined as a by-product of the C matrix codes mentioned in Section 7). The linear system of Eq. (14.2) may be written in matrix form as

$$\Delta E = X \Delta V, \tag{14.3}$$

and inverted to yield the $R$ unknown ECIs:

$$\Delta V = X^{-1} \Delta E. \tag{14.4}$$

Equation (14.4) must be understood in a symbolic sense: It is usually preferable to select more structures $J$ than ECIs $R$, in which case system (14.2) or (14.3) is overdetermined and its "solution" (14.4) must be obtained by a least-squares method, for instance, by singular value decomposition.[132]

Because of its conceptual simplicity, the SIM is a very appealing technique, which has been used successfully for the calculation of alloy properties. The method is also convenient since no specific electronic structure codes need to be developed to calculate cluster expansion coefficients: existing, well-tested computer codes may be used to obtain, to a high degree of accuracy, values for the structural energies (or other properties) appearing on the left of the equal sign in Eqs. (14.2) or (14.3), for example. Actually, what is being done is a parameterization of the

[132]C. L. Lanson, and R. J. Lanson, *Solving Least Squares Problems*, Prentice-Hall, Englewood Cliffs, NJ (1974).

energies of a number $J$ of structures, then to use the derived $\Delta V$'s to calculate, practically "on the back of an envelope," the energy of any other structure described by a set of known $\bar{\xi}_r$ correlation parameters.

One weakness of the SIM is that an *a priori* truncation of the cluster expansion must be chosen. The problem is then "How many $R$ cluster coefficients should one retain, how many $J$ basic structures, so that the cluster expansion will be expected to converge?" Trial and error usually achieves a satisfactory result: Choose a set of clusters (and subclusters) and calculate the energies of a (larger) set of basic structures. Then consider a subset $(J > J' \geq R)$ of these $J$ structures, and solve [symbolically by Eq. (14.4)] for the $R\Delta V_r$ parameters. To test convergence, use these calculated ECIs to evaluate, by cluster expansion, the energies of the remaining $(J - J')$ structures, or test structures, and compare to their energies as calculated directly. If the match is a good one, convergence is acceptable. If not, other sets and/or larger sets of basic structures must be envisaged. Sometimes, different sets of clusters may give equally acceptable results for test structures. In that case, it is useful to select the most orthogonal set of cluster functions,[16,74] i.e., one chooses the set that minimizes the normalized sum of scalar products

$$\frac{1}{J'(J' - 1)} \sum_{j} \sum_{j' \neq j} |\bar{\xi}^{j} \cdot \bar{\xi}^{j'}|,$$

where $\bar{\xi}^{j}$ is the $R$ component vector of orbit-averaged cluster functions for structure $j$.

It has sometimes been argued that the SIM-derived CECs are not especially meaningful since their values, obtained from the inversion procedure of Eq. (14.4), depend on the series truncation level. In direct methods, by contrast, previously calculated CECs remain invariant as new clusters are included in the cluster expansion approximation. This observation is theoretically valid but, in practice, if the set of CECs is well converged, it is also very stable under cluster set enlargements. A recent calculation[15] has demonstrated excellent agreement between ECIs for the Pd-Rh system obtained by both direct and indirect methods.

b. *Structural Relaxation Energy*

For cluster expansion purposes, all structures $(j)$ appearing in Eq. (14.2) must be related to the same underlying lattice. At thermodynamic equilibrium, however, formation energies must be calculated as differences of cohesive energies between structures related to different lattices; for example, the actual formation energy of compound PtV is obtained as the

difference between the $B19$ structure (an hcp-based ordered structure) and the average of the pure fcc Pt and bcc V. The way to reconcile these two sometimes contradictory requirements is to treat each parent lattice and its associated ordered structures separately, then to relate the lattices to one another by calculating the structural energy differences of the pure elements in various crystal structures, in the present example, hcp, fcc, and bcc. The "inversion" process (in the extended sense of subsection a) must thus be carried out separately to obtain sets of ECIs valid for each parent lattice. The structural energy correction just described may be regarded as an example of *postinversion relaxation* (to the ground state lattice), which involves simply a linear transformation of energies as a function of concentration.

The problem of structural relaxation on a given lattice necessarily involves nonlinear corrections and has not been solved in a truly satisfactory manner as yet (1994). First let us classify the types of relaxations that may be encountered (terms in italics are those introduced by Zunger and collaborators[9,39,133]).

1. *Volume deformation.* The unit cell is deformed homogeneously so that only the average atomic volume $\Omega$, or Wigner-Seitz radius, is expanded or contracted.

2. *Cell external relaxation.* When long-range order sets in, symmetry elements are lost and the unit cell of the ordered structure generally acquires additional degrees of freedom. For example, in $L1_0$ ordering the crystal class goes from cubic to tetragonal so that the $c/a$ ratio is "liberated" from its ideal to its equilibrium (relaxed) value.

3. *Cell internal relaxation.* Especially in structures of lower symmetry, or with large unit cells, the reduced symmetry may allow atoms to move away from the lattice sites of the reference lattice, i.e., they may alter their crystallographic coordinates even after cell external relaxation has taken place. An extreme example of this type of relaxation occurs in the disordered phase. There, the unit cell is the whole computational cell, with no particular symmetry, and *all* atoms may relax away from the parent lattice sites.

Often, allowed cell external and internal distortions may be determined by inspection. As a general rule, however, it is preferable to determine from crystallographic tables the space group of the ordered superstructure, the assignment being dictated by atomic occupation. The symmetry class to which the space group belongs then determines which lattice parameter ratios and angles may change and which atomic positions may undergo coordinate changes. These latter positions are those Wyckoff

[133] D. B. Laks, L. G. Ferreira, S. Froyen, and A. Zunger, *Phys. Rev. B* **46**, 12587 (1992).

positions whose coordinates contain at least one arbitrary coordinate value, denoted by $x$, $y$, or $z$ in the international tables.[134] Various methods have been proposed to account for these relaxation phenomena, at least in approximate fashion. Adopting the classification of Carlsson,[34] we have:

(i)  *Complete neglect of relaxation.* All energies $E^{(j)}$ for all structures are calculated for a fixed unit cell size and shape, regardless of average concentration.

(ii)  *Global relaxation.* Energies of all basic structures $(j)$ are calculated at a given atomic volume (with fixed unit cell shape and internal atomic coordinates) to produce $E^{(j)}(\Omega)$ and the matrix inversion process is carried out, leading to ECIs valid for that particular value of $\Omega$. The calculations are repeated likewise for other volumes so as to obtain, perhaps by interpolation, volume-dependent ECIs: $V_\alpha(\Omega)$. Average atomic volume was used as an example of an optimizing variable, but other cell parameters, such as $c/a$ ratio, may be considered as well. For each alloy concentration, the corresponding volume $\Omega(c)$ may be chosen by linear interpolation between the pure state volumes $\Omega_A$ and $\Omega_B$, or the proper volume to use in the ECIs may be chosen by energy minimization, at each concentration, with respect to $\Omega$. Global relaxation may be classified as a *postinversion* method.

(iii)  *Local relaxation.* In this *preinversion* method, all energies appearing on the right-hand side of Eq. (14.1) are calculated in their fully relaxed states (cell volume, external, internal). Matrix inversion may then proceed with these "relaxed" values as input into the linear system (14.1).

The theoretical (and practical) inadequacy of these procedures has been pointed out and alternative schemes have been proposed.[135,136] Here, let us merely describe supplementary corrections that may be applied to the methods just mentioned. Let us begin with method (i). It is clearly very simple to implement and presents certain advantages; for example, the corresponding cluster expansion generally converges rapidly. However, if the fixed unit cell is, for example, chosen to be an equilibrium one at

[134] *International Tables for Crystallography* (T. Hahn, ed.), Vol. A, D. Riedel, Dordrecht (1985).
[135] J. M. Sanchez in *Structural and Phase Stability of Alloys* ( J. L. Morán-López, F. Meija-Lira, and J. M. Sanchez, eds.), pp. 151–165, Plenum Press, New York (1992).
[136] C. Amador, W. R. L. Lambrecht, M. van Schilfgaarde, and B. Segall, *Phys. Rev. B* **47**, 15276 (1993).

$c = 0.5$, the "constrained" ground state energies of pure $A$ and pure $B$ will be larger than their "relaxed" equilibrium energies, and the resulting formation energies, according to Eq. (14.1), will be in error, perhaps even with the wrong sign. Hence an approximate *postinversion* correction is called for. A simple (nonlinear) correction may be described as follows, as applied to volume relaxation only. For *globally* relaxed structures, all referred to the same underlying lattice, let us rewrite Eq. (14.1) in a condensed manner as

$$\Delta E_{form}^x = E^x - (c_A E_A^x + c_B E_B^x), \qquad (14.5a)$$

where the subscript indicates atomic volume relaxation ($x$ for relaxed) for the configuration envisaged and for the pure $A$ and $B$ structures. In the constrained state, which is that of the (fixed) lattice for some structure at concentration $\bar{c}$, we write likewise

$$\Delta E_{form}^c = E^c - (c_A E_A^c + c_B E_B^c), \qquad (14.5b)$$

where now the superscript indicates the constrained state ($c$ for constrained, or coherent). Define also, for convenience

$$\Delta E_I = E_I^x - E_I^c \qquad (I = A \text{ or } B), \qquad (14.6)$$

which are structural energy differences between relaxed and constrained pure states. The various energies introduced in Eqs. (14.5) and (14.6) are shown schematically in Fig. 11 for the case of three ordered superstructures $A_3B$, $AB$, and $AB_3$ along with pure $A$ and $B$. The lower portion of the figure pertains to formation energies, the upper portion to the energies themselves. The lattice of the constrained states is taken to be that of the parent (relaxed) structure at $\bar{c} = 0.5$ so that, assuming atomic volume does not vary appreciably on ordering, we have equality of constrained and globally relaxed energies for structure $AB$. Relaxed energies are given by filled symbols and heavy solid lines, constrained energies by open symbols and heavy dashed lines. Let $D$ denote the difference between relaxed and constrained energies, and $\Delta D$ the corresponding formation energy difference. At the fixed reference concentration $\bar{c}$ we must have

$$\Delta D(\bar{c}) = -(1 - \bar{c}) \Delta E_A - \bar{c} \Delta E_B, \qquad (14.7)$$

along with $\Delta D(0) = \Delta D(1) = 0$. To lowest order, the smooth curve that takes on the correct values of $c = 0$ and 1 is a parabola, which for $\bar{c} =$

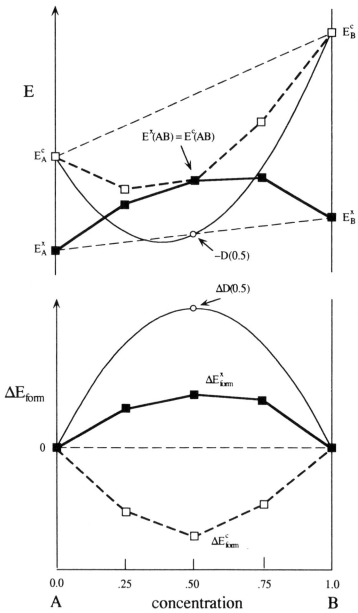

FIG. 11. Schematic energy diagram for hypothetical ordered compounds considered in Fig. 1. Top portion of figure shows absolute energies for relaxed ($x$) and constrained ($c$) states, with $D(c)$ being the quadratic elastic relaxation energy. Lower portion of figure shows relaxed (solid lines, symbols) and constrained (dashed lines, open symbols) formation energies.

0.5 has the explicit form

$$\Delta D(c) \cong -2(\Delta E_A + \Delta E_B)\, c(1 - c). \tag{14.8}$$

The parabolic approximations of $D$ and $\Delta D$ are also plotted in Fig. 11. Approximate expression (14.8) may be used as a crude correction (postinversion) to estimate true (globally relaxed) formation energies from energies calculated on a fixed lattice. Such is the spirit of the so-called $\varepsilon$-$G$ correction suggested by Zunger and coworkers.[137] Going the other way, i.e., from relaxed to constrained states, the $\Delta D$ correction may be used to determine, at least qualitatively, the type of constrained (coherent) equilibria that a system will "see" if it is prevented from reaching relaxed equilibrium. In the hypothetical case of Fig. 11, the system at $\bar{c} = 0.5$ would like to *order coherently* ($\Delta E_{form}^c < 0$), although it actually *phase separates incoherently* ($\Delta E_{form}^c > 0$) at equilibrium. Although elastic relaxations are being discussed here in the context of the structure inversion method, global relaxation (ii) can certainly be applied with direct methods, as shown recently by Wolverton.[15]

The distinction between coherent and incoherent equilibria in the context of first-principles calculations was discussed recently for the Ni-Pt, Au-Pt, and Au-Ni systems.[138,139] The binaries feature $5d$ elements for which relativistic corrections are essential in calculating formation energies. Recent findings pertaining to the Ni-Pt system are reviewed briefly in Section 17. For the Au-Ni case, it was stated[139] that, although the alloy phase separates (incoherently) at equilibrium, $L1_0$ ordering was observed experimentally as a transient state, as might be expected for a situation such as that illustrated schematically in Fig. 11. Actually, Woodilla and Averbach[140] found, on rapid quenching of a 50/50 alloy, diffuse intensity peaks at unusual positions in $k$ space, roughly halfway between Bragg peaks and normal superstructure peaks. A possible explanation[1,141] for this unusual ordering process was reported in article I as being due entirely to coherency strains described by *microscopic* (lattice) elasticity. Whether or not that explanation was valid, it appears that the simple model illustrated in Fig. 11 cannot be invoked without modifications for

[137] A. Zunger, S.-H. Wei, A. A. Mbaye, and G. L. Ferreira, *Acta Metall.* **36**, 2239 (1988).

[138] Z. W. Lu, S.-H. Wei, and A. Zunger, *Phys. Rev. Lett.* **68**, 1961 (1992).

[139] Z. W. Lu, S.-H. Wei, and Z. Zunger, *Europhys. Lett.* **21**, 221 (1993).

[140] J. E. Woodilla and B. L. Averbach, *Acta Metall.* **16**, 255 (1968).

[141] D. de Fontaine and H. E. Cook, in *Critical Phenomena in Alloys, Magnets and Superconductors* (R. E. Mills, E. Ascher, and R. I. Jaffee, eds.), p. 257, McGraw-Hill, New York (1971).

the observed Au-Ni anomaly. It would be interesting to search systematically for systems where opposite signs are observed for incoherent and coherent formation energies. One way would be to look for diffuse short-range order intensity (from critical ordering fluctuations) in a system with large atomic mismatch, quenched rapidly inside an incoherent miscibility gap. A high-intensity synchrotron x-ray source would be required for rapid data collecion, as was used, for example, to locate the ordering spinodal in $Cu_3Au$.[105]

The parabolic correction term of Eq. (14.8) is very reminiscent of the one introduced by Cahn in his theory of coherent spinodal decomposition.[142] The extension of the coherent concept to the ordering case requires "microscopic elasticity," formulated in $k$ space (concentration waves), as was presented in some detail in article I. However, such an approach cannot be readily incorporated into the cluster formalism based on first-principles calculations. To see that, consider the case of $L1_0$ ordering in fcc. According to the concentration wave method, which is a point mean-field approximation, the equilibrium $L1_0$ structure contains elastic energy because pure $A$ and pure $B$ (001) lattice planes are alternatively expanded and compressed. On the other hand, an LDA calculation gives *the* energy of the $L1_0$ structure with, of course, no elastic energy contribution. Thus, the point (in $k$ space) and cluster (in direct space) formalisms are not readily compatible, although a recently proposed $k$ space SIM method may provide a good starting point for a combined approach; the reader is referred to the articles by Zunger and collaborators[9,133] for a complete description of this interesting method. It will not be described further here since it is not clear at present how to incorporate it in cluster methods combined with the CVM.

The local relaxation method (iii), is the only one to use if certain ordered states owe their stability to cell internal or external relaxation. Such is the case for the Ti-Al system described in Section 16(a). The corresponding cluster expansion tends to converge more slowly than for methods (i) or (ii). The task of performing complete local relaxations can be quite daunting, as is described in detail in Section 16. For now, let us note that if a large number of clusters is required for cluster expansions in a given alloy, it will be necessary to calculate a large number of basic structures as well. After the simple ordered structures of high symmetry have been used, the energies of more complex structures with larger unit cells will have to be calculated in *fully relaxed states*. That, in turn, means that a very large parameter space will have to be scanned ($c/a$, $b/a$ ratios, cell angles, internal relaxations) and that, in general, full po-

[142] J. W. Cahn, *Acta Metall.* **10**, 1789 (1962).

tential total energy codes will have to be used since simpler ones, based on atomic sphere approximations, do not handle cell deformations or atomic displacements very satisfactorily. Actually, an appropriate "force theorem" must be used if cell internal relaxations are to be carried out efficiently. Thus, in a full-blown calculation, energy minimization must be performed with full-potential total energy *ab initio* electronic structure codes over several lattice-cell degrees of freedom, for several (ten or more) ordered structures, sometimes with eight or more atoms per unit cell (for an application of the method, see Section 16).

For the purpose of accurately calculating formation energies and ground state diagrams, full potential calculations are indeed the correct ones to perform, and the results are expected to be as reliable as the best experimental ones, in some cases even more reliable than those obtained by calorimetric measurements. But how well are local relaxation effects handled by preinversion method (iii) in partially ordered/disordered phases? The answer to that question is not known at present since there is no simple way of ascertaining how the relaxation procedure "propagates" to the ECIs, hence to the disordered phases, through the highly nonlinear process of matrix inversion (or least-squares analysis).

Surely, by method (iii), some relaxation energy contributions in disordered states are taken into account, but regardless of the precise nature (and validity) of the method, it may also be coupled with a supplementary postinversion correction: the energy of each basic structure may be expressed analytically as a function of cell parameters so that, as in method (ii), all ECIs may be obtained as cell-dependent quantities. Such a method, first proposed by Sluiter,[74,127,143,144] is now described in some detail. Let us consider volume relaxation only for this supplementary correction. If average atomic volumes do not differ too greatly for the various structures envisaged, it suffices to expand the formation energies to second order in $\Omega$ about the 0 K equilibrium volume $\Omega_0^{(j)}$:

$$\Delta E^{(j)}(\vec{\sigma}, \Omega) = a_0^{(j)}(\vec{\sigma}) + a_1^{(j)}(\vec{\sigma})\Omega + a_2^{(j)}(\vec{\sigma})\Omega^2, \qquad (14.9)$$

where the expansion coefficients are given by

$$a_0^{(j)}(\vec{\sigma}) = \Delta E_0^{(j)}(\vec{\sigma}, \Omega_0) + \frac{1}{2}B^{(j)}(\vec{\sigma})\Omega_0^{(j)}(\vec{\sigma}), \qquad (14.10a)$$

[143] M. Sluiter, D. de Fontaine, X. Q. Guo, R. Podloucky, and A. J. Freeman, *Mat. Res. Soc. Symp. Proc.* **133**, 1989.

[144] M. Sluiter, D. de Fontaine, X. Q. Guo, R. Podloucky, and A. J. Freeman, *Phys. Rev.* B **42**, 10460 (1990).

$$a_1^{(j)}(\vec{\sigma}) = -B^{(j)}(\vec{\sigma}), \qquad (14.10b)$$

$$a_2^{(j)}(\vec{\sigma}) = B^{(j)}(\vec{\sigma})/2\Omega_0^{(j)}, \qquad (14.10c)$$

$B^{(j)}$ being the bulk modulus at the minimum formation energy $\Delta E_0^{(j)}$. The $\Omega$ dependence of $\Delta E$ in Eq. (14.9) will induce a quadratic $\Omega$ dependence in the ECIs themselves, which may now be expressed as

$$\Delta V = (X^{-1}A)\,\Omega, \qquad (14.11)$$

where $A$ is the $3 \times J$ matrix of $a_i$ coefficients for the $J$ basic structures and $\Omega$ is the three-component vector of powers 0, 1, and 2 of the atomic volume $\Omega$. Equation (14.11) is strictly valid only if the correlation matrix $X$ is square. If not, Eq. (14.11) must be understood in a symbolic sense, and the coefficients of the powers of $\Omega$ in the ECIs must be determined by least-squares fit.[17-19,35,38,39]

By this procedure, a volume dependence is introduced, via the ECIs, in the CVM free energy. At thermodynamic equilibrium, the free energy should now be minimized not only with respect to the $\xi$ correlation variables, but also with respect to the average volume $\Omega$. Hence, optimal $\Omega$ values can be determined, for any phase (of the parent lattice considered), at any concentration and temperature, as was originally done in the case of the Al-Li system[143,144] and later for the Al-Ti system[17,18] (see Section 16), for example. In principle, formation energies could also be expanded to second order in other relaxation parameters, such as lattice parameter ratios, and the free energy could be minimized with respect to these parameters as well, but it appears that such calculations have not been performed as yet in the form suggested by Eqs. (14.9) and (14.10).

To summarize, we have shown how various relaxation processes could be combined with the structure inversion method (SIM) to generate cluster expansion coefficients, in particular, ECIs. Three types of structural relaxations were described: cell volume, cell shape, and cell internal displacements. All three can of course be lumped into the general category of *cell relaxation*. Three basic methods of relaxation were mentioned: (i) rigid lattice, (ii) global, (iii) local relaxation. Method (ii) is a postinversion relaxation, (iii) is preinversion. Method (i) obviously requires additional postinversion relaxation in order to produce approximately correct formation energies; however, the rigid lattice assumption may be useful to describe *coherent* equilibria, i.e., local stability properties. The postinversion relaxation of method (ii) can be applied in various ways (energy minimization, volume interpolation) and method (iii), the most elaborate, can itself be further supplemented by postinversion correction.

None of these methods treats atomic relaxation in disordered structures correctly, so that much work needs to be done in this field before a truly satisfactory treatment is found. In the meantime, the computational techniques described in this article have found interesting and quite encouraging applications. Examples are given in the next section.

## VII. Selected Applications

The preceding chapters have summarized the cluster formalism developed over the last 10 years or so. Of course, the object of the exercise is to compute thermodynamic properties of real alloy systems in order to make useful quantitative predictions. It would take a separate review article to present critically the vast amount of work that has been carried out recently in this rapidly growing field. Here only a few examples are selected from the work of the present author's collaborators for the purpose of illustrating the concepts presented in the previous chapters. Some applications of direct methods are described in Section 15, followed by two applications of the SIM (Section 16). Section 17 lists other pertinent work.

### 15. APPLICATIONS OF THE DCA

The first computations of ECIs to be performed on real alloys via *direct* methods, i.e., by perturbation of a disordered medium, were all based on the generalized perturbation method (GPM, briefly described in Section 13),[5,95,145–147] in some cases followed up by CVM phase diagram constructions.[148–151] These early studies were performed on transition metal alloys using the tight-binding Hamiltonian given in Dirac notation by

$$\mathbf{H} = \sum_{p,\lambda} |p, \lambda\rangle \, \varepsilon_p^\lambda \, \langle p, \lambda| + \sum_{\substack{p,p' \\ \mu,\mu'}} |p, \mu\rangle \, \beta_{p,p'}^{\mu,\mu'} \, \langle p', \mu'|, \qquad (15.1)$$

where Latin subscripts $(p, p')$ designate lattice sites and Greek superscripts $(\lambda, \mu)$ designate atomic orbitals. The accent on the summation

[145] A. Bieber and F. Gautier, *Physica B* **107**, 71 (1981).
[146] A. Bieber and F. Gautier, *Z. Phys. B* **57**, 335 (1984).
[147] A. Bieber, *Acta Metall.* **34**, 2291 (1986); *Acta Metall.* **35**, 1889 (1987).
[148] C. Sigli and J. M. Sanchez, *Acta Metall.* **36**, 367 (1988).
[149] C. Sigli, M. Kosugi, and J. M. Sanchez, *Phys. Rev. Lett.* **57**, 253 (1986).
[150] P. Turchi, M. Sluiter, and D. de Fontaine, *Phys. Rev. B* **36**, 3161 (1987).
[151] M. Sluiter, P. Turchi, Fu Zezhong, and D. de Fontaine, *Phys. Rev. Lett.* **60**, 716 (1988).

over hopping integrals $\beta$ indicates that distinct sites only ($p \neq p'$) are included. Initially, only $d$ orbitals were considered so that ECI calculations relied only on the $d$ electron numbers and on the diagonal disorder, equal to the difference of the $d$ electron on-site energies, $\delta = \varepsilon_A - \varepsilon_B$ (it is no longer necessary to retain the superscript notation on $\beta$ and $\varepsilon$ in this approximation). Generally, no off-diagonal disorder was considered, i.e., the hopping integrals $\beta$ were assumed to be independent of the nature of the atoms occupying the two neighboring atomic sites considered (off-diagonal disorder was included in Ref. 148, however).

In section 12, we showed how ECIs could be calculated from a knowledge of the local density of states, hence of the diagonal elements of the appropriate Green's functions. For the GPM, likewise, such diagonal elements are required in addition to off-diagonal elements, which may be obtained indirectly in a simple manner.[152] In the context of the tight-binding Hamiltonian, in these early GPM studies, and in the current DCA method, the recursion method[119] was shown to provide an efficient technique for obtaining the required Green's function elements. The recursion process essentially transforms the Hamiltonian matrix to tridiagonal form by means of the Lanczos algorithm: Given a starting vector$|u_0\rangle$, one recursively generates a new set of vectors $|u_i\rangle$ by a Gram-Schmidt orthogonalization process. At step $n$, the recursion expression for the ($n + 1$)'th new vector is

$$H|u_n\rangle = b_{n-1}|u_{n-1}\rangle + a_n|u_n\rangle + b_{n+1}|u_{n+1}\rangle, \tag{15.2}$$

with diagonal and off-diagonal elements of $H$ in the new basis given by

$$a_n = \langle u_n|H|u_n\rangle, \tag{15.3a}$$

and

$$b_n = \langle u_{n-1}|H|u_n\rangle. \tag{15.3b}$$

A continued fraction expansion conveniently gives the diagonal element of the inverse of the tridiagonal matrix $E\mathbf{I} - \mathbf{H}$:

$$\langle u_0|G(E)|u_0\rangle = \cfrac{b_0^2}{E - a_1 - \cfrac{b_1^2}{E - a_2 - \cfrac{b_2^2}{E - a_3 - \ldots}}} \tag{15.4}$$

[152] Christophe H. Sigli, "On the Electronic Structure and Thermodynamics of Alloys," Ph.D. Dissertation, Columbia University (1986) (unpublished).

One usually sets up a finite system of atoms and computes the first few "levels" of the continued fraction [Eq. (15.4)]. Beyond a certain level, the $a$ and $b$ elements are taken to be constant, leading to a quadratic "terminator" for the continued fraction.

Since TB recursion is an extremely efficient real-space method, it was really not necessary to calculate ECIs by perturbing a CPA medium, originally constructed to restore translational symmetry. Hence the DCA method, which avoids the mean-field single-site (CPA) approximation and which naturally incorporates the effects of off-diagonal disorder, was developed,[13,14,49,116,117] as presented in Section 12. In these calculations, $s$, $p$, and $d$ orbitals were considered. The TB parameters, $\varepsilon_I^\lambda$ and $\beta_{I,J}^{\mu,\mu'}(r - r')$ $(I, J = A$ or $B)$ were assumed to depend on the atoms occupying the sites $(p, p')$ and on the lattice distance $(r - r')$ between them. Generally, first and second neighbor hopping integrals were considered. Values of on-site energies and hopping integrals were obtained from the LMTO-ASA formalism recast into two-center TB form following the method of Andersen and coworkers.[153] Scalar-relativistic corrections were incorporated along with (in some calculations) combined correction terms. Unlike-pair hopping integrals were obtained as the harmonic means of the pure element parameters:[153,154]

$$\beta_{I,J}^{\lambda,\mu} = \sqrt{\beta_{I,I}^{\lambda,\mu} \, \beta_{J,J}^{\lambda,\mu}}. \tag{15.5}$$

Average-medium configurations were constructed by randomly selecting $A$ and $B$ atoms with equal probability, which, for a computational region of about 1000 atoms, produced an average concentration departing only insignificantly from the central one, $c = 0.5$, in the spirit of the U-sum scheme of ECI calculations. The computational region, a portion of fcc or bcc lattice, as required, was constructed in the most efficient manner by the "zebra" technique of Dreyssé and Riedinger.[155] Such disordered-medium calculations require certain decisions to be made regarding (1) the atomic volumes at which pure-element LMTO-ASA TB parameters are calculated and (2) the method of handling diagonal disorder $(\delta)$ in the disordered alloy. Regarding point (1), the following procedure was used most often: Total-energy LMTO-ASA calculations were performed

[153] O. K. Andersen and O. Jepsen, *Phys. Rev. Lett.* **53**, 2571 (1984); O. K. Andersen, O. Jepsen and D. Glötzel, in *Highlights of Condensed-Matter Theory* (F. Bassani, F. Fumi, and M. P. Tosi, eds.), pp. 59–176, North-Holland, Amsterdam (1985); O. K. Andersen, O. Jepsen, and M. Sob, *Electronic Band Structure and Its Applications,* Vol. 283 of *Lecture Notes in Physics,* (M. Yussouf, ed.), Springer, Berlin (1987).

[154] H. Shiba, *Prog. Theor. Phys.* **46**, 77 (1971).

[155] H. Dreyssé and R. Riedinger, *J. Phys.* (Paris) **48**, 915 (1987).

on pure $A$ and $B$ at various atomic volumes, the resulting energies were fitted to a third-order polynomial, and the equilibrium atomic volumes $\Omega_A$ and $\Omega_B$ at 0 K were determined from the minimum values of the energy versus $\Omega$ curves. The average atomic volume $\Omega$ at the central concentration was then determined by linear interpolation (Vegard's law), and the alloy parameters were determined from the LMTO-ASA TB formalism at that new volume. A parabolic volume correction was applied later to the calculated ground state energies, as explained in Section 14. That and other approximations are discussed in detail by Wolverton *et al.*,[14,15] along with a comparison of the use of LMTO and band-structure-fitted TB parameters.[156]

Regarding point 2, it is clear that, in general for each orbital $\lambda$, the on-site energies $\varepsilon_I^\lambda$ must be shifted for one of the two elements. The assumption used was that all orbital energies of, say, $I = B$ were to be displaced by the same amount and that displacement was such as to guarantee, on average, zero charge transfer between atoms, an assumption often used for transition metal alloys.[157] This shift procedure and Fermi level determination are arrived at by an iterative self-consistent procedure, as described elsewhere.[14,117]

The flowchart shown in Fig. 12 summarizes the overall DCA procedure: For an alloy $A$-$B$ specified by only the atomic numbers $Z_A$ and $Z_B$, TB parameters are obtained from LMTO density-functional codes, as explained earlier, for a particular lattice (or set of sublattices), say, fcc. Local charge neutrality is imposed on the configurationally averaged random medium (not indicated in the flowchart), then distinct configurations of a selected cluster (*nn* triplets, in the example of Fig. 12) are embedded in the medium. Local density of states (LDOS) are computed by the recursion technique *cum* continued fraction expansion and the effective cluster interaction for that cluster ($\alpha$) is calculated by the formalism described in Section 12, Eq. (12.12) in particular. Other ECIs are calculated, always on the same lattice, until convergence is attained, i.e., until the absolute magnitude of $V_\alpha$ times its multiplicity $m_\alpha$ is considered too small to influence the outcome of ground state or phase diagram calculations.

Ground states themselves are determined by searching for the vertices of the multidimensional configurational polyhedron, as described in Section 7. The search is facilitated here because the ECI for the system and lattice are *known*, so that the Danzig linear programming algorithm converges rapidly on the energy-minimizing vertex. Sometimes, how-

[156]D. A. Papaconstantopoulos, *Handbook of the Band Structure of Elemental Solids*, Plenum Press, New York (1986).

[157]M. O. Robbins and L. M. Falicov, *Phys. Rev. B* **29**, 1333 (1984).

# DCA

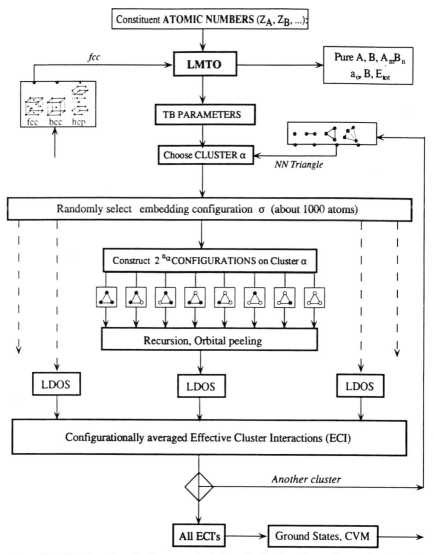

FIG. 12. DCA flowchart leading to calculation of effective cluster interactions [D. de Fontaine and C. Wolverton, *Ber. Bunsenges. Phys. Chem.* **96,** 1503 (1992)].

ever, the vertex coordinates ($\bar{\xi}_\alpha$) do not produce a *constructible* crystal structure, and that vertex must be eliminated from the convex hull. At this stage, free energy functions may be obtained by CVM free energy minimization, as indicated schematically in Fig. 13, where each ground state ordered superstructure produces a free energy curve (as a function of $c$, for given $T$). We may include the free energies of metastable structures as well, i.e., of those structures whose 0 K energies fall inside but close to the vertices and lines of the convex hull. It may actually happen that some phases that are only metastable at low temperature become stable at high temperature, a trivial example being that of the disordered phase.

After stable (or metastable) ordered phases of the parent lattice have been determined, one then selects another lattice (top part of Fig. 13) and returns to the head of the DCA flowchart to start all over again (with bcc, in this example). The various parent lattice ground state structures are then plotted on a formation energy versus concentration master diagram, and the overall convex hull is constructed to determine the expected ground state structures for the *A-B* system in question, regardless of parent lattice. Before thus combining formation energies, however, it is necessary to relate pure states in the different lattices to one another by means of structural energy differences, as explained in Section 14. Since pure *A* and *B* structural energies (calculated directly by the LMTO-ASA method) are plotted at their fully *relaxed* volumes, and ECIs are calculated in a *constrained* state (at $c = 0.5$, generally), it is necessary to apply an elastic energy correction of the type provided by Eq. (14.8), for example. A positive quadratic term (in $c$) cannot introduce new ordered ground states, but can eliminate ones calculated in the constrained state, as in the schematic diagram of Fig. 11.

This may appear to be a roundabout way of doing things but it has distinct advantages. In particular, use of concentration-independent interactions (U-sum) allows one to perform a true ground state search, which returns the lowest energy vertex structures without having to guess which structures would be the likely ones to occur in the system ("rounding up the usual suspects"[9]). The true ground state search with c-independent ECIs can deliver unsuspected structures, and the method is thus really *predictive*.

Some intermetallic compound structures are of course *not* superstructures of some Bravais lattice. We call these structures, such as the *A*15 or various Laves phases, *interloper* structures. They may be placed on formation energy diagrams by direct total energy electronic structure calculations, then compared to ECI-constructed superstructures. If the suspected interloper breaks the superstructure convex hull, it becomes a

# CVM

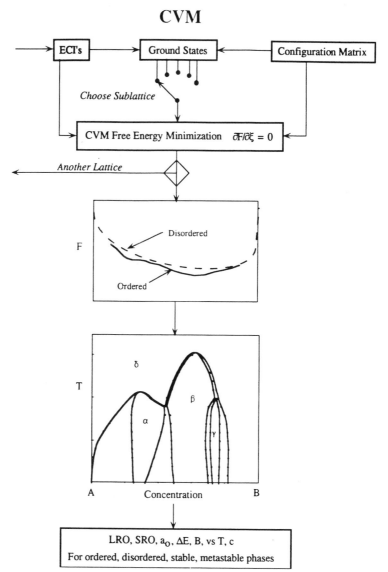

FIG. 13. Flowchart indicating use of ECIs (for example, calculated by DCA technique) in CVM calculations [D. de Fontaine and C. Wolverton, *Ber. Bunsenges. Phys. Chem.* **96,** 1503 (1992)].

*bona fide* ground state. Some examples of these procedures are given next. Note that in all cases to be presented, all ground state structures, except the $A15$'s, were predicted without prior knowledge of their existence. Also, no other parameters but the atomic numbers were entered; no empirical data or fitting parameters were used. Of course, assumptions are made, approximations are used, but the method is indeed a *first-principles* method.

The elements V, Pd, Ti, and Pt form binary alloys whose $(T, c)$ phase diagrams are purported to be "well known."[158] Only the fcc and bcc lattices were considered with 13-, 14-point cluster and 9-, 8-point cluster combinations (bcc cube and two interpenetrating squares,[13] respectively, for the ground state searches). Since the hcp parent structure was not considered in the calculations, no hcp-based superstructures could be predicted. However, energies of corresponding fcc-based superstructures are expected to provide good approximations thereof. Maximal clusters selected allowed for 23 ECIs to be calculated in the fcc case, and 13 in bcc—the largest sets used up until now in such types of calculations.

Commonly occurring fcc and bcc superstructures were depicted in article I (Figs. 28 and 29). Other relevant structures[13] are shown here in Fig. 14; all are superstructures of fcc or bcc lattices, except the $A15$. Calculated formation energy diagrams for Pd-V, Pt-V, and Pt-Ti are given in Figs. 15, 16, and 17, respectively.[13] In all of these diagrams square (round) symbols denote bcc (fcc)-based superstructures, interlopers ($A15$) being represented by triangles. Filled symbols correspond to stable structures and are therefore located at vertices of the (overall: fcc and bcc) convex hull (heavy polygonal line). Open symbols refer to unstable (or metastable) structures inside the convex hull. Dashed-dotted curves represent the energies as a function of concentration of the fully disordered fcc (bcc) states, as calculated by Eq. (5.7). The zero line for $\Delta H$ (formation *enthalpy,* rather than energy; the two are equivalent since the $P\Delta\Omega$ term is small in comparison to the formation energy differences) is obtained from Eq. (14.1), in which $E_A$ and $E_B$ are the energies of the pure elements in their stable structures. From Figs. 15, 16, and 17, it is immediately apparent that structural energy differences (fcc-bcc) are very small and negative for elements Pd, Pt, and Ti, but large ($\sim 0.3$ eV) and positive for V. The effect on combined ground state energy diagrams is to skew and displace the partial convex hulls of the individual parent-lattice-based structures.

[158]T. B. Massalski, ed., *Binary Alloy Phase Diagrams,* 2nd ed., ASM International, Materials Park, OH (1990).

Results for the three binary alloy systems are now briefly described and are discussed in detail elsewhere.[13,14,49]

a. *Pd-V System*

Results of TB-LMTO-ASA-DCA calculations are reported in Fig. 15. Despite the fact that pure vanadium is much more stable in the bcc than in the fcc structure, it is found that ordering energies are much stronger for fcc-based than for bcc-based superstructures for the alloy as a whole. This is partly due to the fact that the *nn* and *nnn* bcc EPIs are of opposite sign and nearly equal in magnitude. Hence, the bcc energy cluster expansion is dominated by (small) triplet interactions, which are responsible for the asymmetry of the disordered state formation energy curve dashed-dotted in Fig. 15. Only the *A*15, and of course pure V itself (but none of the bcc superstructures) break the fcc-dominated convex hull. In particular, the *B*2 energy is found to be much higher than its fcc counterpart $L1_0$ at the central composition. Structure $D0_{22}$ is correctly predicted to be more stable than $L1_2$ at $Pd_3V$ by a small amount, as observed. Prototype

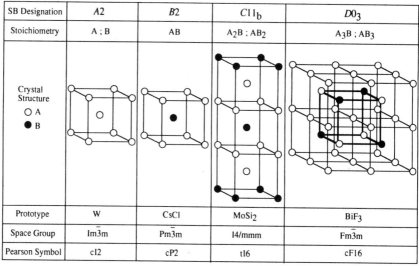

| SB Designation | *A*2 | *B*2 | $C11_b$ | $D0_3$ |
|---|---|---|---|---|
| Stoichiometry | A ; B | AB | $A_2B$ ; $AB_2$ | $A_3B$ ; $AB_3$ |
| Crystal Structure<br>○ A<br>● B | | | | |
| Prototype | W | CsCl | $MoSi_2$ | $BiF_3$ |
| Space Group | Im3̄m | Pm3̄m | I4/mmm | Fm3̄m |
| Pearson Symbol | cI2 | cP2 | tI6 | cF16 |

(a)

Fig. 14. (a) Commonly occurring bcc-based ordered structures. The Structurbericht designation of each structure is given as well as the stoichiometry, crystal structure, prototype, space group symbol, and Pearson symbol. (b) Less common crystal structures occurring in Figs. 15, 16, and 17 [C. Wolverton, Ph.D. Dissertation, University of California, Berkeley, 1993 (unpublished)].

## fcc Superstructures

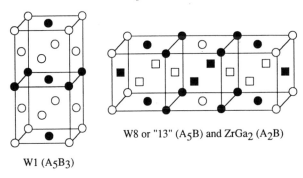

W1 (A₅B₃)

W8 or "13" (A₅B) and ZrGa₂ (A₂B)

## bcc Superstructures

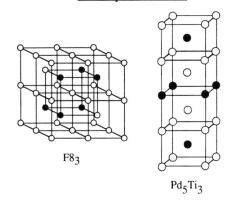

F8₃

Pd₅Ti₃

## Complex Phase

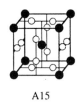

A15

(b)

FIG. 14—(Continued)

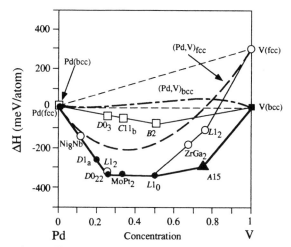

FIG. 15. Ground state diagram of the formation enthalpies for Pd-V alloys. Circles and squares indicate fcc- and bcc-based superstructures, respectively. The *A*15 compound is designated by a triangle. Filled symbols denote structures that lie on the ground state convex hull and therefore are stable. Open symbols indicate structures that do not lie on the convex hull. The dashed-dotted line is the formation enthalpy of disordered fcc (bcc) Pd-V alloys.

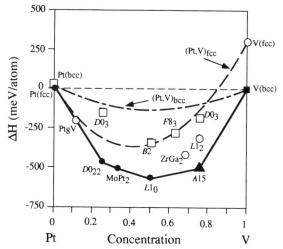

FIG. 16. Ground state diagram of the formation enthalpies for Pt-V alloys. Circles and squares indicate fcc- and bcc-based superstructures, respectively. The *A*15 compound is designated by a triangle. Filled symbols denote structures that lie on the ground state convex hull and therefore are stable. Open symbols indicate structures that do not lie on the convex hull. The dashed-dotted line is the formation enthalpy of disordered fcc (bcc) Pt-V alloys.

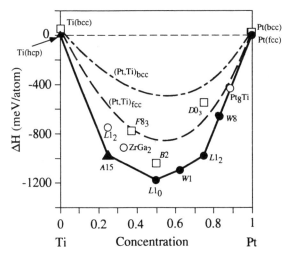

FIG. 17. Ground state diagram of the formation enthalpies for Pt-Ti alloys. Circles and squares indicate fcc- and bcc-based superstructures, respectively. The $A15$ compound and hcp Ti are designated by large and small triangles, respectively. Filled symbols denote structures that lie on the ground state convex hull and therefore are stable. Open symbols indicate structures that do not lie on the convex hull. The dashed-dotted line is the formation enthalpy of disordered fcc (bcc) Pt-Ti alloys.

$MoPt_2$ is also known to be the stable ground state at $Pd_2V$ stoichiometry, as predicted here, but the $D1_a$ structure at $Pd_4V$ has not been observed experimentally. The calculations show that it is only slightly more stable than the two-phase combination $Pd_3V$ + Pd. The most serious discrepancy occurs for $L1_0$, which, in the calculation, breaks the convex hull, whereas experimentally,[158] at least down to about 400°C, no ordering is observed at Pd-V stoichiometry. The spurious $L1_0$ would of course disappear if more accurate calculations showed that either the $A15$ or $MoPt_2$ structures had lower energies than those obtained here. The $Ni_8Nb$ prototype, according to the calculations, barely misses being stable. Also, since the difference between the open-symbol $Pd_8V$ energy and the dashed line for the disordered state at the same concentration is very small, it is expected that, even if this phase were stable, its ordering transition temperature would be very small, perhaps unobservable experimentally without accelerating the kinetics of the reaction. Some evidence exists for $Pd_8V$ ordering at low temperatures, as observed for example under electron irradiation[159,160] below about 400°C. The fcc-based calcula-

[159] J. Cheng and A. J. Ardell, *J. Less-Common Metals* **141**, 45 (1988).

[160] A. J. Ardell, in *Metallic Alloys: Experimental and Theoretical Perspectives* ( J. S. Faulkner and R. G. Jordan, eds.) NATO ASI Series, Vol. 256, pp. 93–102, Kluwer, Dordrecht (1994).

tions for this system indicate that the Pd side is dominated by the $\langle 1\frac{1}{2}0 \rangle$-type special point instability (see article I, also Section 11 here) with its attendant superstructures $MoPt_2$, $D0_{22}$, $D1_a$. The $L1_0$ structure belongs to the $\langle 100 \rangle$ instability family of superstructures. Close competition between these special point instabilities, especially near $Pd_3V$ ($D0_{22}$ and $L1_2$ have almost the same energies) is clearly related to the experimental observation[109] that the short-range order above the $Pd_3V$ transition is of $\langle 100 \rangle$ type, whereas the long-range order ($D0_{22}$) is of $\langle 1\frac{1}{2}0 \rangle$ type. All in all, although some discrepancies do exist, none of the unambiguously (experimentally) observed structures failed to turn up in the theoretical ground state search, and the calculations even provided insight into possible metastabilities in this system.

### b. Pt-V System

The formation energy diagram for Pt-V is shown in Fig. 16. As might be expected, the Pd-V and Pt-V experimentally determined phase diagrams are quite similar except that in the latter a central ordered structure is observed to be stable (where none is found in Pd-V). Correspondingly, the calculated ground state diagrams for those two systems are also similar, with perhaps stronger ordering tendency at $c = 0.5$ for PtV. The experimentally observed PtV intermetallic has the $B19$ structure, not the expected $L1_0$. However, the $B19$ is just the hcp counterpart of $L1_0$, and it could not be predicted here since the hcp parent structure was not included in the calculations. Not only are overall ordering energies higher in the Pt-V system (compare $\Delta H$ scales), but bcc ordering is relatively stronger than it was in the Pd-V system: the bcc disordered phase formation energy is now negative, indicating ordering tendencies, whereas it was positive, asymmetric (and small) for the Pd-V case, indicating phase separation tendencies (for the bcc-based system only, of course). The larger bcc ordering tendencies are still not large enough to bring the $B2$ superstructure into competition with the $L1_0$ (or, more properly, the $B19$). Actually, the Pt-V calculations are in even better agreement with experiment than was the case for Pd-V: As observed in reality, the $D1_a$ structure is no longer found to be stable and the $Pt_8V$ structure comes even closer to being stable than was the case for the $Pd_8V$ structure. Indeed, there is even stronger experimental evidence for that structure's low-temperature stability than for the Pd-based phase.[161,162] In the present system as well, the $D0_{22}$ and $L1_2$ energies at $Pt_3V$ are very close[14] (not shown in Fig. 16). Usually, when such quasi-degeneracy occurs between these two fcc superstructures, it means that the antiphase boundary energy is very

small. That, in turn, means that long-period superstructures may be expected. Remarkably, fcc-based long-period superstructures have indeed been observed near the $Pt_3V$ concentration.[161,162]

c. *Pt-Ti System*

The Pt-Ti formation energy diagram is shown in Fig. 17. From direct LMTO-ASA calculations, the ground state of pure Ti is correctly found to be hcp (denoted by an open triangle in the figure). As for the other systems examined here, actual hcp-based superstructures were calculated based on the fcc lattice instead. Here also, bcc superstructures do not break the convex hull, although now the $B2$ structure comes much closer to doing so, partly because differences between pure-state bcc and close-packed structures for *both* metals are so small. Not surprisingly then, $B2$ PtTi is observed as a stable phase at high temperature, presumably being stabilized with respect to the corresponding close-packed superstructure by vibrational entropy effects, as indeed pure bcc Ti is stabilized at high temperature vis-à-vis hcp. Actually, high-temperature $B2$ TiPt is observed to transform martensitically to $B19$ at about 1000°C, the hcp counterpart of the predicted $L1_0$. The experimentally determined phase diagram of TiPt is rather complex[158] and not very well assessed; many of the phase regions are shown tentatively with dotted lines. Nevertheless, some features are well established, in addition to the $B2 \rightarrow B19$ ($L1_0$) transition just mentioned: $Ti_3Pt$ is the $A15$ structure, in agreement with the present calculation, $TiPt_3$ is $L1_2$, again in agreement with the predicted ground state, and $TiPt_8$ is probably stable at low temperature, its calculated formation energy falling practically on the $W8$-Pt tie line, which is practically the $L1_2$-Pt tie line. The $W8$ structure (see Fig. 14) is not observed experimentally, and the predicted $W1$ [Fig. 14(a)] has the correct stoichiometry of the observed high-temperature phase, $Ti_3Pt_5$, but not the correct crystal structure [Fig. 14(b)]. Curiously, the latter is a bcc-based structure, the former is fcc-based. Both have same crystallographic space groups and same number (8) of atoms per unit cell. In the experimental phase diagram, the $Pt_8Ti$ phase region is shown in dotted lines and is thought to appear by peritectoid reaction at about 1000°C.

[161] D. Schryvers and S. Amelinckx, *Acta Metall.* **34**, 43 (1986).

[162] J. Planès, Thèse de Doctorat d'Etat, Université Paris VI, Paris (1990) (unpublished); J. Planès, A. Loiseau, F. Ducastelle, and G. van Tendeloo, in *Electron Microscopy and Analysis*, Institute of Physics Conference Series No. 90, p. 229, Institute of Physics, Bristol (1987).

The calculated $Pt_8Ti$ is very close to being stable;[14] experimental evidence definitely indicates it to be stable.[160,163]

In summary, the DCA formalism applied to ground state determination turned out to be strikingly successful for these (and other) binary alloy systems. Calculated and measured formation energies (where available) were also found to be in rather good agreement.[13] The test systems were chosen primarily for the following reasons: (1) They involved nonmagnetic transition metal elements for which the TB approximation is expected to give accurate results, and (2) alloys formed from one early and one late element of the transition metal series are expected to order strongly, all the more so that the average $d$ band filling is close to one half.[5,164]

Phase separating systems, such as Pd-Rh, have also been investigated,[15] with a predicted miscibility gap in excellent quantitative agreement with the experimentally determined phase diagram. In addition, these DCA calculations are very efficient and may be carried out on a computer workstation: Once the ECIs have been determined, the formation energies of various ordered superstructures of the parent lattice can be performed by cluster expansion over just a few ECIs and cluster correlation parameters, by means of expansion (7.1), or other similar expansions can be derived from Eqs. (4.4) or (5.1). Only interlopers ($A15$) require separate total energy electronic structure calculations in each case. The success of the calculations reported is partly attributable to the large number of calculated ECIs used in the cluster expansion technique. In other, more computer-intensive studies, the number of ECIs was often quite limited, and did not always suffice to produce (relatively) correct formation energies of competing structures.

The material of this section emphasizes the need to break down the ground state analysis into separate calculations for the different lattices envisioned (here, fcc and bcc). Under those conditions, the *ordered structure* ground state determination can be really predictive, and not rely on assumed or guessed-at structures. Moreover, such a procedure allows one to analyze stability in terms of competition between different parent lattices and, for each lattice, of competition between various types of ordering instabilities (special point "families," see I). Finally, these calculations clearly emphasize the need to perform *global* comparisons; simply evaluating energy differences *locally* (at a fixed composition) is not really meaningful.

[163] D. Schryvers, J. van Landuyt, G. van Tendeloo, and S. Amelinckx, *Phys. Stat. Sol. A* **76**, 575 (1983).

[164] M. Sluiter, P. Turchi, and D. de Fontaine, *J. Phys. F: Met. Phys.* **17**, 2163 (1987).

Not all alloy systems are amenable to the treatment described in this section. In particular, metallic systems whose constituents have very different $d$ band widths often cannot be modeled adequately by a first-order TB Hamiltonian. For example, DCA calculations give the wrong sign for the $nn$ EPI (clustering instead of ordering) in Cu-Pd. Also, although global relaxation may be taken into account,[15] unit cell relaxations (see Section 14) cannot be treated conveniently by the DCA as it presently stands; semiempirical repulsive terms would have to be included to handle atomic displacement. A case in point is the $Al_3Ti$ intermetallic compound, the experimentally observed structure of which is the fcc-based $D0_{22}$, with tetragonal unit cell, the cubic $L1_2$ being a close competitor. Actually, $D0_{22}$ wins in this case only if the $c/a$ ratio is allowed to relax away from its ideal value to its equilibrium one. In such a situation, a different formalism is clearly required, one that takes cell relaxation into account in a very accurate manner. The SIM is such a method, as is demonstrated next.

16. Applications of the SIM

As mentioned in Section 13, the SIM method was originally proposed by Connolly and Williams.[112] It was rapidly applied to calculations of solid-state phase equilibria by Terakura and coworkers,[165] Zunger and coworkers,[9,35,39,166] and Carlsson and Sanchez,[167] who made use of the CVM free energy minimization. The first treatment of combined fcc- and bcc-based phase equilibria appears to have been the application by Sluiter et al. to the Al-Li system.[143,144] Many more applications followed, a partial list of which is given in table form in the next section. Here, we report on very recent studies that illustrate two particular aspects of the method: (1) the necessity of performing full-potential total energy calculations for obtaining ECIs in the difficult but technologically important Ti-Al system[16-18] and (2) the use in the hcp-based Cd-Mg system[16,19] of cluster expansions to describe other configuration-dependent properties such as elastic relaxation and vibrational and electronic free energies. The reader is referred to the original work for detailed descriptions of the calculations.

[165] K. Terakura, T. Oguchi, T. Mohri, and K. Watanabe, *Phys. Rev. B* **35**, 2169 (1987); T. Mohri, K. Terakura, T. Oguchi and K. Watanabe, *Acta Metall.* **36**, 547 (1988); T. Mohri, K. Terakura, S. Takizawa, and J. M. Sanchez, *Acta Metall. Mater.* **39**, 493 (1991).

[166] A. A. Mbaye, L. G. Ferreira, and A. Zunger, *Phys. Rev. Lett.* **58**, 49 (1987).

[167] A. E. Carlsson and J. M. Sanchez, *Solid State Commun.* **65**, 527 (1988).

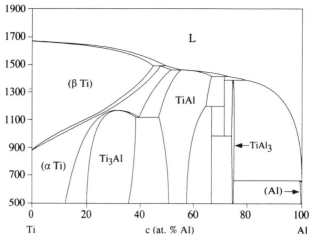

FIG. 18. Ti-Al phase diagram obtained from optimal assessment of available experimental data [U. R. Kattner, J.-C. Lin, and Y. A. Chang, *Met. Trans.* **23A,** 2081 (1992)].

## a. *The Ti-Al System*

Experimental Ti-Al phase equilibrium data were recently assessed by Kattner et al.,[168] resulting in the phase diagram shown in Fig. 18. It is immediately apparent that three different parent structures will have to be included for a complete calculation of the phase diagram by the methods presented in this chapter: cluster expansion *cum* CVM: Al is fcc; Ti is hcp at low temperature and bcc at high temperature. $Ti_3Al$ is an hcp-based ordered structure ($D0_{19}$), TiAl and $TiAl_3$ are fcc-based structures ($L1_0$ and $D0_{22}$, respectively). The phase regions of $TiAl_2$ and $Ti_2Al_5$ are still not well known, so these structures are not considered in this analysis. All ground states are based on close-packed parents; the bcc phase ($\beta Ti$) is stabilized at high temperature only by vibrational entropy and has also been left out, along with the liquid phase, in the present calculation.

Stable equilibrium in this system is thus seen to result from competition between fcc, hcp (and bcc) parents and, within the fcc reference lattice, between $\langle 100 \rangle$ and $\langle 1\frac{1}{2}0 \rangle$ ordering instabilities, since $L1_0$ is a member of the former and $D0_{22}$ of the latter "families" (see article I). This ordering wave competition is also manifest in the close competition between $L1_2$ and $D0_{22}$ structures near the $TiAl_3$ stoichiometry, as revealed by total energy calculations and also by calorimetric measurements.[169,170] More

[168] U. R. Kattner, J.-C. Lin, and Y. A. Chang, *Met. Trans. A* **23A,** 2081 (1992).

[169] R. B. Schwarz, P. B. Desch, and S. Srinivasan, to be published in *Statics and Dynamics of Alloy Phase Transformations* (P. E. A. Turchi and A. Gonis, eds.), NATO ASI Series, Plenum Press, New York.

[170] R. Bormann, private communication (1993).

generally, the electronic factors favoring the relative stability of $L1_2$ and $D0_{22}$ were studied by Carlsson for the aluminides $Al_3M$, $M$ being a $3d$, $4d$, or $5d$ transition metal of groups III, IV, and V.[171] For the group IV elements $M$ = Ti and Zr, the $D0_{22}$ structure is experimentally observed to be the equilibrium ground state, whereas LDA calculations based on the fcc lattice predict $L1_2$. Only if the $c/a$ ratio is allowed to relax away from its ideal value (as in the parent fcc) can one predict theoretically the greater stability of the $D0_{22}$ structure,[17] as was found earlier by Nicholson et al.[172] For SIM purposes, it will not do simply to calculate total energies at experimentally observed lattice parameter ratios, for the following reasons. With only $nn$ ECIs (pair, triangle, tetrahedron), the $L1_2$ and $D0_{22}$ structures are degenerate in energy. Hence, at least $nnn$ EPIs must be included. That, in turn, requires that a rather large number of basic structure energies be calculated. As described in detail elsewhere,[16–18] a total of 11 fcc-based ordered structures were chosen (including fcc Al and fcc Ti), only a few of which, of course, are observed experimentally. These structures (with possible $A/B$ interchange) were described in Fig. 4(a). For the others, no experimental values of lattice parameter ratios are available. For consistency, all ordered structures must be treated similarly; hence, all unit cell sizes and shapes must be calculated *ab initio* and locally relaxed, as explained in Section 14(b), method iii. Atomic sphere (ASA) methods were found to be too unreliable, so that extensive full-potential calculations had to be carried out with full relaxation on all 11 structures. These calculations were performed by van Schilfgaarde[17,18] by means of the full-potential LMTO code developed by Methfessel.[173] SIM and CVM calculations were carried out by Asta,[16–18] who applied the postinversion volume relaxation of Sluiter[74,144] described in Section 16(b). The optimal subset of structures selected for the inversion (least-squares) process was chosen according to the technique described in Section 14(a). For each basic structure, the three coefficients $a_i^{(j)}$ were obtained from Eqs. (14.10) after fitting the calculated values of $\Delta E^{(j)}(\Omega)$ to a third-order polynomial, yielding 0 K equilibrium values $\Delta E_0^{(j)}$, $\Omega_0^{(j)}$, and $B_0^{(j)}$. The $\Delta V$ values of Eq. (14.11) were obtained by least-squares analysis.

In all, formation energies, bulk moduli, average atomic volumes, and, where applicable, $c/a$ and $b/a$ ratios were calculated for 20 structures, a much larger set of structures than previously calculated for this system.

[171] A. E. Carlsson and P. J. Meschter, *J. Mater. Res.* **4**, 1060 (1989).

[172] D. M. Nicholson, G. M. Stocks, W. M. Temmerman, P. Sterne, and D. G. Pettifor, *Mat. Res. Soc. Symp. Proc.* (C. T. Liu, A. I. Taub, N. S. Stoloff and C. C. Koch, eds.), Vol. 133, pp. 17–22 (1989).

[173] M. Methfessel, *Phys. Rev. B* **38**, 1537 (1988).

TABLE IV. STRUCTURAL VALUES FOR SOME TI-AL PHASES

| | | $\Delta E_0$ (kJ/mole) | | $B_0$ (MBar) | | $\Omega_0$ (cm3/mole) | | $c/a$ | |
|---|---|---|---|---|---|---|---|---|---|
| COMPOSITION | STRUCTURE | CALCULATED | EXPERIMENTAL | CALCULATED | EXPERIMENTAL | CALCULATED | EXPERIMENTAL | CALCULATED | EXPERIMENTAL |
| Ti | hcp | 0 | 0 | 1.06 | 1.05 | 9.917 | 10.638 | 1.617 | 1.588 |
| Ti$_3$Al | D0$_{19}$ | −28.7 | −25.3 | 1.26 | | 9.510 | 10.06 to 10.121 | 0.809 | 0.806 |
| TiAl | L1$_0$ | −42.0 | −36.2 | 1.28 | | 9.284 | 9.028 to 9.811 | 1.012 | 1.016 to 1.017 |
| TiAl$_3$ | L1$_2$ | −39.6 | 4 to 5* | 1.18 | | 9.039 | | | |
| TiAl$_3$ | D0$_{22}$ | −41.9 | −37.4 to −36.3 | 1.18 | | 9.178 | 9.596 to 9.569 | 2.240 | 2.227 to 2.235 |
| Al | fcc | 0 | | 0.84 | 0.822 | 9.531 | 9.999 | | |

Calculated and experimentally determined values of formation energy ($\Delta E_0$), bulk modulus ($B_0$), average atomic volume ($\Omega_0$), and $c/a$ ratio (where applicable) for indicated compounds. Calculated values are from the work of Asta et al. [M. Asta, Ph.D. Dissertation, University of California, Berkeley, 1993; M. Asta, D. de Fontaine, M. van Schilfgaarde, M. Sluiter, and M. Methfessel, *Phys. Rev. B* **46**, 505 (1992); M. Asta, D. de Fontaine, and Mark van Schilfgaarde, *J. Mater. Res.* **8**, 2554 (1993)] where full bibliographic reference will be found concerning the experimental data. Starred (*) item gives experimentally measured differences between $L1_2$ and $D0_{22}$ formation energies [R. B. Schwarz, P. B. Desch, and S. Srinivasan, to be published in *Statics and Dynamics of Alloy Phase Transformations* (P. E. A. Turchi and A. Gonis, eds.), NATO ASI Series, Plenum Press, New York; R. Bormann, private communication].

148

Of these structures, only five are observed to be stable; they are listed in Table IV along with the TiAl$_3$ $L1_2$ structure, which, as seen from the table, has energy that differs only slightly from that of the stable $D0_{22}$. Where available, a range of experimentally determined values is also given so that one may judge how well calculated and experimental values agree, and what sort of scatter to expect from measurements. In the original work,[16-18] extensive comparison is also made between values calculated by other investigators. In general, it appears that agreement between theory and experiment is quite good. In particular, calculated $c/a$ ratios lie almost within the experimental scatter, and bulk moduli are predicted accurately. Systematic differences are observed for formation energies and atomic volumes, however: Calculated energies appear to be about 15% too high and volumes less than 10% too low. Some but not all of these discrepancies may be attributed to the fact that the calculations are performed at 0 K, the measurements at room temperature.

Energy differences between $L1_2$ and $D0_{22}$ at TiAl$_3$ stoichiometry were measured to be about 4 to 5 kJ/mole,[169,170] whereas the FPLMTO gave a 2.3 kJ/mole difference. Surprisingly, a previous LMTO-ASA calculation[174] appeared to give better agreement with experiment. This result is somewhat fortuitous, however: The calorimetric measurements almost certainly overestimate the (small) energy difference since the $L1_2$ phase can only be prepared in a highly nonequilibrium manner by ball milling. This operation surely introduces topological defects in the $L1_2$ structure (dislocations, grain boundaries, surfaces), which raise its energy over and above its (unrealizable) relaxed state.

Figure 19 compares graphically calculated Ti-Al ground states and calorimetric experiments of Kubaschewski and Dench.[175] First, note that all well-determined observed structures are calculated correctly, i.e., hcp Ti, $D0_{19}$, $L1_2$, $D0_{22}$, fcc Al. Then, note that experimental data points lie very close to the predicted convex hull. As in the previous section, we have also plotted in Fig. 19 the formation energies of fcc and hcp disordered phases, calculated by Eq. (5.7) from the cluster expansion method. The behavior of these two curves illustrates rather nicely the competition between hcp and fcc in this system: for low Al concentration, hcp dominates, for high Al concentration, fcc does, as expected, the crossover occurring at about equiatomic composition. The ground states shown in Fig. 19 were not obtained by vertex search, as was done in the previous

[174]T. Hong, T. J. Watson-Yang, A. J. Freeman, T. Oguchi, and Jian-hua Xu, *Phys. Rev. B.* **41**, 12462 (1990).
[175]O. Kubaschewski and W. A. Dench, *Acta Metall.* **3**, 339 (1955); O. Kubaschewski and G. Heymer, *Trans. Faraday Soc.* **56**, 473 (1960).

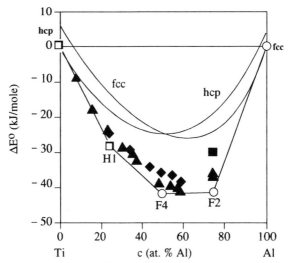

FIG. 19. Calculated (open symbols) and experimentally measured (filled symbols) formation energies for the Ti-Al system. Open squares and circles denote hcp-based and fcc-based structures respectively (see Table I for structure descriptions). Labeled curves indicate fcc and hcp disordered-state formation energies. All theoretical values are obtained by SIM [M. Asta, Ph.D. Dissertation, University of California, Berkeley, 1993 (unpublished); M. Asta *et al.*, *Phys. Rev. B* **46**, 505 (1992); M. Asta, D. de Fontaine, and M. Van Schilfgaarde, *J. Mater. Res.* **8**, 2554 (1993)]. Experimental data are from calorimetric measurements [filled triangles: O. Kubaschewski and W. A. Dench, *Acta Metall.* **3**, 339 (1955); O. Kubaschewski and G. Heymer, *Trans. Faraday Soc.* **56**, 473 (1960); R. Bormann, private communication (1993)].

section. Here, even when each lattice is considered separately, certain structures are stabilized by cell relaxation; for example, $c/a$ relaxation causes the $D0_{22}$ structure to break the fcc convex hull at TiAl$_3$. It follows that, with preinversion relaxation (or with the postinversion global correction, method ii) ground state searches must be conducted by comparing energies of trial structures, suspected to be reasonable ground state candidates. The configuration polyhedron method can only be used on a rigid lattice (method i).

In principle, the CECs having been calculated for formation energies, atomic volumes, and bulk moduli for a given parent structure (here fcc or hcp), we can now obtain the values of these quantities for any state of order characterized by correlation parameters $\xi_\alpha$. Generalizing Eq. (14.2) to any function $f$, standing for $E$, $\Omega$, or $B$, we may write for each phase $\varphi$

$$\Delta f[\xi^{(\varphi)}] = \sum_r^R \Delta F_r \xi_r^{(\varphi)}, \tag{16.1}$$

where the $\Delta F_r$ are the associated CECs defined as in Eq. (5.16) or (14.2). In ordered phases, the cluster orbits are "split" since correlation parameters have different symmetries than they have in the parent structure, hence the sum over orbit indices must be performed differently in the different phases. The values of the correlations themselves may be obtained by free energy minimization, for example, by using the CVM formalism (see Section 9). Thus, it is possible to obtain values of energies, atomic volumes, and bulk moduli for each phase, stable or metastable, as a function of temperature and concentration (or chemical field $\mu$) by inserting equilibrium values of the correlations. The calculated temperature dependence of course does not include that from vibrational entropy contributions. The vibrational free energy can be cluster expanded as well by including it in the hybrid configurational-dependent free energy of Eq. (1.4). Methods for introducing vibrational free energy contributions were proposed by Sanchez et al.[176] and by Asta et al.[16,19] [see Section 16(b)].

A major aim was to calculate, from first principles, the Ti-Al temperature-concentration phase diagram. The fcc and hcp parents were treated separately, each in the TO CVM approximation. A cluster interaction (associated with linear triplets), which was needed in the fcc formation energy's cluster expansion, was not contained in the TO approximation and had to be included approximately by the superposition approximation mentioned in connection with Eq. (5.12a). It is instructive to present separately the fcc-only and hcp-only phase diagrams. These diagrams, calculated by the CVM technique described in Section 9, are shown in Figs. 20(a) and 20(b), respectively. Somewhat surprisingly, the predicted ordering temperatures turn out to be substantially lower for hcp-based than for fcc-based phases, despite the fact that both parent structures are close-packed with similar "frustrating" clusters: triangle and tetrahedron. Of course, the different geometries encountered at the level of *nnn* interactions and the different types of cell relaxations contribute to differentiation between hcp and fcc ordering.

The combined phase diagram is shown in Fig. 20(c). It was obtained by constructing lowest common tangents to sets of free energy curves for both fcc- and bcc-based phases at various temperatures. Whether or not the agreement between experimental (Fig. 18) and theoretical [Fig. 20(c)] phase diagrams is deemed satisfactory depends very much on one's expectations. In the calculated diagram, neither liquid nor bcc phases were included, so a one-to-one comparison obviously cannot be made. What is encouraging in these truly first-principles calculations (only two numbers are input, $Z_{Al} = 13$, $Z_{Ti} = 22$) is that all well-established ground

[176]J. M. Sanchez, J. P. Stark, and V. L. Moruzzi, *Phys. Rev. B* **44**, 5411 (1991).

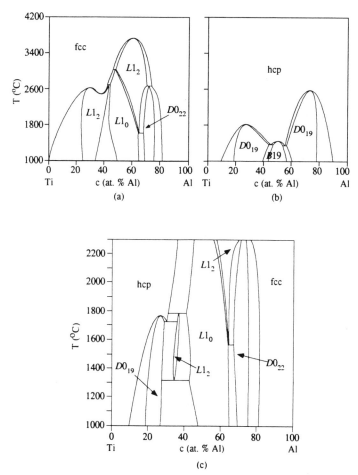

FIG. 20. First-principles calculated Al-Ti crystalline phase diagrams: (a) fcc-based structures only, (b) hcp-based structures only, and (c) fcc- and hcp-based phases combined.
Liquid phase free energies were not calculated [M. Asta, Ph.D. Dissertation, University of
California, Berkeley, 1993 (unpublished); M. Asta, D. de Fontaine, and M. Van Schilfgaarde, *J. Mater. Res.* **8**, 2554 (1993)].

states are predicted correctly, even though calculated energy differences
between certain competing structures are extremely small (less than 3
kJ/mole). Other points of agreement include the fact that $L1_0$ has a rather
wide and $D0_{22}$ a rather narrow phase field, that both remain ordered up
to their melting points, but that the $D0_{19}$ phase shows "congruent ordering" from the disordered hcp phase in both calculated and experimental
phase diagrams. The calculated (first-order) transition temperature for

$D0_{19}$ is about 600 degrees too high, however. This appears to be a major discrepancy, but it must be recalled that very small inaccuracies in calculated energies correspond to very large temperature differences.

Other discrepancies include the appearance of a thin $L1_2$ phase region at about 40 at.% Al, but there again, very small energy changes will eliminate this phase region. More disturbing is the fact that these calculations predict fairly wide solubility on the Al side of the phase diagram, whereas almost none is observed experimentally. The cause of this discrepancy can be seen in Fig. 19, where the calculated energy curve for the completely disordered fcc state actually crosses and falls below the convex hull on the Al side, thereby (erroneously) predicting lower energy for the disordered phase than for the phase mixture $D0_{22}$ + fcc Al. Again, it is observed that the energy differences involved are extremely small.

The calculated phase diagram shown in Fig. 20(c) is probably the most complex first-principles phase diagram obtained to date. Aside from the absence of the bcc phase (left out at this stage of the calculation), the most serious shortcoming of the calculation is the fact that ordering temperatures are too high. Most likely, contributing factors to this discrepancy are that full convergence is not obtained by the set of clusters used in the expansion, and *local* relaxations are not treated correctly in the disordered phases. As a result of the latter factor, the corresponding fcc and hcp "lattice" energies are too large, and therefore so are the differences between disordered and ordered-phase energies, leading to high transition temperatures. Also, vibrational and electronic degrees of freedom in the total free energy have not been taken into account. In the next subsection, these contributions are included in an approximate manner and illustrated for the case of the Cd-Mg system.

b. *The Cd-Mg System*

Results reported in this subsection are taken from the work of Asta *et al.*,[16,19] to which the reader is referred for further details. The Cd-Mg system is an interesting one in the context of this chapter's subject matter for the following reasons. First, although several studies of the ground states of order[12,44,51,61,62] and prototype phase diagrams of the hcp Ising model[12,60,90,91,177] have been performed, very few first-principles calculations of phase diagrams for alloy systems containing hcp-based structures have been undertaken.[19,178] In Fig. 21, the solid state portion of the as-

[177] P. Cénédèse and J. W. Cahn, private communication (1992).

[178] J. M. Sanchez and J. D. Becker, *Mat. Res. Soc. Symp. Proc.* **291**, 1993, p. 27.

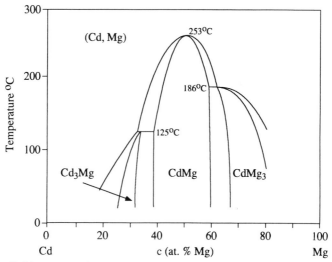

Fig. 21. Solid state portion of experimentally determined Cd-Mg phase diagram [Z. Moser, W. Gasior, J. Wypartowicz, and L. Zebdyr, *Bull. Alloy Phase Diag.* **5**, 23 (1984)].

sessed experimental Cd-Mg phase diagram[179] has been redrawn. At high temperatures (below the melt) continuous solid-solution between hcp Cd and hcp Mg is found. As the temperature is lowered, three ordered phases with hcp-based structures are stabilized in composition ranges around the stoichiometries $Cd_3Mg$, $CdMg_3$, and $CdMg$. The $Cd_3Mg$ and $CdMg_3$ phases form in the $D0_{19}$ structure, while $CdMg$ has the $B19$ structure; these structures were described in Fig. 4(b). The hcp-based $B19$ and $D0_{19}$ structures have the same atomic configurations on close-packed planes as do the fcc-based CuAu and $Cu_3Au$ structures, respectively. Therefore, the Cd-Mg system can be described as the hcp analog of the well-known fcc-based Cu-Au system.

The second reason for performing thermodynamic calculations in the Cd-Mg system is that, since the melting points of elemental Cd and Mg and the transition temperatures of the ordered Cd-Mg phases are low, experimentally measured lattice parameters and thermodynamic properties are readily available for both disordered and ordered alloy phases.[180–182] As shown later, this experimental information can be used

[179]Z. Moser, W. Gasior, J. Wypartowicz, and L. Zabdyr, *Bulletin of Alloy Phase Diagrams* **5**, 23 (1984).

[180]W. Hume-Rothery and G. V. Raynor, *Proc. Roy. Soc.* **A174**, 471 (1940).

[181]R. P. Hultgren, P. D. Anderson, and K. K. Kelley, eds., *Selected Values of Thermodynamic Properties of Metals and Alloys*, p. 604, Wiley, New York (1963).

[182]P. Villars and L. D. Calvert, eds., *Pearson's Handbook of Crystallographic Data for Intermetallic Phases*, 2nd ed., ASM International, Materials Park, OH, 1991.

to evaluate the effects on the calculated phase diagram of nonconfigurational free energy contributions, which arise from vibrational excitations and structural relaxations. It is anticipated that these nonconfigurational effects might play a significant role in determining the shape of the phase diagram of the Cd-Mg system for the following reasons: (1) The Debye temperature of Cd is roughly one-half that of Mg (these Debye temperatures are 209 and 400 K, respectively,[183]) so that the differences between the vibrational free energies of Cd- and Mg-rich alloys should be sizable; and (2) the $c/a$ ratio in elemental Mg is 1.623 [close to the ideal value of $(8/3)^{1/2}$ = 1.632993], whereas for Cd this ratio is highly nonideal at a value of 1.886.[182] Clearly structural relaxations can be expected to give rise to an important contribution to the energy of Cd-rich alloys.

The nine hcp-related structures shown in Fig. 4(b) were used for the structure inversion method: hcp Cd and Mg, the two $H2$'s, the two $H1$'s ($D0_{19}$), $H5$ ($B19$), $H3$, and $H4$. The formation energies of these structures along with 0 K equilibrium atomic volumes and bulk moduli were calculated by the LMTO-ASA method. The energy of each structure was optimized with respect to volume only, assuming close-packed geometry for which the ASA is known to be most accurate. Cell external relaxation was taken into account by an elastic energy correction to be described later. The convex hull construction showed that only hcp Cd, Mg,Cd$_3$Mg, CdMg$_3$ ($D0_{19}$), and CdMg ($B19$) were stable ground states, i.e., occupied the vertices of the convex polygon of formation energies, in complete agreement with experimental findings. Subsequent corrections do not alter the ground state results.

The SIM was used to calculate nine ECIs including in- and out-of-basal plane $nn$ pairs, $nnn$ pair, three distinct $nn$ triplets, and the $nn$ tetrahedron. No postinversion relaxation correction of the type described in Section 14(a) was included since the difference in pure-element atomic volumes, $\Omega_{Cd}$ and $\Omega_{Mg}$, was small. The CVM in the hcp TO approximation was then used to construct the phase diagram shown in Fig. 22. Comparison with the experimentally determined diagram of Fig. 21 reveals that the overall features are fairly well reproduced by this purely first-principles calculation, in particular the congruent ordering of CdMg and the peritectoid reaction for CdMg$_3$. However, the Cd$_3$Mg phase is incorrectly predicted to appear congruently at a high temperature instead of by a peritectoid reaction. The cause of this discrepancy lies in the neglect of the $c/a$ relaxation of Cd and of the Cd-rich hcp solid solution. This cell-relaxation effect could be taken into account by performing full-potential calculations. Here, for simplicity, we apply a semiempirical correction, which

[183] C. Kittel, *Introduction to Solid State Physics*, 6th ed., Wiley, New York (1986).

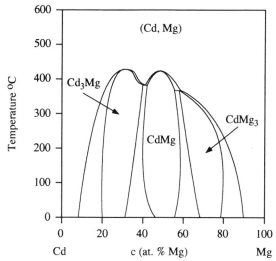

FIG. 22. Calculated (SIM) Cd-Mg phase diagram including configurational contributions only [M. Asta, Ph.D. Dissertation, University of California, Berkeley, 1993 (unpublished); M. Asta, R. McCormack, and D. de Fontaine, *Phys. Rev. B* **48**, 748 (1993)].

adds to the constrained LMTO-ASA electronic structure energy an elastic contribution, which is that required to distort the unit cell at constant volume from its experimentally measured axial ratio to the ideal one. The actual $c/a$ ratios were taken from the experimental measurements of Hume-Rothery and Raynor[180] for Cd-Mg solid solutions at 583 K. The elastic work to perform this axial ratio contraction was calculated by methods of standard elasticity theory with, as input, the elastic moduli of Cd and Mg and their linear interpolation for the intermediate concentrations. To obtain the elastic energy as a function of configuration, a cluster expansion was carried out with CECs calculated from the solid solution elastic energy; use was also made of the fact that the ordered compound $c/a$ relaxation was negligible. The phase diagram calculated with elastic correction included is shown in Fig. 23. Because the $c/a$ relaxation is large at the Cd-rich side, the correction term mainly alters the congruent ordering of $Cd_3Mg$ (Fig. 22) to a peritectoid reaction, in agreement with experiment (Fig. 21). The overall shape of the calculated phase diagram is now quite satisfactory, but the ordering temperatures are still too high.

According to the considerations set forth in Section 1, we still need to take vibrational and electronic free energies into account. Unlike configurational entropy, which requires special treatment (that of the CVM,

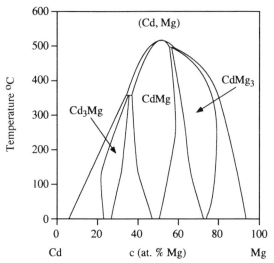

FIG. 23. Calculated Cd-Mg phase diagram with elastic relaxation included [M. Asta, Ph.D. Dissertation, University of California, Berkeley, 1993 (unpublished); M. Asta, R. McCormack, and D. de Fontaine, *Phys. Rev. B* **48,** 748 (1993)].

for example), vibrational and electronic entropies (and energies) may be considered as configuration-dependent functions and may therefore be cluster-expanded by the methods described in this chapter. In the Cd-Mg system, it is sufficient to use the low-temperature approximations for the electronic energy and entropy[19]

$$E_\varepsilon(\vec{\sigma}) = \frac{\pi^2}{6} k_B^2 T^2 \mathcal{N}_F(\vec{\sigma})$$

$$S_\varepsilon(\vec{\sigma}) \frac{\pi^2}{3} k_B^2 T \mathcal{N}_F(\vec{\sigma}),$$

(16.2)

where the notation of Eq. (1.5) has been used and where $\mathcal{N}_F(\vec{\sigma})$ denotes the electronic density of states at the Fermi level. This density of states is obtained as a by-product of the electronic structure calculations for all nine basic structures so that $E_\varepsilon$ and $S_\varepsilon$, along with $\mathcal{N}_F$ itself, can be cluster expanded in the usual way. As an aside, note that $\mathcal{N}(E, (\vec{\sigma})$ for any energy, not merely for $E_F$, can be expanded in like manner so that one could, in principle, obtain full density-of-state curves for any state of order of a (partially) disordered system, without appealing to the CPA. This idea does not appear to have been tested as yet.

The vibrational free energy is more difficult to evaluate. Early studies by Moraitis and Gautier[184] emphasized the influence of configurational order on vibrational entropy. Recently, Moruzzi et al.[185] proposed an interesting procedure whereby first-principles calculated total energies at various volumes were fitted to an empirical Morse potential. From the resulting binding curves it was then possible, by means of some semiempirical expressions, to obtain the Grüneisen parameter, bulk modulus, and Debye temperature for elemental solids. This method was extended to compounds by Sanchez et al.[176,178] and applied very successfully, by cluster expansion means, to thermodynamic equilibrium in Cu-Ag and Zr-Nb. Also, a cluster-variational method has been proposed very recently by Finel[186] for evaluating vibrational entropy of elemental crystals.

The method used here is somewhat different in the sense that it is the Debye temperature $\theta(\sigma)$ itself that is being cluster expanded. The approximation is then made that the expectation value of the vibrational free energy is given by the Debye model free energy expressed as a function of the expectation value $\langle \theta(\vec{\sigma}) \rangle$ of the Debye temperature.[19] Energy and entropy contributions required by Eq. (1.6) are given by:[187]

$$E_\omega(\vec{\sigma}) = \frac{9}{8} k_B \theta(\vec{\sigma}) + 3k_B T D[\theta(\vec{\sigma})/T]$$

$$S_\omega(\vec{\sigma}) = 4k_B D[\theta(\vec{\sigma})/T] - 3k_B \ln[1 - e^{-\theta(\vec{\sigma})/T}]$$

(16.3)

where D is the Debye function. For SIM purposes, the Debye temperatures for various basic structures are taken from known values for elemental Cd and Mg and, for the observed stable compounds, backcalculated from the measured total entropies, configurational plus vibrational (and electronic), the configurational contribution being that obtained from CVM calculations. For the nonequilibrium structures, empirical formulas are used.[16,19] Now that all the relevant CECs have been determined, we have a complete albeit approximate and semiempirical form of $\Psi(\vec{\sigma})$, the hybrid configuration-dependent free energy defined in Eq. (1.4). The thermodynamic calculations proceed as outlined formally in Eqs. (2.3) to (2.6), with the CVM providing the variational framework, as done before. The resulting phase diagram is given in Fig. 24.

[184] G. Moraitis and F. Gautier, J. Phys. F 7, 142 (1977).

[185] V. L. Moruzzi, J. F. Janak, and K. Schwarz, Phys. Rev. B 37, 790 (1988).

[186] A. Finel, Progr. Theor. Phys. ( Japan), in press.

[187] G. T. Furukawa, T. B. Douglas, and N. Pearlman, in American Institute of Physics Handbook, Section 4e, McGraw-Hill, New York (1957).

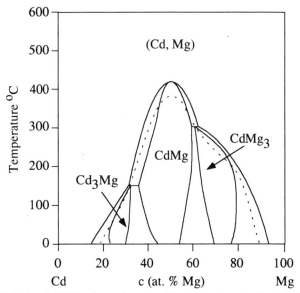

Fig. 24. Calculated Cd-Mg phase diagram with electronic and vibrational contributions in addition to relaxation and configurational contributions. Dashed line is ordered spinodal [M. Asta, Ph.D. Dissertation, University of California, Berkeley, 1993 (unpublished); M. Asta, R. McCormack, and D. de Fontaine, *Phys. Rev. B* **48**, 748 (1993)].

Agreement with the experimental phase diagram (Fig. 21) is now striking. Predicted ordering temperatures are still a bit too high (although, interestingly, vibrational entropy has brought them down), but the overall shape, crystallography of ordered phases, and types of transitions (first-order for CdMg, peritectoid for $Cd_3Mg$ and $CdMg_3$, extent of phase regions, asymmetry, etc.) are reproduced remarkably well. By comparing the successive set of phase diagrams shown in Figs. 22, 23, and 24, it is also gratifying to note that, as more corrections were included, the agreement with the experimental phase diagram (Fig. 21) improved at each step.

If reproducing a known phase diagram were the only objective of these calculations, the justification for such an effort might well be questioned. Actually, much more useful information can be extracted from the computations. For example, the various contributions to the internal energy (or enthalpy), entropy, and free energy at various temperatures and concentrations may be examined individually, which is not readily feasible by experimental techniques. Consider, for example, the normalized enthalpy of formation curves of Fig. 25: long dashed, dot-dashed, short dashed, and solid curves represent the configuration, vibrational (amplified 100 times), relaxation, and total contributions at 600 K, respectively.

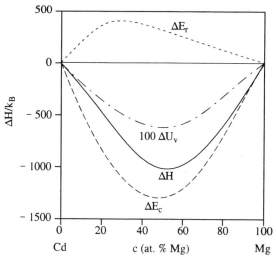

FIG. 25. Calculated Cd-Mg enthalpies of formation (solid curve) decomposed into config-urational (long dashes), vibrational (dot-dashes), and relaxation (short dashes) contribu-tions. Energies are calculated at 600 K, short-range order effects are included [M. Asta, Ph.D. dissertation, University of California, Berkeley, 1993 (unpublished); M. Asta, R. McCormack, and D. de Fontaine, *Phys. Rev. B* **48**, 748 (1993)].

It is seen that, near the $Cd_3Mg$ composition, the relaxation energy of formation is almost as large as the unrelaxed configurational energy, whereas, in this system, the vibrational energy contribution is practically negligible.

Vibrational effects cannot be neglected in the entropy, however, as can be seen in Fig. 26, where the meaning of the curves is the same as in Fig. 25, except that the dot-dashed curve now represents the electronic entropy amplified 10 times (there is no elastic "relaxation entropy"). The configurational contribution still dominates, but $\Delta S_\omega$ is certainly no longer negligible, a conclusion that supports theoretical[176,178] and experimental[188] findings by other investigators. As for the electronic entropy, its effect is small here, but could become more significant for transitional metal elements.[189–191] Free energy ($\Delta G$, Gibbs energy, in solids, practically equal to the Helmholtz free energy $\Delta F$) contributions are shown in Fig. 27 as calculated at 600 K. Solid lines represent the disordered phase,

[188] L. Anthony, J. K. Okamoto, and B. Fultz, *Phys. Rev. Lett.* **70**, 1128 (1993).
[189] R. E. Watson and M. Weinert, *Phys. Rev. B* **30**, 1641 (1984).
[190] F. Willaime and C. Massobrio, *Phys. Rev. Lett.* **63**, 2244 (1989).
[191] O. Eriksson, J. M. Wills, and Duane Wallace, *Phys. Rev. B* **46**, 5221 (1992).

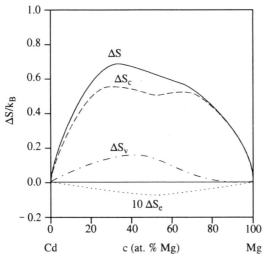

FIG. 26. Calculated Cd-Mg entropies of formation (solid curve) decomposed into configurational (long dashes), electronic (short dashes), and vibrational (dot-dashes) contributions at 600 K [M. Asta, Ph.D. Dissertation, University of California, Berkeley, 1993 (unpublished); M. Asta, R. McCormack, and D. de Fontaine, *Phys. Rev. B* **48**, 748 (1993)].

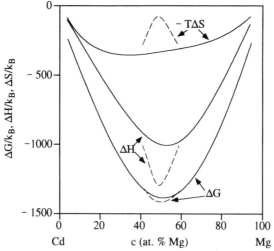

FIG. 27. Free energy of formation ($\Delta G$) for Cd-Mg at 600 K decomposed into enthalpy ($\Delta H$), and entropy ($\Delta S$) contributions for disordered state (solid curves) and ordered B19 phase (dashed curves) [M. Asta, Ph.D. Dissertation, University of California, Berkeley, 1993 (unpublished); M. Asta, R. McCormack, and D. de Fontaine, *Phys. Rev. B* **48**, 748 (1993)].

dashed lines the ordered phase CdMg, which in the calculation has become stable at this temperature. The common tangent construction applied to $\Delta G$ will indeed produce two narrow two-phase fields, as per the
phase diagram of Fig. 24. From the appearance of calculated $\Delta G$ curves
it may be readily appreciated that the computational determination of
phase boundaries is a very delicate business; slight errors in the energies
can lead to very large errors in the resulting phase diagrams.

Other interesting information can be obtained from the calculations.
For example, from the formalism described in Section 11, Eq. (11.5) in
particular, it is possible to determine ordering instabilities, or spinodals.
The relevant one to examine here is the $\langle \frac{1}{2} 00 \rangle$ spinodal, since such is the
ordering wave that corresponds to $B19$ ordering [see Fig. 4(b)]. It is
shown as a dashed line on the calculated phase diagram (Fig. 24). As
expected, because of the first-order character of the CdMg transition,
the spinodal line at the stoichiometric concentration does not reach the
congruent ordering temperature. Short-range order intensity may also be
calculated by a generalization of Eq. (11.8). The generalization[7] is required since this equation, as it stands, is applicable to monatomic structures only. Here, the presence of a two-atom basis in hcp requires four
$k$-space susceptibilities in the expression for $I_{SRO}(\mathbf{k})$: $\chi_{11}$, $\chi_{22}$, $\chi_{12}$, and $\chi_{21}$,
the subscripts 1 and 2 referring to the two atomic positions in the basis.
Short-range order intensity contours have been calculated at the symmetric CdMg composition at 750 K, in the disordered phase. Calculated intensity contours are plotted[16] in Fig. 28, in a (001) reciprocal lattice section; filled circles show positions of reciprocal lattice vectors and the
hexagon indicates the projection of the Brillouin zone on the (001) plane.
We see that $I_{SRO}$ peaks at points of the type $[\frac{1}{2} \frac{1}{2} 0]$. Although points of
the type $[\frac{1}{2} 00]$ on the BZ boundary may be reached from those of the
first type by means of a reciprocal lattice translation, they turn out to
have lower intensity. The fact that $I_{SRO}(\mathbf{k})$ lacks the symmetry of the
reciprocal lattice is due to the two-atom nature of the hcp basis, as discussed in detail by Asta.[16]

These Cd-Mg calculations illustrate clearly the type of thermodynamic
information that may be generated by current theoretical methods featuring cluster expansions. In this instance, empirical information was sup-
plied, so that this is not exclusively a first-principles calculation. In principle, however, the $c/a$ correction could have been implemented by use of
full-potential codes, as described in part (a) of this section for the Ti-Al
system, thereby obviating the need for the $ad$ $hoc$ elastic correction used
in the Cg-Mg case. Vibrational entropy effects could also be handled on
a first-principles basis, along the lines suggested by Moruzzi, Sanchez,
and coworkers,[176,178,185] although these models are still rather crude at
present. For the topic of vibrational entropy, much more work is obvi-

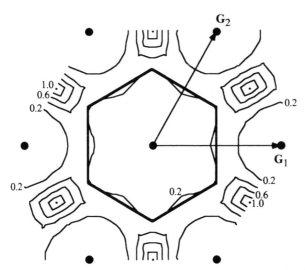

FIG. 28.  Calculated short-range order diffuse intensity in the (001) plane for the disordered Cd-Mg phase at $c$ = 50% Mg and $T$ = 750 K. The step in the contours is 0.2 and the intensity is normalized to have a maximum value of 1.0. The hexagon drawn by the solid thick line is the projection of the first Brillouin zone on the (001) plane. The filled circles indicate reciprocal lattice points. $G_1$ and $G_2$ indicate the two reciprocal lattice vectors in the (001) plane. The diffuse intensity maxima in this figure are located at the points [1/2 − 1 0], [1/2 1/2 0], [1 − 1/2 0], [−1/2 1 0], [−1/2 −1/2 0], and [−1 1/2 0]. Weaker peaks in the diffuse intensity are also located at the points [1/2 0 0], [−1/2 0 0], [0 1/2 0], [0 −1/2 0], [−1/2 1/2 0], and [1/2 −1/2 0]. [M. Asta, Ph.D. Dissertation, University of California, Berkeley, 1993 (unpublished); M. Asta, R. McCormack, and D. de Fontaine, *Phys. Rev. B* **48**, 748 (1993)].

ously needed. Nevertheless, the results of this subsection definitely suggest that vibrational and electronic excitations, mutually coupled or not (along with magnetic excitations, if required), cannot in general be left out in realistic *ab initio* calculations of thermodynamic properties.

17. SURVEY OF APPLICATIONS

The primary objective of this review was to present the formalism of cluster expansions and its application to the calculation of thermodynamic properties of alloys, illustrated by such examples as were most familiar to the author. The intention was not to provide a critical review of the abundant literature describing applications to the large number of alloy systems that have been treated recently. Still a review of the formalism would not be complete without summarizing some of the applications to alloy systems. Primarily those applications which feature cluster

expansions and the CVM are mentioned, which means that phase equilibria obtained by mean-field (Bragg-Williams) or Monte Carlo methods are not included. Also, little mention is made of alloy systems where the ECIs have been obtained by empirical fitting.

The class of systems most copiously studied by methods discussed in this article is that of binary metallic alloys. An earlier survey of systems can be found, in tabular form, in the review article of Inden and Pitsch.[6] Although that article is quite recent (1991), much interesting work has been reported since, so that an update is in order. Such an update is attempted here in Table V, in a surely incomplete manner. The binary (metallic) systems are listed according to the convention adopted in *Binary Alloy Phase Diagrams:*[158] For each system *A-B*, the elements are given in alphabetical order, and in the table, systems are listed by alphabetical order of the first element, then, for a given first element, by alphabetical order of the second. The second column of Table V indicates the parent lattice(s) on which the calculations were based, the third column gives the computational method in abbreviated form, and the last column gives bibliographic references. The acronym LMTO implies ASA (atomic sphere approximation), the letter "F" in front of the acronyms LMTO or LAPW stands for "full potential," and ASW is the acronym for "augmented spherical wave." In accordance with the nomenclature of Section 16, SIM denotes the structure inversion method, often referred to in other work as CWM, or the Connolly and Williams method. "S2" designates the $S^{(2)}$ method mentioned in Section 13, otherwise known as the "concentration wave method" (CWM, note possible confusion with "Connolly and Williams method," and also with the concentration wave approach mentioned in Section 11.) Some early calculations reported in the table were performed by the cluster Bethe lattice method (CBLM). A few ternary (metallic) systems are also listed at the end of the table, with the same type of alphabetical convention as was used for the binaries. Since so few nonempirical ternary system calculations have been reported, Table V includes studies in which ECIs were obtained by fitting to binary system data ("Fit"). Unless otherwise indicated, statistical mechanical calculations were performed by the CVM; the exceptions include mean-field (BW) and Monte Carlo (MC).

A class of systems to which cluster methods have been applied successfully, and not yet mentioned here, is that of semiconductor alloys. Of particular interest are those diamond cubic ternary systems (*A-B-C*) where atoms of, say, type *A* and *B* order on one fcc sublattice while the second sublattice remains occupied exclusively by *C*. In such cases, the ordering problem does not differ formally from that of binary ordering on one fcc lattice, treated in some detail in this review. Work on pseu-

TABLE V. CLUSTER-METHOD CALCULATIONS FOR BINARY AND TERNARY (SUBSTITUTIONAL)
METALLIC ALLOYS.

| SYSTEM | LATTICES | METHOD[a] | REFERENCES[b] |
|---|---|---|---|
| *Binaries* | | | |
| Ag-Au | fcc | ASW-SIM | 1, 2 |
| | fcc | FLAPW-SIM | 3 |
| Ag-Cu | fcc | ASW-SIM | 1, 2 |
| | fcc | FLAPW-SIM | 3 |
| | fcc | LMTO-SIM | 4 |
| Al-Ge | fcc | KKR-CPA-GPM | 5 |
| Al-Li | fcc, bcc | FLAPW-SIM | 6 |
| Al-Ni | fcc | ASW-SIM | 7 |
| | fcc, bcc | TB-CBLM | 8 |
| | fcc, bcc | FLAPW-SIM | 9 |
| | fcc, bcc | LMTO-SIM | 10 |
| | fcc, bcc | KKR-CPA-GPM | 11, 11a |
| Al-Ti | fcc | FLMTO-SIM | 12 |
| | fcc, hcp | FLMTO-SIM | 13 |
| Au-Cu | fcc | ASW-SIM | 1, 2 |
| | fcc | FLAPW-SIM | 3, 9 |
| Au-Ni | fcc | FLAPW-SIM | 14 |
| Au-Pd | fcc | ASW-SIM | 2 |
| | fcc | KKR-CPA-ECM | 15 |
| Au-Pt | fcc | FLAPW-SIM | 14 |
| Be-Fe | bcc | LMTO-SIM | 16 |
| Cd-Mg | hcp | LMTO-SIM | 17 |
| Cr-Fe | bcc | KKR-CPA-GPM | 18 |
| | bcc | KKR-CPA-GPM | 19 |
| Cr-Mo | bcc | TB-CBLM | 20 |
| | bcc | TB-CPA | 21 |
| Cr-Ni | bcc | TB-CPA-GPM | 22 |
| Cr-Ti | bcc | TB-CPA-GPM | 23 |
| Cr-W | bcc | TB-CBLM | 20 |
| Cu-Ni | fcc | TB-CPA-GPM | 24 |
| Cu-Pd | fcc, bcc | FLAPW-SIM | 9 |
| | fcc | KKR-CPA-S2-BW | 25, 25a |
| Cu-Pt | fcc | FLAPW-SIM | 9, 26 |
| | fcc | KKR-CPA-S2 | 27 |
| Cu-Rh | fcc | FLAPW-SIM | 9 |
| Cu-Zn | fcc, bcc | KKR-CPA-GPM | 28, 28a |
| Fe-Ti | bcc | TB-CPA-GPM | 29 |
| Fe-V | fcc, bcc | TB-CPA-GPM | 18, 29 |
| Mo-Nb | bcc | TB-CPA-GPM | 21 |
| Mo-Re | fcc | TB-LMTO-DCA | 30 |
| Mo-Ta | bcc | TB-CPA-GPM | 21 |
| Mo-W | bcc | TB-CBLM | 20 |
| Nb-Ru | bcc, hcp | LMTO-SIM | 31 |
| Nb-Zr | bcc, hcp | LMTO-SIM | 31 |

TABLE V. (CONTINUED)

| SYSTEM | LATTICES | METHOD[a] | REFERENCES[b] |
|---|---|---|---|
| Ni-Pt | fcc | KKR-CPA-S2 | 32 |
| | fcc | FLAPW-SIM | 14, 26, 33 |
| | fcc | FLMTO-SIM | 34 |
| | fcc | LMTO/CPA-GPM | 35 |
| Ni-Ti | fcc, bcc | TB-CBLM | 36 |
| | bcc | KKR-CPA-GPM | 11a |
| Ni-V | fcc | LMTO-SIM | 36a |
| Pd-Pt | fcc | FLAPW-SIM | 26 |
| Pd-Rh | fcc | FLAPW-SIM | 26 |
| | fcc | KKR-CPA-GPM | 37 |
| | fcc | KKR-CPA-ECM | 38 |
| | fcc | TB-LMTO-DCA | 39 |
| Pd-Ti | fcc | TB-LMTO-DCA | 40 |
| Pd-V | fcc | TB-LMTO-DCA | 40, 40a |
| | fcc | KKR-CPA-GPM | 41 |
| | fcc | TB-LMTO-DCA-MC | 42 |
| | fcc, bcc | TB-LMTO-DCA | 43 |
| Pt-Rh | fcc | FLAPW-SIM | 9 |
| Pt-Ti | fcc, bcc | TB-LMTO-DCA | 40 |
| Pt-V | fcc, bcc | TB-LMTO-DCA | 40, 43 |
| Rh-Ti | fcc, bcc | TB-LMTO-DCA | 40 |
| Rh-V | fcc, bcc | TB-LMTO-DCA | 40, 43 |
| Ru-Zr | bcc, hcp | LMTO-SIM | 31 |
| Ti-V | bcc | TB-CPA-GPM | 23 |
| *Ternaries* | | | |
| Ag-Au-Cu | fcc | Fit-CVM | 44 |
| Ag-Pd-Rh | fcc | TB-LMTO-DCA | 45 |
| Al-Co-Fe | bcc | Fit-CVM | 46 |
| $AlNi_3 + X$ | fcc ($L1_2$) | TB-LMTO-DCA | 43, 47 |
| (X = Co,Cu,Pd,Rh,Si,Zn) | | | |
| AlNi-NiTi | bcc | LMTO-LAPW-SIM | 48 |
| Al-Ni-Ti | bcc | LMTO-SIM | 49 |
| | bcc | LMTO-SIM | 50 |
| Cu-Ni-Zn | fcc | PP-Fit-CVM | 51 |
| Fe-Ti-V | bcc | TB-CPA-GPM | 29 |
| Pd-Rh-V | fcc | TB-LMTO-DCA | 43 |
| Rh-Ti-V | fcc | TB-LMTO-DCA | 43 |

[a] Abbreviations: ASW, augmented spherical wave; CBLM, cluster-Bethe lattice method; CPA, coherent potential approximation; CVM, cluster variational method; DCA, direct configurational averaging; (F)LAPW, (full-potential) linear augmented plane wave; (F)LMTO, (full-potential) linear muffin-tin orbital; GPM, generalized perturbation method; KKR, Korringa-Kohn-Rostoker; PP, pseudopotential; S2, $S^{(2)}$ method of concentration waves; SIM, structure inversion method (Connolly-Williams); TB, tight binding; Fit, fitted parameters.

[b]Table references:

[1] K. Terakura, T. Oguchi, T. Mohri, and K. Watanabe, *Phys. Rev. B* **35**, 2169 (1987); T. Mohri, K. Terakura, T. Oguchi, and K. Watanabe, *Acta Metall.* **36**, 547 (1988).

[2] T. Mohri, K. Terakura, S. Takizawa, and J. M. Sanchez, *Acta Metall. Mater.* **39**, 493 (1991).

[3] S.-H. Wei, A. A. Mbaye, L. G. Ferreira, and A. Zunger, *Phys. Rev. B* **36**, 4163 (1987).

[4] J. M. Sanchez, J. P. Stark, and V. L. Moruzzi, *Phys. Rev. B* **44**, 5411 (1991).

[5] P. E. A. Turchi, M. Sluiter, and G. M. Stocks, *Mat. Res. Soc. Symp. Proc.* **291**, 153 (1993).

[6] M. Sluiter, D. de Fontaine, X. Q. Guo, R. Podloucky, and A. J. Freeman, *Mat. Res. Soc. Symp, Proc.* **133**, 1989; *Phys. Rev. B* **42**, 10460 (1990).

[7] A. E. Carlsson and J. M. Sanchez, *Solid State Commun.* **65**, 527 (1988).

[8] C. Colinet, A. Bessoud, and A. Pasturel, *J. Phys. Cond. Matter* **1**, 5837 (1989).

[9] Z. W. Lu, S.-H. Wei, A. Zunger, S. Frota-Pessoa, and L. G. Ferreira, *Phys. Rev. B* **44**, 512 (1991).

[10] A. Pasturel, C. Colinet, A. T. Paxton, and M. van Schilfgaarde, *J. Phys. Cond. Matter* **4**, 945 (1992).

[11] M. Sluiter, P. E. A. Turchi, F. J. Pinski, and G. M. Stocks, *Mat. Sci. Engin. A* **152**, 1 (1992).

[11a] P. E. A. Turchi, M. Sluiter, F. J. Pinski, and D. D. Johnson, *Mat. Res. Soc. Symp. Proc.* **186**, 59 (1991).

[12] M. Asta, D. de Fontaine, M. van Schilfgaarde, M. Sluiter, and M. Methfessel, *Phys. Rev. B* **46**, 505 (1992).

[13] M. Asta, D. de Fontaine, and M. van Schilfgaarde, *J. Mat. Res.* **8**, 2554 (1993).

[14] Z. W. Lu, S.-H. Wei, and A. Zunger, *Europhys. Lett.* **21**, 221 (1993).

[15] P. Weinberger, C. Blaas, B. I. Bennett, and A. M. Boring, *Phys. Rev. B* **47**, 10158 (1993); P. Weinberger, J. Kudrnovsky, J. Redinger, and B. I. Bennett, *Phys. Rev. B* **48**, 7866 (1993).

[16] B. P. Burton and A. Pasturel, to be published in *Statics and Dynamics of Alloy Phase Transformations* (P. E. A. Turchi and A. Gonis, eds.), NATO ASI Series, Plenum Press, New York.

[17] M. Asta, R. McCormack, and D. de Fontaine, *Phys. Rev. B* **48**, 748 (1993).

[18] P. E. A. Turchi, M. Sluiter, G. M. Stocks, *Mat. Res. Soc. Symp. Proc.* **213**, 75 (1991).

[19] L. Reinhard and P. E. A. Turchi, *Mat. Res. Soc. Symp. Proc.* **291**, 407 (1993).

[20] R. J. Hawkins, M. O. Robbins, and J. M. Sanchez, *Phys. Rev. B* **33**, 4782 (1985).

[21] C. Sigli, M. Kosugi, and J. M. Sanchez, *Phys. Rev. Lett,* **57**, 253 (1986).

[22] N. C. Tso, M. Kosugi, and J. M. Sanchez, *Acta Metall.* **37**, 121 (1989).

[23] M. Sluiter and P. E. A. Turchi, *Phys. Rev. B* **43**, 12251 (1991).

[24] M. Sluiter and P. E. A. Turchi, *Mat. Res. Soc. Symp. Proc.* **186**, 77 (1991).

[25] G. M. Stocks, D. M. Nicholson, F. J. Pinski, W. H. Butler, P. Sterne, W. M. Temmerman, B. L. Györffy, D. D. Johnson, A. Gonis, X.-G Zhang, and P. E. A. Turchi, *Mat. Res. Soc. Symp. Proc.* **81**, 15 (1987).

[25a] G. Ceder, D. de Fontaine, H. Dreyssé, D. M. Nicholson, G. M. Stocks, and B. L. Györffy, *Acta Metall. Mater.* **38**, 2299 (1990).

[26] Z. W. Lu, S.-H. Wei, and A. Zunger, *Phys. Rev. Lett.* **66**, 1753 (1991).

[27] J. F. Clark, F. J. Pinski, P. A. Sterne, D. D. Johnson, J. B. Staunton, and B. Ginatempo, in *Metallic Alloys: Experimental and Theoretical Perspectives* ( J. S. Faulkner and R. G. Jordan, eds., NATO ASI Series, Vol. 256, pp. 159–166, Kluwer, Dordrecht (1994).

[28] M. Sluiter, P. E. A. Turchi, D. D. Johnson, F. J. Pinski, D. M. Nicholson, and G. M. Stocks, *Mat. Res. Soc. Symp. Proc.* **166,** 225 (1990).

[28a] P. E. A. Turchi, M. Sluiter, F. J. Pinski, D. D. Johnson, D. M. Nicholson, G. M. Stocks and J. B. Staunton, *Phys. Rev. Lett.* **67,** 1779 (1991).

[29] A. J. S. Traiber, M. Sluiter, P. E. A. Turchi, and S. M. Allen, *Mat. Res. Soc. Symp. Proc.* **291,** 437 (1993).

[30] C. Wolverton, M. Asta, S. Ouannasser, H. Dreyssé, and D. de Fontaine, *J. Chim. Phys.* **90,** 249 (1993).

[31] J. M. Sanchez and J. D. Becker, *Mat. Res. Soc. Symp. Proc.* **291,** 27 (1993).

[32] F. J. Pinski, B. Ginatempo, D. D. Johnson, J. B. Staunton, G. M. Stocks, and B. L. Györffy, *Phys. Rev. Lett.* **66,** 776 (1991); **68,** 1962 (1992).

[33] Z. W. Lu, S.-H. Wei, and A. Zunger, *Phys. Rev. Lett.* **68,** 1961 (1992).

[34] C. Amador, W. R. L. Lambrecht, and B. Segall, *Phys. Rev. B* **47,** 15276 (1993).

[35] P. P. Singh, A. Gonis, and P. E. A. Turchi, *Phys. Rev. Lett.* **71,** 1605 (1993).

[36] D. H. Le, C. Colinet, P. Hicter, and A. Pasturel, *J. Phys. Cond. Matter* **3,** 7895; *ibid.*, 9965 (1991).

[36a] J. Mikalopas, P. E. A. Turchi, M. Sluiter, and P. Sterne, *Mat. Res. Soc. Symp. Proc.* **186,** 83 (1991).

[37] D. D. Johnson, P. E. A. Turchi, M. Sluiter, D. M. Nicholson, F. J. Pinski, and G. M. Stocks, *Mat. Res. Soc. Symp. Proc.* **186,** 21 (1991).

[38] Y. Wang, J. S. Faulkner, and G. M. Stocks, *Phys. Rev. Lett.* **70,** 3287 (1993).

[39] C. Wolverton, D. de Fontaine, and H. Dreyssé, *Phys. Rev. B* **48,** 5766 (1993).

[40] C. Wolverton, G. Ceder, de Fontaine, and H. Dreyssé, *Phys. Rev. B* **48,** 726 (1993).

[40a] C. Wolverton, G. Ceder, D. de Fontaine, and H. Dreyssé, *Phys. Rev. B* **45,** 13105 (1992).

[41] P. E. A. Turchi, G. Stocks, W. Butler, D. Nicholson, and A. Gonis, *Phys. Rev. B* **37,** 5982 (1988).

[42] P. D. Tepesch, G. Ceder, C. Wolverton, and D. de Fontaine, *Mat. Res. Soc. Symp. Proc.* **291,** 129 (1993).

[43] C. Wolverton, "Ground State Properties and Phase Stability of Binary and Ternary Intermetallic Alloys," Ph.D. Dissertation, University of California, Berkeley (1993) (unpublished).

[44] R. Kikuchi, J. M. Sanchez, D. de Fontaine, and H. Yamauchi, *Acta Metall.* **28,** 651 (1980).

[45] C. Wolverton and D. de Fontaine, *Mat. Res. Soc. Symp. Proc.* **291,** 431 (1993).

[46] C. Colinet, G. Inden, and R. Kikuchi, *Acta Metall. Mater.* **41,** 1109 (1993).

[47] C. Wolverton and D. de Fontaine, *Phys. Rev. B* **49,** 12351 (1994).

[48] B. P. Burton, J. E. Osburn, and A. Pasturel, *Phys. Rev. B* **45,** 7667 (1992).

[49] B. P. Burton, W. C. Carter, and A. Pasturel, in *Ordering and Disordering in Alloys* (Y. Yavari, ed.), pp. 223–228, Elsevier, New York (1992).

[50] J. M. Sanchez, Chapter 10 in *Structural and Phase Stability of Alloys* ( J. L. Morán-López, F. Mejia-Lira, and J. M. Sanchez, eds.), Plenum Press, New York (1992).

[51] A. de Rooy, E. W. van Royen, P. M. Bronsveld, and J. Th. M. de Hosson, *Acta Metall.* **28,** 1339 (1980).

dobinary and ternary semiconductors was performed primarily by Zunger and coworkers[166,192] (reviewed in Ref. 9), by Mohri and coworkers,[193] and by Lambrecht and Segall.[194]

A subject that has been investigated extensively by cluster methods is that of oxygen ordering in the high-$T_c$ superconductor $YBa_2Cu_3O_x$ (YBCO) in the concentration interval $6 \leq x \leq 7$. The ordering phenomena occur on the so-called "basal plane" of YBCO (Cu-O plane) between occupied and vacant oxygen sites[59,100] with effective pair interactions $V_1$ > 0 (first neighbor), $V_2$ < 0 (second neighbor, mediated by Cu ion), and $V_3$ > 0 (second neighbor interaction orthogonal to the $V_2$ interaction). The first CVM-derived O-ordering phase diagrams were based on the phenomenological ASYNNNI model (asymmetric next nearest neighbor Ising model).[59,100,195,196] Later, SIM-derived interactions[197] were found to confirm the ASYNNNI inequalities ($V_2$ < 0 < $V_1$ < $V_3$)[59,100] and a CVM phase diagram obtained with the calculated interactions[198] was found to agree remarkably well with available experimental data, as indicated in a review of the subject.[199] Additional long-period ordered structures were also included in the phase diagram.[58,200] Large clusters were used in the "phenomenological" calculation of Morán-López and Sanchez,[201] and *ab initio* EPIs were calculated by a fully relativistic KKR-CPA-ECM method of Szunyogh and Weinberger.[202] Other applications to nonmetallic systems include a CVM-derived phase diagram of He isotope mixtures,[203] a recent SIM study of interstitial ordering in $\beta$-$YH_{2+x}$,[204] and in carbides and nitrides.[205]

[192] S.-H. Wei, L. G. Ferreira, and A. Zunger, *Phys. Rev. B* **45**, 2533 (1992); R. Osório, S. Froyen, and A. Zunger, *Phys. Rev. B* **45**, 14055 (1991); R. Osório and S. Froyen, *Phys. Rev. B* **47**, 1889 (1993); R. Osório, Z. W. Lu, S.-H. Wei, and A. Zunger, *Phys. Rev. B* **47**, 9985 (1993).

[193] T. Mohri, K. Koyanagi, T. Ito, and K. Watanabe, *Jap. J. Appl. Phys.* **28**, 1312 (1989).

[194] W. R. L. Lambrecht and B. Segall, *Phys. Rev. B.* **47**, 9289 (1993).

[195] V. E. Zubkus, S. Lapinskas, and E. E. Tornau, *Physica C* **159**, 501 (1989).

[196] R. Kikuchi and J. S. Choi, *Physica C* **160**, 347 (1989).

[197] P. Sterne and L. T. Wille, *Physica C* **162**, 223 (1989).

[198] G. Ceder, M. Asta, W. C. Carter, M. Kraitchman, D. de Fontaine, M. E. Mann, and M. Sluiter, *Phys. Rev. B* **41**, 8698 (1990).

[199] M. Asta, D. de Fontaine, G. Ceder, E. Salomons, and M. Kraitchman, *J. Less Common Metals* **168**, 39 (1991).

[200] G. Ceder, M. Asta, and D. de Fontaine, *Physica C* **177**, 106 (1991).

[201] J.-L. Morán-López and J. M. Sanchez, *Physica C* **210**, 401 (1993).

[202] L. Szunyogh and P. Weinberger, *Phys. Rev. B* **43**, 3768 (1991).

[203] J.-L. Morán-López and J. M. Sanchez, *Phys. Rev. B* **33**, 5059 (1986).

[204] S. N. Sun, Y. Wang, and M. Y. Chou, *Phys. Rev. B.* **49**, 6481 (1994).

[205] J. Klima, P. Weinberger, P. Härzig and A. Neckel, *Z. Physik B* **90**, 407 (1993); V. Ozolins and J. Häglund, *Phys. Rev. B* **48**, 5069 (1993).

*Important caveat.* Calculations reported in this section (and in Table V) are not equally reliable: Some calculations were performed before accurate methods had been developed or did not include energy contributions that are now known to be important for quantitative predictions to be made. The necessity, for some systems, of performing full-potential calculations and/or of including atomic displacements (elastic and dynamic) was discussed in Section 16. Here, let us reemphasize the need to consider all important contributions by briefly reviewing the "saga of Ni-Pt" in the light of some very recent results.[206]

From Table V, it is seen that the Ni-Pt system has been investigated frequently. To the indicated references one should add the phenomenological study of Dahmani *et al.*,[207] which features a temperature-concentration phase diagram calculated by the CVM in the (fcc) tetrahedron approximation, with ECIs, including magnetic interactions, obtained by fitting to available experimental data. This calculation illustrates quite well the value of semiempirical CVM calculations: The resulting Ni-Pt phase diagram[207] is more complete than the experimentally determined one,[158] hence more useful, and is as good as the experimental data. Furthermore, it could not have been obtained by BW methods. As in the Cu-Au system (and, in the hcp context, the Cd-Mg system, Fig. 21), the Ni-Pt disordered phase transforms to the $L1_0$ ordered phase by a first-order reaction.

In a first-principles $S^{(2)}$ study, Pinski *et al.*[208] found that the disordered fcc Ni-Pt solution at $c = 0.5$, calculated by means of the single-site KKR-CPA, becomes unstable at low temperature to a perturbation by a $\langle 100 \rangle$ ordering wave. These authors therefore concluded that the corresponding long-range ordered state (LRO), i.e., the $L1_0$ structure, would be the predicted equilibrium ground state, in agreement with experiment. However, as was pointed out by Lu *et al.*,[138,139] a *local* ordering tendency, determined by perturbation analysis, does not necessarily predict the correct LRO ground state if the size mismatch of the two elements is large, as is the case for Ni and Pt. In other words, $\Delta E_{ord} = \Delta E_{form} - \Delta E_{dis}$, where $\Delta E_{dis}$ is the formation energy of the disordered state and can be negative for certain ordered configurations without implying $\Delta E_{form} < 0$. Actually, one must consider both constrained ($c$) and relaxed ($x$) equilibria, as shown in Fig. 11. In the example illustrated, the $AB$ ordered

[206]P. P. Singh, A. Gonis, and P. E. A. Turchi, *Phys. Rev. Lett.* **71**, 1605 (1993).

[207]C. E. Dahmani, M. C. Cadeville, J. M. Sanchez, and J. L. Morán-López, *Phys. Rev. Lett.* **55**, 1208 (1985).

[208]F. J. Pinski, B. Ginatempo, D. D. Johnson, J. B. Stanton, G. M. Stocks, and B. L. Györffy, *Phys. Rev. Lett.* **66**, 776 (1991); **68**, 1962 (1992).

phase (which could well be $L1_0$) is stable only with respect to the *constrained* phase-separated state, i.e., $\Delta E^c_{form}$ in Eq. (14.5b) is negative, but $\Delta E^x_{form}$ [Eq. (14.5a)], pertaining to the *relaxed* phase-separated state, is positive. If the formation energies of $L1_0$ Ni-Pt are calculated by a nonrelativistic (NR) FLAPW method, one obtains[138,139,209] formation energies that resemble those represented qualitatively in Fig. 11: At equilibrium, according to NR calculations, Ni-Pt should phase separate, contrary to experimental evidence. By means of arguments based on canonical $d$ band considerations, Tréglia and Ducastelle[210] had shown that late transition metal alloys should exhibit phase-separation tendencies. It was already surmised by these authors that the exceptional ordering behavior of Ni-Pt might be due to relativistic effects, known to play a role for heavy elements, Pt in the present case.

It is indeed found that scalar relativistic (SR) effects do stabilize the ordered states in Ni-Pt, thereby correctly predicting $L1_0$ to be the NiPt ground state when compared to the fully relaxed pure-element states.[138,139,209] Results of the FLAPW calculations are shown in the two central columns of the energy level diagram of Fig. 29, adapted from Fig. 1(b) of Ref. 139. The reference energy level (continuous heavy line) is taken to be that of the fully phase-separated state at 0 K with pure Ni and pure Pt at their respective equilibrium volumes. The phase-separated "constrained" states, with Ni and Pt energies calculated at the atomic volume of NiPt at $c = 0.5$, are indicated by heavy line segments whose correct locations on the energy scale should lie quite a bit higher than they are shown; the "constrained" energy levels have been moved down so as to fit conveniently inside the diagram, as was done in Ref. 139. Ordered phase ($L1_0$) and disordered phase energy levels are indicated by solid and dashed line segments, respectively. The SR-FLAPW calculations not only predict the correct (negative) sign for both $\Delta E^x_{form}$ and $\Delta E^x_{dis}$, but also approximately the correct value for the $L1_0$ formation energy (the experimental value[211] is indicated by a dot-dashed line).

The heading (FLAPW/CE) of the two central columns in Fig. 29 indicates that disordered state energies were calculated by cluster expansions, as in Eq. (5.7), with ECIs obtained by the structure inversion method, the formation energies of ordered structures having been calculated by the FLAPW method. The resulting energy values thus depend to some extent on how well the cluster expansion has converged. It may then be argued that a *direct* method of calculating disordered state energ-

[209] Z. W. Lu, S.-H. Wei, and A. Zunger, *Phys. Rev. Lett.* **66**, 1753 (1991).
[210] G. Tréglia and F. Ducastelle, *J. Phys. F* **17**, 1935 (1987).
[211] R. A. Walker and J. R. Darby, *Acta Metall.* **18**, 1761 (1970).

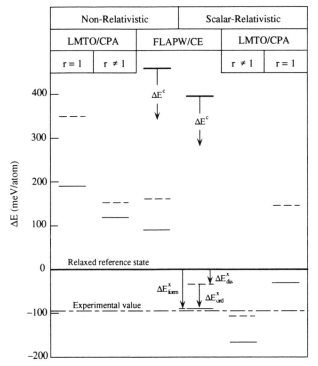

Fig. 29. Formation energies for the Ni-Pt $L1_0$ structure (solid line segments) and disordered state (dashed lines) calculated by various methods: FLAPW/CE (CE = cluster expansion, used for disordered state) [Z. W. Lu, S.-H. Wei, and A. Zunger, *Europhys. Lett.* **21**, 221 (1993)] and LMTO/CPA with equal ($r = 1$) and unequal ($r \neq 1$) sphere radii [P. P. Singh, A. Gonis, and P. E. A. Turchi, *Phys. Rev. Lett.* **71**, 1605 (1993)]. Both relativistic and nonrelativistic results are displayed. The reference state consists of fully relaxed pure Ni and pure Pt at 0 K. The experimentally determined value of the $L1_0$ ordered phase is indicated by a dot-dashed line [R. A. Walker and J. R. Darby, *Acta Metall.* **18**, 1761 (1970)]. Constrained [in the sense of Eq. (14.5b)] formation energies are indicated by heavy line segments, but actually lie higher on the energy scale than shown here (schematically). Relaxed [in the sense of Eq. (14.5a)] formation, ordering and disordered energies, as defined in Fig. 1, are indicated explicitly only for the SR-FLAPW calculations.

ies might be preferable. Such is the viewpoint recently taken by Singh et al.[206] These authors have developed an LMTO-ASA-CPA (or KKR-ASA-CPA) formalism that enabled them to treat both fully ordered and fully disordered energies *on an equal footing* (their terminology), i.e., with basically the same Hamiltonian treated in the same manner. Of course, the direct configurational averaging method does just that, but the TB approximation that was used in the DCA method described in Section 12

makes the numerical results less accurate than those obtained from fully electronically self-consistent methods. Since truly first-principles density-functional methods cannot at present handle arbitrary atomic configurations in suitably large unit cells, homogenization procedures, as provided by the CPA, are attractive alternatives to brute-force configurational averaging. The CPA mean-field approximation neglects fluctuations, in particular local charge fluctuations, however. Johnson and Pinski[212] have taken such fluctuations into account in the KKR-CPA by regarding differently charged sites as separate species in a multicomponent approach.

Singh et al.[206] have chosen to retain the homogeneous medium feature of the CPA while imposing site charge neutrality by varying atomic sphere radii in the ASA framework. The ASA-CPA is computationally efficient and flexible, thus enabling these authors to perform total energy calculations for both ordered and disordered states. Results of these LMTO/CPA (for short) calculations are indicated in the so labeled exterior columns of Fig. 29, the outermost columns corresponding to equal sphere radii (ratio $r = 1$), the next-inner columns to unequal radii ($r \neq 1$) optimized for charge neutrality. Both nonrelativistic and SR calculations were carried out, and the resulting energy levels are indicated in Fig. 29 according to the convention described earlier. Ordered state energies were obtained by the LMTO-ASA method, combined correction terms apparently having little effect.[206] It is observed in Fig. 29 that the agreement between LMTO/CPA ($r \neq 1$) and FLAPW/CE calculations is very close on the NR (left) side, but on the SR (right) side the difference between LMTO/CPA ($r \neq 1$) and FLAPW/CE results is significant.

For all methods illustrated in Fig. 29, all calculated ordering energies are negative, only the SR calculations give the correct (negative) sign for $\Delta E^x_{form}$, and only the FLAPW/CE and LMTO/CPA ($r \neq 1$) calculations give the (presumed) correct (negative) sign for $\Delta E^x_{dis}$. All constained ordering energies are negative, so that local ordering (SRO) tendencies are predicted regardless of the computational method used. Singh et al.[206] conclude that both scalar relativistic and charge neutrality effects must be taken into account for quantitative work relative to the Ni-Pt system.

This conclusion is a very reasonable one, and the disparity of energy values shown in Fig. 29 clearly shows the rather drastic influence of the neglect of various contributions to total energy. Even the optimal SR-LMTO-ASA ($r \neq 1$) $\Delta E_{form}$ calculations do not reproduce the experimentally determined $L1_0$ formation energy [211] as well as do the FLAPW calculations, perhaps because of the atomic sphere approximation em-

[212] D. D. Johnson and F. J. Pinski, Phys. Rev. B **48**, 11553 (1993).

ployed in the LMTO. As for the $\Delta E_{\text{dis}}$ values, there are no experimental data available for comparison: In practice, all disordered states necessarily contain quenched-in SRO. A GPM estimate[206] of the $L1_0$ transition temperature places it far above the experimental one. The fault probably lies in the calculation of the disordered state energy: Local elastic relaxation is completely neglected in the CPA, an effect that is surely important to consider for NiPt alloys for which the size mismatch is substantial. Also, because of large elastic interactions, the cluster expansion is expected to converge slowly, thus necessitating the calculation of a large number of ECIs. Alternatively, the *effective volume* approach of Amador and coworkers[136] may be used, because its application to the problem at hand has produced a very satisfactory Ni-Pt phase diagram.

The Ni-Pt case study concludes this review on a note of optimism and a note of caution. As this example demonstrates, when calculations are performed correctly, good qualitative, even quantitative agreement can be expected, in particular for ground state properties. At the very least, what this example illustrates is that modern alloy thermodynamics is now being performed by solving the Schrödinger equation with relativistic corrections. We have come a long way since the early metallic alloy phase diagram compilations of Hansen and Anderko,[213] for example.

## VIII. Conclusions

The objectives of this review were stated in the introduction. These were, primarily, descriptions of the formalism and applications of cluster expansions to the problem of *ab initio* calculations of thermodynamic properties of crystalline alloys. The success of the method owes much to the parallel developments of statistical and quantum mechanical methods and, of course, to the availability of powerful computational hardware and software.

The cluster expansion techique has provided the essential theoretical tool required to bring together both the statistical and quantum aspects of the problem; *cluster functions* have been shown to constitute a complete orthonormal set, and that basis set has produced a rigorous cluster algebra, which may be used for systems containing an arbitrary degree of configurational order (or disorder). Such is precisely what is necessary for treating the alloy problem.

Cluster methods are, in principle, ideally suited for calculating alloy

[213]M. Hansen and K. Anderko, *Constitution of Binary Alloys,* McGraw-Hill, New York (1958).

phase equilibria. The formalism is rigorous and very general, since any function of configuration can be cluster-expanded, not just the configurational energy. Also, either concentration-independent or -dependent expansion coefficients may be used in alternative but completely equivalent formulations. Serious problems remain, however. The major one perhaps is that rapid convergence of the expansion is generally not guaranteed. We showed in Section 15, for example, that correct ground states could often be predicted only if a fairly large number of ECIs were used. In unfavorable cases, expansions must be extended to fairly large clusters so that combinatorial explosion quickly sets in: the number of atomic configurations increases exponentially with the size (number of points) of the cluster and hence so does the number of cluster interactions to be calculated by electronic structure methods, as does the number of independent variables with respect to which the free energy must be minimized. Even with modern computers, a practical limit to cluster size is rapidly attained. The problem is even more severe for ternary systems than it is for binaries, hence the generalization of cluster methods to technologically relevant multicomponent systems is not as straightforward as the formalism may lead one to believe.

There are some fundamental problems to contend with also. Recent applications have shown (see Section 16, for example) that atomic displacements, both static (elastic) and dynamic (vibrational), played important roles. General and tractable methods of treating these effects in the cluster framework must still be developed or improved, particularly for the case of local elastic relaxations.

Two first-principles methods exist for calculating effective cluster interactions, *direct* and *indirect*. The former includes direct configurational averaging (DCA) and methods based on the CPA (GPM, ECM). The DCA is closest in spirit to the rigorous formalism and is very general and straightforward. It is, however, highly computer intensive, so that it has been implemented thus far only in the TB approximation. Hence, what is gained in fidelity to the formalism may be lost in electronic structure accuracy. The CPA has problems of its own, many of which stem from the mean-field approximation. Also, the KKR-CPA is electronically accurate, but lacks flexibility. It appears that some of the undesirable features of the CPA, such as the neglect of local fluctuations, are currently being taken into account, particularly in the $S^{(2)}$ context.

The most satisfactory results, as measured by comparison with experiment, are often those obtained by the "indirect" SIM method (Connolly-Williams). The advantage of the SIM of course is that one starts with "perfect" structures, the properties of which can be calculated very precisely by density-functional total energy codes. The disadvantage is that

one has little control over cluster expansion convergence. Thus far, among the methods mentioned, no clear winner has yet emerged. Optimally, one would like to do fully electronically self-consistent density-functional DCA calculations. Perhaps new Hamiltonian diagonalization techniques implemented on massively parallel computers would make such calculations feasible.

Clearly much remains to be done. Major effort should go into improving the Hamiltonian portion of the calculations, rather than into improving the statistical mechanical aspects. With the latter, gains of a few percent may be expected; with the former, gains of tens of percent could be achieved. Still, there is cause for optimism. Recent results, some of which have been presented here, are truly impressive. As reliability and generality improve, one can envision the development of a true first-principles thermodynamics of alloys, with significant practical implications for solid state physics and materials science applications.

#### ACKNOWLEDGMENTS

In writing this article, the author has benefited greatly from the help of many colleagues and collaborators. In particular, much of the work described in this review was taken from the work of past and present students: Gerbrand Ceder, Mark Asta, Ryan McCormack, and Christopher Wolverton. The latter three have read critically early drafts of this article and have made invaluable suggestions. The majority of the work performed at the University of California at Berkeley was supported by the Director, Office of Energy Research, Office of Basic Energy Sciences, Materials Sciences Division of the U.S. Department of Energy under contract DE-AC03-76SF00098. A grant from the Nippon Steel Corporation is also gratefully acknowledged.

SOLID STATE PHYSICS, VOL. 47

# The Physics and Mechanics of Brittle Matrix Composites

A. G. EVANS AND F. W. ZOK

*Materials Department, College of Engineering, University of California,
Santa Barbara, California*

## Nomenclature

$a_i$    parameters found in the paper by Hutchinson and Jensen (1990)—Table II

$a_0$    length of unbridged matrix crack

$a_m$    fracture mirror radius

$a_N$    notch size

$a_t$    transition flaw size

$b$    plate dimension

$b_i$    parameters found in the paper by Hutchinson and Jensen (1990)—Table II

$c_i$    parameters found in the paper by Hutchinson and Jensen (1990)—Table II

$d$    matrix crack spacing

$d_s$    saturation crack spacing

$f$    fiber volume fraction

$f_l$    fiber volume fraction in loading direction

$g$    function related to cracking of 90° plies

$h$    fiber pull-out length

$l$    sliding length

$l_i$    debond length

$l_s$    shear band length

$m$    shape parameter for fiber strength distribution

$m_m$    shape parameter for matrix flaw size distribution

$n$    creep exponent

$n_m$    creep exponent for matrix

$n_f$    creep exponent for fiber

$q$    residual stress in matrix in axial orientation

$s_{ij}$    deviatoric stress
$t$    time
$t_p$    ply thickness
$t_b$    beam thickness
$u$    crack opening displacement (COD)
$u_a$    COD due to applied stress
$u_b$    COD due to bridging
$v$    sliding displacement
$w$    beam width
$B$    creep rheology parameter $\dot{\varepsilon}_o/\sigma_o^n$
$C_v$    specific heat at constant strain
$E$    Young's modulus for composite
$E_o$    plane strain Young's modulus for composites
$\bar{E}$    unloading modulus
$E_*$    Young's modulus of material with matrix cracks
$E_f$    Young's modulus of fiber
$E_m$    Young's modulus of matrix
$E_L$    ply modulus in longitudinal orientation
$E_T$    ply modulus in transverse orientation
$E_t$    tangent modulus
$E_s$    secant modulus
$G$    shear modulus
$\mathcal{G}$    energy release rate (ERR)
$\mathcal{G}_{tip}$    tip ERR
$\mathcal{G}_{tip}^o$    tip ERR at lower bound
$K$    stress intensity factor (SIF)
$K_b$    SIF caused by bridging
$K_m$    critical SIF for matrix
$K_R$    crack growth resistance
$K_{tip}$    SIF at crack tip
$I_o$    moment of inertia
$L$    crack spacing in 90° plies
$L_f$    fragment length
$L_g$    gauge length
$L_o$    reference length for fibers
$N$    number of fatigue cycles
$N_s$    number of cycles at which sliding stress reaches steady state
$R$    fiber radius
$\mathcal{R}$    R ratio for fatigue ($\sigma_{max}/\sigma_{min}$)
$\mathcal{R}_c$    radius of curvature
$S$    tensile strength of fiber
$S_b$    dry bundle strength of fibers

$S_c$    characteristic fiber strength
$S_g$    UTS subject to global load sharing
$S_o$    scale factor for fiber strength
$S_p$    pull-out strength
$S_{th}$    threshold stress for fatigue
$S_u$    ultimate tensile strength (UTS)
$S_*$    UTS in presence of a flaw
$T$    temperature
$\Delta T$    change in temperature

*Greek:*

$\alpha$    linear thermal coefficient of expansion (TCE)
$\alpha_f$    TCE of fiber
$\alpha_m$    TCE of matrix
$\gamma$    shear strain
$\gamma_c$    shear ductility
$\delta_c$    characteristic length
$\delta\varepsilon$    hysteresis loop width
$\varepsilon$    strain
$\varepsilon_*$    strain caused by relief of residual stress on matrix cracking
$\varepsilon_e$    elastic strain
$\varepsilon_o$    permanent strain
$\dot{\varepsilon}_o$    reference strain rate for creep
$\varepsilon_\tau$    transient creep strain
$\varepsilon_s$    sliding strain
$\lambda$    pull-out parameter
$\mu$    friction coefficient
$\xi$    fatigue exponent (of order 0.1)
$\kappa$    beam curvature
$\nu$    Poisson's ratio
$\phi$    orientation of interlaminar cracks
$\rho$    density
$\sigma$    stress
$\sigma_b$    bridging stress
$\bar{\sigma}_b$    peak, reference stress
$\sigma_e$    effective stress $\rightarrow \sqrt{(3/2)s_{ij}s_{ij}}$
$\sigma_f$    stress in fiber
$\sigma_i$    debond stress
$\sigma_m$    stress in matrix
$\sigma_{mc}$    matrix cracking stress
$\sigma^o$    stress on 0° plies
$\sigma_o$    creep reference stress

$\sigma_{rr}$    radial stress
$\sigma^R$    residual stress
$\sigma_s$    saturation stress
$\sigma_s^*$    peak stress for traction law
$\sigma_\tau$    lower bound stress for tunnel cracking
$\sigma^T$    misfit stress
$\tau$    interface sliding stress
$\tau_f$    value of sliding stress after fatigue
$\tau_o$    constant component of interface sliding stress
$\tau_s$    in-plane shear strength
$\bar{\tau}_c$    critical stress for interlaminar crack growth
$\tau_{ss}$    steady state value of $\tau$ after fatigue
$\Delta^R$    displacement caused by matrix removal
$\Delta\varepsilon_p$    unloading strain differential
$\Delta\varepsilon_o$    reloading strain differential
$\Gamma$    fracture energy
$\Gamma_i$    interface debond energy
$\Gamma_f$    fiber fracture energy
$\Gamma_m$    matrix fracture energy
$\Gamma_R$    fracture resistance
$\Gamma_S$    steady state fracture resistance
$\Gamma_T$    transverse fracture energy
$\Omega$    misfit strain
$\Omega_o$    misfit strain at ambient temperature

## I. Introduction

### 1. RATIONALE

Various types of brittle matrix composites exist, based on ceramics, glasses, polymers, and intermetallics. The respective designations are CMCs, GMCs, PMCs, and IMCs. The fibers are used to impart sound structural characteristics, particularly to resist the propagation of cracks when either steady or cyclic loads are imposed. However, all of the thermomechanical properties are affected by the fibers—sometimes profoundly. As a result, the approaches needed for design and for assuring reliability are completely different from those used for monolithic metals, ceramics, and polymers. The underlying principles are explored in this chapter. Many of the basic ideas originated with the development of PMCs. In these materials, the matrix has relatively low modulus and strength, but moderate ductility. The fibers enhance the modulus and

strength but reduce the ductility. The mechanisms that dictate the structural performance of PMCs reflect these factors. In CMCs and GMCs, as well as many IMCs, the elastic properties of the fibers and matrix are similar and the matrix has low ductility. Consequently, the mechanisms that operate in response to thermomechanical loads are often quite different from those found in PMCs. The emphasis of this article is on composites exemplified by CMCs, GMCs, and IMCs.

Continuous fiber-reinforced brittle matrix composites have a major advantage compared with the monolithic matrix. They exhibit an ability to retain good tensile strength in the presence of holes and notches.[1-3] This characteristic is important because composite components generally need to be attached to other components, usually metals. At these attachments (whether mechanical or bonded), stress concentrations arise, which dominate the design and reliability. Inelastic deformation at these sites is crucial. It alleviates the elastic stress concentration by locally redistributing stress.[4] Such inelasticity is present in brittle matrix composites.[5-8] In association with the inelastic deformation, various degradation processes occur that affect the useful life of the material. Several fatigue effects are involved:[9,10] cyclic, static, and thermal. The most severe degradation appears to occur subject to out-of-phase thermomechanical fatigue (TMF). In addition, creep and creep rupture occur at high temperatures.[11]

All of the mechanical characteristics that govern structural utility and life depend on the constituent properties (fibers, matrix, interfaces), as well as the fiber architecture. Since the constituents are variables, optimization of the property profiles needed for design and lifetime considerations become prohibitively expensive if traditional empirical procedures are used. The philosophy of this chapter is based on the recognition that mechanism-based models are needed that allow efficient interpolation between a well-conceived experimental matrix. The emphasis is on the

[1] K. M. Prewo, *J. Mater. Sci.* **17**, 3549 (1982).

[2] S. Mall, D. E. Bullock, and J. J. Pernot, to be published.

[3] C. Cady, T. J. Mackin, and A. G. Evans, *J. Am. Ceram. Soc.,* in press.

[4] A. G. Evans, J. M. Domergue, and E. Vagaggini, *J. Am. Ceram. Soc.,* in press.

[5] V. C. Nardonne and K. M. Prewo, *J. Mater. Sci.* **23**, 168 (1988).

[6] R. Y. Kim and N. Pagano, *J. Am. Ceram. Soc.* **74**, 1082–1090 (1991).

[7] H. C. Cao, E. Bischoff, O. Sbaizero, M. Rühle, and A. G. Evans, *J. Am. Ceram. Soc.* **73**(6), 1691–1699 (1990).

[8] A. W. Pryce and P. Smith, *J. Mater. Sci.* **27**, 2695–2704 (1992).

[9] K. M. Prewo, *J. Mater. Sci.* **22**, 2595–2701 (1987).

[10] L. P. Zawada, L. M. Butkus, and G. A. Hartman, *J. Am. Ceram. Soc.* **74**, 2851–2858 (1991).

[11] C. Weber and A. G. Evans, *J. Am. Ceram. Soc.,* in press.

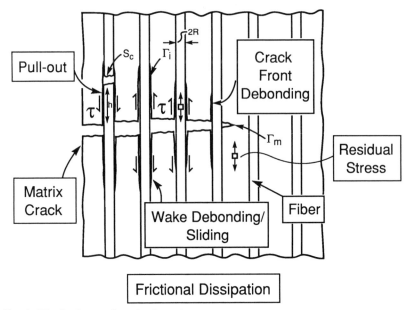

FIG. 1. The fundamental mechanisms that operate as a crack extends through the matrix.

creation of a framework that allows models to be inserted, as they are developed, which can also be validated by carefully chosen experiments.

## 2. OBJECTIVES

The initial intent of this chapter is to address the *mechanisms* of stress redistribution upon monotonic and cyclic loading, as well as the *mechanics* needed to characterize the notch sensitivity.[4,12] This assessment is conducted primarily for composites with 2-D reinforcements. The basic *phenomena* that give rise to inelastic strains are matrix cracks and fiber failures subject to interfaces that debond and slide (Fig. 1).[13-15] These phenomena identify the essential constituent properties, which have the typical values indicated in Table I.

[12]G. Bao and Z. Suo, *Appl. Mech. Rev.* **45**(8), 355–366 (1992).
[13]J. Aveston, G. A. Cooper, and A. Kelly, in *The Properties of Fiber Composites, NPL Conf. Proc.*, pp. 15–26 (1971). IPC Science and Technology, U.K.
[14]W. A. Curtin, *J. Am. Ceram. Soc.* **74**, 2837 (1991).
[15]A. G. Evans, and D. G. Marshall, *Acta Metall.* **37**, 2567–2583 (1989).

TABLE I. CONSTITUENT PROPERTIES OF CMCs AND METHODS OF MEASUREMENT

| CONSTITUENT PROPERTY | MEASUREMENT METHODS | TYPICAL RANGE |
|---|---|---|
| Sliding stress, $\tau$ (MPa) | • Push-out force<br>• Pull-out length, $\bar{h}$<br>• Saturation crack spacing, $\bar{l}_s$<br>• Hysteresis loop, $\delta\varepsilon$<br>• Unloading modulus, $\bar{E}_L$ | 1–200 |
| Characteristic strength, $S_c$ (GPa) | • Fracture mirrors<br>• Pull-out length, $\bar{h}$ | 1.2–3.0 |
| Misfit strain, $\Omega$ | • Bilayer distortion<br>• Permanent strain, $\varepsilon_p$<br>• Residual crack opening | $0–2.10^{-3}$ |
| Matrix fracture energy, $\Gamma_m$ (J m$^{-2}$) | • Monolithic material<br>• Saturation crack spacing, $\bar{l}_s$<br>• Matrix cracking stress, $\bar{\sigma}_{mc}$ | 5–50 |
| Debond energy, $\Gamma_i$ (J m$^{-2}$) | • Permanent strain, $\varepsilon_p$<br>• Residual crack opening, $u_p$ | 0–5 |

Three underlying mechanisms are responsible for the nonlinearity:[16,17] (1) *Frictional dissipation* occurs at the fiber-matrix interfaces, whereupon the sliding resistance of debonded interfaces $\tau$ becomes a key parameter. *Control of $\tau$ is critical.* This behavior is dominated by the fiber coating, as well as the fiber morphology.[18,19] By varying $\tau$, the prevalent damage mechanism and the resultant nonlinearity can be dramatically modified. (2) The matrix cracks increase the *elastic compliance*.[20] (3) The matrix cracks also cause changes in the residual stress distribution, resulting in a *permanent strain*.[20]

The relative ability of these mechanisms to operate depends on the loading and the fiber orientation. It is necessary to address and understand the mechanisms that operate for loadings, which vary from tension along one fiber direction to shear at various orientations. For *tensile loading,* several damage mechanisms have been found, involving matrix

[16] A. G. Evans and F. W. Zok, in *Topics In Fracture and Fatigue* (A. S. Argon, ed.), pp. 271–308 (1992). Springer-Verlag.

[17] E. Vagaggini, J. M. Domergue, and A. G. Evans, *J. Am. Ceram. Soc.,* in press.

[18] J. B. Davis, J. P. A. Löfvander, A. G. Evans, E. Bischoff, and M. L. Emiliani, *J. Am. Ceram. Soc.* **76,** 1249 (1993).

[19] A. G. Evans, F. W. Zok, and J. Davis, *Composites Sci. Technol.* **42,** 3–24 (1991).

[20] M. Y. He, B. X. Wu, A. G. Evans, and J. W. Hutchinson, *Mech. of Mtls.,* in press.

**Class I**

Matrix Cracking + Fiber Failure

**Class II**

Matrix Cracking: No Fiber Failure

Pull-Out Tractions
Redistribute Stress

Matrix Cracks
Redistribute Stress

**Class III**

Shear Damage By Matrix Cracking

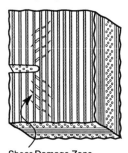

Shear Damage Zone
Redistributes Stress

FIG. 2. Three prevalent damage mechanisms occurring around notches in CMCs. Each mechanism allows stress redistribution by a combination of matrix cracking and fiber pull-out.

cracks combined with sliding interfaces (Fig. 2). These can be visualized by mechanism maps,[21] which then become an integral part of the testing and design activity. One damage mechanism involves mode I cracks with simultaneous fiber failure, referred to as *class I behavior* (Fig. 2). Stress redistribution is provided by the tractions exerted on the crack by the failed fibers as they *pull*.[12,22–24] A second damage mechanism involves

[21] A. G. Evans, *Mat. Sci. Eng.* **A143**, 63 (1991).
[22] B. N. Cox, *Acta Metall. Mater.* **39**(6), 1189–1201 (1991).
[23] B. N. Cox and C. S. Lo, *Acta Metall. Mater.* **40**, 69 (1992).
[24] B. N. Cox and D. B. Marshall, *Fatigue Fracture of Eng. Mtls.* **14**, 847 (1991).

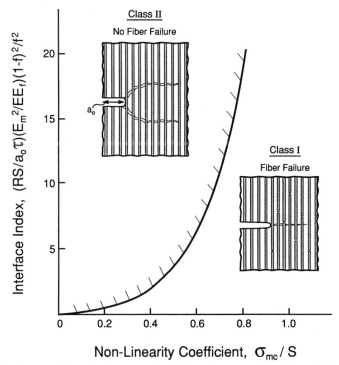

## Non-Linearity Coefficient, $\sigma_{mc}/S$

FIG. 3. A proposed mechanism map that distinguishes class I and class II behavior.

multiple matrix cracks, with minimal fiber failure, referred to as *class II behavior* (Fig. 2). In this case, the plastic deformation caused by matrix cracks allows stress redistribution.[3,4] A schematic of a mechanism map based on these two damage mechanisms (Fig. 3) illustrates another important issue: the use of *nondimensional parameters* to interpolate over a range of constituent properties.* On the mechanism map, the ordinate is a nondimensional measure of sliding stress and the abscissa is a nondi-

---

* For ease of reference, all of the most important nondimensional parameters are listed in a separate table (Table II).

| | |
|---|---|
| Relative stiffness | $\xi \to fE_f/(1-f)E_m$ |
| Sliding index | $\mathcal{T} \to \xi[\tau_o E/\sigma E_f]^{1/2}$ |
| Cyclic sliding index | $\Delta\mathcal{T} \to \xi[\tau_o E/\Delta\sigma E_f]^{1/2}$ |
| Loading index | $\mathscr{E} \to [2R\sigma/f\xi^2 a\tau_o]$ |
| Cyclic loading indices | $\Delta\mathscr{E} \to [2R(\Delta\sigma)/f\xi^2 a\tau_o]$ |
| | $\Delta\mathscr{E}_o \to [2R(\Delta\sigma)/f\xi^2 a_o\tau_o]$ |
| Bridging index | $\mathscr{E}_b \to [2R\sigma_b/f\xi^2 a\tau_o]$ |
| Cyclic bridging indices | $\Delta\mathscr{E}_b \to [2R(\Delta\sigma_b)/f\xi^2 a\tau_o]$ |
| | $\Delta\mathscr{E}_T \to [2RE_f(\alpha_f - \alpha_m)\Delta T/\xi^2 f\tau_o a]$ |
| Misfit index | $\Sigma_T \to \dfrac{\bar{\sigma}_T}{\bar{\sigma}_p} = (c_2/c_1)E_m\Omega/\bar{\sigma}_p$ |
| Debond index | $\Sigma_i \to \dfrac{\bar{\sigma}_i}{\bar{\sigma}_p} = (1/c_1)\sqrt{E_m\Gamma_i/R\bar{\sigma}_p^2} - \Sigma_T$ |
| Hysteresis index | $\mathscr{H} \to b_2(1 - a_1 f)^2 R\bar{\sigma}_p^2/4\bar{l}\tau E_m f^2$ |
| Crack spacing index | $\mathscr{L} \to \Gamma_m(1-f)^2 E_f E_m/f\tau^2 E_L R$ |
| Matrix cracking index | $M \to 6\tau\Gamma_m f^2 E_f/(1-f)E_m^2 RE_L$ |
| Residual stress index | $\mathfrak{Q} \to E_f f\Omega/E_L(1-\nu)$ |
| Flaw index | $\mathscr{A} \to a_o S^2/E_L\Gamma$ |
| Flaw index for bridging | $\mathscr{A}_b \to [f/(1-f)]^2(E_f E_L/E_m^2)(a_o\tau/RS_u)$ |
| Flaw index for pull-out | $\mathscr{A}_p \to (a_o/\bar{h})(S_p/E_L)$ |

$$a_1 = E_f/E$$

$$a_2 = \frac{(1-f)E_f(1 + E_f/E)}{[E_f + (1-2\nu)E]}$$

$$b_2 = \frac{(1+\nu)E_m\{2(1-\nu)^2 E_f + (1-2\nu)[1 - \nu + f(1+\nu)](E_m - E_f)\}}{(1-\nu)E_f[(1+\nu)E_o + (1-\nu)E_m]}$$

$$b_3 = \frac{f(1+\nu)\{(1-f)(1+\nu)(1-2\nu)(E_f - E_m) + 2(1-\nu)^2 E_m\}}{(1-\nu)(1-f)[(1+\nu)E_o + (1-\nu)E_m]}$$

$$c_1 = \frac{(1 - fa_1)(b_2 + b_3)^{1/2}}{2f}$$

$$c_2 = \frac{a_2(b_2 + b_3)^{1/2}}{2}$$

$$c_1/c_2 = \frac{1 - a_1 f}{a_2 f}$$

with

$$E = fE_f + (1-f)E_m$$

$$E_o = (1-f)E_f + fE_m$$

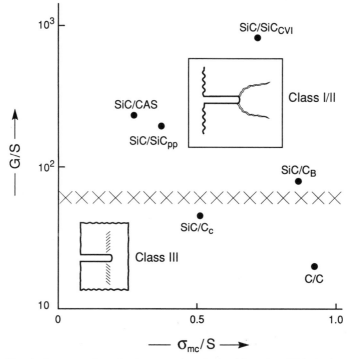

FIG. 4. A proposed mechanism map that distinguishes class III behavior.

mensional *in situ* fiber strength. A third damage mechanism also exists (Fig. 2), referred to as *class III*. It involves matrix shear damage prior to composite failure as a means for redistributing stress. A proposed mechanism map[25] is presented in Fig. 4.

A summary of tensile stress-strain curves obtained for a variety of 2-D composites (Fig. 5) highlights the most fundamental characteristic relevant to the application of CMCs. Among these four materials, the SiC/CAS system is found to be *notch insensitive* in tension,[3] even for quite large notches (~5 mm long). The other three materials exhibit varying degrees of *notch sensitivity*.[26,27] Moreover, the notch insensitivity in SiC/CAS arises *despite relatively small plastic strains*. These results delineate two issues that need resolution: (1) How much plastic strain is

[25] P. A. Brøndsted, F. E. Heredia, and A. G. Evans, *J. Am. Ceram. Soc.,* in press.

[26] F. E. Heredia, S. M. Spearing, P. Mosher, A. G. Evans, and W. A. Curtin, *J. Am. Ceram. Soc.* **75,** 3017–3025 (1992).

[27] F. E. Heredia, S. M. Spearing, M. Y. He, T. J. Mackin, P. A. Brønsted, A. G. Evans, and P. Mosher, *J. Am. Ceram. Soc.,* in press.

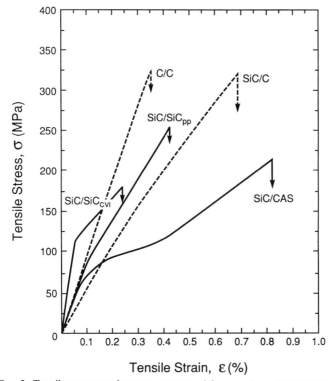

Tensile Strain, $\varepsilon$ (%)

FIG. 5. Tensile stress-strain curves measured for a variety of 2-D CMCs.

needed to impart notch insensitivity? (2) Is the ratio of the "yield" strength to ultimate tensile strength (UTS) an important factor in notch sensitivity? This chapter review addresses both questions.

The *shear behavior* also involves matrix cracking and fiber failure.[25] However, the ranking of the shear stress-strain curves between materials (Fig. 6) differs appreciably from that found for tension (Fig. 5). Preliminary efforts at understanding this difference and for providing a methodology to interpolate between shear and tension are described.

Analyses of damage and failure have established that certain *constituent properties* are basic to composite performance (Table I). These need to be measured independently and then used as characterizing parameters, analogous to the yield strength and fracture toughness in monolithic materials. The six major *independent* parameters are[4] the interfacial sliding stress $\tau$, debond energy $\Gamma_i$, the *in situ* fiber properties, $S_c$ and $m$, the fiber-matrix misfit strain $\Omega$, and the matrix fracture energy $\Gamma_m$, as well as the elastic properties $E$ and $v$. *Dependent* parameters that can often be

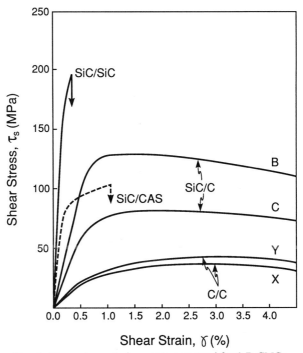

FIG. 6. Shear stress-strain curves measured for 2-D CMCs.

used to infer the constituent properties include the fiber pull-out length,[7,14,28] the fracture mirror radius on the fibers,[29] and the saturation crack spacing in the matrix.[30] Approaches for measuring the constituent properties in a consistent, straightforward manner are emphasized here, and their relevance to composite behavior explored through models of damage and failure. Moreover, the expressions that relate composite behavior to constituent properties are often unwieldy, because a large number of parameters are involved. Consequently, throughout this article, the formulas used to represent CMC behaviors are the *simplest* capable of describing the major phenomena.*

---

* The behaviors represented by these formulas are often applicable only to composites: the equivalent phenomenon being absent in monolithic ceramics. Consequently, the expressions should be restricted to composites with fiber volume fractions in the range of practical interest ( $f$ between 0.3–0.5). Extrapolation to small $f$ would lead to erroneous interpretations, because mechanism changes usually occur.

[28] W. A. Curtin, *J. Mater. Sci.* **26**, 66 (1991).

[29] J. F. Jamet, D. Lewis, and E. Y. Luh, *Ceram. Eng. Sci. Proc.* **5**, 625 (1984).

[30] F. W. Zok and S. M. Spearing, *Acta Metall. Mater.* **40**, 2033 (1992).

In most composites with desirable tensile properties, linear elastic fracture mechanics (LEFM) criteria are violated.[31,32] Instead, various large-scale nonlinearities arise that are associated with matrix damage and fiber pull-out. In consequence, an alternative mechanics is needed to specify the relevant *material and loading parameters* and to establish *design rules*. Some progress toward this objective is described and related to test data. This has been achieved using large-scale bridging mechanics (LSBM) combined with continuum damage mechanics (CDM).[12,22–24] The preceding considerations dictate the ability of the material to survive thermal and mechanical loads imposed for short durations. In many cases, long-term survivability at elevated temperatures dictates the applicability of the material. Life models based on *degradation* mechanisms are needed to address this issue. For this purpose, generalized fatigue and creep models are required, especially in regions that contain matrix cracks. It is inevitable that such cracks exist in regions subject to strain concentrations and, indeed, are required to redistribute stress. In this situation, degradation of the interface and the fibers may occur as the matrix cracks open and close on thermomechanical cycling, with access to the atmosphere being possible through the matrix cracks. The rate of such degradation dictates the useful life.

3. APPROACH

To address the preceding issues, this chapter is organized in the following manner. First, some of the basic thermomechanical characteristics of composites are established, with emphasis on interfaces and interface properties, as well as residual stresses. Then, the fundamental response of unidirectional (1-D) materials, subject to tensile loading, is addressed, in accordance with several subtopics: (1) mechanisms of nonlinear deformation and failure; (2) constitutive laws that relate macroscopic performance to constituent properties; (3) the use of stress-strain measurements to determine constituent properties in a consistent, straightforward manner; and (4) the simulation of stress-strain curves. The discussion of 1-D materials is followed by the application of the same concepts to 2-D materials, subject to combinations of tensile and shear loading. At this stage, it is possible to address the *mechanisms of stress redistribution* around flaws, holes, attachments, and notches. In turn, these mechanisms suggest a *mechanics methodology* for relating strength to the size and shape of the flaws, attachment loading, etc.

[31]D. B. Marshall, B. N. Cox, and A. G. Evans, *Acta Metall.* 33, 2013–2021 (1985).
[32]D. B. Marshall and B. N. Cox, *Mech. of Mtls.* 7, 127 (1986).

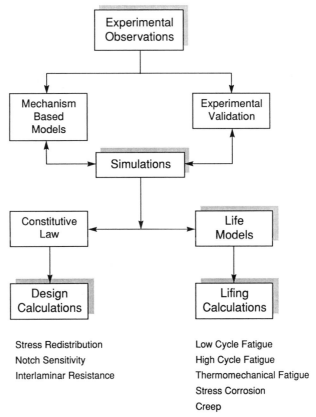

FIG. 7. The philosophy adopted for using models in the design and application of CMCs.

Data regarding the effects of cyclic loading and creep on the life of brittle matrix composites are limited. The concepts to be developed thus draw on knowledge and experience gained with other composite systems, such as metal matrix (MMCs) and polymer matrix (PMCs) materials. The overall philosophy is depicted in Fig. 7.

## II. Interfaces

### 4. THERMOMECHANICAL REPRESENTATION

The thermomechanical properties of coatings at fiber-matrix interfaces are critically important. A consistent characterization approach is neces-

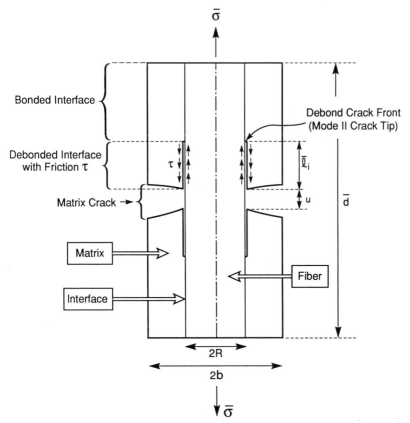

FIG. 8. A schematic indicating the sliding and debonding behavior envisaged in CMCs.

sary. The most commonly adopted hypothesis is that there are two parameters (Fig. 8). One is associated with *fracture* and the other with
*slip*.[33-36] Fracture, or debonding, is considered to involve a debond energy
$\Gamma_i$.[21,37] Slip is expected to occur with a shear resistance $\tau$. A schematic
representation (Fig. 9) illustrates the issues. *Debonding* must be a mode
II (shear) fracture phenomenon. In brittle systems, mode II fracture typically occurs by the coalescence of microcracks within a material

[33] J. W. Hutchinson and H. Jensen, *Mech. of Mtls.* 9, 139 (1990).
[34] R. J. Kerans and T. A. Parthasarathy, *J. Am. Ceram. Soc.* 74, 1585 (1991).
[35] P. D. Jero, R. J. Kerans, and T. A. Parthasarathy, *J. Am. Ceram. Soc.* 74, 2793 (1991).
[36] T. Mackin, P. Warren, and A. G. Evans, *Acta Metall. Mater.* 40(6), 1251–1257 (1992).
[37] M. Y. He and J. W. Hutchinson, *Intl. Jnl. Solids Struct.* 25(9), 53–67 (1989).

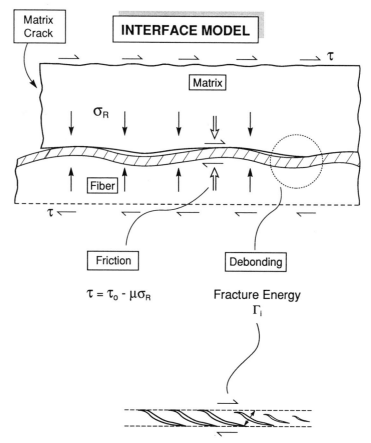

FIG. 9. The fiber sliding model.

layer.[38,39] In some cases, this layer coincides with the coating itself, such that debonding involves a diffuse zone of microcrack damage (Fig. 9). In other cases, the layer is very thin and the debond has the appearance of a single crack. For both situations, it is believed that debond propagation can be represented by a debond energy $\Gamma_i$, with an associated stress jump above and below the debond front.[33] Albeit that, in several instances, $\Gamma_i$ is essentially zero.[40] When a discrete debond crack exists, *frictional slid-*

[38] N. A. Fleck, *Proc. Roy. Soc.* **A432**, 55–76 (1991).
[39] C. Xia and J. W. Hutchinson, Harvard University Report Mech-208, *Intl. Jnl. Solids Structures* **31**, 1133–1148 (1994).
[40] D. B. Marshall and W. C. Oliver, *J. Am. Ceram. Soc.* **70**, 542–548 (1987).

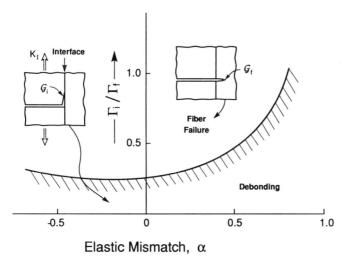

Elastic Mismatch, $\alpha$

FIG. 10. A debond diagram for CMCs.

*ing* of the crack faces provides the shear resistance. Such sliding occurs in accordance with a friction law:[33-36,40]

$$\tau = \tau_o - \mu\sigma_{rr}, \tag{4.1}$$

where $\mu$ is the Coulomb friction coefficient, $\sigma_{rr}$ is the compression normal to the interface, and $\tau_o$ is a term associated with fiber roughness. When the debond process occurs by diffuse microcracking in the coating, it is again assumed (without justification) that the interface has a constant shear resistance, $\tau_o$.

For debonding and sliding to occur, rather than brittle cracking through the fiber, the debond energy $\Gamma_i$ must not exceed an upper bound, relative to the fiber fracture energy $\Gamma_f$.[37] Calculations have suggested that the following inequality must be satisfied (Fig. 10):

$$\Gamma_i \gtrsim (1/4)\Gamma_f. \tag{4.2}$$

Noting that most ceramic fibers have a fracture energy of $\Gamma_f \approx 20 \text{ J m}^{-2}$, Eq. (4.2) indicates that the upper bound on the debond energy is $\Gamma_i \approx 5 \text{ J m}^{-2}$. This magnitude is broadly consistent with experience obtained on fiber coatings that impart the requisite properties.[18,41-44]

[41]R. W. Rice, "BN Coating of Ceramic Fibers for Ceramic Fiber Composites, February 10, 1987"; assigned to the United States of America as represented by the Secretary of the Navy U.S. Patent 4,642,271.

5. MEASUREMENT METHODS

Measurements of the sliding stress $\tau$ and the debond energy $\Gamma_i$ have been obtained by a variety of approaches (Table I). The most direct involve displacement measurements. These are conducted in two ways: (1) fiber push-through/push-in by means of a small-diameter indentor[40] and (2) tensile loading in the presence of matrix cracks.[4,45] Indirect methods for obtaining $\tau$ also exist. These include measurement of the saturation matrix crack spacing[30] and the fiber pull-out length.[14] The *direct* measurement methods require accurate determination of displacements, coupled with an analysis that allows rigorous deconvolution of load-displacement curves. The basic analyses used for this purpose are contained in papers by Hutchinson and Jensen,[33] Liang and Hutchinson,[46] and Jero *et al*.[35] The fundamental features are illustrated by the behavior found upon tensile loading, subsequent to matrix cracking (Fig. 11). The hysteresis that occurs during an unload/reload cycle relates to the sliding stress, $\tau$. *Accurate values for $\tau$ can be obtained from hysteresis measurements.*[4,17,47] Furthermore, these results are *relevant to the small sliding displacements* * that occur during matrix crack evolution in actual composites. The plastic strains contain combined information about $\tau$, $\Omega$, and $\Gamma_i$. Consequently, if $\tau$ is already known, $\Gamma_i$ can be evaluated from the plastic strains measured as a function of load, especially if $\Omega$ has been obtained from independent determinations.[4] The basic formulas that connect $\tau$, $\Gamma_i$, and $\Omega$ to the stress-strain behavior are presented in a subsequent section.

6. SLIDING MODELS

The manipulations of interfaces needed to control $\tau$ can be appreciated by using a model to simulate the sliding behavior. A simplified sliding model has been developed (Fig. 10) that embodies the role of the pressure

---

* Information about $\tau$ at larger sliding displacements is usually obtained from fiber push-through measurements.

[42] R. W. Rice, J. R. Spann, D. Lewis, and W. Coblenz, *Ceram. Eng. Sci. Proc.* **5**(7–8), 614–624 (1984).

[43] B. Bender, O. Shadwell, C. Bulik, L. Incorvati, and D. Lewis, III, *Am. Ceram. Soc. Bull.* **65**(2), 363–369 (1986).

[44] J. J. Brennan, *Tailoring of Multiphase Ceramics* (R. E. Tressler and J. R. Hellman, eds.) Plenum Press, New York **20**, 549 (1986).

[45] D. B. Marshall and A. G. Evans, *J. Am. Ceram. Soc.* **68**, 225–231 (1985).

[46] C. Liang and J. W. Hutchinson, *Mech. of Mtls.* **14**, 207–221 (1993).

[47] T. J. Kotil, J. W. Holmes, and M. Comninou, *J. Am. Ceram. Soc.* **73**, 1879 (1990).

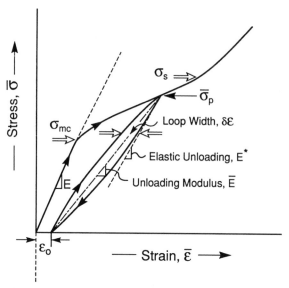

FIG. 11. A typical load/unload cycle showing the parameters that can be measured that relate to the interface properties.

at contact points, due to the combined effects of a mismatch strain and roughness.[35,36] Coulomb friction is regarded as the fundamental friction law operating at contacts. Otherwise, the system is considered to be elastic. The variables in the analysis are (1) the amplitude and wavelength of the roughness; (2) the mismatch strain $\Omega$; (3) the Coulomb friction coefficient $\mu$; and (4) the elastic properties of the constituents. With these parameters as input, the sliding can be simulated for various loading situations. One set of simulations conducted for comparison with fiber push-out tests (Fig. 12) illustrates the relative importance of each of the variables. For this set, the fiber roughness was characterized using a fractal method. The roughness within the section was selected at random, from the measured amplitude distribution, causing some differences in the push-out spectrum for each simulation. By using this simulation, *substantial* systematic changes in the sliding resistance have been predicted when the friction coefficient, the mismatch strain, and the roughness amplitude are changed.* Generally, the mismatch strain and the roughness can be measured independently.[36] Consequently, the comparison between simulation and experiment actually provides an estimate of the

---

* Poisson's ratio causes only minor effects.

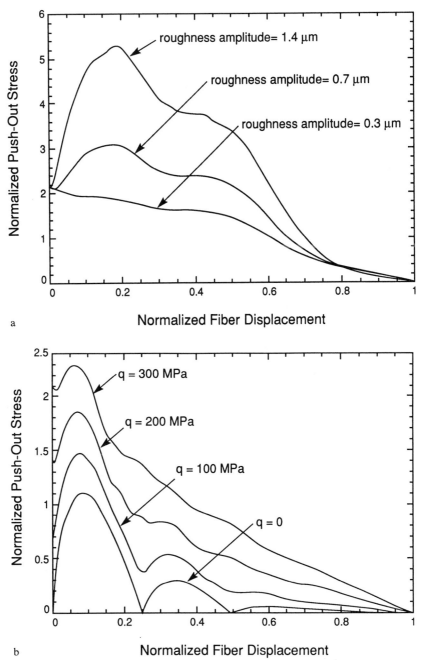

FIG. 12. Simulation of the effects of the key variables on the push-out behavior: (a) roughness, (b) residual stress, and (c) friction coefficient.

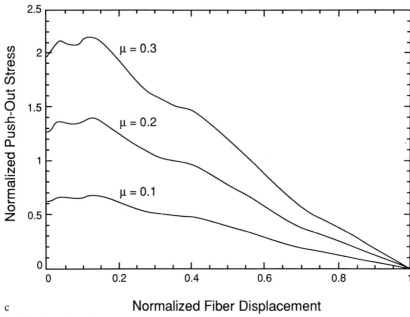

c

Normalized Fiber Displacement

FIG. 12—(continued)

*friction coefficient* $\mu$. If this is found to be within an acceptable range, the inferred $\mu$ is, thereafter, used to predict how $\tau$ can be expected to vary as either the misfit or the roughnesses are changed, if $\mu$ is fixed. This approach indicates that $\mu \approx 0.1$ for either C or BN coatings,[48] whereas $\mu \approx 0.5$ for oxide coatings.[49] Such values are compatible with macroscopic friction measurements made on bulk materials and thus appear to be reasonable. However, much additional testing is needed to validate the sliding model.

## 7. EXPERIMENTAL RESULTS

Most of the experience with brittle matrix composites is on C, BN, or Mo fiber coatings.[18,19,41–44,50] Such coatings usually have a relatively low debond energy $\Gamma_i$ and can provide a range of sliding stresses $\tau$ (Table I), as illustrated by comparison of three different carbon coatings on sapphire fibers in TiAl [Fig. 13(a)]. A considerable range in $\tau$ has even been

[48]J. Lamon, P. Raballiat, and A. G. Evans, *J. Am. Ceram. Soc.*, in press.
[49]T. Mackin, J. Yang, C. Levi, and A. G. Evans, *Acta Metall. Mater.* **41**, 2681–2690 (1993).
[50]J. J. Brennan and K. M. Prewo, *J. Mater. Sci.* **17**, 2371–2383 (1982).

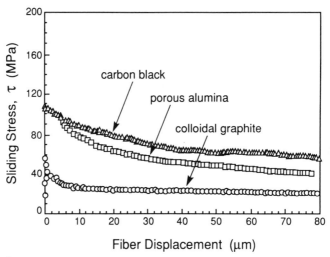

a

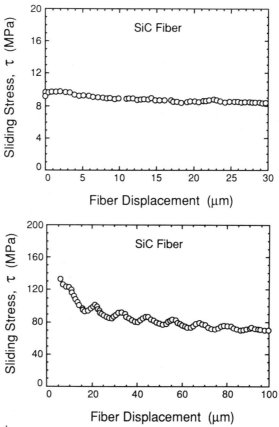

b

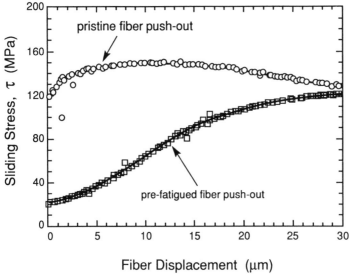

c

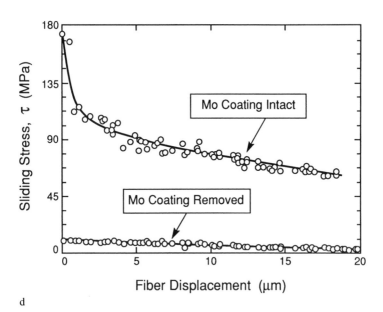

d

Fig. 13. Some typical fiber push-out measurements conducted on CMCs and intermetallic matrix composites: (a) $Al_2O_3/TiAl$ within $C/Al_2O_3$ double coatings, (b) SiC/glass and $Al_2O_3/$ glass showing effect of fiber roughness, (c) SiC/Ti with C coating showing influence of fatigue, and (d) $Al_2O_3/Al_2O_3$ with fugitive Mo coating.

achieved with C coatings. Values between 2 and 200 MPa have been found. Furthermore, this range is obtained even at comparable values of the misfit strain. The different values may relate to fiber roughness. Roughness effects are best illustrated by the sliding behavior of sapphire fibers in a glass matrix. During fiber manufacture, sinusoidal asperities are grown onto the surface of the sapphire fibers. The sinusoidal fiber surface roughness is manifest as a wavelength modulation in the sliding stress during push-out [Fig. 13(b)].[36] However, there must also be influences of the coating thickness and microstructure. A model that includes the effects of the influence of the coating has yet to be developed.

In most brittle matrix composites, the debond energy $\Gamma_i$ has been found to be negligibly small ($\Gamma_i < 0.1$ J m$^{-2}$). Such systems include all of the glass ceramic matrix systems reinforced with Nicalon fibers, which have a C interphase formed by reaction during composite processing. Low values also seem to be obtained for SiC matrix composites with BN fiber coatings. The clear exception is SiC/SiC composites made by chemical vapor infiltration (CVI), which use a C interphase, introduced by chemical vapor deposition.[51] For such composites, the nonlinear behavior indicates a debond energy, $\Gamma_i \approx 5$ J m$^{-2}$ (Table I). The interphase in this case debonds by a diffuse damage mechanism.[52] Moreover, it has been found that the coating behavior can be changed into one with $\Gamma_i \approx 0$, either by heat treatment of the composite (after CVI) or by chemical treatment of the fiber.[51] A basic understanding of these changes in $\Gamma_i$ does not exist.

## 8. Environmental Influences

Temperature and the environment also affect $\tau$ and $\Gamma_i$. There are also effects on $\tau$ of fiber displacement and cyclic sliding [Fig. 13(c)]. These effects can critically influence composite performance. The basic effect of temperature on $\tau$ concerns[53] changes in the misfit strain and friction coefficient, evident from the simulations shown in Fig. 12. Environmental influences can be pronounced, especially in oxidizing atmospheres. The major effects arise either at high temperatures or during fatigue.* When either C or Mo coatings are used, $\tau$ initially decreases upon either expo-

---

\* A consequence of internal heating associated with cyclic frictional sliding at the interfaces.

[51] R. Naslain, *Composite Interfaces* **1**, 253–286 (1993).
[52] X. Buratt, unpublished research at LCTS, Bordeaux (1993).
[53] J. W. Holmes and S. F. Shuler, *J. Mater. Sci. Lett.* **9**, 1290–1291 (1990).

sure or fatigue [Fig. 13(d)] because a gap is created between the fiber and matrix, caused by elimination of the coating, through volatile oxide formation.[7,18,53–55] This process occurs when the *local* temperature reaches ~800°C. The subsequent behavior depends on the fibers. When SiC fibers are used, further exposure causes $SiO_2$ formation.[56] This layer gradually fills the gap, leading to large values of $\tau$. Eventually, a "strong" interface bond forms (with large $\Gamma_i$) that produces brittle behavior, without fiber pull-out. Conversely, oxide fibers in oxide matrices are inherently resistant to this embrittlement phenomenon[18,49] and are environmentally desirable, provided that the matrix does not sinter to the fibers.

## III. Residual Stresses

9. ORIGIN

Many composite properties are sensitive to the residual stress caused by the misfit strain $\Omega$ between fiber and matrix. Measurement of these stresses thus becomes an important aspect of the analysis and prediction of properties. These stresses arise at inter- and intralaminate levels. Within a laminate, the axial stress in the matrix is[57]

$$q = (E_m/E_L)\sigma^T, \qquad (9.1)$$

where $\sigma^T$ is the misfit stress, which is related to the misfit strain by (Table II)[17,33]

$$\sigma^T = (c_2/c_1)E_m\Omega. \qquad (9.2)$$

The average residual stress in a 0/90 laminate, with uniform laminate thickness, $\sigma^R$, depends on constituent properties in approximate accordance with[58,59]

$$\sigma^R \approx \frac{\Omega(1 - f)E_L(1 - E_m/E_L)}{(1 + \nu_{LT})(1 + E_L/E_T)}. \qquad (9.3)$$

[54]J. W. Holmes and C. Cho, *J. Am. Ceram. Soc.* 75(4), 929–938 (1992).

[55]R. Y. Kim and A. P. Katz, *Ceram. Eng. Sci. Proc.* 9, 853–860 (1988).

[56]E. Bischoff, M. Rühle, O. Sbaizero, and A. G. Evans, *J. Am. Ceram. Soc.* 72(5), 741–745 (1989).

[57]B. Budiansky, J. W. Hutchinson, and A. G. Evans, *J. Mech. Phys. Solids* 34, 167–189 (1986).

[58]K. K. Chawla, *Composite Materials Science and Engineering,* Springer-Verlag, New York (1987).

[59]F. W. Zok and A. G. Evans, to be published.

Note that the residual stress $\sigma^R \to 0$ on the elastic properties becomes homogeneous ($E_f = E_m = E_L$). Although connections between the residual stresses and constituent properties are rigorous, experimental determination is still necessary, because $\Omega$ is not readily predictable. In general, $\Omega$ includes terms associated with the thermal expansion difference $\alpha_f - \alpha_m$, as well as volume changes that occur either upon crystallization or during phase transformations. For CVI systems, "intrinsic" stresses may also be present.

The temperature dependence can be assessed from the thermal expansion mismatch, by using

$$\Omega = \Omega_o - (\alpha_m - \alpha_f)\Delta T_R, \qquad (9.4)$$

where $\Delta T_R$ is the temperature change from ambient and $\Omega_o$ is the ambient misfit strain, measured using the procedures outlined next.

## 10. MEASUREMENT METHODS

Several experimental procedures can be used to measure the residual stresses. The four preferred methods involve (1) diffraction (x-ray or neutron), (2) beam deflection, (3) Raman microscopy, and (4) permanent strain measurements. X-ray diffraction measurements give lattice strains. They are limited in that the penetration depth is small, such that only near-surface information is obtained. Moreover, in composites, residual stresses are *redistributed* near surfaces.[46] Consequently, a full stress analysis is needed to relate the measured strains to either $q$ or $\sigma^R$ and the method has not been widely used.

Beam deflection and permanent strain measurements have the advantage that they provide information *averaged* over the composite. The results thus relate directly to the misfit strain $\Omega$. An experimental approach having high reliability involves curvature measurements on beams made from 0/90 composites.[60] For such material, polishing to produce one 0° layer and one 90° layer results in elastic bending (Fig. 14).* The curvature $\kappa$ is related[60] to the residual stress by†

$$\sigma^R = E_L I_o \kappa / t_b^2 w, \qquad (10.1)$$

---

* Unless the material has a plain weave.

† There is a typographical error in Beyerle *et al.*: The width $w$ was omitted in their equation.

[60] D. Beyerle, S. M. Spearing, and A. G. Evans, *J. Am. Ceram. Soc.* **75**(12), 3321–3330 (1992).

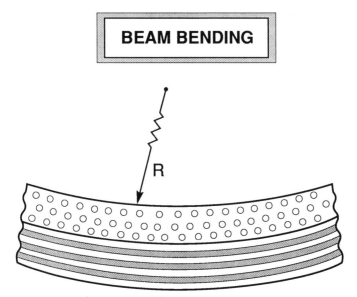

BEAM BENDING

R

FIG. 14. A schematic of the beam bending effect used to evaluate residual stress.

where $I_o$ is the second moment of inertia, $t_b$ the beam thickness, and $w$ the beam width.

When only 1-D material is available, the preferred approach is to measure the displacement $\Delta^R$ that occurs when a section of matrix, of length $L_d$, is removed by dissolution (when possible). The residual stress in the matrix is then[61]

$$q = E_f f \Delta^R / (1 - f) L_d. \tag{10.2}$$

Typical results are plotted on Fig. 15.

The Raman microscope can be used in two different modes to measure the residual stress. Both methods rely on shifts in Raman peaks induced by strain. A fluorescence spectroscopy method[62,63] uses the fluorescence peak created by impurities and dopants (such as Cr) in oxide fibers, particularly $Al_2O_3$. The capability of the method has been demonstrated for $Al_2O_3$ fiber-reinforced materials. The second method applies to ceramic

[61]D. Beyerle, S. M. Spearing, F. Zok, and A. G. Evans, *J. Am. Ceram. Soc.* **75**(10), 2719–2725 (1992).
[62]Q. Ma and D. R. Clarke, *J. Am. Ceram. Soc.* **76**, 1435–1440 (1993).
[63]Q. Ma, H. C. Cao, D. R. Clarke, and A. G. Evans, to be published.

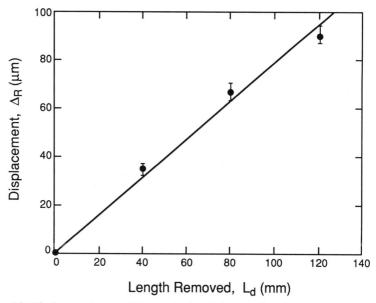

FIG. 15. Displacements caused by matrix dissolution as a function of length removed.

fibers that contain C (such as Nicalon and C itself). It relies on the shifts in the peaks of the Raman spectrum for C.[64] The method has been applied to Nicalon fiber-reinforced CMCs.

The permanent strains that arise following tensile plastic deformation also relate to $\Omega$. Measurement of these strains allows $\Omega$ to be assessed.[17] The relevant formulas are presented in Section 21.

## 11. EXPERIMENTAL RESULTS

Experimental results are mostly consistent with a misfit strain that derives from the thermal expansion difference, $\alpha_m - \alpha_f$, and the cooling range from the processing temperature. Examples for SiC/CAS and SiC/SiC are given in Table III. However, volumetric changes that occur in the matrix contribute to $\Omega_o$ when relatively low temperature processing steps are used. For example, matrix crystallization of glass ceramics can induce substantial misfit.[64]

[64] X. Yang and R. J. Young, *J. Mater. Sci.* **28**, 2536 (1993).

TABLE III. IMPORTANT CONSTITUENT PROPERTIES FOR TWO TYPICAL CMCs:
COMPARISON BETWEEN SiC/SiC AND SiC/CAS[4]

| | MATERIAL | |
| PROPERTY | SiC/CAS | SiC/SiC |
| --- | --- | --- |
| Matrix modulus, $E_m$(GPa) | 100 | 400 |
| Fiber modulus, $E_f$(GPa) | 200 | 200 |
| Sliding stress, $\tau$(MPa) | 15–20 | 100–150 |
| Debond energy, $\Gamma_i$(J m$^{-2}$) | ~0.1 | ~2 |
| Residual stress, $q$(MPa) | 80–100 | 50–100 |
| Fiber strength, $S_c$(GPa) | 2.0–2.2 | 1.3–1.6 |
| Shape parameter, $m$ | 3.3–3.8 | 4.2–4.7 |
| Matrix fracture energy, $\Gamma_m$(J m$^{-2}$) | 20–25 | 5–10 |

# IV. Fiber Properties

## 12. LOAD SHARING

The strength properties of fibers are statistical in nature. Consequently, it is necessary to apply principles of weakest link statistics, which define the properties of fibers *within a composite*. The initial decision to be made concerns the potential for interactions between failed fibers and matrix cracks. It has generally been assumed that matrix cracks and fiber failure are noninteracting and that global load sharing (GLS) conditions are obtained.*[14,18,65,66] In this case, the stress along a material plane that intersects a failed fiber is equally distributed among all of the intact fibers. Experience has indicated that these assumptions are essentially valid for a variety of CMCs.

Subject to the validity of GLS, several key results have been derived. Two characterizing parameters emerge:[67] a characteristic length

$$\delta_c^{m+1} = L_o(S_o R/\tau)^m \tag{12.1}$$

---

* However, a criterion for GLS breakdown has yet to be devised.

[65] L. Phoenix and R. Raj, *Acta Metall. Mater.* **40**, 2813–2828 (1992).

[66] F. Hild, J. M. Domergue, F. A. Leckie, and A. G. Evans, *Intl. Jnl. Solids Structures,* in press.

[67] R. B. Henstenburg and S. L. Phoenix, *Polym. Comp.* **10**(5), 389–406 (1989).

and a characteristic strength

$$S_c^{m+1} = S_o^m(L_o\tau/R), \tag{12.2}$$

where $m$ is the shape parameter, $S_o$ the scale parameter, $L_o$ the reference length, and $R$ the fiber radius. Various GLS results based on these parameters are described later.

When fibers do not interact, analysis begins by considering a fiber of length $2L$ divided into $2N$ elements, each of length $\delta z$. The probability that a fiber element will fail, when the stress is less than $\sigma$, is the area under the probability density curve[68,69]

$$\delta\phi(\sigma) = \frac{\delta z}{L_o} \int_0^\sigma g(S)\, dS, \tag{12.3}$$

where $g(S)\, dS/L_o$ represents the number of flaws per unit length of fiber having a "strength" between $S$ and $S + dS$. The local stress $\sigma$ is a function of both the distance along the fiber $z$ and the *reference* stress $\bar{\sigma}_b$. The survival probability $P_s$ for *all elements* in the fiber of length $2L$ is the product of the survival probabilities of each element:[70]

$$P_s(\bar{\sigma}_b, L) = \prod_{n=-N}^{N} [1 - \delta\phi(\bar{\sigma}_b, z)], \tag{12.4}$$

where $z = n\delta z$ and $L = N\delta z$. Furthermore, the probability $\Phi_S$ that the element at $z$ will fail when the peak, reference stress is between $\bar{\sigma}_b$ and $\bar{\sigma}_b + \delta\bar{\sigma}_b$, *but not when the stress is less than* $\bar{\sigma}_b$, is the change in $\delta\phi$ when the stress is increased by $\delta\bar{\sigma}_b$ divided by the survival probability up to $\sigma_b$, given by[68,69,71]

$$\Phi_S(\bar{\sigma}_b, z) = [1 - \delta\phi(\bar{\sigma}_b, z)]^{-1} \left[\frac{\partial\delta\phi(\bar{\sigma}_b, z)}{\partial\bar{\sigma}_b}\right] d\bar{\sigma}_b. \tag{12.5}$$

Denoting the probability density function for fiber failure by $\Phi(\bar{\sigma}_b, z)$, the probability that fracture occurs at a location $z$, when the peak stress

[68] A. Freudenthal, *Fracture* (H. Liebowitz, ed.), Academic Press, New York (1967).

[69] J. R. Matthews, W. J. Shack, and F. A. McClintock, *J. Am. Ceram. Soc.* **59**, 304 (1976).

[70] H. E. Daniels, *Proc. Roy. Soc.* **A183**, 405 (1945).

[71] H. L. Oh and I. Finnie, *Intl. J. Frac.* **6**, 287 (1970).

is $\bar{\sigma}_b$, is governed by the probability that all elements *survive up to a peak stress* $\bar{\sigma}_b$, but that failure occurs, at $z$, when the stress reaches $\bar{\sigma}_b$.[71-73] It is given by the product of Eq. (12.4) with Eq. (12.5):

$$\Phi_S(\bar{\sigma}_b, z)\delta\bar{\sigma}_b\delta z = \frac{\prod\limits_{-N}^{N}[1 - \delta\phi(\bar{\sigma}_b, z)]}{[1 - \delta\phi(\sigma^-_b, z)]}\left[\frac{\partial\delta\phi(\bar{\sigma}_b, z)}{\partial\bar{\sigma}_b}\right]d\bar{\sigma}_b. \quad (12.6)$$

While these results are quite general, it is convenient to use a power law to represent $g(S)$:

$$\int_0^\sigma g(S) \, dS = (\sigma/S_o)^m. \quad (12.7)$$

Alternative representations of $g(S)$ are not warranted at the present level of development. Using this assumption, Eq. (12.6) becomes[72]

$$\Phi(\bar{\sigma}_b, z) = \exp\left\{-2\int_0^L\left[\frac{\sigma(\bar{\sigma}_b, z)}{S_o}\right]^m\frac{dz}{L_o}\right\}\left(\frac{2}{L_o}\right)\frac{\partial}{\partial\bar{\sigma}_b}\left[\frac{\sigma(\bar{\sigma}_b, z)}{S_o}\right]^m. \quad (12.8)$$

This basic result has been used to obtain solutions for several problems[14,72,74] described later.

## 13. The Ultimate Tensile Strength

When multiple matrix cracking precedes failure of the fibers in the 0° bundles, the load along each matrix crack plane is borne entirely by the fibers. *Nevertheless, the matrix has a crucial role,* because stress transfer between the fibers and the matrix still occurs through the sliding resistance $\tau$. Consequently, some stress can be sustained by the failed fibers. This stress transfer process occurs over a distance related to the characteristic length $\delta_c$. As a result, the stresses on the intact fibers along any plane through the material are less than those experienced within a "dry" fiber bundle (in the absence of matrix). The transfer process also allows the stress in a failed fiber to be unaffected at distance $\gtrsim\delta_c$ from the fiber

[72]M. D. Thouless and A. G. Evans, *Acta Metall.* **36**, 517 (1988).
[73]M. D. Thouless, O. Sbaizero, L. S. Sigl, and A. G. Evans, *J. Am. Ceram. Soc.* **72**(4), 525–532 (1989).
[74]M. Sutcu, *Acta Metall.* **37**(2), 651–661 (1989).

fracture site (Fig. 16). Consequently, composite failure requires[14] that fiber bundle failure occur *within* $\delta_c$. This phenomenon leads to a UTS *independent of gauge length* $L_g$, provided that $L_g > \delta_c$.* The magnitude of the UTS can be computed by first evaluating the average stress on *all* fibers, failed plus intact, along an arbitrary plane through the material. Then, by differentiating with respect to the stress on the *intact* fibers, in order to obtain the maximum, the UTS becomes

$$S_g = f_l S_c F(m),    \qquad (13.1)$$

with

$$F(m) = [2/(m + 1)]^{1/(m+1)}[(m + 1)/(m + 2)].$$

It is of interest to compare this result to that found for a "dry" bundle. Then, the "fiber bundle" strength $S_b$ depends on the gauge length in accordance with[75]

$$S_b = f S_o (L_o/L_g)^{1/m} e^{-1/m}.    \qquad (13.2)$$

In all cases, $S_g > S_b$.

As the load increases, the fibers fail systematically, resulting in a characteristic fiber fragment length. At composite failure, multiple cracks can occur within some fibers. The existence of many fiber fragments is still compatible with a high UTS.† However, a diminished creep strength may ensue, as elaborated later (Section IX).

The preceding results are applicable to *tensile loading*. When a bending moment is applied, the behavior is modified. In this case, the stress is redistributed by both matrix cracking and fiber failure. Predictions of the UTS in pure flexure (Fig. 17) indicate the salient phenomena.[66]

14. FIBER PULL-OUT

In CMCs with good composite properties, fiber pull-out is evident on the tensile fracture surfaces.[73] Various measurements conducted on these

---

* At small gauge lengths ($L_g < \delta_c$), the UTS becomes gauge length dependent and exceeds $S_u$.[66]

† A good analogy being the strength of a wire rope.

[75] H. T. Corten, *Modern Composite Materials* (L. J. Broutman and R. H. Krock, eds.), p. 27, Addison Wesley, Reading, MA (1967).

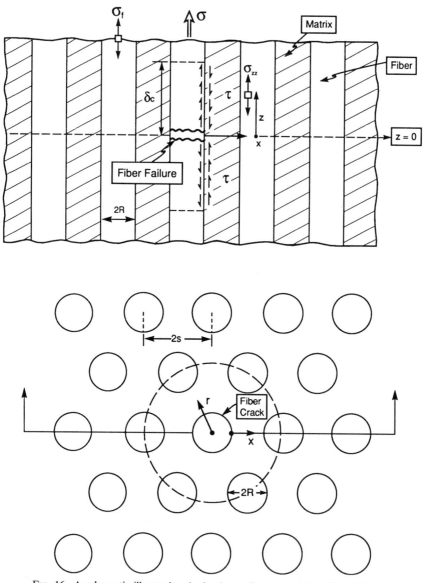

FIG. 16. A schematic illustrating the load transfer process from failed fibers.

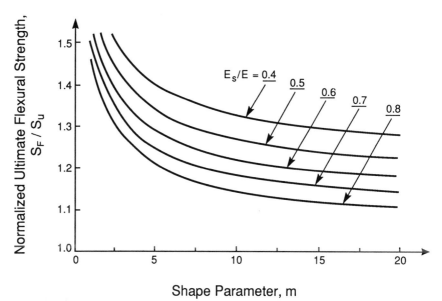

Shape Parameter, m

FIG. 17. Relationship between ultimate strengths measured in flexure and tension.

surfaces provide valuable information. Regions with highly correlated fiber failures and minimal pull-out are indicative of manufacturing flaws. Such flaws often occur in regions where fiber coating problems existed. In zones where fiber failures are *uncorrelated,* the distribution of fiber pull-out lengths provides essential information. The pull-out lengths are related explicitly to the *stochastics* of fiber failure.[14,72] The basic realization is that, on average, fibers do not fail on the plane of the matrix crack, even though the stress in the fibers has its *maximum value* at this site. This unusual phenomenon relies exclusively on statistics, wherein the locations of fiber failure may be identified as a distribution function that depends on the shape parameter $m$. Furthermore, the mean pull-out length $\bar{h}$ has a connection with the characteristic length $\delta_c$. Consequently, a functional dependence exists, dictated by the nondimensional parameters $\tau\bar{h}/RS_c$ and $m$:

$$\bar{h}\tau/RS_c = \lambda(m). \tag{14.1}$$

There are two bounding solutions for the function $\lambda$ (Fig. 18). Composite failure subject to multiple matrix cracking gives the upper bound. Failure in the presence of a single crack gives the lower bound.

Because of pull-out, a frictional *pull-out resistance* exists, which allows the material to sustain load beyond the UTS. The associated pull-out

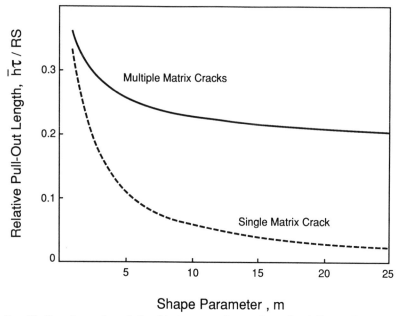

Shape Parameter , m

FIG. 18. Bounds on the relationship between the nondimensional fiber pull-out length and the Weibull modulus.

strength $S_p$ is an important property of the composite (Fig. 19). The strength $S_p$ is given by[76]

$$S_p = 2\tau f\bar{h}/R,$$
$$\equiv 2fS_c\lambda(m).$$
$$(14.2)$$

## 15. INFLUENCE OF FLAWS

The preceding results are applicable provided there are no unbridged segments along the matrix crack. *Unbridged regions* concentrate the stress in the adjacent fibers and weakens the composite.[12,77,78] Simple linear scaling considerations indicate that the diminished UTS depends on a nondimensional *flaw index* (Table IIa):

$$\mathscr{A} = a_o S_g^2/E_L\Gamma,$$
$$(15.1)$$

[76] D. C. Phillips, *J. Mater. Sci.* 9(11), 1874–1854 (1974).
[77] L. Cui and B. Budiansky, *J. Mech. Phys. Solids* 42, 1–19 (1994).
[78] Z. Suo, S. Ho, and X. Gong, *J. Matl. Engr. Tech.* 115, 319–326 (1993).

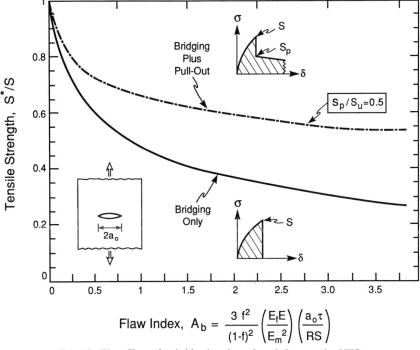

$$\text{Flaw Index, } A_b = \frac{3\,f^2}{(1-f)^2}\left(\frac{E_f E}{E_m^2}\right)\left(\frac{a_o \tau}{RS}\right)$$

Fig. 19. The effect of unbridged regions, length $2a_o$, on the UTS.

where $\Gamma$ is the toughness, reflected in the area under the stress-displacement curve for the bridging fibers, $E$ is Young's modulus, and $2a_o$ is the length of the unbridged segment. The flaw index $\mathscr{A}$ can be specified, based on $\Gamma$, using LSBM. The dependence of the UTS, designated $S^*$, on the flaw index $\mathscr{A}$ can be determined from LSBM by numerical analysis[78] (Fig. 19). The results reveal that the ratio $S_p/S_g$ is an important factor. Notably, relatively large values of the pull-out strength alleviate the strength degradation caused by unbridged cracks.

### 16. IN SITU STRENGTH MEASUREMENTS

In general, composite consolidation degrades fiber properties, and it becomes necessary to devise procedures that allow determination of $S_c$ and $m$ to be evaluated relevant to the fibers *within the composite*. This is a challenging problem. In some cases, it is possible to dissolve the matrix without further degrading the fibers and then measure the bundle

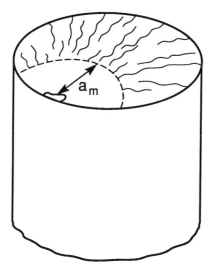

FIG. 20. A schematic indicating a fracture mirror and the dimension used to predict the *in situ* strength.

strength.[79] This is not feasible with most CMCs of interest. The following two alternatives exist.

Some fibers exhibit fracture mirrors when they fail within a composite (e.g., Nicalon). A semiempirical calibration has been developed that relates the mirror radius $a_m$ to the *in situ* fiber tensile strength $S$, given by (Fig. 20),

$$S \approx 3.5 \sqrt{E_f \Gamma_f / a_m},$$  (16.1)

where $\Gamma_f$ is the fracture energy of the fiber.[7,29,80] By measuring $S$ on many fibers and then plotting the cumulative distribution $G(S)$, both the shape parameter $m$ and the characteristic *in situ* fiber strength $S_c$ can be ascertained. Results of this type have been obtained for Nicalon fibers in a variety of different matrices (Fig. 21). This compilation indicates the sensitivity of the *in situ* strength to the composite processing approach. This fiber strength variation is also reflected in the range of UTS found among CMCs reinforced with these fibers (Fig. 4).

A problem with implementing the fracture mirror approach arises when a significant fraction of the fibers does not exhibit well-defined mirrors. Those fibers that do not have mirrors usually have a smooth fracture

[79] K. M. Prewo, *J. Mater. Sci.* **21**, 3590–3600 (1986).
[80] A. J. Eckel and R. C. Bradt, *J. Am. Ceram. Soc.* **72**, 435 (1989).

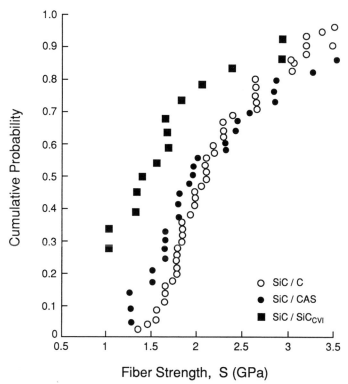

**Fiber Strength, S (GPa)**

Fig. 21. *In situ* strength distributions measured for Nicalon fibers in three CMCs, using the fracture mirror approach.

surface. It has thus been assumed that these are the weakest fibers in the distribution.[61,80] The order statistics used to determine $G(S)$ are adjusted accordingly. This assumption has not been validated.

The only alternative approaches known to the authors for evaluating $S_c$ are based on pull-out and fragment length measurements.[28] Both quantities depend on $S_c$ and $m$, as well as $\tau$. Consequently, if $\tau$ is known, $S_c$ can be determined. For example, $m$ can be evaluated by fitting the distribution of fiber pull-out lengths to the calculated function. Then, $S_c$ can be obtained for the mean value $\bar{h}$ using Eq. (12.4). This approach has not been extensively used and checked.

## 17. EXPERIMENTAL RESULTS

Several studies have compared the multiple matrix cracking GLS prediction $S_g$ [Eq. (13.1)] with the UTS measured for either 1-D or 2-D CMCs.

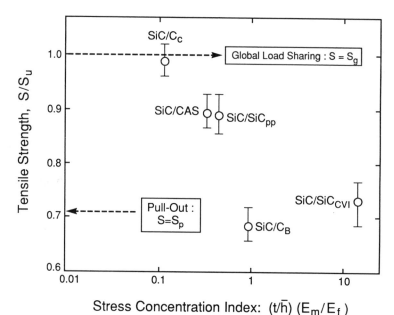

Stress Concentration Index:  $(t/\bar{h})$ $(E_m/E_f)$

FIG. 22. Comparison of the measured UTS with $S_g$ predicted from GLS [Eq. (13.1)] plotted against a stress concentration index. Note that $\bar{h}$ is inversely proportional to $\tau$.

In most cases, the UTS is in the range (0.7–1) $S_g$, as indicated on Fig. 22. The two obvious discrepancies are the SiC/SiC$_{CVI}$ material and one of the SiC/C materials. In these cases, the GLS predictions overestimate the measured values. Moreover, $\tau$ is relatively large for both materials, as reflected in the magnitude of the stress concentration index (Fig. 22). Two factors have to be considered as these results are interpreted: (1) In some materials, the fraction of fibers that exhibit mirrors is not large enough to provide confidence in the inferred values of $S_c$ and $m$. This issue is a particular concern for the SiC/SiC$_{CVI}$ material. (2) In other materials, manufacturing flaws are present that provide unbridged crack segments, which cause the UTS to be smaller than $S_g$ (Section 15).

With the preceding provisos, it is surprising that the UTS measured for several 2-D CMCs is close to the GLS prediction. In these materials, cracks exist in the 90° plies at low stresses and these cracks should concentrate the stress on the neighboring fibers in the 0° plies. The UTS would thus be expected to follow the strength degradation diagram (Fig. 19). That this weakening does not occur remains to be explained. It probably reflects the influence on the strength degradation of elastic anisotropy, as well as pull-out (Fig. 19).

## V. Matrix Cracking in Unidirectional Materials

The development of damage in the form of matrix cracks within 1-D CMCs subject to tensile loading has been traced by direct optical observations on specimens with carefully polished surfaces and by acoustic emission detection,[6,8,55,61] and ultrasonic velocity measurements.[81] Interrupted tests, in conjunction with sectioning and SEM observations, have also been used. Analyses of the matrix damage found in 1-D CMCs provides the basis on which the behavior of 2-D and 3-D CMCs may be addressed. The matrix cracks are found to interact with predominantly intact fibers, subject to interfaces that debond and slide. This process commences at a lower bound stress, $\bar{\sigma}_{mc}$. The crack density increases with increase in stress above $\bar{\sigma}_{mc}$ and may eventually attain a saturation spacing $\bar{d}_s$ at stress $\bar{\sigma}_s$. The details of crack evolution are governed by the distribution of matrix flaws. The matrix cracks reduce the unloading elastic modulus $\bar{E}$ and also induce a permanent strain $\varepsilon_o$ (Fig. 9). Relationships between $\bar{E}$, $\varepsilon_p$, and constituent properties provide the key connections between processing and macroscopic performance, via the properties of the constituents.

The deformations caused by matrix cracking, in conjunction with interface debonding and sliding, exhibit three regimes that depend on the magnitude of the debond stress $\bar{\sigma}_i$. In turn, $\bar{\sigma}_i$ depends on the debond energy through the relationship[33]

$$\bar{\sigma}_i = (1/c_1) \sqrt{E_m \Gamma_i / R} - \sigma^T, \qquad (v.1)$$

which has a useful nondimensional form:

$$\Sigma_i = \bar{\sigma}_i / \sigma. \qquad (v.2)$$

A mechanism map that identifies the three regimes is shown[17] in Fig. 23. When $\Sigma_i > 1$, debonding does not occur, whereupon matrix crack growth is an entirely elastic phenomenon. This condition is referred to as the no debond (ND) regime. When $\Sigma_i < 1/2$, small debond energy (SDE) behavior arises. The characteristic of this regime is that the reverse slip length at the interface, upon complete unloading, exceeds the debond length. In the SDE regime, $\Gamma_i$ is typically small and does not affect certain properties, such as the hysteresis loop width. The term SDE is thus loosely used to represent the behavior expected when $\Gamma_i \approx 0$. An intermediate, large debond energy (LDE) regime also exists, when $1/2 \leq \Sigma_i \leq 1$. In this situation, reverse slip is impeded by the debond.

---

[81] S. Baste, R. El Guerjouma, and B. Andoin, *Mech. of Mtls.* **14**, 15–32 (1992).

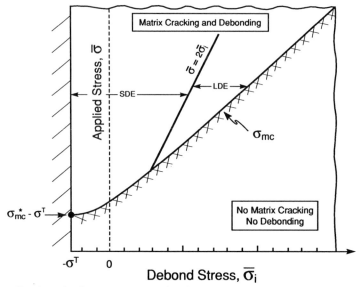

FIG. 23. A mechanism map representing the various modes of interface response.

18. BASIC MECHANICS

The approach used to simulate mode I cracking under monotonic loading is to define tractions $\sigma_b$ acting on the crack faces, induced by the fibers (Fig. 1) and to determine their effect on the crack tip by using the $J$ integral:[31,57]

$$\mathcal{G}_{tip} = \mathcal{G} - \int_0^u \sigma_b\, du, \tag{18.1}$$

where $\mathcal{G}$ is the energy release rate and $u$ is the crack opening displacement. Cracking is considered to proceed when $\mathcal{G}_{tip}$ attains the pertinent fracture energy. Since the fibers are not failing, the crack growth criterion involves matrix cracking only. A lower bound is given by[57,82]

$$\mathcal{G}_{tip} = \Gamma_m(1 - f), \tag{18.2}$$

with $\Gamma_m$ being the matrix toughness. Upon crack extension, $\mathcal{G}$ becomes the crack growth resistance $\Gamma_R$, whereupon

$$\Gamma_R = \Gamma_m(1 - f) + \int_0^u \sigma_b\, du. \tag{18.3}$$

[82]L. N. McCartney, *Proc. Roy. Soc.* **A409**, 329–350 (1987).

A traction law $\sigma_b(u)$ is now needed to predict $\Gamma_R$. A law based on frictional sliding along debonded interfaces has been used most extensively and appears to provide a reasonable description of many of the observed mechanical responses [Eq. (4.1)]. The traction law also includes effects of the interface debond energy $\Gamma_i$.[33] For many CMCs, $\Gamma_i$ is small, as reflected in the magnitude of the debond stress $\Sigma_i$.

For SDE, with a constant sliding stress $\tau_o$, the sliding distance $l$, in the absence of fiber failure, is related to the crack surface tractions, $\sigma_b$, by [13,31]

$$l = [RE_m(1 - f)/2\tau_o E_f f](\sigma_b + \sigma^T). \tag{18.4}$$

For LDE, the corresponding solution is [33]

$$l = [RE_m(1 - f)/2\tau_o E_f f](\sigma_b - \bar{\sigma}_i). \tag{18.5}$$

The sliding length is, in turn, related to the crack opening displacement. The corresponding traction law [31,57] for SDE is

$$\sigma_b + \sigma^T = (2\xi\tau_o E_L f u/R)^{1/2}. \tag{18.6}$$

For LDE, [17] it is

$$\sigma_b - \bar{\sigma}_i = (2\xi\tau_o E_L f u/R)^{1/2}, \tag{18.7}$$

where $\xi$ is defined in Table II. When fiber failure occurs, statistical considerations are needed to determine $\sigma_b(u)$.

The matrix fracture behavior can also be described by using stress intensity factor $K$. This approach is more convenient than the $J$ integral in some cases: particularly for short cracks and for fatigue.[31,83] To apply this approach, it is first necessary to specify the contribution to the crack opening induced by the applied stress, as well as that provided by the bridging fibers. For a plane strain crack of length $2a$ in an infinite plate, the contribution due to the applied stress is [84]

$$u_\infty = (4/E_L)\sigma \sqrt{a^2 - x^2}, \tag{18.8}$$

[83] R. M. McMeeking and A. G. Evans, *Mech. of Mtls.* **9**, 217–227 (1990).

[84] H. Tada, P. C. Paris, and G. R. Irwin, *The Stress Analysis of Cracks Handbook*, Del Research Corporation, St. Louis (1985).

and that caused by bridging is

$$u_b = -(4/E_L) \int_0^a \sigma_b(\hat{x}) H \, d\hat{x}, \tag{18.9}$$

with $H$ being a weight function. The net crack opening displacement is

$$u = u_\infty + u_b. \tag{18.10}$$

The contribution to $K$ from the bridging fibers is obtained using[84]

$$K_b = -2 \sqrt{\frac{2}{\pi}} \int_0^a \frac{\sigma_b(x) \, dx}{\sqrt{a^2 - x^2}}, \tag{18.11}$$

with $\sigma_b$ given by Eqs. (18.4) and (18.5). The shielding associated with $K_b$ leads to a tip stress intensity factor

$$K_{tip} = K + K_b, \tag{18.12}$$

where $K$ depends on the loading and specimen geometry.

A *criterion for matrix crack extension,* based on $K_{tip}$, is needed. For this purpose, to be consistent with the energy criterion [Eq. (18.2)], the critical stress intensity factor is taken to be

$$K_{tip} = \sqrt{E\Gamma_m(1 - f)}. \tag{18.13}$$

Then, the two approaches ($K$ and $\mathcal{G}$) lead to the same steady state matrix cracking stress.

## 19. The Matrix Cracking Stress

The preceding basic results can be used to obtain solutions for matrix cracking.[13,45,57,82,83] Our current understanding involves the following factors. Because the fibers are intact, a steady state condition exists wherein the tractions on the fibers in the crack wake balance the applied stress. This special case may be addressed by integrating Eq. (18.1) up to a limit $u = u_0$. This limit is obtained from Eqs. (18.6) and (18.7) by equating $\sigma_b$ to $\sigma$. For SDE, this procedure gives[57]

$$\mathcal{G}_{tip}^0 = \frac{(\sigma + \sigma^T)^3 E_m^2 (1 - f)^2 R}{6\tau_o f^2 E_f E_L^2}. \tag{19.1}$$

A *lower bound to the matrix cracking stress* $\sigma_{mc}$ is then obtained by invoking Eq. (18.2), such that[57]

$$\bar{\sigma}_{mc} = E_L \left[ \frac{6\tau\Gamma_m f^2 E_f}{(1-f)E_m^2 R E_L} \right]^{1/3} - \sigma^T$$

$$\equiv \sigma_{mc}^* - \sigma^T. \tag{19.2}$$

In some cases,[6] *small* matrix cracks can form at stresses below $\bar{\sigma}_{mc}$. These occur either within matrix-rich regions or around processing flaws. The nonlinear composite properties are usually dominated by fully developed matrix cracks that form at stresses above $\bar{\sigma}_{mc}$. However, these small flaws may provide access of the atmosphere to the interfaces and cause degradation.

Analogous results can be obtained using stress intensity factors.[31,83] For a small center crack in a tensile specimen,* Eqs. (18.11) and (18.13) give a steady state result at large crack lengths of[83]

$$K_{\text{tip}} = \frac{\sigma^* \sqrt{R}}{\sqrt{6\mathcal{T}}}, \tag{19.3}$$

where $\mathcal{T}$ is a sliding index defined in Table II. When combined with the fracture criterion [Eq. (8.13)], the matrix cracking stress $\bar{\sigma}_{mc}$ is predicted to be the same as that given by Eq. (19.2).

The $K$ approach may also be used to define a transition crack length $a_t$, above which steady state applies. This transition length is given by[31,83]

$$a_t/R \approx E_m[\Gamma_m(1 + \xi)^2(1 - f)^4/\tau_o^2 f^4 E_f^2 R]^{1/3}. \tag{19.4}$$

Namely, when the initial flaw size $a_i > a_t$, cracking occurs at $\sigma = \bar{\sigma}_{mc}$. Conversely, when the initial flaws are small, $a_i < a_t$, it has been shown that[83]

$$K_{\text{tip}} \approx K\left(1 - \frac{3.05}{\mathcal{E}}\sqrt{\mathcal{E} + 3.3} + \frac{5.5}{\mathcal{E}}\right). \tag{19.5}$$

where $\mathcal{E}$ is a loading index defined as (Table II):

$$\mathcal{E} = 2R(1 - f)^2 E_m^2 \sigma/E_f E\tau_o a f^2(1 - \nu^2).$$

---

* $K = \sigma\sqrt{\pi a}$.

This result for $K_{tip}$, when combined with Eq. (18.13), gives a revised matrix cracking stress that *exceeds* $\bar{\sigma}_{mc}$.

Analogous results can be derived for the LDE regime. In this case, Eq. (18.7) may be used with Eq. (18.1) to derive an energy release rate, which can be combined with the fracture criterion [Eq. (18.2)] to predict $\sigma_{mc}$. The result is contained within the implicit formula

$$\left[\frac{\sigma_{mc} + \sigma^T}{\sigma_{mc}^*}\right]^3 - 3\left[\left(\frac{\sigma_{mc} + \sigma^T}{\sigma_{mc}^*}\right)\left(\frac{\bar{\sigma}_i + \sigma^T}{\sigma_{mc}^*}\right)^2\right] + 2\left(\frac{\bar{\sigma}_i + \sigma^T}{\sigma_{mc}^*}\right)^3 = 1.$$

(19.6)

The trend in $\sigma_{mc}$ with $\bar{\sigma}_i$ is plotted on Fig. 23.


20. Crack Evolution

The evolution of additional cracks at stresses above $\sigma_{mc}$ is less well understood, because two factors are involved: *screening* and *statistics*.[30,85] When the sliding zones between neighboring cracks overlap, *screening* occurs and $\mathscr{G}_{tip}$ differs from $\mathscr{G}_{tip}^0$. The relationship is dictated by the location of the neighboring cracks. When a crack forms midway between two existing cracks with a separation $2d$, subject to SDE, $\mathscr{G}_{tip}$ is related to $\mathscr{G}_{tip}^0$ by[30]

$$\mathscr{G}_{tip}/\mathscr{G}_{tip}^0 = 4(d/2l)^3 \qquad \text{for } 0 \le d/l \le 1 \qquad (20.1a)$$

$$\mathscr{G}_{tip}/\mathscr{G}_{tip}^0 = 1 - 4(1 - d/2l)^3 \qquad \text{for } 1 \le d/l \le 2 \qquad (20.1b)$$

When $d$ is sufficiently small, $\mathscr{G}_{tip}$ becomes independent of the stress. Once this occurs, $\mathscr{G}_{tip}$ cannot increase and is unable to again satisfy the matrix crack growth criterion [Eq. (18.2)]. This occurs with spacing $\bar{d}_s$ at an associated stress $\bar{\sigma}_s$ (Fig. 11). This saturation spacing is given by

$$\bar{d}_s/R = \chi[\Gamma_m(1 - f)^2 E_f E_m/f\tau_o^2 E_L R]^{1/3}. \qquad (20.2)$$

Note that this result is *independent* of the residual stress, because the terms containing $(\sigma_b + \sigma^T)$ in Eqs. (18.4), (18.5), and (19.1) cancel when inserted into Eq. (20.1a). The coefficient $\chi$ depends on the spatial aspects of crack evolution: periodic, random, etc. Simulations[30] for spatial randomness indicate that $\chi \approx 1.6$.

[85]C. Cho, J. W. Holmes, and J. R. Barber, *J. Am. Ceram. Soc.* **75**(2), 316–324 (1992).

In addition to these screening effects, the actual *evolution of matrix cracks* at stresses above $\sigma_{mc}$ is governed by statistics that relate to the size and spatial distribution of matrix flaws. If this distribution is known, the evolution can be predicted. Such statistical effects arise when the matrix flaws are smaller than the transition size $a_t$ at which steady state commences [Eq. (19.4)]. In this case, the flaw size distribution must be combined with the short crack solution for $K_{tip}$ [Eq. (19.5)] in order to predict crack evolution. At the simplest level, this has been done by assuming an exponential distribution for the matrix flaw size[86]

$$p = \exp(L/L_*)(a_t/a)^\omega, \qquad (20.3)$$

where $p$ is the fraction of flaws in a composite, length $L$, having size larger than $a$, $\omega$ is a shape parameter related to the Weibull modulus for the matrix ($\omega = m_m/2$), and $L_*$ is a scale parameter

$$L_* = \lambda_s l_{mc}, \qquad (20.4)$$

with $l_{mc}$ being the slip distance at $\sigma = \sigma_{mc}$ and $\lambda_s$ a flaw size coefficient. The condition $\lambda_s \lesssim 1$ corresponds to a high density of matrix flaws already large enough to be at steady state. Conversely, $\lambda_s > 1$ refers to a situation wherein most matrix flaws are smaller than the transition size $a_t$.

Simulations can be performed in which the key variables are the shape parameter $\omega$ and the scale parameter $\lambda_s$. The simulated crack densities [Fig. 24(a)] indicate a sudden burst of cracking at $\sigma = \sigma_{mc}$, when $\lambda_s < 1$, followed by a gradual increase with continued elevation of the stress. The saturation stress is similar to that given by Eq. (20.3). In contrast, when $\lambda_s \gg 1$, the cracks evolve more gradually with stress, reaching saturation at substantially higher levels of stress.* These simulated behaviors are qualitatively similar to those measured by experiment [Fig. 24(b)]. Moreover, the values found for $\omega$ are in a reasonable range ($m_m = 2\omega \approx 4$–8). However, since $\omega$ and $\lambda_s$ are not known *a priori*, in practice this approach becomes a fitting procedure rather than a predictive model. Despite this limitation, it has been found that a simple formula can be used to approximate crack evolution in most CMCs,[4] given by [Fig. 24(b)]:

$$\bar{d} \approx \bar{d}_s \frac{(\bar{\sigma}_s/\bar{\sigma}_{mc} - 1)}{(\bar{\sigma}/\bar{\sigma}_{mc} - 1)}. \qquad (20.5)$$

---

* Nevertheless, the saturation spacing remains insensitive to $\lambda_s$.[86]

[86] S. M. Spearing and F. W. Zok, *Jnl. Eng. Mtls. Tech.* **115**, 314–318, (1983).

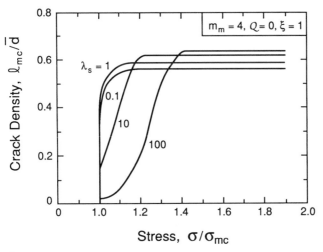

a

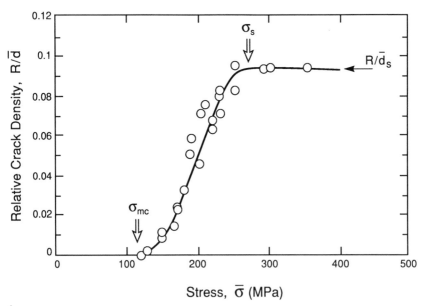

b

FIG. 24. (a) Simulation of crack evolution for various matrix flaw distributions characterized by $\lambda_s$ when the shape parameter $\omega = 2$. (b) Evolution of matrix crack density with
stress for unidirectional SiC/CAS.

Analogous results can be derived for LDE, with the debond length given by Eq. (18.5) and the reference energy release rate by Eq. (19.6). In this case, the saturation crack spacing is smaller than that given by Eq. (20.3).

## 21. CONSTITUTIVE LAW

Analyses of the plastic strains caused by matrix cracks, combined with calculations of the compliance change, provide a constitutive law for the material. The important parameters are the permanent strain $\varepsilon_o$ and the unloading modulus $\bar{E}$. These quantities, in turn, depend on several constituent properties; the sliding stress $\tau$, the debond energy $\Gamma_i$, and the misfit strain $\Omega$. The most important results are summarized next.

Matrix cracks *increase* the elastic compliance. Numerical calculations indicate that the *unloading elastic modulus $E^*$* is given by[20]

$$E_L/E^* - 1 = (R/\bar{d})\mathscr{B}(f, E_f/E_m),\tag{21.1}$$

where $\mathscr{B}$ is the function plotted on Fig. 25. The matrix cracks also cause a permanent strain associated with relief of the residual stress. This strain $\varepsilon^*$ is related to the modulus and the misfit stress by (Fig. 26)[20]

$$\varepsilon^* \equiv \sigma^T(1/E^* - 1/E_L).\tag{21.2}$$

The preceding effects occur *without* interface sliding. The incidence of *sliding* leads to *plastic strains* that superpose onto $\varepsilon^*$. The magnitude of these strains depends on $\Sigma_i$ (Fig. 23) and on the stress relative to the saturation stress $\sigma_s$.

### a. *Stresses below saturation*

(i) Small debond energy

For SDE, when $\sigma < \sigma_s$, the unloading modulus $\bar{E}$ depends on $\tau_o$, but is *independent* of $\Gamma_i$ and $\Omega$. However, the permanent strain $\varepsilon_o$ depends on $\Gamma_i$ and $\Omega$, as well as $\tau_o$. These differing dependencies of $\bar{E}$ and $\varepsilon_o$ on constituent properties have the following two implications: (1) To *simulate* the stress-strain curve, both $\varepsilon_o$ and $\bar{E}$ are required. Consequently, $\tau_o$, $\Gamma_i$, and $\Omega$ *must be known*. (2) The use of unloading and reloading *to evaluate the constituent properties* has the convenience that the hysteresis is dependent *only on $\tau_o$*. Consequently, precise determination of $\tau_o$ is possible. Moreover, with $\tau_o$ known from the hysteresis, both $\Gamma_i$ and $\Omega$

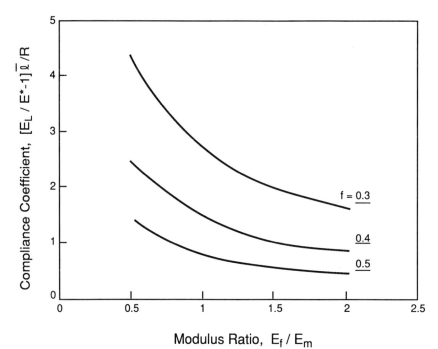

FIG. 25. Effects of modulus mismatch and fiber volume fraction on the elastic compliance.

can be evaluated from the permanent strain. The principal SDE results are as follows.

The permanent strain is[4,8,17]

$$(\varepsilon_o - \varepsilon^*)\mathcal{H}^{-1} = 4(1 - \Sigma_i)\Sigma_T + 1 - 2\Sigma_i^2,\qquad (21.3)$$

where $\mathcal{H}$ is a hysteresis index (Table II)

$$\mathcal{H} = b_2(1 - a_1f)^2 R\bar{\sigma}^2/4\bar{d}\tau_o E_m f^2 \qquad (21.4)$$

and

$$\Sigma_T = \sigma^T/\bar{\sigma}. \qquad (21.5)$$

The maximum width of the hysteresis loop, at half maximum, $\delta\varepsilon_{1/2}$, is (Figs. 9 and 26)

$$\delta\varepsilon_{1/2} = \mathcal{H}/2. \qquad (21.6)$$

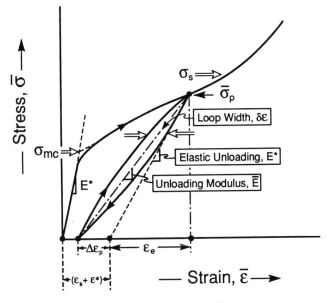

a) Debonding and Sliding Interface

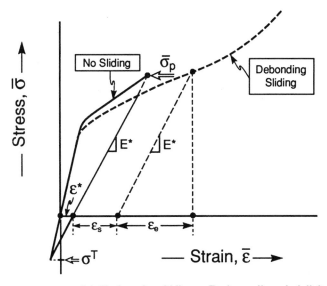

b) Behavior When Debonding Inhibited

FIG. 26. Basic parameters involved in the stress-strain behavior of CMCs: (a) Interfaces that debond and slide subject to SDE and (b) behavior in the absence of debonding and sliding.

The unloading strain is (Fig. 26)

$$\Delta \varepsilon_p = \mathcal{H} \tag{21.7}$$

and the unloading modulus is

$$(\bar{E})^{-1} = (E^*)^{-1} + \mathcal{H}/\bar{\sigma}. \tag{21.8}$$

(ii) Large debond energy

For LDS (Fig. 23), when $\sigma < \sigma_s$, the unloading modulus depends on both $\tau$ and $\Gamma_i$ (Fig. 26). There are also linear segments to the unloading and reloading curves. These segments can be used to establish constructions that allow the constituent properties to be conveniently established. The principal results are as follows. The permanent strain is[17]

$$(\varepsilon_o - \varepsilon^*)\mathcal{H}^{-1} = 2(1 - \Sigma_i)(1 - \Sigma_i + 2\Sigma_T) \tag{21.9}$$

and the unloading modulus is

$$(\bar{E})^{-1} = (E^*)^{-1} + 4\Sigma_i(1 - \Sigma_i)\mathcal{H}/\bar{\sigma}. \tag{21.10}$$

In this case, the hysteresis loop width depends on the magnitude of $\Sigma_i$. For intermediate values, $1/2 \le \Sigma_i \ 3/4$

$$\delta\varepsilon_{1/2} = \mathcal{H}[1/2 - (1 - 2\Sigma_i)^2] \tag{21.11}$$

whereas, for $3/4 \le \Sigma_i \le 1$

$$\delta\varepsilon_{1/2} = 4\mathcal{H}(1 - \Sigma_i)^2 \tag{21.12}$$

b. *Stresses above saturation*

At stress, $\sigma > \sigma_s$, the crack density remains essentially constant. It has thus been assumed that there is no additional stress transfer between the fibers and the matrix. In this case, the tangent modulus is given by[13]

$$E_t \equiv d\sigma/d\varepsilon = fE_f. \tag{21.13}$$

In practice, the tangent modulus is usually found to be smaller than predicted by Eq. (21.13). Two factors are involved: changes in the sliding stress and fiber failure. At high fiber stresses, the Poisson condition of the fiber reduces the radial stress $\sigma_{rr}$. Consequently, whenever the sliding

stress can be represented by Eq. (4.1), $\tau$ decreases as the stress increases. The associated tangent modulus at fixed crack spacing is[33]

$$d\bar{\sigma}/d\bar{\varepsilon} = b_1 E_m \bar{d}/a_3 b_2 R[1 + \vartheta + \exp(-\vartheta)], \qquad (21.14)$$

where $\vartheta = 2\mu b_1 d/R$, with $\mu$ being the friction coefficient.

As the UTS is approached, significant fiber failures occur, which further reduce the tangent modulus. The basic stress relationship is[66]

$$\bar{\sigma} = fE_f\bar{\varepsilon}\left\{1 + \sum_{n \geq 1} \frac{(-1)^n}{2n!}\left[\frac{2 + n(m + 1)}{1 + n(m + 1)}\right](E_f\bar{\varepsilon}/S_c)^{n(m+1)}\right\}. \qquad (21.15)$$

## 22. SIMULATIONS

The preceding constitutive laws may be used to simulate stress-strain curves for comparison with experiments. To conduct the simulations, the constituent properties $\tau$, $\Gamma_i$, and $\Omega$ are first assembled into the nondimensional parameters $\mathcal{H}$, $\Sigma_i$, and $\Sigma_T$. For this purpose, it is necessary to have independent knowledge of $\bar{d}(\bar{\sigma})$. When this does not exist, an estimation procedure is needed, based on Eq. (20.5), through evaluation of $\bar{d}_s$, $\bar{\sigma}_{mc}$, and $\bar{\sigma}_s$. The first step is to use Eq. (20.2) to evaluate the saturation crack spacing $\bar{d}_s$ from the constituent properties. One limitation of this procedure concerns the accuracy with which $\chi$ and $\Gamma_m$ are known. An alternative option exists when crack spacing data are available for another CMC with the *same matrix*. Then, Eq. (5.20a) can be used to *scale* $\bar{d}_s$ in accordance with

$$\bar{d}_s^3 \sim E_f R^2/\tau_o^2 E_L.$$

It is also possible to estimate $\bar{\sigma}_{mc}$ from the constituent properties by using Eqs. (19.2) and (19.6).

When $d(\bar{\sigma})$ has been established in this manner, stress-strain curves can be simulated for 1-D materials on recognizing the need for internal consistency. Notably, both $\bar{d}_s$ and $\sigma_{mc}$ depend on $\tau_o$ and $\Gamma_i$. In addition, $\sigma_{mc}$ depends on the misfit stress $\sigma^T$, whereas $\bar{d}_s$ is $\sigma^T$ independent. Based on this approach, simulations have been used to conduct sensitivity studies of the effects of constituent properties on the inelastic strain. The examples of Fig. 27 indicate the spectrum of possibilities for CMCs.

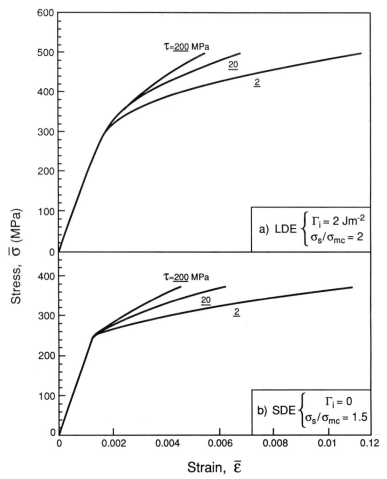

Strain, $\bar{\varepsilon}$

FIG. 27. Simulated stress-strain curves for 1-D CMCs indicating the relative importance of constituent properties.

## 23. EXPERIMENTS

Relatively complete matrix cracking and *inelastic strain* measurements have been made on two unidirectional CMCs:[4,48] SiC/CAS, as well as SiC/SiC (produced by CVI). The stress-strain curves for these two materials (Fig. 28) indicate a contrast in inelastic strain capability, which demands interpretation. Some typical hysteresis measurements for these

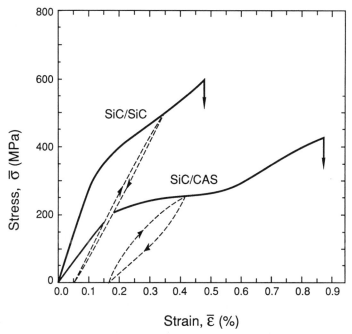

Strain, $\bar{\varepsilon}$ (%)

FIG. 28. Stress-strain curves and typical hysteresis measurements obtained on SiC/CAS and SiC/SiC unidirectional composites.

materials (Fig. 28) reveal major differences, which must reflect differences in constituent properties. There are also considerable differences in the evolution of matrix cracks (Fig. 24). An analysis of the hysteresis loops (Fig. 29) and the permanent strain (Fig. 30), as well as other characteristics, indicates the substantial differences in interface properties summarized on Table III. These differences arise despite the fact that the fibers are the same and that the fiber coatings are C in both cases.*

The constituent properties from Table III can, in turn, be used to simulate the stress-strain curves (Fig. 31). The agreement with measurements affirms the simulation capability, whenever the constituent properties have been obtained from *completely independent tests* (Table I). This has been done for the SiC/CAS material, but not yet for SiC/SiC. While

---

* Analysis of the coating structure by TEM provides a rationale for specifying the differing interface responses in accordance with the basic model (Fig. 9).

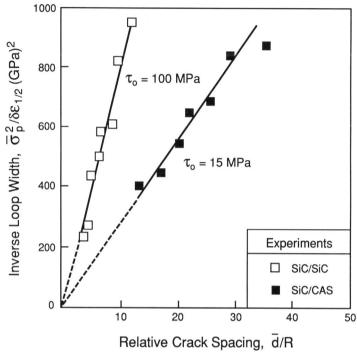

Fig. 29. Analysis of hysteresis loop results for unidirectional SiC/CAS and SiC/SiC.

the limited comparison between simulation and experiment is encouraging, an unresolved problem concerns the predictability of the saturation stress $\sigma_s$. In most cases, *ab initio* determination cannot be expected, because the flaw parameters for the matrix ($\omega$, $\lambda_s$) are processing sensitive. Reliance must therefore be placed on experimental measurements, which are rationalized *post facto*. Further research is needed to establish whether formalisms can be generated from the theoretical results, which provide useful bounds on $\sigma_s$. A related issue concerns the necessity for matrix crack density information. Again, additional insight is needed to establish meaningful bounds. Meanwhile, experimental methods that provide crack density information in an efficient, straightforward manner require development. One possibility involves measurements of the acoustic velocity $v$, which can be conducted continuously during testing.[81] These measurements relate to changes in the elastic modulus $E^*$ as matrix cracks develop ($E^* = \rho_o v^2$). This modulus can be related to the crack spacing through a model [Eq. (21.1)].

Debate has arisen about the *matrix cracking stress* $\sigma_{mc}$ and its interpre-

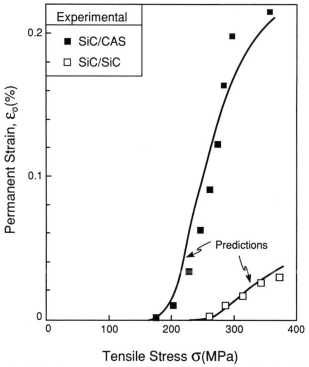

FIG. 30. Analysis of permanent strains for unidirectional SiC/CAS and SiC/SiC.

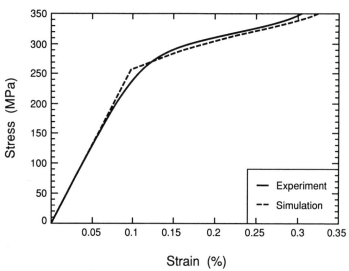

FIG. 31. Simulated stress-strain curve for unidirectional SiC/SiC and comparison with experiment.

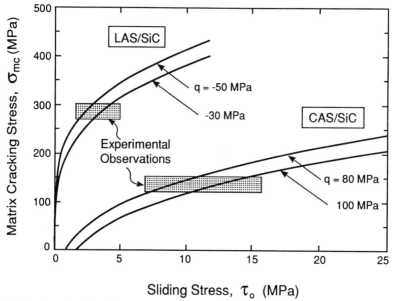

Sliding Stress, $\tau_o$ (MPa)

FIG. 32. A comparison between measured and predicted values of the matrix cracking stress for two unidirectional CMCs.

tation on comparison with experimental measurements. When adequate independent measurements of constituent properties have been measured (Fig. 32), it has been found[61] that the stress at which significant inelastic strain occurs always exceeds $\sigma_{mc}$, given by Eq. (19.6). This stress may thus be interpreted as a lower bound for the stress at which matrix cracking is sufficiently extensive to cause detectable inelastic strain. It thus has a similar interpretation to the yield strength (or proof stress) in metallic systems. It may be used as a basic strength parameter relevant to the simulation of stress-strain curves, as well as calculations of stress redistribution. However, small matrix cracks form[6] at stresses below $\sigma_{mc}$. These arise in heterogeneous regions of the composite, where interactions occur between small matrix flaws and the combined applied/residual field in the composite. Such flaws are most important when atmospheric degradation of the fibers is possible, because they provide pathways for ingress of the degrading species. Again, analogies with yielding in metals may be useful upon appreciating that slip over small distances (within grains) occurs in metals at stresses appreciably below the macroscopic yield strength. Such slip is important in fatigue, etc., but is incidental to the plastic strain that causes stress redistribution.

## VI. Matrix Cracking in 2-D Materials

General loadings of 2-D CMCs involve mixtures of tension and shear. For design purposes, it is necessary to have models and experiments that combine these loadings. Matrix cracking and fiber failure are the basic phenomena that dictate all of the nonlinearities. However, there are important differences between tension and shear. The behavior subject to tensile loading has been widely investigated.[45,53,87-92] The behavior in shear is only appreciated at an elementary level.[25] Furthermore, the intermediate behaviors have had even less study.[88,93] Nevertheless, the basic concept is clear. Matrix cracking, as well as fiber failure, phenomena must be incorporated into the models in a consistent manner, such that *interpolation* approaches can be devised and implemented that interrelate the tensile and shear properties.

### 24. TENSILE PROPERTIES

A general comparison between the tensile stress-strain [$\sigma(\varepsilon)$] curves for 1-D and 2-D materials (Fig. 33) provides important perspective. It is found that $\sigma(\varepsilon)$ for 2-D materials is quite closely matched by simply scaling down the 1-D curves by 1/2. The behavior of 2-D materials must, therefore, be *dominated* by the 0° plies,* because these plies provide a fiber volume fraction in the loading direction about half that present in 1-D material.[4]

The most significant 2-D effects occur at the *initial deviation from linearity*. At this stage, matrix cracks that form either in matrix-rich regions or in 90° plies evolve at lower stresses than cracks in 1-D materials. The associated nonlinearities are usually slight and do not normally contribute substantially to the overall nonlinear response of the material. However, these cracks have important implications for oxidation embrit-

---

* Furthermore, since some of the 2-D materials are woven, the 1/2 scaling infers that the curvatures introduced by weaving have minimal effect on the stress-strain behaviors.

[87] R. F. Cooper and K. Chyung, *J. Mater. Sci.* **22**, 126 (1987).

[88] B. Harris, R. A. Habib, and R. G. Cooke, *Proc. Roy. Soc., Series A* **437**, 109–131 (1992).

[89] K. Prewo and J. J. Brennan, *J. Mater. Sci.* **17**(4), 1201–1206 (1982).

[90] K. M. Prewo and J. J. Brennan, *J. Mater. Sci.* **17**(2), 463–468 (1980).

[91] K. M. Prewo and J. J. Brennan, *J. Mater. Sci.* **17**, 1201–1206 (1982).

[92] T. W. Coyle, M. H. Guyot, and J. F. Jamet, *Cer. Eng. & Sci. Proc.* **7**(7–8), 947–957 (1986).

[93] O. Sbaizero and A. G. Evans, *J. Am. Ceram. Soc.* **69**(6), 481 (1986).

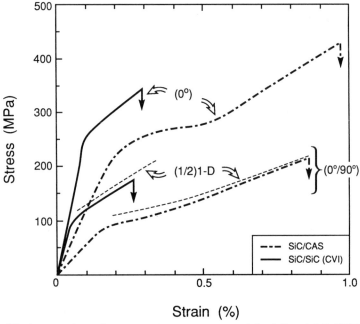

### Strain (%)

FIG. 33. A comparison of stress-strain curves measured for 1-D and 2-D CMCs. The dashed lines labeled 1/2 (1-D) represent the behavior expected in 2-D materials when the 90° plies carry zero load.

tlement and creep rupture and require analysis. Matrix cracking in the 90° plies often proceeds by a tunneling mechanism (Fig. 34). Tunnel cracking occurs[94,95] subject to a lower bound stress $\sigma_t$ given by

$$\sigma_\tau = \sigma_\tau^o - \sigma^R(E_L + E_T)/2E_T \qquad (24.1)$$

with

$$\sigma_\tau^o = [E_o\Gamma_R/t_P]^{1/2} g(f, E_f/E_m)$$

where

$$E_o = E_L(1 + E_L/E_T)/2(E_L/E_T - \nu_L^2).$$

[94] J. W. Hutchinson and Z. Suo, *Appl. Mech. Rev.* **28**, 1–69 (1991).
[95] C. Xia, R. R. Carr, and J. W. Hutchinson, Harvard Univ. Report Mech-202, *Acta Metall. Mater.*, in press.

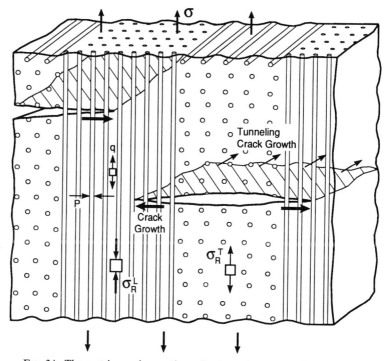

FIG. 34. The matrix crack growth mechanisms that operate in 2-D CMCs.

The function $g$ depends quite strongly on whether the transverse fibers remain in contact with matrix upon loading or separate, as plotted on Fig. 35. The relative unloading modulus associated with such tunnel cracks, $\bar{E}/E$, depends primarily on the crack density $t_p/\bar{L}$, with $\bar{L}$ being the mean crack spacing in the 90° plies.[95,96] The effect when the fibers are contacting is illustrated in Fig. 36. The ratio $\bar{E}/E$ is larger when the fibers separate. Note that at large crack densities a limiting value is reached, which is given by

$$\bar{E}_l/E_o = E_L/(E_L + E_T). \tag{24.2}$$

The corresponding permanent strain is

$$\varepsilon_o = (1/\bar{E} - 1/E_o)\sigma^R(E_L + E_T)/2E_L. \tag{24.3}$$

[96] N. Laws and G. Dvorak, *Jnl. Composite Mtls.* **22**, 900 (1980).

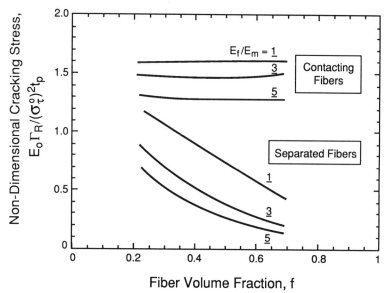

FIG. 35. The effect of elastic modulus ratio and fiber volume fraction on the lower bound stress for tunnel cracking ($\sigma^R = 0$) for contacting and separating interfaces.

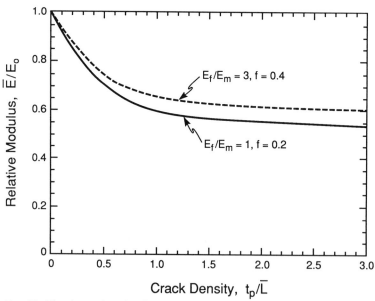

FIG. 36. The change in unloading compliance caused by cracks in the 90° plies.

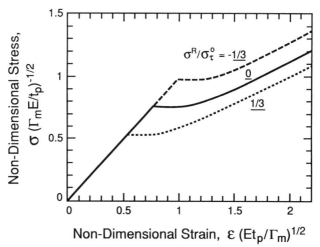

FIG. 37. Simulated stress-strain response for a 2-D CMCs subject to tunnel cracking.

Examples of the overall stress-strain response are summarized in Fig. 37. In practice, the stresses at which these cracks evolve may be larger, because the formation of cracks at stresses above $\sigma_\tau$ depends on the availability of flaws in the 90° plies.

Lateral extension of these tunnel cracks into the matrix of the 0° plies (Fig. 34) results in behavior similar to that found in 1-D material. Moreover, if the stress $\sigma^o$ acting on the 0° plies is known, the 1-D solutions may be used directly to predict the plastic strain. Otherwise, this stress must be estimated.[95] For a typical 0/90 system, $\sigma^o$ must range between $\bar{\sigma}$ and $2\bar{\sigma}$, depending on the extent of matrix cracking in the 90° plies and on $E_T/E_L$. Preliminary analysis has been conducted using $\sigma^o = 2\bar{\sigma}$, as implied by the comparison between 1-D and 2-D stress-strain curves (Fig. 33). Additional modeling on this topic is in progress.

Using this simplified approach, simulations of stress-strain curves have been conducted.[97,98] These curves have been compared with experimental measurements for several 2-D CMCs. The simulations lead to somewhat larger flow strengths than the experiments, especially at small inelastic strains. To address this discrepancy, further modeling is in progress, which attempts to couple the behavior of the tunnel cracks with the matrix cracks in the 0° plies.

[97] X. Aubard, Thèse de Doctorat de L'Université de Paris (Nov. 1992).
[98] J. M. Domergue, E. Vagaggini, and A. G. Evans, *J. Am. Ceram. Soc.,* in press.

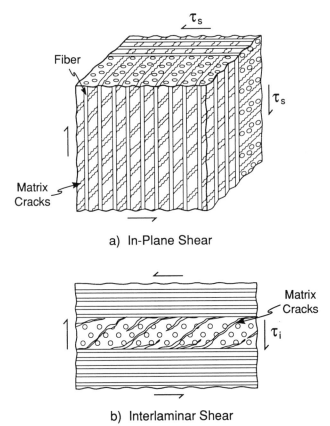

a) In-Plane Shear

b) Interlaminar Shear

FIG. 38. Schematic indicating the two modes of shear damage: (a) in-plane and (b) interlaminar.

## 25. SHEAR PROPERTIES

The matrix cracking that occurs in 2-D CMCs, subject to shear loading depends on the loading orientation and the properties of the matrix. Two dominant loading orientations are of interest in-plane shear along one fiber orientation and out-of-plane (or interlaminar) shear. The key difference between these loading orientations concerns the potential for interaction between the matrix cracks and the fibers (Fig. 38). For the out-of-plane case, matrix cracks evolve without significant interaction with the fibers. Conversely, for in-plane loading, the matrix crack *must interact* with the fibers. These interactions impede matrix crack development. Consequently, *the in-plane shear strength always exceeds the interlaminar shear strength.*

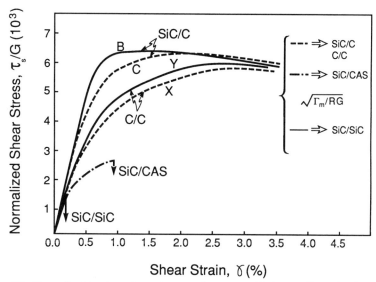

FIG. 39. Normalized in-plane shear stress-strain curves with the nondimensional parameter $\mathcal{W}$ indicated.

## a. *In-plane Shear*

Experiments that probe the in-plane shear properties have been performed by using Iosipescu test specimens.[25] A summary of experimental results (Fig. 6) indicates that the matrix has a major influence on the shear flow strength $\tau_s$ and the shear ductility $\gamma_c$. Moreover, it has been found that the shear flow strengths can be ranked using a parameter $\mathcal{W}$ derived from the matrix cracking stress in the absence of interface sliding,[57] given by (Fig. 39)

$$\mathcal{W} = \sqrt{\Gamma_m/RG}. \tag{25.1}$$

The property of principal importance within $\mathcal{W}$ is the shear modulus $G$, which reflects the *increase in compliance* caused by the matrix cracks. However, a model needs to be developed that gives a complete relationship between the composite strength and the constituent properties.

The shear ductility also appears to be influenced by the shear modulus, but in the opposite sense: high modulus matrices result in low ductility. This behavior has been rationalized in terms of the effect of matrix modulus on the bending deformation experienced by fibers between matrix cracks.[25] As yet, there have been no calculations that address this phenomenon.

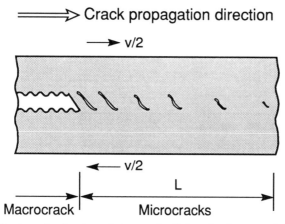

FIG. 40. A schematic showing echelon cracks that evolve into a mode II failure.

## b. *Interlaminar Shear*

The matrix cracks that form upon interlaminar shear loading and provide the plastic strains are material dependent. The simplest case, depicted in Fig. 38(b), involves multiple tunnel cracks that extend across the layer and orient normal to the maximum tensile stress *within* the layer.[93] In other cases, the matrix cracks are confined primarily to the matrix-only layers between plies.[60] A general understanding of these different behaviors does not yet exist.

When the interlaminar cracks form by tunneling, the solutions have a direct analogy within the transverse cracking results described earlier.[39] In shear loading, the tunnel cracks evolve and orient such that a mode II crack develops, as sketched on Fig. 40. The evolution of the echelon array of cracks has been analyzed[39] and shown to occur in accordance with the stress-displacement curve plotted on Fig. 41. There is a critical shear stress $\bar{\tau}_c$ at which interlaminar shear failure occurs, given by

$$\bar{\tau}_c \approx 1.5 \sqrt{G\Gamma_R/t_p} \qquad (25.2)$$

where $t_p$ is now the thickness of the material layer that governs cracking. There must also be effects of residual stress, but these have yet to be included in the model. The form of the critical shear stress relation [Eq. (25.2)] is the same as that for transverse tunnel cracking [Eq. (24.1)], verifying that these two phenomena are interrelated. The elastic properties dictate whether $\bar{\tau}_c$ or $\sigma_\tau$ is the larger: usually $\bar{\tau}_c < \sigma_\tau$ because $G \ll E$.

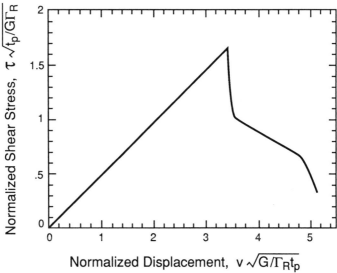

Normalized Displacement, $v\sqrt{G/\Gamma_R t_p}$

Fɪɢ. 41. The stress-displacement relation for interlaminar shear.

## 26. TRANSVERSE TENSILE PROPERTIES

CMCs with 2-D fiber architecture are susceptible to interlaminar cracking in various component configurations (Fig. 42). In such cases, as the crack extends through the component, conditions range from mode I to mode II. Tests and analyses are needed that relate to these issues. Most experience has been gained from PMCs.[99] The major issue is the manner whereby the interlaminar (transverse) cracks interact with the fibers. In principle, it is possible to conduct tests in which the cracks do not interact. In practice, such interactions always occur in CMCs, as the crack front meanders and crosses over inclined fibers.[100,101] These interactions dominate the measured fracture loads in conventional cantilever (DCB) specimens, as well as in flexure specimens.[102,103] Some typical results for the transverse fracture energy (Fig. 43), indicate the large values (compared with $\Gamma_m \approx 20J\ m^{-2}$) induced by these interactions.

Analysis indicates that large-scale bridging (LSB) is involved and the

[99] H. Chai, *Composites* **15**(4), 277–290 (1984).

[100] S. M. Spearing and A. G. Evans, *Acta Metall.* **40**(9), 2191–2199 (1992).

[101] D. A. W. Kaute, H. R. Shercliff, and M. F. Ashby, *Acta Metall. Mater.,* in press.

[102] G. Bao, B. Fan, and A. G. Evans, *Mech. of Mtls.* **13**, 59–66 (1992).

[103] R. Bordia, B. J. Dalgleish, P. G. Charalambides, and A. G. Evans, *J. Am. Ceram. Soc.* **74**(11), 2776–2780 (1991).

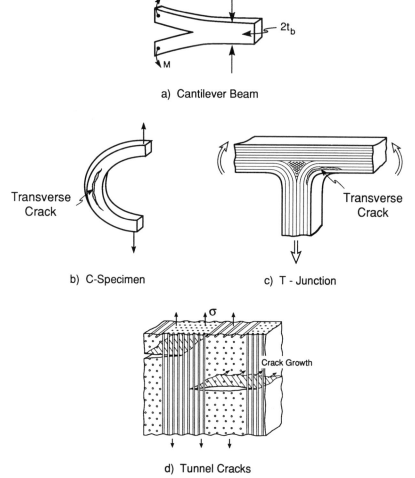

a) Cantilever Beam

Transverse
Crack

Transverse
Crack

b) C-Specimen                    c) T - Junction

Crack Growth

d) Tunnel Cracks

FIG. 42. Schematic of the various modes of transverse cracking in CMCs: (a) cantilever beam, (b) C specimen, (c) T junction, and (d) tunnel cracks.

bridging behavior can be explicitly ascertained from the measured curves.[102] For the particular case of a DCB specimen [Fig. 42(a)], the $J$ integral is explicitly defined in terms of the bending moment $M$ and the traction law.[12] For example, the steady state resistance $\Gamma_s$ for a linear softening traction law is

$$\Gamma_s \equiv 12M_s^2/E_L t_b^3$$
$$= \sigma_s u_s/2 + \Gamma_m \qquad (26.1)$$

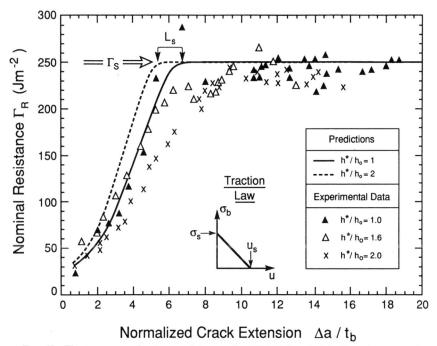

FIG. 43. The transverse fracture resistance of a SiC/CAS material. Also shown are the traction law assumed for inclined bridging fibers upon transverse cracking and the predicted resistance curves.

and the zone length at steady state is

$$L_s = (Eu_s/3\sigma_s)^{1/4} t_b^{3/4} \qquad (26.2)$$

where $2t_b$ is the DCB beam thickness, $M_s$ is the bending moment, with the quantities $\Gamma_s$ and $L_s$ defined on Fig. 43. Experimental measurements made with DCB specimens can be used to evaluate the parameters $\sigma_s$ and $u_s$ by simply fitting the data to Eqs. (26.1) and (26.2). This information can then be used to *predict* $\Gamma_s$ and $\Gamma_R$ for other configurations.

An example is given for SiC/CAS composites (Fig. 43). Experimental results for this material[100] give $u_s \approx 100$ μm and $\sigma_s \approx 10$ MPa. One application of these results is the prediction of the tunnel cracking found in 0/90 laminates [Eq. (24.1)]. The analysis of tunnel cracking[95] has established that for typical laminate thicknesses, the crack opening displacements are small (<1 μm). For such small displacements, there is a *negligible influence of the fibers*. Consequently, $\Gamma_R \approx \Gamma_m(1 - f)$. Other applications to C specimens and T junction are in progress.

An obvious limitation of the procedure is the uncertainty about the manner whereby the matrix crack interacts with the fibers in other geometries and, hence, the universality of $\sigma_s$ and $u_s$. This is a topic for further research.

## VII. Stress Redistribution

CMCs usually have substantially lower notch sensitivity than monolithic brittle materials and, in several cases, exhibit notch insensitive behavior.[2,3] This desirable characteristic of CMCs arises because the material may *redistribute stresses* around strain concentration sites. Notch effects appear to depend on the class of behavior. Moreover, a different mechanics is required for each class, because the stress redistribution mechanisms class operate over different physical scales. Class I behavior involves stress redistribution by fiber bridging/pull-out, which occurs along the crack plane.[12,104,105] Large-scale bridging mechanics (LSBM) is preferred for such materials. Class II behavior allows stress redistribution by large-scale matrix cracking[2] and continuum damage mechanics (CDM) is regarded as most appropriate. Class III behavior involves material responses similar to those found in metals, and a comparable mechanics might be used:[26,27] either LEFM for small-scale yielding or nonlinear fracture mechanics for large-scale yielding. Since a unified mechanics has not yet been identified, it is necessary to use mechanism maps that distinguish the various classes (Figs. 3 and 4).

27. MECHANISM TRANSITIONS

The transition between class I and class II behaviors involves considerations of both matrix crack growth and fiber failure. One hypothesis for the transition may be analyzed using LSBM. Such analysis allows the condition for fiber failure at the end of an unbridged crack segment to be solved simultaneously with the energy release rate of the matrix front. The latter is equated to the matrix fracture energy.[77] By using this solution to specify that fiber failure occurs *before the matrix crack extends into the steady state*, class I behavior is presumed to ensue. Conversely, class II behavior is envisaged when steady state matrix cracking occurs prior

[104] F. W. Zok, O. Sbaizero, C. Hom, and A. G. Evans, *J. Am. Ceram. Soc.* **74**(1), 187–193 (1991).

[105] F. W. Zok and C. L. Hom, *Acta Metall. Mater.* **38**, 1895 (1990).

to fiber failure. The resulting mechanism map involves two indices (Table II):

$$\mathcal{S} = (RS/a_o\tau)(E_m^2/E_L E_f)[(1-f)/f]^2$$
$$\equiv 3/\mathcal{A}_b \tag{27.1}$$

and

$$\mathcal{U} = \sigma_{mc}/S. \tag{27.2}$$

With $\mathcal{S}$ and $\mathcal{U}$ as coordinates, a mechanism map may be constructed that distinguishes class I and class II behavior (Fig. 3). Although this map has qualitative features consistent with experience, the experiments required for validation have not been completed. In practice, the mechanism transition in CMCs probably involves additional considerations.

The incidence of class III behavior is found at relatively small magnitudes of the ratio of shear strength $\tau_s$ to tensile strength $S$. When $\tau_s/S$ is small, a shear band develops at the notch front and extends normal to the notch plane. Furthermore, since $\tau_s$ is related to $G$, the parameter $G/S$ is selected as the ordinate of a mechanism map. Experimental results suggest that class III behavior arises when $G/S \gtrsim 50$ (Fig. 4).

## 28. Mechanics Methodology

### a. *Class I Materials*

The class I mechanism, when dominant, has features compatible with LSBM.[104–106] These mechanics may be used to characterize effects of notches, holes, and manufacturing flaws on tensile properties whenever a single matrix crack is prevalent. For cases wherein the flaw or notch is small compared with specimen dimensions, the tensile strength may be plotted as functions of *both* flaw indices: $\mathcal{A}_b$ and $\mathcal{A}_p$ (Fig. 18). For the former, the results are sensitive to the ratio of the pull-out strength $S_p$ to the UTS.[78] These results should be used whenever the unnotched tensile properties are compatible with global load sharing. Conversely, $\mathcal{A}_p$ should be used as the notch index when the unnotched properties appear to be pull-out dominated.

When the notch and hole have dimensions that are a significant fraction of the plate width ($a_o/b > 0$), *net section* effects must be included.[7,8]

[106] J. Bowling and G. W. Groves, *J. Mater. Sci.* **14**, 43 (1979).

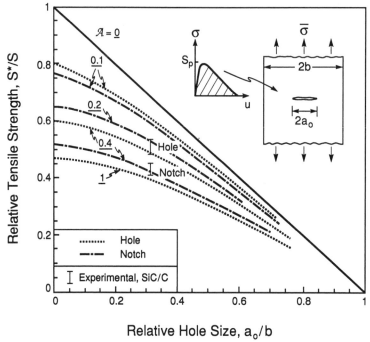

**Relative Hole Size, $a_0/b$**

FIG. 44. Effects of relative notch size on the UTS. Also shown are experimental data for a SiC/C material.

Some results (Fig. 44) illustrate the behavior for different values of the notch sensitivity index $\mathcal{A}$. Experimental validation has not been undertaken, although partial results for one material ($SiC/C_B$) are compatible with LSBM,[27] as shown for data obtained with center notches and holes (Fig. 44). The promising feature is that LSBM explains the difference between notches and holes (upon requiring that $\mathcal{A} \approx 0.8$).

b. *Class II Materials*

The nonlinear stress-strain behavior governed by matrix cracking [expressed through $\bar{E}$, Eq. (21.10), and $\varepsilon_0$, Eq. (21.11)] provides a basis for a CDM approach that may be used to predict the effects of notches and holes. Such developments are in progress.* In practice, several class II CMCs have been shown[33] to exhibit notch insensitive behavior, at notch sizes up to 5 mm. The notch insensitivity is manifest in the effect of the

---

* An important factor that dictates whether continuum or discrete methods are used concerns the ratio of the matrix crack spacing to the radius of curvature of the notch.

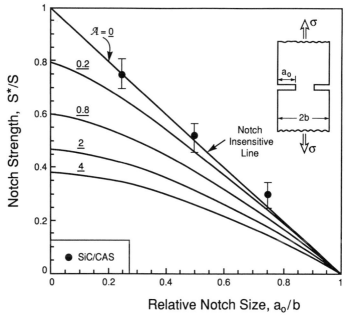

FIG. 45. Experimental results for SiC/CAS indicating notch insensitivity.

relative notch size $a_o/b$ on the ratio of the UTS measured in the presence of notches (designated $S^*$) to the strength in the absence of notches (designated $S$). Results for SiC/CAS are illustrated on Fig. 45. In this material, the nonlinearity provided by the matrix cracks allows sufficient stress redistribution such that the stress concentration is *eliminated*. This occurs despite the low ductility ($<1\%$). A CDM procedure capable of predicting this behavior will be available in the near future, using the stress-strain simulation capability based on constituent properties (Figs. 25, 35, and 36).

## c. *Class III Materials*

Class III behavior has been found in several C matrix composites.[26,27] In these materials, the shear bands can be imaged using an x-ray dye penetrant method. Based on such images, the extent of the shear deformation zone $l_s$ is found to be predictable from measured shear strengths $\tau_s$ (Fig. 6) in approximate accordance with (Fig. 46)

$$l_s/a_o \approx \sigma/\tau_s - 1. \tag{28.1}$$

Calculations have indicated that this shear zone diminishes the stress ahead of the notch (Fig. 47), analogous to the effect of a plastic zone in

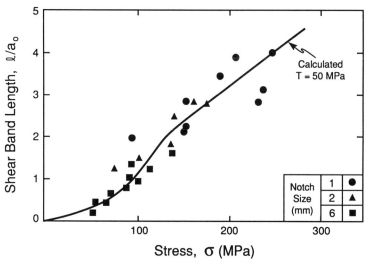

FIG. 46. Relationship between shear band length and stress for a C/C composite. The calculated curve is also shown.

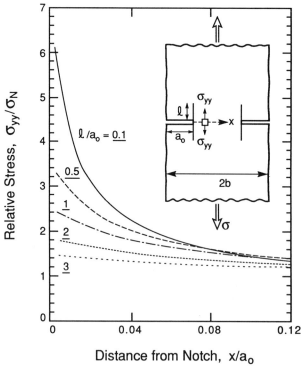

FIG. 47. Effect of shear bands on the stress ahead of a notch.

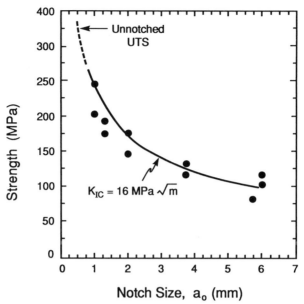

Notch Size, $a_o$ (mm)

FIG. 48. LEFM representation of notch data for C/C.

metals. For C/C materials, it has been found that the shear band lengths are small enough that LEFM is able to characterize the experimental data over a range of notch lengths, such that $K_{IC} \approx 16$ MPa$\sqrt{m}$ (Fig. 48). However, conditions must exist where LEFM is violated. For example, when $l_s/a_o \gtrsim 4$, the stress concentration is essentially eliminated (Fig. 47) and the material must then become notch insensitive. Further work is needed to identify parameters that bound the applicability of LEFM and to establish the requirements for notch insensitivity.

29. MEASUREMENTS

Notch sensitivity data (Figs. 44, 45, and 48) provide an explicit measure of stress redistribution. However, further understanding requires techniques that probe the stress and strain around notches, as CMCs are loaded to failure. Many of the methods have been developed and used for the same purpose on PMCs.[107,108] These techniques can measure both strain and stress distributions.

[107] H. R. Bakis, H. R. Yih, W. W. Stinchcomb, and K. L. Reifsnider, *ASTM STP* **1012,** 66–83 (1989).
[108] W. W. Stinchcomb and C. E. Bakis, in *Fatigue of Composite Materials* (K. L. Reifsnider, ed.), pp. 105–180, Elsevier Science Publishers, New York (1990).

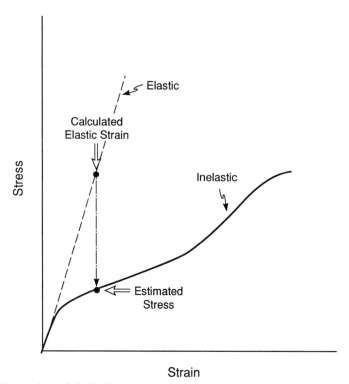

Strain

Fɪɢ. 49. A schematic indicating an approximate method for obtaining the stress by using the strain obtained from elastic calculations.

*Strain* distributions are measured with high spatial resolution by using moiré interferometry. In this method, the fringe spacings relate to the in-plane displacements which, in turn, govern the strains. This technique has had only limited use for CMCs.[109] Preliminary measurements suggest that the inelastic deformations that arise from shear bands result in strains similar to *elastic* strains. Based on such similarity, it may be speculated that the reduced stress concentrations may relate explicitly to the lower stresses that arise upon inelastic deformation at fixed strain (Fig. 49). Further exploration of this simple concept is in progress.

Since strain measurements appear to have minimal sensitivity to the stress redistribution mechanisms operative in CMCs, a technique that measures the *stress* distribution is preferred. One such method involves measurement of thermoelastic emission. This method relies on the *tem-*

[109]M. C. Shaw, D. B. Marshall, M. Dhadkah, and A. G. Evans, *Acta Metall. Mater.* **41**, 3311–3322 (1993).

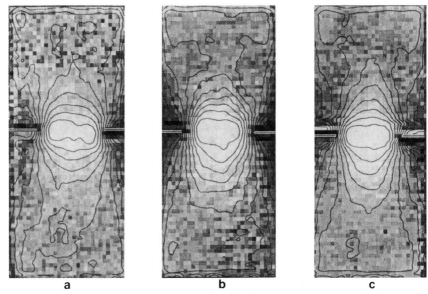

a                                b                                c

FIG. 50. SPATE images obtained from a SiC/CAS composite at three applied loads; (a) to (c). The light regions along the notch plane are the zone at the highest stress. Note that this zone is not at the notch tip, but has displaced toward the center.

*perature rise* $\Delta T$ that occurs when an element of the composite is subject to a *hydrostatic stress* $\Delta \sigma_{kk}$ under adiabatic conditions. The fundamental adiabatic relationship for a homogeneous solid is[110]

$$\Delta \dot{\sigma}_{kk} = (C_v \rho_o / \alpha T_o) \Delta \dot{T} \qquad (29.1)$$

where $C_v$ is the specific heat at constant strain and $\rho_o$ is the density. One experimental implementation of this concept is a technique referred to as *stress pattern analysis by thermoelastic emission* (SPATE).[110] It involves the use of high-sensitivity infrared detectors, which measure the temperature in a lock-in mode as a cyclic stress is applied to the material. This feature essentially eliminates background problems and has good signal-to-noise characteristics. SPATE measurements are conventionally performed at small stress amplitudes, which elicit "elastic" behavior in the material. Experimental results[111] for a class II material (SiC/CAS) have confirmed that the stress concentration can be eliminated by matrix cracks (Fig. 50). In addition, results for a class III material (C/C) have

[110] N. Harwood and W. M. Cummings, *Thermoelastic Stress Analysis*, Adam Hilger IOP Publishing, UK (1991).

[111] T. J. Mackin, A. G. Evans, M. Y. He, and T. E. Purcell, *J. Am. Ceram. Soc.*, in press.

provided a direct measure of the stress redistribution caused by shear bands (Fig. 51).

Another method for strain measurement uses fluorescence spectroscopy.[112] This method has particular applicability to oxides, especially $Al_2O_3$ (either as fiber or matrix). The technique has the special advantage that strains can be measured in individual fibers, such that stress changes caused by matrix cracks can be measured. Such measurements permit the material to be probed at the spatial resolution needed to understand mechanisms in detail.[63]

## VIII. Fatigue

30. BASIC PHENOMENA

Upon cycling loading, matrix cracking and fiber failure occur in brittle matrix composites,[10,54,79,113,114] in accordance with the same three classes found for monotonic loading (Fig. 2). The preceding matrix cracking and fiber failure models still apply, except that some additional factors need to be introduced.[114] The experimental results needed to establish the specific fatigue mechanisms that operate in CMCs are sparse. However, similar mechanisms operate in metal (MMC) and polymer (PMC) matrix composites. Observations, modeling, and measurements performed on these materials provide insights that facilitate and hasten an understanding of the cyclic behaviors of brittle matrix composites.

Among the new features that enter when cyclic loading is used are *degradation mechanisms* and, in some cases, revised *crack growth criteria*. The macroscopic characteristics associated with the degradation mechanisms are fatigue life ($\sigma$-$N$) curves (Fig. 52) and changes in compliance (Fig. 53). In addition, the hysteresis loops change as fatigue proceeds (Fig. 54). Analyses of compliance and hysteresis changes, as well as differences in fiber pull-out, indicate that the interface sliding stress changes upon fatigue. *A cyclic sliding function $\tau_f(N)$ thus becomes a new constituent property.*[114] In some cases, at high temperature and upon thermomechanical fatigue, a particularly low fatigue threshold stress (compared with the UTS) implies fiber strength degradation. Conse-

[112] S. E. Molis and D. R. Clarke, *J. Am. Ceram. Soc.* **73**, 3189 (1990).

[113] C. Q. Rousseau, in *Thermal and Mechanical Behavior of Metal Matrix and Ceramic Matrix Composites, ASTM STP 1080* (J. M. Kennedy, H. H. Moeller, and W. S. Johnson, eds.), American Society for Testing and Materials, Philadelphia, PA (1990).

[114] D. Rouby and P. Reynaud, *Ceramic Matrix Composites, AGARD Conf. Proc.* Antalya, Turkey (1993).

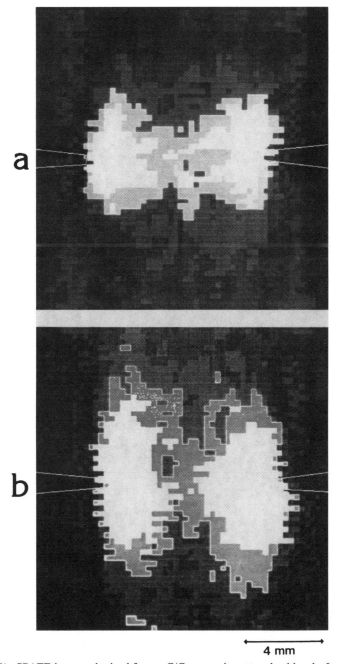

4 mm

FIG. 51. SPATE images obtained from a C/C composite at two load levels. In this case, the regions of highest stress are white. Note that the high stress zone spreads laterally as the load increases from (a) to (b).

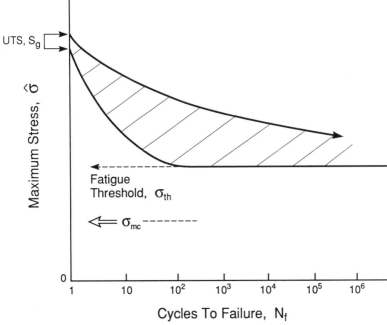

FIG. 52. A schematic of typical isothermal fatigue data for CMCs.

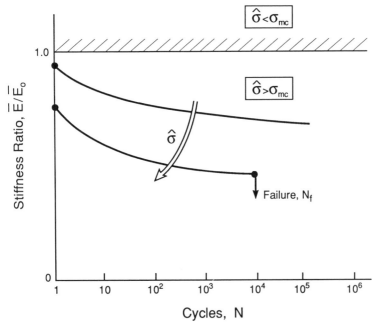

FIG. 53. A schematic of changes in modulus that occur in CMCs upon cycling.

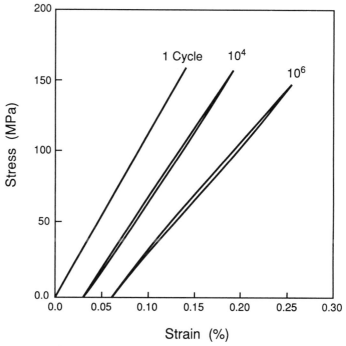

Fig. 54. Hysteresis loop measurements obtained upon fatigue for a unidirectional SiC/ CAS.

quently, a cyclic fiber strength function $S_f(N)$ may also be needed to predict fatigue life.

Several possible matrix *crack growth criteria* are applicable to fatigue. These relate to the conditions at the crack front. When the matrix itself is susceptible to cyclic fatigue, the Paris law relates crack growth in the matrix to the stress intensity *range* at the crack front $\Delta K_{tip}$ by[83]

$$da/dN = \beta(\Delta K_{tip}/E)^{n_f} \qquad (30.1)$$

where $N$ is the number of cycles, $n_f$ is a power law exponent, and $\beta$ is a material-dependent coefficient. In some cases, $n_f$ is sufficiently large that matrix crack growth is dominated by the peak value of either $K_{tip}$ or $\mathcal{G}_{tip}$. Then, the same criterion used for monotonic loading [Eq. (18.2)] may be preferred. Finally, when the dominant mechanism involves stress corrosion, crack growth can be described in terms of $\mathcal{G}_{tip}$ through the commonly used power law:[115]

[115] S. M. Weiderhorn, *J. Am. Ceram. Soc.* **50**, 66–79 (1967).

$$\frac{da}{dt} = \dot{a}_o \left( \frac{\mathcal{G}_{\text{tip}}}{\mathcal{G}_m} \right)^{\eta} \tag{30.2}$$

where $\dot{a}$ is a reference velocity, $\eta$ is the power law exponent, and $\mathcal{G}_m$ is the matrix toughness, taken to be $\Gamma_m(1 - f)$.

### 31. Matrix Crack Growth

When the interfaces are "weak," fibers can remain intact in the crack wake and cyclic frictional dissipation resists fatigue crack growth.[83] The latter has been extensively demonstrated on Ti matrix composites reinforced with SiC fibers.[116–119] The essential features of the weak interface behavior are as follows: Intact, sliding fibers acting in the crack wake shield the crack tip, such that the stress intensity range at the crack tip $\Delta K_{\text{tip}}$ is less than that expected for the applied loads $\Delta K$. Using this approach, a simple transformation converts the monotonic crack growth parameters into cyclic parameters that can be used to interpret and simulate fatigue growth of each matrix crack. The key transformation is based on the relationship between interface sliding during loading and unloading, which relates the monotonic result to the cyclic equivalent through[83]

$$\left( \frac{1}{2} \right) \Delta \sigma_b(\chi/a, \Delta \sigma) = \sigma_b(\chi/a, \Delta \sigma/2) \tag{31.1}$$

where $\Delta \sigma$ is the range in the applied stress. Notably, the amplitude of the *change* in fiber traction $\Delta \sigma_b$ caused by a change in applied stress $\Delta \sigma$ is twice the fiber traction $\sigma_b$, which would arise in the monotonic loading of a previously unopened crack caused by an applied stress equal to half the stress change. *This result is fundamental to all subsequent developments.*[83]

[116] M. Sensmeier and K. Wright, *Proc. TMS Fall Meeting* (P. K. Law and M. N. Gungor, eds.), p. 441, ASME, Pittsburgh (1989).

[117] D. Walls, G. Bao, and F. Zok, *Scripta Metall. Mater.* **25**, 911 (1991).

[118] D. Walls, G. Bao, and F. W. Zok, *Acta Metall. Mater.*, in press.

[119] D. Walls and F. W. Zok, in *Advanced Metal Matrix Composites for Elevated Temperatures* (M. N. Gungor, E. J. Lavernia, and S. G. Fishman, eds.), p. 101, ASM, Metals Park, OH (1991).

The stress intensity factor for bridging fibers subject to cyclic conditions is

$$\Delta K_b(\Delta\sigma) = -2\sqrt{\frac{a}{\pi}}\int_0^a \frac{\Delta\sigma_b(\chi,\Delta\sigma)}{\sqrt{a^2-\chi^2}}\,d\chi \qquad (31.2)$$

which, with the use of Eq. (31.1), becomes

$$\Delta K_b(\Delta\sigma) = 2K_b^{max}(\Delta\sigma/2) \qquad (31.3)$$

where the superscript "max" refers to the maximum values of the parameters achieved in the loading cycle and thus $K_b^{max}$ is the bridging contribution that would arise when the crack is loaded by an applied stress equal to $\Delta\sigma/2$. Furthermore, since $\Delta K$ is linear, Eq. (31.1) is also valid for the tip stress intensity factor:

$$\Delta K_{tip} = 2K_{tip}(\Delta\sigma/2). \qquad (31.4)$$

When the fibers remain intact, a cyclic *steady state* ($\Delta K$ independent of crack length) is obtained when the cracks are long, given[83] by the condition $\Delta\mathscr{E} \leq 4$, where $\Delta\mathscr{E}$ is defined in Table II. The result is*

$$\Delta K_{tip} = \Delta\sigma\sqrt{R}(\sqrt{12}\Delta\mathscr{T})^{-1} \qquad (31.5)$$

where $\Delta\mathscr{T}$ is defined in Table II.

The corresponding crack growth rate is determined by using a crack growth criterion. When a Paris law applies, Eq. (30.1) and (31.5) give[83]

$$\frac{da}{dN} = \beta\left(\frac{\Delta\sigma\sqrt{R}}{\sqrt{6}\,\Delta\mathscr{T}E_m}\right)^{n_f}. \qquad (31.6)$$

When the matrix does not fatigue, such that Eq. (18.2) represents the crack growth criterion, *fatigue crack growth after the first cycle is only possible, provided that $\tau$ reduces upon cycling*, as elaborated on later.

When short cracks are of relevance ($\Delta\mathscr{E} > 4$),

$$\Delta K_{tip} = \Delta\sigma\sqrt{\pi a}\left(1 - \frac{4.31}{\Delta\mathscr{E}}\sqrt{\Delta\mathscr{E}+6.6} + \frac{11}{\Delta\mathscr{E}}\right). \qquad (31.7)$$

---

* For cyclic loading, the residual stress $q$ does not affect $\Delta K_{tip}$.

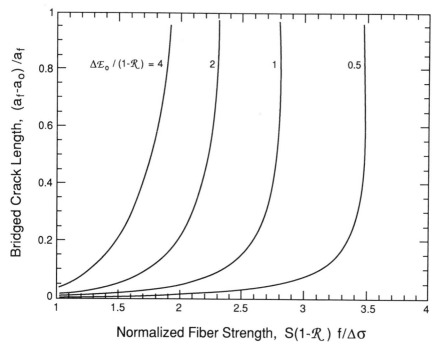

Normalized Fiber Strength, $S(1-\mathcal{R})$ $f/\Delta\sigma$

FIG. 55. The length of matrix crack $a_f$ at first fiber failure as a function of fiber strength for a range of stress amplitudes $\Delta\mathcal{E}$.

Consequently, at fixed $\Delta\sigma$, $\Delta K_{tip}$ increases as the crack extends, and the Paris law matrix crack growth accelerates. However, the bridged matrix fatigue crack always grows at a *slower rate* than an unbridged crack of the same length. Consequently, the composite always has *superior* crack growth resistance relative to the monolith.

To incorporate the effects of fiber breaking into the fatigue crack growth model, a deterministic criterion has been used:[120] The statistical characteristics of fiber failure have yet to be incorporated. To conduct the calculation, once the fibers begin to fail, the unbridged crack length has been continuously adjusted to maintain a stress at the unbridged crack tip equal to the fiber strength. These conditions lead to the determination of the crack length $a_f$ when the first fibers fail, as a function of the fiber strength and the maximum applied load (Fig. 55). Note that when either the fiber strength is high or the applied stress is low, no corresponding value of $a_f$ can be identified and the fibers do not fail.

[120]G. Bao and R. McMeeking, *Acta Metall. Mater.*, in press.

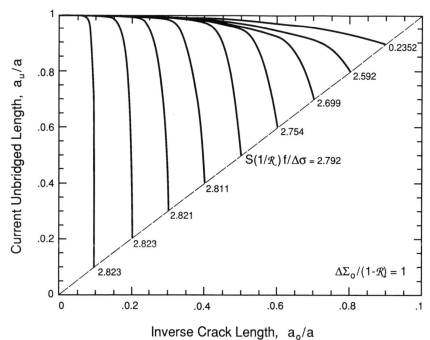

FIG. 56. Fiber breaking rate as manifest in the current unbridged matrix crack length $2a_u$ as a function of total crack length $2a$.

After the first fiber failure, fibers continue to break as the crack grows. Continuing fiber failure creates an unbridged segment larger than the original notch size. However, only the current unbridged length $2a_u$ and the current total crack length $2a$ are relevant[120] (Fig. 56).

If the fibers are relatively weak and break close to the crack tip ($a_o/a \rightarrow 1$), the bridging zone is always a small fraction of the crack length. In this case, there is minimal shielding. If the fibers are moderately strong, the fibers remain intact at first. But when the first fibers fail, subsequent failure occurs quite rapidly as the crack grows. The unbridged crack length then increases more rapidly than the total crack length and the $\Delta K_{tip}$ also increase as the crack grows. When the fibers are even stronger, first fiber failure is delayed. But once such failure occurs, many fibers fail simultaneously and the unbridged length increases rapidly. This causes a sudden increase in the crack growth rate. Finally, when the fiber strength exceeds a critical value, they never break and the fatigue crack growth rate always diminishes as the crack grows. The sensitivity of these behaviors to fiber strength is quite marked (Fig. 56), with the different types

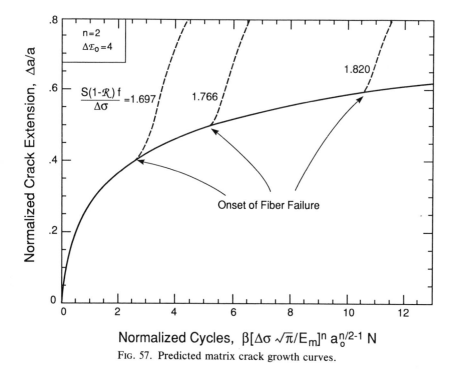

Normalized Cycles, $\beta[\Delta\sigma\sqrt{\pi}/E_m]^n \, a_o^{n/2-1} \, N$

FIG. 57. Predicted matrix crack growth curves.

of behavior occurring over a narrow range of fiber strength. Some typical crack growth curves predicted using this approach are plotted on Fig. 57. Finite geometry effects associated with LSB also exist.[120]

The results of Fig. 55 can be used to develop a criterion for a "threshold" stress range $\Delta\sigma_t$ below which fiber failure does not occur for *any* crack length. Within such a regime, the crack growth rate approaches the steady state value given by Eq. (31.6), with all fibers in the crack wake remaining intact. The variation in the "threshold" stress range with fiber strength is plotted on Fig. 58.

A notable feature of the predictions pertains to the role of the stress ratio $\mathcal{R}_s$ in composite behavior. Prior to fiber failure, the crack growth rate is independent of $\mathcal{R}_s$ (except for its effect on the fatigue properties of the matrix itself). However, $\mathcal{R}_s$ has a strong influence on the transition to fiber failure, as manifested by its effect on the maximum stress. It thus plays a dominant role in the fatigue lifetime.

In many cases, CMCs are subject to multiple matrix cracking upon cyclic and static loading, which leads to reductions in the unloading modulus $\bar{E}$, as well as changes in the hysteresis. The basic mechanics is

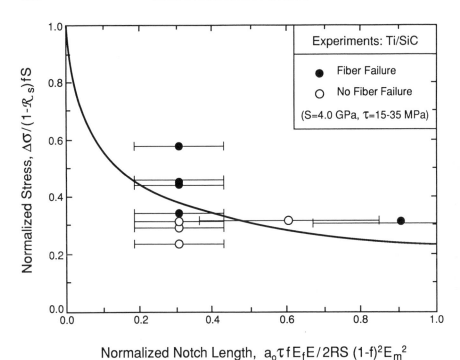

Normalized Notch Length, $a_o \tau f E_f E / 2RS (1-f)^2 E_m^2$

FIG. 58. The threshold stress diagram. Also shown are experimental results for Ti matrix composites.

essentially the same as that described for monotonic loading, except that the matrix crack growth criterion must be changed.

## 32. MULTIPLE CRACKING AND FAILURE

As cycling proceeds and $\tau$ decreases, there is a corresponding decrease in both the matrix cracking stress $\sigma_{mc}$ [Eq. (19.2)] and the UTS (Eq. 13.1). The former effect leads to additional matrix cracking and a diminished modulus. The latter effect dictates the fatigue threshold stress $S_{th}$, provided that *fiber strength degradation does not occur*. Moreover, $S_{th}$ can be substantially larger than $\sigma_{mc}$. Both behaviors can be readily predicted from the corresponding monotonic loading models whenever $\tau_f(N)$ is known.

Upon using the sliding function proposed for SiC/SiC composites,[114] indicated on Fig. 59(a),

$$\begin{align}
\tau_f &= \tau N^{-\xi} \quad \text{for } 1 < N < N_s \\
\tau_f &= \tau_{ss} \quad \text{for } N > N_s
\end{align} \tag{32.1}$$

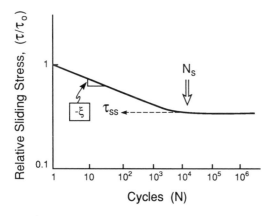

a) Reduction In Interface Sliding Resistance During Fatigue

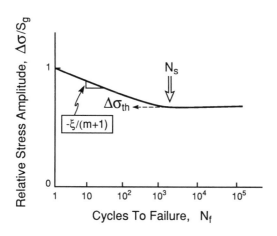

b) Fatigue Curve As A Result Of Interface Degradation

FIG. 59. (a) Effect of fatigue on the interface sliding stress (schematic) and (b) corresponding fatigue ($\sigma$-$N$) curve.

the following predictions can be generated. The threshold stress $S_{th}$, when GLS applies, is given by inserting Eq. (12.2) into Eq. (13.1) with $\tau$ replaced by $\tau_{ss}$,

$$S_{th}/S_g = (\tau_{ss}/\tau)^{1/(m+1)}. \qquad (32.2)$$

This threshold occurs after $N_s$ cycles. At intermediate cycles, $N < N_s$, the retained strength $S_R$ is derived as,

$$S_R/S_g = N^{-\xi/(m+1)}. \qquad (32.3)$$

These results can be combined to yield a fatigue ($\sigma$-$N$) curve [Fig. 59(b)]. Upon comparing with measured fatigue curves (Fig. 52), these predictions provide a straightforward means of determining whether fiber degradation occurs.

Two factors lead to changes in the *modulus* during fatigue. One occurs at fixed crack density. The other involves additional matrix cracking. Both effects are evident from Eq. (21.4) and (21.8). For example, when the sliding resistance $\tau$ has been reduced to steady state $\tau_{ss}$, the reduction in the unloading modulus $\Delta \bar{E}$ is given by

$$\frac{\Delta \bar{E}}{\bar{E}_o} = \frac{(1 - \bar{E}_o/E^*)(\tau \bar{d}/\tau_{ss} \bar{d}_s - 1)}{1 + (1 - \bar{E}_o/E_*)(\tau \bar{d}/\tau_{ss} \bar{d}_s - 1)} \tag{32.4}$$

where $\bar{E}_o$ is the initial unloading modulus and $\bar{d}_s$ is the revised saturation crack spacing. To obtain $\bar{d}_s/\bar{d}$, it is necessary to use Fig. 24, with the revised $\sigma_{mc}$ obtained from Eq. (19.2) upon replacing $\tau$ by $\tau_{ss}$.

## 33. THERMOMECHANICAL FATIGUE

The basic matrix crack growth model can be extended to include thermomechanical fatigue (TMF). This can be achieved by means of another transformation wherein all of the stress range terms in Eqs. (31.1) to (31.7) are replaced as follows:[120]

$$\begin{aligned} \Delta \sigma \Rightarrow \Delta t &= \Delta \sigma + f E_f (\alpha_f - \alpha_m) \Delta T \\ \Delta \sigma_b \Rightarrow \Delta t_b &= \Delta \sigma_b + f E_f (\alpha_f - \alpha_m) \Delta T \end{aligned} \tag{33.1}$$

where $\Delta T$ represents the temperature cycle and $\Delta \sigma$ the stress cycle. With these transformations, it is possible to represent the crack growth using two nondimensional parameters, $\Delta \mathscr{E}_o$ and $\Delta \mathscr{E}_T$ (Table II), that specify the stress cycling and the temperature cycling, respectively. It is immediately apparent that matrix crack growth and fiber failure are expected to be quite different for out-of-phase and in-phase TMF. The salient predictions are presented for both cases.

For materials in which $\alpha_m > \alpha_f$, in-phase TMF causes $\Delta T$ to be *less* than that expected for stress cycling alone and vice versa. These effects are apparent from trends in the stress intensity range $\Delta K_{tip}$ (Fig. 60), calculated for cases wherein fiber failure does not occur. A key result is that, whereas $\Delta K_{tip}$ always reduces upon initial crack extension either for stress cycling alone or for in-phase TMF, it can *increase* for out-of-phase TMF. Furthermore, for extreme ratio of $\Delta \mathscr{E}_T$ to $\Delta \mathscr{E}_o$, $\Delta K_{tip}$ can

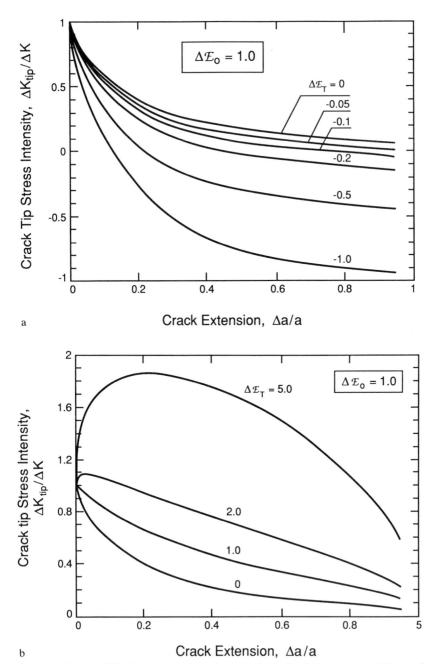

FIG. 60. Effects of TMF on the tip stress intensity factor for (a) in-phase and (b) out-of-phase TMF.

*exceed* that for the monolithic matrix without fibers. This result implies that the crack growth rate also *exceeds* that for the monolith (at the equivalent $\Delta K$). Then, the composite has crack growth resistance *inferior* to the monolithic matrix. The implications for the choice of fiber and the allowable temperature range $\Delta T$ are immediate.

When fiber failure effects are introduced, in-phase and out-of-phase cycling result in behaviors *that oppose* those associated with matrix crack growth. Namely, the crack size $a_f$ at which fiber failure commences is *smaller* for in-phase loading than for out-of-phase loading (Fig. 61). Consequently, to ensure a threshold, the material is required to operate under conditions of fiber integrity. Then, in-phase TMF represents the more severe problem.

## 34. EXPERIMENTAL RESULTS

Experimental measurements performed on CMCs and Ti MMCs reflect features associated with the cyclic degradation of the sliding stresses and fiber strength and also provide a critique of crack growth criteria. These features are manifest in phenomena ranging from the growth characteristics of individual cracks to changes in modulus to fatigue life curves. The salient cyclic and static fatigue characteristics are illustrated using various experimental results.

The growth of individual cracks has been investigated on Ti MMCs, but not on CMCs. The crack growth trends found in Ti MMCs are in broad agreement with the predictions of the matrix crack growth models (Fig. 62) upon using a Paris law applicable to the matrix [Eq. (30.1)]. The results indicate that sliding stress $\tau$ decreases upon cycling, because of "wear" mechanisms operating within the fiber coating.[117–119,121] The reduction in $\tau$ occurs after a relatively small number of cycles ($<1000$) and thereafter remains at an essentially constant value, $\tau_{ss}$, consistent with Eq. (32.1). It is also evident for these materials that the fiber strength *is not degraded by cyclic sliding of the interface*, even after $>10^5$ cycles.

Tensile fatigue testing of CMCs has been conducted under conditions that produce multiple cracking. There are consequent changes in the modulus and hysteresis loop width, which relate to the fatigue life. Such results do not provide a critical test of the matrix crack growth criterion, but clearly illustrate the influence of cycling on the interface sliding stress and the fiber strength. Reductions in unloading modulus $\bar{E}$ are found at fixed *stress amplitude* (Fig. 63).[10,122] In some cases, there is also a small

[121] T. Mackin and F. W. Zok, *J. Am. Ceram. Soc.* **75**, 3169–3171 (1993).

[122] S. M. Spearing, F. W. Zok, and A. G. Evans, *J. Am. Ceram. Soc.* **77**, 562–570 (1994).

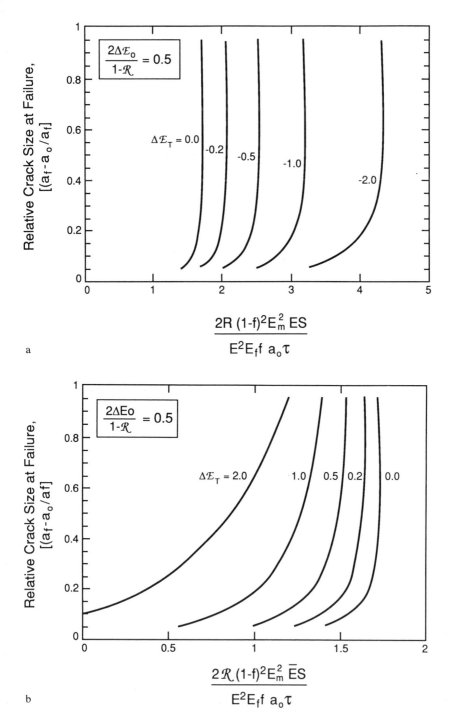

FIG. 61. Effects of TMF on the crack size at which fiber failure occurs for (a) in-phase and (b) out-of-phase TMF.

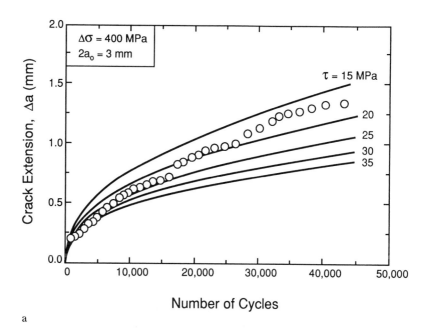

a

b

FIG. 62. Comparison between experimental crack growth results and predictions for unidirectional SiC/Ti composites. (a) small notch; (b) large notch.

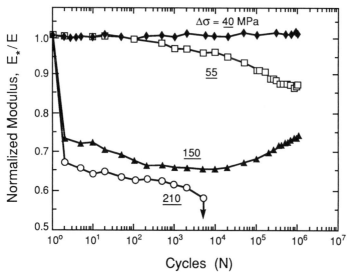

FIG. 63. Modulus reduction found upon fatigue in a glass matrix composite.[10]

subsequent increase. The modulus changes have been analyzed such that constituent properties during fatigue may be obtained. For example, measurements made for SiC/CAS (at frequencies <10 Hz) have been correlated with the crack density (Fig. 64) such that comparisons may be made with predictions based on Eq. (32.4). This analysis indicates a substantial reduction in sliding stress, from $\tau \approx 15$ MPa for the pristine composite[121] to $\tau_{ss} \approx 5$ MPa. Fatigue life data for SiC/SiC (CVI) composites provide similar information.[114] Analysis of $S_{th}$ may be made using Eq. (32.2), subject to the assumption that there is no fiber degradation. The analysis indicates that $\tau_{ss}/\tau \approx 0.38$. This degradation in $\tau$ is similar to that found for SiC/CAS and Ti MMCs and described earlier. A commonality regarding the changes in interface sliding that occur upon fatigue thus appears to be emerging. Note that the fatigue threshold stress $S_{th}$ is a relatively large fraction of the UTS ($S_{th}/S_g \approx 0.7$) when fatigue is accompanied by interface degradation, but does not degrade the fibers. The ratio $S_{th}/S_g$ is larger than that usually found for metals.

At higher frequencies ($\gtrsim 50$ Hz), frictional heating also occurs,[123] accompanied by a *larger reduction* in $\tau$. The hypothesis is that the frictional heating causes the C fiber coating to be eliminated. Such behavior would be consistent with that found upon isothermal heat treatments.[56]

[123] J. W. Holmes, *J. Am. Ceram. Soc.* **74**(7), 639–45 (1991).

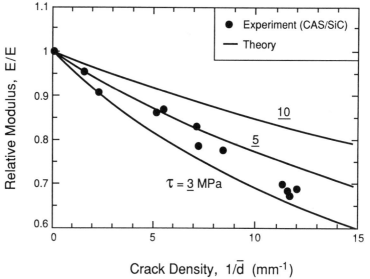

Crack Density, 1/d̄ (mm⁻¹)

FIG. 64. Influence of cyclic loading on modulus reduction as a function of crack density for a unidirectional CAS/SiC composite indicating that τ has been decreased by fatigue.

The occurrence of cyclic fatigue failure at peak stresses substantially lower than the UTS (Fig. 65) has been found at high temperatures and especially for TMF. Such results suggest that the fiber strength systematically diminishes for certain cyclic thermomechanical loadings. The three primary mechanisms of fiber weakening are abrasion, oxidation, and stress corrosion. These mechanisms might be distinguished in the following manner. The strength degradation caused by stress corrosion occurs abruptly, following *time* accumulated at *peak load*.[115] Abrasion occurs systematically with cyclic sliding at the interfaces (Fig. 66) and should be enhanced by out-of-phase TMF, which accentuates the sliding displacement. Oxidation is strictly time and temperature dependent. The strong effect of out-of-phase TMF on the fatigue life at high temperature[2] suggests that fiber degradation by abrasion is an important mechanism, perhaps accentuated by oxide formation at higher temperatures. Much additional study is required on this topic.

In some CMCs, modulus changes and rupture occur at *constant stress*.[122] Substantial matrix crack growth has been found at stresses below that required to produce cracks in short-duration monotonic tensile tests. Furthermore, the crack densities following extended periods under load ($\sim 10^6$ s) are *higher* than those obtained in the short duration tests. The development of cracks with time and stress (Fig. 67) has been consid-

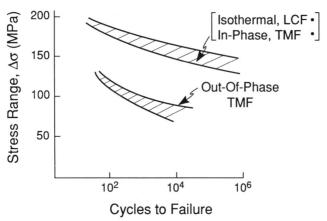

Cycles to Failure

Fig. 65. Isothermal fatigue and TMF data for a glass matrix composite.[2]

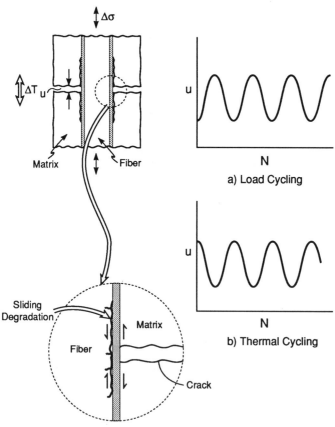

Fig. 66. Mechanism of fiber degradation by fatigue, coupled with oxidation.

273

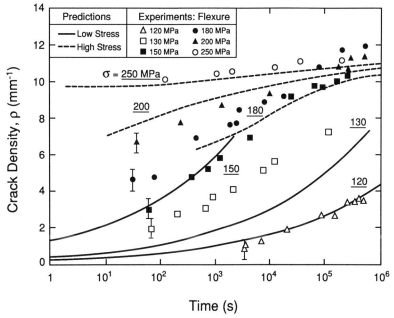

FIG. 67. Experimental measurements and simulations of matrix crack evolution in a SiC/ CAS composite caused by stress corrosion at constant stress.

ered to involve stress corrosion of the matrix. The behavior is consistent with a revised matrix crack growth criterion [Eq. (30.2)] without any changes in the sliding stress. Fiber weakening may also be occurring by stress corrosion.

## IX. Creep

### 35. BASIC BEHAVIOR

The creep behavior and relationships with constituent properties are critically influenced by fiber failure, matrix cracks, and interface debonding. Some of the basic stress-time characteristics are sketched in Figs. 68 and 69. When the fibers and matrix are intact and the interfaces are bonded, the creep deformations of the composite and the constituent properties are related in a straightforward manner.[124,125] When one constituent is elastic (fiber or matrix) and the other creeps, the *longitudinal* creep strain

---

[124] R. M. McMeeking, *International Journal of Solids and Structures,* in press.
[125] M. McLean, *Composites Sci. Technol.* **23**, 37–52 (1985).

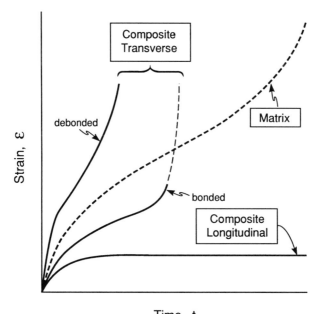

FIG. 68. Schematic indicating creep anisotropy in unidirectional CMCs.

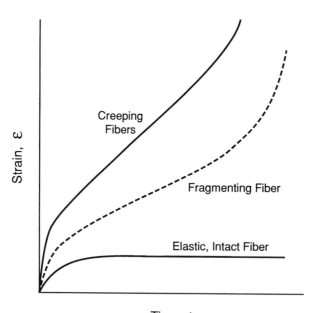

FIG. 69. Schematic indicating effects of intact and creeping fibers, as well as fiber failure on the longitudinal creep.

is *transient* and stops when all of the strain is transferred onto the elastic material (Figs. 68 and 69).[124] The creep law needed to describe this behavior is

$$\dot{\varepsilon}_{ij} = \frac{1}{2G}\dot{s}_{ij} + \frac{1}{9K}\delta_{ij}\dot{\sigma}_{kk} + \frac{3}{2}B\sigma_e^{n-1}s_{ij} + \alpha\delta_{ij}\dot{T} \qquad (35.1)$$

where $\dot{\varepsilon}$ is the strain rate, $\dot{\sigma}$ is the stress rate, $\delta_{ij}$ is the Kronecker delta, $n$ is the creep index, $s_{ij}$ is the deviatoric stress, the effective stress $\sigma_e$ is defined by

$$\sigma_e = \sqrt{\frac{3}{2}s_{ij}s_{ij}}, \qquad (35.2)$$

and $B$ is the rheology parameter for steady state creep:

$$B = \dot{\varepsilon}_o/\sigma_o^n$$

with $\sigma_o$ being the reference stress and $\dot{\varepsilon}_o$ the reference strain rate. If the fibers are elastic and the matrix creeps, the stress in the matrix, $\sigma_m$, evolves at constant applied stress as $(n \neq 1)$:[124,125]

$$\sigma_m(t) = \left\{\frac{(n-1)fE_fE_mBt}{E_L} + \frac{1}{[\sigma_m(0)^{n-1}]}\right\}^{1-n} \qquad (35.3)$$

where $\sigma_m(0)$ is the matrix stress at time $t = 0$. When the $\sigma_m \to 0$, the stress on the fibers increases to $\sigma_f = \sigma/(1 - f)$ such that the transient strain $\varepsilon_t$ is

$$\varepsilon_t = \sigma/E_f(1 - f). \qquad (35.4)$$

Similar results apply when the fibers creep, but the matrix is elastic.

When both the fiber and the matrix creep, the steady state develops in the composite following an initial transient (Fig. 69). The evolution of the matrix stress occurs according to[124]

$$\left(\frac{E}{fE_mE_f}\right)\dot{\sigma}_m = B_m\sigma_m^{n_m} - B_f\left[\frac{\sigma - (1-f)\sigma_m}{f}\right]^{n_f} \qquad (35.5)$$

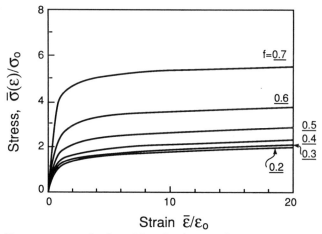

FIG. 70. Transverse strength of a unidirectional composite with a power law hardening matrix.

where $n_m$ and $n_f$ are the creep indices for the matrix and fibers, respectively. When a *steady state* is reached ($\dot{\sigma}_m = 0$) $\sigma_m$ and $\sigma_f$ are related by

$$[\sigma_m^{n_m}(B_m/B_f)]^{1/n_f} + \frac{(1-f)}{f}\sigma_m = \frac{\sigma}{f} \qquad (35.6)$$

and

$$\sigma_m(1-f) + \sigma_f f = \sigma. \qquad (35.7)$$

These formulas can be solved for specific $n_m$ and $n_f$ to obtain $\sigma_m$ and $\sigma_f$. With the stresses known the composite creep rate can be readily obtained.

*Transverse* creep with well-bonded fibers is usually *matrix dominated*. Solutions that have been generated for bonded rigid fibers thus have utility. All such solutions indicate that the creep attains steady state with a creep rate *lower* than that for the matrix alone (Fig. 68). Moreover, strengthening solutions derived for transverse deformation with a power law hardening matrix (Fig. 70) also apply to a power law creeping matrix in steady state.* The reduction in creep rate depends on the power law exponent for the matrix and the spatial arrangement of the fibers. For a composite with a square arrangement of fibers, and a matrix subject to

---

* With the strains becoming the strain rates.

diffusional creep ($n_m = 1$), since there is no creep in the fiber direction $(z)$[124]

$$\dot{\varepsilon}_{yy} = -\dot{\varepsilon}_{xx} = (\sigma_{yy} - \sigma_{xx})k_1(f) \tag{35.8}$$

with

$$k_1(f) = (3/4)[(1 - f)/(1 + 2f)]. \tag{35.9}$$

In essence, $k_1$ gives the *reduction* in creep rate upon incorporating the bonded fibers. For nonlinear matrices, the equivalent results have the form

$$\dot{\varepsilon}_{xx} = -\dot{\varepsilon}_{yy} = B_m(\sigma_{xx} - \sigma_{yy})^{n_m-1}(\sigma_{xx} - \sigma_{yy})k_n(f) \tag{35.10}$$

where $k_n$ is a function of the fiber volume fraction and spatial arrangement. For example, when $n_m = 5$ and a square fiber array is used,

$$k_n = 0.42[(1 - f)/(1 + f^2)]^5 \tag{35.11}$$

36. EFFECT OF FIBER FAILURES

When stresses are applied along the fiber axis in a system with a creeping matrix, the time-dependent stress elevation on the fibers may cause some fiber failures. Following fiber failure, *sliding* would initiate at the interface, accompanied by further creep in the matrix. The time constant for this process is much longer than that for the initial transient (described earlier) and can be analyzed as a separate creep problem.[124] While the process is complicated, several factors are important. If the stress on the fibers reaches their strength $S$, the composite will fail. Moreover, the relevant $S$ is probably that with a *small* $\tau$, associated with creep sliding of the interface. In this limit, composite failure is possible at all stresses above the "dry bundle" strength $S_b$ [Eq. (13.2)]. Conversely, the composite *cannot* rupture at stress below $S_b$, *unless the fibers are degraded by creep*. The dry bundle strength thus represents a "threshold." At stresses below $S_b$, creep must be transient.

At higher stresses, the fibers will fracture and may fragment. Then, steady state creep is possible (Fig. 68), proceeding in accordance with a creep law devised for a material with aligned rigid reinforcements of *finite aspect ratio*. This behavior is represented by the Mileiko

model.[126] The solution for a nonsliding interface is[124,127]

$$\dot{\varepsilon} = B_m \sigma^{n_m} (R/L_f)^{n_m+1} \mathscr{L}(n_m, f) \qquad (36.1)$$

where $L_f$ is the fragment length and

$$\mathscr{L}(n_m, f) = 2^{n_m+1} \sqrt{3} \left[ \frac{\sqrt{3}(2n_m + 1)}{2n_m f} \right]^{n_m} \frac{(1 - f)^{n_m-1)/2}}{(n_m - 1)}.$$

However, the fragment length *decreases* as the stress increases. This occurs in accordance with the scaling[28]

$$L_f/R \sim (S_c/\sigma)^m. \qquad (36.2)$$

Consequently, the steady state creep rate should occur[124] with a large power law exponent, $n_m + m + m n_m$. Such behavior has been reported in composites with discontinuous fibers.[128] The overall behavior is sketched on Fig. 71. In practice, because of the large stress exponent at stress above $S_b$, *adequate creep performance can only be ensured at stresses below $S_b$.*

## 37. INTERFACE DEBONDING

While there are no solutions known to the authors for transverse creep with debonding interfaces, the analogy (noted earlier) between power law deformation and steady state creep provides insight. Calculations of transverse deformation with and without interface bonding (Fig. 72) indicate a major strength degradation when debonding occurs.[129,130] Furthermore, the composite behavior approaches that for a body containing *cylindrical* holes. Creep results for porous bodies may thus provide rough estimates of the transverse creep strength when the interfaces debond.

## 38. MATRIX CRACKING

In some CMCs, the fibers creep more readily than the matrix. Such materials include SiC/SiC and SiC/C. In this case, fiber creep and matrix

[126] S. T. Mileiko, *J. Mater. Sci.* **5**, 254–261 (1970).
[127] A. Kelly and K. N. Street, *Proc. Royal Soc. London* **A328**, 283–293 (1972).
[128] T. G. Nieh, *Metallurgical Transactions A* **15A**, 139–146 (1984).
[129] S. Gunawadena, S. Jansson, and F. E. Leckie, *Acta Metall. Mater.*, in press.
[130] S. Jannson and F. A. Leckie, *J. Mechan. Phys. Solids* **40**, 593–612 (1992).

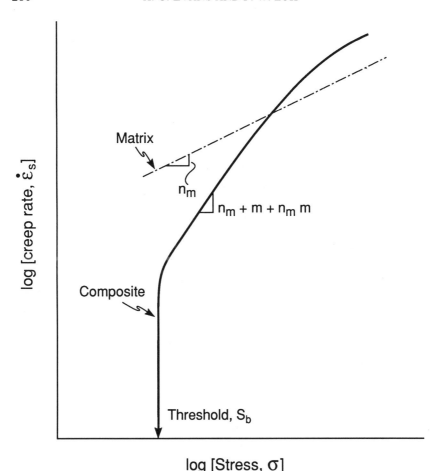

FIG. 71. A sketch indicating the longitudinal creep threshold and the behavior above the threshold.

cracking appear to proceed in a synergistic manner that accelerates the creep and causes premature creep rupture. The basic phenomenon is as follows. Creep in the fiber increases the stress on the matrix, as already described. Above a threshold, the stress on the matrix then exceeds $\sigma_\tau$ [Eq. (24.1)], causing multiple matrix cracks to form in the 90° plies. These cracks gradually extend into the 0° plies, because creep of the fibers relaxes the bridging tractions. As a result, the stress at these locations is borne entirely by the fibers, which creep without impediment, leading to rupture of the composite (Fig. 73). The creep analogy of the tunneling

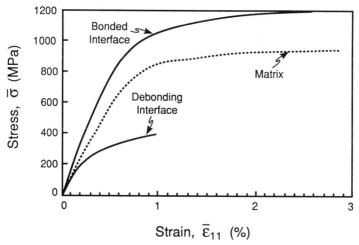

FIG. 72. Comparison of transverse behavior with and without interface debonding.

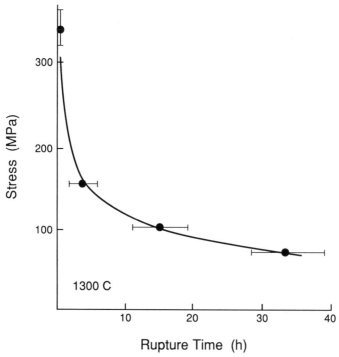

FIG. 73. Creep rupture data for a SiC/C composite, which is susceptible to fiber creep and matrix cracking.

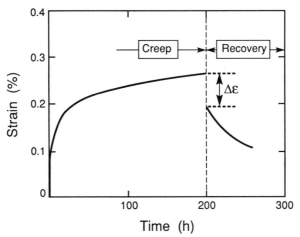

FIG. 74. Creep recovery effects in a SiC/Si₃N₄ with "elastic" fibers and a creeping matrix.[131]

stress, $\sigma_\tau$ [Eq. (24.2)], represents a *threshold stress*. At stresses above $\sigma_\tau$, matrix cracks eventually extend across the composite and the composite fails by fiber rupture. The rupture ductility of polycrystalline ceramic fibers is typically quite low, because of void formation along the grain boundaries. Consequently, matrix cracking often leads to creep rupture with *creep brittle* characteristics.

39. STRAIN RECOVERY

Since creep in composites redistributes stresses between matrix and fiber, strain recovery *must occur when the loads are removed*.[131] This behavior is well established for a system with one elastic constituent and one viscoplastic constituent, in accordance with standard Kelvin concepts. Notably, the elastic stretch in one constituent is gradually relaxed when the load is removed. The specifics depend, of course, on the nature of the viscoplasticity. A simple example illustrates the salient phenomena. A composite with elastic fibers and a creeping matrix, loaded along the fiber direction, has been crept until the stress in the matrix is essentially zero (Fig. 74). The load is then removed. The instantaneous elastic shrinkage $\Delta\varepsilon$ must satisfy

$$\Delta\varepsilon = \frac{\sigma_m}{E_m} = \frac{\Delta\sigma_f}{E_f}. \tag{39.1}$$

[131] J. W. Holmes, *J. Mater. Sci.* **26**, 1808–1814 (1991).

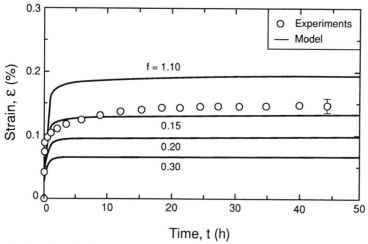

FIG. 75. Transient longitudinal creep in a TiAl matrix composite reinforced with sapphire fibers.[131]

The stresses after elastic unloading are thus

$$\sigma_m = -\frac{f\sigma E_m}{(1-f)E_L}$$

$$\sigma_f = \sigma E_m/E_L$$

(39.2)

Thereafter, holding at temperature causes $\sigma_m$ to relax according to Eq. (35.3), with $\sigma_m(0)$ given by Eq. (39.2).

### 40. EXPERIMENTAL RESULTS

Experimental data for a range of different composites are used to illustrate some of the features described in earlier sections and to anticipate trends. The longitudinal behaviors found when the fibers are elastic are addressed first. Results obtained on TiAl reinforced with sapphire fibers (Fig. 75) establish the existence of transient creep in the longitudinal orientation when the fibers are elastic and intact, but the matrix is subject to creep.[132] At higher loads, when some fibers fail, creep can continue and rupture may occur, as demonstrated by data obtained on a Ti matrix

[132]C. Weber, J. Y. Yang, J. P. A. Löfvander, C. G. Levi, and A. G. Evans, *Acta Metall. Mater.*, **41**, 2681–2690 (1993).

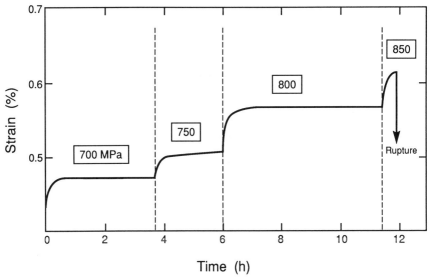

FIG. 76. Transient creep and rupture data obtained for a SiC/Ti composite subject to incremental loading.[133]

composite reinforced with SiC fibers (Fig. 76). Removal of the load after creep results in reverse deformation, as demonstrated for a SiC/Si$_3$N$_4$ composite (Fig. 50). Upon using a creep index applicable to monolithic Si$_3$N$_4$ ($n = 2$), the stress in the matrix relaxes in the manner

$$\sigma_m = \left[ \frac{fE_fE_mBt}{E_L} - \frac{(1-f)E_L}{f\sigma E_m} \right]^{-1} \qquad (40.1)$$

Note that B has units of (stress)$^{-2}$.

The inverse situation may also be important in some CMCs, wherein the fibers creep but the matrix is *elastic*.[132,133] Typical examples include SiC/SiC and SiC/C composites, which have SiC fibers with fine grain size (such as Nicalon). In these materials, matrix cracks are created upon loading above a threshold stress $\sigma_r$. When these cracks exist, fiber creep results in continuous deformation and creep rupture (Fig. 73). However, if the stress is below the threshold, creep will occur in a transient manner.[134]

When both the matrix and fibers creep, and there are no matrix cracks,

[133] F. Abbe, J. Vicens, and J. L. Chermant, *J. Mater. Sci. Lett.* **8**, 1026–1028 (1989).
[134] C. Weber, S. J. Connell, and F. W. Zok, ICCM-9, Madrid, to be published.

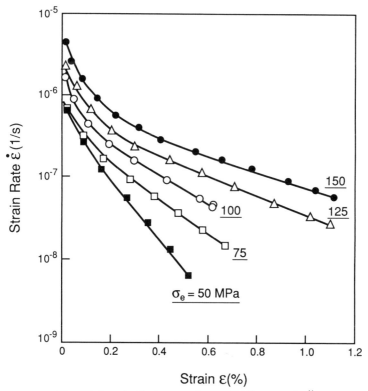

**Strain ε(%)**

FIG. 77. Longitudinal creep of a SiC/CAS composite.[11]

continued deformation of the composite proceeds in the longitudinal orientation.[11] Results obtained on CAS/SiC (Fig. 77) verify that creep continues. However, interpretation is complicated by microstructural changes occurring in the fibers, which lead to creep hardening. The deformation is thus entirely primary in nature. These results identify microstructural stability as an important fiber selection criterion.

## X. Conclusions

Reasonable progress has been made in understanding inelastic strain mechanisms, although the continued development of models and experimental validation is necessary. It is now possible to appreciate how stress redistribution occurs and to characterize the notch sensitivity. The analysis of degradation mechanism is much less mature.

Several challenges and opportunities arise. With regard to short-duration performance, it is necessary to develop simple constitutive laws that can be used with finite element codes in order to calculate stresses around attachments, holes, etc. Mechanism-based models of the inelastic strain are preferred for this purpose. However, our basic understanding is insufficient in terms of the inelastic strains that occur upon *shear loading* and their dependence on constituent properties. Basic inelastic strain models with matrix cracks inclined to the fibers are needed to address this deficiency.

Degradation mechanisms that operate upon cyclic loading in the presence of matrix cracks require concerted study. Interface changes and fiber degradation are both possible. Moreover, there may be detrimental synergistic interaction with the environment. The models developed for MMCs indicate that the retention of fiber strength upon cyclic loading is particularly important, because this strength governs the fatigue threshold. Mechanism and models that predict fiber strength degradation are critically important.

SOLID STATE PHYSICS, VOL. 47

# Defects at Surfaces and Interfaces

R. C. POND

*Department of Materials Science and Engineering, University of Liverpool,*
*Liverpool, United Kingdom*

J. P. HIRTH

*Department of Mechanical and Materials Engineering, Washington State University,*
*Pullman, Washington*

## I. Introduction

Interfaces profoundly affect the mechanical, electrical, and chemical properties of materials and, consequently, are the subject of intensive theoretical and experimental investigation. Microscopic observations of metallic, ceramic, semiconducting, superconducting, and composite materials have confirmed that dislocations are ubiquitous features in interfaces, occurring both as isolated discrete defects and in organized arrays. Moreover, they are known to be involved in a wide variety of solid state processes; for example, they are the agents by which misfit is accommodated in epitaxial films and precipitates, and the mechanisms of twinning, phase transformation, and high-temperature deformation involve the motion of interfacial dislocations. In addition, they can be electrically active, enhancing electron-hole recombination for example, and may also be instrumental in chemical processes such as the growth of oxides. Concurrent with these studies of interfacial defects, various microscopic techniques have been used to investigate other defects inside the bulk of single crystals and on their surfaces. Observations of the interactions between bulk, surface, and interfacial defects imply that the topological properties of these features can be expressed in a unified framework. Thus, the broad objective of this chapter is to set out the underlying principles of such a framework, and to apply the methods developed to interfacial defects in particular. Naturally, this will draw on much established work in this field, and, should link aspects of defect theory that have evolved independently up to now.

Before describing the objective and structure of this chapter in greater detail, we make a few general remarks. First, dislocations and other defects are not material objects, but are *descriptions* of structure expressed with respect to some reference structure. Therefore, modeling an interfacial structure in terms of dislocations is only justified if the resulting description is useful for interpreting experimental observations. In the present work we are concerned with the topological aspects of defects; these are intrinsic geometrical properties, such as the Burgers vectors of dislocations, that are invariant with the direction of line defects (or with the surface orientation in the case of extended defects) and are subject to conservation rules in contiguous material. Such properties form an essential foundation for a more comprehensive theory that would include, for example, the nature of elastic displacement fields and the atomic and electronic core structures of defects. In crystalline materials, defects are discontinuities in the underlying order, and their topological properties are constrained to particular forms either by virtue of the *symmetry* or *structure* of the host object. The properties of the former type of defects

can be deduced on the basis of symmetry arguments, and this is the main theme of our work. We refer to defects of the latter type as being "imperfect"; when the topological properties of such defects are known, they can be incorporated into the general framework presented here, but cannot be predicted in advance on the basis of symmetry theory alone.

Section II is an account of the crystallographic tools and methodology used in this work. It begins with a review of some important (infinite) crystal structures and their space groups, and then outlines the assignment of space groups to (1) crystals exhibiting a planar surface and (2) bicrystals. This provides the crystallographic grounding of our work, and the capability to define reference states for the subsequent characterization of isolated bulk, surface, and interfacial defects.

Defect characterisation was pioneered by Frank[1] who investigated crystal dislocations. He constructed closed circuits around defects and subsequently mapped these circuits into the (reference) crystal lattice; the closure failure of a mapped circuit is the Burgers vector of the defect. Circuit mapping methods have been generalized since this early work and are now used to characterize a broad range of types of solid state defects, as is expressed in homotopy theory.[2] However, for structural defects in crystalline matter, which are the subject of interest here, the only extension to Frank's original work that we need to take into account for a generalized theory is that the reference space (or order parameter space in homotopy theory) is the space group of the reference object rather than merely its lattice. In this method, defects are characterized by symmetry operations in this reference space. We refer to such defects as belonging to the class of "manifest" symmetry, since the symmetry operation in question is manifested by the reference object.

Defects can also arise in dissymmetrized objects, i.e., where the symmetry actually exhibited is lower than some precursor reference structure; defects of this type are said to be in the class of "broken" symmetry. A crystal exhibiting symmetry lower than that of the lattice on which it is based is a simple example of a dissymmetrized object, and domain boundaries are the defects that can arise as a consequence. Surfaces and interfaces are expected to be hosts to defects in this class since, in general, the creation of surface and interfacial structures causes the suppression of some symmetry operations exhibited by the component crystals. The central difference between defects in the manifest and broken symmetry classes is that the latter separate structures that are crystallo-

[1]F. C. Frank, *Phil Mag.* **42**, 809 (1951).
[2]N. D. Mermin, *Rev. Mod. Phys.* **51**, 591 (1979).

graphically equivalent (and therefore energetically degenerate), rather than identical.

The number of variant forms of a dissymmetrized object, and the (broken) symmetry operations that interrelate these, can be established by means of space group decomposition, which is the mathematical expression of the principle of symmetry compensation.[3] Furthermore, by developing the circuit mapping method mentioned earlier, one can show that defects in this class are actually characterized by the broken symmetry operations, which interrelate the two variant structures separated by a defect. Moreover, one finds that symmetry operations characterizing defects in the manifest class can also be obtained using group decomposition arguments, and that they correspond to a special (trivial) case of the more general category of broken symmetry defects. Thus, we have an integrated framework wherein defects in both the manifest and broken symmetry classes can be considered. The group decomposition method requires only the space group of the dissymmetrized and reference structures to be known, i.e., it does not require knowledge of the defect structure that would physically separate variant structures should they coexist in a material specimen. Therefore, it can be used to predict the character of isolated defects that are admissible in the reference object, whether it is a single crystal, a crystal surface, or an interface. We refer to this method of defect characterization by advance prediction as being *a priori*. A visualization of the defect corresponding to a characterizing operation determined in this way can be obtained from the procedure described by Volterra.[4] Volterra originally described the creation of dislocations and disclinations by means of rigid body operations applied to the opposite faces of a cut, but his procedure can be extended to include other line and extended defects.

Circuit mapping is used in practice to characterize isolated defect structures that have already been established by some means, and hence is referred to here as being an *a posteriori* method. It can be carried out graphically or, as is formulated here for the first time, mathematically. Clearly, the *a priori* and *a posteriori* methods of characterizing a given defect must lead to the same result. Being able to express both the *a priori* and circuit mapping methods mathematically enables us to demonstrate readily the equivalence of the two approaches. Circuit mapping by graphical means has its own advantages, providing, for example, a powerful visualization of defect character. Circuit mapping is also invaluable in

[3] A. V. Shubnikov and V. A. Koptsik, *Symmetry in Science and Art*, Plenum Press, New York (1977).

[4] V. Volterra, *Ann. Sci. Ec. Norm. Sup. Paris* **24**, 401 (1907).

the analysis of defect interactions, enabling, for example, a generalization of Frank's node rule[5] for dislocation interactions.

In the analysis of an isolated defect in the bulk of a crystal or on a surface, the reference space into which a circuit is mapped is the space group of the crystal concerned. Where interfaces are concerned, reference spaces are associated with both the component crystals. Although he did not use the present terminology, Bollmann,[6,7] in his theory of interfacial structure, emphasized the significance of considering both crystals. Here, we develop his ideas, constructing a circuit around an interfacial defect and subsequently mapping each of the two distinct crystal segments of this circuit into their corresponding reference spaces.

The topological properties of defects in single crystals are discussed in Section III. Only line defects arise in the class of manifest symmetry, namely, dislocations, disclinations, and dispirations. Defects in the broken symmetry class are all extended, and domain boundaries in sphalerite and translation (antiphase) domains in ordered alloys are discussed as examples. We analyze these defects by both the *a priori* and *a posteriori* methods.

Surface discontinuities are considered in Section IV. All defects in this category are in the class of broken symmetry, and it is convenient to subdivide these into two groups: defects on (1) unrelaxed and (2) reconstructed surfaces. In the former subgroup, crystal symmetry is suppressed by virtue of creating a surface from a previously infinite single crystal, and the resulting discontinuities are steps, demisteps, and facet junctions. When surface reconstruction occurs, further defect types known as *domain lines* arise. The operations characterizing all of these types of defects can be obtained by means of the *a priori* method. Circuits cannot be constructed around a surface feature in the conventional way; however, a circuit confined to the surface that crosses the feature twice can be. As an illustration of the application of these *a priori* and *a posteriori* methods, the defect structure of (001) surfaces of Si is discussed, and the predictions shown to be consistent with experimental observations.

Isolated interfacial defects are discussed in Section V. Dislocations and disclinations can arise in the class of manifest symmetry, but because these are not distinct from those already described in Section III, they are not considered in further detail. A broad range of defect types can arise in the broken symmetry class, and it is convenient to subdivide

[5]W. T. Read, *Dislocations in Crystals*, McGraw-Hill, New York (1953).

[6]W. Bollmann, *Crystal Defects and Crystalline Interfaces*, Springer, Berlin (1970).

[7]W. Bollmann, *Crystal Lattices, Interfaces, Matrices*, Published privately, Geneva (1982).

these into surface-like features (steps, demisteps, and facet junctions), and bulk-like defects (dislocations, disclinations, and dispirations). With the *a priori* approach, one obtains a mathematical expression for the operations characterizing admissible defects in any interface. These operations are shown to be equal to a sequence of two symmetry operations, one belonging to each of the space groups of the adjacent crystals. This expression is completely general, incorporating not only bulk-like defects, but also surface-like ones and crystal defects as special cases. The two component crystal operations in the expression are expressed in the coordinate frame of one of the adjacent crystals, and hence the relative orientation and position of the crystals also appear in the expression. For a pair of crystals with given space groups, variations of the relative orientation and position can break symmetry, and, the greater the extent of such symmetry breaking, the broader the range of admissible defects in the corresponding interface. Interfacial dislocations can arise through four distinct modes of symmetry breaking; an example of each type is discussed in some detail using the *a priori* and *a posteriori* (both graphical and mathematical) methods. Interfacial disclinations and dispirations are not treated in depth here.

In Section VI arrays of interfacial defects are considered. This topic has been covered extensively in earlier works. Hence, the principal aim of this section is to express previous formulations in the present notation and to explore any implications arising from the results obtained in earlier sections. The historical development of this subject began with the work of Frank,[8] who used graphical circuit mapping arguments to establish the total Burgers vector content of grain boundaries. This was later generalized by Bilby,[9] and an expression, known as the Frank-Bilby equation, was derived that relates the total Burgers vector intersected by a probe vector lying in the interface to the correspondence between the two crystal lattices expressed as an affine transformation. This equation can be used to predict the dislocation content of any general interface, and the total Burgers vector is expressed in units of the translation vectors of the reference lattice. We show that the Frank-Bilby equation can be derived from the mathematical formulation of circuit mapping introduced earlier.

In the original derivation of the Frank-Bilby equation, a single reference lattice was used. This can be chosen arbitrarily, but Christian[10] has shown that the use of one of the crystal lattices for this purpose leads to

---

[8] F. C. Frank, in *Symposium on the Plastic Deformation of Crystalline Solids,* p. 150, The Physical Society, London (1950).

[9] B. A. Bilby, *Prog. Solid Mech.* **1,** 329 (1960).

[10] J. W. Christian, *Met. Trans. A* **13A,** 509 (1982).

a simpler formulation of the equation. Bollmann[6] obtained an equivalent formulation in the development of his O-lattice theory, but also emphasized the geometrical aspects of the two crystals when interpenetration is involved. Reexpressing and extending this important idea in the present terminology, we can choose a bicrystal configuration as the reference structure rather than a single crystal, and the two crystal space groups, appropriately disposed, become the reference spaces. Circuit mapping can now be carried out in these two spaces as explained in Section V. Any supplement to the transformation relating the adjacent crystals can now be modeled as being caused by an array of interfacial defects superimposed on the reference bicrystal. Moreover, the density of such defects can be expressed by an equation analogous to the Frank-Bilby equation, except that the supplementary transformation is now used, and the total Burgers vector intersected by the probe vector is expressed in terms of interfacial defects. This equation was first presented by Bollmann,[6] and we show how it can be obtained with the present circuit mapping method.

   Modeling interfacial structures in terms of dislocation arrays is useful when the resulting defects are relatively widely spaced. To illustrate the application of the present method, we briefly consider epitaxial growth on a planar but misfitting substrate. Subsequently, we consider growth on a vicinal substrate, and investigate the consequences of accommodating the additional array of substrate surface features. This example illustrates the value of a generalized framework in which surface features, crystal dislocations, and interfacial defects can be discussed in a unified way.

## II. Crystallographic Tools and Methodology

This section introduces the crystallographic tools and methodology to be employed in our topological treatment of defects. As outlined in the introduction, defects are discontinuities in the otherwise regular order of crystalline materials, and their character is determined either by the symmetry actually manifested by the host object, or by broken symmetry when the host exhibits lower symmetry than some precursor structure. The order exhibited by a crystalline material is concisely expressed by assigning a space group; thus, it is necessary to review briefly space groups for single crystals and bicrystals. However, it is important in the present context to distinguish between symmetry and structure, and hence we begin by emphasizing this distinction.

   Following this overview of structure and symmetry, *a priori* and *a posteriori* methods of defect characterization are introduced. In the case

of manifest symmetry type defects, the necessary tools are already established and widely used. The Volterra procedure provides a visualization of the formation of admissible defects in a crystalline medium (and, hence, the means of *a priori* prediction), and circuit mapping is the *a posteriori* technique. These two methods are also applicable to defects in the class of broken symmetry, but certain generalizations are needed and mathematical formulation is then particularly advantageous. To extend the *a priori* method, one must be able to identify the totality of broken symmetry operations and to elucidate their role interrelating the reference and dissymmetrized structures. Group decomposition is the appropriate tool in this context, and it shows, for example, that operations characterizing defects in the manifest class are a special instance of those in the more general class of broken operations. Regarding the extension of circuit mapping, which currently is invariably applied graphically, significant advantages also follow from developing mathematical formulation. This topic is introduced in this section, but is applied to examples of surface and interfacial defects in the appropriate later sections.

1. THE STRUCTURE OF CRYSTALLINE OBJECTS

Consider first an infinite single crystal; its structure can be conveniently specified in terms of its lattice and atomic basis. By definition, a *lattice* is an array of points each with identical surroundings (i.e., a purely geometrical concept). The atomic basis is the group of atoms that is located at each lattice site. In simple crystals this is a single atom, but the basis may be considerably more complicated in other instances. In the general case, let the $u$ atoms in the basis be located at the endpoints of the vectors $r_i$ where $i$ goes from 1 to $u$. The vectors $r_i$ are usually defined with respect to a coordinate frame associated with the lattice, and the origin is chosen to be a lattice point.

One can create semi-infinite crystals from infinite ones by selecting a surface plane with a particular orientation, specified by its outward pointing unit normal $\mathbf{n}$, and discarding all material beyond this plane. If the chosen plane is rational, it will exhibit periodicity. However, for cases where $u$ is greater than 1, the crystal can be terminated at a multiplicity of locations depending on which atoms in the basis form the outermost layer. This multiplicity is equal to $u^* = u - v$, where $v$ is the number of atom pairs in the crystal's basis parallel to the surface [i.e., pairs for which $\mathbf{n} \cdot (\mathbf{r}_i - \mathbf{r}_j + \mathbf{t}_k) = 0$, $\mathbf{t}_k$ being some translation vector]. The atoms near real surfaces may relax away from their crystal sites. This process is referred to as *reconstruction* when the symmetry of the semi-infinite crystal is thereby modified.

A bicrystal can be imagined to be created by bonding two semi-infinite crystals that have appropriately prepared surfaces. The number of ways in which this can be done is equal to the product of the values of $u^*$ for the two crystal surfaces concerned. In addition, further relaxations, such as a rigid body displacement of one crystal with respect to the other, as well as local atomic relaxations and reconstructions can occur, as is discussed in later sections.

## 2. THE SYMMETRY OF INFINITE CRYSTALS

A prodigious number of different crystal structures exists, but the symmetries exhibited by them fall into a relatively small number of distinctive classes, or space groups. We assume here that the reader is already reasonably familiar with the notions of symmetry operations and groups. Symmetry operators are represented by means of the notation of the International Tables for Crystallography (ed. Hahn et al.);[11] an operation $\mathfrak{W}$ is designated in matrix form as $(\mathbf{W}, \mathbf{w})$, where $\mathbf{W}$ is the orthogonal part, and $\mathbf{w}$ corresponds to any associated displacement. For example, a translation operation is written $(\mathbf{I}, \mathbf{t})$, where $\mathbf{I}$ represents the identity matrix and $\mathbf{t}$ is the translation. Simple rotations and reflections are written as $(\mathbf{R}, \mathbf{0})$ and $(\mathbf{M}, \mathbf{0})$ respectively. (Translations and rotations are referred to as proper operations; reflections and inversions involve lateral and total inversions respectively, and are known as improper operations. For an exposition of the manipulation of symmetry operations using matrix notation, the reader is referred to the International Tables.)[11] Individual operations combine into the 230 admissible space groups; it is convenient to subdivide these into symmorphic and nonsymmorphic groups. The latter contain screw-rotation and/or mirror-glide planes in their generating sets, whereas the former do not; this is an important distinction in defect theory. Another important category is that of nonholosymmetric groups, i.e. those corresponding to crystals with structures that exhibit lower symmetry than that of the lattices on which they are based. Such groups may be symmorphic or nonsymmorphic. Some simple illustrations of distinctive types of groups for crystal structures of interest in the present work are described below.

a. *Symmorphic Groups*

The simple cubic structure is depicted in Fig. 1(a); its lattice is primitive cubic and the basis is a single atom located at $\mathbf{r}_1 = [000]$, and the structure exhibits the symmorphic space group Pm$\bar{3}$m. This space group combines

[11] T. Hahn, ed., *International Tables for Crystallography*, Reidel, Dordrecht (1983).

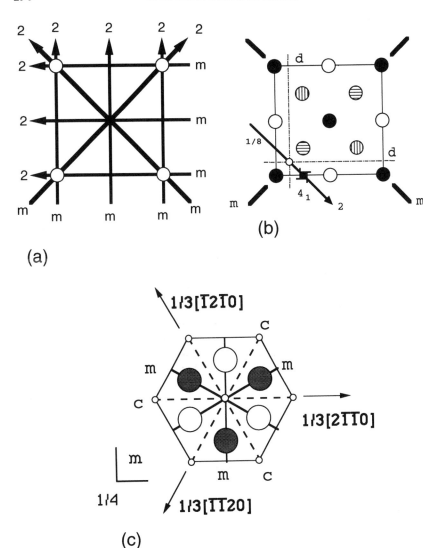

FIG. 1. (a) Projection along [001] of the unit cell of a primitive cubic crystal showing some of the symmetry operations present. (b) Corresponding diagram for a diamond structure crystal; the shading of the symbols represents atomic heights in the diamond structure and, additionally, hatched symbols represent the second atomic species in sphalerite. (c) The [0001] projection of an hcp metal.

TABLE I. SYMMETRY OPERATIONS (EXCLUDING TRANSLATIONS) IN CUBIC GROUPS

| Pm3̄m | Fd3̄m | F4̄3m | NUMBER OF OPERATIONS | ORIENTATION |
|---|---|---|---|---|
| 1 | 1 | 1 | 1 | — |
| 4̄⁺ | 4̄⁺ | 4̄⁺ | 3 | ⟨100⟩ |
| 4̄⁻ | 4̄⁻ | 4̄⁻ | 3 | ⟨100⟩ |
| 2 | 2 | 2 | 3 | ⟨100⟩ |
| m | m | m | 6 | {110} |
| 3⁺ | 3⁺ | 3⁺ | 4 | ⟨111⟩ |
| 3⁻ | 3⁻ | 3⁻ | 4 | ⟨111⟩ |
| 1̄ | 1̄ | — | 1 | — |
| 4⁺ | 4₁⁺ | — | 3 | ⟨100⟩ |
| 4⁻ | 4₁⁻ | — | 3 | ⟨100⟩ |
| 2 | 2 | — | 6 | ⟨110⟩ |
| m | d | — | 3 | {100} |
| 3̄⁺ | 3̄⁺ | — | 4 | ⟨111⟩ |
| 3̄⁻ | 3̄⁻ | — | 4 | ⟨111⟩ |

Entries in the lower half of the table for Fd3̄m have matrices of the form $(\mathbf{W}, \mathbf{w})$ with $\mathbf{w} = \frac{1}{4}[111]$ when the origin is taken to be an atomic site; $\mathbf{w} = \mathbf{0}$ for all other entries.

the infinity of translation operations defining the cubic lattice with 48-point symmetry operations, all of which are listed in Table I and some of which are illustrated in the Figure 1(a). All 48-point operations intersect at certain points and this is the characteristic property of symmorphic groups.

b. *Nonsymmorphic Groups*

An example of a nonsymmorphic symmetry group is Fd3̄m, which is exhibited by the diamond structure, as depicted in Fig. 1(b). In this structure the lattice is face-centered cubic (fcc) and the basis comprises two atoms ($\mathbf{r}_1 = [000]$ and $\mathbf{r}_2 = [1/4, 1/4, 1/4]$). The orthogonal components of the 48 symmetry operations in this group that are listed in Table I are the same as for the previous case; however, some of these operations are now nonsymmorphic. The 24 operations in the point group 4̄3m, which is a subgroup of the present group, intersect at each atomic position, and are therefore represented by matrices of the form $(\mathbf{W}, \mathbf{0})$. Each of the remaining 24 operations has a nonzero displacement $\mathbf{w}$ due either to the intrinsic glide associated with the operation or its location or both (see Table I). If the two atoms in the basis are designated α [open and filled symbols in Fig. 1(b)] and β [hatched symbols in Fig. 1(b)], the

TABLE II. SYMMETRY OPERATIONS (EXCLUDING TRANSLATIONS) IN HEXAGONAL SPACE GROUPS

| $P6_3/mmc$ | $P6_3mc$ | NO. OF OPERATIONS | ORIENTATION |
|---|---|---|---|
| 1 | 1 | 1 | — |
| $\bar{1}$ | — | 1 | — |
| m | m | 3 | $\{2\bar{1}\bar{1}0\}$ |
| 2 | — | 3 | $\langle2\bar{1}\bar{1}0\rangle$ |
| $3^+$ | $3^+$ | 1 | [0001] |
| $3^-$ | $3^-$ | 1 | [0001] |
| $\bar{3}^+$ | — | 1 | [0001] |
| $\bar{3}^-$ | — | 1 | [0001] |
| c | c | 3 | $\{10\bar{1}0\}$ |
| m | — | 1 | (0001) |
| 2 | — | 3 | $\langle10\bar{1}0\rangle$ |
| $2_1$ | $2_1$ | 1 | [0001] |
| $6_3^+$ | $6_3^+$ | 1 | [0001] |
| $6_3^-$ | $6_3^-$ | 1 | [0001] |
| $\bar{6}^+$ | — | 1 | [0001] |
| $\bar{6}^-$ | — | 1 | [0001] |

Entries in the lower half of the table have matrices of the form $(W, w)$ with $w = \frac{1}{2}[0001]$. The origin is taken to be a center of symmetry ($\bar{3}m$) for the group $P6_3/mmc$.

former set of 24 operations relates α atoms to other α atoms and β to β, whereas the latter interrelate α and β.

The space group of hcp metals is $P6_3/mmc$, and the principal symmetry elements (see Table II) are depicted in Fig. 1(c). This shows the projection of the atomic structure viewed along [0001]; the . . . . ABABAB. . . . stacking sequence of the atoms is represented by circular symbols with different shading. A center of symmetry (small open circle) is a convenient choice for lattice points in this structure; with respect to this origin, the two atoms in the basis are located at $r_1 = 1/12[\bar{4}043]$ and $r_2 = 1/12[40\bar{4}\bar{3}]$, and are designated A and B. In Fig. 1(c) mirror planes parallel to $\{11\bar{2}0\}$, and c-mirror-glide planes parallel to $\{1\bar{1}00\}$ have been indicated. Both of these elements pass through the origin. The former, however, relate A type atoms to other A atoms, whereas the latter relate A type to B. Similarly, the rotation operations, $3^+$ and $3^-$, and the screw-rotation operations, $6_3^+$ and $6_3^-$, parallel to [0001], interrelate atoms of the same and different types, respectively. One more symmetry element in the present space group that we wish to draw attention to is the mirror plane parallel to (0001). This element relates A atoms to A type, and B type to B, and we note that it does not pass through the chosen origin, but is located at heights $+1/4$ and $-1/4$.

## c. Nonholosymmetric Groups

Each of the three groups just outlined is holosymmetric. An example of a nonholosymmetric structure is sphalerite. This structure resembles diamond except that the two atoms in the basis are different species [note that fig 1(b) can also represent this structure if distinct symbols correspond to $\alpha$ and $\beta$ atoms]. As a consequence, the 24 operations in the diamond space group with $\mathbf{w} \neq \mathbf{0}$ are suppressed; the remaining operations constitute the symmorphic group $F\bar{4}3m$ (see Table I). Another example of a nonholosymmetric structure is the wurtzite structure. This is closely related to that of hcp metals except that the four atoms in the basis of the material consist of two pairs of atoms of different species, with the consequence that the mirror plane parallel to (0001), for example, is suppressed; the space group of the material is $P6_3mc$, as indicated in Table II.

### 3. The Symmetry of Semi-Infinite Crystals

An unrelaxed crystal surface can be imagined to be created in the manner outlined in Section 1. In general, this procedure suppresses some of the symmetry initially present in the infinite crystal, and it is helpful to be able to express concisely the residual symmetry by the assignment of an appropriate space group (which may have zero-, one-, or two-dimensional translation symmetry). The initial infinite crystal exhibits the space group $\Phi$, but when a surface is introduced, only those operations that leave the semi-infinite object (including the unique surface plane) invariant survive. If the $i$'th operation in the group $\Phi$ is designated $\mathfrak{W}_i$, the operations in the space group of the semi-infinite crystal, $\Phi(s)$, are those for which the following conditions are satisfied:

$$\mathbf{W}_i\mathbf{n} = \mathbf{n}, \qquad (3.1)$$

$$\mathbf{n} \cdot (\mathbf{w}_i + \mathbf{t}_j) = 0. \qquad (3.2)$$

Equation (3.1) shows that rotation axes and mirror planes must be parallel to $\mathbf{n}$, and that roto-inversion axes are not admissible. Equation (3.2) shows that pure translation operations must be perpendicular to $\mathbf{n}$, screw-rotation axes are not admissible, and the total translation associated with a mirror glide plane must be perpendicular to $\mathbf{n}$.

The permissible combinations of the preceding operations form the space groups $\Phi(s)$, and have been tabulated by, for example, Pond and

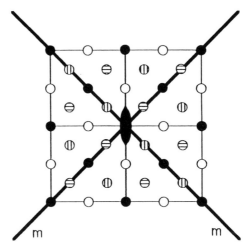

FIG. 2. Schematic plan view of a segment of a semi-infinite Si crystal with an unrelaxed (001) surface, showing the symmetry operations in the layer space group p2mm.

Casey.[12] As an illustration of the assignment of a space group to an unrelaxed semi-infinite crystal, we consider the (001) surface of Si, depicted schematically in Fig. 2. The two shortest independent translation operations satisfying the conditions required by expression (3.2) are $t_1$ = 1/2[110], and $t_2$ = 1/2[1$\bar{1}$0]; of the 48 operations in Table I, only the operations 1, $2_{[001]}$, $m_{(110)}$, and $m_{(1\bar{1}0)}$ satisfy expression (3.1). These operations constitute the layer group p2mm, where the lowercase p implies a primitive two-dimensional lattice. For the case of Si, $u$ is equal to 2 and, for (001) surfaces, $u^*$ is also equal to 2. Therefore, the crystal can be terminated in two different ways, and these both exhibit the same space group as is discussed further in Section III.

## 4. THE SYMMETRY OF BICRYSTALS

The symmetry groups discussed express concisely the order present in infinite and semi-infinite perfect crystals, and they also provide the basis necessary for the characterization of defects on crystal surfaces and in their interiors. To discuss interfacial defects, we need to review briefly the symmetry of bicrystals. First we distinguish the component crystals by designating one black ($\mu$) and the other white ($\lambda$); the $j$'th operation

[12]R. C. Pond and S. M. Casey, in *Equilibrium Structure and Properties of Surfaces and Interfaces* (A. Gonis and G. M. Stocks, eds.), Plenum Press, New York (1993).

in the space group of the white crystal is then written $\mathfrak{W}(\lambda)_j = [\mathbf{W}(\lambda)_j,$ $\mathbf{w}(\lambda)_j]$. The coordinate frames of the two crystals are related by the transformation $\mathfrak{P} = (\mathbf{P}, \mathbf{p})$, where $\mathbf{P}$ will generally involve a rotation and deformation, and $\mathbf{p}$ is defined as the displacement of the black origin away from a position of coincidence with the white.

When the black and white crystal lattices are imagined to interpenetrate, the resulting configuration is known as a *dichromatic pattern*. When the two crystal structures (formally lattice complexes) are imagined to interpenetrate, the resulting configuration is known as the *dichromatic complex*, and its symmetry is a key factor governing the character of defects that can arise in interfaces between the two crystals. Two types of symmetry operation arise; first, black and white crystal symmetry operations of the same form may coincide so that the dichromatic complex as a whole exhibits this symmetry. One can readily find such coincident operations, designated $\mathfrak{W}(c)$, by reexpressing black operations in the white coordinate frame and comparing the result with the set of white operations. In a mathematical description, the $k$'th coincident operation is identical to the $j$'th white and the transformed $i$'th black operation:

$$\mathfrak{W}(c)_k = \mathfrak{W}(\lambda)_j = \mathfrak{P}\mathfrak{W}(\mu)_i \mathfrak{P}^{-1}. \tag{4.1}$$

Two examples of dichromatic complexes are illustrated in Figs. 3(a) and 3(b); the first corresponds to two simple cubic structures relatively rotated by 53.1° about their coincident [001] axis, and the second is formed by two diamond crystals disposed in the same way. For the former, the solutions to Eq. (4.1) include translation vectors defining a tetragonal coincidence-site-lattice, and the point symmetry operations in the group 4/m as listed in Table III. In the second case, the situation is similar except that the coincidence-site-lattice is now body centered, and some of the coincident point operations are nonsymmorphic (see Table III); for example, there is a fourfold screw axis parallel to [001]. Although the illustrations in Fig. 3 are pertinent to grain boundaries, coincident operations can also, of course, arise in the case of interphase interfaces. Also, in more general cases, dichromatic complexes may exhibit periodicity in less than three dimensions.

A second type of symmetry operation arises for dichromatic complexes pertaining to grain boundaries and causes the interchange of black and white crystals. In this circumstance, the transformation $\mathfrak{P}$, or equivalent formulations of it which are given by $\mathfrak{P}\mathfrak{W}(\lambda)_l$, have the form of symmetry operations. These are referred to as *antisymmetry operations* and are distinguished from coincident operations by primed symbols. In Fig. 3(a), antimirror planes arise parallel to side and diagonal faces of the unit cell.

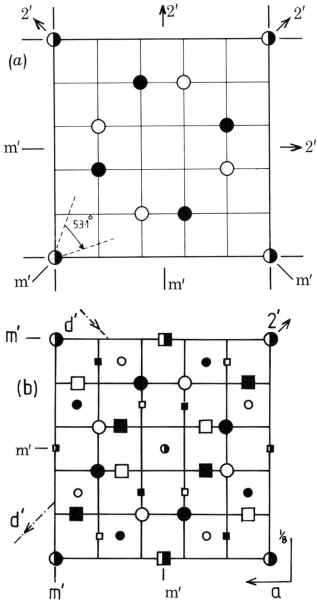

FIG. 3. Projection along [001] of dichromatic complexes: (a) Black and white primitive cubic crystals relatively rotated by 53.1° about [001] and (b) the corresponding diagram for diamond crystals.

TABLE III. THE SYMMETRY OF [001]/53.1° DICHROMATIC
COMPLEXES FOR SIMPLE CUBIC, DIAMOND,
AND SPHALERITE CRYSTALS

| SIMPLE CUBIC | DIAMOND | SPHALERITE |
|---|---|---|
| P4/mmm | I$4_1$/am'd' | I$\bar{4}$2'm' |
| [210] | ½[310] | ½[310] |
| [1$\bar{2}$0] | ½[1$\bar{3}$0] | ½[1$\bar{3}$0] |
| [001] | ½[2$\bar{1}$1] | ½[2$\bar{1}$1] |
| 1 | 1 | 1 |
| $4^+$ | $4_1^+$ | — |
| $4^-$ | $4_1^-$ | — |
| $2_{[001]}$ | $2_{[001]}$ | $2_{[001]}$ |
| $\bar{4}^+$ | $\bar{4}^+$ | $\bar{4}^+$ |
| $\bar{4}^-$ | $\bar{4}^-$ | $\bar{4}^-$ |
| $\bar{1}$ | $\bar{1}$ | — |
| $m_{(001)}$ | $a_{(001)}$ | — |
| $m'_{(210)}$ | $m'_{(310)}$ | $m'_{(310)}$ |
| $m'_{(1\bar{2}0)}$ | $m'_{(1\bar{3}0)}$ | $m'_{(1\bar{3}0)}$ |
| $m'_{(3\bar{1}0)}$ | $d'_{(2\bar{1}0)}$ | — |
| $m'_{(130)}$ | $d'_{(120)}$ | — |
| $2'_{[210]}$ | $2'_{[310]}$ | — |
| $2'_{[1\bar{2}0]}$ | $2'_{[1\bar{3}0]}$ | — |
| $2'_{[3\bar{1}0]}$ | $2'_{[120]}$ | $2'_{[120]}$ |
| $2'_{[130]}$ | $2'_{[2\bar{1}0]}$ | $2'_{[2\bar{1}0]}$ |

Hence, the colored space group of the complex is P4/mm'm' (see Table III for details). The corresponding space group for Fig. 3(b) is I$4_1$/am'd', as summarized in Table III. (A full account of dichromatic symmetry is presented elsewhere.)[13,14] For completeness, we note that Fig. 3(b) can also represent the complex for two sphalerite crystals if the two symbols denoting heights along [001] are taken to signify different atomic species; the space group of the complex is then I$\bar{4}$2'm', which is symmorphic and nonholosymmetric (see Table III).

The creation of a bicrystal from a dichromatic complex can be imagined by choosing the orientation and location of the interface plane and discarding white atoms on one side and black on the other. The unit normal to the interface is designated **n**, and is taken to point into the white crystal. The subset of symmetry operations present in the dichromatic complex that also leave the bicrystal (including the unique interface

[13]R. C. Pond and D. S. Vlachavas, *Proc. R. Soc. London* **386A**, 95 (1983).
[14]R. C. Pond, *Inst. Phys. Conf. Series No. 67*, p. 59, Institute of Physics, London (1983).

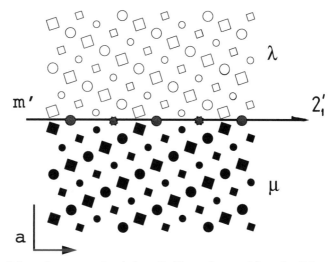

FIG. 4. Schematic cross-sectional view of a bicrystal created from the dichromatic complex shown in Fig. 3(b). The interfacial orientation is (310), and the layer space group of the bicrysal is p2₁'am'.

plane) invariant can readily be identified. Since these may include both coincident and antisymmetry operations, a pair of equations analogous to Eqs. (3.1) and (3.2) can be written, as explained in detail elsewhere.[12] The operations thus established constitute a bicrystal space group $\Phi(b)$ (see Ref. 12 for a tabulation of all possible groups). An example, based on the complex in Fig. 3, is depicted in Fig. 4. However, the symmetry of real bicrystals may be further modified by relocation of the interface plane, atomic relaxation, and reconstruction (see Ref. 15 for more details).

## 5. DEFECT CHARACTERIZATION: THE CLASS OF MANIFEST SYMMETRY

### a. *Volterra's Procedure*

In this section we identify *a priori* the set of line discontinuities that can be introduced into a host structure exhibiting a given space group. This can be achieved by Volterra's method (see Ref. 16 for a more complete review), which was developed originally for the case of discontinuities in

[15] R. C. Pond, D. J. Bacon, A. Serra, and A. P. Sutton, *Met. Trans.* **22A,** 1185 (1991).
[16] F. R. N. Nabarro, *Theory of Dislocations,* Clarendon Press, Oxford, UK (1967).

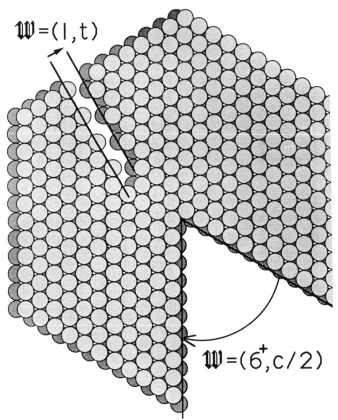

$$\mathbb{W} = (1, t)$$

$$\mathbb{W} = (6^+, c/2)$$

FIG. 5. Schematic illustration of the formation of a dislocation and a dispiration in an hcp crystal by the Volterra procedure.

elastic continua, and applied later to defects in single crystals (see, for example, Burgers[17] and Eshelby[18]) as is described now.

Volterra's procedure is to make a cut over some surface and then to displace the two faces of the cut with respect to each other by some rigid-body operation. After removal or insertion of additional material as necessary, the two surfaces are finally rebonded, creating a defect delineating the perimeter of the cut. Now, for crystalline materials, so that the rebonding process does not lead to the formation of a faulted region over the rebonded surfaces, the admissible rigid-body operations are restricted to proper symmetry operations (translations, rotations, and screw-rotations). This is illustrated schematically in Fig. 5, which shows

[17] J. M. Burgers, *Proc. Kon. Ned. Akad. Wetenschap.* **42**, 293 (1939).
[18] J. D. Eshelby, *Solid State Phys.* **3**, 79 (1956).

two surfaces related by a translation operation $(\mathbf{I}, \mathbf{t})$ in an hcp crystal. The defect created by rebonding these surfaces is a dislocation, and, as demonstrated later by means of circuit mapping, we can readily prove that the defect is characterized topologically by this symmetry operator. Two surfaces related by a $6_3^-$ screw-rotation operation are also shown in Fig. 5; the defect resulting from the rebonding of these surfaces is a dispiration. It is characterized by this screw-rotation operation, and circuit mapping for such defects is considered further in Section III.

In summary, the situation regarding line defects in this class is straightforward. Geometrically admissible line defects are characterized by proper symmetry operations belonging to the space group of the host object. This is true whether the host is a single crystal or bicrystal. (In the latter case, we note that a defect that is admissible in the interface would also be admissible in both of the component crystals since the characterizing operation would be coincident.) When the space group of the host is known, it is therefore straightforward to predict the character of admissible line defects. Finally, we note that line defects in this class cannot arise on the free surfaces of crystals.

### b. *Circuit Mapping*

Once a defective structure has been established, for example, by experimental observation, or visualized through Volterra's procedure, a method is required for the *a posteriori* characterization of the defect. A method that made use of circuit mapping was pioneered in the 1950s by Frank[1] for characterizing dislocations in single crystals, and is depicted schematically in Fig. 6. A closed-circuit PQRSP is constructed around the defect, and is subsequently mapped onto the lattice of the (perfect) host crystal, P'Q'R'S'T'. To define the topological properties of such a line defect fully, we must assign a unit vector $\boldsymbol{\xi}$, tangent to the line, that defines the $\pm$ sense of the defect. In fig. 6, $\boldsymbol{\xi}$ points out of the page, and the circuit is defined as right-handed relative to this vector. The closure failure of the circuit from finish to start, T'P' in the present case, is the Burgers vector, $\mathbf{b}$, as indicated in the figure. This is known as the **RH/FS** convention[19]; the Burgers vector of a right-handed screw dislocation would point in the same direction as $\boldsymbol{\xi}$ using this convention (the opposite convention occasionally appears in the literature). In the case of perfect dislocations, the Burgers vector is a translation vector $\mathbf{t}$ of the crystal's lattice. To ensure that the mapping process is unambiguous, operations in the initial circuit must clearly correspond to operations in the reference space, and

[19] J. P. Hirth and J. Lothe, *Theory of Dislocations*, Wiley, New York (1982).

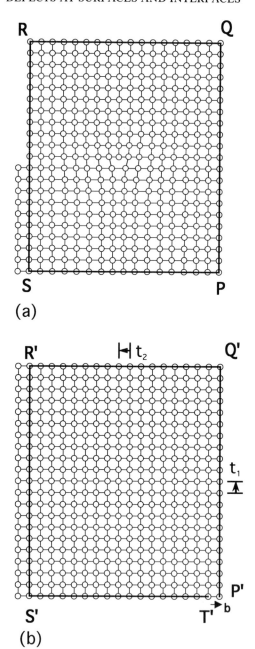

(a)

(b)

FIG. 6. Schematic illustration of (a) a closed circuit constructed around a dislocation and (b) the mapping of this circuit onto the reference lattice. The line direction of the defect $\xi$ is upwards from the page.

hence regions of large strain, such as dislocation cores, must be avoided in the construction of circuits. Conventionally, closed circuits are constructed around a defect of interest, but this is not a necessary condition. Open circuits can be used as long as they subtend $2\pi$ radians in projection about the defect's line direction, $\xi$; the defect is then characterized by the difference between the closure failures in the initial and mapped circuits.

It is often advantageous to formulate circuit mapping mathematically rather than graphically, and we now indicate how this can be done. A mapped circuit, as depicted in Fig. 6(b) for example, can be regarded as a journey consisting of a sequence of symmetry operations imposed on an observer who thereby moves from one point to another equivalent one in the (invariant) reference space. The sequence of operations corresponds to that identified in the closed circuit in the deformed material, and we wish to establish the closure failure of the mapped circuit. Since we can represent an individual symmetry operation $\mathfrak{W}_i$ in mathematical terms as a matrix $(\mathbf{W}_i, \mathbf{w}_i)$, it is also possible to formulate a sequence of operations. Now, by definition, an operation represented by $\mathfrak{W}_i$ acts through the initially chosen (invariant) origin, whereas, in formulating a circuit, we may require some or all of the operations in a sequence to act through some other equivalent position, located by the vector $\mathbf{r}$. Thus, individual operations in a circuit sequence must be reexpressed to act through the relevant position; the operation $\mathfrak{W}_i$ redefined in this way is designated $\mathfrak{W}_i^*$, and is given by $\mathfrak{W}_i^* = (\mathbf{I}, \mathbf{r})\mathfrak{W}_i(\mathbf{I}, \mathbf{r})^{-1}$, and hence a sequence of mapped operations is written (reading from right to left), $\mathfrak{W}_s^* \ldots \mathfrak{W}_3^* \mathfrak{W}_2^* \mathfrak{W}_1^*$. We refer to this total sequence as the *circuit operator,* and designate it $\mathfrak{C}$. In the case of translation operations, $\mathfrak{W}_i = \mathfrak{W}_i^*$ (because translations do not act through a point) and, hence, circuits comprising only translation operations can be formulated simply as $\mathfrak{C} = \mathfrak{W}_s \ldots \mathfrak{W}_3\mathfrak{W}_2\mathfrak{W}_1$. We consider such instances first and return to more general cases later. In the case of fig. 6(b), the circuit is the sequence of translation operations starting at $P'$ and terminating at $T'$, i.e., $\mathfrak{C} = (\mathbf{I}, \mathbf{t}_2)^{-1} (\mathbf{I}, \mathbf{t}_2)^{-1} \ldots (\mathbf{I}, \mathbf{t}_1)^{-1} (\mathbf{I}, \mathbf{t}_1)^{-1} \ldots (\mathbf{I}, \mathbf{t}_2)(\mathbf{I}, \mathbf{t}_2)(\mathbf{I}, \mathbf{t}_2) \ldots (\mathbf{I}, \mathbf{t}_1)(\mathbf{I}, \mathbf{t}_1)$, where the number of operations of type $(\mathbf{I}, \mathbf{t}_1)^{-1}$ is equal to those of type $(\mathbf{I}, \mathbf{t}_1)$, but where there is one more operation of type $(\mathbf{I}, \mathbf{t}_2)$ than $(\mathbf{I}, \mathbf{t}_2)^{-1}$. If we choose the origin to be at the starting point of the circuit, i.e., $P'$, then $\mathfrak{C}$ acting on the null vector locates the endpoint of the observer's journey, $\mathbf{P'T'}$. For this case, the circuit failure is seen to be $\mathfrak{C}^{-1}$, i.e., $\mathfrak{C}^{-1}$ is equal to $(\mathbf{I}, \mathbf{b})$; moreover, the circuit failure is independent of the circuit chosen, and this is characteristic of pure dislocations.

Circuits can be constructed that include point operations or nonsymmorphic operations in appropriate crystals. The formulation of $\mathfrak{C}$ in these circumstances requires that such operations be represented by $\mathfrak{W}_i^*$ rather

than $\mathfrak{W}_i$. For example, it is often convenient to consider a symmetry operation to be defined with respect to the position located by the previous operation in the sequence. In this case, for a circuit comprising both pure translations and other operations, the overall result is that the component translations and displacements are simply added, and the orthogonal contributors are independently combined as though operating through the terminating point of the circuit. The meaning of $\mathfrak{C} = (\mathbf{W}_I, \mathbf{w}_I + \mathbf{t}_m)$ is then that the observer's frame has been rotated or reflected corresponding to the orthogonal operation, and displaced by $\mathbf{w}_I + \mathbf{t}_m$ with respect to the starting point of the circuit, an example of a circuit formulated this way is presented in Section V. In the case of pure disclinations, one can conveniently formulate circuits as sequences of operations acting through an invariant origin (i.e., using operations $\mathfrak{W}_i$) located at the core of the defect, rather than at the starting point of the circuit; an example is discussed in Section III.

## 6. Defect Characterization: The Class of Broken Symmetry

### a. A priori *Method*

Our objective in this section is to introduce the *a priori* method for predicting admissible defects characterized by broken symmetry operations. Such defects arise in crystalline objects that are dissymmetrized with respect to a precursor structure. Therefore, the first step is to review the consequences of dissymmetrization as embodied in the principle of symmetry compensation. The second step is to extend the application of Volterra's method to the case of defects in this class.

The principle of symmetry compensation[3] states that whenever symmetry is suppressed at one structural level it reappears and is conserved at another. Consider first a holosymmetric crystal structure. In this case the existence of the set of basis atoms at each lattice site does not suppress any of the symmetry exhibited by the lattice. However, for nonholosymmetric crystals, some lattice symmetry is suppressed in this way, and, as a consequence, a multiplicity of crystallographically equivalent crystal variants can exist. A simple example of two coexisting variants is a pair of inversion domains in sphalerite, as depicted schematically in Fig. 7. We can argue that the symmetry of the underlying lattice has been reduced when decorated by the diatomic basis. The number of domains that can arise in sphalerite, and their interrelation, is concisely expressed by the decomposition of the space group of the lattice with respect to

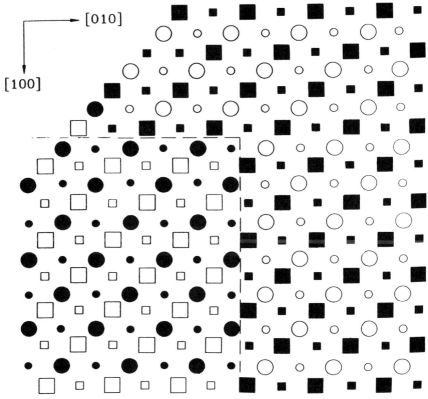

FIG. 7. Projection along [001] of two sphalerite variants separated by an inversion domain boundary.

that of sphalerite. For the purpose of illustration, it is actually simpler to consider a precursor structure isomorphic with the lattice rather than the lattice itself. The diamond structure is a convenient holosymmetric precursor in the present case. Using right cosets, we have

$$Fd\bar{3}m = (F\bar{4}3m)1 \cup (F\bar{4}3m)\,\bar{1}, \qquad (6.1)$$

where the symbol $\cup$ signifies union, and the symmetry operations are as defined in Table I. [Note that, since the precursor group is nonsymmorphic, the decomposition of Eq. (6.1) requires the concept of groups by modulus.][3] Thus, since there are two cosets, two domains can arise, and both exhibit the symmetry group F$\bar{4}$3m. The coset representatives show how a given domain is related to the reference domain. Thus, in this simple case, the reference domain is related to itself by the identity opera-

tion, signified 1 in shorthand notation, and the second domain is related to the reference by the (broken) inversion operation, $\bar{1}$ (hence, the designation of these as *inversion* domains). In fact, the two domains are interrelated by all of the operations in the coset $(F\bar{4}3m)\bar{1}$. These are the broken symmetry operations, the $i$'th being designated $\mathfrak{W}_i^e$. The operations in this set include the 24 in the lower part of Table I. Neither domain exhibits these symmetries, but carrying out any of these operations of one domain transforms it into the other (the superscript "$e$" denotes the "exchange" of the two domains).

We now show briefly that one can obtain operations characterizing defects in the manifest symmetry class using the present method, and that this corresponds to a special case. Consider a holosymmetric crystal such as the simple cubic one illustrated in Fig. 6(b). Because there is no suppression of lattice symmetry in this case, there is only one crystallographically distinct variant. Mathematically, we can write that the decomposition of the lattice's space group, $Pm\bar{3}m$, with respect to that of the crystal (which is also $Pm\bar{3}m$), is

$$Pm\bar{3}m = (Pm\bar{3}m)1. \qquad (6.2)$$

In Eq. (6.2) we have chosen the coset representative to be the identity, but we are free to choose any operation in the group $Pm\bar{3}m$ for this purpose. For example, we can choose a translation operator, and (6.2) becomes

$$Pm\bar{3}m = (Pm\bar{3}m)t. \qquad (6.3)$$

This formulation emphasizes that there is a sense in which a multiplicity of "identical variants" exists, interrelated by "self-exchange" operations, which are simply symmetry operations manifested by the host crystal. The proper operations in this set characterize admissible defects. This consideration is not restricted to holosymmetric single crystals, but applies also to nonholosymmetric crystals and bicrystals.

Returning now to the pair of crystallographically equivalent variants described by Eq. (6.1), we visualize the introduction of a boundary separating the two domains by means of a Volterra-like procedure. We consider first one of the variants, and generate the second by operating the inversion on the first, allowing the two variants to interpenetrate. We now locate an infinite surface (or a curved surface defining a closed volume) and discard the first variant on one side and the second on the other, finally rebonding along the initial surface. This would produce regions of domain boundary as depicted in Fig. 7. We showed in Section

5 that line defects are characterized topologically by the operation involved in their creation in a Volterra process. Extending this notion to the present case, we see that the domain boundary is characterized by the inversion operation, and this is quite independent of the orientation and position of the boundary and the choice of initial variant. (An actual defect might have additional displacement or local atomic relaxations in order to reduce its free energy.) We recall from Eq. (6.1) that the two domains are actually interrelated by all of the operations in the exchange coset, and in the present case this includes proper operations, such as the $4_1^+$ operation along [001], in addition to improper ones like the inversion. This implies that domain boundaries can be introduced into sphalerite by alternative Volterra processes, and can be terminated by line defects (for example, by a disparition if the exchange operation is taken to be $4_1^+$) as illustrated further in Section III.

The particular example of an inversion domain boundary in sphalerite discussed earlier illustrates the more general result that defects in dissymmetrized objects are characterized by broken symmetry operations. In other words, defects in this class separate crystallographically equivalent variants coexisting in a material specimen. At interfaces and surfaces, line defects (i.e., defects without associated extended defects, as in the preceeding example) can arise in this class. These defects separate equivalent regions of interface or surface, and are characterized by broken symmetry operations. However, the physical form of a defect also depends on its location (i.e., whether it is at an internal or external surface) and the mode of symmetry breaking. For example, interfacial dislocations characterized by combinations of black and white translation operations can occur, and can be imagined to be created in a Volterra process analogous to that described in Section 5(a). Interfacial steps can be regarded as a special case where the opposing faces of the Volterra cut are complementary and can be rebonded without any additional rigid-body displacement. These are characterized by translation operations that are coincident in the dichromatic complex, but do not belong to the bicrystal in question, as considered further in Section V. Line defects can also arise that separate interfacial or surface domains where symmetry has been broken through atomic relaxations. Such reconstructed domains may, for example, be related by broken translation operations (coincident ones in the interfacial case), but the resulting defects do not have dislocation character. These can be imagined to be created by a Volterra-like process, but rigid-body operations are not involved in this case. To summarize, the number of distinct variants and the totality of broken operations can be determined by means of group decomposition; hence, we have an *a priori* method for predicting the character of admissible defects in this

class. However, the physical nature of a defect, such as the form of its displacement field, depends not only on the operation characterizing it, but also on the mode of symmetry breaking and its location at an internal or external surface.

### b. A Posteriori *Method*

Defects on crystal surfaces and at interfaces can be characterized *a posteriori* if one uses the circuit method either graphically or mathematically. However, additional considerations arise compared with defects in single crystals, and in the present section we only indicate the nature of these and leave more detailed discussions until later. In the case of surface defects, circuits cannot be constructed in the usual manner. In the case of line defects at interfaces, closed circuits can be constructed around a defect, but these must cross the interface at least twice. In addition, since there are two crystals, we now have two reference spaces, i.e., the space groups of each crystal. In previous treatments, other authors have invoked a common reference space based on the existence of a three-dimensional coincidence site lattice. In particular, Bollmann[6] has defined a lattice of differences between black and white translation vectors, $t(\lambda)_i - Pt(\mu)_j$ (expressed in the white coordinate frame), called the *dsc lattice* (displacement-shift-complete). The present authors have not adopted this approach, preferring to map directly into the component crystal reference spaces. An important feature of the present method is that it enables symmetry operations other than translations to be considered, which is an essential feature for a comprehensive treatment of interfacial defects.

### 7. SUMMARY

The topological properties of defects in the categories of manifest and broken symmetries can be summarized as follows.

Any crystalline object that manifests proper symmetry operations can, in principle, be host to line defects characterized by those operations. Such defects are known as dislocations, disclinations, and dispirations, and can arise inside crystals and at interfaces (when coincident symmetry operations are present), but cannot arise on crystal surfaces.

Crystalline objects that are dissymmetrized with respect to some precursor structure can act as hosts to defects that separate crystallographically equivalent variants. In bulk crystals (either nonholosymmetric, or variant products of a phase decomposition or ordering), extended domain boundaries arise that are characterized by broken symmetry opera-

tions. Domain boundaries can be terminated by line defects within the host crystal if any of the corresponding broken operations are proper. On crystal surfaces and at interfaces, line defects can occur in this class; the range of defect types is particularly wide at interfaces because there are several degrees of freedom in the creation of bicrystals and additional relaxation modes by which the symmetry of the constituent crystals may be suppressed. Thus, defects in this class include dislocations, disclinations, and dispirations at interfaces, while steps, facet junctions, and reconstruction domain lines can occur at interfaces and surfaces. A comprehensive list of all the defect types is postponed until later sections.

In the foregoing, we have used the principle of symmetry compensation to provide a comprehensive framework for predicting the nature of operations characterizing defects in the classes of manifest and broken symmetry. Importantly any dissymmetrization considered so far has not arisen as a consequence of the presence in a specimen of a defect itself. Dissymmetrization has been considered to have arisen either because of the degrees of freedom associated with the creation of a nonholosymmetric crystal, an unrelaxed surface or interface, or due to relaxation processes. However, the presence of defects can in itself also lead to dissymmetrization. For example, the dislocation in Fig. 6(a) breaks all the translation symmetry of the host crystal in the plane of the drawing. In fact, the space group of the dislocated crystal is a p2mm, where the translation symmetry is parallel to the dislocation line, the mirrors are parallel to the "extra half-plane" and the plane of the page, and the twofold axis lies along the intersection of these mirrors. Therefore, according to the principle of symmetry compensation, a multiplicity of equivalent dislocations can exist. Moreover, if two of these variants coexist in the same material specimen, then further defects can arise. For example, let the two variants be related by a primitive translation vector $t$; the new "defect" separating the coexisting "variants" is then a jog or kink depending on the orientation of $t$ with respect to $\xi$. This instance illustrates the application of principle of symmetry compensation at a different structural level compared with the previous discussion of defect characterization. In the following sections we do not pursue this aspect further.

All of the defects considered so far have been characterized by symmetry operations; these are the only types that can be predicted *a priori* on the basis of the principle of symmetry compensation. We refer to these as "perfect" defects in the sense that their motion leaves behind either a structure identical to that encountered (manifest symmetry class) or a crystallographically equivalent (energetically degenerate) one (broken symmetry class). However, other defects also arise in crystals, on surfaces and at interfaces. These are characterized by operations that are

not manifest or broken symmetry operations, and we refer to them as "imperfect" defects. In crystals they are always associated with extended faults, and on surfaces and at interfaces they are line defects separating distinct structures. Such defects sometimes arise as a result of the dissociation of perfect defects. Although these defects fall into the same general categories as perfect ones, the precise nature of the characterizing operations will depend on the atomic structure in each case. If the operation characterizing an imperfect defect is known, it can be incorporated into the present framework, but prediction on the basis of symmetry theory alone is not possible.

Formally, symmetry would be broken by disordered arrangements of point defects such as vacancies or solute atoms. On a finer scale, thermal vibrations could be thought to disrupt symmetry, but such details are ignored here and only extended faults and line defects are considered. Actual dislocations may undergo core extension or dilatation; planar faults may have local displacement fields; and steps, facet junctions, and reconstruction domain lines may have local strain fields. These local effects do not appear in the intrinsic topological properties deduced from symmetry arguments, but can be superposed on the latter if known.

## III. Defects in Single Crystals

In this section we consider defects that arise in the bulk of single crystals. As explained in Section II, line defects arise in the class of manifest symmetry and in various types of domain boundaries in the class of broken symmetry. In addition, extended discontinuities occur in the class of imperfect defects. The nature of these types of defects has been described comprehensively in standard texts (e.g., see Refs. 16, 19, and 20), so here we only summarize their principal topological properties.

8. LINE DEFECTS: THE CLASS OF MANIFEST SYMMETRY

The discussion in Section II demonstrates that perfect line defects (i.e., defects not attached to any extended discontinuity) in the bulk of single crystals are characterized by proper symmetry operations, which belong to the space group of the crystal. Hence the admissible types of defects are limited to dislocations, disclinations, and dispirations, characterized by translation, rotation, and screw-rotation operations, respectively. Dis-

[20] J. Friedel, *Dislocations*, Pergamon Press, Oxford, UK (1967).

locations can arise in any crystal, although only those with a small magnitude of **b** are likely to be important physically because their elastic energy[19] scales as the square of *b*. Disclinations and dispirations can only arise in crystals that exhibit rotation and screw-rotation operations, respectively, in their space groups. For bulk metal and inorganic crystals, usually only dislocations are observed as perfect defects because disclinations and dispirations have too large an elastic formation energy (thin films are an exception). In organic and liquid crystals, disclinations and dispirations are observed as well as dislocations.[21,22] Disclinations are also observed in magnetic flux line lattices, ferromagnetic domain wall patterns, and other domain lattices, but our focus here is on crystal defects.

An example of a dislocation in a simple cubic crystal is illustrated schematically in Fig. 6. The formation of a 90° disclination is shown in Fig. 8. The undistorted crystal, which we can also regard as representing the reference space, is shown in Fig. 8(a) and the final defect in 8(b). One can imagine that such a defect can be introduced into a crystal by a Volterra process whereby a cut is made along a surface like P'U' (or P'V'), rigidly rotating this surface by the 90° rotation operation (4⁺, **0**) normal to the page (clockwise about $\xi$, which is taken to point upwards from the page), removing excess material, and finally bonding to the surface P'Q' (or P'W'). Such defects are known as *positive wedge disclinations*. A *negative wedge disclination* would result if the surface P'U' (or P'V') were to be rotated by the operation (4⁻, **0**) and additional material inserted.

The defect in Fig. 8(b) can be characterized by means of circuit mapping, and we consider first the case where all the component operations in the circuit are chosen to be translations. Two concentric circuits, QRSTQ and WXYZW [Fig. 8(b)], are shown around the disclinations, which become Q'R'S'T'U' and W'X'Y'Z'V' [Fig. 8(a)] when mapped into the reference space. These clearly have different closure failures, U'Q' and V'W', as seen in Fig. 8(a). In fact, no component of the closure failure is independent of the circuit chosen, revealing that the defect does not have dislocation character. However, it is seen that the starting and finishing points for both circuits, Q' and U' and W' and V', are interrelated by the operation (4⁻, **0**) acting through the (invariant) origin P'. In other words, the circuit operator $\mathfrak{C}$, acting on **P'Q'** and **P'W'**, equals **P'U'** and **P'V'**, respectively; hence $\mathfrak{C}^{-1}$ is equivalent to the operation (4⁺, **0**)

[21] G. Friedel, *Ann. de Phys.* **18**, 273 (1922).
[22] W. F. Harris, in *Surfaces and Defect Properties of Solids,* Vol. 3, p. 57, The Chemical Society, London (1974).

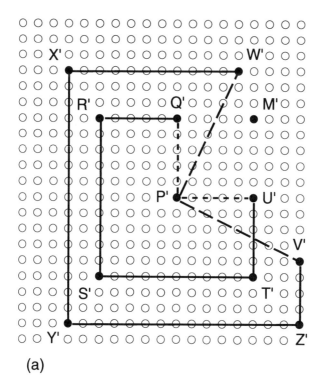

(a)

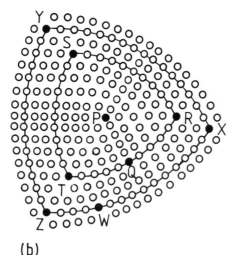

(b)

FIG. 8. Schematic illustration of the introduction of a 90° disclination into a simple cubic crystal: (a) the initial cut and (b) the final defect. Two concentric circuits are indicated in the distorted and reference frames. The line direction of the defect, ξ, is upwards from the page.

irrespective of the circuit chosen. In the case of pure disclinations, it is more straightforward to construct circuits by means of rotation operations; starting at point R, the sequence of points, S, T, and R in Fig. 8(b) map to the points R'S'T'M' in Fig. 8(a), and are interrelated by the sequence of operations $(4^+, 0)$ $(4^+, 0)$ $(4^+, 0)$, i.e., $\mathfrak{C} = (4^-, 0)$. Thus, if we construct symmetric circuits about the defect, $\mathfrak{C}^{-1}$ is equal to the operation $(4^+, 0)$, thereby characterizing the defect as a disclination. (An equivalent formulation using polar vector notation has been presented by Nabarro.[16])

Just as disclinations can be characterized with circuits employing either translation or rotation operations, so also can dislocations. This reflects the fact that dislocations and disclinations are not strictly distinct topological entities; each can be modeled in terms of the other.[2,18] Disclinations can be regarded as walls of dislocations and a dislocation can be viewed as a disclination dipole, but we do not pursue this matter here.

The formation of a 90° dispiration in a diamond crystal is indicated schematically in Fig. 9. The surfaces to be bonded are now related by the 90° screw-rotation operation $4_1^+$ (note that this operation does not act through an atomic site, the origin chosen for the definition of symmetry operators in Table I, but through the point Q). Characterization can be carried out using circuits, but, in addition to the disclination part of $\mathfrak{C}^{-1}$ as in the previous case $(4^+, 0)$, a component $(I, b)$ with $b = 1/4[001]$ corresponding to the dislocation part also arises.

The examples given so far are straight defects. However, all of the defects described previously can also bend gradually or abruptly. (Keep in mind that topological characterization as discussed in this chapter is completely independent of line direction and associated structural variations of the core of a defect.) As with dislocations, which are referred to as screw ($b$ parallel to $\xi$) and edge ($b$ perpendicular to $\xi$), disclinations are designated wedge ($R$ parallel to $\xi$) and twist ($R$ perpendicular to $\xi$).

## 9. EXTENDED DEFECTS: THE CLASS OF BROKEN SYMMETRY

As explained in Section II, extended defects can arise as a consequence of the suppression of symmetry, and are each characterized by a broken symmetry operation $\mathfrak{W}_i^e$. Domain boundaries in sphalerite were used as an illustration in the instance of a nonholosymmetric crystal, $\mathfrak{W}_i^e$ being taken as the inversion operation. However, other operations in the coset of operations characterizing this defect [the second coset in Eq. (6.1)] are proper, implying that domain boundaries in such cases can be terminated by line defects. This can be appreciated if one takes the crystal in

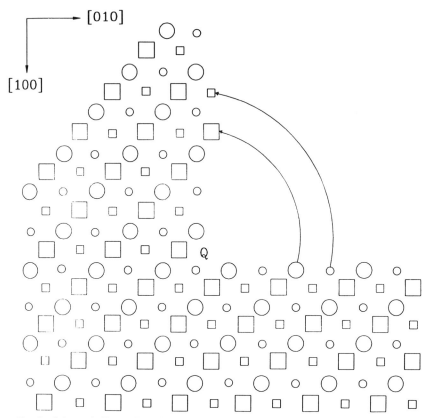

Fıɢ. 9. Schematic illustration of a 90° dispiration in a diamond structure crystal, showing the initial cut before deformation. This diagram also illustrates the introduction of a domain boundary terminated by a dispiration in sphalerite if the square and circular symbols are taken to represent different atomic species.

Fig. 9 to be sphalerite rather than diamond. Now the 90° screw-rotation operation belongs to the set $\mathfrak{W}_i^e$, and, when the indicated surfaces are bonded, an inversion domain boundary is created, which terminates at the dispiration. Another proper operation in this coset is the twofold rotation axis along ⟨110⟩, and hence inversion domains can, in principle, also be terminated by 180° disclinations. Note that there are no simple translation operations in this coset, and hence inversion domains in sphalerite cannot terminate at dislocations. Summarizing the general result, we can identify the coset of operations $\mathfrak{W}_i^e$ characterizing a given domain boundary by carrying out group decomposition. All of these operations are equivalent topological characterizations of the boundary, but certain

distinctions emerge if the boundary is imagined to be introduced into a crystal by a Volterra-like process. In such a process, improper operations can only be used to create domains that are either closed or reach free surfaces. On the other hand, each proper operation in the coset corresponds to the possibility of a distinct line defect terminating the boundary.

An important class of domain boundaries arises in ordered materials, where the higher symmetry of the precursor (disordered) structure is reduced. We consider the $Cu_3Au$ structure to illustrate an example where dislocations can terminate boundaries, in contrast to the earlier case of sphalerite. In the disordered state we can take the space group to be $Fm\bar{3}m$ (assuming that the atomic sites are occupied randomly by Cu and Au in the ratio $3:1$ on a space-averaged basis) whereas the ordered state exhibits the space group $Pm\bar{3}m$. Decomposing the former with respect to the latter, we have

$$Fm\bar{3}m = (Pm\bar{3}m)1 \cup (Pm\bar{3}m)t_1 \cup (Pm\bar{3}m)t_2 \cup (Pm\bar{3}m)t_3, \quad (9.1)$$

where $t_1$, $t_2$, and $t_3$ represent the translation operations $(\mathbf{I}, 1/2[110])$, $(\mathbf{I}, 1/2[101])$, and $(\mathbf{I}, 1/2[011])$, respectively. Thus, four domains arise, and each coset of exchange operations includes both improper and proper operations, the latter including the primitive translations suppressed by the ordering. For this reason, such domains are referred to here as *translation domains*, but are also known as *antiphase domains*. Translation domains may either be closed or terminate on line defects such as $1/2\langle 110 \rangle$ dislocations. An important mechanism for their introduction into ordered crystals is the dissociation of perfect line defects. For example, a superdislocation with $\mathbf{b} = [100]$ can decompose into partial superdislocations with $\mathbf{b}_1 = 1/2[110]$ and $\mathbf{b}_2 = 1/2[1\bar{1}0]$ separated by a segment of translation domain boundary.

## 10. IMPERFECT DEFECTS

It is important to appreciate that the topological analysis of line and extended defects described earlier involves the *symmetry* of crystals as distinct from their *structures*. Topological arguments are concerned with continuity in crystalline materials and, thus, in a sense, increasing structural complexity does not necessarily complicate an analysis; it is only the *symmetry* of the crystal that is relevant. However, the actual atomic structure of a crystal does, of course, have a bearing on the nature of defects. In particular, the core energies of line and extended defects and the elastic constants of materials are determined by structure. Thus, per-

fect line defects are known to decompose into partial line defects bounding extended faults.

A simple example is the formation of a stacking-fault between two partial dislocations in an fcc metal; such defects are characterized by an operation of the type $(\mathbf{I}, 1/6\langle 211 \rangle)$. Another example would be the dissociation of a dispiration into its component disclination and dislocation parts connected by a planar fault. In addition, an important class of planar stacking-faults and crystallographic shear-faults arises in crystals by other mechanisms such as the condensation of point defects.

Although all of these imperfect defects can be characterized *a posteriori* by circuit methods (e.g., see the discussion of stacking-faults in fcc metals by Frank[23] for an early treatment), they are not characterized by symmetry operations of the undistorted crystal structure or of some precursor structure, and cannot be predicted *a priori* by symmetry arguments.

As a corollary to the structural specificity of extended defects in this class, they are normally favorable only on certain planes. This fault behavior is in striking contrast to the case for domains in the class of broken symmetry, which generally exhibit continuously curving morphologies (except where they arise by dissociation of line defects). In other words, irrespective of the orientation of a domain boundary, the operation characterizing the defect, and hence relating the variants, ensures that the underlying structure is continuous across a boundary and that it is only the allocation of atomic species to precursor lattice sites that changes. Actually, in real crystals, there may be additional relaxations at domain boundaries, and these would vary with orientation of the boundary. One can analyze these effects and the additional defect character thereby introduced at domain and structural faults by treating the defects as interfaces and using the methods presented in Section V. Additionally, point defects such as vacancies or solute atoms could segregate to boundaries and lower their free energy, which would tend to stabilize them. Such thermodynamic considerations are additional to symmetry considerations and are not treated here.

## IV. Surface Discontinuities

In Section II we introduced the crystallography of surfaces in terms of their space groups $\Phi(s)$. Such groups can exhibit proper symmetry operations, and hence it might be expected that crystal surfaces would act as

[23] F. C. Frank, *Disc. Faraday Soc. London* **25**, 1 (1958).

hosts to defects in the class of manifest symmetry, i.e., dislocations, disclinations, and dispirations. However, such defects cannot lie at free surfaces because their displacement fields collapse. Thus, all surface defects can be regarded as belonging to the class of broken symmetry, and it is convenient to subdivide this range of defects into two categories depending on how symmetry has been suppressed. In the first category, defects arise on unrelaxed surfaces, the precursor object being the infinite crystal, and symmetry suppression having arisen due to the creation of the unrelaxed surface. In the second, suppression has occurred by virtue of surface reconstruction. The character of possible defects in these two categories is first treated by means of group decomposition, and then the specific case of the (001) surface of Si is considered. This is followed by a discussion of the interaction of surface defects with other surface defects and with bulk defects, and circuit mapping is shown to be helpful in this regard.

## 11. DEFECTS DUE TO BROKEN SYMMETRY ON UNRELAXED SURFACES

The procedure for establishing the character of all the admissible discontinuities on a given unrelaxed surface, represented by its unit normal $\mathbf{n}$ (a dimensionless parameter), is as follows. First, the space group of the infinite crystal $\Phi$, which consists of the individual operations $\mathfrak{W}_i$, is decomposed with respect to that of the surface group $\Phi(s)$, comprising the group of operations $\mathfrak{W}_j(s)$, i.e.:

$$\Phi = [\Phi(s)]\mathfrak{W}_1^{se} \cup [\Phi(s)]\mathfrak{W}_2^{se} \cup \ldots [\Phi(s)]\mathfrak{W}_q^{se}. \tag{11.1}$$

This decomposition determines the number of variants $q$ and the cosets of broken symmetry operations where the superscript "$se$" denotes surface exchange operations, and $\mathfrak{W}_1^{se}$ is the identity. The operations in each coset (represented by $\mathfrak{W}_k^{se}$) characterize a discontinuity separating energetically degenerate surfaces, which can be classified into five principal types as described next.

1. *Steps:* These are characterized by broken translation operations, $\mathfrak{W}_k^{se} = (\mathbf{I}, \mathbf{t}_k^{se})$ [modulo any translation vector parallel to the surface, i.e., in the group $\Phi(s)$]. They can arise on surfaces with any orientation, $\mathbf{n}$, and the step height $h_s$ is equal to $\mathbf{n} \cdot \mathbf{t}_k^{se}$. Note that $h_s$ is independent of the particular choice of $\mathfrak{W}_k^{se}$ and the line direction of the step. The surfaces on either side of a step are identical structures except for their location in space. We assign a line direction $\boldsymbol{\xi}$ to a step, so that the

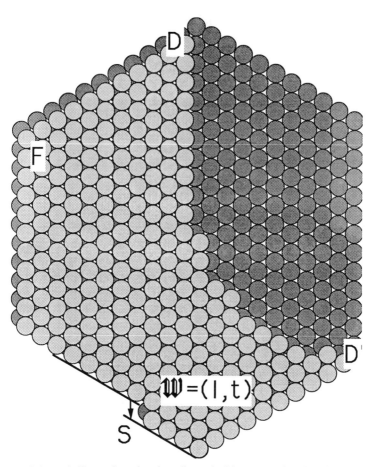

FIG. 10. Schematic illustration of surface discontinuities on unrelaxed surfaces of an hcp crystal; a facet junction is shown at F, a step at S, and a demistep at DD'.

meaning of $\mathfrak{W}_k^{se}$ is that it transforms the structure to the left of the step into that on the right (i.e., the direction $\boldsymbol{\xi} \times \mathbf{n}$). An example of a step seen end-on with $\mathbf{t}_k^{se} = 1/3[\bar{1}\bar{1}20]$ on a $(\bar{1}010)$ surface of an hcp crystal is depicted in Fig. 10; $\boldsymbol{\xi}$ is taken to point out of the diagram and $h_s$ is equal to the spacing of the $(\bar{1}010)$ planes. Real steps may have displacement fields associated with them, but these do not have the form characteristic of, for example, single dislocations.

2. *Demisteps:* These can arise only on certain surfaces of nonsymmorphic crystals. They are characterized by operations $\mathfrak{W}_k^{se} = (\mathbf{W}_k^{se}, \mathbf{w}_k^{se})$ such that $\mathbf{W}_k^{se}\mathbf{n} = \mathbf{n}$, i.e., the orientation of the surface in question is left

invariant by the point operation, and the step height $h_d$ is equal to $\mathbf{n} \cdot \mathbf{w}_k^{se}$. An important distinction between steps and demisteps is that the equivalent (energetically degenerate) surfaces separated by the latter are interrelated by a point symmetry operation, $\mathbf{W}_k^{se}$, rather than the identity as in the former case.

An example of a demistep on the (0001) surface of an hcp metal is designated DD' in Fig. 10. In this case, $\mathbf{n}$ is parallel to [0001], and $\mathfrak{W}_k^{se}$ can be taken, for example, as the screw axis $6_3^+$ or a $c$-mirror-glide plane; $h_d$ is equal to $c/2$, and is clearly independent of $\xi$, which varies between D and D'. The surfaces on either side of the demistep are interrelated by a rotation of 60° about [0001] or reflection across $\{10\bar{1}0\}$, for example. In hcp crystals, such demisteps can only arise on $\{hkil\}$ surfaces where $l$ is not zero.

3. *Facet junctions:* These are characterized by surface exchange operations $\mathfrak{W}_k^{se} = (\mathbf{W}_k^{se}, \mathbf{w}_k^{se})$ where $\mathbf{W}_k^{se}$ represents a rotation, roto-inversion, or a mirror operation. Such features separate equivalent surfaces with normals $\mathbf{n}$ and $\mathbf{W}_k^{se}\mathbf{n}$, as depicted schematically at F in Fig. 10, for example. In this case the operation $\mathfrak{W}_k^{se}$ can be taken as $3^-$, and the junction separates equivalent $(\bar{1}010)$ and $(10\bar{1}0)$ facets. In the general case, if $\mathbf{n} \cdot \mathbf{w}_k^{se}$ is not zero, a demistep is coincident with the facet junction.

4. *Nonholosymmetric crystals:* In this case a domain boundary in the bulk of the crystal, characterized by $\mathfrak{W}_f^e$, may emerge onto the surface. This operation belongs to the space group of the crystal's parent structure, but does not belong to the crystal group $\Phi$ or the surface group $\Phi(s)$, and the discontinuity delineating the line of emergence is characterized by $\mathfrak{W}_f^e$. The surface feature separates equivalent surfaces, and is either a facet junction, step, or demistep depending on the form of $\mathfrak{W}_f^e$.

5. *Imperfect defects:* Steps and facet junctions separating distinct surfaces can also arise. For example, just as partial dislocations can bound surfaces of different fault nature, so can partial steps or imperfect facet junctions. In addition, just as stacking-faults, once characterized by other means, can be described in the present methodology, so can imperfect surface features.

## 12. Defects Due to Broken Symmetry on Reconstructed Surfaces

Reconstruction at surfaces reduces the symmetry of the surface group $\Phi(s)$. Therefore, the number of variant surface structures increases and additional discontinuities can arise. Let the space group of the recon-

structed surface be $\Phi(rs)$; the additional variants are given by the decomposition

$$\Phi(s) = [\Phi(rs)]\mathfrak{W}_1^{re} \cup [\Phi(rs)]\mathfrak{W}_2^{re} \cup \ldots [\Phi(rs)]\mathfrak{W}_\nu^{re}, \qquad (12.1)$$

where $\mathfrak{W}_i^{re}$ is the $i$'th exchange operation due to surface reconstruction. These exchange operations characterize surface domain lines, and are referred to as translation domain lines when surface translation symmetry is broken $[\mathfrak{W}_i^{re} = (\mathbf{1}, \mathbf{t}_i^{re})]$ and rotation or mirror domain lines when point symmetry $\mathfrak{W}_i^{re} = (\mathbf{W}_i^{re}, \mathbf{w}_i^{re})]$ is broken. Facet junctions, steps, or demisteps are not intrinsically associated with these features since they correspond to operations in the unrelaxed surface group $\Phi(s)$. Defects of this type have been reported in the literature, particularly with the advent of scanning tunneling microscopy; examples observed on the (001) surface of silicon are discussed in the next section. Imperfect domain lines can also arise in cases where more than one type of reconstruction is thermodynamically stable.

## 13. DEFECTS ON (001) SURFACES OF SILICON CRYSTALS

The unrelaxed structure of this surface is shown in Fig. 2, and its surface space group $\Phi(s)$ is the layer group p2mm. Decomposing the crystal space group $\Phi = Fd\bar{3}m$ with respect to the surface group, we find that there are 12 variant surfaces related to the initial one by point operations $\mathfrak{W}_q^{se}$, in addition to an infinity of broken translation operations characterizing admissible steps. The 12 variants correspond to a pair of surfaces separated by demisteps on each of the six {001} faces of a cube. Figure 11 is a schematic illustration of a step on the (001) surface characterized by $\mathfrak{W}_p^{se} = (\mathbf{I}, \mathbf{t}_p^{se}) = (\mathbf{I}, 1/2[101])$, reacting with two demisteps, both characterized by a fourfold screw operation oriented along [001], for example, $\mathfrak{W}_q^{se} = (\mathbf{W}_q^{se}, \mathbf{w}_q^{se}) = (4^+, 1/4[\bar{1}\bar{1}\bar{1}])$ and $\mathfrak{W}_r^{se} = (\mathbf{W}_r^{se}, \mathbf{w}_r^{se}) = (4^-, 1/4[\bar{1}1\bar{1}])$. The height of the step $h_s$ is $a/2$, and that of the demisteps $h_d$, is $a/4$. Note that the environment of surface atoms rotates by 90° on crossing a demistep (as revealed in Fig. 11 by the orientation of the back-bonds to the subsurface atoms for example), but is unrotated across a step. All the surfaces illustrated in the figure are energetically degenerate, but, of course, the step and demistep energies are distinct.

The (001) surface of silicon is known to reconstruct, and the modified (2 × 1) structure is shown schematically in cross section in Fig. 12, and the new space group is $\Phi(rs)$ = p1m1. Both translation {i.e., [$\mathbf{I}$, $\mathbf{t}_u(s)$] = [$\mathbf{I}$, 1/2[110]} and point symmetry {i.e., $\mathfrak{W}_\nu(s) = [\mathbf{W}_\nu(s), \mathbf{w}_\nu(s)] = [\mathbf{M}_{(110)}, \mathbf{0}]$}

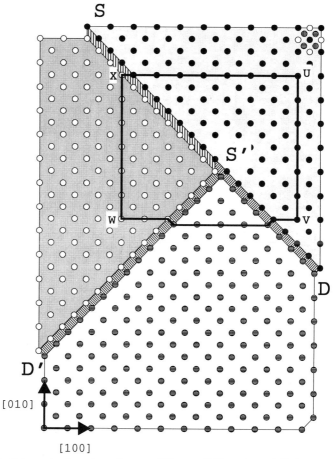

FIG. 11. Schematic plan view of a step SS' on a (001) surface of Si decomposing into two demisteps, D and D'.

operations are broken by this relaxation, and hence become exchange operations, $\mathfrak{W}_j^{re}$ and $\mathfrak{W}_k^{re}$, characterizing surface domain lines. Figure 13 is a schematic illustration showing translation domain lines, characterized by $\mathfrak{W}_j^{re} = (\mathbf{I}, \mathbf{t}_j^{re}) = (\mathbf{I}, 1/2[110])$, and mirror domain lines, characterized by $\mathfrak{W}_k^{re} = (\mathbf{W}_k^{re}, \mathbf{w}_k^{re}) = [\mathbf{M}_{(110)}, \mathbf{0}]$. Steps and demisteps are also shown in the figure, and it is interesting to note how the reconstruction rotates by 90° on crossing a demistep, but not across a step. These surface features are consistent with experimental studies.[24]

[24] B. S. Swartentruber, Y. W. Mo, and M. G. Lagally, *Appl. Phys. Lett.* **58**, 822 (1991).

[110]

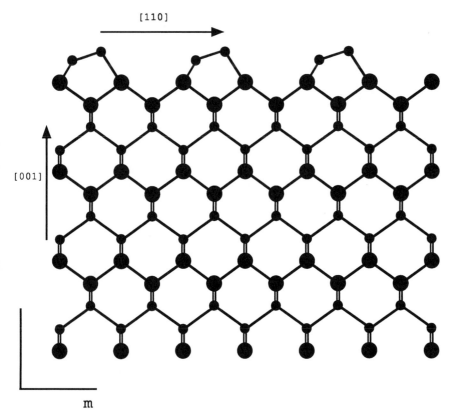

m

FIG. 12. Schematic cross-sectional view of the (2 × 1) reconstructed (001) Si surface, showing the residual symmetry elements.

14. CONSERVATION OF TOPOLOGICAL PROPERTIES

The topological properties associated with defects in contiguous materials are conserved in reactions between them. In the present section we discuss this point briefly, and illustrate it by reference to reactions between surface steps and demisteps, and interactions of bulk defects with external surfaces. The principal tool used is circuit mapping. Consider the surface of Si as depicted in Fig. 11 where a step SS' is shown decomposing into two demisteps, D and D'. The step SS' is characterized by the translation operation $\mathfrak{W}_p^{se} = (\mathbf{I}, \mathbf{t}_p^{se}) = (\mathbf{I}, 1/2[101])$, and the step height $h_s = \mathbf{n} \cdot \mathbf{W}_p^{se}$ is equal to $a/2$. If the line directions of the demisteps are defined to point away from the node, as indicated in Fig. 11, D and D' are characterized by $(4^+, 1/4[\bar{1}\bar{1}\bar{1}])$ and $(4^-, 1/4[\bar{1}1\bar{1}])$, respectively, their

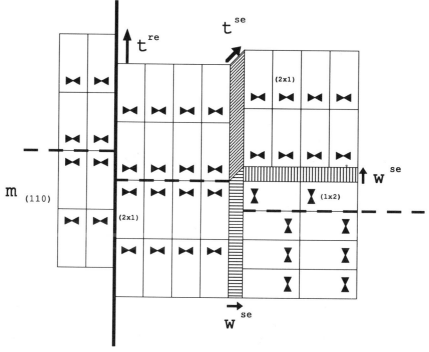

FIG. 13. Schematic plan view illustration of a reconstructed (001) Si surface showing the arrangement of (2 × 1) cells near a translation domain line, a mirror domain line, a step, and demisteps. The "bow-tie" symbols represent the presence of mirror symmetry parallel to the long axis of the (2 × 1) cell, and its absence parallel to the short axis.

heights $h_d$ being equal to $a/4$. Now consider the closed circuit UVWXU, which encircles the nodal reaction, with no other discontinuities linked by the circuit. This circuit lies on the crystal surface and passes through the cores of the surface defects. However, this does not introduce ambiguity in the mapping procedure because the strains involved are small. The demisteps are characterized by operators involving rotations, and hence, in formulating the circuit mathematically, we use the transformed operators, $\mathfrak{W}_i^*$, so that they are defined with respect to the location specified by previous operations (see Section II). After mapping into the reference space, the circuit operator $\mathfrak{C}$ is found, after cancellation of opposing translation operations, to reduce to the operations characterizing the demisteps and the step, i.e.,

$$\mathfrak{C} = (\mathbf{I}, 1/2[101])\,(\mathbf{4}^+, 1/4[\bar{1}1\bar{1}])^*\,(\mathbf{4}^-, 1/4[\bar{1}\bar{1}\bar{1}])^*, \qquad (14.1)$$

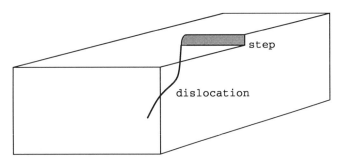

FIG. 14. Schematic illustration showing the emergence of a dislocation from the bulk to become a surface step.

which is equal to the identity $(\mathbf{I}, \mathbf{0})$. In other words, the circuit closes in the reference space and the topological properties of the discontinuities are conserved at the nodal reaction. This conservation condition is analogous to Frank's rule for conservation of the Burgers vector at a node.

Similarly, we can investigate the situation where a surface step, such as $SS'$, is connected to a bulk dislocation, as shown in Fig. 14. Let the line direction $\boldsymbol{\xi}$ of the dislocation and step be parallel at their point of contact; the step is characterized by $(\mathbf{I}, \mathbf{t})$. For a surface circuit encircling the point of dislocation emergence, the circuit operator $\mathfrak{C}$ is equal to $(\mathbf{I}, \mathbf{t})^{-1}$; the fact that this does not equal the identity reflects the fact that the circuit links a further discontinuity (in addition to the step) characterized by $\mathfrak{C}^{-1}$, i.e., the dislocation. In other words, the step and dislocation are characterized by the same operation, i.e., $\mathbf{b} = \mathbf{t}$.

We recall that, whereas bulk defects are characterized uniquely by an operation, surface features are not. Thus, all the distinct dislocations with Burgers vectors equal to $\mathbf{b}$ modulo some translation vector parallel to the surface would produce the identical step on reaching the surface. However, when a surface defect is attached to a bulk defect, as in Fig. 14, it is meaningful to choose the same operator to characterize both features. This is analogous to the characterization of line defects terminating extended defects in the bulk, as discussed in Section 9. The preceding discussion of a crystal dislocation emerging onto a surface illustrates the more general point that discontinuities that pass from the bulk onto a surface (or interface) preserve their intrinsic topological character despite the fact that there may be dramatic changes of structure. Thus, dislocations emerging onto surfaces become steps with $h_s = \mathbf{n} \cdot \mathbf{b}$, or translation domain lines on reconstructed surfaces when $\mathbf{b}$ is equal to $\mathbf{t}_i^{re}$. Similarly, one can show that a disclination, characterized by the rotation $(\mathbf{R}, \mathbf{0})$ emerging onto a surface $\mathbf{n}$ leads to a facet junction on unrelaxed surfaces

(unless $\mathbf{Rn} = \mathbf{n}$), or to rotation domain lines on relaxed surfaces where $\mathbf{Rn} = \mathbf{n}$. A dispiration is similar to a disclination except that an additional demistep arises unless $\mathbf{n} \cdot \mathbf{w}_i = 0$.

## V. Interfacial Discontinuities

In this section we discuss interfacial defects using *a priori* and *a posteriori* methods. The *a priori* approach leads to an expression that specifies the operations characterizing all defects admissible in any given interface; these include defects in both the manifest and broken symmetry classes. However, defects in the former class must also be admissible in the bulk of the adjacent crystals because they are characterized by (proper) coincident symmetry operations. In other words, such dislocations and disclinations can thread from the white crystal into the interface itself and on into the black crystal. Defect motion through the interface would not modify the interfacial structure or create steps or facet junctions. In all other respects, the topological properties of these defects are as discussed in Section III, and hence we do not consider them further here. A broad range of defects is possible in the class of broken symmetry, since a considerable number of the symmetry operations exhibited by the component crystals may be suppressed when a bicrystal is created. As might be expected, this range includes defects similar to surface and bulk discontinuities, and it is convenient to consider these separately in the following discussion.

### 15. *A PRIORI* CHARACTERIZATION

Our starting point is an interface characterized by the space groups of the adjacent crystals $\Phi(\lambda)$ and $\Phi(\mu)$, their relative orientation and position $\mathfrak{P} = (\mathbf{P}, \mathbf{p})$, and the interface normal $\mathbf{n}$. An admissible defect would separate crystallographically identical (manifest class) or equivalent (broken symmetry class) regions of interface, and these would therefore be energetically degenerate in both cases. We assume that the introduction of a single such defect does not modify the crystallographic parameters of the interface listed earlier. (This is in contrast to the next section, where an interface is itself modeled as an array of defects.)

Our task now is to obtain an expression that enables the character of admissible discontinuities to be determined *a priori*. We could proceed by means of group decomposition to find the equivalent bicrystals that can be created from the set of equivalent dichromatic complexes, and hence identify the operations characterizing admissible defects as the

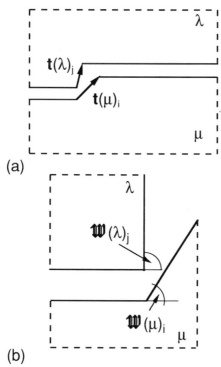

Fig. 15. Schematic illustration showing the formation of interfacial discontinuities by a Volterra process: The surfaces of the black and white crystals exhibit (a) steps and (b) facet junctions.

exchange operations interrelating these variants. However, a simpler method, leading to the same result, is to use a Volterra-like procedure to introduce defects into the bicrystal of interest. This bicrystal can be regarded as having been created by bringing together the black and white crystals, with the required surfaces having been prepared, and then bonding these together. This is our reference object, and the black and white space groups constitute our reference spaces. Now, we make a cut along the interface (this is the simplest choice), thereby reexposing portions of the initial black and white surfaces as the faces of the cut. Next, we create from these exposed surfaces equivalent new surfaces, as illustrated in Fig. 15(a) for the case of steps and in 15(b) for facet junctions.

After the necessary rigid-body displacement is applied, these variant surfaces can be rebonded to form an interface degenerate with the initial one. This is the displacement that characterizes the defect, and can be formulated in terms of the operations characterizing the free-surface fea-

tures. Let $\xi$, the line direction of the black and white surface features and the resulting interfacial defect, be taken to be directed out of the page, and we choose the interface normal, $\mathbf{n}$, to point into the white crystal. The translation and rotation operations relating the variant surfaces to the initial ones are indicated in Figs. 15(a) and 15(b). (Note that these are actually the inverses of the operations that would be used for features on black and white free surfaces with normal $\mathbf{n}$. However, the white free surface would actually have its normal parallel to $-\mathbf{n}$. The convention adopted here leads to a consistent characterization of bulk and interfacial defects.)

The operation required to bring the new black surface onto the new white one in order to form an interface degenerate with the initial one is simply the inverse of the black operation, i.e., $\mathfrak{P}\mathfrak{W}(\mu)_i^{-1}\mathfrak{P}^{-1}$ expressed in the white frame, followed by the white operation $\mathfrak{W}(\lambda)_j$ (see Ref. 25). We refer to this overall operation as $\mathfrak{Q}_{ij} = (\mathbf{Q}_{ij}, \mathbf{q}_{ij})$, and hence we have

$$\mathfrak{Q}_{ij} = \mathfrak{W}(\lambda)_j \mathfrak{P}\mathfrak{W}(\mu)_i^{-1}\mathfrak{P}^{-1}. \tag{15.1}$$

This equation shows that interfacial defects are characterized by a sequence of two symmetry operations, one from each of the space groups of the adjacent crystals. This is a general expression encompassing both manifest and broken symmetry defects. Defects in the former class correspond to the case where one of the two crystal operations is the identity, for example, if $\mathfrak{W}(\mu)_i = (\mathbf{I}, \mathbf{0})$, and $\mathfrak{W}(\lambda)_j$ is a proper operation belonging to the bicrystal group (or vice versa). In the broken symmetry class, it is convenient to consider two categories corresponding to surface-like and bulk-like defects, as outlined next.

1. The first category is when substitution into Eq. (15.1) leads to the identity, i.e., $\mathfrak{Q}_{ij} = (\mathbf{I}, \mathbf{0})$, and hence the associated discontinuities do not exhibit dislocation or disclination character. This arises when the two symmetry operations involved are pairs of coincident operations that do not belong to the bicrystal group, i.e., $\mathfrak{W}(\lambda)_j = \mathfrak{W}(\mu)_i = \mathfrak{W}(c)_k$, or antioperations, $\mathfrak{W}'$. The discontinuities in this category correspond to surface-like features, i.e., interfacial steps, demisteps, or facet juntions, analogous to those described in the previous section. In other words, the black and white surface features depicted in Fig. 15 are complementary, and no rigid-body displacement is necessary to bond the new surfaces in order to form an interface degenerate with the initial one. These defects are examined later in greater detail in Section 17.

[25]R. C. Pond, in *Dislocations in Solids* (F. R. N. Nabarro, ed.), Vol. 8, North-Holland, Amsterdam (1989).

2. The second category is when $\Omega_{ij}$ corresponds to a proper operation, and hence characterizes bulk-like defects, i.e., interfacial dislocations, disclinations, or dispirations. In this case $\mathfrak{W}(\lambda)_j$ and $\mathfrak{W}(\mu)_i$ must both be proper or improper, but not mixed. These defects are considered further in Section 18.

### 16. A POSTERIORI CHARACTERIZATION

#### a. Graphical Method

Circuit mapping is a useful method of *a posteriori* defect characterization, and is used in this section for the analysis of illustrations of distinct types of defects. Circuits are constructed around a feature of interest as a sequence of crystallographically equivalent white points followed by a sequence of equivalent black points. The only features additional to those previously discussed are first that there are now two crystal reference spaces, and second that a closed circuit must cross the interface at two points. Operations interrelating white points are mapped into the white reference space, and a similar procedure is followed for the black. The closure failure of a right-handed circuit after mapping (finish to start) identifies the topological character of the defect considered.

#### b. Mathematical Method

Each operation carrying the observer from one position to an equivalent one is represented in the reference space by the corresponding symmetry operation, $\mathfrak{W}(\lambda)_l$ or $\mathfrak{W}(\mu)_k$. The black and white points chosen in the formation of a circuit are equivalent to the origins selected in the two crystals for the definition of the symmetry operators, as in Tables I and II, for example. In principle, any point can be chosen for this purpose, but points of high symmetry offer the advantage of simpler formulations of the displacements $w(\lambda)_j$ or $w(\mu)_i$ associated with symmetry operations. Since the relative position of the two crystals, $\mathbf{p}$, is specified in terms of the black and white origins selected, it follows that the parameters $\mathbf{p}$ and $\mathbf{w}$ are not independent in any particular case. In the formulation of a circuit operator $\mathfrak{C}$ crossing the interface from white to black corresponds to a displacement operation $(\mathbf{I}, \mathbf{p})$; it also alerts the observer to change reference spaces.

In the case of defects in the manifest class, the interfacial structures on either side of the defect in question are identical, so that the second crossing of the interface (black to white) corresponds to $(\mathbf{I}, \mathbf{p})^{-1}$; hence these two contributions to $\mathfrak{C}$ cancel each other.

For defects in the broken symmetry class, the interfacial structures on either side of a defect are interrelated by a broken symmetry operation $\mathfrak{W}_i$; in this case the circuit in the deformed material will cross the interface by two symmetry related displacements, i.e., $(\mathbf{I}, \mathbf{p})$ and $(\mathbf{I}, \mathbf{W}_i\mathbf{p})^{-1}$.

Closed circuits around surface-like defects in interfaces map to closed circuits, i.e., these defects exhibit no dislocation or disclination character, and we do not present any examples of such circuits in the present work. On the other hand, circuits around bulk-like defects lead to circuit failures $\mathfrak{C}^{-1}$, after mapping, and examples concerned with bulk-like defects are illustrated later. We show that the *a priori* and *a posteriori* treatments of a given defect lead to the same characterisation. In other words, $\mathfrak{Q}_{ij}$ and $\mathfrak{C}^{-1}$ are identical, and $\mathfrak{C}^{-1}$ can be regarded as the closure failure of an irreducible circuit.

## 17. INTERFACIAL DEFECTS IN THE CLASS OF BROKEN SYMMETRY: SURFACE-LIKE DISCONTINUITIES

Defects in this category can be predicted *a priori* using Eq. (15.1); as already mentioned, these defects correspond to the special case where coincident symmetry or antisymmetry operations exist in the complex but are broken by formation of the particular bicrystal. Substitution of these coincident operations into Eq. (15.1) leads to the identity, showing that these features exhibit no dislocation or disclination character. For completeness, we show how these discontinuities can also be characterized by group decomposition in a manner analogous to that described by Eqs. (11.1) and (12.1) for unreconstructed and reconstructed surfaces, respectively. In the former case, it is necessary to decompose the space group of the dichromatic complex, $\Phi(\lambda\mu)$, with respect to that of the bicrystal in question, $\Phi(b)$, as follows:

$$\Phi(\lambda\mu) = [\Phi(b)]\mathfrak{W}_1^{be} \cup [\Phi(s)]\mathfrak{W}_2^{be} \cup \ldots [\Phi(b)]\mathfrak{W}_q^{be}. \qquad (17.1)$$

The bicrystal exchange operations, $\mathfrak{W}_q^{be}$, correspond to coincident or antisymmetry operations, $\mathfrak{W}(c)_k$ or $\mathfrak{W}'$, respectively, which do not leave the particular bicrystal invariant. These operations therefore characterize interfacial facet junctions, steps, or demisteps as summarized next.

1. *Interfacial facet junctions:* These are characterized by rotation, rotoinversion, or mirror operations. The discontinuity separates the interface with normal $\mathbf{n}$ from the crystallographically equivalent one with orientation $\mathfrak{W}_p^{be}\mathbf{n} = \mathbf{W}(c)_k\mathbf{n}$, or $\mathbf{W}_i'\mathbf{n}$. An example, derived from the dichromatic pattern illustrated in Fig. 3, is shown in Fig. 16.

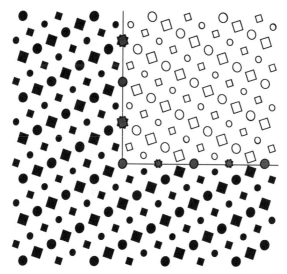

FIG. 16. Schematic illustration of an interfacial facet junction based on the dichromatic complex in Fig. 3. The interfaces have {310} orientations and are related by the coincident fourfold screw axis parallel to [001].

2. *Interfacial steps:* These are characterized by coincident translation operations, $\mathfrak{W}_n^{be} = [\mathbf{I}, \mathbf{t}(c)_k]$, and exhibit heights equal to $\mathbf{n} \cdot \mathbf{t}(c)_k$. An example is shown in Fig. 17 (antitranslations cannot arise if the adjacent crystals have different orientations).

3. *Interfacial demisteps:* These are characterized by nonsymmorphic exchange operations. In general, they arise at facet junctions, but can occur on planar interfaces in the special cases where $\mathbf{W}(c)_k \mathbf{n} = \mathbf{n}$, or $\mathbf{W}'_I \mathbf{n} = \mathbf{n}$, and the heights are then equal to $\mathbf{n} \cdot \mathbf{w}(c)_k$ and $\mathbf{n} \cdot \mathbf{w}'_I$, respectively (see Ref. 25 for a more complete discussion of the operation of antisymmetry operators). A schematic illustration is shown in Fig. 18. Here the interfacial regions on either side of the demistep are related by the (001) mirror-glide plane parallel to the page. Displacement fields may be associated with relaxed interfacial facet junctions, steps, or demisteps, but these will not have the characteristic form of single dislocations or disclinations. This can be understood in terms of bonding together black and white surfaces each exhibiting a free-surface feature; in the present case these two features are exactly complementary and fit together without the need for rigid-body displacements. Imperfect defects can exist in principle in this category, but seem improbable. For example, in the case of steps, one or both of the free surface crystal steps would have to be imperfect, but their heights would need to be identical. Even where the

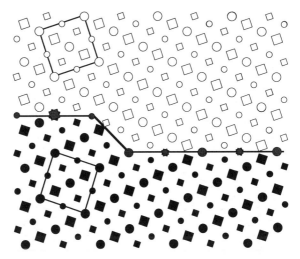

Fig. 17. Schematic illustration of an interfacial step in a (310) interface, derived from Fig. 3.

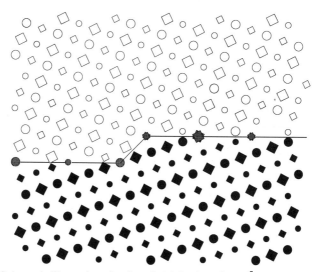

Fig. 18. Schematic illustration of an interfacial demistep in a (2̄10) interface derived from Fig. 3, characterized by the coincident mirror-glide plane parallel to (001).

heights are identical at some temperature, differences between the thermal expansion coefficients of the adjacent crystals imply that they would not be the same at other temperatures. This latter consideration is also valid for perfect steps at interphase boundaries.

Reconstruction, leading to the breaking of coincident and antisymmetry operations in a bicrystal group, are known to occur at interfaces (we do not include rigid-body displacements $\mathbf{p}$ in the present discussion because these lead to dislocations as considered later). For example, {211} twin boundaries in Ge, for which the space group of the unrelaxed structure is p2'mm', reconstruct to a centered $2 \times 2$ configuration,[26,27] and dimerization has been detected in $CoSi_2 : Si$ interfaces.[28] To find the possible discontinuities resulting from reconstruction, it is necessary to decompose $\Phi(b)$ with respect to the group of the reconstructed bicrystal $\Phi(rb)$, i.e.,

$$\Phi(b) = [\Phi(rb)]\mathfrak{W}_1^{re} \cup (\Phi(rb))\mathfrak{W}_2^{re} \cup \ldots [\Phi(rb)]\mathfrak{W}_v^{re}. \quad (17.2)$$

The exchange operations are coincident or antisymmetry operations belonging to $\Phi(b)$, which are broken by the interfacial reconfiguration, and characterize interfacial domain lines summarized as follows.

1. Translation domain lines can arise when a coincident translation operation exhibited by the unrelaxed interface is broken by reconstruction, and are characterized by an exchange operation, $\mathfrak{W}_k^{re} = (\mathbf{I}, \mathbf{t}_k^{re})$. Although such domain lines are characterized by translation operations, we emphasize that these discontinuities are not dislocations; they are analogs of the surface features discussed earlier and involve relaxations and strains localized to the interface region. Displacement fields may arise, but will not have the special form characteristic of dislocations.

2. Rotation or mirror domain lines can arise if the appropriate coincident or antioperation is broken by the reconstruction (as before, we exclude rigid-body displacements $\mathbf{p}$ from this consideration). As far as the authors are aware, such symmetry breaking relaxations have not been reported in the literature.

3. Imperfect domain lines can also arise in principle if regions of interface with distinct reconstructions coexist.

[26] A. Bourret, L. Billard, and M. Petit, *Inst. Phys. Conf. Ser.* **76**, 23 (1985).
[27] A. Bourret and J. J. Bacmann, *Proc. Jap. Inst. Met. I. S.* **4**, 64 (1985).
[28] D. Loretto, J. M. Gibson, and M. Yalisove, *Thin Solid Films* **184**, 309 (1990).

18. INTERFACIAL DISLOCATIONS IN THE CLASS OF BROKEN
    SYMMETRY

The character of interfacial dislocations can be predicted *a priori* using
Eq. (15.1) and correspond to the case where $\mathfrak{Q}_{ij}$ is a translation $(\mathbf{I}, \mathbf{q}_{ij})$,
and the Burgers vector $\mathbf{b}_{ij}$ is equal to $\mathbf{q}_{ij}$. A special case in this category
is when one of the two crystal operations is the identity; for example, if
$\mathfrak{W}(\mu)_i = (\mathbf{I}, \mathbf{0})$, then $\mathfrak{Q}_{ij}$ is equal to a proper (but not coincident) crystal
symmetry operation, $\mathfrak{W}(\lambda)_j$. In other words, this subset of defects is the
same as those that arise in the bulks of the adjacent crystals, as discussed
in Section III. Therefore, any defect that is admissible in the black or
white crystals is also admissible in the interface between them. We do
not investigate this subset further here, but concentrate on dislocations
that are normally observed only at interfaces. It is convenient to discuss
these in terms of the cause of symmetry breaking; there are four distinct
ways in which this can arise, as considered in the following subsections.

a *Broken Translation Symmetry*

When the component crystal operations in Eq. (15.1) are both transla-
tions, $[\mathbf{I}, \mathbf{t}(\lambda)_j]$ and $[\mathbf{I}, \mathbf{t}(\mu)_i]$, the resulting Burgers vector is given by

$$\mathbf{q}_{ij} = \mathbf{b}_{ij} = \mathbf{t}(\lambda)_j - \mathbf{Pt}(\mu)_i. \qquad (18.1)$$

Note that this expression is independent of $\mathbf{n}$, implying that such defects
can arise regardless of the interfacial orientation. It is also independent
of $\mathbf{p}$ since the interfacial structures on either side of the defect are identical (except for their location) and hence there is no change of $\mathbf{p}$ on either
side of the defect. A schematic illustration of a defect of this type in an
interface between an fcc (white) and hcp (black) crystal is shown in Fig.
19(a); the translation $\mathbf{t}(\lambda)_j = 1/2[112]$ and $\mathbf{t}(\mu)_i = [0001]$, to be substituted
into Eq. (18.1) are also shown. The Burgers vector of the defect, $\mathbf{b}_{ij}$, is
equal to $1/2[(1 - v), (1 - v), (2 - v)]$ in the general case, where $v = 4c/3^{1/2}a_c$ and $c$ and $a_c$ are lattice parameters of the hcp and fcc crystals,
respectively, and takes the value $1/6[\bar{1}\bar{1}2]$ in the special case illustrated
in Fig. 19 where $c/a_h$ is ideal and $a_c = 2^{1/2}a_h$.

The Burgers vector assigned to the defect in Fig. 19 can be confirmed
by circuit mapping. Since the line direction of the defect $\boldsymbol{\xi}$ points out of
the figure, the circuit PQRSTUVWP in Fig. 19(a) is right-handed; this is
shown mapped into the reference spaces in 19(b), and the closure failure
P″P′ is seen to be equal to $\mathbf{b}_{ij}$. (Note that the origin chosen in the white
crystal is an atomic site, whereas that in the black is a center of symmetry.) The circuit operator $\mathfrak{C}$ can be formulated as the sequence of white

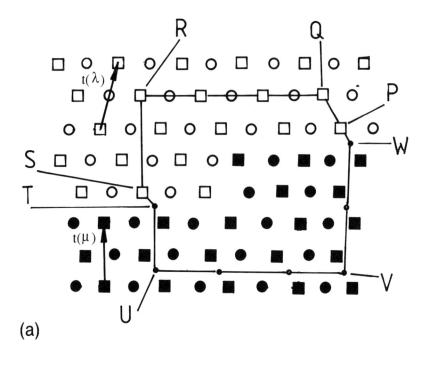

(a)

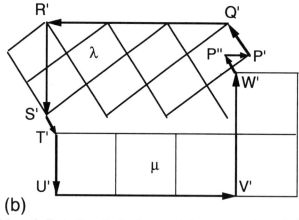

(b)

FIG. 19. Schematic illustration of a (broken translation symmetry) interfacial dislocation in a (111)/(0001) interface between fcc (white) and hcp (black) crystals. The square and circular symbols in (a) represent atoms at different projected heights along [1$\bar{1}$0] and [11$\bar{2}$0], respectively. Atomic sites are chosen as the origin in the white crystal and centers of symmetry, indicated by small circles, in the black. The circuit shown in (a) is depicted after mapping into the reference spaces in (b); the closure failure P″P′ is the Burgers vector of the dislocation.

translation operations transporting the observer from P' through Q', and R' to S', followed by the displacement $(\mathbf{I}, \mathbf{p})$ taking the observer across the interface to T', and then black translations to U' and on to V' and W', and finally recrossing the interface to P" by the displacement $(\mathbf{I}, \mathbf{p})^{-1}$.

Figure 19 shows graphically that the closure failure P"P' corresponds to $\mathbf{b}_{ij}$; mathematically, $\mathfrak{C}^{-1}$ can also be seen to be equal to $(\mathbf{I}, \mathbf{b}_{ij})$, after cancellation of opposing translations. The contributions $(\mathbf{I}, \mathbf{p})$ and $(\mathbf{I}, \mathbf{p})^{-1}$ clearly cancel; this result can be seen in a more general way for defects of this type as follows.

Let the sequence of translation operations in the white segment of the circuit sum to $\mathfrak{W}(\lambda)_r$, and similarly those in the black segment to $\mathfrak{W}(\mu)_s$. Expressed in the white frame, $\mathfrak{C}$ is therefore given by

$$\mathfrak{C} = (\mathbf{I}, \mathbf{p})^{-1}\mathfrak{P}\mathfrak{W}(\mu)_s\mathfrak{P}^{-1}(\mathbf{I}, \mathbf{p})\mathfrak{W}(\lambda)_r, \tag{18.2}$$

and this simplifies to

$$\mathfrak{C} = (\mathbf{P}, \mathbf{0})\mathfrak{W}(\mu)_s(\mathbf{P}, \mathbf{0})^{-1}\mathfrak{W}(\lambda)_r, \tag{18.3}$$

which is independent of $\mathbf{p}$. The particular value of $\mathbf{p}$ chosen in Fig. 19 leads to the maintenance of perfect crystal nearest neighbor separations for the atoms in the vicinity of the interface.

Associated with each dislocation core may be a relocation of the interface; such interfacial steps are somewhat more complicated to characterize than surface steps because of the presence of the dislocation. We distinguish two aspects of such features and refer again to Fig. 19. First, we define the black and white free-surface step heights, $h_s(\mu)_i$ and $h_s(\lambda)_j$, which have heights equal to $\mathbf{n} \cdot \mathbf{Pt}(\mu)_i$ and $\mathbf{n} \cdot \mathbf{t}(\lambda)_j$, respectively, as shown in Fig. 19(a). If these two step heights are not equal, then the dislocation formed at the interface will have a component of $\mathbf{b}_{ij}$ normal to the interface equal to the difference between these heights, i.e., $\mathbf{n} \cdot [\mathbf{t}(\lambda)_j - \mathbf{Pt}(\mu)_i]$. In this circumstance, there will be a change of the interface location, which includes elastic buckling due to the presence of the defect. This will depend on the elastic constants of the adjacent crystals, and, for the case where these are similar, the height of the interface step, designated $h_{ij}$, is given approximately by $h_{ij} = \mathbf{n} \cdot [\mathbf{t}(\lambda)_j + \mathbf{Pt}(\mu)_i]/2$, i.e., the average of the heights of the black and white surface steps associated with $\mathbf{t}(\lambda)_j$ and $\mathbf{t}(\mu)_i$, with proper account of their senses. For the special case illustrated in Fig. 19, the black and white crystal steps have equal heights, $h_s(\mu)_i = h_s(\lambda)_j$, and hence $h_{ij}$ has this value also. In the motion of an interfacial dislocation along an interface, the amount of material required in the climb process is related to the normal component of $\mathbf{b}_{ij}$.

Many examples of dislocations in this class have been reported in the literature; their crystallographic origin can be regarded as being due to the breaking of translation symmetry. Grain boundaries in cubic materials have been studied in considerable depth, for example, see the work of Babcock and Balluffi.[29] In these materials, periodic interfaces are thought to have special properties, and the Burgers vectors of admissible dislocations, as given by Eq. (15.1), correspond to dsc vectors in Bollmann's nomenclature for such cases.

As a further illustration of defects in this important category, we consider dislocation in $(11\bar{2}\bar{2})$ twin boundaries in hcp metals. The dichromatic complexes for such bicrystals exhibit periodicity parallel to the interfacial plane, but none perpendicular to it. Figure 20 shows three $[1\bar{2}10]$ projections of computer-simulated defects taken from the work of Serra et al.[30] The crystal translation operations used in the calculation of the Burgers vectors [Eq. (15.1)] are shown, and the arrows in the vicinity of the cores denote hydrostatic stress. The step heights $h_{ij}$ are one, three, and four $(11\bar{2}2)$ planes in Figs. 20(a), (b), and (c), respectively.

b. *Broken Coincident Symmetry*

Dislocations can also arise if coincident operations are orientationally aligned, i.e., $\mathfrak{W}(\lambda)_j = \mathbf{P}\mathfrak{W}(\mu)_j\mathbf{P}^{-1} = \mathfrak{W}(c)_k$, but where the translational alignment is broken due to the local relative displacement of the crystals, $\mathbf{p}$. In this case, substitution into Eq. (15.1) leads to

$$\mathbf{q}_{ij} = \mathbf{b}_{ij} = [\mathbf{W}(c)_k - \mathbf{I}]\mathbf{p}. \tag{18.4}$$

In other words, such dislocations separate domains of interface characterized by the (broken) symmetry related displacements $\mathbf{p}$ and $\mathbf{W}(c)_k\mathbf{p}$. In general, such dislocations are expected to arise at facet junctions, but can arise on planar interfaces in the special case where the interfacial orientation is such that $\mathbf{W}(c)_k\mathbf{n} = \mathbf{n}$. For these dislocations, the free-surface and interface step heights are equal and given by $h_{ij} = \mathbf{n} \cdot \mathbf{w}(c)_k$.

Experimental observations of such defects in the (001) interface between Al and GaAs have been reported,[31] as illustrated in Figure 21. In this case the maximum possible symmetry of the bicrystal is p2mm, but the actual space group is only p1 due to the relative position of the crystals. The interfacial structures on either side of the defect are related by

[29] S. E. Babcock and R. W. Balluffi, *Phil. Mag. A* **55**, 643 (1987).
[30] A. Serra, R. C. Pond, and D. J. Bacon, *Acta Met. Mater.* **39**, 1469 (1991).
[31] C. J. Kiely and D. Cherns, *Phil. Mag. A* **59**, 1 (1989).

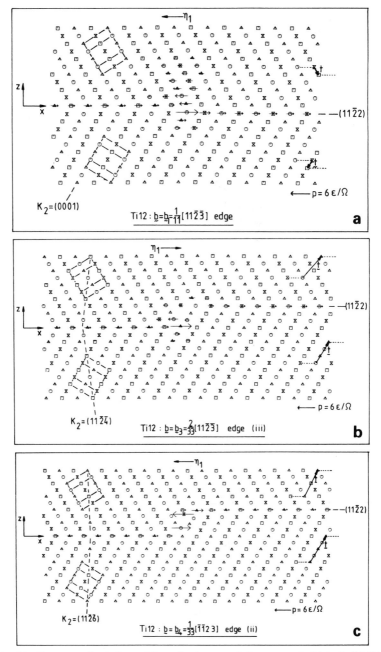

Fig. 20. Computer simulations of three (broken translation symmetry) interfacial dislocation in a (11$\bar{2}$2) boundary viewed along [1$\bar{1}$00]. The arrows represent the magnitude of the local hydrostatic pressure, those pointing to the right represent tensile stresses, and compressive to the left. The translation vectors characterizing the free-surface steps are also indicated.

342

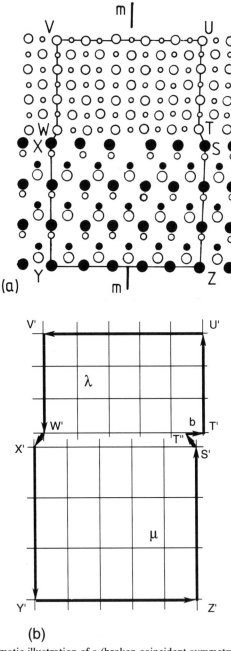

**(a)**

**(b)**

FIG. 21. (a) Schematic illustration of a (broken coincident symmetry) interfacial dislocation in edge orientation in a (001) interface between GaAs and Al. The thick vertical line
represents the broken coincident mirror. The circuit shown in (a) is mapped into the reference spaces in (b), and the closure failure, **T″T′** is the Burgers vector.

343

one of the broken (coincident) (110) mirror planes. No step arises at the core in this case because $\mathbf{n} \cdot \mathbf{w}(c)_k = 0$ in this case. A circuit TUVW-XYZST has been indicated around the defect in Fig. 21(a), where the components WX and ST correspond to the displacements involved in crossing the interface, and the origins of the two crystals are taken to be atomic sites. The circuit is shown mapped into the reference spaces in Fig. 21(b), and the closure failure T″T′ is seen to be equal to $\mathbf{b}_{ij}$. In mathematical terms the circuit operator would have been the identity if the interface had been crossed in equivalent ways at ST and WX since the translation operations UV cancel with YZ. However, since the displacements $(\mathbf{I}, \mathbf{p})$ and $[\mathbf{I}, \mathbf{m}_{(1\bar{1}0)}\mathbf{p}]^{-1}$ corresponding to WX (white to black) and ST (black to white), respectively, are included, $\mathfrak{C}$ becomes $[\mathbf{I}, \mathbf{m}_{(1\bar{1}0)}\mathbf{p}]^{-1} (\mathbf{I}, \mathbf{p}) = [\mathbf{I}, \mathbf{p} - \mathbf{m}_{(1\bar{1}0)}\mathbf{p}]$, and hence $\mathfrak{C}^{-1} = [\mathbf{I}, \mathbf{m}_{(1\bar{1}0)}\mathbf{p} - \mathbf{p}] = (\mathbf{I}, \mathbf{b}_{ij})$.

### c. Frustrated Symmetry Dislocations

A third way in which dislocations can arise is when nonsymmorphic operations exist in one or both of the two crystals such that $\mathbf{W}(\lambda)_j = \mathbf{P}\mathbf{W}(\mu)_i\mathbf{P}^{-1}$, but where $\mathbf{w}(\lambda)_j$ is not equal to $\mathbf{P}\mathbf{w}(\mu)_i$. In other words, where the orthogonal parts are coincident but the associated translations, either by virtue of an intrinsic difference or orientation, are not. According to Eq. (15.1), these dislocations have

$$\mathbf{q}_{ij} = \mathbf{b}_{ij} = \mathbf{w}(\lambda)_j - \mathbf{P}\mathbf{w}(\mu)_i + [\mathbf{W}(\lambda)_j - \mathbf{I}]\mathbf{p}. \qquad (18.5)$$

Similar to the preceeding case, such defects can only arise on planar interfaces when the interfacial orientation is such that $\mathbf{W}(\lambda)_j\mathbf{n} = \mathbf{n}$. The interface step height is given by $h_{ij} = \mathbf{n} \cdot [\mathbf{w}(\lambda)_j + \mathbf{P}\mathbf{w}(\mu)_i]/2$, and the free-surface step heights are equal to $\mathbf{n} \cdot \mathbf{w}(\lambda)_j$ and $\mathbf{n} \cdot \mathbf{P}\mathbf{w}(\mu)_i$. One example of such a defect is a glissile dislocation in $\{11\bar{2}1\}$ twin interfaces in hcp metals studied by computer simulation.[32]

Another example of a defect in this category arises in interfaces between $NiSi_2$ and Si, and has been studied experimentally in detail.[33] These defects are generally observed at facet junctions and only occur on planar interfaces where $\mathbf{W}(\lambda)_j\mathbf{n} = \mathbf{n}$, as predicted by theory. A schematic visualization of a frustrated symmetry dislocation in the (001) interface is illustrated in Fig. 22(a). The Burgers vector of such defects can be obtained by means of Eq. (15.1). The white and black operations to be substituted

[32] A. Serra, D. J. Bacon, and R. C. Pond, *Acta Met.* **36**, 3183 (1988).
[33] R. C. Pond and D. Cherns, *Surf. Sci.* **152**, 1197 (1985).

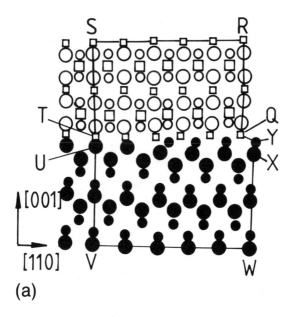

**(a)**

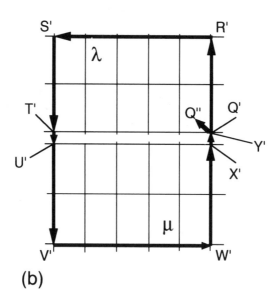

**(b)**

Fig. 22. (a) Schematic illustration of a (frustrated symmetry) interfacial dislocation in the (001) interface between NiSi$_2$ (white) and Si (black). Si atoms are represented by circular symbols and Ni atoms by square ones. In the circuit indicated, the origin in the white crystal is taken to be a Ni site and a Si site in the black. This circuit is mapped into the reference spaces in (b), and the closure failure $\mathbf{Q''Q'}$ is the Burgers vector.

in this case can be taken, for example, as the fourfold rotation, $\mathfrak{W}(\lambda)_j =$ (**4**⁺, **0**), in the NiSi₂ and the fourfold screw-rotation parallel to [001], $\mathfrak{W}(\mu)_i = (\mathbf{4}^+, 1/4[\bar{1}11])$, in the Si (the origin of the white crystal is taken to be a Ni site, and the black at a Si site). We can regard these as the operations characterizing surface features (bearing in mind the conventions adopted earlier for interfaces). The former belongs to the group $\Phi(s)$ and hence represents an unperturbed (001) NiSi₂ surface, and the latter characterizes a demistep on the Si surface. We can take $\mathbf{P} = \mathbf{I}$ since the black and white lattices are parallel, and their parameters are equal (to a very good approximation).

The crystals are translationally aligned in such a way that the atomic coordination of the Ni-Si bonds is conserved in the interface region (in symmetry related ways on either side of the defect). Referring to the indexing of Fig. 22, we can therefore take the displacement across the interface, e.g., **TU** in Fig. 22(b), to be $\mathbf{p} = 1/4[1\bar{1}\bar{1}]$. Substitution into Eq. (15.1) then gives $\mathfrak{Q}_{ij} = (\mathbf{I}, 1/4[11\bar{1}])$, i.e., the resulting Burgers vector is $1/4[11\bar{1}]$, which is also consistent with observations.

The Burgers vector of the defect in Fig. 22 can alternatively be confirmed by circuit mapping; a circuit QRSTUVWXYQ around the dislocation is shown in Fig. 22(b), and this is right-handed if $\xi$ is taken to point out of the diagram, i.e., parallel to $[1\bar{1}0]$. The circuit is shown after mapping into the reference spaces in Fig. 22(b), and the closure failure $\mathbf{Q''Q'}$ is seen to be equal to $\mathbf{b}_{ij}$. The horizontal translations RS and VW cancel, as do the vertical components QR and ST in the white crystal and UV and WX in the black. Thus, the sequence of operations taking the observer around the circuit reduces to the displacement across the interface TU, the black screw-rotation operation XY, and the (broken) symmetry related displacement across the interface YQ. The circuit operator is then given by

$$\mathfrak{C} = (\mathbf{4}^-, 1/4[\bar{1}\bar{1}1]) = (\mathbf{I}, \mathbf{4}^+\mathbf{p})^{-1}(\mathbf{4}^-, 1/4[\bar{1}11])^* (\mathbf{I}, \mathbf{p}). \quad (18.6)$$

The meaning of $\mathfrak{C}$ is that, at the end of the mapped circuit, the observer's frame has been rotated 90° in addition to a displacement of $1/4[\bar{1}\bar{1}1]$. This, of course, is because the interfacial structure on either side of the defect is related by the (broken) fourfold operation. Thus, in order to map the initial closed circuit in the general sense, i.e., to be in the same rotational state at the beginning and end, a final operation (**4**⁺, **0**)* must be carried out at Q″ to return the observer to his or her initial frame in the white crystal (without displacement). Thus, finally, $\mathfrak{C}$ is equal to (**4**⁺, **0**)* (**4**⁻, $1/4[\bar{1}\bar{1}1]) = (\mathbf{I}, 1/4[\bar{1}\bar{1}1])$, and hence $\mathfrak{C}^{-1} = (\mathbf{I}, 1/4[11\bar{1}])$, giving the Burgers vector to be $1/4[11\bar{1}]$ as previously.

This Burgers vector has components both parallel and perpendicular to the (001) interface, and consequently the dislocation can only move by climbing in this interface. The set of special interfacial orientations in which such defects can arise is {hk0}, i.e., where at least one Miller index is zero; this is the set for which at least one of the broken operations leaves the orientation of **n** invariant. It follows that such defects can move without climbing on {110} interfaces.

### d. *Broken Antisymmetry Dislocations*

The final way in which interfacial dislocations can arise is due to the breaking of antisymmetry $\mathfrak{W}'_k$. Defects in this category do not arise because of incompatible surface features, as envisaged in Fig. 15, but are characterized by a very similar formulation wherein $\mathfrak{W}(\lambda)_j$ and $\mathfrak{W}(\mu)_i$ are replaced by $\mathfrak{W}'_k$. The resulting expression for the Burgers vector is

$$\mathbf{b} = (\mathbf{W}'_k - \mathbf{I})\mathbf{p}, \tag{18.7}$$

and these defects can only arise on planar interfaces when the interfacial orientation is such that $\mathbf{W}'\mathbf{n} = \mathbf{n}$. The interfacial step height $h_{ij}$ is given by $\mathbf{n} \cdot \mathbf{w}'$. An example of such a defect in a (121) twin grain boundary in Al has been studied experimentally[34] and is schematically illustrated in Fig. 23. The broken symmetry operation $\mathbf{W}'_k$ in this case can be taken to be the antimirror parallel to the interfacial plane $\mathbf{m}'_{(121)}$; this has been broken due to **p** having a component parallel to the interface, designated $\mathbf{p}^*$, equal to $0.44[\bar{1}\bar{1}\bar{1}]$ in the present case. A circuit PQRSTUVWP is shown comprising black and white translation operations, and the displacements across the interface, ST and WP. Note that the interfacial structures in the regions of ST and WP are degenerate and interrelated by the broken antimirror. Moreover, these displacements are also seen to be symmetry related, i.e., $\mathbf{p} = \mathbf{ST}$, and $\mathbf{W}'_k\mathbf{p} = \mathbf{PW}$, respectively. [Because of their color reversing nature, antioperations act on displacements such as **p** in a manner complementary to the action of ordinary symmetry operations; in the present case the antimirror acts to invert the component of **p** responsible for breaking the symmetry, i.e., $\mathbf{p}^*$, and leaves invariant the normal (expansion) component, which does not break symmetry; the reader is referred to Ref. 25 for further details.]

The particular defect in Fig. 23 can be imagined to be created by a Volterra process in the following way. A cut is made along part of the initial interface (characterized by $\mathbf{p}^*$), and the two faces of the cut dis-

[34]R. C. Pond, *Proc. Roy. Soc. London A* **357**, 471 (1977).

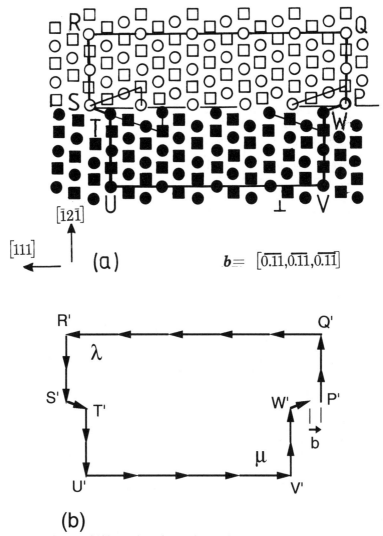

FIG. 23. (a) Schematic illustration of a (broken antisymmetry) interfacial dislocation in a (1$\bar{2}$1) interface between twinned crystals of Al. Circles and squares represent atoms at different heights projected along [$\bar{1}$01]. The circuit indicated in (a) is shown in (b) after mapping into the reference spaces, and the closure failure is the Burgers vector.

placed by $\mathbf{W}'_k\mathbf{p}^* - \mathbf{t}(b)_n$, and then rebonded, where $\mathbf{t}(b)_n = [111]$, which is a translation operation of the reference bicrystal. The resulting Burgers vector is given by Eq. (18.7) modulo $\mathbf{t}(b)_n$, i.e., $\mathbf{b} = (\mathbf{W}'_k - \mathbf{I})\mathbf{p} - \mathbf{t}(b)_n$. In the present case $\mathbf{p}^* = 0.44[\bar{1}\bar{1}\bar{1}]$, and hence $\mathbf{b} = 0.11[\bar{1}\bar{1}\bar{1}]$. This result is confirmed graphically in Fig. 23(b), which shows the mapped circuit and the closure failure $\mathbf{P}''\mathbf{P}' = \mathbf{b}$. The circuit operator can also be formulated readily; the vertical translations PQ and RS, and TU and VW cancel, the difference between QR and UV is [111], and hence $\mathfrak{C}$ reduces to

$$\mathfrak{C} = (\mathbf{I}, 0.11[111]) = (\mathbf{I}, \mathbf{W}'_k\mathbf{p})^{-1}(\mathbf{I}, [111])(\mathbf{I}, \mathbf{p}), \qquad (18.8)$$

and therefore $\mathfrak{C}^{-1} = (\mathbf{I}, \mathbf{b})$.


## 19. Other Interfacial Defects

In this chapter, we concentrate on interfacial dislocations, and only outline other possible defects.

### a. *Interfacial Disclinations*

For this case $\mathfrak{Q}_{ij}$ is a pure rotation; these defects can arise if point symmetry operators are orientationally misaligned in the two crystals. Small angular misalignments can occur, for example, during epitaxial growth on vicinal or rough substrates, and this has been described in more detail elsewhere.[35] A schematic illustration of the formation of an interfacial disclination is shown in Fig. 24; mirror planes in the two crystals are misaligned by $\phi$, and substitution of these operations into Eq. (15.1) leads to $\mathfrak{Q}_{ij}$ being the rotation of $2\phi$ as indicated in the figure. One can characterize the defect graphically by circuit mapping in the manner discussed for disclinations (see Fig. 8), or by formulating a circuit operator, but this is not pursued here.

### b. *Interfacial Dispirations*

These are characterized by operations $\mathfrak{Q}_{ij}$, which comprise both rotation $\mathbf{Q}_{ij}$ and translation $\mathbf{q}_{ij}$. For a more complete discussion of these defects, the reader is referred to other work;[25] an example of a dispiration in the interface between Ti and TiH has been studied experimentally and is described in that work.

[35]R. C. Pond, *Mat. Res. Soc. Symp. Proc.* **56**, Materials Research Society, Boston (1986).

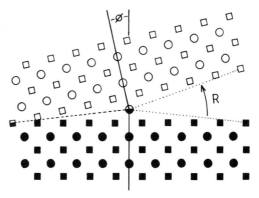

FIG. 24. Schematic illustration of the formation of a disclination in an interface between fcc crystals. The projection direction is [001], and misoriented crystal ($1\bar{1}0$) mirror planes are indicated. After bonding the surfaces on the right of the diagram, mirror symmetry is restored.

### c. Domain Boundary-Interface Intersections

The nature of the line discontinuity that delineates the intersection of a domain boundary (in a nonholosymmetric crystal) with an interface can be readily included in the present scheme. In this case, the exchange operator characterizing the domain boundary is substituted into the expression for $\mathfrak{Q}_{ij}$ instead of $\mathfrak{W}(\lambda)_j$ or $\mathfrak{W}(\mu)_i$, as appropriate. Depending on the form of the exchange operator, the resulting discontinuity will exhibit characteristics resembling those of a surface-like or bulk-like interfacial defect.

### d. Imperfect Defects

Imperfect defects separate distinct interfacial structures. Some examples of dislocations have been studied experimentally;[36,37] these appear to have formed by decomposition of perfect interfacial dislocations.

## VI. Interfaces Modeled as Dislocation Arrays

In Section V the topological character of isolated interfacial defects was discussed; we assumed that the crystallographic parameters specifying the interface were not modified by the presence of the defect. When

[36] W. Bollmann, G. Silvestre, and J. J. Bacmann, *Phil. Mag. A.* **43**, 201 (1981).
[37] C. P. Sun and R. W. Balluffi, *Phil. Mag. A.* **46**, 63 (1982).

defects are present in arrays, this assumption is no longer valid. In fact, any interface can itself be modeled as an array of defects, and the purpose of this section is to review briefly the dislocation content of interfaces modeled in this way.

The dislocation content of grain boundaries was first set out by Frank,[38] and later generalized by Bilby,[39,40] who showed how the net content may be defined for a general interphase interface. In these works, the dislocation content of an interface is defined in a reference lattice, from which the crystal lattices are obtained by affine transformations. The Frank-Bilby equation has been presented in terms of circuit mapping by Christian;[10] a closed circuit sampling both crystals near the interface is mapped into the reference lattice, and this is reviewed briefly here. In addition, mapping into the component crystal reference spaces disposed in some chosen relative orientation is discussed, bearing in mind the generalizations introduced in previous sections. As an illustration of the latter, we consider the technologically important case of epitaxial growth, and the consequences of using vicinal substrates.

### 20. Mapping Into a Single Reference Space: The Frank-Bilby Equation

We outline the derivation of the Frank-Bilby equation in the manner presented by Christian.[41] First, a reference lattice is defined, as shown schematically in Fig. 25(a). (In order to use the terminology of earlier sections, a reference crystal and reference space need to be identified. However, only translation symmetry operations were considered in earlier work, and hence only a reference lattice need be defined.) The black and white crystal lattices are obtained from the reference by the transformations $P_\lambda$ and $P_\mu$, as indicated in Figs. 25(b) and (c), respectively (for simplicity, p is taken to be zero). A closed right-handed circuit, RSTUR, is constructed as shown in Fig. 25(d), the line direction of the encircled dislocations at the interface being taken as pointing out of the page.

The circuit segment in the white crystal, RST, corresponds to a sequence of white translation operations, and the total translation is equal to RT, which we represent by the vector $v^r$ (expressed in the reference

[38] F. C. Frank, in *Symposium on the Plastic Deformation of Crystalline Solids*, The Physical Society, London (1950).

[39] B. A. Bilby, R. Bullough, and E. Smith, *Proc. Roy. Soc. A.* **231**, 263 (1955).

[40] B. A. Bilby and E. Smith, *Proc. Roy. Soc. A* **236**, 481 (1956).

[41] J. W. Christian, *The Theory of Transformations in Metals and Alloys*, Pergamon Press, Oxford, UK (1975).

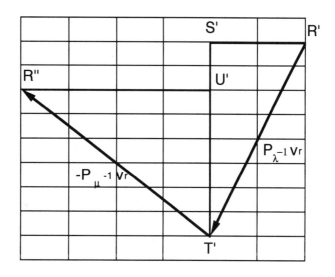

(a)

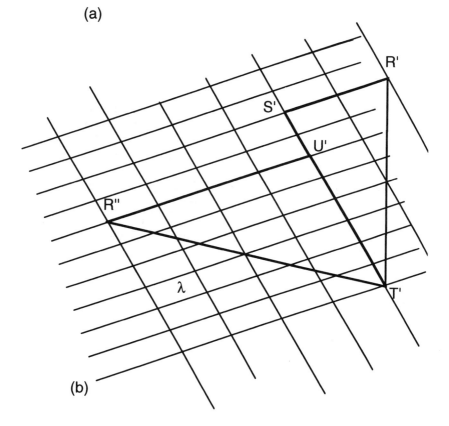

(b)

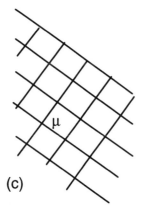

(c)

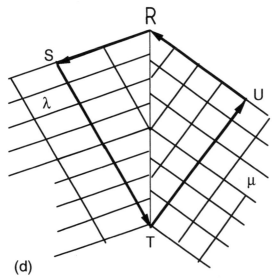

(d)

FIG. 25. Schematic illustration of the dislocation content of an interface (after Christian[41]); see text for details.

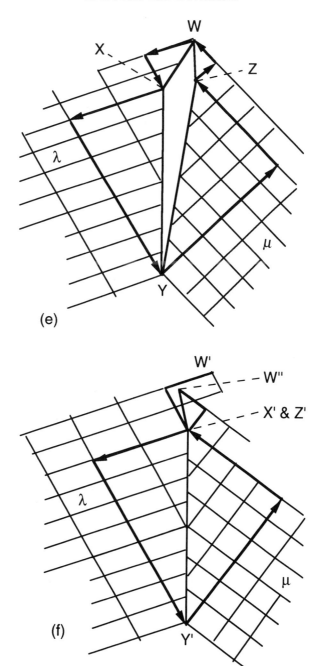

(e)

(f)

FIG. 25—(continued)

coordinate frame as signified by the superscript). Similarly, the partial circuit in the black crystal, TUR, corresponds to a sequence of black translation operations, equal in total to **TR**, i.e., $-\mathbf{v}^r$. When mapped from their respective crystal lattices into the reference space, these two vectors are $\mathbf{P}_\lambda^{-1}\mathbf{v}^r$ and $-\mathbf{P}_\mu^{-1}\mathbf{v}^r$, respectively, as indicated in Fig. 25(a). In other words, they have the same indices in the reference lattice as in their respective crystal lattices. Thus, expressed in the reference frame, the closure failure $\mathbf{R}''\mathbf{R}'$, which is equal to the total Burgers vector of the dislocations encircled, designated $\mathbf{b}^r$, is given by

$$\mathbf{b}^r = (\mathbf{P}_\mu^{-1} - \mathbf{P}_\lambda^{-1})\mathbf{v}^r. \tag{20.1}$$

This formulation of $\mathbf{b}^r$ is written in terms of $\mathbf{v}^r$, which is known as the probe vector; the meaning of $\mathbf{b}^r$ is therefore the total Burgers vector of the interface dislocations intersected by the probe vector.

The probe vector chosen in the analysis of an interface of interest should be large compared with the magnitudes of translation vectors in the reference frame. We also note that the probe vector in Fig. 25 joins points where black and white crystal origins coincide; this condition can always be met to any required degree of accuracy if one chooses a sufficiently large probe vector.

As described in the present terminology, the circuit operator $\mathfrak{C}$ is the operator expressed in the reference frame that relates the starting point R' in the mapped circuit to the endpoint R", as indicated in Fig. 25(a). Let the translation **RT** correspond to the operation $[\mathbf{I}, \mathbf{t}(\lambda)_q]$ in the white crystal (expressed in the white frame), and similarly let $[\mathbf{I}, \mathbf{t}(\mu)_r]$ be this translation in the black frame. First, if these operations are transformed into the reference frame, they become $\mathbf{P}_\lambda[\mathbf{I}, \mathbf{t}(\lambda)_q]\mathbf{P}_\lambda^{-1}$ and $\mathbf{P}_\mu[\mathbf{I}, \mathbf{t}(\mu)_q]^{-1}\mathbf{P}_\mu^{-1}$, respectively, and, secondly, if they are mapped into the reference lattice, they finally become $\mathbf{P}_\lambda^{-1}\mathbf{P}_\lambda[\mathbf{I}, \mathbf{t}(\lambda)_q]\mathbf{P}_\lambda^{-1}\mathbf{P}_\lambda = [\mathbf{I}, \mathbf{t}(\lambda)_q]$ for the white, and similarly $[\mathbf{I}, \mathbf{t}(\lambda)_q]$ for the black (where these are now operations in the reference frame). Hence,

$$\mathfrak{C} = [\mathbf{I}, \mathbf{t}(\mu)_q]^{-1}[\mathbf{I}, \mathbf{t}(\lambda)_q] = [\mathbf{I}, \mathbf{t}(\lambda)_q - \mathbf{t}(\lambda)_r]. \tag{20.2}$$

The vectors $\mathbf{t}(\lambda)_q$ and $\mathbf{t}(\mu)_r$ can be identified with $\mathbf{P}_\lambda^{-1}\mathbf{v}^r$ and $\mathbf{P}_\mu^{-1}\mathbf{v}^r$ in Eq. (20.1), and, as mentioned above, corresponding pairs have the same indices in the crystal and reference lattices. It then follows that $\mathfrak{C}^{-1} = (\mathbf{I}, \mathbf{b}^r)$.

The choice of reference lattice is arbitrary, but a selection of one of the crystal lattices may be convenient. If we choose the white lattice, the mapped circuit is as shown in Fig. 25(b), and Eq. (20.1) has

the simpler form

$$\mathbf{b}^\lambda = (\mathbf{P}^{-1} - \mathbf{I})\mathbf{v}^\lambda. \tag{20.3}$$

The interpretation and application of Eqs. (20.1) and (20.3) have been discussed in detail by Christian,[10] and are only reviewed briefly here. They give the dislocation content of an interface, but this is not unique because of the multiplicity of affine transformations, which will generate one lattice from another (as consequences of additional homogeneous deformations or symmetry operations that leave the lattices invariant). Thus, formally there is an infinity of descriptions of the net Burgers vector content for a given interface, and only descriptions where the component discrete dislocations are relatively widely spaced are useful. However, the best description need not necessarily be that with smallest $\mathbf{b}^\lambda$; for example, a symmetrical tilt grain boundary in centrosymmetric crystals can be generated by a rotation about the tilt axis or a reflection across the interface plane. The latter does not identify the dislocation content of the boundary, whereas the former leads to an array of distinct edge dislocations if the tilt is small. We note that if such a boundary is terminated at a line defect inside the material, the defect must be characterized uniquely by a proper rotation operation (not a crystal symmetry operation), which also characterizes the boundary. This is analogous to the situation regarding planar faults discussed in Section III.


21. MAPPING INTO A DICHROMATIC COMPLEX

Consider again the interfacial configuration depicted schematically in Fig. 25(d). Let this represent a reference bicrystal structure; the two crystal space groups in the appropriate relative disposition, i.e., the dichromatic complex, are the reference spaces. The closed circuit RSTUR is comprised of the white and black segments RST and TUR as discussed earlier. However, these components are now mapped into their corresponding crystal spaces. If the white segment is equal overall to the operation $\mathfrak{W}(\lambda)_k$, and the black to $\mathfrak{W}(\mu)_l$, then the circuit operator $\mathfrak{C}$, expressed in the white frame, is equal to $\mathfrak{P}\mathfrak{W}(\mu)_l\mathfrak{P}^{-1}\mathfrak{W}(\lambda)_k$. Since we are mapping these segments into the reference dichromatic complex, the circuit remains closed, i.e., $\mathfrak{C} = (\mathbf{I}, \mathbf{0})$, and there is no dislocation content with respect to the reference structure. Now imagine that the bicrystal is modified, as indicated schematically in Fig. 25(e); a closed circuit WXYZW constructed in this configuration will lead to a closure failure when mapped into the reference complex. This implies the presence of addi-

tional interfacial defects in the modified interface. To identify the density and nature of these additional defects, we need to consider the set of defects admissible in the reference bicrystal, and the magnitude of the closure failure, as addressed separately in the following subsections.

### a. *The Set of Admissible Defects*

The interfacial defects that form the admissible set in a given interface are characterized by the operations $\mathfrak{Q}_{ij}$, as explained in Section V. This set depends on the extent to which the symmetry elements of the black and white crystals coincide; we refer to this property as the extent to which the adjacent crystals are connected. It is helpful in the present discussion to consider briefly the two extremes of this condition. Completely connected crystals exhibit the same space group (but not necessarily the same structure) and the correspondence between their coordinate frames, $\mathfrak{P}$, is the identity $(\mathbf{I}, \mathbf{0})$, i.e., the two lattices have identical parameters and orientation. The opposite extreme of completely disconnected crystals means that no symmetry operations at all are coincident in the two crystals. In the former case, i.e., when Eq. (4.1) is satisfied for all the black and white symmetry operations, Eq. (15.1) becomes

$$\mathfrak{Q}_{ij} = \mathfrak{W}(\lambda)_j \mathfrak{P} \mathfrak{W}(\mu)_i^{-1} \mathfrak{P}^{-1} = \mathfrak{W}(c)_j \mathfrak{W}(c)_i^{-1} = \mathfrak{W}(c)_l. \qquad (21.1)$$

In other words, the discontinuities that can exist in the bicrystal, including those at the interface, are, from the topological point of view, the same as those that can arise in either of the single crystals, irrespective of the interfacial orientation. Now consider departures from complete connection. The greater the extent to which the symmetry of the crystals is no longer coincident, the greater the extent to which the sets of crystal discontinuities differ, and, according to Eq. (15.1), the wider the range becomes of distinct admissible interfacial features. Departures from complete connection arise either if the crystals have distinct space groups or the correspondence between the two coordinate frames is not the identity (due to differences of lattice parameters, relative orientations, or positions).

Whatever the extent of connectivity between two adjacent crystals, the set of admissible defects predicted by Eq. (15.1) is independent of the choice of $\mathfrak{P}$ (unlike the dislocation content of the interface with respect to a single reference lattice as described earlier). This can be seen if one substitutes into Eq. (15.1) transformations equivalent to $\mathfrak{P}$, which are given by $\mathfrak{W}(\lambda)_q \mathfrak{P} \mathfrak{W}(\mu)_p$. (We do not include unimodular transformations other than symmetry operations since they dissymmetrize the complex.)

Using this expression in Eq. (15.1), we obtain

$$\mathfrak{Q}_{ij} = \mathfrak{W}(\lambda)_j\mathfrak{W}(\lambda)_q\mathfrak{P}\mathfrak{W}(\mu)_p\mathfrak{W}(\mu)_i^{-1}\mathfrak{W}(\mu)_p^{-1}\mathfrak{P}^{-1}\mathfrak{W}(\lambda)_q^{-1} \qquad (21.2)$$

As a consequence of the properties of groups and excepting automorphic transformations, this reduces to

$$\mathfrak{Q}_{rs} = \mathfrak{W}(\lambda)_s\mathfrak{P}\mathfrak{W}(\mu)_r^{-1}\mathfrak{P}^{-1}, \qquad (21.3)$$

which predicts the same set of defects as Eq. (15.1).

b. *Closure Failure*

We now return to the closure failure of circuit WXYZW when mapped into the dichromatic complex, illustrated in Figs. 25(e) and (f). The new probe vector corresponds to WY, and the two circuit segments to WXY and YZW. However, the component XY corresponds to the probe vector used in the reference bicrystal [Fig. 25(d)] and YZ to the negative of this. The other components, WX and ZW, are supplements to the white and black circuit segments, respectively. These components are shown mapped into the reference complex in Fig. 25(f), and it is seen that X'Y' superimposes on Z'Y'. In other words, the closure failure, W"W', can be expressed in terms of the supplementary components only. The circuit operator $\mathfrak{C}$ relates the point W' to W" and is equal to the sequence of white operations taking the observer from W to X, designated $\mathfrak{W}(\lambda)_t$, followed by the sequence of black operators taking the observer from Z to W, designated $\mathfrak{W}(\mu)_u$, expressed in the white reference frame, i.e., $\mathfrak{C} = \mathfrak{P}\mathfrak{W}(\mu)_u\mathfrak{P}^{-1}\mathfrak{W}(\mu)_t$. Thus, the defects encircled by the circuit WXYZW correspond to the operation $\mathfrak{C}^{-1}$, which is seen to be an operation in the set of admissible ones, $\mathfrak{Q}_{ij}$, for the reference bicrystal.

Alternatively, we can derive an expression for the total defect content in terms of the new probe vector **WY** in Fig. 25(e), which we write as $\mathbf{v}_2^\lambda$. Let the actual correspondence relating the black and white frames in the modified bicrystal be written $\mathfrak{S}\mathfrak{P}$, where $\mathfrak{S}$ describes the supplementary affine transformation. As indicated in Fig. 25(f), the closure failure is given by **W"Y'** + **Y'W'**, i.e.,

$$\mathbf{b}^\lambda = (\mathfrak{S}^{-1} - \mathbf{I})\mathbf{v}_2^\lambda. \qquad (21.4)$$

This expression is analogous to Eq. (20.2) and gives the total Burgers vector of the interfacial defects intersected by the probe vector. It was first obtained by Bollmann[6] for the case where the unit Burgers vectors

belong to the dsc lattice associated with a coincidence site lattice. In the present work, $\mathbf{b}^\lambda$ is regarded as a combination of defects in the admissible set specified by Eq. (15.1) for the chosen reference bicrystal, which includes the case visualized by Bollmann as a special instance. The formulation in terms of $\mathfrak{S}^{-1}$ has more general validity since symmetry operations other than translations can be incorporated in the analysis. In addition, the presence of finite displacements $\mathbf{p}$, and symmetry related forms, can also be included in the mapping of circuits as described previously in Section V. Equation (21.3) is subject to the same qualifications as discussed above for Eqs. (20.1) and (20.2). In particular, $\mathfrak{S}$ cannot be defined uniquely, but descriptions leading to relatively widely spaced dicrete interfacial defects superimposed on the reference bicrystal are the most useful. Also, a reference bicrystal must be chosen, and this is not always straightforward. Considerable success has been achieved in the analysis of grain boundaries in cubic materials; periodic interfaces are chosen as reference structures and Eq. (21.3) is used to find the additional defect content when $\mathfrak{S}$ corresponds to a small supplementary rotation (see Ref. 42 for example).

## 22. Dislocation Content of Epitaxial Interfaces

### a. Growth on Low-index Substrates

In this section we illustrate the analysis of epitaxial interfaces by mapping into a dichromatic complex. For simplicity, we choose the case of two misfitting primitive cubic structures with space groups $Pm\bar{3}m$, which adopt parallel orientation when growth takes place on the (001) plane of the (black) substrate crystal. The structure illustrated in Fig. 26(a) is chosen as reference because it exhibits no displacement field near the interface, and the two crystals exhibit their relaxed lattice parameters. For simplicity, the interface initially considered is periodic (nonperiodic cases are discussed later); for this interface $\mathbf{P} = 8/7(\mathbf{I}, \mathbf{0})$ and $\mathbf{n} = [001]$. The set of admissible interfacial defects predicted by Eq. (17.2) comprises (broken translation symmetry) dislocations only, with Burgers vectors given by

$$\mathbf{b}_{ij} = \mathbf{t}(\lambda)_j - \mathbf{Pt}(\mu)_i, \tag{22.1}$$

expressed in the white crystal frame. One can obtain the smallest magnitude Burgers vector by substituting, for example, $\mathbf{t}(\lambda)_j = [100]^\lambda$ and

[42] E. Kvam and R. W. Balluffi, *Phil. Mag. A* **56**, 137 (1987).

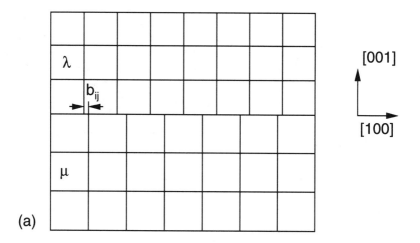

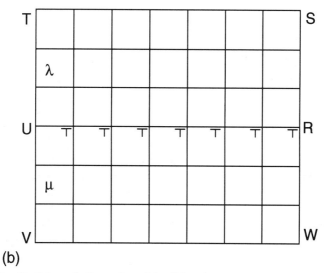

FIG. 26. Schematic illustration of the dislocation content of epitaxial interfaces; see text for details.

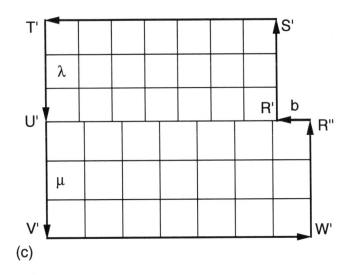

(c)

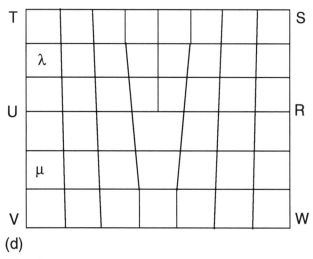

(d)

FIG. 26—(continued)

$t(\mu)_i = [100]^\mu$, giving $\mathbf{b}^\lambda_{min} = 1/7[\bar{1}00]^\lambda$, as indicated in Fig. 26(a). No interfacial steps are associated with such defects because $\mathbf{n} \cdot t(\lambda)_j$ and $\mathbf{n} \cdot \mathbf{Pt}(\mu)_i$ are both zero. The set of Eq. (22.1) also includes translation vectors of the two crystals, i.e., crystal dislocations are admissible in the interface; those with $\mathbf{b}$ parallel to the interface are not associated with interfacial steps, and vice versa.

Consider a supplementary deformation that homogeneously expands the white crystal and contracts the black so that the lattice parameters of the two crystals become identical; the modified bicrystal is depicted in Fig. 26(b), and has been referred to as a coherent interface by Olsen and Cohen,[43] for example, and is known as a *commensurate interface*. In a linear elastic viewpoint, a more convenient deformation that gives the same information with respect to defect content is to treat the supplementary deformation that homogeneously expands the white crystal so that the two lattice parameters become identical. The supplementary deformation is represented by $\mathfrak{S} = 7/8(\mathbf{I}, \mathbf{0})$, and hence the overall transformation relating the black and white coordinate frames is $\mathfrak{S}\mathfrak{P} = (\mathbf{I}, \mathbf{0})$. We can now find the dislocation content of the modified interface with rspect to the reference by determining $\mathfrak{C}^{-1}$, or equivalently by using Eq. (21.4). Taking $\xi$ to be parallel to $[0\bar{1}0]$, we define the right-handed circuit RSTUVWR, shown in Fig. 26(b), and its mapping into the dichromatic complex in Fig. 26(c). The circuit operator $\mathfrak{C}$ is seen to be $\mathbf{P}(\mathbf{I}, [700]^\mu)\mathbf{P}^{-1}(\mathbf{I}, [700]^\lambda)$ after cancellation of the vertical translations, RS and TU, and UV and WR, in the white and black crystals, respectively. Thus, $\mathfrak{C}^{-1} = (\mathbf{I}, [\bar{1}00]^\lambda)$, and therefore the total Burgers vector encircled is $[\bar{1}00]^\lambda$. We obtain the same result from Eq. (21.4) by taking the probe vector to be $\mathbf{v}^\lambda_2 = \mathbf{RU}$ in Fig. 26(b), i.e., $[\bar{7}00]^\lambda$; substituting then leads to

$$\mathbf{b}^\lambda = [8/7(\mathbf{I}, \mathbf{0}) - (\mathbf{I}, \mathbf{0})][\bar{7}00]^\lambda = [\bar{1}00]^\lambda. \qquad (22.2)$$

To be consistent with the atomic configuration shown in Fig. 26(b), this total Burgers vector can be modeled formally as comprising seven interfacial dislocations, each with Burgers vector $\mathbf{b}^\lambda_{min}$, having separations equal to the period of the modified interface, as shown in Fig. 26(b).

In reality, a case where the lattice mismatch was such that the interface structure exhibited a short periodicity, as in Fig. 26, would be very rare (at least for thick films). In terms of $\mathfrak{P}$ and $\mathfrak{S}$, however, one can describe any interface iteratively, a procedure that is particularly useful for interfaces that are very close to a periodic structure. Consider, for example, a configuration analogous to Fig. 26(a) but where the period along the

[43] G. B. Olsen and M. Cohen, *Acta Metall. Mater.* **27,** 1007 (1979).

interface is $801[100]^\lambda$ (or $700[100]^\mu$), i.e., $\mathfrak{P} = 801/700(\mathbf{I}, \mathbf{0})$ and $\mathbf{n} = [001]$. This structure forms a new reference bicrystal and has an associated dichromatic complex and set of broken translation symmetry dislocations. The configuration illustrated in Fig. 26(a) can be obtained from the new reference by homogeneous expansion, i.e., $\mathfrak{S} = 800/801(\mathbf{1}, \mathbf{0})$, and the method described can be used to determine its dislocation content. Putting $\mathbf{v}_2^\lambda = 800[\bar{1}00)^\lambda$, and substituting into Eq. (21.4) one finds $\mathbf{b}^\lambda = [\bar{1}00]^\lambda$. Dislocations of this type would be distributed along the interface as an array of (broken translation symmetry) interfacial dislocations. The analysis of the dislocation structure for the interface with period $[800]^\lambda$ (or $[700]^\mu$) would then proceed as before to yield regularly spaced interface dislocations with $\mathbf{b}_{min}^\lambda = 1/7[\bar{1}00]^\lambda$. Evidently, even for an irrational match between the two lattices, one could iterate to describe the interface within any given small residual $\mathfrak{S}$ that would be infinitesimal in the limit. Similar considerations would apply for stepped interfaces arising from overgrowths, treated later, or in phase transformations.

The free energy of homogeneously strained epitaxial layers, such as the white crystal in Fig. 26(b), can be reduced by the introduction of crystal dislocations, generally referred to as *misfit dislocations*, into the interface.[44] By this means, the long-range strain of the white crystal can be relieved so that its lattice parameter returns to the equilibrium value; such a configuration is shown schematically in Fig. 26(d). One can confirm that the circuit RSTUVWR remains closed when mapped into the complex, i.e., $\mathfrak{C} = \mathbf{P}(\mathbf{I}, [700]^\mu)\mathbf{P}^{-1}(\mathbf{I}, [\bar{8}00]^\lambda) = (\mathbf{I}, \mathbf{0})$ after cancellation of the vertical translations. Similarly, substitution into Eq. (21.4) gives the same result with $\mathbf{v}_2^\lambda = \mathbf{RU}$ in Fig. 26(d), i.e., $[\bar{8}00]^\lambda$ and $\mathfrak{S} = (\mathbf{I}, \mathbf{0})$. Thus, the relaxed configuration [Fig. 26(d)] has zero dislocation content, the same as the reference bicrystal [Fig. 26(a)]; however, the displacement field near the interface is usefully described in terms of an array of discrete misfit dislocations. For the case of the long-period interface mentioned earlier, an extra crystal dislocation must be introduced every 800 white lattice periods (or 700 black lattice periods).

## b. *Growth on Vicinal Substrates*

Epitaxial films are frequently grown on substrates with surfaces cut slightly off low-index orientations. Such substrates are known as *vicinal* and exhibit arrays of surface steps or demisteps[45] as described in Section

[44]J. W. Matthews, in *Dislocations in Solids* (F. R. N. Nabarro, ed.), Vol. 2, p. 461, North-Holland, Amsterdam (1979).

[45]A. Zangwill, *Physics at Surfaces*, Cambridge University Press, Cambridge (1988).

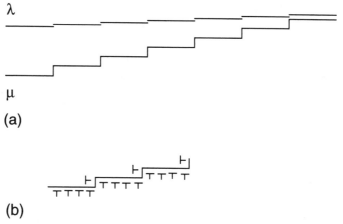

FIG. 27. (a) Schematic illustration of a vicinal substrate surface and the opposing over-layer surface before bonding. The dislocation structure of the interface after bonding is shown schematically in (b).

IV. When growth of the overlayer takes place, these substrate surface features must be accommodated, and we now briefly investigate the topo-logical consequences of this. Consider first the misfitting crystals just discussed. A schematic view of a step on the black substrate surface, characterized by $\mathfrak{W}(\mu)_i = (\mathbf{I}, [001]^\mu)$ overgrown by a coherent epilayer exhibiting a corresponding step characterized by $\mathfrak{W}([\lambda)_j = (\mathbf{I}, [001]^\lambda)$, is shown in Fig. 27(a). One can confirm, either by mapping into the complex or substitution into Eq. (15.1), that each initial surface step is transformed into a (broken translation symmetry) dislocation. If the Burgers vector is designated $\mathbf{b}_s^\lambda$, then substitution into Eq. (15.1) gives

$$\mathbf{b}_{ij} = \mathbf{t}(\lambda)_j - \mathbf{P}\mathbf{t}(\mu)_i = \mathbf{b}_s^\lambda = [001]^\lambda - \mathbf{P}[001]^\mu = 1/7[00\bar{1}]^\lambda. \quad (22.3)$$

If the vicinal substrate surface initially exhibited a regular array of steps separated by terraces of length $x[700]$, where $x$ is some integer, the vicinal angle, $\theta_v$ is equal to $\tan^{-1}1/7x$. For coherent films, the total dislocation content of the interface can be taken as in Fig. 27(b), i.e., with an array of $\mathbf{b}_{min}^\lambda$ dislocations on the terraces and one $\mathbf{b}_s^\lambda$ dislocation at each interfacial step. The total dislocation content along each terrace/step, $\mathbf{b}$, is now equal to $1/7[\overline{7x}, 0, \bar{1}]^\lambda$, and we note that this has no component perpendicular to the new interfacial orientation ($\mathbf{n}$ is now parallel to $[\bar{1}, 0, 7x]^\lambda$). In other words, while the two crystals remain coherent, the function of the dislocation array is to accommodate the misfit between the crystals along their interface, irrespective of the in-

terfacial orientation. However, if the misfit along the terraces is relieved, by incoming crystal dislocations, for example, the normal component of **b** may no longer be zero. Consider the case where the terrace misfit is relieved completely; the normal component of **b** along each terrace/step is then equal to $\mathbf{b}_s^\lambda \cos\theta_v$. If the upper surface of the epitaxial film is unrestrained, this dislocation array will also cause the film to become rotated clockwise about $[0\bar{1}0]$ with respect to the substrate. This misorientation angle $\theta_m$ is given approximately by $(\mathbf{b}_s^\lambda \cos \theta_v)/7x$, and is hence correlated to the vicinal angle. Moreover, since the sign of the perpendicular component of $\mathbf{b}_s^\lambda$ depends in general on whether $h_s(\lambda)$ is larger or smaller than $h_s(\mu)$, the sense of the rotation about $[0\bar{1}0]$ will also be determined by these relative heights. Misorientations correlated in this way with vicinal angles have been observed in several heteroepitaxial semiconductor films.[46]

Finally, we mention the consequences of the black and white crystals in heteroepitaxial layers having different symmetries, i.e., being disconnected to some extent. Even if the two crystal lattices match exactly, Eq. (15.1) shows that interfacial defects can arise. The discussion of (frustrated symmetry) dislocations in $NiSi_2 : Si$ interfaces in Section 18(c) is an example. Thus, the substrate may exhibit demisteps rather than (or in addition to) steps, for example, and these must be accommodated by the overlayer. A possible consequence when the overlayer is nonholosymmetric or ordered is that domains are nucleated at these interfacial features, as discussed elsewhere.[47] The *a priori* and *a posteriori* methods for characterizing defects described in this work can be applied to such problems.

## ACKNOWLEDGMENTS

The authors are grateful to Prof. J. W. Christian and Dr. A. P. Sutton for valuable discussions, to the SERC for the financial support of RCP and to the NSF for the support of JPH under grant DMR 9119342.

[46] M. Aindow and R. C. Pond, *Phil. Mag. A* **63**, 667 (1991).
[47] R. C. Pond, *J. Cryst. Growth* **79**, 946 (1986).

SOLID STATE PHYSICS, VOL. 47

# Giant Magnetoresistance in Magnetic Layered and Granular Materials*

PETER M. LEVY

*Physics Department New York University New York, New York*

## I. Introduction

Magnetoresistance is the change in electrical resistance of a material in response to a magnetic field. All metals have an inherent, albeit small, magnetoresistance (MR) owing to the Lorentz force that a magnetic field exerts on moving electrons. However, metallic alloys containing magnetic atoms can have an enhanced MR because the scattering that produces the electrical resistance is controlled by a magnetic field. Today,

* This work was supported in part by the Office of Naval Research.

367

for example, permalloy (a mixture of nickel and iron) is used as a magnetoresistive sensor in reading heads used in magnetic hard disk drives in computers. Recent experiments on layered and granular materials have shown an even more dramatic MR effect that makes these structures candidates for reading heads in the next generation of information storage systems.

Although earlier studies reported unusual magnetoresistive effects in layered structures,[1] it was discovered in 1988 that the application of magnetic fields to atomically engineered materials known as *magnetic superlattices* greatly reduced their electrical resistance;[2] that is, superlattices had a *giant* magnetoresistance (Fig. 1). A similar, albeit diminished effect, was simultaneously recorded for a magnetic sandwich structure.[3]

Superlattices are a special form of multilayered structures, artifically grown under ultrahigh-vacuum conditions by alternately depositing on a substrate several atomic layers of one element, say, iron, followed by layers of another, such as chromium. With molecular beam epitaxy, one can grow single-crystal ultrathin films of each element. By stacking magnetic atoms into layers and alternating them with nonmagnetic layers, magnetic superlattices have been formed whose electrical resistances are readily controlled by magnetic fields that reorient (align) the moments of the magnetic layers relative to one another.

The original observation of giant magnetoresistance was made on iron-chromium superlattices with nearly perfect crystallinity, which were grown by molecular beam epitaxy (MBE). Subsequently, by using sputtered samples that are grown much more rapidly than the MBE samples, it was possible not only to reproduce these results but also to observe oscillations in the magnetoresistance as the thickness of the nonmagnetic spacer layers was varied (Fig. 2); these oscillations mirror changes in the coupling between the magnetic layers.[4] At first it was thought the antiferromagnetic coupling was tied to the giant magnetoresistance. It was later shown, however, that although nonparallel alignment is needed to obtain magnetoresistance, the antiferromagnetic coupling is not a prerequisite.[5] In the past five years, other combinations of magnetic and nonmagnetic

[1]H. Sato, P. A. Schroeder, J. M. Slaughter, W. P. Pratt, Jr., and W. Abdul-Razzaq, *Superlattices Microstruct.* **4**, 45 (1987); E. Velu, C. Dupas, D. Renard, J. P. Renard, and J. Seiden, *Phys. Rev. B* **37**, 668 (1988).

[2]M. N. Baibich, J. M. Broto, A. Fert, F. Nguyen Van Dau, F. Petroff, P. Etienne, G. Creuzet, A. Friederich, and J. Chazelas, *Phys. Rev. Lett.* **61**, 2472 (1988).

[3]G. Binash, P. Grünberg, F. Saurenbach, and W. Zinn, *Phys. Rev. B* **39**, 4828 (1989).

[4]S. S. P. Parkin, N. More, and K. P. Roche, *Phys. Rev. Lett.* **64**, 2304 (1990).

[5]V. S. Speriosu, B. Dieny, P. Humbert, B. A. Gurney, and H. Lefakis, *Phys. Rev. B* **44**, 5358 (1991).

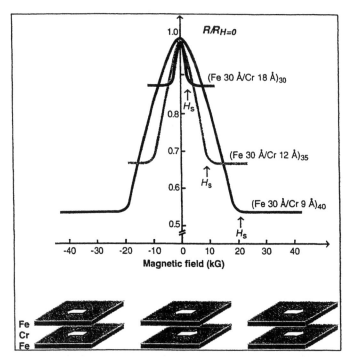

FIG. 1. Resistivity (normalized to its value in zero field) versus magnetic field for three iron-chromium superlattices at $T$ = 4.2 K. The thickness of the ferromagnetic iron layer is held fixed at 30 Å, while the nominally nonmagnetic chromium layer thickness varies from 9 to 18 Å. The resistivity is maximum when the magnetic moments of successive iron layers are antiparallel (see the schematic of the two representative layers below the curve at $H$ = 0 kG). It drops off as the applied field aligns the magnetic moments, denoted by the right and left diagrams for positive and negative fields, respectively. As the thickness of the chromium layer decreases, the magnetoresistance increases as well as the field $H_s$ needed to align the moments. [Adapted from M. N. Baibich et al., Phys. Rev. Lett. **61**, 2472 (1988).]

metallic multilayered structures have been studied. Recent studies[6] on sputtered samples of cobalt-copper revealed magnetoresistances at room temperatures that are from three to four times larger than those for iron-chromium, and *thirteen* times greater than those for permalloy films currently used as magnetoresistive sensors, for instance, in magnetic reading heads.

[6]S. S. P. Parkin, R. Bhadra, and K. P. Roche, Phys. Rev. Lett. **66**, 2152 (1991); D. Mosca, F. Petroff, A. Fert, P. A. Schroeder, W. P. Pratt, Jr., R. Loloee, and S. Lequien, J. Magn. Magn. Mater. **94**, L1 (1991); S. S. P. Parkin, Z. G. Li, and D. J. Smith, Appl. Phys. Lett. **58**, 2710 (1991).

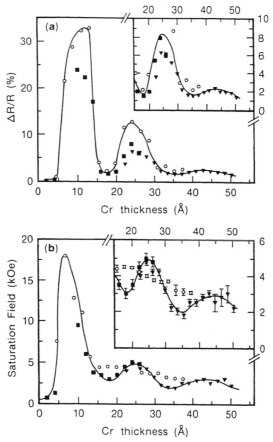

FIG. 2. Oscillations in the magnetoresistance that reflect those in the interlayer coupling or alignment of the magnetic layers: (a) Transverse saturation magnetoresistance (4.5 K) and (b) saturation field (4.5 K) versus Cr layer thickness for three series of structures of the form Si(111)/(100 Å) Cr/[(20 Å) Fe/$t_{Cr}$ Cr]$_N$/(50 Å) Cr, deposited at temperatures of $\Delta$, ■, 40°C ($N$ = 30); o, 125°C ($N$ = 20). [From S. S. S. Parkin, N. More, and K. P. Roche, *Phys. Rev. Lett.* **64**, 2304 (1990).]

In the past year, a new window on giant magnetoresistance has been opened with the announcement of large effects for ferromagnetic granules in nonmagnetic metal films, such as cobalt precipitates in copper or silver.[7] These results raise the possibility of the development of materials

[7] A. Berkowitz, J. R. Mitchell, M. J. Carey, A. P. Young, S. Zhang, F. E. Spada, F. T. Parker, A. Hutten, and G. Thomas, *Phys. Rev. Lett.* **68**, 3745 (1992); J. Q. Xiao, J. S. Jiang, and C. L. Chein, *Phys. Rev. Lett.* **68**, 3749 (1992).

that are simpler to grow than the multilayered structures and that will exhibit giant magnetoresistance. Today numerous experimental and theoretical studies are under way to understand better the origins of the giant magnetoresistance in metallic superlattices and nonmagnetic metallic matrices containing magnetic granules (granular films).

Our current understanding is that the giant magnetoresistance observed in layered and granular structures arises from the dependence of the resistivity on their internal (local) magnetic configuration. The use of "giant" refers to the origin of the MR effect; it does not always refer to the magnitude of the effect. This effect can be distinguished from the ordinary MR coming from the direct action of the magnetic field on the electron trajectories, the Lorentz force; and from the anisotropic MR, which comes from dependence of the resistivity on the relative orientation of the magnetization to the current. The role of the external magnetic field is to change the internal magnetic configuration; in cases where this is not possible, e.g., if the layers are coupled ferromagnetically, or so strongly antiferromagnetically coupled that ordinary fields cannot rotate one layer relative to another, giant MR does not appear. For this reason, ordinary magnetic metals do not display this MR effect, and it is necessary to separate magnetic regions from one another so as to be able to reorient their magnetizations. Compositional layering of these structures (magnetic layers with nonmagnetic spacer layers) was the first method to produce this result. More recently, precipitating out magnetic granules in a nonmagnetic metallic matrix also produces the physical separation of the magnetic entities. This separation permits an external field to rotate the local magnetic regions *relative* to one another as they orient themselves in the direction of the field.

Spin-dependent scattering of the condition electron produces a dependence of the resistance on the magnetic configuration; this dependence is amplified or attenuated by the spin-dependent potentials in these magnetic structures. In the absence of spin-dependent scattering, the giant MR effect is nonexistent for currents in the plane of the layers (CIP), while it does appear for currents perpendicular to the plane of the layers (CPP) (Fig. 3). The scattering producing this effect is elastic and occurs primarily at the interfaces between magnetic and nonmagnetic regions (layers or granules and matrix), although for magnetic regions consisting of alloys, e.g., permalloy, intrinsically spin-dependent scattering exists in the bulk itself. The strength of the spin-dependent scattering, which determines the magnitude of the MR, depends on the roughness of the interfaces and on the interfacial magnetism; quenching the latter kills the effect.

For the reorientation of the magnetization to produce an MR effect for

Current In the Plane

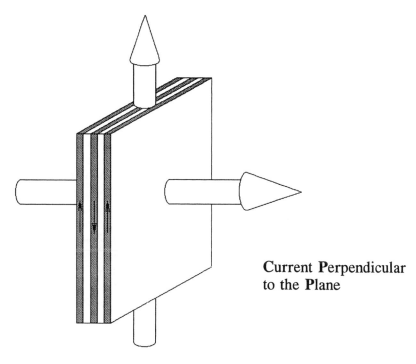

Current Perpendicular
to the Plane

a     Magnetic Multilayer

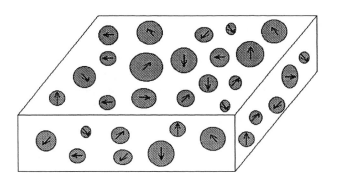

b     Magnetic Granular Film

FIG. 3. Different realizations of the giant magnetoresistance effect in layered and granular structures: (a) For multilayered structures the resistance and magnetoresistance depend on the orientation of the layers relative to the current, CIP versus CPP. (b) For granular films the response is relatively isotropic, although for epitaxially grown granular films there is a slight dependence on orientation; see Fig. 8 (d).

CIP, it is necessary for the mean free path of the electrons to be larger than the spacing between the magnetic layers.[8] For CPP, one *always* obtains a magnetoresistive effect because, independently of their mean free paths, the electrons comprising the current traverse the entire multi-layered structure. Similarly, for granular solids the current samples the magnetic regions that produce the giant MR.

A trilayered structure consisting of two magnetic layers separated by a nonmagnetic one is sufficient to produce the giant MR effect; variants of this effect known as spin-valve or exchange-biased structures[9] have a sufficiently high sensitivity (change in resistance divided by the magnetic field required to achieve it) such that they are prime candidates for use in the magnetic reading heads of the next generation of hard disk drives in computers. However, large MR ratios are achieved on multilayered structures with many repeats of a basic magnetic layer–nonmagnetic layer "unit cell"; these structures are known as *metallic superlattices*. Also the analysis of their transport properties is simpler than for sandwich structures; the role of edge effects such as shunting of the current by substrates and overlayers is minimized and the periodicity allows one to use Bloch or plane wave states rather than the more cumbersome states describing the partial confinement of electrons in a sandwich structure.

Both the semiclassical and quantum treatments of transport in inhomo-geneous magnetic materials are able to reproduce the *gross* features ob-served for the giant MR effect. However, the semiclassical approach is unable to account properly for the strong scattering at interfaces (quan-tum interference effects) and the nonlocality of the effects of scattering on transport phenomenon, i.e., the transport lifetime of an electron in

---

[8]This result can be understood when one relates the mfp to the spatial extent over which the velocity or momentum of the plane waves that represent the electrons remains well defined. For currents parallel to the layers, electrons sample in the *transverse* direction to the current those layers within a mean free path $\lambda$ from their center. Therefore, if $\lambda \gg d_{in}$ (the characteristic length scale for the inhomogeneities in the multilayered structure), it is irrelevant where one places the electron, because one always samples the same distribution of inhomogeneities. When the mfp is small compared with the spacing between magnetic layers, an electron does not sample more than one magnetized layer *within its mean free path $\lambda$*. As one is free to choose the axis of spin quantization for the conduction electron's spin parallel to the magnetization of that individual layer which the electron samples, the application of an external magnetic field will not alter the conductivity of a superlattice in this limit. In other words, an electron must sample within its mfp two or more magnetized layers, which reorient themselves relative to one another, in order for there to be a magneto-resistive effect. A *uniform* rotation of all the magnetized layers, without any internal re-arrangement, does not produce magnetoresistance.

[9]The term *spin-valve* was coined by Virgil Speriosu's group; see Refs. 5 and 18. S. S. P. Parkin uses the phrase *exchange-biased;* see, for example, his article in Ref. 41.

one layer depends on the scattering in neighboring layers as well as from the interfaces. These effects can be accounted for in a quantum treatment of transport by using a nonlocal self-energy for the one-electron propagators. This nonlocality has been implemented in the momentum space quantum treatment of transport, albeit in an approximate way, but has not yet been attempted in the real-space approach. Quantum interference effects have been neglected in the present treatments of transport; they are particularly important to include in the real-space treatment of the mixed layers representing the interfacial regions between layers.

The theory developed in this article contains the ingredients essential to an understanding of transport in magnetically inhomogeneous media. What is necessary in the future is to work out in detail the magnetotransport properties. It is important to emphasize that the proper approach to a theory of transport in inhomogeneous magnetic media is quite separate from the mechanisms that produce the spin-dependent scattering. While there is little correlation between the magnitude of the spin scattering asymmetries $\alpha$ found from studies on bulk magnetic alloys and the $\alpha$ needed to explain the MR of magnetic multilayers, this discrepancy should not be too surprising. The spin-dependent potentials amplify or attenuate the effective $\alpha$'s needed to fit the MR data on multilayers.

Finally, equivalent resistor network models, while they provide reasonable heuristic interpretations of the giant MR effect, are no substitute for more realistic treatments of the magnetotransport properties of inhomogeneous magnetic structures. Most of the multilayers have mean free paths and inhomogeneity lengths $d_{in}$, which are neither in the local or homogeneous limits for which the simpler resistor network models apply.

We begin by reviewing the experimental data that illustrate the diverse features of giant MR in its various manifestations. The theoretical formulation is reviewed from both the semiclassical and quantum mechanical viewpoints. We then discuss the mechanisms that can produce this effect. The quantum linear response theory of magnetotransport in layered and granular structures is fully developed in the following sections, and we present some fits of the theory to data. We conclude by indicating directions for future work on this effect. The study of giant magnetoresistance in inhomogeneous structures will be seen to broaden our understanding of electrical transport in magnetic media. The formalism developed to study MR is useful in the study of spin-polarized conduction through nonmagnetic metals and the detection of these currents in ferromagnetic detectors.[10] Giant MR and spin-polarized transport are challenging physics problems that hold tremendous potential for future applications in emerging technologies.

[10] M. Johnson, *Science* **260**, 320 (1993); *Appl. Phys. Lett.* **63**, 1435 (1993).

## II. Survey of Experimental Data

The prehistory of the giant MR effect has its antecedents at the intersection of two separate areas: exchange-coupled films[11] and electrical transport in ferromagnetic metallic alloys.[12] Following some ideas of Néel, a group in Grenoble in the early 1960s grew Fe/Cu/Fe sandwiches, in which the ferromagnetically magnetized layers of iron were to be magnetically coupled through the nonmagnetic copper spacer layer. Thin layers in those days were about 400 Å, and experimentalists found that even at those large thicknesses the iron layers were always coupled in parallel, i.e., ferromagnetically. After some false speculations that there was a monotonic ferromagnetic interlayer coupling through the copper, the realization was made that ferromagnetic bridges of iron formed in the copper layer and provided the coupling between the iron layers.[13]

It was not until 1985 that the art of growing ultrathin metallic layered structures advanced to the point where one could convincingly demonstrate a true interlayer coupling due to the intervening electron gas (itinerant electrons). Peter Grünberg et al.[14] was able to grow Fe/Cr/Fe sandwiches in which the chromium spacer layer was sufficiently thin (of the order of 10 Å), so that the coupling was at the same time antiferromagnetic and large enough to overcome anisotropies and orient the magnetic layers. As an antiparallel alignment of the iron layers ruled out ferromagnetic bridges, it was finally possible to demonstrate that two magnetic layers could be coupled magnetically through an intervening nonmagnetic metallic layer.[15] This was the first step toward producing giant MR; it was realized only later[5] that the coupling *per se* was not needed to produce the effect. All that is necessary is that the magnetic layers *not* be locked

[11] J-C Bruyère, O. Massenet, R. Montmory, and L. Néel, *Comptes Rendus Acad. Sci. Paris* **258**, 1423 (1964); *IEEE Trans. Magnetics* **MAG-1**, 10 (1965); J. C. Bruyère, G. Clerc, O. Massenet, D. Paccard, R. Montmory, L. Néel, J. Valin, and A. Yelon, *IEEE Trans. Magnetics* **1**, 174 (1965); A. Yelon, in *Physics of Thin Films* (M. Francombe and R. Hoffman, eds.), Vol. **6**, p. 205, Academic Press, New York (1971).

[12] A. Fert and I. A. Campbell, *J. Phys. F* **6**, 849 (1976); *J. de Physique* **32** (Colloque) C1, 46 (1971); I. A. Campbell, A. Fert, and O. Jaoul, *J. Phys. C: Metal Physics Suppl.* **1**, S95 (1970); O. Jaoul, I. A. Campbell, and A. Fert, *J. Magn. Magn. Mater.* **5**, 23 (1977); A. Fert, *Physica. B* **86-88**, 491 (1977).

[13] H. J. Juretschke, *Bull. Am. Phys. Soc.* **11**, 110 (1966); O. Massenet, F. Biragnet, H. Juretschke, R. Montmory, and A. Yelon, *IEEE Trans. Magnetics* **MAG-2**, 553 (1966).

[14] P. Grünberg, R. Schreiber, Y. Pang, M. B. Brodsky, and H. Sowers, *Phys. Rev. Lett.* **57**, 2442 (1986).

[15] Similar results, and indeed an oscillatory coupling, were found in rare-earth superlattices; see C. F. Majkrzak, J. W. Cable, J. Kwo, M. Hong, D. B. McWhan, Y. Yafet, J. V. Waszczak, and C. Vettier, *Phys. Rev. Lett.* **56**, 2700 (1986).

together ferromagnetically, and that they be easily reoriented relative to one another by an external field.

The second step in producing giant MR was the study of the electrical resistivity of ferromagnetic transition metal alloys containing various impurities. From a systematic study of the variation of the resistivity as a function of the type and concentration of impurities, Fert and Campbell[12] concluded that conduction electrons in these magnetic metals were scattered differently depending on whether their spin was parallel or opposite to the magnetization. In other words, impurity scattering in magnetic metals is spin dependent.

Following these lines, magnetoresistance measurements produced unusually large values on two different realizations of iron-chromium multilayered structures: Peter Grünberg's group found a 4% decrease in the resistivity in a trilayered Fe/Cr/Fe structure when the initial antiferromagnetic configuration was aligned in parallel (saturation);[3] by using an Fe/Cr superlattice (40 repeats), Albert Fert and his group found a nearly 50% drop in the resistivity as an external field aligns ferromagnetically a magnetic superlattice that is antiferromagnetically aligned in zero field (Fig. 1).[2] It is this latter number, with a change of the resistivity of $\Delta\rho \cong$ 23 $\mu\Omega$ cm, that has now been named *giant magnetoresistance*. One usually quotes the ratio of this change to the resistivity in either zero field $R_0$ or at saturation $R_s$. (The former is preferred by theorists because it bounds the ratio between zero and one; the latter by experimentalists because in many cases the magnetic state of the sample is ill defined at zero field.)

Subsequent to the discovery of this effect, developments have occurred on several fronts. While the initial layered structures were grown by MBE, one found that similar and possibly even larger effects could be produced with sputtered samples. Because sputtered samples can be grown much more rapidly than by MBE, Stuart Parkin was able to survey a considerably larger range of layer thicknesses and was the first to observe oscillations in the MR as the thickness of the nonmagnetic spacer layer is varied; these oscillations mirrored changes in the coupling between the magnetic layers[4] (Fig. 2). He confirmed that a large MR was present when antiferromagnetic coupling existed between the layers, and a very small MR otherwise.

The quest for larger MR ratios led to sputtered Co/Cu superlattices that did produce higher values.[6] Indeed, by using sufficiently thin layers of cobalt and copper, an MR ratio (normalized to the resistivity at high field) of 115% for currents in the planes of the layers was achieved (Fig. 4). In this figure, the data for Co/Cu grown on an iron buffer layer are compared to the data on ruthenium; as one can see, buffer layers play a

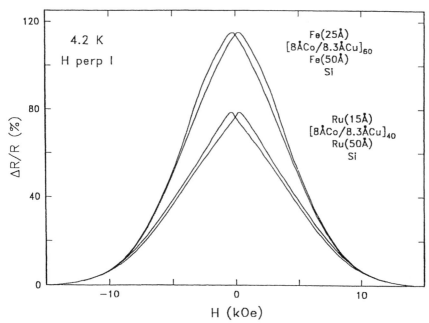

FIG. 4. Effect of substrate on magnetoresistance. The superlattice with the iron buffer layer has a 50% higher MR ratio than the one grown on ruthenium. [From S. S. P. Parkin, Z. G. Li, and D. J. Smith, *App. Phys. Lett.* **58**, 2710 (1991).]

crucial role in endowing the superlattice grown on top of it with the structural properties necessary to maximize its MR. The variation of the MR of Co/Cu with an increasing thickness of copper (Fig. 5) revealed that the MR was rising in regions where, from data on the coupling, one would expect it to be small. The resolution of this conundrum was that at the larger layer thicknesses of copper, the interlayer coupling was not sufficiently strong to dictate the alignment of adjacent layers;[16] thus, as the copper layer thickness increased, the amount of randomness in the alignment of the weakly coupled layers increased. The impact of these random alignments on MR is developed in the following sections.

Recently, Bader's group reported a maximum CIP-MR of 150% at 4.2 K (28% at room temperature) for Fe/Cr superlattices [Fig. 6(a)].[17] They

[16] S. Zhang and P. M. Levy, in *Magnetic Surfaces, Thin Films and Multilayers* (S. S. P. Parkin, H. Hopster, J-P. Renard, T. Shinjo, and W. Zinn, eds.), *Mat. Res. Soc. Symp. Proc.*, Vol. 231, p. 255; *Phys. Rev. B* **47**, 6776 (1993).

[17] E. E. Fullerton, M. J. Conover, J. E. Mattson, C. H. Sowers, and S. D. Bader, *Appl. Phys. Lett.* **63**, 1699 (1993).

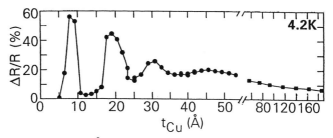

FIG. 5. The MR for Co (10Å)/Cu($t_{Cm}$). For thin spacer layer thicknesses, the MR oscillations reflect those of the interlayer coupling; eventually they die out and the MR is that for an uncoupled structure or random alignment of magnetic layers; see the text. [From S. S. P. Parkin, R. Bhadra, and K. P. Roche, *Phys. Rev. Lett.* **66**, 2125 (1991).]

were epitaxially grown by dc magnetron sputtering onto single-crystal MgO (100) substrates, whereas Fert's samples, with an MR ratio of ≈75%, were MBE grown on GaAs (100).[2] Bader's group's largest $\Delta\rho$ = 21 $\mu\Omega$ cm is comparable to the $\Delta\rho$ = 23 $\mu\Omega$ cm found by Fert.[2] However, the resistivity at saturation $\rho_s$ = 14 $\mu\Omega$ cm is less than Fert's (≈31 $\mu\Omega$ cm).

Antiferromagnetic coupling was initially thought to be tied to giant MR; although it is true that in layered structures with large MR, there is a strong antiferromagnetic coupling, the converse is not true, i.e., it is not necessary to have this coupling to produce giant MR. All that is necessary is that the layers *not* be ferromagnetically aligned; that coupling is not necessary to produce giant MR was shown in at least three ways. Virgil Speriosu and his group developed the "spin-valve" structures[18] in which a magnetic layer is pinned to an antiferromagnetic one by exchange anisotropy forces while another magnetic layer is free to be oriented by an external field [Fig. 7(a); there is little to no coupling between the magnetic layers]. Velu *et al.*,[1] Shinjo and his group,[19] and Chaiken *et al.*[20] used two magnetic layers with different coercivities to achieve antiparallel and parallel alignment as a function of field and, as seen in Fig. 7(c) (Shinjo's data), achieved quite respectable MRs. What is particularly noteworthy

[18] B. Dieny, V. S. Speriosu, S. Metin, S. S. P. Parkin, B. A. Gurney, P. Baumgart, and D. R. Wilhoit, *J. Appl. Phys.* **69**, 4774 (1991); B. Dieny, V. S. Speriosu, B. A. Gurney, S. S. P. Parkin, D. R. Wilhoit, K. P. Roche, S. Metin, D. T. Peterson, and S. Nadimi, *J. Magn. Magn. Mater.* **93**, 101 (1991).

[19] T. Shinjo and H. Yamamoto, *J. Phys. Soc. Japan* **59**, 3061 (1990); H. Yamamoto, T. Okuyama, H. Dohnomae, and T. Shinjo, *J. Magn. Magn. Mater.* **99**, 243 (1991); T. Shinjo, H. Yamamoto, T. Anno, and T. Okuyama, *Appl. Surf. Sci.* **60-61**, 798 (1992); H. Yamamoto, Y. Motomura, T. Anno, and T. Shinjo, *J. Magn. Magn. Mater.* **126**, 437 (1993).

[20] A. Chaiken, P. Lubitz, J. J. Krebs, G. A. Prinz, and M. Z. Harford, *Appl. Phys. Lett.* **59**, 240 (1991), *J. Appl. Phys.* **70**, 5864 (1991).

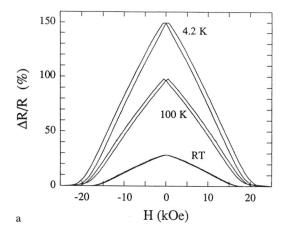

a

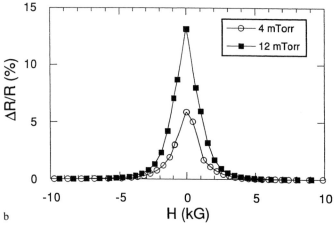

b

FIG. 6. The influence of growth conditions on the MR of sputtered Fe/Cr superlattices: (a) By taking particular care in the growth of sputtered samples, the group at Argonne National Laboratory has achieved a *record* 150% CIP-MR at $T = 4.2$ K for Cr(100Å) [Fe(14Å)/Cr(8Å)]$_{50}$. This was achieved by lowering the resistivity of the sample rather than increasing the change in resistivity $\Delta\rho$. [From E. E. Fullerton *et al., Appl. Phys. Lett.* **63**, 1699 (1993).] (b) By varying the argon sputtering pressure the MR ratio can be increased nearly 2.5 times. [From E. E. Fullerton *et al., Phys. Rev. Lett.* **68**, 859 (1992).]

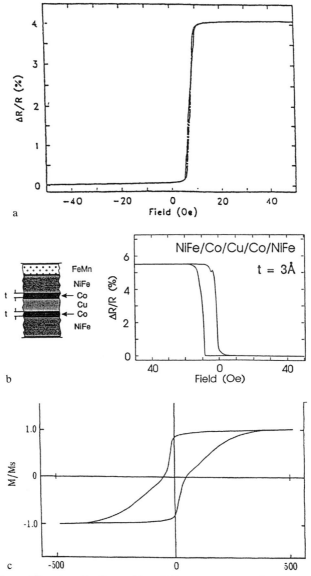

Fig. 7. Three different realizations of low-field giant magnetoresistance structures: (a) An exchange anisotropy biased or "spin-valve" structure Si/2 × (50 Å Ta/62 Å NiFe/22 Å Cu/40 Å NiFe/70 Å FeMn)/50 Å Ta; magnetoresistance for field swept between ±50 Oe at *room temperature*. [From B. Dieny *et al.*, *J. Appl. Phys.* **69**, 4774 (1991).] (b) Exchange biased structure similar to (a) but with a thin layer of cobalt added at interfaces [Si/Ni$_{81}$ Fe$_{19}$ (53 Å)/Co (3 Å)/Cu (32 Å)/Co (3 Å)/Ni$_{81}$ Fe$_{19}$ (22 Å)/Fe Mn (90 Å)] at room temperature. (Courtesy of S. S. P. Parkin.) (c) A structure with two magnetic layers with different coercivities; magnetic hysteresis curve and MR both at 300 K for [Co (30 Å)/Cu (50 Å)/Ni Fe (30 Å)/Cu (50 Å)] × 15. (d) Individual magnetization processes of the two magnetic components estimated from the result in (c), and the field dependence of resistance; only the results with increasing field are shown and the spin structures are schematically illustrated. [From T. Shinjo and H. Yamamoto, *J. Phys. Soc. Japan* **59**, 3061 (1990).]

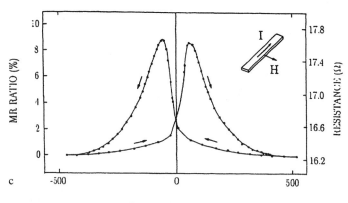

c

EXTERNAL FIELD (Oe)

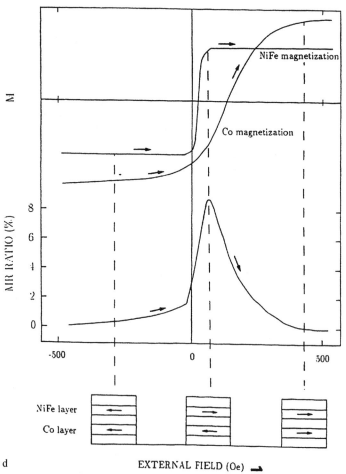

NiFe magnetization

Co magnetization

NiFe layer

Co layer

d

EXTERNAL FIELD (Oe)

381

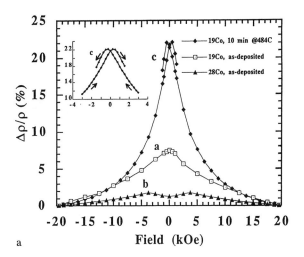

a

## 26vol% Co-76 vol% Ag

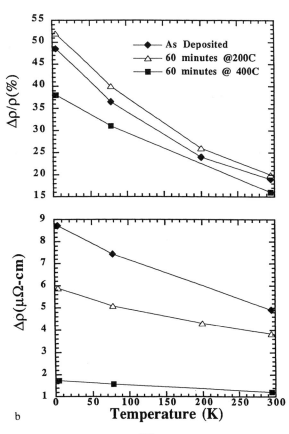

b

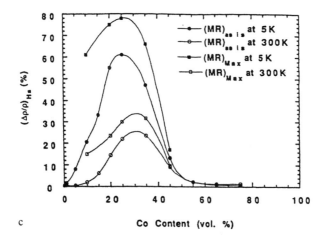

c

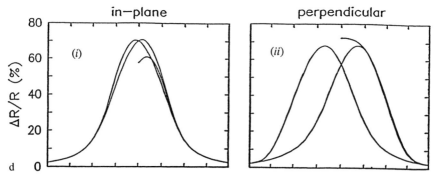

FIG. 8. Magnetoresistance of granular films: (a) Cosputtered sample of CoCu; field dependence of $\Delta\rho/\rho = (\rho_{He} - \rho_{H=20kOe})/\rho_{H=10kOe}$ for the three types of curves obtained. *Inset:* Details of curve c. Curves *a* and *b* measured at $T = 100$ K; curve *c* measured at 10 K. [From A. E. Berkowitz *et al., PRL* **68**, 3745 (1992); see also J. Q. Xiao, J. S. Jiang, and C. L. Chien, *et al., PRL* **68**, 3749 (1992).] (b) Magnetoresistance data for the Co(26%)Ag sample as-deposited and after annealing at 473 and 673 K, with $\Delta\rho/\rho$ versus temperature and $\Delta\rho$ versus temperature. [From M. J. Carey *et al., Appl. Phys. Lett.* **61**, 2935 (1992).] (c) Giant magnetoresistance at 5 K (closed symbols) and 300 K (open symbols) of CoAg as a function of Co volume fraction. The as-prepared samples ($T_s = 300$ K) and the annealed samples that exhibit maximum GMR are denoted as circles and squares, respectively. [From C. L. Chien *et al., J. Appl. Phys.* **73**, 5309 (1993)]. (d) MBE grown CoAg film: field dependence, at 4.2 K, of saturation magnetoresistance $R_s$ for a 940-Å-thick (111) oriented $Co_{0.26}Ag_{0.74}$ MBE-grown film. (i) $R_s$ for field orthogonal to measuring current, in the plane of the film. (ii) $R_s$ for field perpendicular to the film plane. Note the slightly different behaviors for these orientations. [From S. S. P. Parkin *et al., Europhys. Lett.* **22**, 455 (1993).]

of these results on uncoupled layered structures is the sensitivity of their MR, i.e., the change in resistivity or resistance compared to the field required to produce the change. While the MR found in antiferromagnetically coupled Fe/Cr superlattices is large, the fields needed to achieve this MR are quite large, of the order of 1 to 2 T (Fig. 1), and the quotient $\Delta\rho/H^{\text{sat}}$ is $\sim 10^{-3}$ $\mu\Omega$ cm G$^{-1}$. For the uncoupled structures [Fig. 7(a)] one is able to produce[21] a $\Delta\rho = 0.88$ $\mu\Omega$ cm with only 2 G, i.e., a $\Delta\rho/\Delta H = 0.44$ $\mu\Omega$ cm G$^{-1}$. For technological applications the latter is far more impressive; however, as we will see, superlattices with a large number of repeats lend themselves more readily to analysis, because the fraction of the structure that is not actively involved in producing the MR is negligible.

A third type of uncoupled structure was developed in 1992: magnetic granular films.[7] These consist of a nonmagnetic matrix with varying concentrations of an immiscible magnetic metal that precipitates into granules. Depending on the miscibility, and conditions for growth and annealing, these granules range in size upward from 20 Å. If they are smaller, the granule's magnetic moment is not fixed (spatially) and the sought-after MR effect disappears. Although the granules may not be magnetically coupled, the saturation fields required to produce the giant MR (as large as in layered structures) were very large in the first films studied (Fig. 8). If this field can be substantially reduced, the sensitivity of granular films might be an attractive alternative to that of sandwiched structures. Another difference between uncoupled layered and granular structures is that the zero or coercive field configuration of the magnetic granules is random (noncollinear) while for the layered structures the magnetic moments are *nominally* antiparallel (collinear).

While vertical transport (CPP) is the common mode for using semiconducting superlattices, it has been largely shunned in metallic layered structures for a good reason. For a given resistivity the resistance depends on the size of a sample as $l/A$ where $l$ is the length parallel to current and $A$ is the cross-sectional area. A typical layered structure is 1 mm$^2$ in the plane of the layer and 1 $\mu$m thick in the direction of layer growth. For current in the plane of the layers, $l/A = 10^3$ mm$^{-1}$, whereas for CPP, $l/A = 10^{-3}$ mm$^{-1}$; thus, simply due to its geometry, the resistance is one million times *smaller* for CPP than CIP for the same sample. The small CPP resistance is hard to measure by conventional methods; however, by incorporating their multilayered structures as part of a superconducting quantum interference device, a group at Michigan State

---

[21] See Fig. 1 of Ref. 18 (B. Dieny *et al.*, *J. Appl. Phys.*). The resistivity of the structure is $\rho = 22$ $\mu\Omega$ cm; V. S. Speriosu, private communication, July 1993.

University (MSU) has achieved an MR ratio of 170% for CPP in sputtered Co/Cu superlattices[22] (Fig. 9). This value refers to the drop in resistivity from the initial (as-grown) state. The MSU group has also pointed to two problems: (1) the peaks in the resistivity as a function of field do not occur at the coercive field and (2) the initial (as-grown) resistivity is not reproducible; it is either higher or lower than the peak resistivity as the layered structures goes through its hysteresis cycle.

Other attempts at measuring the CPP-MR[23] are aimed at increasing the $l/A$ ratio of the sample by reducing the cross-sectional area $A$ by means of lithographic techniques. We can anticipate considerable progress in this area. One advantage of this method over the superconducting technique is that it is not limited to low temperature (usually below 10 K) so that one can gain information on the temperature dependence of the CPP-MR relative to that of the CIP-MR.

Indeed the temperature dependence of the magnetoresistance is of critical importance to its applications, which ideally are at room temperature, while the experimental data reviewed until now have been mostly at 4.2 K. For Fe/Cr superlattices, Petroff et al.[24] showed that the structures with the higher MR ratios at low temperatures also had a stronger temperature dependence, e.g., the MR ratio dropped by about 60% in going from 4.2 K to room temperature for a Fe/Cr superlattice (Fig. 10). Similar results on the temperature dependence have been obtained on Co/Cu and Cu/Co/Cu/Ni(Fe) superlattices.[6,25] The true temperature dependence of the MR may be masked by the temperature dependence of the resistivity of the nonmagnetic overlayers and underlayers surrounding the multilayered structures.[26]

[22] W. P. Pratt Jr., S.-F. Lee, J. M. Slaughter, R. Loloee, P. A. Schroeder, and J. Bass, *Phys. Rev. Lett.* **66**, 3060 (1991); W. P. Pratt Jr., S.-F. Lee, Q. Yang, D. Holody, R. Loloee, P. A. Schroeder, and J. Bass, *J. Appl. Phys.* **73**, 5326 (1993); *J. Magn. Magn. Mater.* **126**, 406 (1993); P. A. Schroeder, J. Bass, P. Holody, S.-F. Lee, R. Loloee, W. P. Pratt, Jr., and Q. Yang, in *Magnetism and Structure in Systems of Reduced Dimension,* (R. F. C. Farrow et al., eds.), NATO ASI Series (B-Physics), Vol. 309, p. 129, Plenum Press, New York (1993).

[23] M. A. M. Gijs, S. K. Lenczowski, and J. B. Giesbers, *Phys. Rev. Lett.* **70**, 3343 (1993).

[24] J. Barnaś, A. Fuss, R. E. Camley, P. Grünberg, and W. Zinn, *Phys. Rev. B* **42**, 8110 (1990); F. Petroff, A. Barthélémy, A. Hamzić, A. Fert, P. Etienne, S. Lequien, and G. Creuzet, *J. Magn. Magn. Mater.* **93**, 95 (1991); J. E. Mattson, M. E. Brubaker, C. H. Sowers, M. Conover, Z. Qui, and S. D. Bader, *Phys. Rev. B* **44**, 9378 (1991); A. Chaiken, T. M. Tritt, D. J. Gillespie, J. J. Krebs, P. Lubitz, M. Z. Harford, and G. A. Prinz, *J. Appl. Phys.* **69**, 4798 (1991); M. A. M. Gijs and M. Okada, *Phys. Rev. B* **46**, 2908 (1992).

[25] H. Yamamoto, T. Okuyama, H. Dohnomae, and T. Shinjo, *J. Magn. Magn. Mater.* **99**, 243 (1991); see also data on permalloy based spin-valves by B. Dieny, V. S. Speriosu and S. Metin, *Europhys. Lett.* **15**, 227 (1991).

[26] A. Fert, private communication, August 1993.

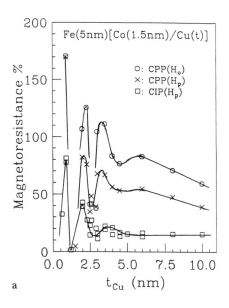

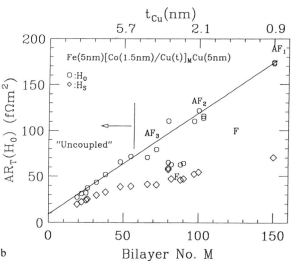

FIG. 9. The magnetoresistance of Co/Cu at $T = 4.2$ K as a function of the thickness of copper layers for currents *perpendicular* to the plane of the layers (CPP) for the change in resistance measured from its zero-field (as-grown) value to saturation ($H_0$), and from its reproducible *peak* value after recycling through the hysteresis curve ($H_p$). (a) Compared to the CIP-MR values measured from the reproducible peak values. (b) The "sheet" resistance for CPP at zero-field ($H_0$) and at saturation ($H_s$) of Co/Cu superlattices as a function of the number of bilayers, holding the overall thickness of the superlattice $L$ constant. The straight line connecting data on both AF coupled and uncoupled structures indicates that the resistance is a function of $1/t_{Cu}$ alone, so that the *resistivity* is the same for AF and uncoupled structures for CPP; both have $\bar{M} = 0$. (Courtesy of the Michigan State University group.)

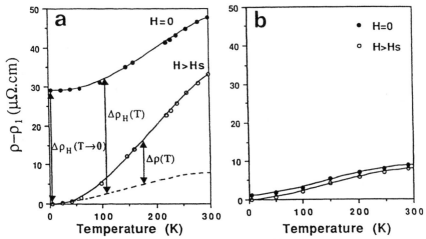

FIG. 10. Temperature dependence of the resistivity of Fe/Cr superlattices in the ferromagnetic ($H > H_s$) and antiferromagnetic ($H = 0$) configurations for: (a) (Fe 16 Å/Cr 12 Å)$_{18}$ (sample with large magnetoresistance) and (b) (Fe 16 Å/Cr 11 Å)$_{30}$ (sharper interfaces and small magnetoresistance). The figures represent ($\rho - \rho_1$) versus $T$ where $\rho$ is the resistivity at $T$ (at $H > H_s$ and at $H = 0$) and $\rho_1$ is the resistivity at $T \rightarrow 0$ and $H > H_s$ [$\rho_1 = 41$ μΩ cm and 26 μΩ cm for (a) and (b), respectively]. The dashed line in (a) represents the nonenhanced temperature dependence taken from (b). $\Delta\rho(T)$, $\Delta\rho_H(T)$, and $\Delta\rho_H(T \rightarrow 0)$ are defined in the figure (a). [From F. Petroff *et al.*, *J. Magn. Magn. Mater.* **93**, 95 (1991).]

A major source of MR is the interface between magnetic and nonmagnetic regions.[27] Several studies characterize the features of this region, which determine its influence on the MR of layered and granular structures. Noninvasive probes such as nuclear magnetic resonance[28] (which gives the number of magnetic neighbors to the nuclei undergoing resonance) and grazing incidence anomalous small angle x-ray scattering[29]

[27] S. S. P. Parkin, *Phys. Rev. Lett.* **71**, 1641 (1993).

[28] C. Mény, P. Panissod, and R. Loloee, *Phys. Rev. B* **45**, 12269 (1992); C. Mény, P. Panissod, P. Humbert, J. P. Nozières, V. S. Speriosu, B. A. Gurney, and R. Zehringer, *J. Magn. Magn. Mater.* **121**, 406 (1993); H. Yasuoka in *Metallic Superlattices* (T. Shinjo and T. Takada, eds.), Chap. 5, p. 51, Elsevier, Amsterdam (1987); A. Goto, H. Yasuoka, H. Yamamoto, and T. Shinjo, *J. Magn. Magn. Mater.* **124**, 285 (1993); *J. Phys. Soc. Japan* **62**, 2129 (1993); Y. Saito, K. Inomata, A. Goto, and H. Yasuoka, *J. Phys. Soc. Japan,* **62**, 1450 (1993); *J. Magn. Magn. Mater.* **126**, 466 (1993); K. LeDang, P. Veillet, E. Vélu, S. S. P. Parkin, and C. Chappert, *Appl. Phys. Lett.* **63**, 108 (1993).

[29] S. S. P. Parkin, R. F. C. Farrow, T. A. Rabedeau, R. F. Marks, G. R. Harp, Q. H. Lam, C. Chappert, M. F. Toney, R. Savoy, and R. Geiss, *Europhys. Lett.* **22**, 455 (1993); T. A. Rabedeau, M. F. Toney, R. F. Marks, S. S. P. Parkins, R. F. C. Farrow, and G. R. Harp, *Phys. Rev. B* **48**, 16810 (1993); Y. Fujii, in *Metallic Superlattices* (T. Shinjo and T. Takada, eds.), Chap. 2, p. 33, Elsevier, Amsterdam (1987).

yield information on the structure of the interfacial regions. Other probes of the magnetic and structural characteristics of metallic multilayers include polarized neutron diffraction and reflection studies[30] and Mössbauer spectroscopies.[31] Neutron studies provide information about the magnetic configuration of the layered structures, whereas Mössbauer spectroscopy is a local probe of magnetism in the layers.

Invasive methods (those that alter the nature of the interface) have also been used to study the role of interfaces in producing giant MR. These include studies that selectively dope an interfacial region with ternary impurities, and others in which a monolayer or two of a ternary element has been inserted[32] (for example, a monolayer of cobalt at the interface between permalloy and copper layers). These monolayers of cobalt have been found to enhance significantly (double) the MR ratio of permalloy-

[30] A. Barthélémy, A. Fert. M. N. Baibich, S. Hadjoudj, F. Petroff, P. Etienne, R. Cabanel, S. Lequien, F. Nguyen Van Dau, and G. Creuzet, *J. Appl. Phys.* **67**, 5908 (1990), see Fig. 4 and discussion; S. S. P. Parkin, A. Mansour, and G. P. Felcher, *Appl. Phys. Lett.* **58**, 1472 (1991); Y. Y. Huang, G. P. Felcher, and S. S. P. Parkin, *J. Magn. Magn. Mater.* **99**, L31 (1991); S. S. P. Parkin, V. Deline, R. Hilleke, and G. P. Felcher, *Phys. Rev. B* **42**, 10583 (1990); N. Hosoito, K. Mibu, S. Araki, T. Shinjo, S. Itoh, and Y. Endoh, *J. Phys. Soc. Japan* **61**, 300 (1992); Y. Endoh and C. F. Majkrzak, in *Metallic Superlattices* T. Shinjo and T. Takada, eds.), Chap. 3, p. 81, Elsevier, Amsterdam (1987); G. P. Felcher, *Phys. Rev. B* **24**, 1595 (1981); M. Loewenhaupt, W. Hahn, Y. Y. Huang, G. P. Felcher, and S. S. P. Parkin, *J. Magn. Magn. Mater.* **121**, 173 (1993); also in *Physics of Transition Metals* (P. M. Oppeneer and J. Kübler, eds.), Vol. 1, p. 438, World Scientific, Singapore (1993); J. E. Mattson, E. E. Fullerton, C. H. Sowers, Y. Y. Huang, G. P. Felcher, and S. D. Bader, *J. Appl. Phys.* **73**, 5969 (1993); J. A. C. Bland, R. B. Bateson, N. F. Johnson, V. S. Speriosu, B. A. Gurney, and J. Penfold, *J. Magn. Magn. Mater.* **123**, 320, (1993).

[31] T. Shinjo, *Surf. Sci. Rep.* **12**, 49 (1991), see also his article in *Metallic Superlattices* (T. Shinjo and T. Takada, eds.), Chap. 4, p. 107, Elsevier, Amsterdam (1987); C. J. Gutierrez, Z. Q. Qiu, M. D. Wieczorek, H. Tang, and J. C. Walker, *J. Magn. Magn. Mater.* **43**, 326, 369 (1991); H. Tang, M. D. Wieczorek, D. J. Keavney, D. F. Storm, C. J. Gutierrez, Z. Q. Qui, and J. C. Walker, in *Magnetic Surfaces, Thin Films, and Multilayers* S. S. P. Parkin *et al.*, eds.), *Mat. Res. Soc. Symp. Proc.* **231**, 405 and 411 (1992); Ch. Sauer, J. Landes, W. Zinn, and H. Ebert, in Magnetic Surfaces, Thin Films, and Multilayers (S. S. P. Parkin *et al.*, eds.), *Mat. Res. Soc. Symp. Proc.* **231**, 153 (1992); D. M. Kelly, E. E. Fullerton, F. T. Parker, J. Guimpel, Y. Bruynseraede, and I. K. Schuller, in *Physics of Transition Metals* (P. M. Oppeneer and J. Kübler, eds.), Vol. I, p. 419, World Scientific, Singapore (1993).

[32] For studies on Fe/Cr, see B. A. Gurney, D. R. Wilhoit, V. S. Speriosu, and I. L. Sanders, *IEEE Trans. Magnetics* **26**, 2747 (1990); P. Baumgart, B. A. Gurney, D. R. Wilhoit, T. Nguyen, B. Dieny, and V. S. Speriosu, *J. Appl. Phys.* **69**, 4792 (1991); B. A. Gurney, P. Baumgart, D. R. Wilhoit, B. Dieny, and V. S. Speriosu, *J. Appl. Phys.* **70**, 5867 (1991). For NiFe/Cu and Co/Cu, see S. P. P. Parkin, *Appl. Phys. Lett.* **61**, 1358 (1992); and A. Fert, Ref. 41. For ternary elements *in* Co or Cu layers, see N. Kataoka, K. Saito, and H. Fujimori, *J. Magn. Magn. Mater.* **121**, 383 (1993).

copper multilayered structures.[27] The introduction of ternary elements produces a panoply of effects and alters many of the structure parameters in an uncontrolled manner.

By varying the growth conditions and the subsequent anneals, one can also influence interfacial regions as well as the structural integrity of the layers. For MBE-grown samples, extensive work has been done on Fe/Cr and Co/Cu interfaces.[33,34] Ironically, much of the thrust behind this work has been in obtaining flatter-smoother interfaces so as to establish the existence of short-wavelength oscillatory interlayer coupling in Fe/Cr/Fe structures,[33] and in the case of Co/Cu structures, to establish the existence of long-range antiferromagnetic oscillatory interlayer coupling in the (111) direction. Kamijo and Igarashi[33] carried out a particular careful study of MR on Fe/Cr superlattices to obtain "extremely flat interfaces." For sputtered samples the focus has been on varying the growth (sputtering) conditions so as to optimize the change in resistivity $\Delta\rho$ (between zero field and saturation), lower the resistivity, and obtain the highest MR ratio. Whereas for Fe/Cr multilayered structures, rougher interfaces produce higher MR ratios[24,35] (up to the point where they are so rough that either the interfacial magnetization or layering is lost), for Co/Cu it seems that flatter-smoother interfaces produce higher MR ra-

[33] See Refs. 2, 3, and 24 (Barnaś et al. and Petroff et al.); P. Etienne, J. Chazelas, G. Creuzet, A. Friederich, J. Massies, F. Nguyen Van Dau, and A. Fert, J. Crystal Growth 95, 410 (1989); P. Etienne, S. Lequien, J. Massies, R. Cabanel, A. Fert, and A. Barthélémy, J. Appl. Phys. 67, 5400 (1990); A. Kamijo and H. Igarashi, J. Appl. Phys. 71, 2455 (1992); J. Appl. Phys. 72, 3497 (1992); J. Unguris, R. J. Celotta, and D. T. Pierce, Phys. Rev. Lett. 67, 140 (1991).

[34] Several papers were presented at the spring meeting of the Materials Research Society on the interlayer coupling for MBE grown Co/Cu (111), see Magnetic Ultrathin Films (B. T. Jonker et al., eds.), Mat. Res. Soc. Sym. Proc. 313 (1993); see also A. Cebollada, R. Miranda, C. M. Schneider, P. Schuster, and J. Kirschner, J. Magn. Magn. Mater. 102, 25 (1991); S. S. P. Parkin, R. F. Marks, R. F. C. Farrow, G. R. Harp, Q. H. Lam, and R. J. Savoy, Phys. Rev. B 46, 9262 (1992); J. P. Renard, P. Beauvillian, C. Dupas, K. LeDang, P. Veillet, E. Vélu, C. Marlière, and D. Renard, J. Magn. Magn. Mater. 115, L147 (1992); A. Kamijo and H. Igarashi, Jpn. J. Appl. Phys. 31, L1058 (1992); M. T. Johnson, R. Coehoorn, J. J. de Vries, N. W. E. McGee, J. aan de Stegge, and P. J. H. Bloemen, Phys. Rev. Lett. 69, 969 (1992); D. Greig, M. J. Hall, C. Hammond, B. J. Hickey, H. P. Ho, M. A. Howson, M. J. Walker, N. Wiser, and D. G. Wright, J. Magn. Magn. Mater. 110, L239 (1992); G. R. Harp, S. S. P. Parkin, R. F. C. Farrow, R. F. Marks, M. F. Toney, Q. H. Lam, T. A. Rabedeau, and R. J. Savoy, Phys. Rev. B 47, 8721 (1993).

[35] E. E. Fullerton, D. M. Kelly, J. Giumpel, I. K. Schuller, and Y. Bruynseraede, Phys. Rev. Lett. 68, 859 (1992); Y. Obi, K. Takanashi, Y. Mitani, N. Tsuda, and H. Fujimori, J. Magn. Magn. Mater. 104-107, 1747 (1992); K. Takanashi, Y. Obi, Y. Mitani, and H. Fujimori, J. Phys. Soc. Japan 61, 1169 (1992).

tios.[36] For Co/Cu, growth conditions determine the existence of pinholes in copper and the integrity of the structure more than the roughness of interfaces. It is possible that the MR in Co/Cu is more dependent on the coupling due to pinholes than on the roughness of interfaces. Figure 6(b) shows the MR changes for Fe/Cr superlattices with variation of the pressure of the argon sputtering gas as measured by Schuller's group.[35] The influence of deposition temperature on the MR of Fe/Cr multilayers has also been studied.[37]

Hylton et al.[38] studied NiFe/Ag multilayers, which in their as-prepared state did not show a giant MR effect. After annealing they find MR ratios of the order of 4% to 6% in fields of 5 to 10 Oe at room temperature (Fig. 11); their multilayers yield a change in the MR ratio per unit field of 0.8%/ Oe, which is close to the "largest sensitivity reported in any multilayer or alloy giant MR structure." The appearance of the giant MR in these samples comes from the breakup of the permalloy layers into islands. Rodmacq et al.[39] also have studied the MR of annealed NiFe/Ag multilayers. Initially, their samples of $NiFe(12.5 \text{ Å})/Ag(10.5 \text{ Å})$ show a MR ratio of 17% with $H_s = 300$ Oe at room temperature. After annealing there is a threefold increase in their sensitivity, primarily due to a large decrease in the saturation field. Finally, Parker et al.[40] reported on the MR for a "bad" multilayer of $Ni_{66}Fe_{16}Co_{18}/Cu$, which is quasigranular, with "virtually no hysteresis and very low saturation field."

Other surveys of the experimental data on giant MR are listed in Ref. 41.

[36] R. J. Highmore, W. C. Shih, R. E. Somekh, and J. E. Evetts, J. Magn. Magn. Mater. **116**, 249 (1992); R. J. Highmore, R. E. Somekh, W. C. Shih, I. M. McLoughlin, and J. E. Evetts, Appl. Surf. Sci. **65**, 124 (1993); Y. Saito, S. Hashimoto, and K. Inomata, Appl. Phys. Lett. **60**, 2436 (1992); J. Kohlhepp, S. Cordes, H. J. Elmers, and V. Gradmann, J. Magn. Magn. Mater. **111**, 231 (1992). For permalloy-copper spin valve structures, see V. S. Speriosu, J. P. Nozières, B. A. Gurney, B. Dieny, T. C. Huang, and H. Lefakis, Phys. Rev. B **47**, 11579 (1993); J. P. Nozières, V. S. Speriosu, B. A. Gurney, B. Dieny, H. Lefakis, and T. C. Huang, J. Magn. Magn. Mater. **121**, 386 (1993).

[37] S. S. P. Parkin and B. R. York, Appl. Phys. Lett. **62**, 1842 (1993).

[38] T. L. Hylton, K. R. Coffey, M. A. Parker, and J. K. Howard, Science **261**, 1021 (1993).

[39] B. Rodmacq, G. Palembo, and Ph. Gerard, J. Magn. Magn. Mater. **118**, L11 (1993).

[40] S. Hossian, D. Seale, G. Qiu, J. Jarratt, J. A. Barnard, H. Fujiwara, and M. R. Parker, J. Appl. Phys. **75**, 7067 (1994); M. Parker, J. Barnard, D. Seale, M. Tan, S. Hossain, and H. Fujiwara, I.E.E.E. Trans. on Magn. **30**, 358 (1994).

[41] See articles by A. Fert and P. Bruno, and S. S. P. Parkin, in Ultra-Thin Magnetic Structures (B. Heinrich and J. A. C. Bland, eds.), Vol. 2, Springer-Verlag, Berlin (1993). The proceedings of several conferences are excellent sources of data. For example, see Mat. Res. Soc. Sym. Proc. **151** (1989), **221** and **232** (1991), **231** (1992), and **313** (1993); J. Magn. Magn. Mater. **93** (1991), **104-107** (1992), **121** and **126** (1993); and Magnetism and Structure in Systems of Reduced Dimension, (R. F. C. Farrow et al., eds.) NATO ASI Series (B-Physics), Vol. 309, Plenum Press, New York (1993).

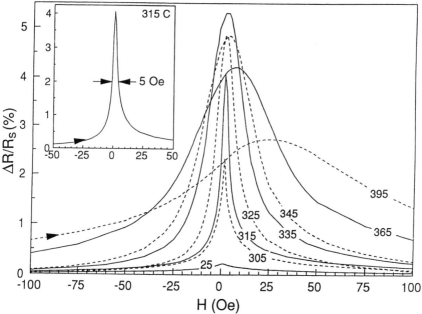

Fig. 11. The magnetoresistance ratio $\Delta R/R_s$ versus $H$ for a sample Ta(100 Å)/Ag(20 Å)/[NiFe(20 Å)/Ag(40 Å)]$_4$/NiFe(20 Å)/Ag(20 Å)/Ta(40 Å)/SiO$_2$(700 Å)/Si. The field is in the plane of the sample and perpendicular to the current. Arrows indicate the ramping direction of the field. Unannealed samples show only a small anisotropic MR effect, but for annealing temperatures above 300°C, a large giant MR effect is evident. Large sensitivites of order 0.8%/Oe are achieved in the sample annealed at 315°C (*inset*). [From T. L. Hylton *et al.*, *Science* **261**, 1021 (1993) © AAAS.]

## III. Theoretical Formulations of Transport

The theory of the giant MR effect was first formulated within a semiclassical approach by Camley and Barnaś,[42] and subsequently by using quantum linear response theory. More recently, real-space versions of the quantum approach have been put forward, as well as calculations based on the Landauer-Büttiker formulation of conductance. *Ab initio* calculations of the MR based on realistic superlattice band structures are just beginning to appear. Here we review the various approaches and their interrelations.

[42] R. E. Camley and J. Barnaś, *Phys. Rev. Lett.* **63**, 664 (1989).

1. SEMICLASSICAL APPROACH

Of central importance to the electrical transport in magnetic layered and granular structures is the inhomogeneous distribution of the scattering centers, which differs in the magnetic and nonmagnetic regions and may well be concentrated at interfaces. We introduce length scales $d_{in}$, which characterize the spatial inhomogeneity of the scattering. In multilayered structures one has reasonable control over the layer thicknesses and thereby $d_{in}$; for granular films it is harder to specify ad control $d_{in}$. The intergranular distance and size of the granules serve as rough measures for $d_{in}$.

In discussing electrical transport in structures where the size of the inhomogeneities is comparable to the mean free path, it is not possible to replace the distribution of scatterers by one that is homogeneous. This problem was tackled for thin films where scattering from the boundaries contributes to the overall resistivity of the structure. Fuchs[43] and later Sondheimer[44] solved the Boltzmann equation for electron transport in these reduced geometries, and represented the scattering due to surface roughness by a reflection coefficient $p$ (not to be confused with the $p$ introduced later to represent the ratio of spin-dependent to spin-independent scattering), which is zero for rough surfaces and one for perfectly smooth ones. While $p = 1$ does not produce any additional resistance, $p = 0$ contributes an additional boundary resistance to the structure, above that coming from scattering within the bulk. The deviation of the electron distribution function in the presence of a uniform external field from the equilibrium Fermi distribution, $g(\mathbf{k}, \varepsilon, z)$, is a function of the distance $z$ from the boundary for finite geometries. Excellent discussions of the physics behind the Fuchs-Sondheimer approach are given by Ziman[45] and Fert.[46]

To adapt this approach to metallic multilayers, e.g., Pd//Au, Carcia and Suna[47] extended the idea of Fuchs and Sondheimer to composites by neglecting differences in potential between layers so that there is no specular reflection at interfaces. As in the Fuchs-Sondheimer theory,

[43] K. Fuchs, *Proc. Philos. Camb. Soc.* **34**, 100 (1938).

[44] E. H. Sondheimer, *Adv. Phys.* **1**, 1 (1952).

[45] J. M. Ziman, *Electrons and Phonons*, pp. 451–469, Oxford University Press, London (1972).

[46] A. Fert in *Metallic Multilayers*, Materials Science Forum, Vols. **59-60**, p. 439, Trans. Tech. Publications, Zürich (1990); A. Fert, *Science and Technology of Nanostructured Magnetic Materials* (G. C. Hadjipanayis and G. A. Prinz, eds.), NATO ASI Series (B-Physics), Vol. **259**, p. 221, Plenum Press, New York (1991).

[47] P. F. Carcia and A. Suna, *J. Appl. Phys.* **54**, 2000 (1983).

they introduced a probability $p$ of coherent transmission across an interface. Camley and Barnaś[42] extended the Fuchs-Sondheimer-Carcia-Suna idea by introducing spin-dependent coefficients $T^\sigma$ to represent the fraction of electrons coherently transmitted (instead of $p$), whence $(1 - T^\sigma)$ is the fraction diffusely scattered at an interface. One additional parameter was introduced to describe the spin-dependent scattering in the magnetic layers. Based on these ideas and by making some approximations applicable to real systems, Barthélémy and Fert[48] derived simple analytic expressions for the MR, which allowed them to analyze the effects of varying the parameters such as layer thickness, mean free path, and $T^\sigma$ on the MR. Reference 48 contains an illuminating exposition of the Camley-Barnaś approach; in particular, their Fig. 1 shows how the distribution function $g(\mathbf{k}, \varepsilon, z)$ is matched at interfaces and varies across the multilayer. In addition, analytic expressions for the MR ratio are given in limiting cases in terms of the parameters mentioned earlier. One of the main conclusions of Ref. 48 is that one set of parameters cannot be used to *simultaneously* fit the MR ($\Delta\rho$) and the resistivity $\rho$ for a magnetic multilayer; this conclusion is ascribed to the restriction $T^\sigma \leq 1$ in the Camley-Barnaś model.

This difficulty with the semiclassical approach to the giant MR was overcome partially by two modifications. The approximation of neglecting differences in the potentials between the layers was removed by Hood and Falicov,[49] who introduced spin-dependent reflection in addition to transmission coefficients. The other modification was more directly related to the restriction $T^\sigma \leq 1$; it was recognized that the scattering at interfaces should be treated on the same basis as the scattering in the layers. In reality, the interface between two layers is not a perfect plane because of its roughness. Johnson and Camley[50] observed that it is more accurate to represent this interface by a mixed layer whose thickness is given by that of the interfacial region, i.e., at least two to four monolayers (MLs) wide. The mean free path (mfp) of electrons for the mixed layer used in the analysis of Ref. 50 ($\sim$6 Å) is comparable to the inverse of the Fermi momentum $k_F^{-1}$, which is of the order of a lattice constant. Consequently, quantum interference effects may occur due to strong scattering in this layer and there will be corrections to the semiclassical description of electron transport in the mixed layer.Therefore, the parameters obtained from fits that use this theory will have to be reexamined eventually.

[48] A. Barthélémy and A. Fert, *Phys. Rev. B* **43**, 13124 (1991).
[49] R. Q. Hood and L. M. Falicov, *Phys. Rev. B* **46**, 8287 (1992).
[50] B. L. Johnson and R. E. Camley, *Phys. Rev. B* **44**, 9997 (1991).

Valet and Fert[51] have extended the development of the semiclassical description to the case of CPP where the internal electric field is no longer uniform as it is for CIP. As they emphasize, the spin diffusion length $\lambda_{sdl}$, which is related to the average distance traveled by an electron before its spin is flipped, is a new length scale in CPP that controls the distance over which the two-*independent*-current model holds.[52] When the inhomogeneity length scale $d_{in}$ is small compared to $\lambda_{sdl}$ they agree with the result first found on the basis of a quantum approach that neglected spin-flips:[53] that $\lambda_{mfp}$ is no longer a relevant length scale for the CPP-MR, even though $\lambda_{mfp}$ does enter the expressions for resistivity. The meaning of "length scale" in this context is clarified later. In the opposite limit, $d_{in} \gg \lambda_{sdl}$, the CPP-MR decreases as $\exp(-d_{in}/\lambda_{sdl})$.

By working within the paradigm outlined, Visscher[54] considered within the semiclassical Boltzmann approach *both* the differences in potentials in going from one layer to another, and the MR for CIP and CPP geometries. Because there are a large number of parameters (eight) in his approach, the variety of behavior of the MR as the parameters are varied is quite impressive; at this time only a few regions of parameter space have been explored.

Fert[55] has stressed the role of electron-magnon scattering in mixing the two spin conduction currents at finite temperature. This effect undoes the mechanism that creates the giant MR effect. As temperature increases so does this scattering, so that the MR decreases faster than one would predict from the decrease of the magnetization alone.

## 2. QUANTUM THEORY

When electrons are subject to changes in the scattering potential that occur over distances comparable to the lattice constant of the metal, it is not possible[56] to assign a unique scattering rate to the electron in a local region, as the use of the local relaxation-time approximation in the

[51] T. Valet and A. Fert, *J. Magn. Magn. Mater.* **121**, 378 (1993); *Phys. Rev. B.* **48**, 7099 (1993).

[52] I. A. Cambell and A. Fert, in *Ferromagnetic Materials* ( E. P. Wohlfarth, ed.), Vol. 3, p. 769, North-Holland, Amsterdam (1982).

[53] S. Zhang and P. M. Levy, *J. Appl. Phys.* **69**, 4786 (1991).

[54] P. B. Visscher, *Phys. Rev. B* **49**, 3907 (1994). See also P. B. Visscher and H. Zhang, *J. Magn. Magn. Mater.* **121**, 449 (1993); *Phys. Rev. B* **48**, 6672 (1993).

[55] For CIP-MR, see F. Petroff *et al.*, Ref. 24; for CPP-MR, A. Fert, private communication, August 1993.

[56] N. W. Ashcroft and N. D. Mermin, *Solid State Physics*, Chaps. 12, 13, and 16, W. B. Saunders, Philadelphia (1976).

Boltzmann equation implies. Tešanović *et al.*[57] observed that by using the Fuchs-Sondheimer approach, one predicts the nonphysical result that, in the absence of scattering in the bulk of a film, scattering off random surfaces does not produce any resistivity. A fully quantum mechanical approach was necessary to resolve this discrepancy.[57] The quantum Boltzmann equation (Keldysh),[58] the Landauer approach,[59] and the Kubo formalism[60] are all appropriate. The latter has been adapted to metallic multilayers and granular films in real (position) and momentum space representations.

In position space, multilayered and granular structures are viewed as composites of separate entities. Their transport properties are solved in each region and then matched at the interfaces to assure continuity. In momentum space the structure is considered in its entirety, so that one first determines wave functions for the whole structure, and then evaluates the effects of the scattering in the bulk and at the interfaces as if the gas of conduction electrons is subject to this inhomogeneous distribution of scatterers.

Underlying the quantum theory of transport in solids is the concept of the random impurity average by which the actual distribution of scatterers is replaced by a random distribution when calculating the effects of the scattering on the electron propagators.[61] One can begin to appreciate some of the complications arising in the quantum theory of conduction in our inhomogeneous structures by realizing that, while impurity averages are done *locally,* there is no *global* averaging of the scattering distribution in our treatment of this problem. As we will see, conduction in these structures, i.e., the two-point conductivity tensor we introduce in Section 6, is *sample specific*—it depends on the spatial distribution of the scattering centers.[62] Therefore, as one varies the thicknesses of the layers or reorients the magnetic layers relative to one another for layered structures (or changes the composition or annealing conditions of granular films), one is varying the spatial distribution of scatterers and, concomitantly, the two-point conductivity tensor $\sigma(r, r')$. In this respect, an

[57] Z. Tešanović, M. Jarić, and S. Maekawa, *Phys. Rev. Lett.* **57**, 2760 (1986).

[58] Two excellent reviews on the quantum Boltzmann equation are J. Rammer and H. Smith, *Rev. Mod. Phys.* **58**, 323 (1986) and G. D. Mahan, *Phys. Rep.* **145**, 251 (1987).

[59] D. S. Fisher and P. A. Lee, *Phys. Rev. B* **23**, 6851 (1981).

[60] R. Kubo, M. Toda, and N. Hashitsume, *Statistical Physics II. Non-Equilibrium Statistical Mechanics,* Springer Series in Solid-State Sciences, Vol. **31**, Chaps. 4 and 5, Springer-Verlag, Berlin (1985), R. Kubo, *J. Phys. Soc. Japan* **12**, 570 (1957).

[61] W. Kohn and J. M. Luttinger, *Phys. Rev.* **108**, 590 (1957).

[62] P. A. Lee and T. V. Ramakrishnan, *Rev. Mod. Phys.* **57**, 287 (1985); J. Rammer, *Rev. Mod. Phys.* **63**, 781 (1991).

analogy exists with transport in mesoscopic systems where the conductivity depends on the specific spatial distribution of scattering. In the same way that the magnetoconductance of mesoscopic systems has been used to observe the sample-specific "fingerprints" of the scatterers,[63] the giant MR can be used to identify the "magneto-fingerprint" of inhomogeneous magnetic structures.

The development of the quantum approach to transport in magnetic multilayers has been mostly limited to $T = 0$ K. The additional scattering at finite temperatures leads to (1) self-energy corrections of the one-particle propagators, which can be readily evaluated, and (2) vertex corrections of the electron-hole propagators, which are quite difficult to evaluate. The effects of localized spin-flips on the temperature dependence of the MR have been taken into account, and at least for Fe/Cr, we are able to fit the data.[64] Magnon scattering of electrons and the attendant spin-flips and "spin mixing" of the two conduction channels from this extended source are accounted for by vertex corrections to the electron-hole propagators entering the Kubo expression for the conductivity.[60] Although a formal expression can be written for these corrections, there have not been any calculations of the temperature dependence of the MR in magnetic multilayers due to vertex corrections coming from magnon scattering. Hasegawa has studied the temperature dependence of the giant MR by extending to multilayers a finite-temperature theory of bulk magnetism based on the Hubbard model.[64]

Another approach to CPP transport is to use the Landauer formula for conductance;[65] in this approach, the conductance is proportional to the number of conducting channels in the structure. Bauer has estimated how this number changes as the "potential landscape" for spin-up and spin-down electrons is altered by realigning an antiferromagnetically configured multilayered structure into a ferromagnetically aligned one. By making the ansatz that the transmission is zero for electrons whose kinetic energy normal to the layers is smaller than the barrier potential, he derives a rather simple formula for the change in the conductance due to the "superlattice" potential in the CPP geometry. For CIP, this mechanism is irrelevant and produces nearly zero MR.[66] To make comparisons

[63]G. Bergmann, *Phys. Rep.* **101**, 1 (1984); P. A. Lee and A. D. Stone, *Phys. Rev. Lett.* **55**, 1622 (1985); P. A. Lee, A. D. Stone, and H. Fukuyama, *Phys. Rev. B* **35**, 1039 (1987).

[64]S. Zhang and P. M. Levy, *Phys. Rev. B* **43**, 11048 (1991); H. Hasegawa, *J. Magn. Magn. Mater.* **126**, 384 (1993); *Phys. Rev. B* **47**, 15080 (1993).

[65]G. E. W. Bauer, *Phys. Rev. Lett.* **69**, 1676 (1992).

[66]P. M. Levy, Z.-P. Shi, S. Zhang, H. E. Camblong, and J. L. Fry, *J. Magn. Magn. Mater.* **121**, 357 (1993).

with real multilayers and previous theoretical work on the CPP-MR, he includes the effects of the interface roughness and bulk scattering. In the limit of large superlattices, he retrieves the CPP-MR originally found by using the Kubo formulaism.[53]

## IV. Sources of Magnetoresistance

Resistivity is not an indigenous property of metals; rather, it comes from impurities and defects that scatter the conduction electrons. The sources of scattering in multilayered and granular structures are grouped into those originating within the layers (bulk) and those occurring at the interfaces between layers. The former include the ions of one element that stray into the layer of another element, grain boundaries, and other structural defects that occur in compositionally layered materials grown at "low" temperatures. Scattering at interfaces comes from their "roughness,"[57,67,68] i.e., compositional disorder of the length scale of the mean free path of the electrons. For periodic multilayered structures, i.e., superlattices, perfectly flat interfaces are not sources of scattering; however, the difference in the lattice potential in going from one layer to another does affect the scattering coming from other sources.[69] Therefore, even perfect interfaces indirectly affect the resistivity of metallic superlattices.

Magnetoresistance has several origins; the most common one in metals, the effect of magnetic fields on the trajectory of the electrons (the Lorentz force), does not contribute much to metallic layered and granular films because of their high residual resistivity. The frequent scattering of an electron does not allow the magnetic field to act long enough to curve its trajectory.

As a multidomain sample is magnetized, domain walls are erased. This effect contributes to the MR observed in pure iron whiskers;[70,71] however, the change in resistivity produced by this effect is dwarfed by the resistivity of the multilayered structures themselves, so that this cannot be the origin of their giant MR ratios. Anisotropic magnetoresistance,

[67]N. Trivedi and N. W. Ashcroft, *Phys. Rev. B* **38**, 12 298 (1988).

[68]G. Fishman and D. Calecki, *Phys. Rev. Lett.* **62**, 1302 (1989).

[69]M. B. Stearns, *J. Magn. Magn. Mater.* **104-107**, 1745 (1992); A. C. Ehrlich, *Phys. Rev. Lett.* **71**, 2300 (1993).

[70]G. R. Taylor, A. Isin, and R. V. Coleman, *Phys. Rev.* **165**, 621 (1968).

[71]G. G. Cabrera and L. M. Falicov, *Phys. Status Solidi (b)* **61**, 539 (1974); *Phys. Status Solidi (b)* **62**, 217 (1974); L. Berger, *J. Appl. Phys.* **49**, 2156 (1978); *J. Appl. Phys.* **55**, 1954 (1984).

i.e., the variation of the resistivity with the angle between the current and magnetic field, has been observed in magnetic multilayers;[72] although it is the origin of the MR in the permalloy films currently that is used in magnetoresistive reading heads[73] and can produce an MR ratio of several percent, it is an order of magnitude too small to explain the giant MR observed in multilayered structures. In addition, the MR observed in multilayers and granular films is almost entirely *isotropic;* therefore, anisotropic MR cannot be its origin.

### 3. ORIGIN OF GIANT MAGNETORESISTANCE

As first proposed by Fert,[2] spin-dependent scattering of conduction electrons, i.e., a different scattering cross section for spin-up and spin-down electrons, is the primary source of the giant MRs observed in layered and granular structures. This mechanism is not an intrinsic property of the host metal, but depends on the specific impurity producing the scattering;[74] in the case of scattering at interfaces, it depends in addition on the varying lattice potential in that region. This scattering is not a source of MR unless the scattering rate of the electrons is changed by an external field. The relation of the change in scattering rate to the spin-dependent scattering is arrived at through the following line of reasoning. The scattering of electrons in the spin-up or majority (parallel to the magnetization) conduction band of transition-metal ferromagnetic alloys, $V_{\text{scat}}^{\uparrow}$, is different from that for electrons in the spin-down or minority band, $V_{\text{scat}}^{\downarrow}$.[12,52] Instead of writing $V_{\text{scat}}^{\uparrow}$ and $V_{\text{scat}}^{\downarrow}$ for the majority and minority electron *scattering* potentials, one could write in a rotationally invariant form in spin-½ space,

$$V_a = v_a + j_a \hat{M}_a \cdot \hat{\sigma}, \tag{3.1}$$

where $\hat{M}_a$ is a unit vector corresponding to the local magnetic region (layer or granule) or interface at which the scattering occurs, and $\hat{\sigma}$ is a

[72] See Ref. 12 and T. R. McGuire and R. I. Potter, *IEEE Trans. Magnetics* **MAG-11,** 1018 (1975); P. Ciureanu, in *Thin Film Resistive Sensors* P. Ciureanu and S. Middelhoek, eds.), p. 253, Institute of Physics Publishing, Bristol (1992).

[73] T. Miyazaki, T. Ajima, and F. Sato, *J. Magn. Magn. Mater.* **81,** 86 (1989); T. Miyazaki and T. Ajima, *J. Magn. Magn. Mater.* **81,** 91 (1989); T. Tanaka, I. Kobayashi, M. Takahashi, and T. Wakiyama, *IEEE Trans. Magnetics* **MAG-26,** 2418 (1990); T. Tanaka, I. Kobayashi, M. Takahashi, M. Kunii, and T. Wakiyama, *J. Magn. Soc. Japan* **14,** 225 (1990) (in Japanese).

[74] See A. Fert and P. Bruno, Ref. 41.

vector-like entity whose components are the Pauli spin matrices, e.g.,

$$\sigma_z = \begin{pmatrix} 1 & 0 \\ 0 & -1 \end{pmatrix}.$$

By choosing the spin axis of quantization for the electron parallel to the magnetization, one obtains a diagonal $2 \times 2$ matrix whose components are $v \pm j$; these are synonymous with the $V_{scat}^{\uparrow}$ and $V_{scat}^{\downarrow}$ introduced earlier. When Eq. (3.1) is applied to bulk ferromagnetic alloys, the application of an external field does not alter the magnetization of a saturated ferromagnet (we are confining ourselves to low temperatures), and the scattering rates are unchanged. In magnetic multilayers and granular films, an external field rearranges the local magnetization $\hat{M}(r)$ spatially in these structures, and we find from Eq. (3.1) that the scattering potential of the electrons is altered by the field; this change provides a plausible source of the giant MR.

In making this argument we have assumed that the spin axis of quantization for the electron does not follow the local internal field (magnetization). This assumption is jus⸱ʼfied as long as the time spent by the electron in any one region of magnetization is small compared with the time it takes the electron's axis of quantization to reorient itself parallel to that magnetization.[75,76] This approximation is valid for layered and granular structures where the size of the regions over which the magnetization changes is small. However, it would not be correct in cases where the magnetization changes gradually, such as in ɑ domain wall.

The spin-dependent scattering represented by Eq. (3.1) should be distinguished from spin-flip scattering off paramagnetic impurities; whereas it is represented by the Hamiltonian-like Eq. (3.1), the classical unit vector representing the magnetization $\hat{M}$ is replaced by a quantum-mechanical spin-operator $S$ representing the internal degrees of freedom of a paramagnetic impurity. The distinction between the two is best seen in systems where the magnetization is collinear (either parallel or antiparallel); in this case one chooses the spin axis of quantization along the magnetization. For spin-dependent scattering there is no spin mixing, i.e., no transitions from spin-up to spin-down or vice versa because the components of the magnetization $\hat{M}_x$ and $\hat{M}_y$ of the spin-flip operators $\sigma_x$ and $\sigma_y$ are zero for the natural axes. However, for paramagnetic impuri-

[75] See A. Messiah, *Quantum Mechanics*, Vol. II, pp. 739–759, North-Holland, Amsterdam (1961).
[76] See L. Berger, Ref. 71, and E. Salhi and L. Berger, *J. Appl. Phys.* **73**, 6405 (1993).

ties the operators $S_x$ and $S_y$ produce spin-flips. While spin-dependent scattering *produces* the giant MR, spin-flip scattering *diminishes* this effect.[77]

At finite temperatures phonons can increase the MR *if* one has strongly spin-dependent densities of states to evaluate this scattering, e.g., for cobalt-based structures.[78] However, in general, phonons do not produce spin-dependent scattering, and therefore reduce the MR, e.g., Fe/Cr. Scattering by magnons reduces $\Delta\rho$ and increases $\rho$. The reduction in the MR comes from two sources: (1) the spin-dependent scattering[64] decreases with the magnetization and (2) magnons create spin-flips that mix the two spin bands or currents.[77]

While scattering takes place in both the bulk (layers) and at the interfaces between layers, there is invariably more scattering at the interfaces of metallic structures. Whether this produces spin-dependent scattering depends on the interface magnetism; where it exists one can anticipate strong spin-dependent scattering from the interfacial regions of these structures. Indeed, some treatments of the giant MR have focused on this mechanism alone, with reasonably good results.[79]

All the layered and granular structures that display giant MR are made of at least two different metals, one of them magnetic. Thus, the band structure changes from one metal to another. If the length scale associated with this inhomogeneity is less than the mfp due to other scattering, the different metals becomes a source of scattering, e.g., for granular films with small ($\sim$15-Å) magnetic precipitates. Since superlattices are periodic, their band structure change would not be a source of scattering.

Of far greater import than the scattering caused by compositional differences is the change in the wave functions they cause. The conduction bands for composites are different from those of the constituents. These differences affect the scattering of conduction electrons by other sources. In layered and granular structures, the external field reorients one magnetic region relative to another and thereby alters the composite band structure. In driving a system from antiferromagnetic to ferromagnetic, one changes the band structure from one in which the majority and minority spin bands alternate to one in which they remain constant as one goes from one region to another. The dependence of the wave functions on the magnetic configuration of the composite structure changes the conduction electron scattering rates, even when one evaluates a scattering event that by itself is independent of spin. We conclude that compositional

[77] A. Fert, *J. Phys. C* **2**, 1784 (1969); see also A. Fert and I. A. Campbell, Ref. 12.

[78] B. Loegel and F. Gautier, *J. Phys. Chem. Solids* **32**, 2723 (1971).

[79] S. S. P. Parkin, A. Modak, and D. J. Smith, *Phys. Rev. B* **47**, 9136 (1993).

differences in these structures, although they may not be a source of scattering, have a profound effect on how scattering events are felt by the condition electrons through their wave functions and thereby are a potential source for the giant MR observed in layered and granular structures.[69]

In summary, giant MR in inhomogeneous magnetic structures has at least two origins: (1) scattering events that are different for the spin-up and spin-down conduction bands, i.e., spin-dependent scattering, and (2) conduction band wave functions that depend on the magnetic configuration of the composite structure and determine the effect of a scattering event on the resistivity. The first mechanism can produce giant MR by itself (both in CIP and CPP); the second *cannot*. However, in the presence of spin-dependent scattering, the second mechanism can amplify or attenuate the MR due to the first mechanism.

4. CALCULATIONS OF SCATTERING

In current formulations of electrical conduction in inhomogeneous magnetic structures, scattering is characterized by phenomenological parameters that are determined by fitting theoretical expressions for the resistivity and MR to data. Here we review three different calculations of the basic scattering parameters.

Maekawa and his group[80] have evaluated the scattering potentials for two series of structures: iron or cobalt magnetic layers with nonmagnetic transition metal layers [Fe(Co)/TM] and ferromagnetic-copper (FM/Cu) multilayers. In the first series, the $d$ band is at the Fermi level and strongly contributes to the conduction in Fe(Co)/TM multilayers. Maekawa's group uses a tight-binding $d$-band model with on-site Coulomb interactions between electrons of opposite spin. By using the Hartree-Fock approximation, they calculate the random spin-dependent exchange potential, defined as the difference between the potential for an impurity and the unperturbed potential of the site on which the impurity is located. These scattering potentials have been self-consistently calculated for impurities in the first atomic monolayer in Fe or Co, as well as in the TM layer, for a series of transition metals ranging from scandium to palladium. They find the scattering potential for minority electrons is approxi-

[80] J. Inoue, A. Oguri, and S. Maekawa, *J. Phys. Soc. Japan* **60**, 376 (1991); J. Inoue and S. Maekawa, *Prog. Theor. Phys. Suppl.* **106**, 187 (1991); J. Inoue, H. Itoh, and S. Maekawa, *J. Phys. Soc. Japan* **61**, 1149 (1992); *J. Magn. Magn. Mater.* **121**, 344 (1993); H. Itoh, J. Inoue, and S. Maekawa, *Phys. Rev. B* **47**, 5809 (1993).

mately zero for Fe/Cr and Co/Ru, and the magnetic impurities at the interfaces retain their magnetic moments. These results provide some basis for understanding the large MR seen in these multilayered structures. With their calculated scattering potentials, and by using expressions for the MR ratios that are applicable to multilayers in which the mfp is large compared to the thickness of the layers, they predicted the variation of the MR ratio across the TM series for both Fe and Co. At the present time not enough data are available to corroborate these predictions.

For FM/Cu multilayers, Inoue *et al.*[80] consider that the carriers are primarily the *s*-like conduction bands in the copper layers. These electrons are scattered through the *s-d* mixing interaction by the magnetic atoms randomly distributed near interfaces. The mixing parameter $V_{sd}$ was determined from the magnetic moment for cobalt in copper, and the variation of $V_{sd}$ with the number of *d* electrons $n_d$ of the magnetic ions was taken into account. They calculated the MR ratio for FM/Cu multilayers as a function of $n_d$ and found a maximum around $n_d \sim 7.5$, i.e., between iron and cobalt.[80] Their results are supported by the large MR observed in Co/Cu multilayers;[6] however, the results to date on Fe/Cu multilayers are ambiguous.[81]

One calculation of the giant MR from first principles has been made; Butler *et al.*[82] have used the layer Korringa-Kohn-Rostoker[83] (LKKR) technique to determine the electronic structure of Co/Cu and NiFe/Cu superlattices. Their calculation of the electrical resistivity is based on a coherent potential approximation (CPA) to evaluate the Green's functions entering the Kubo linear response expression for the conductivity. For Co/Cu superlattices, they assumed all the scattering arises from the atomic layers that border the interfaces in which 1% of the cobalt atoms are randomly interdiffused into the neighboring copper layer and vice versa. The MR ratio they find, about 16 or 1600%, is an order of magni-

[81] F. Pétroff, A. Barthélémy, D. H. Mosca, D. K. Lottis, A. Fert, P. A. Schroeder, W. P. Pratt, R. Loloee, and S. Lequien, *Phys. Rev. B* **44**, 5355 (1991); O. Durand, J. M. George, J. R. Childress, S. Lequien, A. Schuhl, and A. Fert, *J. Magn. Magn. Mater.* **121**, 140 (1993). While most of the MR studies on Fe/Cu find MR ratios considerably smaller than for Co/Cu, there has been one unpublished report by L. Smardz (abstract CDI-4 for Symposium on Magnetic Ultra-Thin Films, Multilayers and Surfaces, September 7–10, 1992, Lyon, France) that the MR in Fe/Cu is as large as that for Co/Cu.

[82] W. H. Butler, J. M. MacLaren, and X.-G. Zhang, in *Magnetic Ultrathin Films* (B. T. Jonker *et al.*, eds.), *Mat. Res. Soc. Sym. Proc.* **313**, 59 (1993).

[83] J. M. MacLaren, S. Crampin, D. D. Vvedensky, and J. B. Pendry, *Phys. Rev. B* **40**, 12164 (1989).

tude larger than observed in Co/Cu superlattices;[6,22] undoubtedly this ratio will be reduced when other scattering mechanisms, e.g., scattering arising in the bulk of the layer, are taken into account. For NiFe/Cu superlattices, scattering arises within the permalloy layers, which are assumed to be random alloys. The MR ratios they calculate are about three orders of magnitude (one thousand times) larger than those observed in NiFe/Cu superlattices.[84] Butler et al.[82] note that their calculation omits a scattering mechanism that significantly affects the majority spin electrons and that, if properly accounted for, would considerably reduce their estimate of the CPP-MR ratio. These results are extremely encouraging and indicate one direction for future work on the understanding of the giant MR effect in inhomogeneous magnetic structures.

A third type of numerical calculation of the MR is based on a tight-binding model of the superlattice in which the potential along the growth direction is explicitly taken into account. Based on this model, Maekawa's group[85] calculated the conductance for the CIP and CPP geometries for finite two- and three-dimensional lattices by using the Landauer formula with the transfer matrix method. The size of the systems (approximately 2300 lattice sites) is limited by the time it takes to run these calculations. The Landauer expression for the conductance, given in terms of the transmission matrix for a given electronic structure, has been derived from the Kubo formula[59] so that the conductances calculated by the two methods are, in principle, the same. Asano et al.[85] find that (1) the *conductance* for CIP is larger than for CPP because the effects of the potential, i.e., the band structures and gaps, are primarily experienced by electrons in the CPP geometry;[66,86] (2) the CIP-MR is increased by interface roughness (spin dependent) and suppressed by bulk impurity scattering (spin independent); and (3) the CPP-MR is larger than the CIP-MR. These results are encouraging; in three dimensions they are currently limited to a layered structure with four layers (two magnetic, two nonmagnetic), and therefore with only three interfaces. They compare favorably to MR data on comparable Fe/Cr structures.[3]

[84] B. Dieny, Europhys. Lett. 17, 261 (1992); J. Phys.: Condens. Matter 4, 8009 (1992), B. Dieny, V. S. Speriosu, J. P. Nozières, B. A. Gurney, A. Vedyayev, and N. Ryzhanova, in Magnetism and Structure in Systems of Reduced Dimension (R. F. C. Farrow et al., eds.), NATO ASI Series (B-Physics), Vol. 309, p. 279, Plenum Press, New York (1993).

[85] A. Oguri, Y. Asano, and S. Maekawa, J. Phys. Soc. Japan 61, 2652 (1992); Y. Asano, A. Oguri, and S. Maekawa, Phys. Rev. B. 48, 6192 (1993).

[86] S. Zhang and P. M. Levy, in Magnetic Ultrathin Films (B. T. Jonker et al., eds.), Mat. Res. Soc. Sym. Proc. 313, 53 (1993).

## V. Quantum Theory of Magnetoresistance[87]

5. HAMILTONIAN

To calculate the conductivity and MR of inhomogeneous magnetic structures in a quantum approach it is necessary to write down the Hamiltonian that describes the conduction electrons. By making some separation between conduction and localized (core) electrons the one-electron model Hamiltonian is

$$\mathcal{H} = \mathcal{H}_0 + V_{\text{scat}}, \tag{5.1}$$

where

$$\mathcal{H}_0 = \frac{p^2}{2m} + V_{\text{pot},M}(\mathbf{r}, \sigma),$$

and

$$V_{\text{scat}} = \sum_a (v_a + j_a \hat{M}_a \cdot \hat{\sigma}) \, \delta(\mathbf{r} - \mathbf{r}_a). \tag{5.2}$$

We have taken the range of this scattering potential to be zero; this simplifies our treatment of the local scattering without altering the effect we are modeling. The roughness of the interfaces is modeled as a scattering potential in Eq. (5.2); because the scattering is confined to a narrow region we have represented it as random in the plane of the interface and a $\delta$ function in the third dimension (direction of layer growth). This is the same potential that results from the unitary transformation used by Tešanović et al.[57] to map the rough boundary problem into one with flat surfaces; however, in multilayers it is more correct to think of this scattering plane representing the interfacial region, e.g., the mixed layer of Johnson and Camley,[50] than resulting from the unitary transformation.

Although we have included the Coulomb interaction of the conduction electrons with the background $V_{\text{pot}}$ and use it to calculate the wave functions and one-electron propagators, here we neglect it between conduction electrons themselves as this enters the vertex corrections to the conductivity, which we do not *explicitly* consider. Also we are primarily

---

[87]The quantum formulation of transport in inhomogeneous magnetic structures outlined here has been developed in collaboration with my former students Horacio E. Camblong and Shufeng Zhang, and with Albert Fert.

interested in transport at $T = 0$ K, so that processes that occur at finite temperature are omitted. Here $V_{pot}$ represents the spin-dependent potentials of the electrons in the different regions; for layered structures, its effects on the MR have been considered by several groups,[49,54,69,85] and we discuss our approach[66,86] in Section 11. In granular films, this potential is random, and there have been no attempts to include its effect on conduction. Because sufficient complications arise from the scattering potential, most of the theoretical development to date has been confined to taking $V_{pot} = $ constant (zero).[88]

For the nonmagnetic regions, $j = 0$; whereas at interfaces and in magnetic regions (granules or layers), $j \neq 0$. The majority of the data on the giant MR effect has been on metallic structures with two active ingredients: one magnetic and one nonmagnetic element. If we exclude the substrates, buffer and capping layers, and layers that are used to pin the magnetic layers in spin-valve structures, there are *five* parameters that characterize the scattering: At the interfaces we have $v^s$ and $j^s$; for the bulk the parameters we have $v^m$, $j^m$, and $v^{nm}$, where $m \equiv$ magnetic and $nm \equiv$ nonmagnetic. Alternatively we can use $v^s$, $v^m$, and $v^{nm}$ to set the strength of the scattering in the different regions and $p^s$ and $p^m$ for the spin dependence, where $p \equiv j/v$.

The scattering potential $V_{scat}$ [Eq. (5.2)] refers to the scattering of a single electron by a particular configuration of impurities. Although transport properties of very pure systems, e.g., mesoscopic systems, depend on the specific configuration,[62] Kohn and Luttinger showed that their mean square deviations from the mean value, normalized by their mean value, tend to zero as the number of impurities tends to infinity.[61] Therefore, for all but the purest systems in which the transport is "ballistic," and specifically for metallic layered and granular structures in which giant MR has been observed, transport properties are described by functions, such as the self-energy and one-particle propagators, which have been

---

[88] The magnetic multilayers studied to date have ratios of $d/\lambda_{mfp} \gtrsim 1$ where $d$ is the thickness of the *entire* structure. Therefore, the conduction is impurity dominated: The roughness of the *outer* surfaces does not dominate the resistivity and those quantum effects coming from confinement are not of paramount importance. If differences in the potentials between layers are sizable compared to the Fermi energy, one should use wave functions that are eigenstates of the multilayer potential, and then evaluate the scattering by using these wave functions. It would be incorrect to consider the quantum wells arising from potential differences between layers as confinement potentials. If indeed they confined electrons to wells, one would not have conduction perpendicular to the plane of the layers, which is inconsistent with the data on the systems studied to date in the CPP geometry. Therefore, the thickness $d$ entering the ratio $d/\lambda_{mfp}$ to indicate whether one is in the impurity- or surface-dominated scattering regime is *not* the thickness of an individual layer but that of the entire multilayer.

averaged over all possible configurations of impurities. This "impurity average" eliminates the dependence of transport properties on the specifics of the impurity configuration.

Because there is no mechanism for dissipation of the electron's energy in the Hamiltonian of Eq. (5.1), Chester,[89] Doniach and Sondheimer,[90] and Trivedi and Ashcroft,[67] among others, have stressed the crucial role of the impurity-averaging procedure in *defining* a resistance for systems modeled by *elastic* scattering events, as we have[91] at $T = 0$ K. In homogeneous samples where the dimensions are large compared to the coherence length of the electron's wave function, the conditions are satisfied for calculating transport properties from impurity-averaged functions. That is, there is no difference between the resistance one calculates when the electrons sample an ensemble of impurity distributions, and the resistance found by using impurity-averaged electron propagators. For samples where the characteristic dimensions $L$ are less than $\lambda_{inel}$ (inelastic mfp), the dissipation occurs in the leads (reservoirs) rather than the sample itself. In "pure" systems where the elastic mfp is comparable to $\lambda_{inel}$, and $\lambda_{mfp} \approx \lambda_{inel} > L$, one has entered the mesoscopic regime where the sample-specific impurity configuration dictates the resistance, and impurity averaging is *not* valid. The multilayered and granular structures that display the giant MR effect have $\lambda_{mfp} \ll \lambda_{inel} < L$, i.e., conduction is dominated by impurity scattering; if they were homogeneous structures, using impurity-averaged functions to calculate their transport properties would be indubitably valid. However, they are *inhomogeneous* structures and as the size of the inhomogeneities becomes small, it becomes questionable whether *local* averages in the Kohn-Luttinger sense can be established.

Camblong[92,93] has considered impurity averaging for multilayered structures and finds that, as the in-plane cross-sectional areas for the

[89] G. V. Chester, *Rep. Progr. Phys.* **26**, 411 (1963).

[90] S. Doniach and E. H. Sondheimer, *Green's Functions for Solid State Physics*, Chap. 5, pp. 96–98, Benjamin/Cummings Pub. Co., Reading, MA (1974).

[91] The argument goes as follows (see Ref. 67): Electrons retain coherence in elastic collisions so that within its coherence length $\lambda_{inel}$ (inelastic mfp) one can solve for the electron's eigenstates for a given configuration of impurities. Within $\lambda_{inel}$ the system is reversible; however, as the electrons are coupled to sources of dissipation (e.g., phonons, albeit weakly at low temperatures), phase coherence of the electrons is destroyed on length scales of the order of $\lambda_{inel}$. The eigenstates prepared in one region for one impurity configuration are subsequently scattered in the next region by a different realization of the impurity configuration; however, this time it is *irreversible* as the electron has lost its coherence. Therefore, the electron samples different configurations of impurities, and it is this averaging effect that leads to resistance.

[92] H. E. Camblong, Ph.D. Thesis, New York University (1993) (unpublished).

[93] H. E. Camblong and P. M. Levy, *Phys. Rev. Lett.* **69**, 2835 (1992); *J. Magn. Magn. Mater.* **121**, 446 (1993); *J. Appl. Phys.* **73**, 5533 (1993).

layers are large, i.e., of the order of 1 mm$^2$, and as there are many impurities in each monolayer, the conditions are met for a meaningful impurity average in each monolayer. He concludes that (1) it is possible to define local *in-plane* impurity-averaged self-energies and propagators for multilayered structures, and therefore (2) it is meaningful to calculate the two-point conductivity $\sigma(z, z')$ [see Eq. (7.3)] by using these impurity-averaged quantities. Thus, in the case of multilayers, one does a partial averaging over impurities in the plane, but the distribution of impurities in the longitudinal $z$ direction is *not* averaged over; then, one considers the specific distribution of impurities in the growth direction. It is questionable whether one can construct an impurity-averaged *local* theory for granular films; if the size of the granules is small, of the order of 20 Å, it is not possible to represent transport in regions of this size by impurity-averaged propagators; there are not enough impurities and lattice sites to have a statistically meaningful "local" average. Fortunately, the giant MR effect observed in granular films (as well as for layered structures in the CPP geometry) depends on a *global* rather than on a local average, as we now discuss.

For layered structures in the CPP geometry, the electron current samples all the different scattering potentials in the structure. Therefore, one could *effectively* use self-energies and propagators for which the impurity average has been taken over the *entire structure* to represent *global* transport in this geometry. This is an example of a transport property that does *self-averaging* of an inherently inhomogeneous structure.

However, it should be pointed out that even though this effectively works for some structures, in general it is conceptually wrong to perform the impurity average over the whole three-dimensional structure. In effect, for layered structures in the CIP geometry the current lines do *not* sample all the scattering in the structure; rather, they sample only the scattering that is within a mfp of the center of the wave packet describing the electron. Therefore, transport in this geometry is *not* self-averaging; while the electron's trajectory samples all the different impurity configurations within a set of atomic planes for CIP (determined by the size of the mfp), it does not sample the impurity potential outside this region. Therefore, to calculate the transport properties of multilayered structures in the CIP geometry, it is essential to use self-energies and propagators that are defined in terms of *in-plane* impurity averages.

To calculate the conductivity in the quantum approaches we outline in Sections 9 and 10, it is necessary to obtain the impurity-averaged one-electron propagators or Green's functions $\langle G(\varepsilon) \rangle_I$ (angular brackets denote impurity-average). This function is defined as[92,93]

$$\langle G(\varepsilon) \rangle_I = G_0 + G_0 \langle T(\varepsilon) \rangle_I G_0, \tag{5.3}$$

where $G_0 = (\varepsilon - \mathcal{H}_0 + iO^+)^{-1}$ is the unperturbed one-particle propagator, and

$$\langle T(\varepsilon) \rangle_I = \langle V \rangle_I + \langle VG_0(\varepsilon)T(\varepsilon) \rangle_I \tag{5.4}$$

is the $T$-matrix; $V = \Sigma_a V_a$ is the scattering potential [Eq. (5.2)]. The one-particle irreducible self-energy $\Sigma$ ($\varepsilon$) for the impurity-averaged Green's function satisfies Dyson's equation:

$$\langle G(\varepsilon) \rangle_I = [\varepsilon - \mathcal{H}_0 - \Sigma(\varepsilon)]^{-1}. \tag{5.5}$$

The energy $\Sigma$ ($\varepsilon$) is calculated by placing Eq. (5.4) in Eq. (5.3) and identifying it as the irreducible insertion in this series.

The self-energy is related to the set of diagrams that defines the one-site $t$-matrix

$$t_a(\varepsilon) = V_a + V_a G_0(\varepsilon) t_a(\varepsilon). \tag{5.6}$$

This can be rewritten as

$$t(\mathbf{r}) = \frac{\lambda(\mathbf{r})}{1 - \lambda(\mathbf{r}) \mathrm{Tr}[G_0(\varepsilon)]}, \tag{5.7}$$

where $\lambda(r)$ is the scattering strength at position $r$, which is obtained from Eq. (3.1), $\lambda_a \equiv v_a + j_a \hat{M}_a \cdot \hat{\sigma}$. Transport properties are related to the imaginary part of this $t$-matrix; for weak scattering this is

$$-\mathrm{Im}[t(\mathbf{r})] = \pi\rho(\varepsilon_F)[v^2(\mathbf{r}) + j^2(\mathbf{r}) + 2v(\mathbf{r})j(\mathbf{r})\hat{M}(\mathbf{r}) \cdot \hat{\sigma}], \tag{5.8}$$

where $\rho(\varepsilon_F)$ is the density of states per unit volume at the Fermi level, and $\hat{M}(\mathbf{r})$ is a unit vector in the direction of local magnetization.

Two different quantum approaches can be taken to calculate the one-electron propagators and conductivity that use the same *one-site t*-matrix [Eqs. (5.7) and (5.8)]. One is based on the *local* self-energy, which is applicable to the dilute and weak scattering limit of impurities (if one does not demand self-consistency); a real-space representation is used to find, without further approximation or limits, the propagators and the *two*-point conductivity for multilayers, Eq. (7.3).[92–94] In this approach one concludes that the semiclassical approach for multilayers and the real-space quantum treatments, based on a local self-energy, produce

[94] A. Vedyayev, B. Dieny, and N. Ryzhanova, *Europhys. Lett.* **19**, 329 (1992).

the same magnetotransport properties, provided the effect of quantum interference and quantum size effects can be neglected.[92,93,95] The second approach uses a *nonlocal* self-energy built from the one-site $t$-matrix [Eqs. (5.7) and (5.8)]; here one attempts to take into account distant but strong scattering from interfaces. With this approach, *approximate* solutions are found for the *one*-point conductivity, Eq. (7.6), for multilayered structures by using the Kubo formalism in momentum space.[96,97]

## 6. Linear Response

The current at a point $r$ is related to the *static* electric field at $r'$ through the two-point conductivity

$$\mathbf{j}(\mathbf{r}) = \int d^3\mathbf{r}' \, \sigma(\mathbf{r}, \mathbf{r}') \cdot \mathbf{E}(\mathbf{r}'), \tag{6.1}$$

where $\mathbf{E}(\mathbf{r}')$ is the internal electric field in the solid and $\sigma(\mathbf{r}, \mathbf{r}')$ is the microscopic conductivity given by Kubo's linear response formalism,[98,99] as a current-current correlation function:

$$\sigma(\mathbf{r}, \mathbf{r}') \propto \langle [\hat{\mathbf{j}}(\mathbf{r}), \hat{\mathbf{j}}(\mathbf{r}')] \rangle, \tag{6.2}$$

where $\hat{\mathbf{j}}(\mathbf{r})$ is the quantum-mechanical current operator.

Electrical transport in metals leads to a redistribution of space charge if the rate at which the electrons are scattered varies from one region to another. For this reason, the field $E(r')$ is not the same as the field applied externally. For example, while one might apply a uniform electric field, the internal field is nonuniform in inhomogeneous media. Transport in magnetic metals with spin-dependent scattering or spin-polarized currents leads to a spatial redistribution of spin as well as charge;[100] this is referred to either as *spin accumulation* or *nonequilibrium* (current-driven) magnetization. To account for either spin-dependent scattering or spin-polarized conduction, it is necessary to introduce the spin variables referring to

[95] B. Dieny, A. Vedyayev, and N. Ryzhanova, *J. Magn. Magn. Mater.* **121**, 366 (1993).
[96] P. M. Levy, K. Ounadjela, S. Zhang, Y. Wang, C. B. Sommers, and A. Fert, *J. Appl. Phys.* **67**, 5914 (1990); P. M. Levy, S. Zhang, and A. Fert, *Phys. Rev. Lett.* **65**, 1643 (1990).
[97] S. Zhang, P. M. Levy, and A. Fert, *Phys. Rev.* B **45**, 8689 (1992).
[98] G. D. Mahan, *Many-Particle Physics*, Secs. 7.1 and 7.3, Plenum, New York (1981).
[99] G. Rickayzen, *Green's Functions and Condensed Matter*, in particular Chap. 4, Academic Press, London (1980).
[100] R. H. Silsbee, *Bull Magn. Reson.* **2**, 284 (1980); M. Johnson and R. H. Silsbee, *Phys. Rev. Lett.* **55**, 1790 (1985); *Phys. Rev.* B **35**, 4959 (1987); *Phys. Rev.* B **37**, 5312, 5326 (1988).

the conduction electrons in the constitutive relation that relates fields to currents. To introduce spin variables we start from the bare external field $E_{ext}(r')$, not from the internal field defined in Eq. (6.1).

When considering spin-dependent interactions in the electron's Hamiltonian, the electron propagators, currents, and internal fields are spin dependent. To obtain a covariant description for arbitrary choices of the quantization axis, we introduce quantities with definite spinor character. This leads to the definition of the generalized spin-dependent current densities $j_{\alpha\beta}(r) = \langle \hat{j}_{\alpha\beta}(r) \rangle$, which are expectation values of the spinor current operators[101]

$$\hat{j}_{\alpha\beta}(r) = \frac{e\hbar}{mi} \Psi_\alpha^+(r) \overset{\leftrightarrow}{\nabla}_r \Psi_\beta(r), \tag{6.3}$$

where $\overset{\leftrightarrow}{\nabla}_r = (\overset{\rightarrow}{\nabla}_r - \overset{\leftarrow}{\nabla}_r)/2$ is the antisymmetric gradient operator, $\Psi_\alpha(r)$ is the real space one-electron field operator, and greek indices label the two spin channels. By introducing this spinor notation, we find the spinor current at point 1 is related to an electric field at point 3 by[102]

$$j_{\alpha\beta}(1) = \int d3 \, \sigma_{\alpha\beta}(13) \cdot E_{ext}(3)$$

$$= \int d2 \, d3 \, d4 [G_{\alpha\gamma}(12) \overset{\leftrightarrow}{\nabla}_1 \Gamma_{\gamma\delta}(234) G_{\delta\beta}(41)] \cdot E_{ext}(3), \tag{6.4}$$

and where the Feynman diagram associated with this expression is given in Fig. 12(a). In Eq. (6.4), as well as in all subsequent equations in this section, summation over repeated greek indices is implied. Here $G(12)$ is a one-electron propagator; it is a $2 \times 2$ spin matrix, inasmuch as it satisfies a differential equation that includes a $2 \times 2$ spin scattering matrix, which represents the impurity-averaged self-energy. The vector vertex function $\Gamma(234)$ is represented by a $2 \times 2$ spin matrix, which is given by the integral equation[102] [Fig. 12(b)]

$$\Gamma(234) = \overset{\leftrightarrow}{\nabla}_3 1 \delta(2,3)\delta(4,3) + V(24) \int G(2,2') \Gamma(2'34') G(4',4) d2' \, d4'$$

$$+ \delta(2,4) \int V(25) G(5,2') \Gamma(2'34') G(4',5) d2' \, d4' \, d5, \tag{6.5}$$

---

[101] Spinor currents were introduced by J. Slonczewski, *Phys. Rev. B* **39**, 995 (1989) to study transmission through tunneling barriers.

[102] This is an extension of the Kubo formula for conductivity, see G. Rickayzen, Ref. 99, to include the spin variables.

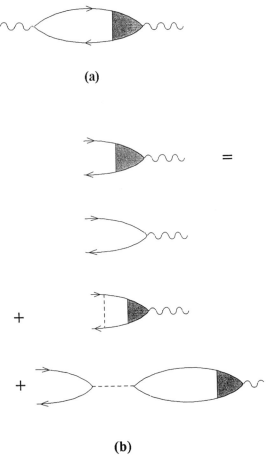

(a)

(b)

FIG. 12. (a) Feynman diagram for the conductivity of Eq. (6.4) consisting of electron and hole propagators coupled at the right end to an electric field through a *dressed* vertex. (b) The shaded portion represents the vertex correction of Eq. (6.5). This term consists of three parts: the bare vertex; the corrections due to interactions between electrons, and those coming from the impurity averaging, that couple the electron and hole propagators; and polarization corrections, which modify the field seen by the electrons.

where the $V$'s represent interactions not accounted for in the one-particle propagator $G$, matrix multiplication is implied, 1 is a $2 \times 2$ unit matrix, and $\delta(1, 2)$ stands for the Dirac delta function $\delta(\mathbf{r}_1 - \mathbf{r}_2)$. The first term is the bare vertex; the second represents vertex corrections to the electron-hole propagators (two-particle Green's functions), which represent correlations due to scattering at different sites that are lost when one uses Green's functions with impurity-averaged self-energies; and the

last term accounts for polarization effects in the medium that contribute to the total internal field as distinguished from the external field $\mathbf{E}_{\text{ext}}(3)$.[103]

Once the Green's functions $G$ are known, the integral equation for the vertex function can be solved (in principle at least); however, this is rarely done. What is important about Eq. (6.5) is that it allows one to check that conserving approximations have been made.[104] Some of the relations that define these approximations are referred to as Ward identities.[98,99]

While the first term in Eq. (6.5) represents the interaction of an electron with the external field, the other terms represent the effects of the *other* electrons that have rearranged themselves in response to the field. By using the vertex function, we define the effective *local* field acting on an electron in response to an external field as follows. First, we define a scalar vertex function[98]

$$\Gamma_{\gamma\delta}(234) \equiv \overset{\leftrightarrow}{\nabla}_2 \Gamma_{\gamma\delta}(234), \tag{6.6}$$

where the gradient operates on the Green's function when it is placed in Eq. (6.4). Then, we write

$$\int \Gamma_{\gamma\delta}(234)\mathbf{E}_{\text{ext}}(3)\,d3 \equiv \mathbf{E}_{\gamma\delta}(2)\delta(2,4), \tag{6.7}$$

where we have confined the corrections in the second term of the vertex function [Eq. (6.5)], to those that can be represented by a *local* field, i.e., where 2 and 4 are one and the same position in space. For example, to lowest order in the density of scatterers, vertex corrections due to impurity averaging are local[98,99] (the applicability of this to interfaces requires further study). Upon placing Eq. (6.7) in Eq. (6.4) we find

$$\mathbf{j}_{\alpha\beta}(1) = \int d2[G_{\alpha\gamma}(12)\overset{\leftrightarrow}{\nabla}_1 \overset{\leftrightarrow}{\nabla}_2 G_{\delta\beta}(21)] \cdot \mathbf{E}_{\gamma\delta}(2). \tag{6.8}$$

This can be put in the form of Eq. (6.1), but now with spin indices,

$$\mathbf{j}_{\alpha\beta}(\mathbf{r}) = \int d^3r'\, \boldsymbol{\sigma}_{\alpha\beta,\gamma\delta}(\mathbf{r},\mathbf{r}') \cdot \mathbf{E}_{\gamma\delta}(\mathbf{r}'), \tag{6.9}$$

[103] See G. D. Mahan, Ref. 98, pp. 205–208, and G. Rickayzen, Ref. 99, pp. 127–129, for a discussion of the difference between total and external electric fields.

[104] G. Baym and L. P. Kadanoff, *Phys. Rev.* **124**, 287 (1961). They showed that the conservation laws for transport imply relationships between the vertex functions and one-electron propagators, and that it is necessary to respect them so that the vertex used satisfies the conservation laws.

where $\sigma_{\alpha\beta,\gamma\delta}(\mathbf{r}, \mathbf{r}')$ is a two-point fourth-rank spinor conductivity. It represents the terms in the brackets in Eq. (6.8), which contain only the contribution from the bubble diagram in the Kubo formula; this is the diagram in Fig. 12(a) *without* the vertex correction [Fig. 12(b)], i.e., with just a bare vertex. Equations (6.4) through (6.8) are to be interpreted as Matsubara Green's functions; when properly analytically continued, they lead to combinations of retarded and advanced Green's functions. The two-point spinor conductivity is explicitly written as[105]

$$\sigma_{\alpha\beta,\gamma\delta}(\mathbf{r}, \mathbf{r}') = -\frac{2}{\pi}\frac{e^2}{\hbar}\left(\frac{\hbar^2}{2m}\right)^2 A_{\beta\gamma}(\mathbf{r}, \mathbf{r}')\overleftrightarrow{\nabla}_r\overleftrightarrow{\nabla}_{r'}A_{\delta\alpha}(\mathbf{r}', \mathbf{r}), \qquad (6.10)$$

where

$$A_{\alpha\beta}(\mathbf{r}, \mathbf{r}') = \frac{1}{2}[G^{\text{ret}}_{\alpha\beta}(\mathbf{r}, \mathbf{r}') - G^{\text{adv}}_{\alpha\beta}(\mathbf{r}, \mathbf{r}')]$$

is the density of states function. This spinor conductivity is proportional to the bubble part of the current-current correlation of the spinor currents, i.e.,

$$\sigma_{\alpha\beta,\gamma\delta}(\mathbf{r}, \mathbf{r}')\alpha\langle[\hat{\mathbf{j}}_{\alpha\beta}(r), \hat{\mathbf{j}}_{\gamma\delta}(\mathbf{r}')]\rangle.$$

From Eqs. (6.7) and (6.9) it is clear that the charge and spin accumulations attendant to conduction in inhomogeneous magnetic structures are accounted for in the effective internal field $\mathbf{E}_{\gamma\delta}(\mathbf{r})$ [Eq. (6.7)], which has absorbed the vertex corrections [the third term in Eq. (6.5)]. It would be incorrect to include such effects when calculating the conductivity $\sigma_{\alpha\beta,\gamma\delta}(\mathbf{r}, \mathbf{r}')$ if one uses the effective fields defined in Eq. (6.7);[106] it would be tantamount to including polarization effects to evaluate the current-current correlation function when one is relating the current to the *total* electric field.[103] In fact, by starting with the vertex equation [Eq. (6.5)], and making a Taylor series expansion for points 2' in the neighborhood of 2, we have shown[107] that the vertex function $\Gamma_{\gamma\delta}(232)$ [4 = 2 from Eq.

[105] H. E. Camblong, S. Zhang, and P. M. Levy, "Theory of Magnetotransport in Inhomogeneous Magnetic Structures," *J. Appl. Phys.* **75**, 6906 (1994).

[106] It has been incorrectly assumed (see Refs. 23 and 65) that spin accumulation effects have been ignored in theories of the CPP-MR, which are based on Eq. (6.9), e.g., Refs. 53, 114, and 120.

[107] See Ref. 92 and P. M. Levy, H. E. Camblong, and S. Zhang, "Effective Internal Fields and Magnetization Buildup for Magnetotransport in Magnetic Multilayered Structures," presented at the Conference on Magnetism and Magnetic Materials, Minneapolis, MN, Nov. 15–18, 1993; *J. Appl. Phys.* **75**, 7076 (1994).

(6.7)] at large distances 3 from 2 satisfies the diffusion equation that has been used in semiclassical treatments of transport in inhomogeneous magnetic structures to account for spin and charge accumulation.[51,108]

Finding the global or measurable conductivity, i.e., the net current density across the boundaries of a sample for an applied potential, for inhomogeneous structures from the local conductivity Eq. (6.10) is by no means straightforward. The main difficulty arises from the lack of symmetry in general, which leads to complicated distributions (magnitudes and directions) for both current densities and internal fields. If one could evaluate the internal field $E_{\gamma\delta}(r)$ from the vertex function [Eq. (6.7)], one could find the current density from Eq. (6.8); this is equivalent to solving the conductivity in Eq. (6.4) when the field $E$ is simply related to the applied potential. Provided one has taken care to use current-conserving approximations for the vertex function, one is assured that the steady state current density, i.e., the trace over spin space of the spinor current density $j(r) = \text{Tr}[j(r)] = \Sigma_\alpha j_{\alpha\alpha}(r)$, is conserved.[104] Thus,

$$\nabla \cdot j(r) = 0, \qquad (6.11)$$

because $\partial\rho/\partial t = 0$ in the steady state. The *spinor* current densities satisfy the equation

$$\nabla \cdot j_{\alpha\beta}(r) = p_{\alpha\beta}(r), \qquad (6.12)$$

where

$$p_{\alpha\beta}(r) = \frac{\partial\rho_{\alpha\beta}(r)}{\partial t}$$

and

$$\rho_{\alpha\beta}(r) \sim e\langle \Psi_\alpha^\dagger(r) \Psi_\beta(r)\rangle$$

is the spinor charge density that represents the charge buildup or loss from spin-flip processes. We define spin-flip processes as those that give rise to finite $p_{\alpha\beta}(r)$; conversely when $p_{\alpha\beta}(r) = 0$ we say these are no spin-flip processes. It will be important to distinguish those situations

[108] P. C. van Son, H. van Kempen, and P. Wyder, *Phys. Rev. Lett.* **58**, 2271 (1987); M. Johnson and R. H. Silsbee, *Phys. Rev. Lett.* **60**, 377 (1988), and Ref. 100.

where $p_{\alpha\beta}(\mathbf{r}) \neq 0$, which reduce the giant MR effect due to spin mixing[51,77] from those where the off-diagonal elements of the spinor current density $\mathbf{j}_{\alpha\beta}(\mathbf{r})$ are due to one's using quantization axes at an angle to the direction of the magnetization in a region [see Eq. (3.1)]. In this latter case, $p_{\alpha\beta}(\mathbf{r}) = 0$ and the steady state current density is conserved for each spin component:

$$\mathbf{\nabla} \cdot \mathbf{j}_{\alpha\beta}(\mathbf{r}) = 0. \tag{6.13}$$

Kane *et al.*[109] have shown directly from the Kubo formula that $\vec{\mathbf{\nabla}}_r \cdot \sigma(\mathbf{r}, \mathbf{r}') = 0$ and $\sigma(\mathbf{r}, \mathbf{r}') \cdot \vec{\mathbf{\nabla}}_{r'} = 0$, so that the equation of continuity is trivially satisfied, independently of the electric field distribution $\mathbf{E}(\mathbf{r}')$ in Eq. (6.1).[110] Similarly one can show that the spinor conductivity $\sigma_{\alpha\beta}(\mathbf{r}, \mathbf{r}')$ is divergenceless when there are *no* spin-flip processes.[111] However, the bubble conductivity of Eq. (6.10) and its equivalent when taking the spin trace of Eq. (6.10) are *not* divergenceless. Therefore, imposing the constraint of Eq. (6.12) or of Eq. (6.13) on the current density given by Eq. (6.9) provides a set of equations that allows one in some cases to determine the effective internal fields $\mathbf{E}_{\gamma\delta}(\mathbf{r}')$:[111]

$$\int d^3r' \vec{\mathbf{\nabla}}_r \sigma_{\alpha\beta, \gamma\delta}(\mathbf{r}, \mathbf{r}') \cdot \mathbf{E}_{\gamma\delta}(\mathbf{r}') = p_{\alpha\beta}(\mathbf{r}). \tag{6.14}$$

Another condition comes from the definitions of the internal field [Eq. (6.7)] and the vertex function [Eq. (6.5)]. One can show that

$$\int_C \mathbf{E}_{\gamma\delta}(\mathbf{r}') \cdot d\mathbf{r}' = V\delta_{\gamma\delta}, \tag{6.15}$$

where $V$ is the potential applied to the outer boundaries of the structure and the line integral is the current path $C$ from one boundary to the other.[111] In cases where there is some symmetry (layered structures), we will show that one can solve for the fields and currents. For more complicated geometries (granular films), we resort to an ansatz based on some degree of randomness to find the measured resistivity and MR.

[109] C. L. Kane, R. A. Serota, and P. A. Lee, *Phys. Rev. B* **37**, 6701 (1988).

[110] This is true provided that one uses the complete two-point conductivity $\sigma(\mathbf{r}, \mathbf{r}')$, i.e., not just the bubble approximation to $\sigma(\mathbf{r}, \mathbf{r}')$, in which case a spin-independent but undetermined electric field $\mathbf{E}(\mathbf{r})$ develops.

[111] H. E. Camblong, P. M. Levy, and S. Zhang, in press.

## 7. SIMPLIFICATIONS DUE TO SYMMETRY

In cases where there are spatial or spin symmetries, or in certain limits of the characteristic length scales $d_{in}$, which describe the inhomogeneity of the structure, the general constitutive relation between field and current [Eq. (6.9)] simplifies, and it is possible to evaluate explicitly the global conductivity (resistivity) and MR. We first consider the simplifications due to geometrical and magnetic symmetries.

### a. *Layered Structures*

We designate the layers to lie in the *x-y* plane and the growth direction to be the *z* axis. We do not focus on the atomic potentials, and as random impurity averages are taken over the *x-y* planes of the layers (see Section 5), the planes are homogeneous. The conductivity, Eq. (6.4) or Eq. (6.10), can be written as

$$\boldsymbol{\sigma}(\mathbf{r}, \mathbf{r}') = \boldsymbol{\sigma}(\boldsymbol{\rho} - \boldsymbol{\rho}'; z, z')$$
$$= 1_{\parallel}\sigma^{\parallel}(\boldsymbol{\rho} - \boldsymbol{\rho}'; z, z') + \hat{e}_z\hat{e}_z\sigma^{\perp}(\boldsymbol{\rho} - \boldsymbol{\rho}'; z, z'), \tag{7.1}$$

where $\boldsymbol{\rho} = (x, y)$, $1_{\parallel}$ is the unit dyadic in the plane of the layers, $\hat{e}_z$ is a unit vector along the *z* axis, and we have temporarily suppressed the spin indices. By taking the Fourier transform with respect to $(\boldsymbol{\rho} - \boldsymbol{\rho}')$, we find Eq. (6.9) is written as

$$\mathbf{j}_{\alpha\beta}(\mathbf{k}, z) = \int dz' \, \boldsymbol{\sigma}_{\alpha\beta, \gamma\delta}(\mathbf{k}; z, z') \cdot \mathbf{E}_{\gamma\delta}(\mathbf{k}, z'). \tag{7.2}$$

We are interested in cases where the fields are uniform over the layers and we assume the magnetic domains in the layers are large compared to the mfp's. Thus, we take $\mathbf{k} = 0$ and suppress this index, so that Eq. (7.2) is written as

$$\mathbf{j}_{\alpha\beta}(z) = \int dz' \, \boldsymbol{\sigma}_{\alpha\beta, \gamma\delta}(z, z') \cdot \mathbf{E}_{\gamma\delta}(z'), \tag{7.3}$$

and we are left with a *one-dimensional* problem for the spatial dependence of currents and fields.

For fields parallel to the plane of the layers (CIP), the electric field $\mathbf{E}_{\gamma\delta}(z)$ is a constant. From condition (6.15) we find,

$$\mathbf{E}_{\gamma\delta}^{CIP} = \frac{V}{L_T}\delta_{\gamma\delta} \equiv E\delta_{\gamma\delta}, \tag{7.4}$$

when $L_T$ is the length of the sample in the transverse direction, i.e., the square root of the cross-sectional area of the multilayered structure. Therefore, the current density for CIP,

$$j_{\alpha\beta}(z) = \sigma^{\parallel}_{\alpha\beta}(z)E,$$

(7.5)

is proportional to the one-point conductivity

$$\sigma^{\parallel}_{\alpha\beta}(z) = \sum_{\gamma} \int dz' \, \sigma^{\parallel}_{\alpha\beta,\gamma\gamma}(z, z'),$$

(7.6)

where $\sigma^{\parallel}$ denotes the in-plane component of the conductivity tensor. The measured current per unit area, or average current density $\langle j \rangle = I/A$, where $j = \mathrm{Tr}[j] = \Sigma_{\alpha} j_{\alpha\alpha}$, is

$$\langle j \rangle = \frac{1}{L} \int dz j(z) \equiv \sigma_{\mathrm{CIP}} E,$$

(7.7)

where $\sigma_{\mathrm{CIP}}$ is the global or measured CIP conductivity

$$\sigma_{\mathrm{CIP}} = \frac{1}{L} \int \int dz \, dz' \sum_{\alpha,\gamma} \sigma^{\parallel}_{\alpha\alpha,\gamma\gamma}(z, z')$$

$$= \frac{1}{L} \int \int dz \, dz' \, \mathrm{Tr}[\sigma^{\parallel}(z, z')],$$

(7.8)

and $L$ is the length of the sample in the $z$ direction. In Eq. (7.8) Tr is shorthand for the double partial trace explicitly shown. The remarkable feature of these results for CIP is that one can determine the resistivity and MR, for this particular geometry, because the field distribution is trivial. The result, Eqs. (7.7) and (7.8), reinforces the point of Dieny et al.[112] that it is more relevant to talk about conductivities than resistivities for CIP.

For currents perpendicular to the plane of the layers (CPP), the internal field $E_{\gamma\delta}(z)$ is *not* constant. However, from the continuity equation [Eq. (6.12)] one gains information on the current density. Therefore, it is better to express the electric field in terms of the current, i.e., to invert Eq. (6.9),

$$E_{\alpha\beta}(z) = \int dz' \rho^{\perp}_{\alpha\beta,\gamma\delta}(z, z') j_{\gamma\delta}(z'),$$

(7.9)

[112] B. Dieny, J. P. Nozières, V. S. Speriosu, B. A. Gurney, and D. R. Wilhoit, *Appl. Phys. Lett.* **61**, 2111 (1992).

where $\rho^\perp$ is the perpendicular component of the resisitivity tensor. The Kubo formula yields the conductivity; in order to find the two-point resistivity, one must solve the integral equation

$$\int dz'' \sigma_{\alpha\beta,\gamma\delta}(z, z'') \rho_{\gamma\delta,\alpha'\beta'}(z'', z') = \delta(z - z')\delta_{\alpha\alpha'}\delta_{\beta\beta'}, \qquad (7.10)$$

that is, invert the matrix

$$\rho_{\alpha\beta,\gamma\delta}(z, z') = \sigma^{-1}_{\alpha\beta,\gamma\delta}(z, z') \neq [\sigma_{\alpha\beta,\gamma\delta}(z, z')]^{-1}, \qquad (7.11)$$

which is unwieldy. In limiting cases one need only invert a *one*-point conductivity, $\sigma_{\alpha\beta,\gamma\delta}(z)$, which reduces to inverting a $4 \times 4$ spin matrix; if there is sufficient spin symmetry present so that no spin indices are necessary, the one-point resistivity $\rho(z)$ is just $1/\sigma(z)$.

The voltage drop per unit length of the sample or average electric field $\langle E_{\alpha\beta} \rangle$ is, from Eqs. (7.9) and (6.15),

$$\langle E_{\alpha\beta} \rangle = \frac{1}{L} \int dz\, E_{\alpha\beta}(z),$$

$$= \frac{1}{L} \int \int dz\, dz'\, \rho^\perp_{\alpha\beta,\gamma\delta}(z, z') j_{\gamma\delta}(z'), \qquad (7.12)$$

$$= \langle E \rangle \delta_{\alpha\beta},$$

where

$$\langle E \rangle = \frac{V}{L} = \frac{1}{L} \int \int dz\, dz'\, \rho^\perp_{\alpha\alpha,\gamma\delta}(z, z') j_{\gamma\delta}(z'),$$

is independent of $\alpha$ (but a sum over $\gamma$ and $\delta$ is implied). The current density $j_{\gamma\delta}(z')$ for the CPP geometry satisfies the ordinary differential equation [see Eq. (6.12)]:

$$\partial_z j_{\alpha\beta}(z) = p_{\alpha\beta}(z). \qquad (7.13)$$

One trivial solution is for $p_{\alpha\beta} = 0$, i.e., for the case of no spin-flips or no spin mixing of the two spin channels. In this case, $j_{\alpha\beta}(z)$ is a *constant*, and Eq. (7.12) reduces to

$$\langle E \rangle = \rho^{CPP}_{\gamma\delta} j_{\gamma\delta}, \qquad (7.14)$$

where

$$\rho_{\gamma\delta}^{\text{CPP}} = \frac{1}{L} \int \int dz \, dz' \, \rho_{\alpha\alpha,\gamma\delta}^{\perp}(z, z'),$$

is a reduced $2 \times 2$ resistivity matrix. Because the voltage drop across the sample is independent of the spin direction $\alpha$ of the conduction electrons [Eq. (7.12)], this resistivity matrix $\rho^{\text{CPP}}$ is independent of the spin index $\alpha$. The total current is

$$j = \text{Tr}[j] = \sum_{\gamma} j_{\gamma\gamma}$$

$$= \langle E \rangle \sum_{\gamma} ([\rho^{\text{CPP}}]^{-1})_{\gamma\gamma}, \tag{7.15}$$

where the square brackets indicate one is taking the inverse of a spin matrix. Thus the conductivity for CPP when $p_{\alpha\beta} = 0$ [see Eq. (7.13)] is

$$\sigma_{\text{CPP}}(p = 0) = \sum_{\gamma} ([\rho^{\text{CPP}}]^{-1})_{\gamma\gamma}. \tag{7.16}$$

By comparing Eqs. (7.8) and (7.16) one notes that the two conductivities are quite different. The CIP global conductivity is a complete sum of the local conductivities over the entire sample *and* over all spin indices; in some limiting cases it is analogous to conduction for a set of resistors in *parallel*. The CPP conductivity [Eq. (7.16)] is a sum over the conductivities for each spin channel $\gamma$. The conductivity in each channel comes from taking the inverse of the resistivity $\rho^{\text{CPP}}$ [Eq. (7.14)], which is arrived at by summing over the local resistivities. It is analogous to a set of resistors in *series,* for a specific spin index.[113]

b. *Granular Films*

For magnetic precipitates in nonmagnetic matrices, there is no symmetry, other than a certain degree of randomness in the positions and shapes of the granules (precipitates). Here one is left with the general *three-dimensional* (spatial) problem where the field distribution is unspecified and the only constraint on the current density is given by either Eq. (6.12) or Eq. (6.13). We present a real-space quantum approach to this problem

---

[113] Because resistivity is proportional to the scattering of conduction electrons, when one takes the average of the resistivities as in Eq. (7.14), one is, at some level, taking the average of the scattering; therefore, it seems intuitively plausible that $\rho^{\text{CPP}}$ is proportional the *average* of the scattering and does not depend on how it is spatially distributed.

in Sections 9 and 12, which shows that conduction in granular films is analogous to that for CPP in layered structures.[105]

One can intuit as follows why this analogy is plausible. The one condition on transport in granular films is on the current density. Therefore, it is preferable to express the electric field in terms of the current (for the reason outlined in the previous subsection) and to invert Eq. (6.9):

$$\mathbf{E}_{\alpha\beta}(\mathbf{r}) = \int d^3 r' \, \boldsymbol{\rho}_{\alpha\beta,\gamma\delta}(\mathbf{r}, \mathbf{r}') \cdot \mathbf{j}_{\gamma\delta}(\mathbf{r}'). \tag{7.17}$$

By integrating both sides along a current path $C$ we find, by using Eq. (6.15),

$$V\delta_{\alpha\beta} = \int d^3 r' \left[ \int_C d\mathbf{r} \cdot \boldsymbol{\rho}_{\alpha\beta,\gamma\delta}(\mathbf{r}, \mathbf{r}') \right] \cdot \mathbf{j}_{\gamma\delta}(\mathbf{r}'). \tag{7.18}$$

If one now considers, due to the randomness of this structure, that the current density and resistivity function in square brackets at a point $\mathbf{r}'$ are not correlated, one averages over them separately and arrives at a result analogous to that for CPP in multilayered structures [see Eq. (7.14)]. This hypothesis provides an *upper* limit to the resistivity; the actual resistivity is *less* because the current takes the path of least resistance. Therefore there is some correlation between the current density and resistivity function in Eq. (7.18).

### c. Collinear Magnetic Structures

When we limit ourselves to structures with collinear magnetization configurations, e.g., ferromagnetic and antiferromagnetic configurations, we can choose the quantization axis for the electron's spin parallel to the magnetization vectors. In this case, the spin-dependent scattering potential [Eq. (5.2)] contains only diagonal elements, and if there are no spin-flip processes, the electron's self-energy, propagator (Green's function), and vertex function are all diagonal in spin space. From this, and from the definitions of the spinor current density, conductivity, and effective internal field [see Eqs. (6.4) through (6.9)], it follows that $\mathbf{j}_{\alpha\beta}(\mathbf{r}) = \delta_{\alpha\beta}\mathbf{j}^\alpha(\mathbf{r})$, $\mathbf{E}_{\alpha\beta}(\mathbf{r}) = \delta_{\alpha\beta}\mathbf{E}^\alpha(\mathbf{r})$, and $\boldsymbol{\sigma}_{\alpha\beta,\gamma\delta}(\mathbf{r}, \mathbf{r}') \propto \delta_{\beta\gamma}\delta_{\alpha\delta}$ are diagonal in spin space. Then, the constitutive relation (6.9) is written in the simplified form

$$\mathbf{j}^\alpha(\mathbf{r}) = \int d^3 r' \, \boldsymbol{\sigma}^\alpha(\mathbf{r}, \mathbf{r}') \cdot \mathbf{E}^\alpha(\mathbf{r}'), \tag{7.19}$$

where $\boldsymbol{\sigma}^\alpha(\mathbf{r}, \mathbf{r}') = \boldsymbol{\sigma}_{\alpha\alpha,\alpha\alpha}(\mathbf{r}, \mathbf{r}')$ and no sum over $\alpha$ is implied here.

This simplification for collinear structures does not have much of an impact on the CIP conductivity for layered structures [Eq. (7.8)]; however, it does reduce the CPP conductivity [Eq. (7.16)] to

$$\sigma_{CPP}(p = 0)|_{collinear} = \sum_{\gamma} \frac{1}{\rho_{CPP}^{\gamma}}. \tag{7.20}$$

This follows from the fact that the inverse of a diagonal matrix is a diagonal matrix whose elements are the inverse of the original matrix elements.

The form of the constitutive relation Eq. (7.19) and $\mathbf{j} = \Sigma_{\alpha} \mathbf{j}^{\alpha}$ constitute the two-current model originally introduced by Fert and Campbell to discuss transport in ferromagnetic metals.[12] In their case, the electric fields are uniform, and the condition (6.15) requires the fields to be also *independent* of spin. The appropriate generalization of the two-current model to inhomogeneous magnetic structures is Eq. (6.9) and $\mathbf{j} = \text{Tr}[\mathbf{j}] = \Sigma_{\alpha} \mathbf{j}_{\alpha\alpha}$.

## 8. LIMITING CASES

The effective internal field and current density are determined by the conductivity and boundary conditions, i.e., the applied potential. In the last section, we considered the role of geometry and boundary conditions; here we focus on the conductivity and on its dependence on the points $\mathbf{r}$ and $\mathbf{r}'$. Although we could discuss this dependence for noncollinear magnetic configurations in random structures, the additional complications in spin indices (matrix notation) and the three-dimensional nature of the problem tend to obfuscate the simplifications from considering limiting cases. For this reason, in this section, we limit our discussion to transport in layered structures with collinear magnetic configurations.[105,114] In this case the effects of the simplifications on the measurable transport properties can be described succinctly, and their extension to granular structures and noncollinear magnetic configuration are transparent, albeit somewhat tedious, e.g., one is always left with inverting $4 \times 4$ spin matrices to obtain the resistivity from the conductivity.

The form of the two-point conductivity is controlled by (1) the distribution of the scatterers and (2) the intensity of the scattering. The first is dictated by the layering and is characterized by $d_{in}$ (for granular films it is the average distance between granules and their sizes); the second is characterized by the mean free path $\lambda$ (where we drop the subscript mfp

[114] H. E. Camblong, S. Zhang, and P. M. Levy, *Phys. Rev. B* **47**, 4735 (1993).

because there is no confusion here), which represents the *average* of the scattering encountered over the distances $d_{in}$. There are two limits for which $\sigma(z, z')$ of Eq. (7.3) is simple: (1) when $\lambda \gg d_{in}$ and (2) when $\lambda \ll d_{in}$.

When $\lambda \gg d_{in}$, the conductivity is "self-averaging" and the layering or granularity is not important. This limit resembles the case in homogeneous alloys and will be referred to as such. In this case the inhomogeneities are irrelevant and translational invariance is restored; therefore one can write

$$\sigma(z, z') = \mathbf{1}F(z - z') = \mathbf{1}f\left(\frac{z - z'}{\lambda}\right), \tag{8.1}$$

whose range dependence is scaled by the average $\lambda$ (arising from the average scattering) as a characteristic length scale. In this limit the conductivity tensor is a *scalar*. In reciprocal space, the two-point conductivity is diagonal:

$$\sigma(v, v') = \mathbf{1}\sigma(v)\delta(v - v'), \tag{8.2}$$

with $\sigma(v)$ being the Fourier transform of the real-space conductivity kernel [Eq. (8.1)]. By writing Eq. (7.3) for collinear structures [see Eq. (7.19)] in reciprocal space, we find in the homogeneous limit that

$$j^{\alpha}(v) = \int dv'\, \sigma^{\alpha}(v)\delta(v - v')E^{\alpha}(v') = \sigma^{\alpha}(v)E^{\alpha}(v). \tag{8.3}$$

For a divergenceless current ($j^{\alpha}$ = constant), this implies that $v = 0$ and that the electric field is a constant and unique as mentioned at the end of Section 7. In this case there is *no* distinction between CPP and CIP. From Eq. (8.2) we note that the conductivity matrix is readily inverted in reciprocal space, so that

$$\rho^{\alpha}(v) = \frac{1}{\sigma^{\alpha}(v)}, \tag{8.4}$$

and that

$$\sigma_{CPP}\big|_{\lambda \gg d_{in}} = \sum_{\alpha = \uparrow, \downarrow} \sigma^{\alpha}(v = 0) = \sigma_{CIP}, \tag{8.5}$$

as can be seen by placing Eq. (8.4) in Eq. (7.20) and comparing it with Eq. (7.8). This result is reasonable inasmuch as the layering or granularity is imperceptible in this limit, and we have taken the impurity scattering to be isotropic.

When $\lambda \ll d_{in}$, which we call the *local* limit, the conductivity (each component, and where we drop the indices) is a one-point function,

$$\sigma(z, z') = \sigma(z)\delta(z - z'), \tag{8.6}$$

for points $z$ and $z'$ separated by distances $|z - z'| \gg \lambda$. Notice that, in the local limit, for distances $|z - z'| \lesssim \lambda$, the two-point conductivity exhibits its nonlocal structure

$$\sigma(z, z') = f\left[\frac{z - z'}{\lambda(z)}\right], \tag{8.7}$$

whose functional form is like that of Eq. (8.1), but scaled with the local mean free $\lambda(z)$ [related to the one-point conductivity $\sigma(z)$] rather than with the average mean free path $\lambda$. By placing Eq. (8.6) in Eq. (7.3), appropriately adapted to CPP and for collinear structures [see Eq. (7.19)], we find that the electric field for CPP with $p = 0$ (no spin-flips) is proportional to the inverse of the one-point conductivity $\sigma(z)$.[53] In this case the spin-dependent internal electric fields are

$$E^\alpha(z) = \frac{j^\alpha}{\sigma^\alpha(z)}, \tag{8.8}$$

where $j^\alpha$ is the constant current density in the $\alpha$ conduction channel. In this limit the conductivity is a *diagonal* matrix, which is easily inverted, so that

$$\rho^\alpha(z, z') = \frac{1}{\sigma^\alpha(z)}\delta(z - z'). \tag{8.9}$$

Actually, this is true *only* when the linear response of the system is probed over distances $|z - z'| \gg \lambda$ (otherwise, it would be nonlocal); this is precisely the case for multilayers, when the external field is uniform, because the nonuniformity of the internal field arises from the layering (length scales $d_{in}$). By placing this result in Eq. (7.20), we find that in the local limit[53,114]

$$\sigma_{CPP}(p = 0)|_{\lambda \ll d_{in}} = \sum_{\alpha = \uparrow, \downarrow} \left[ \frac{1}{L} \int_0^L \frac{dz}{\sigma^\alpha(z)} \right]^{-1}. \qquad (8.10)$$

In this limit the CPP conductivity is different from the CIP conductivity, which is found by placing Eq. (8.6) in Eq. (7.8):

$$\sigma_{CIP}|_{\lambda \ll d_{in}} = \sum_{\alpha = \uparrow, \downarrow} \frac{1}{L} \int_0^L dz \, \sigma^\alpha(z). \qquad (8.11)$$

In the local limit of the CIP geometry and with the local character of the conductivity [Eq. (8.6)], we find the global conductivity [Eq. (8.11)] is independent of the orientation of the magnetization of one layer relative to another. Note that $\Sigma_\alpha \, \sigma^\alpha(z)$ enters Eq. (8.11) before integration. This is not the case for CPP, where, in Eq. (8.10), the sum over spin is taken only *after* one has evaluated the global conductivity for each spin channel; the latter *is* sensitive to average magnetization in the layered structure. From this we conclude that no magnetoresistance exists in the local limit for CIP; however, it *does exist* for CPP with $p = 0$.

In the *local* limit it is meaningful to talk about the conductivity or resistivity of each layer independent of the neighboring layers.[97] Thus, it is appropriate to make analogies with resistor networks to understand whether or not the resistivity changes in going from an antiferromagnetic or random configuration to a ferromagnetic alignment of the magnetic layers. In Fig. 13(a), we show the appropriate network corresponding to four layers—two magnetic and two nonmagnetic—in CIP [Eq. (8.11)]. We see that the resistivities are the same for the ferro (F) and antiferromagnetic (AF) configurations, so that there is no CIP-MR in this limit. For CPP ($p = 0$), where there is *no* mixing of the currents (for electrons with spin-up with those of spin-down), the resistances of the individual layers for each spin direction are added in series, while those for the two channels are added in parallel. In Fig. 13(b) we note that in the ferromagnetic configuration the resistance is less in one branch than in the other, producing a "short-circuit" effect, while in the antiferromagnetic configuration they are equal. Thus, we have magnetoresistance for CPP ($p = 0$). However, when the currents are mixed via spin-flips, $p \neq 0$,

FIG. 13. Resistor network analogies for the (a) CIP and (b) CPP resistances of the ferromagnetic (F) and antiferromagnetic (AF) configurations in the local limit $\lambda \ll d_{in}$. The $R_+$, $R_-$, and $R_{nm}$ stand for the resistances of the magnetic layers for spin parallel and antiparallel to the local magnetization, and of the nonmagnetic layers. In CIP (a) the current-density vector **j** is perpendicular to the growth direction $z$, while for CPP (b) they are parallel. [From H. E. Camblong et al., Phys. Rev. B **47**, 4735 (1993).]

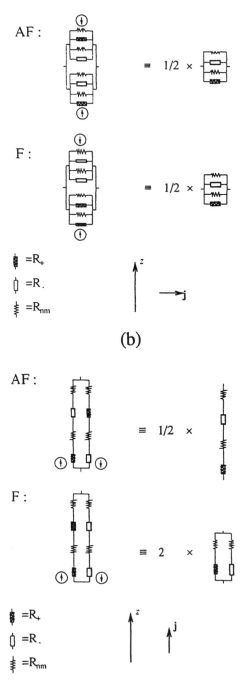

the resistors are coupled and the effect of the short circuit is reduced so that the CPP-MR is diminished.

Without explicit expressions for the conductivity, we cannot say more about the field and current distributions in inhomogeneous structures. We now determine the conductivity in the real and momentum space approaches.

## 9. REAL-SPACE FORMULATION

This approach has been proposed by Vedyayev et al.[94] and Camblong[92,93,115] for quasi-one-dimensional layered structures. Here we present a real-space quantum approach to transport in inhomogeneous three-dimensional structures;[105] it is an extension of Camblong's formulation for multilayered structures. In this treatment we take $\mathcal{H}_0$ in Eq. (5.1) to be that of free electrons and we neglect the differences in the potentials between regions, i.e., we set $V_{pot}$ = constant (zero).

The conductivity [Eq. (6.1)], which depicts the linear response to an electric field, is given by Kubo's formula, which in the limit of zero frequency is[98,99]

$$\sigma(\mathbf{r}, \mathbf{r}') = \lim_{\omega \to 0} \frac{\pi(\mathbf{r}, \mathbf{r}', \omega)}{\omega}, \tag{9.1}$$

where $\pi(\mathbf{r}, \mathbf{r}', \omega)$ is the frequency-dependent current-current correlation function

$$\pi(\mathbf{r}, \mathbf{r}', \omega) = \int_0^\infty d\tau e^{i\omega\tau} \langle [\hat{\mathbf{j}}(\mathbf{r}, t + \tau), \hat{\mathbf{j}}(\mathbf{r}', t)] \rangle. \tag{9.2}$$

This function is independent of $t$ due to time-translation invariance. By placing the spinor current operators of Eq. (6.3) in Eqs. (9.1) and (9.2) we arrive at the two-point spinor conductivity [Eq. (6.10)] defined in Section 6; it is given in terms of one-particle propagators $G_{\alpha\beta}(\mathbf{r}, \mathbf{r}')$. As defined by Eq. (6.9), they are impurity-averaged Green's functions. Parenthetically, if one used the Green's function for one specific impurity configuration, no vertex corrections would enter Eq. (6.5) from impurity-averaging; this would simplify expression (6.7) for the internal field, albeit at the expense of a more complicated Green's function $G_{\alpha\beta}$.

The one-particle Green's function satisfies Dyson's equation (5.5). For weak scattering and in the dilute limit of impurity concentration, the self-energy is given by the same set of diagrams that defines the one-site

[115] H. E. Camblong and P. M. Levy, J. Appl. Phys. 73, 5533 (1993).

$t$-matrix [Eqs. (5.6) and (5.8)]. If one does not demand that the self-energy be solved self-consistently, it is *local*, i.e.,

$$\langle \mathbf{r}|\Sigma(\varepsilon)|\mathbf{r}'\rangle = \delta(\mathbf{r} - \mathbf{r}')\Sigma(\mathbf{r}), \tag{9.3}$$

where

$$\Sigma(\mathbf{r}) = n_{\text{imp}}(\mathbf{r})\,t(\mathbf{r}),$$

$n_{\text{imp}}(\mathbf{r})$ is the local density of scatterers. Thus in real space for *dilute* (local self-energy) and weak scattering, Dyson's equation is written as[116]

$$\left[\left(\varepsilon_F + \frac{\hbar^2}{2m}\nabla_r^2\right)1 - \Sigma(\mathbf{r})\right]G(\mathbf{r}, \mathbf{r}') = \delta(\mathbf{r} - \mathbf{r}')1 \tag{9.4}$$

where

$$G(\mathbf{r}, \mathbf{r}') = \langle \mathbf{r}|\langle G(\varepsilon)\rangle_I|\mathbf{r}'\rangle,$$

and 1 is a unit matrix in spin space, whereas the self-energy $\Sigma(\mathbf{r})$ and Green's function $G(\mathbf{r}, \mathbf{r}')$ are $2 \times 2$ matrices in spin space, so that matrix multiplication is implied in Eq. (9.4).

To describe transport properties, one focuses on the imaginary part of the self-energy; the real part will be subsumed in $\mathcal{H}_0$ [see Eq. (5.5)]. By performing the local impurity averages over the different regions in a structure (layers, granules, matrix, or interfaces)[92,93] one finds, in the dilute and weak scattering limits, that

$$\begin{aligned}\Delta(r) &= -\operatorname{Im}[\Sigma(\mathbf{r})]\\ &= n_{\text{imp}}(\mathbf{r})\{-\operatorname{Im}[t(\mathbf{r})]\},\end{aligned} \tag{9.5}$$

where $\operatorname{Im}[t(\mathbf{r})]$ is given by Eq. (5.8). By defining

$$g(\mathbf{r}, \mathbf{r}') = \left(\frac{\hbar^2}{2m}\right)G(\mathbf{r}, \mathbf{r}'), \tag{9.6}$$

we find Eq. (9.4) is written as

$$\{\nabla_r^2 + [k_F^2 + i2m\Delta(r)/\hbar^2]\}g(\mathbf{r}, \mathbf{r}') = \delta(\mathbf{r} - \mathbf{r}'), \tag{9.7}$$

[116]In general the self-energy [Eq. (9.3)] is not diagonal in real space, and a *nonlocal* self-energy enters Dyson's equation.

where we have suppressed the unit $2 \times 2$ matrix to make the equation more transparent. One solves this equation by using the WKB approximation[92,93]

$$g(\mathbf{r}, \mathbf{r}') \approx \frac{-1}{4\pi|\mathbf{r} - \mathbf{r}'|} \exp\left[i \int_{\Gamma[\mathbf{r}, \mathbf{r}']} ds'' k''(\mathbf{r}'')\right], \qquad (9.8)$$

where $k(\mathbf{r}) = [k_F^2 + i2m\Delta(\mathbf{r})/\hbar^2]^{1/2}$ and the integral extends along the straight line $\Gamma(\mathbf{r}, \mathbf{r}')$ that connects the points $\mathbf{r}$ and $\mathbf{r}'$. In effect, Eq. (9.8) describes an electron propagating with a complex wave number $k(\mathbf{r})$. When $\varepsilon_F \gg \Delta(\mathbf{r})$ the electron singles out quasiclassical trajectories; then

$$g(\mathbf{r}, \mathbf{r}') \approx -\frac{1}{4\pi|\mathbf{r} - \mathbf{r}'|} \exp(ik_F|\mathbf{r} - \mathbf{r}'|)$$
$$\times P_{\mathbf{r}'\to\mathbf{r}} \exp\left[-\frac{1}{2}\xi(\mathbf{r}, \mathbf{r}')|\mathbf{r} - \mathbf{r}'|\right], \qquad (9.9)$$

where

$$\xi(\mathbf{r}, \mathbf{r}') = \left(\frac{2m}{\hbar^2 k_F}\right)\frac{1}{|\mathbf{r} - \mathbf{r}'|}\int_{\Gamma[\mathbf{r}, \mathbf{r}']} ds'' \Delta(\mathbf{r}''), \qquad (9.10)$$

and $P_{\mathbf{r}'\to\mathbf{r}}$ is the *path-ordering* operator that reorders the noncommuting $2 \times 2$ scattering matrices in the exponential series from point $\mathbf{r}'$ to point $\mathbf{r}$ and from right to left. This noncommutativity is characteristic of noncollinear magnetization configurations, and the corresponding Green's function is *not* symmetric under the exchange of the points $\mathbf{r}$ and $\mathbf{r}'$. In the presence of spin-dependent scattering [Eq. (5.2)], the one-particle propagator $G(\mathbf{r}, \mathbf{r}')$ and the self-energy $\Sigma(\mathbf{r})$, as well as $\Delta(\mathbf{r})$ and $\xi(\mathbf{r}, \mathbf{r}')$ are $2 \times 2$ spin matrices. Then, from the Kubo formula of Eq. (6.10), we find in the limit of large $k_F$ that

$$\sigma_{\alpha\beta,\gamma\delta}(\mathbf{r}, \mathbf{r}') = \frac{3C_D}{4\pi}\frac{\hat{n}\hat{n}}{|\mathbf{r} - \mathbf{r}'|^2}\left\{P_{\mathbf{r}'\to\mathbf{r}} \exp\left[-\frac{1}{2}\xi(\mathbf{r}, \mathbf{r}')|\mathbf{r} - \mathbf{r}'|\right]\right\}_{\beta\gamma}$$
$$\times \left\{P_{\mathbf{r}\to\mathbf{r}'} \exp\left[-\frac{1}{2}\xi(\mathbf{r}, \mathbf{r}')|\mathbf{r} - \mathbf{r}'|\right]\right\}_{\delta\alpha}, \qquad (9.11)$$

where $C_D = e^2 k_F^2/(6\pi^2\hbar)$ and $\hat{n}$ is a unit vector from $\mathbf{r}$ to $\mathbf{r}'$.

To apply Eq. (9.11) to local transport the regions in between and including the points $\mathbf{r}$ and $\mathbf{r}'$ have to be sufficiently large so that impurity averages in the Kohn-Luttinger sense can be applied to them. Therefore, it is questionable whether *local* transport in granular films with small precipitates can be described by the impurity-averaged propagators of Eq. (9.9), and thus the local conductivity of Eq. (9.11), which is based on these propagators.

For the particular case of multilayers, the layer-wise impurity averages described in Section 5 lend credence to the applicability of the impurity-averaged propagator of Eq. (9.8) to *local* transport in these systems. Multilayers are characterized by in-plane translational invariance [see Eqs. (7.1), (7.2), and (7.3)], so that the two-point conductivity is given by[93]

$$
\sigma_{\alpha\beta,\gamma\delta}(z, z') = \frac{3C_D}{2} \int_1^\infty dt \left[ \frac{1}{2}\left( \frac{1}{t} - \frac{1}{t^3} \right) 1_\parallel + \frac{1}{t^3}\hat{e}_z\hat{e}_z \right]
$$

$$
\times \left\{ P_{z'\to z}\exp\left[ -\frac{t}{2}\int_{z<}^{z>} dz'' \, \xi(z'') \right] \right\}_{\beta\gamma} \qquad (9.12)
$$

$$
\times \left\{ P_{z\to z'}\exp\left[ -\frac{t}{2}\int_{z<}^{z>} dz'' \, \xi(z'') \right] \right\}_{\delta\alpha},
$$

where the substitution $t = |\mathbf{r} - \mathbf{r}'|/|z - z'|$ has been made, $\xi(z) = (2m/\hbar^2 k_F)\Delta(z)$, $1_\parallel$ is the unit tensor in the plane of the layers, $\hat{e}_z$ is the unit vector in the $z$ direction, $z < (z >)$ is the smaller (larger) of $z$ and $z'$, and integration with respect to the in-plane azimuthal angle has rendered the tensor diagonal. For collinear magnetizations, the scattering matrix $\xi(\mathbf{r}, \mathbf{r}')$ is diagonal so that the path-ordering operator $P_{z\to z'}$ can be suppressed and spin indices can be contracted as in Eq. (7.19)

$$
\sigma^\alpha(z, z') = \frac{3C_D}{2} \int_1^\infty dt \left[ \frac{1}{2}\left( \frac{1}{t} - \frac{1}{t^3} \right) 1_\parallel + \frac{1}{t^3}\hat{e}_z\hat{e}_z \right]
$$

$$
\times \exp\left[ -t \int_{z<}^{z>} dz'' \, \xi^\alpha(z'') \right]. \qquad (9.13)
$$

The two-point conductivities for CIP geometries are[93]

$$
\sigma_\alpha^\parallel(z, z') = \frac{3C_D}{4} \{ E_1[\phi_\alpha(z, z')] - E_3[\phi_\alpha(z, z')] \}, \qquad (9.14)
$$

and

$$\sigma_\alpha^\perp(z, z') = \frac{3C_D}{2} E_3[\phi_\alpha(z, z')],$$

where

$$\phi_\alpha(z, z') = \int_{z<}^{z>} dz'' \xi^\alpha(z'')$$
$$= |z - z'| \xi_\alpha(z, z'), \tag{9.15}$$

and $E_n(x)$ is the exponential integral function of order $n$,[117]

$$E_n(x) = \int_1^\infty \frac{dt}{t^n} e^{-tx}. \tag{9.16}$$

These results for metallic multilayered structures, based on the semiclassical limit of the real space quantum transport approach, are in agreement with the Boltzmann equation approach applied to magnetic multilayers.[42,50,93] There is, of course, the caveat that the scattering at interfaces does not introduce quantum interference corrections.

Without explicitly making quantum corrections to the scattering from interfaces, one can make a rather important correction to the conventional treatment of transport in the semiclassical approach. Transmission of an electron through a region of interfacial disorder can be modeled by a thin mixed layer,[50] and can be subsumed into the real-space formulation of transport by considering it on a par with the other layers. To make the connection with the coefficients that are used in the semiclassical approach to describe the coherent transmission and diffuse scattering at interfaces, one can replace the real interfacial regions by infinitely thin interfaces with internal structure.[93] To account for the exponential decay of the electron propagators through an interface layer, one must use an effective coherent transmission coefficient, $T(t) = \exp(-\Lambda t)$, where $\Lambda = a/\lambda_{mfp}$, $a$ = thickness of interfacial layer, $t = (\cos\theta)^{-1}$, and $\theta$ is the angle of the electron's trajectory with respect to the axis perpendicular to the plane of the layers. In this picture of geometric electron propagation, $[1 - T(t)]$ represents the diffuse scattering from the interface. From this analysis Camblong concluded that, at the very least, *angle-dependent*

[117] M. Abramowitz and I. A. Stegum, *Handbook of Mathematical Functions*, Chap. 5, Dover Publications, New York (1965).

transmission coefficients should enter into the semiclassical approach to conduction in multilayers.[42,47] This angle-dependent transmission is needed even if the interfacial disorder was so small that quantum interference effects could be neglected (as they are in the semiclassical approach).

For CPP and collinear magnetic structures with $p_{\alpha\beta} = 0$, we find from Eq. (7.13) that $j_\alpha(z) = j_\alpha$ = constant, so that the internal electric field $E(z)$ is the solution of the integral equation [see Eq. (7.19)]

$$j_\alpha = \int dz' \, \sigma_\alpha^\perp(z, z') E_\alpha(z'). \tag{9.17}$$

The replacement $E_\alpha(z) \propto \xi^\alpha(z)$ converts this equation into an identity,[93] because, from Eqs. (9.14) and (9.15),

$$t \int dz' \, \xi^\alpha(z') \exp\left[ -t \int_{z<}^{z>} dz'' \xi^\alpha(z'') \right] = 2. \tag{9.18}$$

As $\int dz \, \xi^\alpha(z)$ is the average scattering in the layered structure, CPP resistivity is *self-averaging,* not just for the local and homogeneous limits discussed in Section 8, but for all length scales.[118]

10. MOMENTUM SPACE FORMULATION

The first quantum treatment of transport in multilayered structures was developed in momentum space to explain the giant MR found in the CIP geometry.[96,97] One of the central issues, according to Fert, was to be able to account for scattering from interfaces at points in the layers removed from the interfaces. This is reminiscent of the problem posed and solved by Tešanović et al.:[57] how to account for the *finite* conductivity due to boundary scattering in a thin film with no scattering in the bulk. In this case, the semiclassical (Fuchs-Sondheimer) result was that the resistivity was zero due to the short circuit created in the bulk; the quantum treatment produced a finite resistivity proportional to $\hbar$.[119] We have included

---

[118]This result was originally predicted by Zhang, Ref. 53, and was later confirmed experimentally; see Fig. 9(b) and Ref. 22.

[119]To ameliorate the semiclassical treatment of conduction in thin films or wires with rough surfaces, Tešanović' et al., Ref. 57, made a unitary transformation that mapped the problem of a Hamiltonian with complicated boundary conditions on one with simpler boundary conditions, but with an effective Hamiltonian containing additional surface scattering potentials. This approach made it possible to determine the effects of surface roughness on

these *nonlocal* effects of the scattering in our self-energy [see Eqs. (10.5) through (10.10)] by solving for this energy *self-consistently*. Solutions for the one-electron propagator and conductivity for this self-energy are ambitious projects and we have made three crucial approximations: (1) We have considered only one subset of diagrams that contributes to our nonlocal self-energy [Eq. (10.10)]. (2) We limit ourselves to the one-point conductivity [Eq. (7.6)]. (3) We have made a decoupling approximation to evaluate this one-point conductivity.

In our treatment we have focused our attention on obtaining the global or measurable CIP conductivity [Eq. (7.8)]; no attempt has been made to determine the local conductivity [Eq. (7.3)], although a Fourier-transformed version of Eq. (7.6) appears in the calculation. By making plausible arguments, the formalism we now develop has been extended to find the global conductivity and MR for CPP in multilayers,[53,120] and for random three-dimensional granular films.[121] We present here the approach for quasi-one-dimensional structures; this approach probably

---

the lifetime of electron states by using perturbation theory to evaluate the effects of the additional scattering generated by the transformation. For the special case of a particle in a box potential, they were able to find the complete one-electron Green's function, and by using the Kubo formula, they found the single-loop contribution to the conductivity. Its inverse, the resistivity, represented the residual resistivity coming from the roughness of the bounding surfaces. It vanished with Planck's constant $\hbar$, which demonstrated that it was a quantum effect. The classical zero resistivity thus arises because of ballistic electron trajectories that are parallel to a rough surface, which exist when there is no scattering in the bulk of the film. Quantum mechanical zero-point motion excludes momentum states that are entirely confined to the plane parallel to the boundary surface and this results in a finite resistivity even for no scattering in the bulk of the film. In the presence of impurities in the bulk, they find that the total film resistivity, as a function of the ratio $d/\lambda_{mfp}$ of the film thickness to the mfp, deviates from the semiclassical Fuchs-Sondheimer result as one goes from the impurity dominated region ($d/\lambda_{mfp} \gg 1$) to the thin film (quantum) regime ($d/\lambda_{mfp} \ll 1$) where surface scattering dominates.

These results have been verified (see Ref. 68) and extended to surface roughness on different length scales. Trivedi and Ashcroft (Ref. 67) have accounted for variations in film thickness $d$ on length scales shorter than the mfp by using a quantum approach with the unitary transformation of Ref. 57. Large-scale fluctuations of the film thickness (over distances of the coherence length of the electron) are described semiclassically by dividing the film into segments, which are treated as independent units so that the total resistance of the film is a sum of resistances of the individual segments. By focusing on the quantum size effects associated with the confinement of electrons to small thickness, Trivedi and Ashcroft show that the conductivity has oscillations as a function of the film thickness with a period of half the Fermi wavelength (quantum well effects).

[120] S. Zhang and P. M. Levy, *Phys. Rev. B* **47**, 6776 (1993).

[121] S. Zhang, *Appl. Phys. Lett.* **61**, 1855 (1992); S. Zhang and P. M. Levy, *J. Appl. Phys.* **73**, 5315 (1993).

could be extended to three-dimensional cases by using a three-dimensional Fourier transform instead of the one-dimensional transform we employ. However, in this case one would have to find the two-point conductivity $\sigma(q, q')$, the double transform of Eq. (6.9) or of Eq. (6.4), and it is not immediately obvious how to extend the decoupling procedure we use[97] to find an explicit solution; in addition, one must be concerned about properly defining the impurity averages in inhomogeneous three-dimensional systems with small inhomogeneities [see Section 5].

### a. Calculation of Conductivity

The calculation of the one-point conductivity $\sigma(z)$ in momentum space is given in detail in Ref. 97; here we review the essential ideas. The one-point conductivity of Eq. (7.6) for a *layered* structure in reciprocal space is defined as

$$\sigma(\bar{v}) = \frac{1}{L} \int e^{-i\bar{v}z} \sigma(z) \, dz, \tag{10.1}$$

where $L$ is the thickness in the growth ($z$) direction of the structure. It is given in terms of the Kubo formula as[90,98]

$$\sigma^\parallel_{\alpha\beta}(\bar{v}) = -\lim_{\omega \to 0} \left[ \frac{1}{\omega} \operatorname{Im} \Pi^\parallel_{\alpha\beta}(\bar{v}, \omega) \right], \tag{10.2}$$

where the current-current correlation function

$$\Pi^\parallel_{\alpha\beta}(\bar{v}, \omega) = \frac{1}{2}\left(\frac{e}{m}\right)^2 \sum_{k\sigma,\sigma'} k^2 \sum_{v,v'} \frac{1}{\beta} \sum_{iv_m}$$
$$\times G^{\beta\gamma}_{v+\bar{v}v'}(k, iv_m + i\omega_m) G^{\gamma\alpha}_{v'v}(k, iv_m)\big|_{i\omega_m = \omega + i0}, \tag{10.3}$$

is given in terms of Matsubara Green's functions $G^{\beta\gamma}_{vv'}(k, i\omega)$, which are diagonal in $k = (k_x, k_y)$ but have off-diagonal elements $vv'(k_z, k'_z)$. This property follows directly from translational invariance of the superlattices in directions parallel to the layers. To arrive at the electron-hole correlation function $\Pi(\bar{v}, \omega)$ we *assumed* there are no vertex corrections, i.e., that the function can be written as the product of electron and hole correlation functions. Equation (10.3) is appropriate for the CIP conductivity $\sigma^\parallel(\bar{v})$.

The off-diagonal Green's function $G^{\alpha\beta}_{vv'}$ satisfied Eq. (5.3), which in

momentum space is

$$G^{\alpha\beta}_{\nu\nu'}(k, \omega) = G^0_\nu(k, \omega)\delta_{\nu\nu'}\delta_{\alpha\beta} + G^0_\nu(k, \omega)T^{\alpha\beta}_{\nu\nu'}(k, \omega)G^0_{\nu'}(k, \omega), \quad (10.4)$$

where we have used $G^{\alpha\beta}_{\nu\nu'}(k, \omega) = G^0_\nu(k, \omega)\delta_{\nu\nu'}\delta_{\alpha\beta}$ for *free* electrons, i.e.,
(1) we neglect the effect of the magnetic field on the conduction electrons;
only the effect of the field on the local moments is considered in $T^{\alpha\beta}_{\nu\nu'}$,
and (2) we neglect for now the different potentials in the magnetic and
nonmagnetic layers; this is addressed in Section 11.

The self-energy [Eq. (5.5)] is *nonlocal*:

$$\Sigma(\nu, \nu') = \langle\nu|\langle VG(\varepsilon)V\rangle_I|\nu'\rangle \neq \Sigma(\nu - \nu'), \quad (10.5)$$

where we have taken the average of the scattering potential $V$ to be zero.
The angular brackets refer to the average over the random distribution
in the planes parallel to the layers. Note that $G(\varepsilon)$ is the *full* Green's
function and not the unperturbed $G_0(\varepsilon)$. Therefore, on taking the Fourier
transform we find in real space this is a nonlocal self-energy $\Sigma(z, z')$, and
not the local $\Sigma(z)$ of Eq. (9.3).

While similar in some aspects to the surface scattering problem solved
by Tešanović *et al.*[57] [see their Eq. (5)], the presence of several scattering
interfaces in this multilayer problem does not allow us to write the scattering potential of Eq. (5.2) in a separable form. Therefore, to obtain
a solution of Eq. (10.4), we separate the self-energy into *diagonal* and
*off-diagonal* parts (reverting to operator form instead of matrix elements)

$$\Sigma = \hat{\Sigma} + \Sigma' \quad (10.6)$$

so that the Green's function Eq. (10.4) is written as

$$G = (1 - \hat{G}\Sigma')^{-1}\hat{G}, \quad (10.7)$$

where

$$\hat{G} \equiv [(G^0)^{-1} - \hat{\Sigma}]^{-1}. \quad (10.8)$$

By placing Eq. (10.7) in Eq. (10.5) we find

$$\Sigma = \langle VGV\rangle_I = \langle V(1 - \hat{G}\Sigma')^{-1}\hat{G}V\rangle_I, \quad (10.9)$$

which is similar, but not identical to Eq. (4) of Ref. 57. *One* subset of all
contributions to the self-energy can be rewritten in terms of the one-site
*t*-matrix [Eq. (5.7)] as

$$\Sigma = t(1 - \hat{G}\Sigma')^{-1}. \tag{10.10}$$

To second order in the scattering, the Fourier transform of the one-site $t$-matrix for multilayers, near the Fermi surface, is:

$$t_{\bar{v}} = \frac{1}{L}\int e^{-i\bar{v}z}t(z)\,dz = \sum_{a=t,l} t_a(\hat{\sigma})e^{-i\bar{v}z_a}, \tag{10.11}$$

where the imaginary parts of the $t$-matrices for the layers ($t$) and interfaces ($l$) are given as in Eq. (5.8) but with $\mathbf{r}$ or $z$ replaced by $z_a$, the site of the impurity or interface scattering. The $t$-matrix $t_{vv'}$ of Eq. (10.11) depends only on the difference $\bar{v} \equiv v - v'$; it contains *diagonal* ($v' = v$, $\bar{v} = 0$) and *off-diagonal* ($v' \neq v$, $\bar{v} \neq 0$) elements. On expanding the denominator of Eq. (10.10), we find that while $t$ is local, $\Sigma$ is nonlocal, because the propagator $\hat{G}$ couples different sites, i.e.,

$$\langle t\hat{G}t\rangle_{vv'} = \sum_{v''} \langle t_{vv''}\hat{G}_{v''}t_{v''v'}\rangle \neq f(v - v'). \tag{10.12}$$

By making a decoupling approximation, outlined in Ref. 97, one obtains the conductivity

$$\sigma_{\alpha\beta}^{\parallel}(z) = \frac{ne^2}{2m}\left[\frac{a^{-\alpha}(z)\delta_{\alpha\beta} - b^{\alpha}(z)(1 - \delta_{\alpha\beta})}{a^{\alpha}(z)a^{-\alpha}(z) - b^{\alpha}(z)b^{-\alpha}(z)}\right], \tag{10.13}$$

where

$$a^{\alpha}(z) = \frac{1}{\lambda^{\alpha}}\sum_{a=t,l} \text{Re}\,\Delta_{\alpha}^{\alpha\alpha}e^{-|z-z_a|/\lambda^{\alpha}}, \tag{10.14}$$

and

$$b^{\alpha}(z) = \frac{1}{\lambda^{\alpha}}\sum_{a=t,l} \text{Re}\,\Delta_a^{\alpha-\alpha}e^{-|z-z_a|/\lambda^{\alpha}}.$$

From Eq. (5.8),

$$\text{Re}\,\Delta_a^{\alpha\beta}(\varepsilon_F) = -\frac{1}{\pi}\langle\alpha|\text{Im}[t(r)]|\beta\rangle$$

$$= w_a\langle\alpha|(1 + p_a^2 + 2p_a\hat{\sigma}\cdot\hat{M}_a)|\beta\rangle, \tag{10.15}$$

$p \equiv j/v$, $w_a = \rho(\varepsilon_F)\langle v_a^2\rangle$, and the mfp is derived from the *diagonal* part of the $t$-matrix

$$\lambda^{\alpha} \equiv \frac{k_F}{m\bar{\Delta}^{\alpha}(\varepsilon_F)}, \tag{10.16}$$

where

$$\bar{\Delta}^\alpha = \frac{1}{L} \left\{ \sum_{t \in L} \mathrm{Re}\, \Delta_t^{\alpha\alpha} + \sum_{l \in L} \mathrm{Re}\, \Delta_l^{\alpha\alpha} \right\} \equiv \bar{\Delta}_b^\alpha + \bar{\Delta}_s^\alpha, \qquad (10.17)$$

represents the bulk and surface scattering contributions to $\lambda^\alpha$. Equation (10.17) is the average of the scattering in the *entire* structure, as if one performed the random impurity average over all scatterers. A more accurate decoupling procedure has been recommended by Camblong;[122] this procedure leads to replacing the exponentials $e^{-|z-z_a|/\lambda^\alpha}$ in the coefficients $a^\alpha$ and $b^\alpha$ by $E_1(|z - z_a|/\lambda^\alpha)$, where

$$E_1(x) = \int_x^\infty \frac{e^{-y}}{y}\, dy$$

is the exponential integral of the first order.[117]

  In the conductivity of Eq. (10.13) we note that both bulk $\Delta_b$ and surface $\bar{\Delta}_s$ scattering contribute on *equal* footing. From Eqs. (10.16) and (10.17) we note they both contribute to the mfp; this mfp is determined only from the diagonal part of the $t$-matrix. The *off-diagonal* parts of the $t$-matrix control the position dependence of the conductivity and resistivity. For layered structures it is this off-diagonality that describes their inhomogeneities. The CIP conductivity of Eq. (7.8) is found by averaging the local conductivity of Eq. (10.13) over the length $L$ of the sample, and by taking the trace in spin space,

$$\sigma_{\mathrm{CIP}} = \frac{1}{L} \sum_\alpha \int dz\, \sigma_{\alpha\alpha}^\parallel(z). \qquad (10.18)$$

  In the CPP geometry the two-point *resistivity* [see Eq. (7.9)] is needed; this is not given in terms of the usual Kubo linear response function. We can, however, take the inverse of Eq. (10.13), and apply it to limiting cases, e.g., the local limit [see Eq. (8.9)], to find the CPP conductivity of Eq. (8.10). For a spherical Fermi surface when we replace $\frac{1}{2}k^2$ by $v(v + \frac{1}{2}\bar{v})$ we arrive at the same one-point conductivity as Eq. (10.13), $\sigma^\perp(z) = \sigma^\parallel(z)$.[97] Its *inverse* yields the one-point resistivity

$$\rho_{\alpha\beta}^\perp(z) = \frac{2m}{ne^2} [a^\alpha(z)\delta_{\alpha\beta} + b^\alpha(z)(1 - \delta_{\alpha\beta})]. \qquad (10.19)$$

[122] H. E. Camblong, private communication, November 1991.

This is just the denominator of the expression for the conductivity before one does the inversion of the $2 \times 2$ matrix to obtain Eq. (10.13) [see Eq. (3.23) of Ref. 97]. By averaging over the length of the sample [see Eq. (7.14) or Eq. (8.10)] we find

$$
\rho_{\alpha\beta}^{CPP} = \frac{2m}{ne^2} \frac{1}{L} \int_0^L [a^\alpha(z)\delta_{\alpha\beta} + b^\alpha(z)(1 - \delta_{\alpha\beta})]dz,
$$

$$
= \frac{2m}{ne^2} \bar{\Delta}^\alpha \delta_{\alpha\beta},
$$

(10.20)

where the average of $b^\alpha$ vanishes by an appropriate choice of the axis of quantization for the spin so that, among other things, the mfp of Eq. (10.16) is diagonal in spin space.[97] Thus the resistivity in each spin channel is given by the total scattering in that channel [Eq. (10.17)]. The CPP conductivity [Eq. (7.16)], is

$$
\sigma_{CPP}(p = 0)|_{collinear} = \frac{ne^2}{2m} \sum_\alpha \frac{1}{\bar{\Delta}^\alpha}.
$$

(10.21)

This expression is far simpler than the CIP conductivity of Eq. (10.18).

b. *Magnetoresistance of Multilayered Structures*

As mentioned in the introduction, the extraordinary magnetoresistance found in multilayered structures comes from the *reorientation* of the magnetization of the layers. In the present treatment the effect of an external magnetic field on the conductivity enters through the orientation of the magnetizations in the scattering terms [see Eq. (10.15)]; i.e., we do not consider any effect of the field on the orbits of the conduction electrons, or in altering the magnetization of the layers.

The expressions for the position-dependent conductivity [Eq. (10.13)] for arbitrary angles $\theta$ of the magnetization of the layers with respect to the field and for all ranges of layer thickness compared to mfp are unwieldy; in Section VI we present some numerical results. However, in the limiting cases treated in Section 8, $\lambda \gg d_{in}$ and $\lambda \ll d_{in}$, there are relatively simple results. When $\lambda \ll d_{in}$ the magnetoresistance is *zero*, because the spin scattering in each region can be considered independently of the others. For $\lambda \gg d_{in}$ the $z$ dependence of the conductivity disappears, as the structure looks homogeneous for electrons with extremely long mfp's.

In this limit ($\lambda \gg d_{in}$) the scattering is given by $\Delta^\alpha$ [Eq. (10.17)]; for a *bipartite* lattice such as Fe/Cr we can replace the sum over the entire lat-

tice by summing over one period of the magnetic unit cell $T \equiv 2(a + b)$. For magnetic layers of thickness $a$,

$$\Delta_b^m = w_m(1 + p_m^2 + 2\sigma p_m \cos \theta_m). \qquad (10.22)$$

For nonmagnetic layers of thickness $b$, where $p = 0$,

$$\Delta_b^{nm} = w_{nm},$$

and for the interfaces

$$\Delta_s = w_s(1 + p_s^2 + 2\sigma p_s \cos \theta_s),$$

where $\theta$ is the angle the magnetization in the layers makes with respect to the axis $\hat{\sigma} \| \hat{H}$, and we assume $\theta_s = |\theta_m|$. For the conductivity of Eq. (10.18) we find

$$\sigma(H) = \frac{ne^2}{m} \frac{\gamma}{\gamma^2 - \beta^2 \cos^2 \theta(H)}, \qquad (10.23)$$

where

$$\gamma = \frac{1}{a + b}[(a/a_0)(1 + p_m^2)w_m + b/b_0 w_{nm} + 2(1 + p_s^2)w_s],$$

$$\beta = \frac{2}{a + b}[(a/a_0)p_m w_m + 2p_s w_s],$$

and $a_0$, $b_0$ are the distances between atomic planes so that $a/a_0$, $b/b_0$ are the number of the atomic planes or monolayers in the layers of thickness of $a$ and $b$. In the absence of anisotropy, one finds $\cos \theta$ is proportional to $H$ and one would predict $\rho(H) \sim A - BH^2$ where $\rho(H)$ is the inverse of $\sigma(H)$. However, from the existing data on $\rho(H)$, this is by and large not observed, and we conclude that one should not use the simple relation $\cos \theta \sim H$. If one models the magnetic layers as uniformly and rigidly ordered, one can use the experimentally observed magnetization versus field curves to obtain $\theta(H)$ from the relation $M(H) = 2M_0 \cos \theta(H)$. In Ref. 97, some results are given on $\rho(H)$ for realistic cases when $\lambda$ is the same order as $d_{in}$.

A measure of the magnetoresistivity is its amplitude,

$$R_0 \equiv \frac{\rho(H = 0) - \rho(H = H_s)}{\rho(H = 0)} = \frac{\rho(\theta = \pi/2) - \rho(\theta = 0)}{\rho(\theta = \pi/2)}, \qquad (10.24)$$

where $H_s$ is the field required to align the magnetic layers in parallel, i.e., to saturate the sample.[123] In the limit that we are considering, $\lambda \gg d_{in}$, we find from the inverse of Eq. (10.23),

$$R_0 = \frac{\beta^2}{\gamma^2}.$$ (10.25)

The magnitude of $R_0$ is governed by the parameter $p = p_m = p_s$ [see Eq. (10.23)]. This magnitude is related to the ratio $\alpha \equiv \rho_\downarrow / \rho_\uparrow$ of the resistivities for electrons with spin antiparallel to the magnetization to that for electrons with spin parallel.[52] In the absence of potential differences between layers (see the next section) one has

$$p = \frac{1 - \sqrt{\alpha}}{1 + \sqrt{\alpha}}.$$ (10.26)

The minimum $R_0 = 0$ occurs for $p = 0$, while the maximum for $p = \pm 1$ (as $\alpha \to 0$ or $\infty$) yields

$$R_0(p = \pm 1) = \left\{ 1 + \frac{(b/a_0)w_b}{2[(a/a_0)w_b + 2w_s]} \right\}^{-2},$$ (10.27)

where we set $w_b = w_m = w_{nm}$. As $b \to 0$ or $w_b \to 0$, we obtain $R_0 = 1$. Other limiting cases are (1) if $w_b = 0$ (only interfacial roughness scattering),

$$R_0(w_b = 0) = \frac{4p^2}{(1 + p^2)^2} = \left( \frac{1 - \alpha}{1 + \alpha} \right)^2 = \frac{\rho_\downarrow - \rho_\uparrow}{\rho_\downarrow + \rho_\uparrow},$$ (10.28)

and (2) if $w_s = 0$ (only bulk scattering),

$$R_0(w_s = 0) = \frac{4p^2}{(1 + p^2 + b/a)^2}.$$ (10.29)

The presence of the ratio $b/a$ is understandable because it represents the proportion of the multilayered structure that is *magnetically* inert, i.e.,

---

[123] Another definition of the MR ratio is to use $\rho(H = H_s) = \rho(\theta = 0)$ in the denominator; with this definition the ratio $R_s$ is larger than the $R_0$ given by Eq. (10.24): $0 \leq R_s < \infty$. While one might prefer the definition of Eq. (10.24) because it is bounded, $0 \leq R_0 \leq 1$, the state $\rho(H = 0)$ does not necessarily correspond to $\rho(\theta = \pi/2)$, i.e., the zero-field configuration may be ill defined. For this reason some prefer expressing the ratio with the resistivity at saturation in the denominator.

the nonmagnetic layers have $p = 0$ and they do not contribute to the magnetoresistance. This ratio does not appear in Eq. (10.29) because all the interfacial scattering is spin dependent in our model.

## 11. EFFECT OF SUPERLATTICE POTENTIAL ON MAGNETOTRANSPORT

Up until now, we have used a free-electron Hamiltonian $\mathcal{H}_0$ to represent the conduction electrons in multilayered structures, i.e., we neglected the spin-dependent potentials in the different layers [see Eq. (5.1)]. To determine their effect on the scattering, and hence on the resistivity, it is necessary first to find the eigenstates of $\mathcal{H}_0$ and then evaluate the scattering [Eq. (5.2)] in these states. For aperiodic structures the description of the eigenstates is complicated; for periodic arrays, i.e., superlattices, they are of the Bloch form and relatively simple. Because the conduction band wave functions appropriate to transition metal magnetic superlattices are not reliably known, we resort to the Stoner description, which postulates that conduction electrons in ferromagnetic layers have different potentials for majority and minority spins. To ascertain the role of spin-dependent potentials on the magnetoresistance of multilayers, we use a Kronig-Penney potential in the growth direction $z$ and a constant potential in the plane of the layers.

The potentials we consider consist of a *periodic* array of barriers of thickness $a$ with height $U$ and wells of thickness $b$; the Fermi level is at energy $E_F$ from the bottom of the wells. For the ferromagnetic configuration of the layers, the potential for the majority (spin-up) electrons has $a = t_{nm}$ and $b = t_m$, where $t_{nm}$ is the thickness of nonmagnetic layers and $t_m$ of magnetic layers. For the minority electrons $b = 0$, i.e., there are no wells, and the Fermi level is at $E_F - U$. By taking into account putative differences in the potentials for minority electrons in the layers we engender additional parameters; we neglect these differences here. For antiferromagnetic configurations the potentials for spin-up and spin-down electrons are the same but shifted in space relative to one another: $a = 2t_{nm} + t_m$ and $b = t_m$. This description of the superlattice potentials is believed to be reasonable at least for Fe/Cr superlattices.[124] The wavefunctions for the periodic potential in a specific magnetic configuration $M$, e.g., ferromagnetic or antiferromagnetic, can be written in Bloch form

$$\phi_M(\boldsymbol{k}, \sigma; \boldsymbol{r}) = e^{i(k_x x + k_y y)} \phi_M(\nu, \sigma; z),$$
$$\phi_M(\nu, \sigma; z) = e^{i\nu z} u_M^\sigma(\nu; z), \tag{11.1}$$

[124] K. B. Hathaway and J. R. Cullen, *J. Magn. Magn. Mater.* **104-107**, 1840 (1992).

where

$$u_M^\sigma(v; z + a + b) = u_M^\sigma(v; z),$$

and energy eigenvalues are of the form

$$\varepsilon_M(\boldsymbol{k}, \sigma) = \varepsilon_\parallel(k_\parallel) + \varepsilon_M(v, \sigma), \tag{11.2}$$

where $\varepsilon_\parallel(k_\parallel) = \hbar^2(k_x^2 + k_y^2)/2m$, and $v = k_z$. These Bloch functions exist over a length scale known as the quantum coherence length (inelastic mfp); at low temperatures this length is quite long, of the order of 1 μm, and the thickness of most multilayered structures do not exceed it. Therefore the functions of Eq. (11.1) are the appropriate ones to use to calculate transport properties as long as the coherence of the electron wave functions can be maintained over several repeat distances of a periodic superlattice.

To determine the magnetoresistance, we evaluate the conductivity given by Eqs. (10.18) and (10.21) for the simple cases in which the layers are ferromagnetically and antiferromagnetically aligned. Since we wish to illustrate the influence of the superlattice potential on the MR, we consider only the case where the mfp is much larger than the layer thickness. In this limit, we can neglect the off-diagonal $t$-matrix entering the expression for the global conductivity [Eqs. (10.13) and (10.18)]; $a^\alpha = \Delta^\alpha$ and $b^\alpha = 0$. With this simplification, the conductivity is written as

$$\sigma_M = \frac{e^2}{2m} \sum_{k_\parallel v \sigma} \frac{\xi(k_\parallel, v)\delta(\varepsilon_F - \varepsilon_{k_\parallel v}^\sigma)}{\bar{\Delta}_M^\sigma(v)}, \tag{11.3}$$

where $\xi(k_\parallel, v) = k_\parallel^2/2$ for CIP while for CPP $\xi(k_\parallel, v) = [(m/\hbar^2)\partial\varepsilon_v^\sigma/\partial v]^2$, and where

$$\bar{\Delta}_M^\sigma(v) = \pi \sum_i |V_M^\sigma(i)u_M^\sigma(v, z_i)|^2 \rho_M^\sigma(\varepsilon_F, z_i),$$

$$\rho_M^\sigma(\varepsilon_F, z_i) = \sum_{k_\parallel v'} |u_M^\sigma(v', z_i)|^2 \delta(\varepsilon_F - \varepsilon_{k_\parallel v'}^\sigma), \tag{11.4}$$

and the $V_M^\sigma(i)$ are given by Eq. (3.1). The salient differences between this result and previous expressions for plane waves [Eqs. (10.14) through (10.17)] are (1) $\Delta$ depends on the momenta $v$ and (2) the dependence on

the magnetic configuration $M$ and spin $\sigma$ enters in *two* places: in the scattering $V_M^\sigma$ *and* in the wave functions $u_M^\sigma$.

The effects of superlattice potentials on the MR are found from Eqs. (11.3) and (11.4). These equations are applicable to CPP with no restrictions (assuming there are no spin-flips) and to CIP for $\lambda \gg t_m + t_{nm}$; in the limit $\lambda \ll t_m + t_{nm}$, the CIP-MR is zero. At least eight parameters are involved in the conductivity expression. They are scattering rates in nonmagnetic layers, in magnetic layers for spin-up and down electrons, and at interfaces for spin-up and down electrons, the potential barrier height relative to Fermi energy, and layer thicknesses for nonmagnetic and magnetic layers. The magnetoresistance is a complicated function of these parameters. Here we mention some of the salient results found in Refs. 66 and 86.

First, in the *absence* of spin-dependent scattering the wave functions Eq. (11.1) appropriate to the superlattice potential have little effect in producing the giant MR observed in the CIP geometry. When we neglect the spin dependence of the scattering $V_M^\sigma$, and the $\nu$ and $\sigma$ dependence of the scattering, $\tilde{\Delta}_M^\sigma = \Delta$, the CIP conductivity is proportional to the total number of conduction electrons.[125] Because this number does not depend on the magnetic configuration, the CIP-MR is *zero* under these conditions. However, the same argument does *not* hold for CPP, because the CPP conductivity is *not* related to the total number of electrons. This difference between CIP and CPP is plausible when one thinks of CIP as waves traveling parallel to layers, so that reflections off the steps in the potential at the interfaces cancel on average; however, for waves perpendicular to the layers, the reflections are cumulative and affect the transmission and thereby the conductance. When the scattering is not uniform throughout the structure, i.e., $\tilde{\Delta}_M^\sigma \neq \Delta$, we find a very small CIP-MR ratio, of the order of 1% to 2%, while the CPP-MR, even for uniform scattering, can be about 15% to 30%. Because the experimental MR ratios that are observed in magnetic superlattices are in the range of 20% to 170%, we conclude that the spin and configuration dependence of the superlattice wave functions do not *by themselves* contribute much to the CIP-MR, while they *do* play some role in the CPP-MR.

Second, because the conduction electron density $|u_M^\sigma(\nu; z)|^2$ is not uniform, the self-energy $\tilde{\Delta}_M^\sigma(\nu)$ of Eq. (11.4) depends on the positions of the scatterers in the superlattice unit cell as much as on their strengths, i.e., the resultant MR is sensitive to the *position* of the scatterers *relative* to that of the potentials. Therefore, the lattice potential can amplify or attenuate the effect of the scattering on the MR.

---

[125] The proof for this statement was given by S. Zhang, Ref. 66.

Third, the dependence of the MR on the thickness of the layers is controlled by the scattering, *not* by the potentials. If one assumed the MR were due solely to superlattice potentials with no spin-dependent scattering ($p = 0$), both the CIP-MR and CPP-MR would be weakly dependent on the thicknesses of the layers; this conclusion is not supported by data on the MR of multilayers. Therefore, spin-dependent scattering is necessary to explain the observed dependence of the MR on layer thicknesses.

Fourth, the contributions of the spin-dependent potential and spin-dependent scattering to the MR are intertwined. In the presence of a superlattice potential, the ratios $\alpha = \rho_\downarrow/\rho_\uparrow$ of the resistivity of minority (spin-down) to majority (spin-up) electrons for the magnetic layers and interfaces are[126]

$$\alpha = \frac{E_F}{E_F - U} \cdot \frac{(1 - p)^2}{(1 + p)^2}, \tag{11.5}$$

where $p$ is estimated from impurity scattering in ferromagnetic alloys.[52] In our work in Section 10 we neglected the effects of superlattice potentials, which is synonymous to setting $U = 0$ [see Eq. (10.26)]. If we define an effective $p$ as $p_{\text{eff}} \equiv (1 - \sqrt{\alpha})/(1 + \sqrt{\alpha})$ we can find the $p_{\text{eff}}$'s needed to explain MR data in layered structures. For example from Ref. 86 we see that a CIP-MR of, say, 100% can be achieved with $p_m = p_s = 0.42$ *in conjunction with* a potential with $U/E_F = 1/3$. This is equivalent to a $p_{\text{eff}} = 0.48$ with no potential $U = 0$. Equivalently with $U = 0$, $p = 0.42$ produces a CIP-MR of only 73%. Therefore, the superlattice potential assumes the role of amplifying *or* attenuating the MR coming from the spin dependence of the impurity (interface) scattering. It may take smaller values of $p$ than those estimated on the basis of unpolarized plane wave states to explain the MR ratios observed in multilayered structures with conduction electron bands that are spin-polarized at the Fermi surface.

Fifth, for multilayered structures with transition metal magnetic and nonmagnetic layers, e.g., iron and chromium, the potential wells exist in the magnetic layers; the nonmagnetic layers act as barriers. However, if a noble metal, e.g., copper, is the nonmagnetic layer, *the roles are reversed*; the copper layer now contains the well states,[127] and the magnetic layers are the barriers. If the barrier height for *one* spin direction is above

[126] S. Zhang, private communication, June 1993.
[127] F. J. Himpsel, *Phys. Rev. B* **44**, 5966 (1991); J. E. Ortega and F. J. Himpsel, *Phys. Rev. Lett.* **69**, 844 (1992).

the Fermi level, there is no conduction for CPP in the antiferromagnetic configuration, while in the ferromagnetic state one of the spin channels still conducts. In this case, the CPP-MR is limited only by the size of the spin diffusion length relative to the mfp. At low temperatures the spin diffusion length is an order of magnitude larger than the mfp.[51] Because this behavior has not been observed in the CPP experiments done to date on Co/Cu, Co/Ag,[22] and Fe/Cr,[23] we conclude that *both* quantum well and continuum states are needed to describe their transport properties.

In conclusion, while spin-dependent potentials alone cannot account for the large magnetoresistance observed in layered structures, they do strongly affect the MR in the presence of spin-dependent scattering. A quantitative comparison between theory and experimental data should include *both* mechanisms. Also, precise superlattice band structures will be needed to understand better the interplay between spin-dependent scattering and spin-dependent potentials.[82]

Recently Vedyayev et al.[128] have taken into account the differences in the lattice potentials between layers in their real-space approach for CIP. They conclude that spin-dependent scattering gives the main contribution to the giant MR effect in the permalloy spin-valve structures they have modeled. When the mfp's for the spin-up and spin-down electrons are significantly different, they find that the presence of potential barriers (spin-dependent or not) can only *decrease* the CIP-MR, whereas we have found that for a fixed potential, depending on the sign of the spin-dependent scattering, the MR can be enhanced *or* attenuated by the scattering.[86] Their results are strongly influenced by quantum size effects ($k_F L$ is not large compared to one for their spin-valve structures), therefore they find well-defined oscillations in the MR as a function of the thicknesses of the layers. This arises from the quantization of the momentum perpendicular to the layers.

## 12. Global Conductivity for Inhomogeneous Structures[105]

Finding the global or measurable conductivity for inhomogeneous structures from the local conductivity is by no means straightforward. The main difficulty arises from the lack of symmetry, which leads to complicated distributions for both current densities and internal fields. As a first step toward determining the global conductivity for inhomogeneous structures, we consider the *homogeneous* limit, which is defined as the limit when all mfp's are much larger than all inhomogeneity length scales.

[128] A. Vedyayev, C. Cowache, N. Ryzhanova and B. Dieny, *J. Phys.: Condensed Matter* **5**, 8289 (1993).

a. *Homogeneous Limit*

In the homogeneous limit, for both multilayers and granular solids, the two-point function $\xi(\mathbf{r}, \mathbf{r}')$ [Eq. (9.10)] has a *unique limit*, independent of $\mathbf{r}$ and $\mathbf{r}'$, when $R = |\mathbf{r} - \mathbf{r}'| \to \infty$, with the possible exception of a subfamily of paths $\Gamma[\mathbf{r}, \mathbf{r}']$ in the plane of the layers for multilayers; in other words, the *average* of the *scattering* $\Delta(\mathbf{r})$ is well defined for almost all paths. In actuality, in defining spatial averages, $R$ has an upper bound set by the size $L$ of the sample; therefore, what is characteristic of self-averaging systems is the existence of a minimum length scale $D_{sa}$, such that for $D_{sa} \lesssim R \ll L$, the function $\xi(\mathbf{r}, \mathbf{r}')$ becomes asymptotically a constant. For *magnetic* metallic systems, the function $\xi(\mathbf{r}, \mathbf{r}')$ is a spin matrix; its self-averaging limit is of the form $\bar{\xi} = \bar{\xi}_0 + \bar{\xi} \cdot \hat{\sigma}$. As a consequence of this definition, for any region $\mathfrak{R}$ of dimensions of the order of $D_{sa}$ (or greater), the average of the scattering over a volume $V$

$$\bar{\Delta} = \frac{1}{V[\mathfrak{R}]} \int_{\mathfrak{R}} d^3 \mathbf{r} \Delta(\mathbf{r}) = \bar{\Delta}_0 + \hat{\sigma} \cdot \bar{\mathbf{\Delta}}, \qquad (12.1)$$

is independent of the chosen region $\mathfrak{R}$ for both multilayers and granular solids. In Eq. (12.1),

$$\bar{\Delta}_0 = \pi \rho(\varepsilon_F) \int \frac{d^3 r}{V} n(\mathbf{r}) [v^2(\mathbf{r}) + j^2(\mathbf{r})], \qquad (12.2)$$

$$\bar{\mathbf{\Delta}} = 2\pi \rho(\varepsilon_F) \int \frac{d^3 r}{V} n(\mathbf{r}) v(\mathbf{r}) j(\mathbf{r}) \hat{M}(\mathbf{r}). \qquad (12.3)$$

and $n(\mathbf{r})$ is the density of scatterers.

When all the local mfp's are much larger than all inhomogeneity length scales (homogeneous limit), the two-point conductivity of Eq. (9.11) becomes effectively a function of only $R = |\mathbf{r} - \mathbf{r}'|$ [see Section 8, especially Eqs. (8.1) through (8.4)]. More precisely, choosing a quantization axis that diagonalizes $\bar{\Delta}$, and considering that the internal field varies over distances of the order of the inhomogeneity length scales (which are much smaller than the effective mfp's), Eq. (6.9) is reduced to

$$\mathbf{j}_{\alpha\beta} = \delta_{\alpha\beta} \left[ \sum_{\gamma} \int d^3 r' \, \boldsymbol{\sigma}_{\alpha\alpha,\gamma\gamma}(\mathbf{r}, \mathbf{r}') \right] \cdot \bar{\mathbf{E}}$$
$$= \delta_{\alpha\beta} (\bar{\rho}_\alpha)^{-1} \bar{\mathbf{E}}, \qquad (12.4)$$

where $\bar{E}$ stands for the average field. From the homogeneous limit of Eq. (9.11) the electrical resistance for each spin channel is completely determined by the average scattering $\bar{\Delta}$ in the medium, via

$$\bar{\rho}_\alpha = \left(\frac{2m}{\hbar^2 k_F}\right)[(\bar{\Delta}^{-1})_{\alpha\alpha}]^{-1}. \tag{12.5}$$

This equation is valid provided the spin diffusion length is much larger than both the elastic mfp's and the inhomogeneity length scales; under this condition the steady state current density is *constrained* to satisfy the continuity equation for *each* spin component [Eq. (6.13)].

### b. *Local Limit*

The opposite limiting case, the local limit, corresponds to the regime when all local mfp's are much smaller than the inhomogeneity length scales, in which case the linear response of Eq. (6.9) becomes local; the local conductivity can be written as the product of a one-point conductivity and the delta function $\delta(\mathbf{r} - \mathbf{r}')$ [see Section 8, Eqs. (8.6) through (8.10)]. We have calculated the local resistivity by inverting the conductivity and by expressing the electric field as the product of the local resistivity and the current density.[111] With the constraint of Eq. (6.13), we find the global resistivity is $\bar{\rho}_\alpha$ [Eq. (12.5)] along a typical current line, *provided* that the local resistivity and the current are uncorrelated.[129]

### c. *Multilayers*

For the particular case of multilayers, which are characterized by in-plane translational invariance, the two-point conductivity with its arguments $z$ and $z'$ can be easily obtained by integrating the in-plane coordinates $\boldsymbol{\rho} - \boldsymbol{\rho}'$ of the conductivity [see Eqs. (9.12) and (9.14)]. For CIP the internal electric field induced by an external uniform field is uniform, due to the in-plane *translational invariance* of the multilayers. The global conductivity can be found by integrating the two-point conductivity of Eq. (9.11) twice, with respect to both arguments, $z$ and $z'$ [see Eq. (7.8)]; the resulting CIP conductivity exhibits a characteristic *exponential dependence* with respect to the thicknesses of the different layers, and the magnetoresistance vanishes exponentially in the local limit.

The solution for the CPP conductivity is obtained by rewriting the current density $\mathbf{j}(\mathbf{r})$, from Eqs. (6.9) and (9.11), as an angular average and a radial average, weighted with the conductivity kernel. A possible

---

[129] See Section 7(b) also. Actually, there is some correlation, and this hypothesis yields an *upper* limit to the resistivity.

solution for the internal field, from Eqs. (6.9) and (9.11), is that $E_{\alpha\beta}(r)$ is proportional to the local scattering rate $\Delta_{\alpha\beta}(r)$, as follows from the formula

$$\int_0^\infty dR\left\{P_{r'\to r}\exp\left[-\frac{R}{2}\xi(r,r')\right]\right\}_{\alpha\gamma}\Delta_{\gamma\delta}(r')\left\{P_{r\to r'}\exp\left[-\frac{R}{2}\xi(r,r')\right]\right\}_{\delta\beta}=\delta_{\alpha\beta}$$

(12.6)

where $R = |r - r'|$ [see Eqs. (9.10) and (9.11)]. This local solution can be implemented *only* when the current density is a constant $j_{\alpha\beta}$, which is precisely the case for CPP: $E(r) = 2m\Delta(r)j/\hbar^2 k_F$, in agreement with Eqs. (12.4) and (12.5), where the fields, currents, and strength of scattering are matrices, and a matrix product is implied. Thus, for the CPP geometry, the corresponding global resistivity is proportional to the *average scattering* for each spin channel; thus, the CPP geometry for multilayers exhibits a self-averaging behavior (all transport properties are determined by the average scattering) not only in the homogeneous limit, but for *all* length scales, and the magnetoresistance is scale independent and does not vanish in the local limit.[118] This result can be described with the aid of the following *current line picture*: current lines sample all the scattering in the medium; later this picture will be generalized to granular solids, for which we will see that there are some restrictions.

The case of multilayers illustrates that there are two radically different behaviors for the magnetoresistance: (1) when it vanishes exponentially with respect to the average distance between magnetic regions (as for the CIP geometry of multilayers) and (2) when it does not vanish exponentially and is independent of average distance between magnetic regions (as for the CPP geometry of multilayers). We will refer to the latter category as *magnetically self-averaging* systems.

### d. Granular Solids: Magnetically Self-Averaging Systems

Our theory leads us to postulate that granular solids are magnetically self-averaging due to *randomness* in the distribution of granules. As a first step, note that the current line picture suggests that the global resistivity is proportional to the *average scattering* $\bar{\Delta}_\alpha$ sampled in each spin channel by the current lines, as in the CPP case.[129a] However, in the local limit for granular solids, current lines do not necessarily sample all the scattering in the medium with equal weight; the relative weight depends on the local resistivity differences.[130] This exclusion does not in any way

---

[129a] This hypothesis provides an *upper* limit to the resistivity; the actual resistivity is *less* because the current takes the path of least resistance.

[130] Only if the current lines do not undergo significant refraction at the interfaces, namely, when the relative differences in local conductivities are small, can one safely assume that

alter the conclusion that the system is magnetically self-averaging. In general, in the local limit, the average scattering includes that from the matrix and interfaces (interfaces are probed regardless of the relative values of the local resistivities) and only a fraction of the scattering in the granules, due to partial penetration of the current lines. The only difference between the two limiting cases is at most the contribution from the granules. Thus, while the magnetoresistance depends exponentially on the size of the granules, it does not depend exponentially on the average distance between adjacent granules and it does not vanish in the local limit. It is in this sense that granular solids are magnetically self-averaging.

e. *Magnetoresistance of Magnetically Self-Averaging Systems*

We now turn to a discussion of the magnetoresistance of magnetically self-averaging systems. Based on the "current line picture" the global conductivity for a given magnetic configuration $M$ of the system is the sum of the conductivities of the individual spin channels,

$$\sigma^M = \sum_\alpha \sigma_\alpha^M = \sum_\alpha (\bar{\rho}_\alpha^M)^{-1} \propto \mathrm{Tr}(\bar{\Delta}_M^{-1}), \qquad (12.7)$$

where Tr stands for the trace in spin space. The dependence of the resistivity on the magnetic configuration $M$ is determined by $\bar{\Delta}$ of Eq. (12.3). For antiferromagnetic and random configurations the average magnetization $\bar{M}$ is zero and $\bar{\Delta}(\bar{M} = 0) = 0$, while for the ferromagnetic configuration the magnetization $\bar{M}$ reaches its saturation value $M_s$, and $\bar{\Delta}(\bar{M} = M_s) = \bar{\Delta}[\hat{M}(\mathbf{r}) = \hat{H}]$ is given by Eq. (12.3) with $\hat{M}(\mathbf{r})$ along the direction of the magnetic field $H$. For any magnetically self-averaging system, i.e., magnetic granular systems and layered structures in the CPP geometry, the maximum magnetoresistance ratio, found by using Eqs. (12.2) through (12.5) and (12.7), is identical to that previously found for the CPP geometry,[53] i.e.,

$$R_s \equiv \frac{\rho(\bar{M} = 0) - \rho(\bar{M} = M_s)}{\rho(\bar{M} = M_s)} = \frac{|\bar{\Delta}|^2}{\Delta_0^2 - |\bar{\Delta}|^2}. \qquad (12.8)$$

---

the global resistivity is proportional to the average scattering in the whole system. Instead, if the local resistivity in the granules is much larger than that of the matrix and the mfp is much smaller than the size of the granules, the current lines tend to avoid the granules and only partial penetration into the granules occurs. Therefore, in the limit of very large relative differences in local conductivities, the global resistivity again becomes an average scattering, but one that includes only contributions from the matrix and the interfaces.

Equation (12.8) shows that, although the mfp is *not* a relevant length scale for the MR of magnetically self-averaging systems, it nevertheless enters the expression for the MR through the *average* scattering $\bar{\Delta}$, since it sets the scale for the resistivity.

Until now, the giant MR (GMR) effect has been observed mostly in multilayered structures for the CIP geometry for which the resistivity $\bar{\rho}_\alpha^M$ depends exponentially on the thickness of the layers relative to the mfp's [$\bar{\rho}_\alpha^M$ is not given by Eqs. (12.1) through (12.5)], and the MR vanishes in the local limit. The fact that this is *not* a magnetically self-averaging configuration has led to the erroneous impression that the GMR effect intrinsically depends on the dimensions of the magnetic and nonmagnetic components relative to the mfp.

The actual ratio $R_s$ will be reduced by spin diffusion processes inherent in magnetic granular films[130a] that are not taken into account in the hypothesis that the current density and resistivity are uncorrelated.[129,129a] Also, one can create mixing of currents in the spin channels, for example, by electron-magnon interactions at higher temperatures, in which case our analysis has to be modified.[51] Finally, it is conceivable that magnetic granular films grown epitaxially might not be magnetically self-averaging, either due to the shape of the granules or the patterned way in which they could be deposited.[29,38–40]

## VI. Discussion of Results

A *minimum* of six parameters are used in the theories discussed in Section V that refer to the constituent materials; *five* that refer to the *scattering* in the bulk of the structure ($v_m$, $p_m$, $v_{nm}$) and for the interfaces between the magnetic and nonmagnetic regions ($v_s$, $p_s$), and *one* for the *potential* differences between layers ($U/E_F$). In addition, one must specify the sizes of the magnetic and nonmagnetic regions, e.g., for a bipartite superlattice the thicknesses $t_m$ and $t_{nm}$ of the magnetic and nonmagnetic layers. To help determine these parameters for layered structures, data exist for the resistivity $\rho$ or conductivity, and ($\Delta\rho$ or $R$) for CIP and, in some cases, CPP. These data are available as a function of $t_{nm}$ for fixed $t_m$, and in some studies as a function of $t_m$ for fixed $t_{nm}$, so that one may have up to eight sets of data on a multilayered structure to compare with the theoretical predictions in Section V.

In comparing data to theory, it is necessary to know the magnetic state of multilayers. If the layers are ferromagnetically (F) aligned in zero field, there is no possibility of reorienting them in a field and therefore no

MR effect from the mechanism we are considering. If the layers are antiferromagnetically (AF) aligned in zero field, the comparison with the theory in Section 10 is rather direct. However, as the interlayer coupling weakens, it cannot completely align the layers antiparallel, and the zero field or coercive field magnetic configuration of the multilayer is *ill defined*. This poses a problem for interpreting data taken for CIP because the resistivity and MR are sensitive to the precise configuration of the magnetic layers relative to one another in this geometry. This uncertainty introduces additional approximations and parameters when one tries to fit the theory to data.

For granular solids, the sizes of the magnetic and nonmagnetic regions are more difficult to control; while one specifies the concentration of magnetic material, the distribution in size of the magnetic granules $f(V_\alpha)$ is determined by the conditions of growth and the subsequent anneals. It has been determined[121] that if one uses the resistivity data to fix the mfp's ($v_m$, $v_{nm}$, $v_s$), it is a reasonable working approximation to take the spin-dependent scattering parameters ($p_m$, $p_s$) to be the same as those found in multilayered structures because they have the same physical origins. Two size distributions have been considered:[121] one in which all the granules have the same size; another in which there is a broad distribution such that the product $Vf(V)$ is constant, where $V$ is the volume of a granule. The former is applicable to samples annealed at high temperatures with large granules; the latter better reflects the nature of the as-deposited samples where there is a large number of very small granules. No reasonable attempt has been made up until now to take account of the difference in potentials between the granules and the matrix in these random systems.

Here we review the general trends in the conductivity (resistivity) and MR predicted by the theory outlined in Section V; due to the large number of unknown parameters, fits to the data are suggestive of trends alone. The actual values of the parameters used are not that meaningful, because the approximations we have made may be forcing the parameters to compensate for effects or interactions we have neglected. For example, if we neglect the differences in potentials between layers, i.e., set $U = 0$, [see Eq. (11.5)] we find that the *effective* spin-dependent scattering parameter $p_{eff}$ needed to fit the MR data is larger than the $p$ needed when the differences in potentials are taken into account.

## 13. GENERAL TRENDS

If one focuses on the spin-dependent scattering at interfaces as the origin of the giant MR observed in multilayered structures, one finds from Eqs.

[130a] S. Zhang and P. M. Levy, *Phys. Rev. B* **50** (1994), in press.

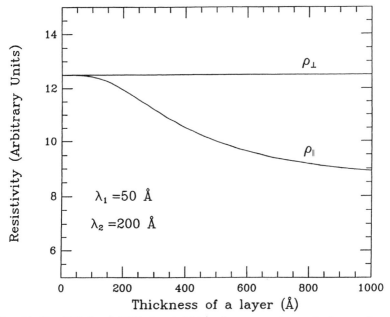

FIG. 14. The CIP($\rho_{\parallel}$) and CPP($\rho_{\perp}$) resistivities of *nonmagnetic* superlattices made up of metals with different mean free paths $\lambda_1$ and $\lambda_2$. We take the interface scattering to be zero. [From S. Zhang and P. M. Levy, *J. Appl. Phys.* **69**, 4786 (1991).]

(10.14) through (10.17) that as the thickness of the nonmagnetic layer $t_{nm}$ increases, the position-dependent scattering $a^{\alpha}(z)$ of Eq. (10.14) and average scattering $\bar{\Delta}_s^{\alpha}$ of Eq. (10.17) decrease. The first goes approximately as $a^{\alpha}(z) \sim (1/t_{nm}) \exp(-|z - z_a|/\lambda^{\alpha})$, while $\bar{\Delta}_s^{\alpha} \sim 1/t_{nm}$. Because the CIP conductivity and MR depend on $a^{\alpha}(z)$, as well as $\bar{\Delta}^{\alpha}$ [see Eqs. (10.13) and (10.18)], the CIP-MR goes as $(1/t_{nm}) \exp(-t_{nm}/\lambda)$, i.e., the mfp is a characteristic length scale over which the MR for transport parallel to the layers decays. However, from Eq. (10.20) it is clear that $a^{\alpha}(z)$ does *not* enter the CPP resistivity or MR, only $\bar{\Delta}^{\alpha}$ enters; and the CPP-MR is simply proportional to $1/t_{nm}$ so that the mfp is *not* a relevant *length scale* for this geometry even though it enters by setting the magnitude of the scattering and thus resistivity.

These trends are brought out in Figures 14 through 18, where we have chosen some typical values for the parameters entering the expressions for the conductivity and resistivity in Section 10. To underscore the independence of the CPP properties from mfp length scales, we show in Fig. 14 the CIP and CPP resistivities of a *nonmagnetic* superlattice made up of metals with different mfp's. So as to remove the $1/t_{nm}$ "dilution ef-

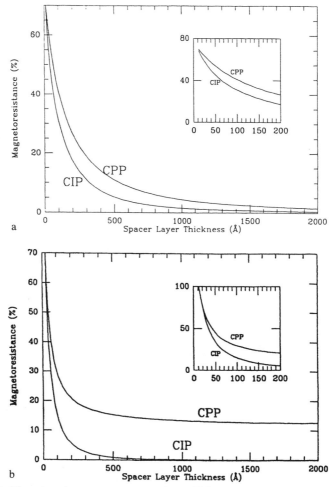

Fig. 15. Magnetoresistance versus spacer layer thickness $t_{nm}$: (a) for fixed magnetic layer thickness $t_m = 30$ Å and (b) for equal layer thicknesses $t_m = t_{nm}$. The parameters used for these curves are $\lambda_m = 40$ Å, $\lambda_{nm} = 200$ Å, $\lambda_s = (t_m + t_{nm})/0.6$, $p_s = 0.5$, and $p_b = 0.2$. These are the mfp's for the magnetic and nonmagnetic layers and interface, and the ratio of spin-dependent to spin-independent scattering potentials for the interface and the bulk, respectively. [From H. E. Camblong et al., Phys. Rev. B **47**, 4735 (1993).]

fect,"[79,96] we have considered only bulk scattering. We see that the CPP resistivity is indeed *constant*, whereas CIP decreases as one goes from the homogeneous limit $t \ll \lambda$ where $\rho^{\parallel} = \rho^{\perp} = (k_F/2ne^2)[(1/\lambda_1) + (1/\lambda_2)]$, to the local limit $t \gg \lambda$, where $\rho^{\parallel} = (2k_F/ne^2)(\lambda_1 + \lambda_2)^{-1}$.

The variation of the MR as a function of the spacer layer thickness $t_{nm}$ is shown in Fig. 15. The parameters used are close to those we have

found by fitting data on the resistivity and MR of Co/Cu and Co/Ag for the CIP and CPP geometries; specifically, we included a representative small amount of spin-dependent scattering in the bulk of the layers. The MR ratios in this section are all defined with respect to the resistivity at saturation. The magnetoresistance behaves differently if the thickness of the magnetic layer $t_m$ is constant, as compared to when it varies in size so as to be equal to this thickness of the nonmagnetic layer $t_{nm}$.

When $t_m$ is held fixed, both CIP-MR and CPP-MR approach zero as $t_{nm}$ increases, but for different reasons [see Fig. 15(a)]. The decrease in the CIP-MR comes from the inability of the electrons to sample more than one magnetic layer within the distance of the mean free path $\lambda_{mfp}$, as the thickness of the nonmagnetic layer $t_{nm}$ increases. For CPP, there is no decay from mfp's; rather the CPP-MR decreases due to the reduced spin-dependent scattering per unit length as $t_{nm}$ increases.

When $t_m = t_{nm}$ [see Fig. 15(b)] the CPP-MR reaches a finite asymptote, which comes from the spin-dependent *bulk* scattering per unit length. This is held *constant*, because as we increase $t_{nm}$ we also add $t_m$ so as to maintain the equality of the two. We note from Fig. 15(b) that the CPP-MR with $t_m = t_{nm}$ provides a sensitive test for the presence of spin-dependent bulk scattering. If this scattering is not present, the CPP-MR goes to zero as $t_{nm}$ increases in much the same way as in Fig. 15(a). The curve for the CPP-MR in Fig. 15(b) is predicated on the assumption that all the distances $t_n + t_{nm}$ are less than $\lambda_{sdl}$. Once $t_n + t_{nm} \gtrsim \lambda_{sdl}$ the magnetoresistance goes to zero. In other words, the CPP-MR maintains its plateau only as long as $d_{in} < \lambda_{sdl}$.

Additional curves depicting the variation of the CIP-MR as a function of layer thicknesses can be found in Refs. 48, 97, and 131. Dieny[84] has given a quantitative interpretation of the CIP-MR in permalloy-based spin-valve structures, based on the semiclassical approach, and shows the variation of *conductance, magnetoconductance*, and MR ratio as a function of the thickness of the permalloy layer. In contrast to other systems, spin-dependent scattering in the *bulk* of the layers is believed to be a dominant source of the MR in these permalloy structures.[84,132] Semiclassical and real-space quantum predictions for the conductance and CIP-MR as a function of layer thicknesses are plotted in Ref. 95.

The implicit assumption in the MR curves in Fig. 15 and those referenced earlier is that the structure is antiferromagnetically aligned in a zero or coercive field; however, for multilayered structures the interlayer

---

[131] See M. A. M. Gijs and M. Okada, Ref. 24.

[132] From recent experimental data, S. S. P. Parkin concludes that in permalloy-based multilayered structures spin-dependent bulk scattering is *not* the dominant sources of MR. Private communication, June 1993.

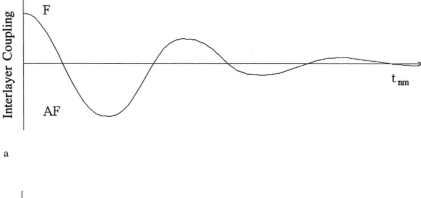

a

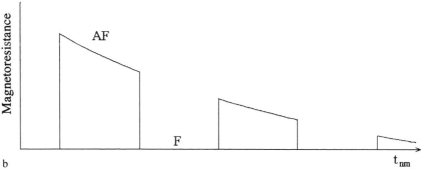

b

FIG. 16. (a) A sketch of the interlayer coupling in multilayered structures as a function of the thickness of the nonmagnetic layers $t_{nm}$. (b) What one expects for the magnetoresistance of the multilayered structure if the coupling is sufficiently strong to align the magnetic layers. When the coupling is ferromagnetic and sufficiently strong to align the layers the magnetoresistance coming from the giant MR mechanism is *zero*, because an external field does not reorient the layers relative to one another.

magnetic coupling oscillates between F and AF as a function of the nonmagnetic spacer layer.[133] In this case, instead of the curves in Fig. 15, we would expect the curve shown in Fig. 16 where the ferromagnetically aligned regions give zero MR, and the AF aligned the maximum MR shown in Fig. 15. However, this is not what is seen experimentally (see Fig. 5); except for the first F minimum in the MR, which is close to zero, the others are nonzero. This leads us to conclude that the layers are not entirely ferromagnetically aligned. By inference, if the coupling is not

[133] P. Grünberg, S. Demokritov, A. Fuss, R. Schreiber, J. A. Wolf, and S. T. Purcell, *J. Magn. Magn. Mater.* **104-107**, 1734 (1992), and references therein; R. Coehoorn, *Europhys. News* **24**, 43 (1993), and references therein.

sufficiently strong to dictate the alignment of the layers in these regions, the MR peaks (other than the first one) cannot be identified as coming from *completely* AF aligned layers. When the spacer layer thickness is large, the coupling is weak and the layers are randomly aligned; nonetheless we note that the MR is not zero. These considerations lead us to analyze MR data not only on the basis of F and AF alignments, but also for randomly aligned "uncoupled" magnetic layers.[16,120]

The antiferromagnetic and random configuration both have a total magnetization for the multilayered structure of zero, $M = 0$. What distinguishes them is the internal arrangements of the layers relative to one another. For example, if we have four layers all with $M = 0$, there are six different configurations, two of which are sequentially up-down, i.e., AF. The other four are up–2 down–up, 2 up–2 down, and their mirror images (time-reversed states). For 10 layers with $M = 0$ there are 252 configurations; only 2 of which are AF. Many have locally ferromagnetic regions, e.g., 5 up–5 down, or 1 up–5 down–4 up. In the CIP, geometry transport properties are sensitive to the local magnetic configuration *within a mfp* of the electrons; therefore, while all 252 configurations of 10 magnetic layers have the same total $M = 0$, their CIP conductivities or resistivities are *different*. Those configurations with locally ferromagnetic regions have higher conductivities than AF regions, because locally the scattering of the electrons will be less for one spin direction than the other and, as the two channels conduct *in parallel*, a short-circuit effect is produced.[2] Thus the statistical average over all configurations with $M = 0$ yields a CIP conductivity or resistivity *in between* that for the AF and F aligned configurations of a multilayer, and the CIP-MR ratio will be less than the maximum based on an AF alignment [see Eq. (10.24)].

In Fig. 17(a) we fit our expressions for the CIP-MR [Eqs. (10.13), (10.18), and (10.24)] to data on Co/Cu as a function of the copper layer thickness. They were fit so that the AF curve goes through the first (AF coupled) peak in the MR, the uncoupled (random alignment) curve matches the MR data at large thickness of copper, and the F curve is the baseline of zero. From this fit, we infer that the second and subsequent peaks in the CIP-MR curves are for $M = 0$ configurations that are *not* completely AF aligned; similarly the second and succeeding minima are not ferromagnetically aligned. If we interpreted the MR peaks as that from AF aligned configurations, the parameters we find lead to a resistivity (at saturation) for Co(15 Å)/Cu(9 Å) of $\rho(H_s) = 37$ $\mu\Omega$ cm, which is more than twice as large as the one measured 17.1 $\mu\Omega$ cm.[16,134] With

[134] See D. Mosca *et al.*, Ref. 6.

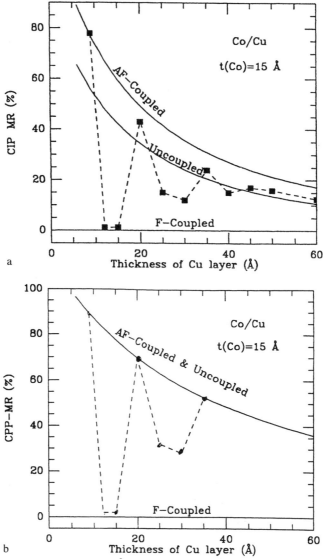

FIG. 17. (a) CIP-MR for Co(15 Å)/Cu($t$) as estimated by taking the layers F and AF aligned and mixtures of the two with $M = 0$. The latter is labeled as "uncoupled." The squares represent data at $T = 4.2$ K. [From D. Mosca *et al., J. Magn. Magn. Mater.* **94,** L1 (1991) and A. Fert (private communication).] The parameters we use in the fits are $\lambda_{Co}$ = 40 Å, $\lambda_{Cu}$ = 75 Å, $w_s$ = 0.3, $p_{Co}$ = 0.2, and $p_s$ = 0.52. [From S. Zhang and P. M. Levy, *Phys. Rev. B* **47,** 6776 (1993).] (b) The CPP-MR for Co(15 Å)/Cu($t$) predicted from Eq. (12.8) and the parameters used in the fit to the CIP-MR. In CPP there is no difference between AF and uncoupled layer configurations as long as the average magnetization is zero. In regions where the coupling is not sufficiently strong to impose antiferromagnetic alignment of the layers, e.g., between 23 to 33 Å as seen from the CIP-MR in part (a), we project a CPP-MR that is in the same proportion of the uncoupled and ferromagnetically aligned MRs as that found from the CIP-MR in part (a). On comparing our predictions to the recent results on Co/Cu [see Fig 9(a)], one notes a reasonable resemblance.

the parameters used in our fit in Fig. 17(a), we find $\rho(H_s) = 20 \ \mu\Omega$ cm, which is a considerable improvement.

There is another motivation for introducing randomly aligned magnetic configurations: Although CIP transport is sensitive to the *local* magnetic environment, the CPP properties are not. Only the global magnetization enters the CPP transport; therefore, the CPP-MR curves for AF and randomly aligned ($M = 0$) configurations are one and the same.[120] We have used the parameters obtained from the fit to the CIP-MR and resistivity for Co/Cu (see caption for Fig. 17) to predict the CPP-MR ratios [see Fig. 17(b)]. Because the CIP data are given for *reproducible* values of the peak in the resistivity as a function of field $H_p$ (close to the coercive field $H_c$), one must compare our prediction to the comparable CPP-MR curve in Fig. 9(a). On comparing Figs. 9(a) and 17(b), we find the overall fit is encouraging, but there is room for improvement.

One prediction, based on Eq. (10.20), that the CPP resistance depends only on the *global* magnetization and not on the internal arrangement of the magnetic layers[53] has been confirmed by data on Co/Cu.[22] In Fig. 9(b), the CPP resistance of as-deposited samples at zero field is plotted as a function of the copper layer thickness. The straight line through the data points represent a $1/t_{Cu}$ variation in the resistance, which is precisely that predicted from Eq. (10.17) if one considers that interface scattering is dominant (see the discussion at the beginning of this section). The data that fall on this line come from multilayered structures with different internal magnetic configurations; those at the bottom left of the figure are from uncoupled layers, while at the upper right end, the layers are AF coupled. Because all of these nominally $M = 0$ configurations fall on one straight line, one confirms with these data that the CPP resistance and the CPP-MR do not depend on the internal or local arrangement of the layers.

The MR of *granular* solids has been analyzed by Zhang. The generic trends in the MR($\Delta\rho$) and MR ratio $R$ are given in Ref. 121; they agree with the original MR data taken on granular films,[7] as well as more recent data.[29] This overall agreement lends support to the conjecture that the origin of the MR observed in granular solids is the same as in multilayered structures (see Section 12).

Finally we plot in Fig. 18 the one-point in-plane conductivity $\sigma^{\parallel}(z) = \Sigma_\alpha \sigma^{\parallel}_{\alpha\alpha}(z)$, where $\sigma^{\parallel}_{\alpha\alpha}(z)$ is given by Eq. (10.13), for the two limiting cases considered in Section 8. In the local limit $\lambda \ll d_{in}$ [Fig. 18(a), the curve labeled AF], the conductivity has a large variation from one region to another, while in the homogeneous limit $\lambda \gg d_{in}$ [Fig. 18(b)], it is nearly flat, i.e., independent of position. We also note that the MR, i.e., the difference in the CIP conductivities [Eq. (10.18)] for the F and AF con-

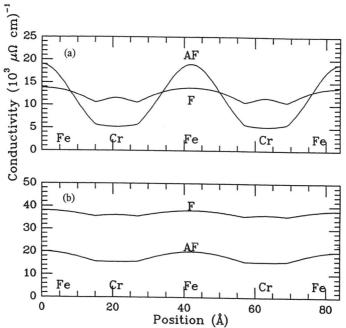

FIG. 18. The position-dependent CIP conductivity $\sigma^{\parallel}(z)$ of a magnetic superlattice with $t_m = a = 30$ Å, and $t_{nm} = b = 12$ Å for one magnetic unit cell $T = 2(a + b) = 84$ Å. (a) Close to the local limit where we choose for input parameters $\lambda_b = 12$ Å, $\lambda_s' = 0.8$, and $p = 0.55$. In the AF configuration the mfp is $\lambda_{AF} = 5.6$Å; while $\lambda_F^{\uparrow} = 3.2$Å and $\lambda_F^{\downarrow} = 20.9$Å so that the mfp in the F configuration is $\lambda_F = 12.1$Å. (b) Near the homogeneous limit $\lambda_b = 40$ Å, $\lambda_s' = 2$, and $p = 0.55$. See Ref. 97 for the meanings of the parameters. In the AF configuration the mfp is $\lambda_{AF} = 16$ Å; while $\lambda_F^{\uparrow} = 10$ Å and $\lambda_F^{\downarrow} = 61$ Å so that the mfp in the F configuration is $\lambda_F = 35.5$ Å. When the mfp's are small compared to the inhomogeneity length scale $d_{in} = T$, the conductivity varies considerably from one region to another. When $\lambda \gg d_{in}$ it approaches the conductivity of a homogeneous system, i.e., it is uniformly flat. In the local limit the average of the CIP conductivities $\sigma_{CIP}$ for the F and AF configurations are nearly the same, thus the MR is close to zero; in the homogeneous case the difference is large and the MR ratio is about 100%. [From S. Zhang *et al.*, *Phys. Rev. B* **45**, 8689 (1992).]

figurations of the multilayers, is nearly zero in the local limit and large in the homogeneous limit.

## VII. Future Directions

### 14. EXPERIMENTAL WORK

The structural, magnetic and transport properties of layered and granular structures are sensitive to the conditions under which they are prepared;

these include the deposition method (sputtering and MBE), temperature of growth, and substrate including the buffer layer. Considerable work has been started on this, but many variables and combinations of them must be manipulated in searching for materials with more desirable transport features, e.g., large MRs and smaller fields to achieve them. Further characterization of the structure (grain size), interfaces, magnetization, scattering centers, and domains are all necessary to understand better the mechanisms that produce the giant MR and the best ways to optimize this effect.

The correlation of growth conditions and the structural and magnetic characterizations with measurements of the physical properties one is trying to optimize continues to be a major thrust of the experimentalists. The structure (roughness) and magnetization of interfaces are critical to the size of the MR; nuclear magnetic resonance, grazing incidence small-angle x-ray scattering, and Mossbauer spectroscopy can provide useful information on these features of interfaces. The magnetic domain pattern in the layers needs further study by polarized neutron diffraction, the magneto-optical Kerr effect, and Brillouin light scattering. This is particularly important for $H \approx 0$ and at coercive fields to characterize these states. The distribution of grain sizes and their orientations in sputtered and MBE-grown samples merit attention. The nature of scattering centers in the layers (besides those at interfaces) has not received much attention because these scatterers are believed to be similar to those in bulk materials; however, the grains in layered and granular structures are different and the origins of scattering in the bulk of these structures are worth studying. This is particularly true of the boundaries between grains and the walls between magnetic domains; in these regions scattering does take place but little is known about these grain boundaries and walls in multilayers.

The resistance of layered and granular structures at low fields depends on their magnetic and temperature history, about which little is known. As seen in Fig. 9(a), the MR ratio can change by a factor of 2, depending on the history of the sample. Clearly, this hysteretic behavior requires some concerted efforts between structural and magnetic characterizations and transport measurements. Knowledge of the magnetization in the individual layers, and of how these magnetizations rotate as a function of applied fields, is necessary to correlate the expressions for the resistivity or conductivity [given as a function of the orientation of the magnetic layers with respect to the field direction; see Eq. (10.23)] to the field. The fields needed to saturate the MR effect $H_s$ seem to be different from those for the magnetization (this is particularly true of granular solids). This difference must be understood better. In addition, ways of lowering $H_s$

are needed if we are to use these materials in applications with low sensing fields, e.g., computer technologies.

For two-component layered and granular structures—one magnetic and one nonmagnetic—the giant MR effect is usually negative inasmuch as the short circuit effect lowers the resistivity when a field drives the magnetic configuration from random or AF to ferromagnetic [see Eqs. (10.24) and (10.25)]. There may be some exceptions to this expectation for binary systems, either due to conditions predicted in Refs. 66 and 97 or those recently found by Parkin.[135] However, for structures with more than two components, one can produce conditions such that the giant MR is positive.[136] This follows immediately from the theory based on spin-dependent scattering when one has two types of scattering with different *signs* of $p$ [see Eqs. (8.26) and (11.5)]. This effect has been observed in recent experiments,[137] but the magnitude of the positive MR has been smaller than expected. This point needs clarification because it might indicate that there are some other mechanisms that produce the giant MR effect.

Spin-flip scattering, e.g., due to paramagnetic impurities, reduces the MR effect. Some studies have been initiated along these lines;[138] these data are important for gaining an understanding of the role of spin-flip scattering on MR, as well as for validating the two-current model of transport in magnetic media.

Finally, new structures consisting of combinations of nonmagnetic and magnetic metals with spin-polarized conduction bands, such that the Fermi surface is below a barrier in the AF state but not for one spin channel in the F state, can produce a CPP-MR much larger than currently measured. Their CPP-MR would be limited only by the spin-diffusion length. Other combinations of semiconducting and magnetic metals are worth considering for enhancing the effects of quantum well states and their putative effects on the MR.

[135] S. S. P. Parkin, *Appl. Phys. Lett.* **63,** 1987 (1993).

[136] Two independent sources of spin-dependent scattering with opposite signs of $p$ are needed [Eq. (10.26)].

[137] J. M. George, A. Barthélémy, O. Durand, J. L. Duvail, A. Fert, P. Galtier, O. Heckmann, L. G. Pereira, F. Petroff, and T. Valet, *Magnetic Ultrathin Films* B. T. Jonker *et al.,* eds.), *Mat. Res. Soc. Sym. Proc.* **313,** 737 (1993).

[138] J. Bass, Q. Yang, S.-F. Lee, P. Holody, R. Loloee, P. A. Schroeder, and W. P. Pratt Jr., "How to Isolate Effects of Spin-Flip Scattering on Giant Magnetoresistance in Magnetic Multilayers," presented at Conference on Magnetism and Magnetic Materials, Minneapolis, MN, Nov. 15–18, 1993; *J. Appl. Phys.* **75,** 6699 (1994); Q. Yang, P. Holody, S.-F. Lee, L. L. Henry, R. Loloee, P. A. Schroeder, W. P. Pratt Jr., and J. Bass, *Phys. Rev. Lett.* **72,** 3274 (1994).

15. THEORETICAL ADVANCES

For most of the magnetic multilayers in which giant MR has been observed, the disorder at the interfaces is stronger than in the bulk of the
layers; this is inferred from the scattering parameters used to fit data
(see Section VI). For example, Dieny et al.[95] have used the mixed layer
description of Johnson and Camley[50] to fit the MR data on Fe/Cr multilayers. For the strong scattering they impute to the mixed layer, they use a
mfp for minority spin electrons of 4 Å so that $k_F \lambda_{mfp}$ is *not* that large
and quantum interference effects might have to be taken into account as
corrections to the quasiclassical results. These corrections are left out in
the semiclassical approach of Section 1, and have not yet been incorporated in the quantum approaches to transport in metallic multilayers. The
effects of scattering at interfaces have not been fully explored. Some
treatments have assumed this scattering is so strong as to disrupt the
*coherent* scattering from the interfaces, and therefore treat scattering
from the potential steps at interfaces individually (rather than collectively).

The theory can be improved in several ways: by including more diagrams in the self-energy; by using better decoupling schemes in the momentum space approach outlined in Section 10; by using a nonlocal self-
energy and including quantum interference effects in the real-space
approach given in Section 9; by introducing more realistic treatments of
interface scattering, e.g., by considering the putative in-plane structure
of interfaces, and evaluating the vertex corrections this would engender;
and by taking into account spin-mixing of the two currents due to paramagnetic impurities, spin-orbit scattering and the electron-magnon interaction. The electron-magnon and -phonon interactions are important
when discussing the temperature dependence of the resistivity and MR;
little has been done to include these interactions until now. Inclusion of
these effects involves vertex corrections to the electron-hole propagators
entering the expressions for the conductivity; these corrections are non-
trivial. For example, it is difficult to calculate the temperature dependence of the resistivity of normal metals (nonmagnetic) due to phonon
scattering.[98]

The inability of the semiclassical Boltzmann approach to explain the
existing data on magnetotransport in magnetic multilayers has been
traced to the use of the local relaxation-time approximation, not necessarily to quantum corrections. Therefore, one could try to find solutions of
the Boltzmann equation for multilayers that do not make this approximation.

Although some general studies have been made of the effects of using

proper wave functions on the MR (see Section 11), no attempts have been made at fitting data when one accounts for the presence of the spin-dependent potential differences between layers. Proper fits to the data require the wave functions for the multilayered structures; band structure calculations are beginning to provide wave functions for magnetic superlattices.[82,83] These *ab initio* calculations are potentially capable of determining the one-electron propagators by *self-consistently* calculating the wave functions and scattering so that one can find the conductivity for different magnetic configurations and hence the magnetoresistance.

The suggestion has been made that quantum well states affect the MR of metallic multilayers; the characteristic oscillations associated with these states have not been observed until now. Further study is warranted, both to find new combinations of materials where the effects due to quantum well confinement might show up, and theoretically to understand why they might be suppressed. Finally, the current understanding is that giant MR comes from spin-dependent scattering of electrons; the conduction electrons need not be spin polarized. However, there is an emerging interest in the transport of spin-polarized currents through nonmagnetic layers in other contexts than giant MR.[139] The theory developed in Section V, particularly Sections 6 and 9 for noncollinear structures, will be useful in understanding the depolarization effects of nonmagnetic layers when one includes the spin-flip process ($p_{\alpha\beta} \neq 0$) in our theory.

The theory is still in a somewhat preliminary state, although the developments presented in this chapter are a significant beginning.

## ACKNOWLEDGMENTS

Many of the theoretical developments covered in Section V were carried out with my former students Horacio E. Camblong and Shufeng Zhang. Without their invaluable input, the theory would not have evolved into its present form. The initial development of the theory was completed with Albert Fert whose seminal contributions to the entire field are recognized. In addition, I want to acknowledge and thank Sam Bader, Ami Berkowitz, Cia-Ling Chien, Bernard Dieny, Hiroyasu Fujimori, Martin Gijs, Peter Grünberg, Bruce Gurney, Sadamichi Maekawa, Stuart Parkin, Ivan Schuller, Peter Schroeder, Virgil Speriosu, Teruya Shinjo, and Koki Takanashi who identified key papers and issues. Finally, I acknowledge with gratitude grants from the Office of Naval Research N 00014-91-J-1695, NATO 5-2-05/RG No. 890599, and the Technology Transfer Fund of New York University under which this work was completed.

---

[139] G. A. Prinz, ARPA/ONR Workshop on Spin-Polarized Transport, Arlington, VA, Sep. 13–14, 1993; see also Ref. 10.

# Author Index

Numbers in parentheses are reference numbers and indicate that an author's work is referred to although his or her name is not cited in the text.

## A

aan de Stegge, J., *389*
Abbe, F., *284*
Abdul-Razzaq, W., *368*
Abraham, F. F., *4*, 10(27–29)
Abramowitz, M., *430*, 436(117)
Aindow, M., *365*
Ajima, T., *398*
Allen, S. M., *65*, 72(41), 165(29), *168*
Amador, C., *123*, 166(34), *168*, 174(136)
Amelinckx, S., 142(161), *143–144*
Anderko, K., *174*
Andersen, H. C., *28*
Andersen, O. K., *132*
Anderson, P. D., *154*
Andoin, B., *218*, 233(81)
Anno, T., *378*
Anthony, L., *160*
Araki, S., *388*
Ardell, A. J., *141*, 144(160)
Asano, Y., *403*, 405(85)
Ashby, M. F., *3*, *244*, 246(100)
Ashcroft, N. W., *394*, *397*, 406(67), 432(67)
Asta, M., *37–38*, 39(16), *49*, 52(28), 57(28, 30), *73*, 73(12), 74(12), 78(12), 92(12), 94(12), 104(16), *105*, 111(29), *113*, 117(30), 121(16), 129(17–19), 145(16–19), 147(16–18), *148*, 149(16–19), *150*, 151(16, 19), *152*, 153(12, 16, 19), *156–157*, 157(19), 158(16, 19), *159–161*, 162(16), *163*, 165(12, 13, 17, 30), *167–169*, 169(58)
Aubard, X., *240*
Averbach, B. L., *126*
Aveston, J., *183*, 220(13), 221(13)
Ayers, J. D., *27*

## B

Babcock, S. E., *341*
Bacmann, J. J., *337*, *350*
Bacon, D. J., *304*, *341*, *344*
Bader, S. D., *377*, 379(17), *385*, *388*, 389(24)

Baibich, M. N., *368*, 376(2), 378(2), *388*, 389(2), 398(2)
Bakis, C. E., *252*
Bakis, H. R., *252*
Balluffi, R. W., *341*, *350*, *359*
Banavar, J. R., *4*, 10(31)
Bao, G., *183*, 185(12), 191(12), 213(12), *244*, 245(12, 102), 247(12), *259*, *261*, 262(120), 263(120), 266(120), 268(117, 118)
Barber, J. R., *223*
Barker, J. A., *75*
Barnard, J., *390*, 449(40)
Barnaś, J., *385*, 389(24), *391*, 393(42), 430(42), 431(42)
Barthélémy, A., *385*, 387(24), *388–389*, 389(24), *393*, 394(24), *402*, 453(48), *460*
Bass, J., *385*, 403(22), 431(22), 444(22), 447(22), 457(22), *460*
Baste, S., *218*, 233(81)
Bateson, R. B., *388*
Bauer, G.E.W., *396*, 413(65)
Baumgart, P., 373(18), *378*, 380(18), 384(18), *388*
Baym, G., *412*, 414(104)
Beauvillian, P., *389*
Becker, J. D., *153*, 158(178), 160(178), 162(178), 165(31), 166(31), *168*
Bender, B., 195(43), *196*, 199(43)
Bennett, B. I., 165(15), *167*
Berera, A., *111*, 112(117), 132(117), 133(117)
Berger, L., *397*, *399*, 399(71)
Bergmann, G., *396*
Berkowitz, A., *370*, 383(7), 384(7), 457(7)
Bernal, J. D., *2*
Bessoud, A., 165(8), *167*
Beyerle, D., *204–205*, 216(61), 218(61), 235(61), 243(60)
Bhadra, R., *369*, 376(6), *378*, 385(6), 402(6), 403(6)
Bichara, C., *73*, 74(60), 78(60), *79*, 153(60)
Bieber, A., *130*
Bilby, B. A., *292*, *351*

463

# Subject Index

## A

Al–Li alloy, 127, 145, 165
Alloys, *see also* Binary alloy systems; Ternary alloy systems
  effective cluster interactions
    calculations, 108–130
    DCA method, 130–145
    SIM method, 145–163
  ferromagnetic, 375
  giant magnetoresistance, 367
  global ground state search, 68
  ground state analysis, 64–79
  lattices, 71
  order–disorder transformations, cluster approach, 33–174
  phase diagrams
    Cd–Mg alloy, 153–163
    Ti–Al alloy, 146–153
  phase equilibrium, 36
  semiconductor alloys, 164, 169
Al–Ti alloy, 127, 145, 165
  phase diagrams, 146–153
  transient creep, 283
Aluminum alloys
  Al–Li, 127, 145, 165
  Al–Ti, 127, 145–153, 165, 283
Antiferromagnetic coupling, 378
Antiphase domains, 320
Antisymmetry operations, 301, 347–349
Au–Cu system, 320
Augmented spherical wave method, 119
Au–Ni alloy, 126, 127, 165
Au–Pt alloy, 126, 165
Average cluster functions, 108
Axial stress, brittle matrix composites, 203

## B

bcc crystals, ground state studies, 71–72
bcc phase diagrams, 92, 137
Bicrystals
  mapping, 356–359
  symmetry, 300–304

Binary systems
  alloys, 164
    Al–Li, 127, 145, 165
    Al–Ti, 127, 145, 146–153, 165
    Au–Cu, 320
    Au–Ni, 126, 127, 165
    Au–Pt, 126, 165
    Cd–Mg, 145, 153–163, 165
    cluster functions, 51–52, 53
    configuration variables, 43–47
    Cu–Pd, 145, 165
    CVM phase diagrams, 90
    effective cluster interactions, 55–58
    Ni–Pt, 126, 166, 170–174
    Pd–Rh, 121, 144, 166
    Pd–V, 137, 138, 140–142, 166
    Pt–V, 137, 140, 142–143, 166
    Ti–Pt, 117, 127, 137, 141, 143–145, 166
  superlattices
    Co/Cu, 369, 376, 385, 389–390, 402
    Fe/Cr, 368, 376–378, 385, 389–390, 402, 437, 440
Bragg–Williams method, 35, 79, 89, 91, 103
Bravais lattice, 39, 102
Brittle matrix composites, 177–286
  creep, 274–285
  fatigue, 255–274
  fiber properties, 207–217
  interfaces, 192–203
  matrix cracking
    in 2-D materials, 236–247
    in unidirectional materials, 218–235
  residual stresses, 203–206
  stress redistribution, 247–255
Broken symmetry, 322
  antisymmetry, 347–349
  coincident symmetry, 341–344
  defects
    characterization, 309–313
    extended, 318–321
    interfacial, 334–337
    reconstructed surface, 324–325
    unrelaxed surfaces, 322
  translation symmetry, 338–341

# Cumulative Author Index, Volumes 1–47